Andrew MacAllan is the pseudonym for James Leasor, whose Dr Jason Love adventure novels have been published in nineteen countries. He is also well known for his factual books, such as *Green Beach* and *Boarding Party*, filmed with Roger Moore and Gregory Peck.

Several would-be writers claimed it was impossible for a newcomer to break into publishing. To prove them wrong, Leasor submitted his novel *Succession* to Headline under the name of Andrew MacAllan. *Succession* was an instant hit, as was its sequel *Generation*, which the *Sunday Express* hailed as 'an epic saga and an epic success'.

Also by Andrew MacAllan

Succession
Generation

Diamond Hard

Andrew MacAllan

KNIGHT

Copyright © 1991 Andrew MacAllan

The right of Andrew MacAllan to be identified as the Author of
the Work has been asserted by him in accordance with the
Copyright, Designs and Patents Act 1988.

First published in 1991
by HEADLINE BOOK PUBLISHING PLC

First published in paperback in 1991
by HEADLINE BOOK PUBLISHING PLC

This edition published 2003 by
Knight an imprint of The Caxton Publishing Group

10 9 8 7 6 5 4 3 2

ISBN 1 86019 6225

Typeset in 10/12½ pt Plantin
by Colset Private Limited, Singapore

Printed and bound in Great Britain by
Cox & Wyman Ltd, Reading, Berkshire

Caxton Publishing Group
20 Bloomsbury Street
London
WC1B 3QA

FROM THE WRITER TO THE READER

Diamond Hard is for all those indomitable diggers who never found a diamond, but who helped to make a nation.

I am indebted to many people for their generous help in my researches, especially to H E Rae Killen, former South African Ambassador to the United Kingdom, and Dr J C Moll, former Counsellor, Cultural Affairs, South African Embassy in London.

I would also like to express my warm thanks and gratitude to members of the staff of De Beers and associated companies, who helped me in various ways, especially to Mr Andrew Lamont of CSO Valuations AG in London; Mr John Imrie, Mr P Bunkell and Mrs Rosemary Burke of the Chamber of Mines of South Africa, in Johannesburg; Mr Dennis Knox of De Beers Consolidated Mines Limited in Kimberley; Mrs Estrilita Forbes and Mr Ivan Morrow of CDM (Proprietary) Limited in Oranjemund, and Mr Gino Noli in Luderitz and Kolmanskop; and to Mr Stephen Flower of the Brooklands Museum.

I would like to acknowledge my debt to various publications on diamond mining published by De Beers, and to the following books: V Alexandrov *The End of the Romanovs* translated by W Sutcliffe (Hutchinson); O Doughty *Early Diamond Days* (Longmans); K Fitzlyon and T Browning *Before the Revolution* (Allen Lane); L G Green *Like Diamonds Blazing* (Robert Hale); A Hammer *The Quest of the Romanoff Treasure* (The Paisley Press); S Jackson *The Great Barnato* (Heinemann); S Joel *Ace of Diamonds* (Frederick Muller); M Kochan *The Last Days of Imperial Russia* (Weidenfeld & Nicolson); H Liepmann *Rasputin: A New Judgment* (Frederick Muller); S W Martins *A Great Estate at Work* (Cambridge University Press); P O'Higgins *Madame* (Weidenfeld & Nicolson); R Pethybridge *Witnesses to the Russian Revolution* (George Allen & Unwin); M Rasputin & P Barham *Rasputin: The Man Behind the Myth* (W H Allen); B Roberts *Cecil Rhodes* (Hamish Hamilton); B Roberts *Kimberley – Turbulent City* (David Philip); H Rubinstein *My Life for Beauty* (The Bodley Head); L Trotsky *Lenin* (George G Harrap); G & H Weber *Lenin: Life and Works* (Macmillan).

Any errors are my own.

I returned, and saw under the sun, that the race is not to the swift, nor the battle to the strong, neither yet bread to the wise, nor yet riches to men of understanding, nor yet favour to men of skill; but time and chance happeneth to them all.

For man also knoweth not his time: as the fishes that are taken in an evil net, and as the birds that are caught in the snare; so are the sons of men snared in an evil time, when it falleth suddenly upon them.

This wisdom have I seen also under the sun, and it seemed great unto me.

Ecclesiastes 9

DIAMOND HARD

Diamond: A very hard and brilliant precious stone, consisting of pure carbon crystallised in regular octahedrons and allied forms (in the native state usually with convex surfaces), and either colourless or variously tinted. It is the most brilliant and valuable of precious stones and the hardest substance known.

Hard: A primary adjective expressing consistency of matter: That does not yield to blows or pressure; not easily penetrated or separated into particles; firm and resisting to the touch; solid, compact in substance and texture. The opposite of soft.

Oxford English Dictionary
Second Edition Clarendon Press Oxford 1989

CONTENTS

ONE

Kolmanskop Revisited

Three thousand square miles of shimmering sand rose on end as Jamie Baird's private plane came in to land.

Unknown generations before, the Hottentots had called this remote desert in South West Africa the Namib, meaning the 'Place of No People'. Largely empty of people and animals it still might be, yet Jamie knew how this vast burning land on the edge of a freezing sea possessed a strange and fearful life all its own.

In the trembling blurred heat of early afternoon, dunes stretched to a hazy infinity, moving restlessly and ceaselessly as tireless winds changed their shape, their size, by the hour, even by the minute. Individual grains of sand, multiplied many million, million times, constantly rasped against each other, producing a curiously sinister and disturbing sound. It increased with the rising wind, and became like a raging storm at sea. And indeed, thought Jamie, that is what it was – not a sea of water but an infinitely more treacherous and hostile sea of sand.

Beneath the aircraft, along hundreds of miles of desolate coast, giant waves pounded lonely beaches. No one ever bathed here, no one walked along these shores. Winds and waves and currents were too strong, too merciless; the Atlantic, rolling in majestically from the Antarctic, was always too bitingly cold.

1

The icy sea combined with the smouldering sand to guard and conceal a buried treasure beyond all accounting: the world's richest source of diamonds.

For the past two decades, more than one million carats of diamonds had been mined here every year. Nor was this the end of the prodigious supply, or indeed anything like the end; some said it was still barely the beginning.

Jamie's flight up from Cape Town, roughly six hundred miles south, had given him his first chance of seeing the Namib from the air. Previously, he had only seen it, and crossed it, on the ground. With every step he took then, his shoes had instantly sunk through a thin and deceptively crisp crust of sand into treacherous quicksand softness underneath. If a car on one of the few surfaced roads briefly put one wheel only inches off the highway into the desert, that car could vanish under the sand. And the driver, going in search of help, might find that in the few minutes since he left his car, the road had also disappeared beneath millions of tons of sand suddenly blown over it by the relentless wind.

This wind blew on nearly every day of every year, always sculpting the sand into new, sometimes frightening shapes. A house which at evening was one of a group, surrounded by solid dunes, seemingly permanent as the hills of Rome, could by dawn be left naked and alone in a plain or a valley of sand.

Over the pilot's shoulder, under straggling clouds stretched thin as ragged cotton against the cobalt sky, a neat brick building edged with white came into view: Lüderitz airport. Several cars, painted white against the heat, were parked on its shady side. Jamie saw a man near a pick-up look up at the plane, shielding his eyes with his hand against the glare.

As the plane banked for its last run-in, Jamie thought of the Bushmen who had originally lived here until driven out by more aggressive black tribes moving from the north hundreds of years ago. Bushmen stood barely five feet tall. They could

2

survive for days without food – and then would gorge themselves on meat from a kudu or an eland. Bushmen could run with the speed of a wild animal, and pace their quarry for twenty miles or more without showing signs of fatigue. When the beast wearied, they would move in for the kill, firing arrows poisoned with snake venom from their primitive bows. They could hit a moving target 150 yards away with all the accuracy of a modern sniper using a sighted rifle at half that range. Strangest of all, they possessed mental telepathy so sophisticated that they could tell what other Bushmen, maybe fifty miles away, were thinking and planning to do. It was also said that after a violent death, the spirit of a dead Bushman would haunt his former home – and whoever had killed him.

The only water to sustain life here came from morning dew and mists blown in from the ocean, so every living thing, including humans, must adapt to the heat or die. Beetles, which elsewhere had shiny black shells, here grew white shells. Other insects developed grotesquely long legs to keep sensitive bodies clear of sand which every day burned hot as an open oven. Plants hid prudently beneath the sand to avoid the heat, only allowing the tips of their leaves to be above the ground. Others adopted protective camouflage; the lithops, or stone plants, were often mistaken for pebbles. Still others had a protective wax coating on their stems. When cut and dried, the stems would burn steadily, hence their name: Bushman's candles.

The pilot brought the plane down neatly in a three-point landing, taxied past the building, turned it round, cut his engine. When the aircraft stopped, he lowered a set of portable steps from the cabin.

The heat hit Jamie with the force of a fist as he came out through the door; he had forgotten just how hot it could be here. Unexpectedly, there was no wind. He must have chosen one of the few days in all the year when for a few hours, at least, the wind was still. On his previous visit, years ago, in a world at

3

war, the wind had blown constantly at gale force. Hot driving sand had burned his face and hands, roughened his throat, stung his eyes and scraped the inside of his nostrils. By the end of the trip his whole body had felt as though it had been systematically sand-papered.

Jamie walked slowly towards the airport building. 'Welcome to Lüderitz' was written on a blue and white board in Afrikaans, English and German. On his earlier visit, Lüderitz had been totally German, the most important port in the colony of German South West Africa, prime source of diamonds for all the Kaiser's empire. There had been no welcoming sign then, no airport and, indeed, only one aircraft in the entire Namib.

The man who had been standing by the side of the pick-up now came forward to meet Jamie. He was young, with a pleasant face; an uncomplicated character, Jamie guessed, and envied him this gift. Complications came when you grew older – and richer.

'Mr Provost?' the man asked him hesitantly.

'Yes,' said Jamie. They shook hands.

'I am Max Greening. I will be your guide while you are here and show you round.'

Jamie Baird was travelling under an alias he used when, for personal, political or financial reasons, he wished to keep secret his true identity. His second passport, in the name of John Provost, described him as a dental surgeon, although his only acquaintance with this profession had been as a patient in a dentist's chair.

The bland, anodyne description shielded Jamie from the intense curiosity, even panic, that could arise when strangers knew his real identity. If – at least according to the newspapers – you were one of the world's richest men, even a social visit or, as now, a largely sentimental one, could cause share prices to rise or flutter or fall. Commentators in a dozen countries would read into harmless actions all manner of sinis-

4

ter motives: the takeover of one company, closure of another, restructuring of a third.

The young man looked at Jamie quizzically, not quite sure what to make of his visitor. He saw a tall man, slimly built, with dark hair now going grey. He was light on his feet, like a runner or a fighter. He wore a superbly cut lightweight suit and desert boots; Greening guessed Provost knew the sort of place he was visiting. Had he been here before? The young man wondered, but did not like to ask outright. A high-priority memo had come from head office to say that every consideration must be paid to all Mr Provost's wishes. Clearly, he was very important, and important people did not always care to answer questions: they asked them.

'I have booked you in at the Bay View Hotel in Lüderitz, sir,' Greening said. 'Your pilot is at Kapps Hotel, as your secretary asked.'

Jamie nodded his approval.

'I understand, sir, you want to visit Kolmanskop?' Greening continued. 'A ghost town, these days, but visitors always want to see it. We frequently get descendants of the original German colonists, coming to see for themselves what it must have been like, living here. In fact we had some visitors this morning. They found something rather interesting.'

'Really? What was that?'

'I'll show you when we get there, sir.'

They climbed into Greening's pick-up. Someone loaded Jamie's overnight bag. They set off.

'Years ago it was very busy and thriving, I understand?' said Jamie conversationally.

'Very much so. When this was a German colony, three hundred Germans lived there, and at least forty pupils attended the local school. Kolmanskop was then the heart and focus of German diamond mining. That has since moved to Oranjemund, where we've actually driven back the ocean to dig for diamonds below sea level.'

5

'I sometimes wonder if there is a curse on diamonds,' Jamie said casually. He had often thought this. Had it yet affected him – or was this still to come? Maybe the curse was due to the fact that so many people who wanted diamonds so desperately would literally do anything, willingly commit any crime or cruelty, simply to possess them.

When the first diamonds were discovered, because they were so hard and rare, kings and emperors believed that they could personally absorb these qualities from the glittering stones. Diamonds represented wealth, and wealth meant power.

They were measured against the weight of dried carob seeds which, strangely, but conveniently, all weighed the same. Gradually the name changed to carat from the Greek word for the carob, *keration*. One carat weighed one fifth of a gram, and probably the world's most famous diamond, the Koh-i-Noor, weighed 280 carats. The name was Persian for The Mountain of Light. A Persian Emperor acquired it from the King of Delhi – and was murdered for its possession. Others who subsequently seized it were blinded, tortured, imprisoned, starved until they surrendered this unique diamond.

When the East India Company acquired the Koh-i-Noor in the nineteenth century, Queen Victoria requested it for the Crown Jewels. The ship bringing the stone to England was nearly wrecked, the crew decimated by cholera, and when an officer finally presented the diamond to the Queen, he suddenly went mad and attacked her. Nor did it bring good luck to Queen Victoria. Her husband, Albert, died early, so did her haemophiliac son, Leopold. She spent the last forty years of her life as a widow, ordering her consort's clothes to be laid out for him every morning – in case he returned from the dead to put them on.

'Diamonds come from the heart of the earth, the centre of the world,' said Greening. 'There was a German missionary, Hermann Heinrich Kleft, who discovered them long before the

Diamond Rush. He threw them away. He said they would only bring tragedy to the country.'

Jamie nodded, looked out across the desert. At intervals, beside the straight white road, triangular road signs gave laconic warnings of hazards: 'Wind' or 'Sand'. A few yards further into the desert, other notices spelled out in black letters the German message: 'Sperrgebiet – Forbidden Territory.' And underneath, in four languages: 'No entry without permit. Trespassers will be prosecuted.'

'You get many trespassers?' Jamie asked.

Greening shook his head. 'Not too many,' he said. 'There's a constant motor patrol linked by radio going up and down the road, and, of course, helicopters above. If anyone's spotted, they're stopped immediately. If they have a genuine reason to be there – say they've accidentally run off the road or something – that's all right. But they will always be escorted back to the road.'

'Many diamonds smuggled out these days?'

Greening shrugged; he did not wish to be drawn on this delicate subject. 'Security's very tight and very good. Electronic stuff. Body searches. Lie-detectors. X-rays. Did you know that only uncut diamonds show up on an X-ray screen?

'In the early days, so many diamonds were just lying about in the sand there was no need to dig for them. German prospectors simply went down on their hands and knees to pick them up like sea shells on a beach. They used to put natives in a line, lying on their bellies, arms spread out, fingers just touching. Then, on the word, they would all crawl forward slowly and pick up any diamonds they saw within their arm span.

'In Kapps Hotel in Lüderitz, where your pilot's staying, the diamond diggers didn't pay cash for their drinks. They would just take out a handful of small diamonds from a jacket pocket. The proprietor would weigh them on a tiny pair of scales he kept in a cigar box. Then he would take diamonds to whatever

7

he thought was the value of their drinks. Lüderitz had two brothels then, the Green House and the Brown House, and diamonds were the currency there, too.

'In those days, security meant herding native workers in a pen and dosing them with castor oil to see whether they'd swallowed any diamonds to try and smuggle them past the guards. Sometimes they swallowed stones worth thousands of pounds. It was worth a try, they thought. No hard feelings on either side. You win some, you lose some. A simpler world, then, sir.'

'In every way,' Jamie agreed.

That morning, he had visited Oranjemund, where the diamond company, CDM (Proprietory) Ltd – formerly Consolidated Diamond Mines, which had taken over the German mines – now concentrated their enormous activities. It was an astonishing contrast to the early days of shovel and sieve which he remembered. Here, a giant machine, the size of several houses, with a bucket wheel weighing 450 tons, moved 1,000,000 tons of sand and gravel every month. Other huge machines of equal complexity and power then dug down to a depth of 60 feet to extract the diamond-bearing ore. Finally, squads of Namibian labourers, working with what seemed like dustpans and soft brushes, swept the bedrock from end to end in case any tiny diamond grains remained trapped in cracks and crevices. These men had no pockets in their blue overalls, to diminish the opportunity of stealing even the smallest stones. All this work went on beneath sea level, as Greening had pointed out. A two-mile-long wall of sand held back the sea for a quarter of a mile so that the sea bed could be dredged.

This mechanisation represented an astonishing, almost unbelievable growth from the days when a vicar's son, Cecil Rhodes, with the German-born Alfred Beit and the Cockney Barney Barnato had first combined their mines and talents in Kimberley to form De Beers, which now owned CDM and much more besides. The name De Beers came from two brothers who had originally owned the land, Vooruitzigt farm, 700 miles north of Cape Town, where excavations revealed diamonds. The first few diamonds soon became a flood; thousands of pounds became millions, then hundreds of millions. Now the De Beers company employed tens of thousands of people of many races, colours and creeds, and indirectly provided work for hundreds of thousands more. The enterprise, shrewdness and vision of the founders, and of the Oppenheimers, father and son, who nurtured the company's growth, had brought prosperity to a nation and transformed a colony's pastoral economy to make South Africa a powerful industrialised nation.

And all this had come about through the immensely skilful mining and marketing of tiny sparkling stones extracted from the earth. 'All for the vanity of women,' Lord Randolph Churchill had remarked on seeing a pile of diamonds in a Kimberley sorting shed. To which the wife of a De Beers manager retorted quickly: 'And for the depravity of man.'

They came up towards Kolmanskop. Jamie had first seen the town at night when the houses had all been lived in. Lights burned in windows then, music poured from clockwork gramophones in front parlours: Brahms, Bach, Wagner. Trains were starting and stopping, and a German band rehearsed in the casino. Now, the place was lifeless. Most of the people he had seen then were probably dead, killed in the war, or dispersed across Europe. The railway lines had long since been taken up and sold to Japanese scrap dealers. A few old railway trucks remained, raw and red with rust, half buried in sand. Driven by almost ceaseless winds, year after year, sand had steadily eaten away the brick walls of the houses. In many, only hardened cement remained, giving a curious impression of concrete honeycombs. Paint on doors and window frames was powdered white by sun, or rubbed down to the wood by wind and sand.

Salt air blowing constantly from the ocean had eroded iron girders, once thick as a man's thigh, and left them thin and weak, perforated by rust.

Greening stopped the pick-up. About a hundred yards away, several men wearing lightweight shirts and trousers stood outside the shell of a house, talking earnestly. Two cars were parked near them. The men had a vaguely official look: they could be senior company officials, or policemen out of uniform.

As Jamie and Greening climbed out of their vehicle, hot, unseen eddies of air, harsh and fierce as a furnace blast, began to alter the face of the dunes around them, sculpting them into strange shapes and outlines.

'They're starting to run,' said Greening.

Jamie nodded.

An uneasy miasma seemed to brood over Kolmanskop, worse than blinding white fog from the sea or corroding sandstorms from the land. Or had Jamie brought this feeling with him? Kolmanskop was no longer a living township; it was simply a gigantic graveyard. He would book into his hotel in Lüderitz, and have a couple of large whiskies to wash away ghosts more difficult to dislodge than sand.

Jamie followed Greening across the sand, crisp as a pastry crust on top, so soft underneath that their shoes instantly sank in and filled with fine, abrasive grains. The men looked up as they approached, nodded to the guide. They glanced at Jamie curiously, wondering who he was, why Greening had brought a stranger here.

He took Jamie round one side of the house. Here, wind had completely blown away the mountain of sand which previously had concealed the entire wall. Now, a hole the size of a newly dug grave gaped at their feet. In that hole, bleached and blasted by a moving, immeasurable weight of sand, lay the skeleton of a man. The bones gleamed white and smooth as an elephant's ivory tusks. Only shreds of leather boots remained, with bright metal heels and toe-caps. A man's skeleton; no woman would wear heavy boots like those.

Jamie took a step nearer. The skeleton's hands were by his side, the skull pressed face down into the pit. On the little finger of the left hand, a tiny glint of gold reflected the afternoon sun.

'He's wearing a gold ring,' Jamie said flatly.

'Yes. That's been photographed. The police say there's a crest or an emblem of some sort on it. Or there was. The sand has almost totally obliterated it, apparently.'

'Any idea who he was?'

'Not yet. But probably some poor fellow who lost his bearings – and only literally yards from a house. That's the worst thing. Yet it's terribly easy to do out here when the sand's blowing. And that's not the only skeleton, sir,' Greening went on, almost proudly, like a conjuror promising an even greater surprise. 'There's another one, just ten metres away.'

'*Another?*' Jamie's surprise sharpened his voice.

Again, he followed Greening, wading through the sand to a shallow trough, half exposed by the afternoon wind. In it lay a second set of bleached human bones, smaller and lighter than the first.

Jamie looked at the skeleton in silence.

'Probably a Bushman, sir.'

Jamie nodded. He could not trust himself to speak, for fear of what he might say. Suddenly, he decided to leave. He no longer felt like having a good look round the place, as he'd originally intended.

They walked back to the pick-up. 'I don't expect you've seen anything like that before, sir, have you?' Greening chattered on, pleased at being able to show this important Mr Provost something so unusual.

Jamie shook his head. 'Perhaps they'll identify the first skeleton by the ring,' he said as they climbed into the vehicle.

Greening nodded. 'But I don't expect we'll ever know who the Bushman was. I don't think they all had names.'

As he spoke, Jamie wondered what Greening would say if he told him there was no need to check the crest on the skeleton's ring to discover his identity.

Jamie knew who the man was.

He also knew when and how he and the Bushman had died.

Most important of all, he knew who had killed them. And why.

At four o'clock precisely, on every afternoon throughout the summer months, Lady Doncaster's dark blue Rolls-Royce turned into the car park of the St James Hotel in the seaside village of St James. The hotel stood on the main coast road from Muizenberg to Simonstown, east of Cape Town. A special parking space was permanently reserved for her car.

The black chauffeur opened the rear door, bowed obsequiously as Lady Doncaster, of indeterminate age, slim, beautifully dressed, with a face totally unwrinkled and the complexion of a woman in her very early forties, walked up the white stone steps to the elegant terrace overlooking the road and the sea.

As on every afternoon, Lady Doncaster's arrival was instantly noted. Staff and guests could set their watches by it; she was never early, never late. The same table was always laid for her to one side beneath a blue sunshade, under a cluster of flags the manager displayed to show the international character of the hotel's guests. Arabella Doncaster sat, as always, beneath the Union Jack.

One waitress brought her a plate of egg sandwiches, cut very thin from brown bread; another, a pot of Indian tea. Lady Doncaster poured out the tea herself, sipped it without milk or sugar, and then looked about her. Some other people, also taking tea, smiled at her rather nervously, and she smiled back politely. Everyone knew who she was, but very few actually knew her well, and so they felt reluctant to start a conversation. She never encouraged any approach from a stranger; as in the phrase popular when she was a girl, Lady Doncaster liked to keep herself to herself.

She found a curious comfort in the total predictability of her four o'clock routine. In a world of frightening, often terrible changes, nearly all unwelcome, this ritual would not change so long as she wished it to continue. Yet this afternoon, for the first time, she had actually been on the point of cancelling her table. She had phoned Jamie's hotel in Lüderitz, but he had not checked in. Had she been able to reach her twin brother, she probably would have cancelled her visit to St James, because something had happened that put even her sacrosanct arrangements into second place.

A total stranger had called to see her, bringing news that filled her with amazement and delight, but still just slightly tinged with a vague and quite irrational apprehension. Jamie, she knew, would be thrilled at what she had to tell him. She would try to reach him again this evening. But now, before she need seriously consider how both their lives would change totally as a result of her visitor, she could retreat, if only temporarily, into the comfort of her daily routine. In its utter familiarity, she found peace – and a sense of safety.

If anyone asked her why every afternoon she drove fifty miles from her great house along the coast, why it was so important to her to arrive here at the same time every day, Lady Doncaster might reply that it was because she liked to sit on this terrace and look at the sea. This was true, but not the whole truth.

As she watched now, the afternoon sun obediently transformed a lapis-lazuli ocean to one of deep Circassian blue. Wreaths of mist moved on the face of mountains to the right of False Bay, now revealing, now concealing tall and silent peaks.

They are like our lives, she thought; Jamie's and mine. Some of our activities are out in the open, for public scrutiny and approval, but many more are deep secrets that must always remain carefully shrouded.

Between the road outside the hotel and the sea lay a railway line, and along these tracks, single-decker electric trains of brown and grey carriages ran regularly between Cape Town and Simonstown. Lady Doncaster had originally chosen this particular table because from it she could see the roof of St James's station, built across the road in the Dutch style like a neat red-tiled farmhouse.

The platforms at St James's, where the trains sometimes stopped, were always clean. Flowers gave them the appearance of a sunny English Edwardian garden. Their fences were freshly painted, bright under the bluest of skies, with no hint of the soot and smoke of a railway station she remembered under a darker, sombre sky in another colder country.

As she raised her second cup of tea to her lips, she heard the familiar clatter of metal wheels. A train was approaching. Like her, it was always on time. She lowered the cup, saw faces briefly – white, brown, black – through the thick glass of their compartment windows.

Where were they all going? What strange, or routine, journeys were they just starting or ending? These thoughts always fascinated her. Most probably, the passengers were only making some prosaic excursion from office or factory or shop to a modest suburban home. But this, of course, was not necessarily so; that was to her the intriguing possibility.

Lookers-on, years earlier, might have thought that she, her brother Jamie and their father were also only making a hum-drum train journey from Manchester. But they would have been wrong. That beginning had led them all to destinations unimagined and indeed unimaginable on that afternoon long ago. Perhaps some people on this train rattling through St

14

James were also setting out, all unknowing, on what might become an Odyssey.

This was the real reason Lady Doncaster came to the hotel at the same time every afternoon; she wanted to see the train go by. And in seeing it, in hearing the reassuring, so well-remembered rumble of iron wheels on iron rails, she could briefly return to the start of another fateful journey – and recall with warmth and regret an innocence and love lost long since . . .

TWO

Exchange Station, Manchester

On the afternoon of their sixteenth birthday, Arabella and Jamie Baird hurried with their father, each holding his hand tightly, beneath the sooty archways of Exchange Station in Manchester. Exchange was an imposing memorial to Victorian railway engineers. Locals were proud of the station's size; it boasted the longest platforms of any in England. Huge fretted metal girders, studded with dome-headed rivets, supported a vast glass roof made opaque by smoke that hung in perpetual billowing, black clouds from the locomotives. The smoke had a sulphurous smell which Arabella always recalled whenever she ate an egg sandwich. She associated it with a journey, the start of an adventure. How strange, she would often think, that a single word, a name, a smell of smoke in a now almost smoke-less world, could immediately unlock the door of memory.

Ahead of them, a porter pushed a four-wheeled trolley. On this lay a ship's cabin trunk of varnished wood, with a slightly domed top, bound by black metal straps. This was the gift of Uncle Don, her father's brother. It contained all their belongings. Uncle Don had served at sea for several years as first mate aboard an East Indiaman, before he retired to become landlord of the Silent Witness inn on the Hyde Road, outside Manchester.

Tacked to the trunk was a label which the steamship company had provided: 'Mr Hamish Baird and family, E Deck, Wanted on Voyage. Liverpool to Cape Town.' Arabella felt very proud of this notice; it advertised their importance. It showed they were not merely short-distance travellers using a stretch of insignificant suburban railway line to go to a mill, or an office. It marked them as emigrants, pioneers, colonists, exchanging the smoke and damp cabbage smells of Manchester, where even rain fell stained with soot, for the bright, sun-burned skies of Cape Colony.

Arabella felt so excited at the prospect that, as always at such moments, she walked on tiptoe, to give her extra speed and silence. Unnecessary noise might somehow shatter the dream. But this, she kept assuring herself, was not a dream; this at last was reality. Within hours, they would be embarked at Liverpool. By this evening, when the train that had taken them there had returned to Exchange Station, they would have begun a voyage to a new country, to a totally new and (so everyone assured them) golden life.

'You will be wanting something to read?' her father asked.

Arabella nodded. She was a keen reader and at the kiosk all sorts of papers and magazines could be bought for a penny. In liking books, she took after her father, who from the twins' childhood had impressed on them the importance of the written word. There were few free libraries in Scotland then, where they had lived before coming to Manchester, but people in the village who possessed books, men like the local doctor, the dominie, as the schoolteacher was called, even Hamish Baird's employer, the local laird, were pleased to lend books. Hamish always returned them, and was eager to borrow more. In their pages, he could escape from the drab routine of mending doors and wooden window frames and chests of drawers in cottages on a great Scottish estate, and travel the seven wide seas in search of adventure and fulfilment. Jamie did not take after his father in this, and was neither a reader nor a dreamer. He did not want simply to read about exciting places; he wanted to visit them.

Hamish gave his daughter three pennies. She crossed to the station bookstall and looked at the covers of magazines she had never seen before, and about which she knew nothing. Finally, she bought *Great Friends* simply because the coloured cover attracted her. It showed a girl, about her own age, holding a hoop and wearing a frilly skirt, and in the background a village church and a lawn.

Arabella had never seen a church and a lawn like that in Scotland. There, the landscape was sombre and bleak on all but the sunniest summer days. The grim Grampian Hills on one side and the Sidlaws on the other gave an added soberness to the view. And there were certainly no such country scenes around Manchester. This picture, she somehow felt, symbolised what would be their new life in South Africa: space, sunshine, freedom.

She hurried back to her father and brother, having spent only one penny.

'It's a pity Uncle Don and Aunt Hannah cannot be with us to say goodbye here,' said Hamish sadly.

Arabella agreed. All around them, other families were starting on journeys that could not possibly be one fraction as exciting as theirs, yet they had hampers, baskets of fruit, newspapers and friends and relations to wish them well. But then they were probably not like Uncle Don and Aunt Hannah, working people.

Mornings were a busy time at the Silent Witness, because Aunt Hannah had to cook for customers who wanted hot dinners at twelve noon sharp. Her husband and a hired potman between them would meanwhile wash the floors, swill out the lavatories, check the beer engines were not drawing up air, see that all casks and barrels were full, every glass clean and polished, and a new fire burning in a freshly black-leaded grate.

Running a public house left little free time. If you were not actually open for trade, then you were preparing for it, or clearing up after it.

Hamish and his two children stood in the midst of scurrying crowds. Wealthier passengers followed servants or porters, who carried or wheeled portmanteaux and wicker baskets. Others, less elegant, had wrapped their belongings in brown paper or crammed them into string bags. Whistles blew, guards waved green flags importantly, and everywhere steam and smoke arose in choking acrid clouds, as the ponderous engines moved out slowly, pulling strings of freshly washed cream-and-chocolate-coloured carriages.

Arabella looked closely at everyone and everything, trying to imprint the scene on her mind so that in the future she could remember exactly what it was like only minutes before she set off on their last journey in England. Her father consulted the German silver turnip watch his employer had given to him as his farewell present; only minutes to go.

They walked towards the platform barrier. The trellis gate at the end of the platform was wide open. The shelter on its right, where the ticket collector usually waited to punch tickets, was empty and people were walking through the open gate on to the platform. They were in plenty of time; their train had not even arrived.

'First or third?' their porter asked them brusquely.

He guessed the answer, of course, from their ready-made clothes, their sensible boots, and so he did not address Hamish Baird as 'sir'. The railway company did not offer second-class carriages. Passengers either sat in a compartment with a patterned carpet under their feet and starched white covers on the back of each seat, known as anti-macassars, because they would absorb the thick macassar oil with which so many men dressed their hair, or they endured harder springs and rougher cushions, without any carpet, in third-class coaches.

19

'Third,' said Baird briefly.

The porter halted about twenty yards along the platform. 'The thirds stop here,' he explained and heaved their trunk off the trolley.

Baird took out a silver threepenny bit and gave this to the man. He spat on it, touched the shiny peak of his cap, then pushed the trolley back through the open gate into the main hall of the station.

Thirty yards behind them, near the station entrance arches, a large crowd of young men suddenly appeared. Several wore formal morning dress; others, dark suits. All had red roses in their lapels, and pink, cheerful faces, flushed with alcohol. They formed up in two lines and began to sing 'The more we are together, the merrier we'll be'. They were merry already, Arabella thought as she watched them empty green bottles, with necks bound in crinkly gold foil, into long-steamed glasses; but they were not unpleasantly drunk, simply enjoying themselves as a wedding party should. Arabella had seen many customers in the saloon bar of the Silent Witness in this state, but none so smartly dressed as these young men.

Hamish Baird glanced at them and frowned. He could not abide drunkenness. He looked away from them, along the platform.

'Good. The train's coming in,' he said thankfully.

Arabella and Jamie turned to watch the engine approach the platform, trailing a frond of thick black smoke. Steam hissed and roared around the domed condenser cover. Pipes, coiled like polished copper serpents, encircled the shining, brassbound boiler. The locomotive's livery of green and dark red briefly caught the light before it came on into the gloomy cavern of the station.

For an instant, the polished bull's-eye lenses of oil lamps above the buffers reflected the sun like heliograph signals. Bright metal spokes on the wheels, polished and oiled steel connecting rods gleamed briefly in the sun.

20

As the train slowed alongside the platform, the young men in the entrance hall gave a great cheer, and raised their glasses high above their heads in a mock salute.

'Come on, boys!' cried one excitedly. 'Let's give them a *proper* welcome!'

Each holding a champagne bottle by the neck in one hand, a glass in the other, they sprinted across the hall, through the open trellis gate and swarmed on to the platform, shouting incoherently as they ran.

Passengers already waiting on the platform turned in surprise – some in alarm – at this sudden invasion by so many young and noisy men.

Oblivious of them all, eyes fixed on carriage doors already opening, the young men poured past. People hurriedly grabbed their luggage and jumped out of their way, as others, also dressed for a wedding, also holding champagne bottles and shouting greetings, began to leap from the moving train.

'A society wedding, I suppose,' said Hamish Baird vaguely, as if that explained it all.

The engine was now within feet of the Bairds, slowing down with a roar of escaping steam. Metal brake shoes squealed against wheels; sparks sprayed from hot rims. Close to, the engine, with its cab for soot-stained driver and fireman, loomed up alarmingly large, the size of a house trundling past them.

'Look out!' Arabella cried suddenly in warning.

A carriage door swung open. She saw the notched leather strap inside it for lowering the window. A young man stood framed in the doorway for a second and then he jumped out and ran along the platform. He had been so close that his face was only feet away.

At Arabella's shout, Hamish Baird turned, and saw half a dozen revellers racing down the platform straight towards the man, like forwards breaking from a rugger scrum. Their collars were undone, cravats loosened, coat tails flying like dark wings.

21

Hamish hurriedly dragged Arabella and Jamie out of their way. In doing so, he took a pace nearer to the edge of the platform, and then turned, his back to the train. For this reason, he did not see the open door on the leading carriage. It struck him on his shoulder.

He gave a gasp of surprise and pain and staggered back. Then a second door swung open and hit his other shoulder. He almost fell, struggled to stand, totally lost his balance, and dropped sideways into the narrow space between the moving train and the edge of the platform.

He had a sharp view of giant chains linking the carriages just above his head; of huge screw couplings and heating pipes that leaked scalding white beards of steam. Then he was down on his back on the track between the coal tender and the leading carriage. He knew he had to move at once, before the slowly turning wheels reached him, but the fall had stunned him. His brain seemed numb, incapable of sending the urgent, desperate message to the muscles in his legs. For a second that seemed to last for hours, he saw axles, and wheels polished by miles of rail. Then he screamed: 'Help! *Help!*'

But no one could help him; no one could even see him as the train moved ponderously on over the last few yards to the buffers with all the heavy progress of a hundred thousand tons of steel.

The shining flanges of the leading wheels bit like razors into Hamish Baird's legs beneath the knees. He felt bones crunch and crush and then saw two lengths of trouser, and the bloodied ends of bones, raw with pink marrow as they fell, severed, to one side of the nearest rail. Wheels turned again, and now he saw blood on them, blood and flesh, his blood and flesh. And yet there was still no pain, only bewilderment, total disbelief that this could be happening to him, that he was even in any way involved.

Oil-caked axles, rusty springs were passing above and

beyond his head and he smelled sweat, soot and blood. And then the pain came, and he writhed, gasping in unspeakable agony. He could not speak. His breath seemed trapped in his throat, like his voice, choking him. He gasped for air and mercy and help.

Dimly, as from a great distance, he heard Jamie shouting frantically: 'My dad's under there! *Stop the train!*' But no one listened. The merrymakers were now cheering each other wildly, waving bottles. Someone threw an empty bottle down on the track beside Baird: the glass shattered like a bomb bursting.

Arabella ran along the platform, caught up with the driver's cab. The fireman, his face grimy with coal dust, streaked with sweat, stared down at her with reddened, uncomprehending eyes. He had been shovelling coal for the two hours' run from Liverpool; he felt exhausted, drained of all effort. After the thunder of the engine and the rattle of the wheels, he could barely hear what the girl was saying.

'The train's run over my father!' she shouted in despair. 'Back there!'

She pointed up along the platform.

The engine driver heard her. Horror and disbelief creased his face. He spun a brass control wheel, gripping its shining rim through a square of oily rag. Passengers now came running along the platform to catch up with the engine.

'There's a man down there!' one shouted. 'Got hit by a carriage door. You'll have to reverse.'

Slowly, slipping wheels striking sprays of sparks from shining rails, the train began to go backwards.

Arabella had a sudden distorted vision of strange, almost disembodied faces staring at her, then turning to peer down ghoulishly between the moving carriage step and the edge of the platform, horrified and yet fascinated by what they might see. As in a dream, she realised the young man who had opened the door had disappeared. His companions, still holding their bottles and glasses, still cheering wildly, were now all running through the open gate at the end of the platform. Within seconds, they were out of sight, with most of the arriving passengers. A porter came towards her and Jamie.

'What's the matter?' he asked. 'What's all the shouting for?'

'There's a man down there. The train's gone over him,' a middle-aged man explained. 'He may be dead.'

There was still no sound from Hamish Baird. *Was* he dead?

'Hurry! *Please* hurry!' cried Jamie to the engine driver, in anguish at the delay. 'It's our father.'

A sudden rush of steam from the exhaust, the sharp, heart-jerking metallic clang as buffers on one coach punched buffers on another, and the train began to move more quickly. Halfway up the platform, it stopped. Now they could see Hamish Baird lying on his back in a greasy trough of cinders between the rails. He was still alive and still conscious. His hands and arms moved slowly as though with a life of their own. His face was so contorted with pain he looked like a living, breathing gargoyle. His boots, the turn-ups of his trousers, and a gory mass of flesh and bone lay on the far side of the rails.

Other porters came at a run, led by the deputy station master, who wore a top hat and frock coat. A guard blew his whistle. Two porters ran up with a luggage trolley. They jumped down between the rails, picked up Hamish between them, and stag-gered with him to the edge of the platform. Then they lifted him, dripping blood, on to the trolley and began to push. Behind them came another porter, carrying his boots with feet still in them.

'Make way there, make way there!' the deputy station master called out importantly. Crowds in the main hall, waiting for other trains, fell back on either side as the grisly procession came through. A woman saw the boots and fainted. Mothers turned their children away from the sight, or covered their eyes with their hands. Jamie and Arabella trotted behind the trolley.

'Where are you taking him to?' Jamie asked the deputy station master.

'The infirmary. Who are you?'

'His son.'

'You'd better come along then.'

And still Hamish Baird did not speak. On the dirty boards of the trolley, his body twitched slightly as though he had no control over his muscles. Blood spouted and dribbled from the stumps of his legs with every beat of his heart. Out of the station, into the courtyard, where hansom cabs stood drawn up in line, waiting. Horses with heads down in nosebags glanced up briefly, and went on munching.

Across the road, dodging a horse tram with its furiously clanging bell, the trolley's iron-tyred wheels struck sparks from cobble stones. Then they were in a side street and through a narrow door into the infirmary, a high solid block of sooty yellow bricks and sash windows. Arabella would never see these colours again on any public building without remembering this terrible day.

'A man's been run over by a train,' the porter told a nurse who came out to see what the commotion was about.

'In here, quickly,' she told him, and then turned to Jamie. 'You keep out, sonny, this isn't for you.'

'It is. He's my father,' Jamie retorted.

'And mine,' said Arabella.

'Then you'd better wait here. Where's your mother?'

'She's dead.'

'Any other relations?'

'Only Uncle Don and Aunt Hannah.'

'Where are they?'

'They run the Silent Witness in the Hyde Road.'

A policeman appeared, mustachioed, tall and grave, wearing

on his blue uniform brightly coloured medal ribbons of distant, long-forgotten wars.

'What's all this?' he asked ponderously.

The porter explained.

'I'll get a message through for them to come at once,' the policeman promised.

'Can't we see our father?' Jamie asked. 'Please.'

'Not yet, sonny. The doctor is with him.'

'Will he be all right?' asked Arabella. Even as she spoke, she realised the futility of the question. How could he emigrate to a new country and start a new career without legs? Many times she had seen men, often old soldiers or sailors, who had one wooden leg, but never anyone with two. How could a man keep his balance on two wooden stumps? And if their father could not go, how could they leave him here, crippled and unable to work?

'You sit down and I'll get you a cup of tea,' another nurse said sympathetically.

Arabella and Jamie sat on a bench. It did not have a back, and the legs were uneven.

'There's no need for you other people to wait, unless you are relations or witnesses,' said the nurse sharply. A handful of men who had followed the trolley now sheepishly melted away. One tall man in a dark overcoat remained. He had a sallow face and a moustache with thickly waxed ends, twirled to points. He looked like a circus ringmaster out of uniform. He stroked the points reflectively as he regarded Jamie and Arabella.

The nurse brought them cups of tea on a tray, and then hurried away into the side room. Tea had slopped into the saucers. The twins drank mechanically, not really wanting to at first, but then grateful for the warm sweet drink.

'Are you with these young people?' the nurse asked the tall man.

'In a sense. I was in the train that caused the accident.'

26

'You are a witness, then? You saw what happened?'

'I saw nothing,' he replied stiffly.

'Then what is your interest here?'

'I am a solicitor,' he explained. 'Mr Snakesby.'

He took out his wallet, removed a card, handed it to Arabella. She read: 'Mr Bevis Snakesby, representing Tatham, Snakesby and Woolfolk, Solicitors, Commissioners for Oaths'. There was an address in Hyde, not far from the Silent Witness. She knew the road well enough: small shops, a branch of the District Bank, dingy offices of coal merchants and builders and decorators, with faded gold lettering painted on blacked-out bow windows.

'You may have a case against the railway company,' Mr Snakesby explained.

'I don't understand you,' said Arabella, puzzled. What was a case? What did the man mean?

'I will await the arrival of your uncle and aunt, and explain it to them.'

The nurse returned.

'How is our father?' Jamie asked her.

'He's been given laudanum. He's drowsy, but not in pain any more, I'm very glad to say. That's the important thing. Wonderful what they can do in accident cases these days,' she added brightly.

They waited, the twins on the bench, Mr Snakesby walking up and down the tiled corridor, sniffing the carbolic-laden air, twirling the ends of his moustache, until Uncle Don and Aunt Hannah arrived.

'You poor things,' were Aunt Hannah's first words. She was a plump, motherly person. She opened her arms and the twins ran to her. The nurse came out of the side room, looked at them inquiringly.

'You with the injured party?' she asked.

'I'm his sister-in-law,' Aunt Hannah explained.

'His brother,' said Uncle Don.

The nurse pursed her lips, glanced sharply at the twins, then gave a brief jerk of her head.

'You had better come in then, but leave them here. For the moment, at least.'

The nurse opened the door. Aunt Hannah and Uncle Don followed her inside. She closed the door quickly behind them before the twins could see their father. He lay on a casualty stretcher resting on two trestles. His body looked ludicrously truncated under a red blanket. A wire cage kept its weight off the stumps of his legs. His face was white as his pillow.

'Is he conscious?' asked Uncle Don in a whisper.

'Off and on. But not now.'

'What happened?'

'Got run over by a train at Exchange Station. Standing too close to the edge of the platform apparently, and hit by a carriage door. Someone opened it and jumped out while the train was still moving.'

'There's notices in the carriages about waiting till the train stops.'

'People don't heed them.'

'So it seems. Will he recover?'

The nurse did not answer, but busied herself with some phials of liquid on a side table.

'It's the shock to the nervous system,' she explained, not looking at them. 'The doctors say that's as bad as any actual injury. He's lost both legs below the knee, you see, and also a lot of blood.'

Uncle Don and Aunt Hannah stood looking down at Hamish, awed by the deepening shadow of approaching death. They still felt unable to comprehend how, barely an hour earlier, they had been wishing him Godspeed on his journey. They did not speak. Hamish Baird opened his eyes slightly, looked up at them. Aunt Hannah leant over the stretcher and touched his shoulder; his hands were somewhere under the blanket.

28

'It's going to be all right,' she assured him with a conviction she did not feel. 'Just you get some rest, Hamish lad. You'll be out and about before you can say Jack Robinson.' Then she turned away before he should see her tears.

Hamish gave no sign that he had heard. His lips, blue now in a face wan as a waxwork, moved slightly, forming words in a whisper so soft that Uncle Don would not have heard them had he not bent low over his face.

'Jamie and Arabella,' he said, and paused. Speech demanded a supreme effort of will over weakness. His voice seemed to be coming from far away, like a faint echo diminished by distant wind.

'Are those the children?' asked the nurse in a matter-of-fact voice. Aunt Hannah nodded. A single tear rolled down her cheek and dropped on the red blanket.

The nurse opened the door.

'You two can come in now,' she said briskly. 'Your father is asking for you.'

They stood at the bottom of the stretcher, uneasy in the strange room with its yellow walls, tiled floor, stretchers stacked in one corner. A notice on the far wall caught Arabella's eye: 'Prevention of Consumption – Do Not Spit.'

They moved to the head of the stretcher and bent low to hear their father's words. The pallor of his face horrified them. His whole body seemed to have shrunk, not just through the loss of his feet, but in its shape. He appeared to be diminishing before their eyes.

'I want you to go on,' he said weakly. 'As we planned. To the Cape.'

'Without you, Dad?' asked Jamie hoarsely. How could they conceivably continue the journey on their own?

'Yes. Bairds never give up. You know the Baird clan's motto – *Dominus fecit* – The Lord Made. What has happened to me must be His doing, so good will come out of it. Do not

29

forget that. Now, you must go on together, on your own. I may not be there with you, not so you can see me, at least. But I will always be with you in spirit, wishing you both well, watching you do all the things I hoped we could have done together. Remember that. Always.'

He spoke slowly, measuring out each word individually as though the effort was almost beyond him. Jamie and Arabella realised then that their father was dying. He was still in this world, but barely of it. His words floated on a mist of laudanum. Arabella looked up and saw the nurse catch Aunt Hannah's eye and shake her head slightly. There was no hope, Arabella knew. No one could survive these terrible injuries and loss of blood, not even their father.

'Can't you give the poor fellow a blood transfusion?' asked Uncle Don. 'I read something in the paper about that the other day. It's quite common now, apparently.'

'Not in this hospital,' the nurse replied. 'We've sent out for the equipment, but it has to come from the other side of Manchester. We're waiting for it to arrive.'

Jamie and Arabella looked at each other, and then at their father. He had closed his eyes and his face glistened with a patina of sweat. The nurse leaned forward, put her hand beneath the coverlet to feel his pulse, and frowned. She lifted his left eyelid and then turned away.

'He's gone?' asked Uncle Don anxiously.

'Yes,' she said. 'Very quickly and, as you see, very peacefully. The shock to the system must have been too great. It's a blessing in a way. He would have been totally crippled if he had lived.'

She put her hands on the twins' shoulders, shepherded them out of the room into the hall. A drunk, who had fallen down in the street outside and cut his face, was being manhandled into the building, singing loudly and out of tune. Two companions holding him upright turned away as he collapsed on the floor, vomiting. A steaming yellow pool of urine spread across the chequered tiles.

'You come back with us,' said Aunt Hannah quickly.

'Our trunk is still at the station,' Arabella said mechanically.

'I'll see to that,' promised Uncle Don, glad of something positive to do. As he walked towards the door, Mr Snakesby approached, bowed.

'Am I to understand, sir,' he asked Uncle Don, 'that you are with the injured party in the next room?'

'Yes. Who are you?'

'A solicitor, sir.' He produced another visiting card with a theatrical flourish.

'Well, what do you want?'

'To help these young people, sir. To see justice done. I feel that the injured party has a very strong case against the railway company. For negligence, gross negligence. The platform gate should have been closed until the train arrived.'

'Maybe. But it's too late now. He's dead.'

'I am very sorry indeed to hear that, sir, and offer you and your lady and the young people here my deepest condolences. But while we most regrettably cannot help the dead, I believe we can help the living. While no monetary consideration could ever adequately recompense them for the loss of a loving father, at least grief can be more easily borne by survivors if they do not also have pecuniary concern.

'I understand that the deceased party was waiting on the platform when a crowd of young men rushed through the open barrier to greet others arriving on the train. In their haste, they pushed him nearer the edge of the platform and an open carriage door hit him.'

'He wasn't pushed. He moved to get out of the way,' Arabella corrected him.

'Precisely. A different form of words.'

'So how are the railway company involved?' asked Aunt

31

Hannah. She had an instinctive distrust of lawyers. To her they meant trouble, expense, just as telegrams never brought good news, only intimations of distant death, injury, calamity of some serious kind.

'The company, madam, have a statutory duty, laid down in the bye-laws – which are available for everyone to read and in which all staff are rigorously instructed – that ticket barriers must be manned at all times when trains are expected to depart or arrive. The barrier should not have been open and a collector should have been on duty to see that no one went on to the platform until arriving passengers had left the train.'

'We just walked through,' said Arabella.

'As did the other people,' said Snakesby, nodding his disapproval. He turned to Uncle Don. 'Will you allow me to take this up, sir, and favour me with your instructions? I think we may be able to extract considerable monetary advantage from the company, which will help these two young people.'

'I suppose it can do no harm.'

'None whatever, sir. Quite the reverse. Very likely, a great deal of good. Now, are you related?'

'His brother,' replied Uncle Don. 'His wife's dead.'

'So these young people are left on their own? Orphans?'

'We will take care of them,' Aunt Hannah said indignantly, putting her arms round their shoulders.

'I am glad to hear that, ma'am. Can I take it then that I have your instructions?'

He glanced from one to the other.

'If you mean you will see what you can do to get some money to help bring them up, yes,' said Uncle Don. He gave his address and Snakesby noted it down.

'I will be in touch,' he promised. Then he bowed, stepped carefully over the snoring drunk, and went out into the street.

'You come home with us,' Aunt Hannah told Jamie and Arabella.

'What about Daddy?' asked Arabella. 'Is he really dead? For ever?' Jamie still had not spoken; he seemed numb with shock.

'Yes,' her aunt said simply. 'He's dead.'

'But he was alive an hour ago, less than that. He gave me money to buy this magazine.'

'What a lovely picture,' said Aunt Hannah, admiring the church and the meadow.

'It's the last thing he gave me,' said Arabella, beginning to cry.

'Come along. We'll have a nice meat tea,' said Aunt Hannah. 'Uncle will bring your luggage.'

In silence they followed Aunt Hannah down the stone steps, out of the hospital. From behind the corner of the building, Mr Snakesby watched her hail a passing four-wheeled cab.

This was the first time Arabella had ever ridden in a cab. She could clearly recall its strange smell, an amalgam of camphor and leather oil, and the special feel of shiny cracking leather under her hands.

She often glanced now at the magazine cover. It did not seem so colourful or enticing as it had then. The print was poor and the green in the field had slipped slightly in the printing. But it still possessed a kind of magical significance as the last link with her father whom she had loved with an intensity she believed she could never feel for anyone else.

Her Dorset estate now embraced the village that contained the church in the illustration. Sometimes she would tell her chauffeur to stop the car in exactly the same place where, so many, many years earlier, a photographer had set up his plate camera on a tripod and thrown a black cloth over his head so that he could focus the picture. Then she would sit and admire the view.

Everyone's memory, she realised, was, at its worst, defective, and at its best only selective. When you were young, summer days crowded closely one on another in a season of seemingly perpetual sunshine. Equally, it always snowed at Christmas, deep and crisp and even, as in the carol. Winter days were rarely wet and cold and foggy. For the same reason, viewed through the rose-tinted glasses of retrospect, the row of terraced houses in Hyde, facing each other across a cobbled street, the Silent Witness on one corner, front doorstep whitened, brass door handles brightly polished, windows wiped clean every morning, possessed a peculiar homely magic all its own.

The reality of sooty summer rain in a northern suburb, of slushy snow in winter, brown from horse droppings, under a fog thick and foul as a dragon's breath, had no part in Arabella's recollections. There may have been such days, of course, but they were so few that now they only served to highlight the pleasures of past good times.

Arabella had never seen a dead person before, and the memory and the vision of her father's face, his pallid, hollow cheeks and sunken eyes, would for years waken her in the night. She would lie listening to her brother's breathing in the bed they shared in the back room of Uncle Don's two-bedroomed living quarters above the public house. From the saloon beneath them she would hear the hum of conversation, like a distant dynamo, and sometimes laughter or the twang of a ukulele, played by an out-of-work music hall performer, who, for the price of a couple of pints of bitter, came in on Friday and Saturday nights to lead singsongs.

Hamish Baird's funeral was a hurried affair. He had not been a regular churchgoer, and the parson of the nearest church, suffering from a heavy cold, kept sniffing, wiping his long nose, dabbing red-rimmed eyes as he intoned the burial service. As he led the little party from the cold, bleak church into the graveyard, he sonorously intoned the psalm: 'Men fade away suddenly like the grass. In the morning it is green, and groweth up; but in the evening it is cut down, dried up and withereth.'

I wonder if *you* are watching all this, Daddy, Arabella thought, I can't believe it's *you* in this box going down into the deep dark grave.

Later came meetings with Mr Snakesby in his office above a bank off the High Street. Its walls were lined with law books bound in red leather-cloth. Photographs of past partners, all bearded, all sombre, looked down on Mr Snakesby and his clients. Snakesby's desk was cluttered by papers and piles of beige files bound with pink ribbons. He handed Uncle Don letters he had received from the railway company, each heavily engraved with their title and a list of directors: dukes, an earl, lords, knights, a handful of generals and admirals. How could Mr Snakesby, in this shabby room, persuade such rich and important people, who personally had no knowledge whatever of events on a Saturday afternoon at Exchange Station, that they should pay money to two young people whose existence they had also not known until Mr Snakesby informed them?

Arabella thought Mr Snakesby's optimism was unfounded. She wondered what she would do if, instead of trying to extract money from a rich and powerful company, she owned that company and had to consider this request. She came to the quick conclusion that she would fight most vigorously to avoid paying a penny. If she did not, if she agreed to pay compensation, who could say how many other people would come forward with all manner of claims against her?

Days became weeks, and weeks stretched into months. Lawyers do not care for haste in their deliberations, nor do they encourage it. A dispute that could be quickly resolved by a meeting of all involved could not possibly command such high fees as a case that lasted for months or, conceivably for years. Mr Snakesby was not a man eager to go against this ancient legal custom. Then, one morning, he told them that the case would be heard on the following Thursday.

'Who pays for all these meetings we've been having?' Aunt Hannah asked him nervously. Customers had frightened her with harrowing accounts of people they claimed to know who had been ruined by lawyers' fees.

'In the end, madam, the railway company. We have a cast-iron case against them. Gross negligence on the part of their servant, the ticket collector, whose instructions were to keep the gate shut until all incoming passengers had left the train. They have no answer to that.

'The court will give costs against them, plus a handsome sum to be placed in trust for the deceased's family until they reach the age of discretion. I may say that my firm operates a very efficient trust department, and, if you allow us to handle the monies, be assured we will use our best endeavours to extract the highest income for you, with total safety.'

'But what if the company doesn't pay?' asked Jamie.

Mr Snakesby frowned. 'In that unlikely case, I would, of course, have to look to you for reimbursement of my fees.'

'But we have no money,' Arabella pointed out.

Mr Snakesby allowed himself a smile, twirling his moustache, as though amused by this frank admission. 'I would not look to you *personally* for the money, of course, but to your aunt and uncle. After all, they instructed me. You, as minors, could not do that.'

'We can't afford a lot of lawyers' fees,' said Uncle Don shortly. 'Indeed, we can't afford any. The licensed trade is not very profitable at the moment, and we are only tenants. Hamish had raised some money by selling furniture and so on when he left his employment. But that would not amount to a great deal. We are not wealthy people, Mr Snakesby.'

'Who is, these days?' Mr Snakesby asked him rhetorically. 'But such an unhappy situation, I can almost certainly assure you, will never arise. However, you asked me a fair question, and I gave you a frank answer. Now, let us prepare ourselves for our appearance in court.'

In the years between then and now, Arabella had several times appeared in court to protect her own interests, and always successfully; it had never been in her nature to be on the losing side. She could, of course, afford to engage the best solicitors, and the most distinguished counsel, because money had become totally unimportant to her. And every other consideration was immediately subordinate to her one aim in any controversy or legal case: victory – uncompromising, and on her own terms.

Even so, whenever she entered a court of law in New York, in Cape Town, London or Paris, always accompanied by her lawyers, her personal secretary, and more recently by her bodyguard, she was instantly transported back to her first visit to a court, in Manchester. Uncle Don accompanied her and Jamie; Aunt Hannah had to stay behind to prepare the Silent Witness for opening time.

The law courts reminded Arabella of the infirmary; yellow brick walls, high ceilings. A similar chill, stale wind blew ceaselessly through open doorways and down long, cold, tiled corridors, but it did not rid the building of the peculiar smell she always associated with such legal hearings: the odour of unwashed bodies and the sweat of fear.

Mr Snakesby had advertised in the *Evening Chronicle* for anyone who witnessed the accident. Two people who had been travelling on the train, far back, replied. Both recalled seeing a carriage door open near the front and Baird stagger to one side and fall between the platform and the carriage. None of the young men in the wedding party had replied to the advertisement, nor had whoever opened the carriage door while the train was still moving. Jamie was puzzled by this. His father had always insisted that everyone should accept responsibility for their actions. If you threw a stone and it broke a window, then you owned up and accepted any punishment with a good grace. You were responsible for your own deeds, your own mistakes. Hadn't these wealthy young men been told that by their fathers?

In court, Mr Snakesby, looking, Arabella thought, like some strange bird of prey in his dark clothes, talked in whispers to counsel, a much younger man, who kept moving his wig slightly backwards and forwards as though to relieve an itchy scalp.

The appearance of the judge, Mr Justice Donovan, in his red robes and long wig filled her with unease. On this man's decision her future and the future of her brother depended. What savings their father had accumulated were, of course, already bespoken for legal fees. If the railway company did not live up to Mr Snakesby's assurances and pay compensation, they would be virtually destitute.

Uncle Don and Aunt Hannah had assured them they would look after them as if they were their own children, but this could only mean a life of drudgery. Arabella might find work somewhere as a tweeny, an untrained housemaid who ran between the floors of a big house, helping more senior servants. Jamie could possibly become a messenger boy. But while these jobs could help for a few months or even for a few years, what lay ahead after that?

Proceedings passed with the speed of a pageant – or, as she sometimes thought on such occasions, a pantomime. The two witnesses were called, swore nervously that they would tell the truth and nothing but the truth, so help them God, and were sharply cross-examined by a much older counsel on behalf of the railway company.

To each reply they made, he shook his head gravely, as though in total disbelief. At last, both sides summed up their case. Counsel for the Bairds claimed that the railway company was directly to blame for the death of Hamish Baird because their paid servant, the ticket collector, had not made certain the platform gate was closed before the train arrived – as was laid down clearly in the railway company's book of rules. So that there could be no doubt whatever about this part of the man's duties, he read the rule aloud to the court.

Counsel for the railway company, having attempted unsuccessfully to argue that the gate had in fact been closed but that somehow passengers had entered the platform in spite of this, fell back on a second line of defence. The deceased person – what an odd way of referring to our father, thought Arabella – should in any case not have been on the platform, regardless of whether the gate was shut or open. There then followed a tedious argument as to whether he could have been trespassing on the property of the railway company interspersed with such phrases as 'My learned friend' . . . 'If I may put it to you' . . . 'With the deepest respect.'

Why can't they just get on with it? thought Arabella with increasing impatience. How could her father be a trespasser when he had a railway ticket? The idea was so absurd, she could scarcely keep silent. At last Mr Justice Donovan, pressing the tips of his fingers together with such force that he seemed to drain the blood from his hands, announced he would sum up.

At that moment, the defence counsel stood and bowed deeply towards him.

'If it please your lordship, and with your lordship's permission, certain information has just come into my possession which I think your lordship may wish to see.'

'In connection with what, pray?' asked Mr Donovan testily.

The barrister did not reply, but instead approached the judge, bowed as though in front of an altar, and handed a sealed envelope to him. Mr Donovan broke it open, read the note inside, slipped the paper back into the envelope, put it in a pocket of his robe. Then he looked round the court.

'In view of the complexities of this case and indeed the

39

seriousness of the whole matter, I have decided to pronounce judgment tomorrow, in this court, at ten o'clock.'

There were cries from the ushers: 'Be upstanding!' and the judge left the court.

In the cold entrance hall, people were hurrying to and from other courts: barristers holding papers, carrying on their shoulders blue bags that contained their wigs, solicitors clutching briefcases, clients – either worried or elated – trailing along a few paces behind them.

Uncle Don buttonholed Mr Snakesby.

'What's the meaning of that, exactly?' he asked bluntly.

'I have no idea,' Mr Snakesby admitted, frowning. 'There should have been a complete disclosure of documents. Our counsel is trying to see his opposite number, but he seems to have left.'

'You mean, you – or he – should have seen the note, if it referred to this case?'

'Yes.'

'Well, why haven't you? It must involve us. He isn't just asking the judge out for a pint, is he?'

Mr Snakesby did not reply, but his face showed his concern. He no longer appeared as confident as at their earlier meetings, and Arabella felt a physical pain in her stomach, as if she had swallowed a lump of lead. They were going to lose their case; the certain win was certain no more.

'You must excuse me, I have other matters to attend to,' Mr Snakesby said shortly. 'I will see you here tomorrow at five to ten.'

The following morning, there was no delay in the judge's deliberations. He dwelt briefly on the sadness of the situation. Here was a father, he said, a widower, with two young children to support, cut down in the prime of his life. He was using his meagre savings so that they could all begin a new life in Cape Colony. Now this could never take place.

'Can anyone withhold a tear at such a grievous situation?' he asked. 'On the other hand, it must be borne in mind that the deceased was himself largely instrumental in causing this terrible accident in which, most sadly, he lost his life.

'That, in my opinion, is possibly the most grievous and ironic part of this tragedy. While it is indeed true that the ticket barrier should have been closed, as learned counsel has argued most eloquently, the ticket collector was unexpectedly called away to help an unfortunate lady passenger who had fallen down and broken her leg. To aid any injured passenger must take priority over other concerns. And he was away from the platform only for minutes, as learned counsel has informed us.

'In leaving to help this injured passenger, the ticket collector was, of course, relying – as anyone involved in working on the railways must rely – on company bye-laws. One of these specifically declares that no passenger is allowed on the platform – *for whatever reason* – when a train is arriving, until all passengers on that train have left the platform.

'If by some means they gain entry to the platform on their own initiative, before this has happened, then they do so at their own risk. It could be argued that not all passengers are aware and fully cognisant of this supremely important bye-law. But each ticket the railway company issues has printed on its reverse side the statement that every ticket is sold subject to the company's bye-laws – a copy of which is readily available for inspection in mainline stations such as Exchange.

'Thus, although I extend the deepest sympathy of this court to these two young people at the loss of their father, I would be lacking in my judicial duty if I did not make this point absolutely clear, distasteful as it is for me to have to do so. I therefore find in favour of the London and North Western Railway Company. Costs to be equally apportioned.'

*   *   *

Outside the court, Mr Snakesby addressed Jamie and Uncle Don.

'They have won. We have lost,' he said bluntly.

'I understand that. But how could we lose?' Uncle Don protested. 'You were convinced that our case was virtually fool-proof. And we were in the right.'

'I have to tell you that rights and wrongs do not, unfortunately, figure largely in the processes of law.'

'I thought that was what the law was all about,' said Uncle Don.

'That, I fear, is a widely held misapprehension in the lay community.'

'So it appears. Well, what do we do now?'

'You can appeal. Take it on through several courts if need be, each court higher than the last, right up to the House of Lords.'

'But what will that cost?'

'I am sorry to say, a great deal of money. Hundreds, perhaps even thousands of pounds.'

'We haven't any more money,' said Uncle Don shortly. 'We have already spent most of what my brother saved to begin a new life in the Cape.'

'In that case, sir, I am sorry, but you will have to accept this court's verdict.'

'This isn't justice,' said Uncle Don bitterly.

'I must say, I would agree with you,' Mr Snakesby replied. 'But it is the law.'

THREE

The Silent Witness

A letter from Mr Snakesby arrived a week after the court hearing. Very few letters were delivered to the Silent Witness, and these were mostly bills or receipts for wines and spirits. The lawyer's letter looked altogether more important. The envelope was large and thick and sealed with red wax. Uncle Don took a knife from the cutlery drawer in the bar to open it. Then he put on a pair of steel-rimmed glasses.

Jamie saw his face crease into lines of disbelief and horror. He let the letter flutter down to the floor, as though he could no longer bear to hold it. Jamie picked it up and read the neat copperplate writing of the lawyer's clerk: 'Preliminary attendance . . . receiving instructions and taking particulars . . . conferring and advising . . . perusing and considering documents, attendance on Counsel . . . appearing in court . . . petty and miscellaneous disbursements.' The phrases had a majestic ring to them that rather appealed to Jamie. Then he read the figure on the bottom line: £333.16.9.

'It's a fortune,' said Uncle Don in a hoarse voice. 'A bloody fortune.'

Jamie had never heard him swear before.

'We will have to find it,' his uncle went on. 'But heaven knows how. If we don't, Snakesby will sue for the debt. He could put the bailiffs in, take our furniture, anything we own until his fee is paid.'

'I thought he was on our side?'

'He's on his own side,' replied Uncle Don.

'Daddy paid for the tickets,' said Arabella. 'Now that we're not going to South Africa, can we get a refund? That would help a bit.'

'The steamship company won't do that. I've asked them already. All they will do is allow three people to travel to South Africa on one of their ships at some future date – steerage class, of course, and provided accommodation is available.'

'I could earn some money and help towards the bill,' said Jamie.

Uncle Don smiled, and shook his head sadly. 'To earn this sort of money, you'd have to work for a long time, boy. I pay you ten shillings a week helping in the bar. At that rate it would take you years to pay it off. And while the bill is unpaid, the lawyer will want interest at four per cent – at least.'

'I'll take another job,' said Jamie.

'You'll be lucky to get one up here. There's only the mills and, I tell you, if you once start there, you'll never escape. You'd be paid just enough to buy food and shelter so that you can continue working there. That's no life, boy. That's not what your father had in mind for you. He wanted to give you a chance to spread your wings in a wide country, not go into a cage. That's all the mill is. Look at the people who work there.'

Jamie had seen them, streams of men in shabby clothes and women in drab skirts, wearing clogs, with shawls over their heads, filing silently in the early morning through cobbled streets towards the mill gates. Every morning at six o'clock, the workers were woken by hooters. If any bedroom window did not show a light that indicated the occupant was awake and dressing, the knocker-uppers, older men with long sticks, would tap on the glass to waken them. Mill workers each paid them a few coppers a week for this service; it was a wise insurance, for many could not afford alarm clocks, and to miss the shift could mean they also lost their jobs. The machines must never be allowed to stop during a shift. At half past six in the evening and one o'clock on Saturdays, the mill-workers walked home.

Usually, youngsters started at the mill as soon as they left school, at twelve or thirteen, perhaps even younger, and stayed until they were too old, or too ill, to work any more.

Black clouds of sulphurous smoke poured from every mill's long thin chimney, inlaid with white tiles spelling out the name of that particular mill – Flowering Field, Rose Hill, Daisy Dell – names cruelly evocative of a countryside and flowers that had existed all around before the mills were built.

'I might be able to wangle a job for you with the brewery,' said Uncle Don thoughtfully. 'But, again, they will pay you almost nothing. And you're a slightly built lad, you could easily rupture yourself moving barrels of beer. The trouble with that job, too, is that when you start delivering beer, every publican feels he must offer you a pint, and so you're a drunk before you know where you are.'

'How much more do we need to find on top of what is left from Father's savings?' Jamie asked.

'If we sell everything, including his clothes, we will still owe about fifty pounds. Maybe I can pawn something if he insists we pay him in full now – as he may. You never see a thin lawyer, Jamie.'

'I will pay that money.'

'How?'

'I don't know yet. But I'll find a way. I must.'

Uncle Don patted him on the shoulder. 'You're a good lad,' he said. 'Your father would be proud of you.'

'I was proud of him,' said Jamie. He remembered his father's

45

words when he first told them they were all going to the Cape.

'Since your mother died, I have been waiting for a sign to show me the way ahead. I've wanted to try one of the colonies for a long time, because opportunities seem so much better overseas. The countries aren't crowded, there's more room to breathe – and move. Your mother couldn't face the voyage, and the fact we'd all be so far away from her own folk. So we stayed, but then, when she fell ill and died, I felt the way was now open for us. That was a sign to me. We should sail away.

'So when you face a problem, son, and you can't see any way out, forwards or sideways, but never running away from it, stop worrying and relax. You will see a sign somewhere, somehow. You may have to watch closely for it, or you may not recognise your opportunity – and that is the saddest thing of all, for then it passes you by. Chances only come once. If you don't make the most of them, be sure someone else will.'

Now, Jamie could see no sign in any direction, but one would come. He was certain of that; his father had told him so, and he had faith in what his father said.

Usually, supper was a fairly jolly occasion. They ate early before the pub filled up, but on this evening, they sat dejectedly, shoulders dropping. No one felt hungry.

'Come on,' said Aunt Hannah at last. 'Cheer up. We may have lost a battle, but we haven't lost the war.'

'How do you make that out?' asked her husband crossly. 'We haven't the money to fight another round. That battle was our war, and we've lost – unless we find some fairytale godfather who's going to back us with his money.'

'I'll make some money,' Jamie said confidently.

'So you tell me, and good for you, lad,' replied Uncle Don. 'But you won't make it here, I'm sorry to say.'

Aunt Hannah served the meal she had cooked especially to cheer them up: Cumberland sausages and stove potatoes; a

46

Scottish dish of mashed potatoes mixed with onions, carrots, turnips, butter and cream.

'Keeps the cold out, sticks to your ribs,' she told them as cheerfully as she could. The stovies did both these things, but nothing could dispel their feeling of gloom and defeat.

The Silent Witness had one spare bedroom apart from the one used by Uncle Don and Aunt Hannah. Before Jamie and Arabella came to stay, the bed was always made up in case a visitor might wish to use it. Sometimes, a commercial traveller, delayed in Hyde for some reason and unable to catch the last train, would take it, but now Jamie and his sister occupied it. There was a double bed under a gas mantle, a small chest of drawers, a marble-topped table with a ewer of water and a china bowl and soap dish. Aunt Hannah made the bed with a bolster down the middle.

'They call that a Dutch wife,' she explained, but she didn't say why, and they didn't like to ask her.

That night, Jamie and Arabella lay awake on either side of the long cold bolster.

Jamie spoke first. 'We will never get anything from the railway company.'

'No,' agreed his sister. 'If we could take it right up to the House of Lords as Mr Snakesby said, then we might win something. But it would probably only be enough to pay the legal fees. I had no idea going to law was so expensive.'

'I meant what I said about making money,' Jamie assured her earnestly. 'I'll get it one day, and then maybe we'll take it to the House of Lords. I don't see any reason why not. Do you think old Snakesby did his best?'

'I think so. Something in that note passed to the judge made Mr Donovan change his mind. I don't know what. Nor did Mr Snakesby. But that is what lost us the case. The judge's behaviour I can't forget – or forgive.'

'Me, too,' agreed Jamie.

'One day I will repay that judge in his own coin,' Arabella said grimly. 'If he's done that to us, we won't be the only ones he has betrayed.'

'You'll have to wait until we're rich before you can do that,' her brother said.

'I'll wait,' Arabella replied shortly.

Next morning, Jamie went out of the side entrance of the pub, early. He walked across cobbles, greasy with rain. A tinker was pushing his cart along the street, crying out hopefully for knives to sharpen, pots to mend. He was an old man with a limp. A black and white mongrel followed him at the end of a string tied to the cart. None of the front doors of the terraced houses opened to him. His cries had all the melancholy of despair. Perhaps, Jamie thought, he was also looking for a sign. Or perhaps it had appeared, and he had not recognised it?

Jamie came into the main street: rows of small shops – a haberdasher's with check jackets of shoddy cloth and blue rain-coats displayed on hangers outside under a faded canvas awning; a butcher's shop, a fishmonger, a pawnbroker, a herbalist. He went into each one. The shopkeepers did not know him, of course – he had not lived there long enough. They greeted him pleasantly, assuming he wished to buy something. When they discovered that he was hoping for work, their attitude changed immediately, but not unkindly. They would help him if they could, but in these hard times, they couldn't.

'Nowt here for you, lad.'

'Nothing at all, son. Sorry, trade's too bad.'

In the case of the pawnbroker, the Jew who ran it, Sammy Rosen, did not reply at first, but came out from behind his counter. Unredeemed pledges, watches with gilt chains, cheap necklaces, silver-plated picture frames filled the shelves behind him and hung on the wall. He regarded Jamie with a steady eye. He was in his early thirties and helped his father who,

Jamie knew, suffered from what locals called 'his chest'.

As Jamie waited hopefully, he could hear the old man coughing behind a door at the back of the shop, then a retch, the sound of spitting into a bowl, and a gasp for air.

'I'd like to help you,' said Rosen, 'but you're the first person who's been in the shop today. That's what business is like. If it weren't for my father, I'd have sold out already – if I could have found a buyer. I'd be off to South Africa. Join the diamond rush I've been reading about in the papers – or any other rush that offers a chance of money.'

'I need money,' said Jamie simply, taking to the older man's friendly response.

'Don't we all?' replied Rosen, putting his head on one side. 'My tragedy is I should have been born rich. Yours too, eh?'

'I mean to be rich one day,' Jamie replied. 'The question is, how? I help my uncle in the pub, but he can't pay me a proper wage.'

'That I can believe. He's feeling the pinch, too. We all are. But tell me, do you mind what you do?'

'No.'

'So why don't you walk along the road a couple of hundred yards and have a word with old Yeung Lee.'

'What does he sell?'

'Junk, mostly. I shove things on to him I can't get rid of myself. He's not a bad bloke for a Chinaman. Must be pretty lonely for him here, I often think. He has a few visitors who come off ships from Liverpool, but apart from them, there aren't many Chinese about. I mean, have you ever seen another one here, eh? So he must be lonely. Stands to reason. Anyway, he might be able to give you something. Tell him I sent you. He owes me a favour. I sold him a vase last week for five bob and I heard he'd sold it on the same day for half a quid.'

Jamie walked on to Yeung Lee's shop. A bell on a curved spring tinkled above the door as he entered. The interior was very dark, lit by an oil lamp in a sooty globe. Brightly coloured prints of pagodas, with men and women standing, hands concealed in the wide sleeves of strange robe-like garments, lined the walls. Under a glass-topped counter a dozen wooden masks grinned up at him; faces of ageless evil smiling in uncontrollable mirth.

Jamie thought the shop must be empty until a small man, wearing a robe like those in the pictures on the wall, stood up in one corner. He had been sitting on a high stool, smoking a long clay pipe. His face was sallow, eyes small, his hair gathered back into a long plaited pigtail. He was the first Chinese Jamie had seen. He did not speak, but simply raised his eyebrows questioningly and waited.

'I wonder if you would have any sort of job for me?' Jamie asked him hopefully. 'Sammy Rosen suggested I should ask you.'

'So. Who are you?'

'Jamie Baird. My father was killed in a train accident at Exchange Station. It was in the paper. My sister and I are staying with relations who run the Silent Witness. I have to get a job.'

'What can you do?'

'Whatever I have to, to make some money. Clean out the shop, wash windows, anything.'

'What hours could you spend doing – anything?'

'At present, I help in the pub from twelve till two and from six every evening until closing time. Apart from these times, I am free.'

'You already work long hours, yes?'

Jamie shrugged. He had never thought of it in that way. 'Not really. My uncle and aunt have been very kind to us.'

'All right,' said Mr Lee slowly. 'We shall see. I have some logs of wood too big for my stove. You come tomorrow morning at eight o'clock and saw them up, and we'll see how we get on. If we get on.'

'How much for?'

'Two shillings. Until a quarter to twelve. Give you time to get back to your uncle's place.'

'Thank you.'

Jamie held out his hand. Yeung Lee looked at the hand in surprise, then shook it.

'You are the first person here to shake hands with me,' he said thoughtfully.

'A handshake seals our bargain.'

'So it does,' agreed Yeung Lee. 'I will see you at eight o'clock sharp.'

Jamie walked back to the Silent Witness wondering whether he should have accepted such a small return for nearly four hours of manual work. It would take a year and a half's work every morning to make £50. It was not a very promising proposition, but at least it was a start – and it might even be the sign his father had mentioned.

Jamie sawed the logs into neat lengths and piled them up in the shed at the back of the shop. He worked so hard that Yeung Lee said he could come and help in the shop each afternoon, as well as in the mornings, and for this he would pay him another two shillings. So in the weeks ahead, Jamie polished brass ornaments, the likenesses of unknown gods and goddesses, scrubbed the floor every day, painted the outside of the shop, and persuaded Yeung Lee to have two larger oil lamps inside to show the goods to better advantage.

Yeung Lee seemed at first amused by Jamie's suggestions and then impressed by them – as he was impressed by his hard work. He had served for years in the merchant navy, and by buying a few trinkets in Hong Kong, or Shanghai, or wherever his ship docked, and then selling them on his return to England, he had gradually built up a small business. Then he left the merchant navy and rented his shop. He often spoke of returning to China, but he made no attempt to do so. He was a loner and happy to be on his own.

As well as dealing in all manner of merchandise, Yeung Lee had a considerable local reputation as a healer of small sick animals and birds. Few mill hands kept dogs as pets because they required feeding, and most households found it difficult enough to feed their families, let alone an animal. A number of men did keep greyhounds and whippets, however, and on Saturday afternoons they were raced against each other for small bets on open patches of ground.

Women tended to have cats, because they were independent and could forage for themselves. They also kept down rats and mice. Others kept budgerigars and parrots in wicker or wire cages; while some younger men had tame blackbirds, and split their tongues to try and make them utter simple words. Yeung Lee usually had several brightly plumaged birds in cages hanging from the ceiling of his shop. He treated them for various ailments, and they added a splash of bright colour to the drab room. One parrot greeted Jamie every morning with the question: 'How are you today?'

Sometimes birds were brought in too late for any treatment, and these Yeung Lee would dissect on a newspaper spread out on the wooden draining board by the sink. He used small scissors to clip their feathers, and a set of minute scalpels to open up their tiny bodies to discover why they had died, whether through old age or from something they had eaten.

In a tin box, Yeung Lee kept items he had discovered in birds' stomachs: an imitation gem from an earring, a small nail, a metal nut, a leather washer.

'These birds certainly pick up some unusual things,' said Jamie, turning over the oddments.

'Sometimes very useful things,' Yeung replied. 'In Brazil, for example, the poor Portuguese folk living near the gold fields keep swarms of chickens – but not just for their eggs. They deliberately let them loose and watch over them like a shepherd so they don't stray, for chickens pick up anything that glitters and catches their eye.

'When they have gorged themselves, their owners squat on the ground, grip the birds between their knees, and slit open their craws with sharp knives. Then they pull out whatever they find, and if the chicken is not too badly injured, they sew it up with a needle and thread and back it goes to work. This way they collect gold dust. If they have enough chickens in the right place, day after day after day, they pick up quite a lot.

'Their throats expand,' Yeung Lee explained. 'I have seen bigger birds with stones in their stomachs as large as eggs. And, of course, in your Bible there's the story of the whale that swallowed the unfortunate voyager, Jonah.'

'But a whale's a fish,' Jamie pointed out.

'No,' Yeung Lee corrected him. 'A mammal. Just like you and me – except they live in water. Although with all the rain we're having up here, we are moving towards that ourselves.'

This was the only time Jamie ever heard Yeung Lee attempt to tell a joke, and he sensed he only did so now because the Chinaman trusted him and liked him.

Sometimes people came knocking at Yeung Lee's front door after hours when his shop was shut. They would bring him some little item wrapped in a page of newspaper. He would examine it carefully and say what he would give for it. They would reply that they did not want money but in exchange sought his advice about a sore they might have, or a spot, a wart, a cut that would not heal. The local chemist and the doctor would need to be paid in cash. Yeung Lee would give his opinion for some piece of bric-a-brac.

He had no medical qualifications, of course, but an abiding interest in the powers of herbs and oils and unguents of the East, and local country specifics. He had learned, for example, that grooms in charge of the mill horses could cure septic cuts by rubbing white mould from damp saddles and harness into them. No one knew why or how, but the treatment worked. To soothe cuts and chafing, Yeung Lee made up a creamy paste which he sold by the spoonful at a penny a time. He also made up pills and potions said to ease minor afflictions from a sore throat to unlikely cases of sunburn for people with unusually sensitive skin.

Trade of all kinds slowly increased, and Yeung Lee began to make regular visits to Liverpool to buy specific items for which there seemed a local demand – cheap vases, imitation willow pattern plates and cups. He no longer relied only for his stock on unwanted curios that sailors might offer him.

When he was away, Jamie looked after the shop on his own. At first, he felt rather nervous at the responsibility, carefully counting out change for all the purchases and, on Arabella's suggestion, writing down in a notebook exactly what he had sold and for how much. She had a methodical mind; she liked figures, while he found excitement in simply making a sale. Time and again she told him it was essential for him to know the real profit on everything he sold, and also the lowest price at which he could afford to sell and still show a profit. She suggested that he kept a record of these bottom prices in the notebook, using a simple code of letters instead of figures. This he did.

Arabella also advised him to mark up prices for the most popular items, so that when he offered a customer something at a discount, the shop would actually be making a larger profit. Jamie soon learned that people generally believe what they want to believe, and in dealing with a foreigner's shop, they wanted to believe they were cheating the foreigner.

Arabella then suggested that whenever Jamie made a bigger profit, above the percentage Yeung Lee might have expected at the original price, he should personally pocket the difference.

'I couldn't do that,' Jamie told her. 'It doesn't seem fair.'

'Why not? Old Lee makes what he thinks is enough. So you

are entitled to whatever you can get on top. You're not robbing him. After all, remember, you – or rather, *I* – thought of this scheme. You owe it to yourself – and to me.'

Jamie could see logic in her argument, but he would not follow her advice. Yeung Lee had helped him by giving him a job; he owed him loyalty in return.

On the third occasion Jamie was left alone, three men came into the shop late in the afternoon as he was about to light the oil lamps. He recognised two of them. For the past week they had been in the public bar of the Silent Witness, ready for the price of a pint to run with illegal betting slips to the local bookmaker. The third was a stranger, broadly built, with a red choker round his neck and a flat cap pulled down over his eyes. All three were unshaven and clearly had been drinking heavily.

'Where's the Chink?' the stranger asked Jamie roughly.

'Mr Yeung is not here,' replied Jamie. 'Can I help you?'

'By giving us the contents of the till, yes, you can,' the man said. The others sniggered; he was clearly the leader.

'What do you want to buy?' asked Jamie, ignoring the remark, telling himself it must be intended as a joke.

'Nothing. Like I said, we want the money.'

'There's nothing in the till,' said Jamie.

'Let's see,' said the man. He took a pace forward, ripped open the wooden drawer. All it contained were a few sixpences and pennies.

'Where is it, then? He's a rich man, the Chink. There's more than this. Must be. A lot more. And we want it.'

Suddenly, the little shop seemed heavy with menace. The men crowded against the glass-topped counter, staring at Jamie, waiting for his next move.

'If I lean on this counter,' the man went on, 'I'll break the glass. That'll cost the Chink a few bob to replace. Then we could break a few plates, a vase or two, couldn't we? Just to show we were here.' He turned to the others for confirmation. They nodded their heads vigorously. 'But that won't be necessary if you give us the cash, son. Where is it?'

'You've come to the wrong place,' said Jamie. 'There's no money here except what you see in the till.'

The man clenched his right fist and punched it into the palm of his left hand.

'Don't want to spoil your good looks now, do we, eh? So don't tell me lies. Give us the money and that's it. No harm to you, no trouble.'

Yeung Lee kept a thick ash walking stick beneath the counter, but Jamie knew he could not reach it; they were watching him too closely.

'Don't try anything clever, or you'll get a broken nose,' said the leader sharply, seeing Jamie's eyes stray. 'So give us the bloody money – now.'

'It's outside,' said Jamie lamely. If he could get them all in the back yard, he might be able to lock the door in the rear of the shop, and keep them there. Then maybe someone in the next shop might hear or see them and send for a policeman. This did not seem a very likely possibility, but at least the men could do less harm in the yard. Inside the shop, they could destroy the stock in a matter of minutes.

'Thought you'd have a bit of sense,' said the big man triumphantly. 'You've got a good head on your shoulders, you have. Wouldn't want it knocked off now, would you?'

Jamie led them through the back room. Birds in painted metal cages fluttered brightly coloured wings in disapproval at being disturbed. The outside door led into a tiny back yard. In its far wall a heavy wooden door opened on to a wide area covered with cinders. The yard, barely twelve feet square, was empty, except for a clothes line. One of Yeung Lee's shirts fluttered damply in the afternoon breeze.

'Well?' said the man. 'Where's the money?'

'In there,' said Jamie, pointing towards the brick privy built in one corner. He opened the door, invited the big man to look inside. He pushed his head carefully into the tiny closet built above an underground drain.

'Where?' he demanded.

'Down there,' said Jamie, pointing towards the wooden seat on its brown china bowl. 'Where no one would think of looking.'

The man took a step forward to look at the bowl and Jamie gave him a shove. He staggered forward, but regained his balance. One of his companions had put his boot against the door so that Jamie could not shut it.

'You bastard!' roared the big man, coming out of the privy. He had lost face with his companions; this kid had tricked him, made him look a fool. 'Tried to screw me, did you? I'll teach you.'

He seized Jamie by the coat lapel, butted his head against his nose. Jamie reeled away, dizzy with pain, blood streaming down his face.

'Give us the bloody money!' the man shouted.

As in a nightmare, Jamie could see three sets of angry eyes staring at him. Then, beyond them, Jamie suddenly saw a fourth face, hazy, as though glimpsed through a dense and drifting fog, but still familiar.

'You wish something?' asked Yeung Lee quietly.

The three men turned in surprise. They had not heard him come out of the shop silently in his slippered feet. The big man jumped at him.

Yeung Lee's arms moved with astonishing speed. They seemed to come together like scissor blades, and suddenly the big man was sailing over their heads, his arms and legs flailing uselessly against the sky. He dropped heavily on the cobbles, and lay on his back, screaming in pain.

'My arm! You've broken my bloody arm!'

Yeung Lee turned to face the other two, looking thin and frail against them. They came in together, meaning to kick him in the crotch and then run. What had initially seemed to be a very simple in-and-out job had somehow gone wrong. As they attacked, Yeung Lee pivoted on his right foot like a ballet dancer and struck one man a ferocious blow in his stomach with his left leg. He dropped, gasping for air, clutching his belly with both hands in a vain attempt to ease the giant and unexpected agony.

The third man cautiously kept his distance, not quite sure how to attack. Yeung Lee took a quick step towards him. Instinctively, the man backed away – and aimed a kick at Lee's groin. Lee dodged the boot, gripped his opponent's foot, turned it sharply to the left, then the right – and pulled with all his strength. The man lost his balance and fell forward. As he fell, Yeung Lee brought a knee up into his face. Jamie heard the man's nose crack like a dry twig breaking. He dropped on to the cobbles and lay there.

Yeung Lee turned to Jamie. 'They attacked you?'

'Yes.'

'Why? What had you done to them?'

Blood was dripping from Jamie's nose down the lapels of his only suit. He dabbed at the stains with his handkerchief.

'They wanted money. Said they'd break up the shop if I didn't give it to them. I got them out here. Nearly trapped the leader in the privy, but he was too quick.'

'For you, maybe,' Yeung Lee agreed. 'But fortunately not for me.'

He walked over to the big man and looked down at him contemptuously.

'Get up!' he ordered. The man shook his head weakly. Yeung Lee jabbed him in the groin with his slippered foot. The man cried out in agony, crawled to his feet, his left arm swinging uselessly in his sleeve.

58

'I could go to your policemen,' Yeung Lee told him quietly, 'but that would take time, and for fat fees lawyers would speak and nothing much would happen to you. But maybe you red-bristled barbarians have learned a lesson. If not, call again – when I am at home. I am willing to continue your instruction.'

He moved across to the far wall, slipped the bolt on the wooden door, opened it. The three men crawled out on to the grey cinders outside. Yeung Lee bolted the door, turned to Jamie.

'Come inside. Wash your face. I think the damage probably looks worse than it is.'

'But not worse than it feels.'

Yeung Lee filled the zinc basin in the back room with cold water. Jamie ducked his face in it. Above his head, the caged birds fluttered uneasily on their perches.

'Hello! Hello! How are you today?' the parrot asked him.

'Not too bright,' Jamie admitted.

Yeung Lee felt his nose. 'At least it's not broken,' he said. 'I have some cream to rub on it which will take away the pain. Now, what made you think you could tackle three men, all bigger and older and much stronger than you?'

'I didn't think about it. I wanted to protect your shop. It was no more than that. I don't like bullies – or thieves.'

'Nor do I. So let us have a drink to celebrate victory. Special rice wine from Shanghai. Not something you see every day in Hyde, eh? Sarsaparilla or dandelion and burdock is more like it here. But I bought a bottle in Liverpool today from a sailor off a ship. It will steady you.'

Yeung Lee poured out two glasses of straw-coloured fluid, handed one to Jamie. He drank thankfully; liquid fire immediately raced through his blood.

'They could have killed you,' Yeung Lee said.

'But they didn't. You stopped them.'

'If I had not been there, it might have been a different story.

You must be quick on your feet, or they would have landed more blows. It may be that they will return, though I doubt it. But in case they do, I will show you how to protect yourself. I will teach you the ancient arts of China which enable one man to face a dozen – whether they attack from the front or from behind him – and overcome them all, without injury to himself.'

'That's not possible,' said Jamie.

'But it is. You saw me deal with three opponents in a single minute. I did not pit my strength against theirs. That would have been futile, one against three – and big heavy barbarians at that. Instead, I borrowed *their* strength, *their* weight and used that to topple them.

'For example, a bully tries to kick you – as that man aimed a kick at me. Instead of just jumping out of the way, you go towards the man, grip his foot, as I did, twist it with all your strength to the left. He will tense his muscles to fight this, so you let him help you when you reverse your force and twist to the right, crack the joints – and pull. So. His own weight brings him down.

'Another bigger man swings a blow at you. If that blow lands, you could be dead. But you do not let it land, so you live. You duck beneath it, grasp his wrist and toss him over your shoulder. You have used *your* shoulder as a fulcrum for *his* arm, which is a lever to defeat him. He overbalances. You could not lift one of his feet off the ground, he is so heavy. But by this means you do not have to. He lifts himself. So you win – because you use your brain. Attackers use their brawn, rarely thinking how easily it can be turned against them.

'Remember the words of Sun Tzu, who wrote the earliest book ever known on the art of war, and one which has lessons for everyone: "When torrential water tosses boulders, it is because of its momentum. The momentum of one skilled in war is overwhelming, because his attack is precisely regulated. His timing is the release of the trigger." '

'You make it all sound very easy.'

'That which is well taught and well practised should always appear simple to the beholder.'

'But how can I learn this?' asked Jamie.

'I will teach you every day. The disciple will soon become as skilled as his tutor. And then you need never feel you are on your own. Your hands and your feet will be your protection – and those who seek to attack you, your bodyguard.'

So, morning after morning, when Jamie arrived in the shop, Yeung Lee took him out into the back yard, and for half an hour each day demonstrated the principles of Chinese martial arts. As the lessons became more complex, he would carry out an old mattress and put this down on the cobbles to break Jamie's fall – or his own when Jamie progressed sufficiently to practise his skills on him.

After several months, Yeung Lee pronounced himself satisfied that Jamie had at least mastered what he called the rudiments of his skills. But Jamie lacked confidence in himself and in his abilities. It all seemed so easy, so logical when he followed Yeung Lee's teaching, but would his technique work in an emergency when he was faced by an eighteen-stone angry man? Until he had proved it would, he remained doubtful. In the meantime, he did not tell anyone about his lessons; he was afraid they would laugh at him.

His chance to put into practice what he had learnt came unexpectedly one Saturday night in the Silent Witness. Uncle Don rang a hand bell five minutes before closing time and called: 'Time, gentlemen, please. Drink up, please.'

Usually, drinkers would finish their pints or half-pints of beer or stout or porter, and then, with mutual expressions of goodwill, shuffle out into the street.

On this occasion, however, two strangers refused to go. They banged their tankards on the counter. The men were fairground workers. They travelled from town to town, never staying long anywhere. The fair arrived every summer in Hyde

61

for 'Wakes Week', the one week in August when all mills in the area shut down by agreement and declared an unpaid holiday for the workpeople.

'Fill 'em up, landlord,' one ordered roughly.

'No. Sorry. Against the law,' Uncle Don replied.

'Bugger the law!' the man retorted. 'Fill 'em up or I'll smash your face in.'

Others in the bar, regulars, nervous of becoming involved in a brawl, began to sidle away. The reputation of the fairground people was fearsome. They liked a rough house because they believed they were tougher than any other opponent. If they fought, they fought dirty – with boots, knees, knives.

'Now, now, gentlemen,' said Uncle Don soothingly. 'I don't make the laws, but we all have to obey them.'

'Bollocks!' retorted the taller of the two. He had been drinking more heavily than his companion. Beer had slopped down his greasy serge waistcoat.

'If you want me to go, put me out, then.'

'That's stupid talk,' said Uncle Don. 'You know the rules.'

'I make my own rules, mister,' the man retorted, and threw his empty pewter tankard into Uncle Don's face.

'Fill it up!'

The tankard caught Uncle Don on the cheek. Its hard metal edge drew blood. He staggered, lost his balance on the beer-sodden sawdust that covered the floor, slipped and fell. The gypsy brought back his boot to kick him.

Afterwards, no one seemed quite clear what happened next. Some said they remembered seeing Jamie Baird take a step forward. Others recalled that he had been wiping a glass with a towel, and they distinctly saw him toss the towel over his shoulder. The next moment the man followed the towel. He sailed through the air, his arms and legs waving uselessly. He landed on the floor on his head, rolled over and lay still. Two elderly regulars stared in disbelief at this sudden reversal of fortune.

Jamie turned to the other gypsy. 'You going out on your legs or on your back?' he asked him.

'I'm just drinking up,' replied the man quickly, chin thrust out. 'I won't give you no trouble.'

Jamie called to the two regulars. 'Give me a hand with this.'

They picked up the unconscious man, carried him through the swing doors and threw him out on the pavement.

'He was that heavy, it was all the three of us could do to pick him up,' one of them said to Jamie in amazement. 'Yet he went over your shoulder like a bullet from a gun. What did you do to him?'

'Nothing,' Jamie replied with a grin. 'I simply stopped him from doing something to us.'

FOUR
First Steps

Arabella had left school at fourteen, along with almost all her contemporaries at the village school in Burrelton, outside Perth. Fourteen was the leaving age in Scotland; in England, schooling could end a year earlier, so she counted herself fortunate in having had the extra year.

A few pupils went on to a secondary school, and one was actually clever enough, or her parents rich enough, or both, to go on to Edinburgh University to train as a doctor. The overwhelming majority of boys and girls, however, went out to work to help with family finances. Further training for a trade or a profession meant that for years they would be unable to make any real contribution to the upkeep of the home.

Boys usually worked on farms or were apprenticed to carpenters or housepainters. Most of the girls went into domestic service. Their mothers would write – or if they could not write well enough themselves would persuade a neighbour to write a letter for them – to the lady of the nearest large house. If she had a vacancy for a maid, an appointment would be made. The girl, washed, scrubbed, wearing her neatest dress, boots well cleaned, hair severely brushed until it glowed, would be taken to meet her. If she impressed the lady of the house as a potential maid, and her housekeeper agreed, she would be taken on to learn the trade of a maidservant.

There was a lot to learn: how to clean brass, silver, copper; how to carry ewers of hot water to the bedrooms every morning without spilling a drop on stair carpets; how to lay a fire and black-lead a grate. Although Arabella was only in service for a few months, what she learned, she never forgot. And when she came to hire servants herself, she made sure that they all lived up to the high standards she had been taught.

Arabella was sorry to leave school because, in her last year, she found she had a gift which none of the other boys and girls of her age seemed to possess to anything like the same extent. None could approach her when it came to dealing with figures. She did not realise that this was at all unusual in a young girl – until she saw classmates poring over sums she could work out in her head. Addition, subtraction, division, even long division; none held any terrors for her. She would sit with the slate on her desk, chalk poised in hand, biting her lower lip in concentration while the dominie, Miss Pringle, set some mathematical problem. Often, Arabella would have scratched the answer to the sum before others in the class had quite understood what the question was about.

This gift stayed with her all her life. When she became involved in negotiations which grew increasingly complex, and others would need calculators or at least had to scribble figures on their notepads, her mind instantly gave her the answer.

Because she had left school so early, and because, except for this gift of simple mathematics, her knowledge seemed so slight, she liked in later life to surround herself with highly qualified people. She saw no reason to engage anyone who had only a second- or third-class degree. The best was barely good enough for her. Arabella wanted only first-class brains. By a process of osmosis, or just close association, she felt she could learn from them without appearing to learn, and without ever admitting her own lack of education, about which she always remained sensitive.

For three months after the death of her father, Arabella helped her uncle and aunt in the Silent Witness. At first, she washed and dried glasses, then set them out attractively on their shelves. She polished pewter tankards for the regulars, and hung them from hooks on the wall behind the bar. But gradually she found a use for her skill with figures, especially on Saturday nights.

Friday was payday, so Saturday was the busiest night of the week. Mill hands, pit workers, all kinds of men who could not afford to spend any other evening in the pub would come in, sometimes on their own, sometimes with a group. They would order a number of different drinks – and then change their minds. Some would query the cost as a matter of pride; not because they really thought they were being overcharged by a ha'penny or a penny, but just to show who was boss.

With only two people serving behind the bar and perhaps thirty clamouring to be served, it was sometimes difficult to remember who had given a florin, who a shilling, and for what drinks. But Arabella remembered. She memorised the cost of every drink in the bar, and when a mixture was ordered, such as one gin and water, two port and lemon, two halves of porter and a gill of old-and-mild, she calculated the cost mentally as she served them. And even when customers challenged her totals, they never found her a penny out.

But although she was accurate when it came to adding up items on a bill, and took pride in this ability, she did not like her job.

Regularly on Sunday afternoons, after the last lunchtime clients had gone, Arabella would also leave the Silent Witness and take a long walk to clear from her lungs the heavy, stale smell of beer and smoke and the cottonseed oil used for frying chips.

She would go down the road by the side of the mill, past stables where the horses were kept to pull the mill carts, past huge sheds for steam tractors that could each tow two or three trailers full of cotton bales. She liked to stroke the horses. She also liked the smell of the big Foden and Aveling Porter steam engines. Their drivers kept fires burning beneath the boilers throughout each weekend so that, early on Monday morning, they would need only perhaps half an hour with the trap doors fully opened to have sufficient head of steam to start. Arabella found something friendly about the horses, and also, perhaps perversely, about the engines. All were solid and heavy and comfortable; homely, was how she would describe them. And from someone who felt acutely the fact that she had no proper home, this was praise indeed.

The road led down to a canal which ran behind the backs of the terraced houses. Here, men and boys would sit for hours on stools or boxes, fishing rods in their hands, jam jars of worms for bait by their feet. Arabella had never seen any fish larger than a tiddler in the water, which was much polluted by discharges from the mills. The dyeing sheds would void unwanted dyes, and vivid streams of blue, red, green, white would suddenly colour a patch of water, and then fade away on the slowly moving current.

On weekdays, carthorses would tow barges along the tow-path. On Sundays, it became a local promenade where people in their best clothes would walk slowly for about a mile in each direction, taking the air, savouring a brief respite from the noise and drudgery of the mills or, in Arabella's case, the inn.

On this particular Sunday Arabella felt more than usually dejected. She remembered a picture in a book her father had once given her, showing the customs of many lands. One illustration stayed in her mind vividly – a bullring in Spain. The horses of the picadors, who goaded the fighting bull until the star matador could dispatch the animal, wore such heavy rugs that the audience never knew whether the bull had gored them or not. Outwardly, the horses stayed smartly apparelled, perfectly groomed, but beneath the drapes they could be bleeding to death from unseen and mortal wounds.

There's a moral here, she thought. Whatever I feel like inside, however lonely or insecure, no one else must ever know. For the first time since the death of her father, Arabella had come to terms with herself. Now she must come to terms with her future.

It was easy enough to decide this, but the obstacles seemed daunting. They still owed Mr Snakesby money, which would have to be paid somehow. She lacked any training, any qualifications whatever, so how could she ever earn enough to pay him? The classic way to wealth would be to marry a rich man, but she would never meet anyone of means in a run-down public house. And, even if she did, she did not wish to marry yet. She wanted to achieve her aims on her own, to be beholden to no one else.

Arabella remembered the Baird motto 'The Lord Made', and her father's assurance that one day she and her brother would see a sign to the way ahead. She did not know when or why or where or how this would happen, but she believed that it would. She *must* recognise it, not let it pass her by, for it might never come again.

She saw this sign quite unexpectedly one Monday evening in the private bar. Trade was always slack on Mondays and the private bar was usually empty. This was a small room, less than a quarter the size of the public bar. The drinks were more expensive here than those in the public bar, but the extra ha'pennies bought a quieter atmosphere.

No darts were played here, and no shove-ha'penny boards were allowed. The private bar had class. Its walls were papered in maroon flock. The fireplace surround was not black-leaded but of highly polished brass. A pile of neatly sawn logs lay near it, with small lumps of coal in a shining copper bucket. There were four round tables in the bar. On this particular evening, three were empty.

At the fourth table sat a man of late middle age wearing a black coat, his hat and gloves on a chair beside him. Arabella recognised Mr Beaumont, agent for Lord Rosael, who owned about a third of the town, including the brewery with sixty public houses, of which the Silent Witness was one, and fifty thousand acres of land. Jephthah Beaumont kept the books, ensured that tenants in houses, shops and farms paid their rent on time, supervised the cost of repairs and breakages.

Spread out on the table in front of Mr Beaumont, next to his glass of whisky and water, were a number of papers and an open ledger. His mouth was pursed as he totted up figures on a pad. Arabella could see his lips move slightly as he counted.

'Just thought I'd see if the fire's all right, sir,' she said respectfully when he had jotted down the total.

He looked up at her, and smiled kindly. 'Very good, my child.' He took a sip of whisky, looked up at her, glad of the excuse to stop working. 'You're the landlord's niece, I suppose? Arabella Baird?'

'I am, sir.'

'I remember reading in the paper about that very sad business with your father. An extraordinary judgment the court came out with, I thought. But then they've been doing that for hundreds of years. The law is an ass, according to Queen Victoria. Lawyers say it's open to all – like the Ritz Hotel. But I say, keep away from it.'

'After that experience, sir, I'm not likely to wish to get close again.'

'Good for you. You work here all the time?'

'Yes, sir. But I don't want to work here all the time, sir,' she went on. 'Not *all* my life.'

'What do you want to do, then? A pretty girl like you will get married. It's different for men. We're lucky to get a job – any job, often – and we keep at that all the time till we die. Or if we're very lucky, we may be pensioned off.' He wiped his hand across his mouth. 'Which I think will come to me soon.'

'Oh no, sir. You're not old.'

'I am when it comes to these sums,' he said. 'I used to be able to race through them like a rabbit through a wood. But now the figures seem to jump about on the page. Extraordinary. I've known this happen to clerks, and given them the rough edge of my tongue in my time. I thought they were putting it on. Now I know they weren't, poor devils, for it's happening to me.'

'Could I help you, sir?' Arabella asked tentatively.

Beaumont turned one of the sheets towards her with a condescending smile, amused by her earnest offer of help. His amusement changed to surprise when she didn't push the sheet back to him in embarrassed confusion.

Arabella frowned as she went through the figures. Lord Rosael's estate was borrowing money from a bank at seven per cent interest to build cottages for farm workers on which the estimated yield would be four per cent. A loss, surely, of £3 for every £100?

'Well, sir,' she said when she had read the paper, 'you're spending seventy pounds a year, and only making forty, a very poor situation. But if you can only make four per cent from the tenants, on your figures you can't really do anything else.'

'Precisely. So you cannot help me, eh?'

'Can I ask a question, sir, before I give you my answer?'

'Anything you like, girl.'

'How many rotations of crops will be in use on the farm or farms to which these figures refer?'

'You know about crop rotation?' Beaumont asked. What an extraordinary barmaid, he thought.

'Only what I've heard people say in the bar.'

70

'I see. Well, we'll do four or five. Say four.'

'That would mean you would possibly start with turnips, then barley, then peas and wheat?'

'What of that? It's pretty routine.'

'Of course, sir. But if you persuaded the farmers to have six crops – turnips, barley as before, then two years hay, peas and then wheat, you should make more profit.'

'Well, that's possible, I agree. It's possible.'

'And I would not accept four per cent on the return of the capital to build the cottages, sir. I would accept three per cent. But tie this return into the profits the farmers are likely to make.'

'How, exactly?' Beaumont looked up at her with new respect. He had forgotten he was in the bar of an inn talking to the maid.

'By giving them a share, sir. A small share would instil in them the feeling they were working not just for his lordship but also for themselves. They would then work much harder – and make more money for themselves and, of course, for their landlord.'

'I don't know about that,' said Beaumont slowly. 'But you've certainly given me food for thought. Where did you go to school?'

'The village school, sir. In Scotland.'

'They taught you well.'

'I like figures.'

'So I see. Well . . .' Beaumont looked down at the papers again thoughtfully, smoothed them with his hands, then looked at Arabella. 'I'm on my own in Lord Rosael's Estate Office,' he said at last. 'There's a lot of figure work to do. I'll have a word with your uncle. Perhaps you could be spared from here to help me from time to time?'

'I'd be very pleased to help you, sir.'

'It might even become more permanent. All depends on

how it works out. You'd be paid a maid's wage, ten shillings a week, and your keep. What do you get here?'

'Half that, sir.'

'Well, then, you would make a one hundred per cent improvement in your salary. Maybe you could go on to even better things. There are very few people who understand figures, in my experience, and almost no women. What do you say, girl?'

'I say yes, sir,' replied Arabella fervently.

The fairground booths and swings filled a field rented for the week on the outskirts of Hyde. The weather had been poor for several days beforehand, and a constant traffic of horses' hooves and caravan wheels and hundreds of visitors had pounded the grass into a muddy swamp. This did not deter crowds of people of all ages arriving, determined to enjoy themselves.

After dark, the field, which was relatively quiet during the day, exploded into noisy, colourful life. Tents and booths that appeared tawdry in daylight now took on a magical appearance. They became brightly lit pavilions, entrances surrounded with coloured lights, or caves of mystery where Madame Romany would tell fortunes, or the bearded lady outstare those who paid a penny to examine and comment on her deformity.

In the background, the brassy bellow of a huge steam organ drowned the cries of vendors of candy floss and toffee apples. The fair provided a brief and colourful escape from the dull drabness of working lives. For the rest of the year, a treat might be a pennyworth of chips with salt and vinegar, eaten out of a newspaper, or a meat tea with tripe and onions. But the fair came from far away and so brought with it an exciting sense of strangeness; why, some of the sideshows were run by foreigners, Frenchmen and Italians. And once there was even a German band, all in uniform, smart as Guardsmen.

Tonight, the biggest crowd gathered outside the largest tent in the field. Over the entrance, where a man was busily collecting three pennies each from people who filed through it, four words were spelled out in flickering, coloured electric bulbs: The Human Cannon Ball.

Inside the tent, which was long and narrow for its size, a net had been erected at the far end. The onlookers sat on benches or stood at the other end of the tent around a strong wooden structure about eight feet high. This provided the base for a highly polished brass cannon with a gigantic barrel, three feet wide. The cannon was decorated with polished metal castings showing heads of lions, tigers, dragons.

A stocky man, broad-shouldered, wearing a leopardskin leotard and a red silk turban like an Indian prince, stood grim-faced, arms folded, by the side of the cannon. When the last person had been squeezed into the tent, the man who had been taking the money climbed up on to the platform to address the crowd.

'Gentlemen all!' he cried, 'I give you the Flying Bombardier! He has served with the Colours for fifteen years in India, the Cape and the Far East. Now, the Bombardier who has discharged so many shells at Her Majesty's enemies in so many far battles, takes on the role of cannon ball himself in a feat that defies danger and a terrible death.

'I will fire the Bombardier as a human cannon ball across this tent into the net. Those who have weak hearing should cover their ears with their hands the moment I apply this taper to the charge.'

He held up a long wax taper, lit it with a flourish.

'You are about to see a phenomenon that has puzzled the greatest scientists of the age. A man will fly through the air like a bird – or a cannon ball – and land safely at his target.'

He turned to the man in the leotard.

'Are you ready to take the risk, Bombardier?' he asked him solicitously. The Bombardier nodded. Amid a storm of clapping, he put a wood block under the cannon's mouth, stood on it, and swung himself into the barrel, with only his head and shoulders protruding.

Jamie watched him closely. He appeared perfectly composed, calm. His colleague applied the taper to a small hole to the rear of the cannon. The thunder of the explosion blew out the walls of the tent like a ship's sails in a Force 10 gale. The Bombardier hurtled through the air, hit the net with his head, dropped lightly to his feet on the ground. He saluted the crowd, took off his turban, and bowed.

Everyone cheered and clapped and stamped their feet. Then they filed out into the warm darkness, and the Bombardier's colleague took up his position again outside.

Jamie walked on and joined another crowd outside a slightly smaller tent.

Here, a man in shirtsleeves was charging sixpence to see what he kept repeating was 'the chance to win a month's wages in five minutes'. Sixty or seventy young men, smoking pipes and cigarettes, stood around a boxing ring set up inside on a wooden platform six feet off the ground. Struts supporting the platform were concealed by Union Jack flags and the flags of British Empire colonies, with huge likenesses of the Queen.

To one side of the ring was a booth, its entrance plastered with framed photogravure likenesses of famous pugilists of the past: Mendoza, Gentleman Jackson, John L. Sullivan. Huge naphtha lights with polished metal reflectors cast a shadowless blaze on the sawdust boards of the ring. Beyond them, night moths fluttered nervous wings on the edge of darkness.

A plump, overweight man, his moustaches waxed and twirled to needle-sharp points, stepped importantly from the booth. He wore a seedy dinner jacket and trousers, a shabby shirt, an overfingered ready-made bow tie. Under the brilliant lights, his lapels glowed green with age.

At his appearance, spectators close to the ropes began to jeer and clapped their hands slowly and stamped their feet, as audiences liked to hiss the villain in a pantomime or melodrama. The man did not attempt to stop them, but stood, nodding his head and smiling as though in approval. He liked to see the punters happy. After a few moments, he raised both hands above his head in an appeal for silence.

'Sportsmen all!' he cried, his voice hoarse from tobacco, slurred by drink. 'I offer you Maxie Monrova, the Mexican Typhoon, the undefeated champion of South America, who has fought in nearly every country in the world, *and* before the crowned heads of Europe.

'Now, by special request, and at enormous expense, I, as his manager, have persuaded him to appear before you tonight to fight for a purse with any man here who is brave enough to challenge him. Who will he be?'

He paused, his face glistening with sweat. His eyes, sharp and hard as polished beads, and just as small, flickered hopefully over the faces of the spectators, silent now and pale under the glaring lights, as he searched for a likely challenger.

'Is it you, sir?' he asked a middle-aged man, who shook his head sheepishly.

'Or you, sir?'

A thin, weedy youth at the back of the crowd shouted back: 'Not on your nelly!'

'What's in it if we do?' asked another man.

'I will tell you, sir. A purse of five golden sovereigns. That is the prize. And here it is.'

He took five coins from his back pocket and slowly dropped them, one after the other from his left hand to his right. The sovereigns had been specially polished and glittered with feverish brightness in the harsh light.

'The man who can survive one five-minute round with the Mexican Typhoon – only one, mark you, not two, not three, only one – is the winner and will be the richer by these five gold sovereigns. Now, gentlemen, sportsmen all, I give you Maxie Monrova, the Mexican Typhoon. And who will challenge him? Who will collect five gold sovereigns for five minutes of his time? A pound a minute, gentlemen, a pound a minute.'

The canvas flaps of the booth parted. A very large man, wearing leopardskin shorts, laced-up boxing boots and black leather boxing gloves came into the ring and bowed stiffly to left and right. He was just beginning to run to fat. Tattooed serpents writhed on his forearms. Across his back was a two-headed eagle, and on his chest the red and blue face of a tiger, teeth bared, mouth wide open. The man's hair was cropped so short it resembled a dusting of steel filings on his head. His moustache sprouted with a curiously unexpected luxuriance. The Mexican Typhoon punched one fist into his other palm and looked expectantly around the crowd.

'Come on, gentlemen, I say,' called the manager. 'Who is for five pounds – a fortune, a month's wages – for five minutes' sport?'

There was an uneasy stirring in the crowd. No one wanted to volunteer. The Mexican Typhoon was clearly a tough customer, a seasoned fighter. His livelihood depended on his skill; he was not likely to be an easy opponent – or a fair fighter.

Then, from the back of the crowd, a man called out, 'I'm for a fight! Gangway!'

Obediently, the crowd parted and everyone started to clap. A tall man in a cloth cap and wearing a dark, high-buttoned suit stepped briskly towards the ring.

'I'll challenge him,' he said.

'And who are you, sir? What name do you fight under?'

'My own. George Evans of Hyde.'

'What is your trade, sir?'

'I'm a blacksmith at Johnson Brothers.'

This was one of the largest cotton mills in the district; everyone had heard of Johnson Brothers. As Evans spoke, he took off his cap, peeled off his jacket and his shirt, handed them over to a spectator.

'Your boots, sir,' said the manager. 'You cannot fight in those boots.'

'Then I'll fight in my stockinged feet,' said Evans dourly. 'I have no other shoes.'

'Here are your gloves.'

A boy came out of the tent holding two boxing gloves. Evans looked at them, pushed his hands into them. The manager laced them up. The boy handed him a small alarm clock with a brass bell.

'When I strike the bell,' the manager explained, 'the round begins. When I strike it again, the fight is over. Either party out for the count of ten – for *whatever* reason – means the other is the winner. No appeals. No argument. Is that clear? Right, then. To your corners, gentlemen.'

The two boxers moved to opposite corners of the ring. The Mexican Typhoon rubbed the soles of his boots on the boards, as much to show his professionalism and to alarm his opponent with this evidence of expertise, as for any other reason. He fought six or eight fights every night, more on Saturdays; he knew the wisdom of unsettling every challenger before the fight began.

The blacksmith stood, arms loosely by his side, watching him. Strong muscles rippled in his forearms and on his back, but his pale body seemed strangely vulnerable under the hissing shadowless lights.

The manager struck the bell, and the boxers advanced

77

slowly towards each other, briefly touched their gloves in the approved fashion to show that this was a contest undertaken by sportsmen. As they parted, Monrova aimed a tremendous right at Evans's head. The blacksmith sidestepped neatly and the blow went uselessly over his shoulder. Then he hit Monrova hard with his right fist, just under his heart.

Jamie could see a spasm of shock and pain, almost disbelief, pass over Monrova's face. He suddenly seemed older; a tiring man who for a bare living had to fight a continual stream of new, younger opponents, each one desperate to win a month's wages by knocking him out.

Every week there would be a new venue and new challengers, while he grew older and increasingly had to rely on the wiles of experience, the quick jab below the belt away from the crowd, the right elbow in an eye, sometimes with gloves dusted with pepper to blind an unsophisticated opponent. The challengers might be fighting for the fun of it, in the hope that they could win the prize money; the Mexican Typhoon was fighting for simple survival.

For the first time in his life, Jamie sensed the terror that growing old could hold for people who had no trade, no savings, who had to rely on their physical strength. It was a disturbing realisation, and he became determined never to join their number. He would use his brains as well as his strength while he was young.

Monrova danced around the ring with astonishing agility for so heavy a man, but his face was already varnished with sweat. His bare flesh shone under the lights. Evans was deliberately allowing Monrova to tire himself, and then, suddenly, he attacked. Instead of retreating, tucking in his elbows to protect himself from Monrova's jabs, he began to fight back solidly. His arms slogged like tireless pistons, powered by muscles hardened through years of hammering white-hot metal on an anvil.

He was in charge now, letting the crowd scent victory with all that this meant, not only for him but, more important in their view, for them. They were all up there with him in spirit, cheering the amateur about to pound the professional into the boards; their own man hammering the life out of a stranger. Evans's victory would be theirs.

With each vicious blow, Monrova swayed. Soon he was obviously in pain, gasping for breath. Beads of sweat sprayed like tears from his face as Evans punched him relentlessly and often. Then, suddenly, the Mexican Typhoon went down on one knee, sobbing for air. He felt a great pain swell in his chest, as though he had somehow swallowed a balloon that was now filling with air, choking him.

The cheering became deafening. He must get up, he must not give way. Wearily and unwisely he stood up to fight on. His mind was dazed, his eyes out of focus, his body one enormous bruise, his adversary merely a vague shape always just out of his reach. The older man's reactions became reflex; a duck here, a feint there, an uppercut, a quick right hook. But somehow his blows did not always connect, and when they did, they lacked force.

Evans danced tantalisingly away from his outstretched arms, then hit him twice, once in the chest as the Typhoon lurched forward, arms sagging, and then on his jaw. Monrova dropped on to the boards and lay still, eyes closed. Saliva trickled out of his open mouth into the sawdust.

His manager stared at him in amazement, horrified, unable to believe that he could have been knocked out. This had happened only once before while they had been together. Now both their earnings could be endangered, both their livelihoods put at risk.

Evans walked across the ring and peered closely at his opponent.

'He's out!' he shouted triumphantly, as though this fact

had been in dispute. 'Now, where's your money?'

The manager pressed his bell and snapped his fingers as though the matter was of no concern to him. The boy came out of the tent carrying a small canvas purse. The manager held it up so that all could see it, and then deliberately dropped in the five gold coins, shaking the bag so that the coins jingled attractively. He handed the bag to Evans. The crowd began to clap, but spasmodically. They would have liked the fight to have been longer, to see more blood spilled. The manager turned to the boy.

'Get Rob over here,' he told him in an urgent whisper.

'I'll be back tomorrow night for a return fight!' Evans shouted threateningly.

The manager said nothing, but lifted the rope so that he could leave the ring. As the crowd drifted away, the manager knelt down by his boxer's side.

'You all right?' he asked him.

Monrova moaned, moved slowly, threshing his arms about feebly like a swimmer against a strong current. He shook his head to try to clear his brain.

'I'm done,' he said hoarsely. 'I'm seeing double. I've got gut's ache like I've never had before. I'm buggered.'

'You'll be all right in ten minutes,' the manager assured him hopefully. 'We've five more shows tonight. That was a full house. I was actually turning them away.'

'No,' said Monrova wearily. 'I can't fight again tonight. I'm done, all in.'

He stood up groggily, almost fell. Then, holding the top rope, he began to move shakily and unsteadily towards the booth.

The boxer might or might not be fit by tomorrow, but it was obvious to Jamie that he could not face another challenger tonight with any hope of victory. This could be the sign about which Jamie's father had spoken. He made up his mind, climbed up into the ring, and walked purposefully across the boards towards the booth.

An oil lamp burned on a wooden trunk. The boxer sat on a cane chair, shoulders hunched, his head in his hands. A bottle of brown ale and a glass stood on an upturned box by his side. The manager was lighting a cigarette; Jamie noticed that his hand trembled. Then he saw Jamie.

'Who the hell are you?' he asked belligerently. 'Get out of here. It's bloody private.'

'Your man won't fight again tonight,' Jamie told him flatly.

'Who says he won't, eh?'

'I do. So do you – if you're honest. In his condition, he couldn't last a minute. He could even be killed. I'm here to make you a proposition. For a fee, I'll take his place.'

'*You?* Those buggers out there could eat you for breakfast, son.'

'At boxing, maybe. But not at all-in fighting.'

The manager's eyes narrowed. He blew out the match; the flame was singeing his fingers. 'What d'you mean, exactly?' This kid might just be worth listening to.

'What I say. I'll take on any challenger, with no holds barred for either of us. No Queensberry Rules, no fouls or fair fighting. Just a scrap, a dog fight, if you like. That would be something new for people to see.'

'You mean you'll kick the challengers in the balls?'

'No. But they will probably try to kick me there, which should appeal to the crowd even more. Except I'll have them on their backs before they can put the boot in.'

'You've got a bloody hope, haven't you? There are some rough folk out there. That blacksmith was only one of them. There are plenty more where he comes from. Navvies, smiths, hod-carriers, using their muscles all day. Maxie here's been boxing since he was a kid and even he got felled. You wouldn't stand a chance.'

'Try me.'

'You could get killed,' said the manager, not as though he cared, simply stating a fact.

Just then the young boy came in through a side flap in the tent.

'Did you get Rob?' the manager asked him.

'Yes. He says he'll fill in for Maxie's next fight. But only for that, no more.'

'Bring him in then. We've got another fight in ten minutes.'

The big man Jamie had thrown in the bar of the Silent Witness came into the tent. He recognised Jamie instantly, and his eyes narrowed.

'What d'you want here, you bastard?' he asked him.

'Maybe the chance to teach you some manners,' retorted Jamie.

'You know each other?' the manager asked, surprised.

'We had a barney in a bar,' the big man admitted grudgingly.

'And I won,' said Jamie.

'That so?' asked the manager.

Rob nodded reluctantly. 'He knows some sort of foreign tricks. Didn't fight fair.'

'Rubbish. You were about to kick my uncle who was down on the floor. I stopped you.'

'How?' the manager asked Jamie.

'I threw him over my shoulder.'

'Did you now? Over your shoulder? Is that a fact?' he asked Rob, obviously impressed.

'Sort of, yes.'

'You must be tougher than you look, son. Rob weighs in at sixteen stone. Right. I'll give you a trial. But if you lose, you're out. What d'you want in money?'

'What's the boxer getting?'

'We split.'

'Equally?'

'No. I've got all the overheads to meet, remember. He gets ten per cent of what we take after that. In his hand.'

82

'Not the most generous division, but at least you know each other. You don't know me – and I don't know you. You could be paying me ten per cent of nothing. I'll do you five bouts a night, at one pound a fight. In advance before each fight. Win or lose.'

'A bloody hard deal,' said the manager.

'You got a better one?' Jamie asked him quietly.

'Make it three.'

'I said five. If you're not interested, I'll leave. But remember, you've just lost a fiver on the Mexican. You'll lose much more if you don't have a fighter to put in the ring.' Jamie turned towards the door.

'Don't be so bloody spiky, son,' said the manager in the sharp tone of one whose bluff has been called. 'All right, make it five. Just for tonight. You're a greedy young bastard.'

'Young, but not greedy,' said Jamie. 'Nor a bastard. And I'll trouble you to keep a civil tongue in your head. We're in business together now, remember.'

'Will you be wanting me, then?' asked Rob.

The manager shook his head. 'No,' he said. 'Not unless this kid is all piss and wind and can't deliver.'

Rob nodded, went out of the tent. The manager crossed to a black metal cash box chained to the main pole, unlocked it, took out a £1 note, relocked the box.

'I'll pay you this later.'

'No. Now,' Jamie told him.

The manager frowned, spat on the note, handed it over reluctantly. 'What are you going to wear to fight?'

'Any clothes you can give me.'

'I've none. Maxie's shorts won't fit you.'

'Then I'll have to fight in my vest and trousers and socks. If we go on after tonight, you can fix me up with something.'

'If. What name you fighting under?'

'None. Mr Nemo. The unknown. Just say I'll take on

83

anyone. But at their own risk. People could get hurt if I throw them out of the ring. So make that point in your spiel. You don't want any trouble if they break arms or legs. And it adds to the attraction for the crowds. They only come in the hope of seeing some damage done.'

'You've got it all thought out, haven't you?'

'Not all,' Jamie admitted. 'But I'm working on it.'

He stripped off his jacket and shirt, removed his shoes, wrapped his necktie round his waist to hold up his trousers.

'Ready when you are,' he said, and followed the manager out into the ring.

Jamie fought five challengers that night and beat them all. By the third bout, he felt confident enough to indulge in some play-acting. He realised that it would be unwise to dismiss each challenger too quickly. That made the fight look easy, and the crowd had paid to see a struggle, not just an immediate victory. In a five-minute round, Jamie reckoned he could afford to give them three minutes of action, and then put his man down in the fourth.

The fairground closed at eleven o'clock; one by one the lights in the booths dimmed and went out, the merry-go-rounds stopped turning. It was time to go.

The manager was having a beer in his tent with another man when Jamie came in to put on his clothes.

'You did all right,' said the manager grudgingly. 'I must say, I wouldn't like to come up against you on a dark night.'

The other man nodded. There seemed something vaguely familiar about his build.

'Meet my old friend, Bombardier Jackson,' said the manager, introducing them.

'I saw your show tonight. The Human Cannon Ball,' Jamie told him. 'First class.'

'Glad you liked it. I saw yours, too. You're pretty nifty on your feet. Could you teach me those tricks?'

'In time. If you could teach me how to be fired from a cannon!'

'It's very simple,' said the Bombardier modestly. 'And the turban protects my head when I hit the net.'

'But how are you certain you *will* hit the net, and not go above or beyond it, or fall short and land on your head on the ground?'

'A matter of science. First of all, my manager weighed me against a sack of sand. Then he shot the sack out from the gun with different strengths of explosive charge behind it. When he got exactly the right one, we knew we had an act. Science is what counts. Like you, throwing people over your shoulder, using their strength against themselves.'

'Enough of this back-scratching,' said the Mexican Typhoon's manager sourly.

'How's Monrova doing?' Jamie asked him.

'Not very good. In fact, I'd say he's right poorly. This is only the second defeat he's ever had. The first was only last week in Ashton-under-Lyne. Two so close together is very bad news. He knows that, and so do I. Once the customers suspect he's not unbeatable, he's through. I reckon he's punch drunk, poor sod. He's getting old and relies on his size and his weight, but his reactions are slow now, and that bugger Evans tired him. I limit his fights to five minutes to try and give him some help. But, even so . . .'

The manager shrugged as though he had already written off the Mexican Typhoon.

'How long are you here for?' Jamie asked him.

'All week.'

'I could come here every night. Five fights, though. Not six. Same price. What do you say?'

Six nights at five pounds a night – a profit of £30, a prodigal return.

'What about afternoon shows?' the manager asked him.

85

'Impossible. I would if I could, but I have to work elsewhere then.'

'Right,' said the manager. 'Be here, five tomorrow sharp, and we have a deal.'

They shook hands, and Jamie walked back to the Silent Witness, his heart pounding with excitement. This was not because he had floored five opponents, but because he knew that, at the end of the week, he would have so much money to his credit. In one week, he would have made more than Uncle Don paid him for a year's work. It seemed incredible, but the really astonishing fact was that it was true.

And this, Jamie assured himself, was only the beginning.

FIVE

The Big House

Arabella got on so well with Jephthah Beaumont that after a couple of weeks working for him part-time he saw Uncle Don and suggested that she should work for him full-time. Uncle Don readily agreed, and Arabella moved her few belongings into what was known locally as the Big House.

Here, Arabella shared a bedroom with Janet, a maid about her own age, whose job was to see that fires were lit in the bedrooms each morning before the occupants got up, and then to carry in polished copper cans of hot water so they could wash in their rooms. Janet was a cheerful, uncomplicated country girl who believed she was in love with an under-groom. The little room they shared contained two narrow beds, two chests of drawers, and one wash bowl with a ewer of water and a lidded china bucket for the waste.

The main part of the Big House had electricity supplied from a generating plant powered by an idiosyncratic petrol engine. When everyone was in bed and all lights had been turned off, the charging plant would stop automatically. But if anyone switched on a light during the night, it would immediately start again with a great banging and backfiring from the engine.

Staff quarters were lit by oil lamps; Arabella's room always smelled of sooty wicks and lamp black. It was chilly and the blankets were so thin she spread her coat over her bed. Uncomfortable and cold as she often was, this was still a step up the ladder. When she had been in the Silent Witness, she felt she was simply marking time. Now, she assured herself, sometimes repeatedly to make herself believe it, she really was going ahead.

The two girls were in bed by ten o'clock each night. Both had to start work early, but they did not always go to sleep quickly; they would lie talking. One day, Janet asked, 'Have you seen the Honourable Orlando Sutton yet?'

'No, who's he?'

'The son of the house. He'll be Lord Rosael when his father dies. Then he'll own the whole estate. Everything. Lucky him!'

'Where is he? Is he away working?'

'I wouldn't call it that. Nor would his parents either, I'd say. He's up at Oxford. He was rusticated – sent home, that means – because he got into some sort of scrape there. A girl in the town, a waitress in a tearoom, I think. He had to spend a year away before he was allowed back.'

'What did he do?'

'Her, I imagine. They sent him out of the country, to Germany. Heidelberg University – so he could learn the language, they said, but there was more in it than that. I didn't hear myself, but Jane, my lady's maid, she told me. Her ladyship was very worried about it, Jane said. There was a lot of talk, lawyers were involved. They had to pay the girl money. Otherwise she was going to make a fuss and it would all be in the papers.'

'You know him?' asked Arabella.

'I don't *know* him, but he's tried to be familiar with me.'

'How?'

'Oh, when I'm laying the fire, he'll come up behind me, put a hand on my bottom, try to get it under my skirt. I don't like him. It'd be different if it was John doing it. Quite different.

But there's something funny about Master Orlando. I don't like him at all. Nor do too many other people, I would say. There was an odd business about the girl who slept in your bed before you came. Kathleen.'

'What happened to her?'

'Well, I know for a fact that he tried a lot with her. I think he really had his way with her, if you ask me, not once but many, many times. She didn't like him either, but she was afraid she'd lose her place if she made a fuss.'

'So what happened?' asked Arabella.

'Kathleen was a girl of spirit, Irish. She finally told him straight to his face that if he didn't leave her alone she would tell her ladyship, and she meant it. And he knew she meant it. She told me so herself, right here in this room. She'd had enough. She sat on the bed where you're lying now, and she cried her eyes out for she guessed this wasn't the end of the matter, and she'd no one to turn to. Then the housekeeper came up and she said: "A very serious thing has happened. Her ladyship has lost a valuable ring."

' "Well, what about it?" asked Kathleen. "Nothing to do with me."

' "Apparently you were seen in her bedroom."

' "Rubbish," said Kathleen. "I've never been in her bedroom in my life. I do the other side of the house. You know that."

' "Well, it's what Master Orlando says. He says he saw you there."

' "Then he's lying."

' "Anyhow, it's your word against his, and her ladyship has asked me to look through your box."

' "But they're only my things in there. My clothes."

' "I've got to tell her I've looked, as she asked me."

'So they pulled her box out from under the bed and opened it and there, in one corner, in a twist of newspaper, was the ring. I

89

guessed it would be there, because it was the sort of dirty trick Master Orlando would think of. Mean, deceitful. He'd put it there deliberately, so it would be found.'

'What happened then?'

'Well, Kathleen got very angry, said she had never seen it before, and the housekeeper pursed her lips, and believed her, or wanted to believe her, but what could she say? Right in front of her was the evidence.

'There was some coming and going. Finally, her ladyship said that so long as Kathleen went within the hour, she would do nothing. Why, she could have gone to gaol. For years, I don't doubt. That ring was worth hundreds of pounds. So I'm telling you, you're new here, if he starts anything, be very careful. His mother dotes on him. I don't know what his lordship thinks, but he finds it easier to go along with what his wife says. So I'm warning you.'

'Thank you, I'm very grateful,' said Arabella, but it was a long time before she fell asleep, and when finally she did, a spider called Orlando, and as big as a man, chased her through her dreams.

Every day, Arabella worked in the Estate Office with Mr Beaumont. He kept the accounts in a very simple way: double entry, all money that came in set down against all money that went out. Arabella would check his sums, and Beaumont found she did this so quickly that soon he had to quicken his own calculations in order to keep up with her.

Next morning, she asked him for his opinion of the Honourable Orlando. He put down his pen, looked across the desk at her.

'Don't get involved with him,' he said sharply. 'He's partial to young girls. Most men are. But he, as they say in the army, pulls his rank. There was a young girl just before you came who left under a cloud. Her ladyship thought she'd stolen an eternity ring. It was found in the girl's box.'

'Do you think she stole it?'

'I don't know,' he said. 'She seemed a nice, honest, cheerful girl to me, not someone who'd touch anything that did not belong to her. She's dead now, poor thing.'

'*Dead?*'

Janet had not said anything about Kathleen being dead.

'She found she was expecting. She'd no one to turn to – so she killed herself. Threw herself in the river. I know her father slightly. He'd been a tenant here in one of the shops, then moved off to better himself. He blamed the son of the house. Orlando. He'd had his way with her. Often, so I heard.'

'Do the rest of the staff know she killed herself?'

'Of course. Bad news always travels like a forest fire, my dear. Good news comes slowly, like a one-legged messenger – if it comes at all.'

Each morning and afternoon in the Big House, a page collected the mail, which was delivered at the back door, and took it to Beaumont. He put aside all letters addressed to Lord Rosael or his wife for the butler to present to them on a silver tray in the morning room. Beaumont opened business letters, but any addressed to the Honourable Orlando Sutton he put on one side to await the young gentleman's return from Oxford at the end of term. He had given strict instructions that none were to be forwarded on to him.

'He says they're mostly bills and they can wait,' Beaumont explained to Arabella.

'And if they're not bills?'

'They can wait, too. A very determined young man is Master Orlando. Determined to do as little work as possible and to let others wait on his pleasure for his reply. But then, Arabella, he has no need to work for a living. Not like the rest of us.'

Orlando was due home on the Friday evening, and that morning, Beaumont told Arabella to take all his letters up to his dressing room.

'Is it all right for me to go through that part of the house?' she asked.

'Of course. I've given you instructions to go. He should be back here this evening about nine o'clock. He has a desk in his dressing room where he likes all his letters to be put in a neat pile, largest envelopes at the bottom, smaller ones on top. Like a pyramid. You take them now, there's a good girl.'

Arabella walked up the staff staircase, along bare corridors, then through two sets of swing doors and on to a landing from which the main bedrooms opened. Here the carpets were thick and the curtains heavy, held back on each side of the windows by gilded ornamental hooks.

She crossed the landing, following Beaumont's instructions, and stopped outside Orlando's dressing-room door. She knocked. There was no answer. She did not expect one, for no one should be inside, but she still felt bashful about entering the room without first making certain. The luxury of this part of the huge house, and the wealth it represented, made her unsure of herself. This is how I'd live if I were rich, she thought, and then corrected herself. *When* I'm rich. There was no doubt about that, she reminded herself sharply.

Arabella opened the door, closed it carefully behind her. The room was furnished in a florid style; heavy dark red curtains, painted chairs, an unexpected abundance of tapestried footstools. Full-length mirrors in thick gilded frames reflected her pale, tense face. Pictures showed eighteenth-century hunting scenes: the chase, the kill, gone to ground. Under the window was a large leather-topped desk.

Arabella crossed the carpet towards it, her feet sinking silently into its rich, soft, golden pile. She put the letters neatly on the desk, and stood for a moment, looking around her. She had never seen a room like this. It opened on to a bedroom and then to a tiled bathroom with a huge bath. Nickel-plated taps controlled the flow of water through a silver dolphin's mouth.

She walked round the room, examining the pictures on the walls, and came to a side table piled with old newspapers,

92

copies of sporting magazines, letters, half in, half out of their envelopes, and a pile of photographs.

Idly, she picked up one photograph. A group of young men in morning dress smiled out of the sepia print. She picked up another; the same young men, but much clearer. As she looked at each face in turn she had a strange feeling that somewhere she had seen them all before, standing like this, smiling, but not at the camera.

Suddenly, with a shock as sharp as a blow to her heart, Arabella realised that they were the young men who had rushed through the barrier at Exchange Station on to the platform where she and Jamie and her father had been waiting for their train.

The recollection made her feel sick. She closed her eyes, held her breath in case she would faint. Then she opened her eyes and, with her heart pounding like a drum, she examined all the photographs. In two of them, one face seemed to leap out of the sepia background at her: it belonged to that unknown young man on the train who had opened the door that hit her father.

Carefully, Arabella replaced the photographs in the order she had found them, and hurried back to Mr Beaumont's Office.

'You found it all right?' he asked her, meaning the dressing room.

'Yes, sir,' she assured him, meaning the photograph.

The Honourable Orlando Sutton strolled into the Estate Office a week later.

'You're new here?' he said to Arabella, without introducing himself. He stubbed out a half-smoked Turkish cigarette on an ashtray Beaumont had placed on her desk in anticipation of this visit.

Arabella stood up and bowed, suddenly afraid to look at him. She kept her head down, her eyes on the ashtray; the cigarette was still smouldering.

'Yes, sir.'

'Hm. Got a pretty face, too. Look at me, girl. Nothing to be afraid of. I won't bite you.'

He turned to Beaumont. 'Does she *really* help you?' he asked sceptically.

'Oh, most definitely, sir. She has a wonderful head for figures.'

'Quite a good figure, too, as well as a head for them, eh?'

Arabella looked up then at Orlando. His soft face, mean eyes set too close together, the wet, full lips, was barely a foot from her. She had only to reach out and she could strike him, knock the sneering smirk from his face. As she had guessed, he was the man in the photograph. Were it not for him, her father would still be alive, and she and her brother would be in Cape Colony with him. She had to hold on to the desk to stop herself from screaming.

'You all right, Arabella?' asked Beaumont anxiously, looking at her sharply.

'Oh, yes, sir. Perfectly.' She sat down, her composure returning.

Orlando stood there looking at her, a smile on his face. 'Where are you from?'

'Hyde, sir.' Arabella's voice sounded faint and far away, like the echo of someone calling down a deep well.

'Ah yes. Of course. Dreadful place, I think. Where were you before that?'

'In Scotland, sir. With my father.'

'And what does he do?'

'He was chief carpenter on the Duke of Coupar's estate.'

'Really? I was up there with his son last August. For the grouse. He and his father are both damn good shots. You never came across them, I suppose? Socially, I mean?'

'No, sir. Not socially. I never did.'

Orlando took out another cigarette from a silver case in the breast pocket of his jacket, lit it, stood staring at her, blowing smoke towards her.

'Funny,' he said. 'I've a feeling I've seen you somewhere

before. You weren't up in Scotland after the twelfth, were you?'

'No, sir.'

'Well, there it is. They say everyone's got a double, a *doppelgänger* as our German cousins told me in Heidelberg. Must have been someone else I saw who you remind me of.'

He walked slowly towards the door, puffing his cigarette, a frond of pale blue expensive smoke drifting behind him. At the door, he turned.

'It *is* damned odd, though. I could swear I've seen you somewhere. Not just someone like you, but you. Strange, eh?'

And Arabella thought: I saw you, you swine. You haven't the guts to admit you opened a door and killed a man, and ruined the future for my brother and me. You don't know I know what you did. But you will. My God, you will!

The clerk in Mr Snakesby's outer office shook his head adamantly. He had a very small head and narrow shoulders. He smelled of old stale sweat and unwashed clothes. His teeth were small and yellow and pointed, like a rodent's.

'It is impossible to see Mr Snakesby,' he said importantly. 'He is engaged with a client.'

'I'll wait,' said Arabella.

'He will be engaged all afternoon.'

'I have all afternoon,' Arabella replied. This was true. She had exchanged her usually free Saturday afternoon for this Tuesday. 'It is a matter of the gravest importance.'

'To him, or to you?'

'To both of us. He is, after all, my solicitor.'

At that moment, the door behind the counter opened and Snakesby put out his head. He did not see Arabella.

'Nip round the corner, sharpish like,' he told the clerk. 'Bring me a ham sandwich from the pub and a pint of porter.'

He gave the clerk half a crown, then saw Arabella standing there.

'Hello,' he said, not unkindly. 'What do you want?'

'To see you, Mr Snakesby. I was told you were engaged with a client all afternoon.'

Snakesby did not bother to deny this fiction, but held the door open for her, closed it behind her.

'Take a seat.'

Arabella sat down on a hard, high-backed wooden chair facing the desk. Snakesby looked at her inquiringly. 'Now, what's the trouble, young lady? Must be something, or you wouldn't come to see a lawyer.'

'It's about our case.'

'I have had a communication from your uncle, with some of my bill. But there's still about thirty pounds overdue. Have you come to settle up?'

'No,' she admitted. 'But I want to tell you something. I have found the man who opened the door on the train that killed my father.'

'Really? And how did you do that?'

Snakesby lit a cheroot, blew smoke at the ceiling, looked at her quizzically.

'I saw a photograph of the young men who were on the platform going to a wedding. I saw his face clearly, as he opened the door. I recognised him at once.'

'I see. Who is he?'

'The son of Lord Rosael. The Honourable Orlando Sutton.'

'Are you absolutely positive?'

'Yes.'

'He might deny it.'

'Possibly. But then he would be telling a lie.'

'Most witnesses lie,' said Snakesby easily. 'It's the judge's job to decide which side is telling the most lies.'

'I am not lying.'

'Hm. Did anyone else see and recognise him?'

'I don't know. I asked my brother, Jamie. He didn't see him.

96

He was looking at the men running towards us on the platform. But I saw his face. I was standing closer to him than I am to you now.'

'So it's really only your word, the word of a girl now in Lord Rosael's employment – so your uncle tells me – against Lord Rosael's heir. Is that it?'

'Yes. That's it, as you say.'

'We couldn't make it stick.'

'We should try,' said Arabella. 'I've come to you because you're a lawyer – *my* lawyer – and you know the law.'

'I couldn't take your case,' Snakesby replied firmly.

'Why not? My brother would pay you. He has recently made some money unexpectedly.'

'Then his first charge should be to pay what I am still owed. Anyhow, I would not wish to go against his lordship. As a matter of fact, he is my landlord. Indirectly, of course, through the estate, he owns this street, and half a dozen more on either side. It would be most imprudent for me to get into litigation with him. I am at the moment in the middle of protracted negotiations trying to have my rent reduced, you see.'

'I see. What you mean is that you hope to make more from him than you would from us?'

'Yes,' Snakesby admitted bluntly. 'That's the situation in a nutshell. You're sharp for a servant girl.'

He stood up, crossed the room, and then paused, looking down at her.

'But I could perhaps be prepared to waive the monies owing to me, and might possibly introduce you to another solicitor, who would take your case on my say-so.'

'Why would you do that?' asked Arabella, surprised.

'If you could help me.'

'In what way?'

'This way.'

Snakesby picked up her left hand folded in her lap, held it

97

against his thigh. She felt his phallus move like a warm living thing, a throbbing serpent head through the rough cloth of his trousers. She squeezed gently. It grew under her touch.

'You see. You understand these things.'

'I think, Mr Snakesby, I understand you as I understand the Honourable Orlando Sutton. You both imagine you can use a girl just as you like simply because she happens to be someone without money or influence. You disappoint me.'

'Why?' Snakesby asked, moving slightly to ease himself more fully into the grip. 'You're doing fine. Keep on.'

Arabella squeezed roughly, with all her strength. Then she pulled.

Snakesby gave a shriek of astonishment and pain. He doubled up sharply and hit his head on his desk. He staggered to one side, still bent over, gasping for breath, both hands pressed into his groin.

'You little bitch!' he sobbed. 'You little bitch! I'll make you pay for this. If it's the last thing I do.'

Arabella stood up. She had summoned power and composure and dignity from she knew not where. All she knew was that she hated and despised this creature, as she hated and despised Master Orlando. Let him do what he wished. She was unafraid. She would get even with them both somehow, somewhere, some day. She had been naive ever to imagine Snakesby would help her. He had named his price, and she was not prepared to pay it. There would be no deal, now or ever.

Snakesby sat down, groaning. She left the office. The clerk leered at her. He had returned with the porter in a jug and a sandwich on a plate.

'Didn't have long in there, did you?' he said. 'You annoyed Mr Snakesby, then?'

He had heard the lawyer's cry and wondered at the cause.

'I wouldn't get on the wrong side of him,' the clerk continued. 'He's a hard man, is Mr Snakesby.'

'And I'm a hard woman!' Arabella retorted. 'Diamond-hard.'

Arabella walked out into the street. She had never imagined men could be like this, bullying, bargaining, threatening. Now she knew, and in knowing, she formed a plan.

Next morning, Beaumont had to inspect some repair work just completed on one of the two lodges at the main gate of the estate. He said he would be away from the office for at least an hour. Hardly had he left than Master Orlando came into the room.

Uneasy at seeing him again so soon, and fearful he might remember where and when they had been face to face before, Arabella stood up.

'Sit down, girl,' he told her, stubbing out his cigarette in the ashtray. 'No need to stand up all the time. What are you doing today?'

'Some figures for Mr Beaumont about the new tenancy in Upper Farm. He has increased the rent by one pound a week.'

'Really? How boring that sounds. A pound a week. Barely enough to buy a bottle of decent champers. D'you like champagne, girl?'

'I've never tasted it,' Arabella admitted.

'You poor girl. Then you've got some good things coming to you, I don't doubt.'

He cast his eyes over Arabella, mentally undressing her. She would probably wear very unexciting, threadbare underwear. But then what could you expect from a girl who just did adding up, who was probably paid only a few shillings a week – and glad of the job?

She was a good-looking girl, Orlando admitted that at once. She had dark hair, deep blue eyes set far apart, a full figure, nice hands. She had something else about her, too – character. She wasn't the sort of kid he would expect to find just adding up columns of figures. Give her some decent clothes, a few jewels and she would be far more attractive than most of the other girls he knew. She wouldn't be interested in gossip either – if indeed she knew any – or feminine fripperies of that kind. Looking at her, he realised Arabella had a strong will of her own, much stronger than his. He would mess about with her at his peril; that, of course, added to the attraction. Orlando crossed the room, picked up a chair, carried it to her table, sat down beside her.

'Now show me,' he told her.

'There is very little to show,' she said. 'It's just a matter of percentages.'

'Still, show me, eh?'

He put an arm round her shoulder. She tried to shrug it off, but his hand did not move. Instead, the pressure on her shoulder increased slightly. She felt her flesh crawl beneath his soft fingers.

'Please,' she said. 'I don't like that.'

'Really? No girl I've known has ever told me that. Fact is, I don't care what you like, or don't like. You're an employee.'

'I'm paid to work for Mr Beaumont, sir.'

'You're paid to do what you're told. You know who I am, don't you?'

'Yes, sir. I know.'

Arabella moved her chair slightly to one side. Orlando moved his after her. The legs of his chair scraped slightly on the stained wooden floor.

'Oh, we are hoity-toity, aren't we? Who's the little virgin, then? Well, if you don't want to play, I don't want to play,' he said peevishly. Then he stood up and walked out of the office.

He would be back, Arabella knew, and he was, the next day and the day after that. Every morning, if Beaumont was out, riding around the farms, examining properties, work to do on them or work done, Orlando would come into the office. Always he brought the chair up to Arabella's table and sat close to her. At first, he simply caressed her shoulder. Then he gradually grew bolder. One hand would touch her thigh, slowly sliding the dress up above her knee until his fingers touched the bare warm flesh beneath. And then his other hand would drop from her shoulder, under the armpit and cup her breast. Arabella wriggled free.

'*Please*,' she said, 'please. Don't do that. I don't like it.'

'*I* do,' he retorted sharply.

Now he pulled the dress up, roughly pushed his fingers between her legs. She clamped her knees and tried to move her body away, but he held her fast, his fingers forcing their way into her. Then he kissed her, his mouth slobbering with saliva, his tongue like a searching serpent seeking hers. His breath smelled of tobacco smoke and brandy. With strength born of fear and revulsion, she pushed him away, jumped up and back, and slapped him hard across the face.

'How dare you!' she cried.

'How dare *you*, you little bitch! You know who I am, don't you?'

'You keep asking me,' she said. 'And I keep telling you. *Yes*. Of course I know. But I don't have to put up with this.'

'And who the hell are you? A little tweeny dragged in from some one-up, one-down terraced house! You'll do what *I* say, when *I* say it.'

'And if I won't?'

'Then you'll pretty smartly find yourself out of this house and out of a job. And whenever you try to get another, they'll come to me for a reference, and I'll tell them all about you and your stuck-up ways.'

'I warn you, if you touch me again, I will tell your mother, her ladyship.'

'Will you really? Then let me tell you that another little

tweeny, just like you, threatened to do that, and she went out very quickly indeed.'

'So I heard. And then the poor creature took her own life because she was expecting. But I'll still tell her ladyship. Maybe the other girl couldn't stand up for herself. I can, and I intend to.'

Orlando looked at Arabella and suddenly felt uneasy. Her eye were cold and hard, like chips of blue diamond. This little tart just *might* tell his mother. That last business of the tweeny, coming so soon after the waitress in Oxford, could have been nasty. His mother had not been entirely certain Kathleen was guilty of stealing her eternity ring. She had come with a very good reference, and had always appeared honest and trustworthy. All the other members of the staff, inside and outside, had liked her. None of them were likely to have put the ring in her box. For one thing, they did not have access to his mother's bedroom and her jewel case. But then neither did Kathleen. And now Kathleen was dead.

This new girl was devilish attractive, thought Orlando, but altogether tougher. She wouldn't kill herself. Would his mother accept Arabella's word against his? He had to admit that, in view of these recent instances, and others in the past, it was just possible that she might.

Orlando stood up and walked out of the room.

When Beaumont came back, he saw Arabella's flushed face, noticed the nervous movements of her hands.

'What's the matter?' he asked her.

'Nothing,' she said. 'Nothing.'

'That young sprig, Master Orlando, been here?'

'Yes,' Arabella admitted reluctantly. 'He comes in whenever you're not here.'

'Does he try anything untoward?' he asked bluntly.

'Yes,' she admitted. She liked Mr Beaumont and she trusted him. 'But so far, I've managed to push him off.'

'You'll never get rid of him. He's too used to having his own way. His mother's spoiled him since the day he was born. Like so many mothers, she tries to mould him into her idea of the perfect man, maybe the sort of man she thinks she should have married. But a child has to be trained. No child knows right from wrong in the beginning. That has to be taught. No one has ever bothered to do that with him. They sent him to fancy schools and colleges, and if he didn't like it, he came back home and then was packed off to another one. They've had a governess, a tutor, all kinds. But he's bad inside, that one. I have to tell you that. He's bad.'

That evening, Arabella went upstairs to her room early, before Janet finished work. She pulled out her box from under the bed, lit the oil lamp and began to go through her things. In one corner, as she had half suspected, she saw a twist of newspaper, torn from the previous day's *Morning Post*. She unwrapped this carefully. Inside lay two earrings, each alive with a single diamond. The stones caught the light and glittered harshly, as though they had a secret, inner life of their own, flames captive within the stones. So Orlando was trying the same trick on her he had played on the Irish maid.

She had to move fast, or she would be sacked in disgrace. What a story to tell Aunt Hannah and Uncle Don: that her box had been searched and Lady Mandeville's diamond earrings had been discovered! Would they believe that she was innocent? Would anyone?

Arabella made up her mind on her course of action, put the jewels back in the paper. Then she opened the top drawer in the chest. Each drawer had newspapers folded beneath her clothes. She wrapped a piece of a page round the twist of paper, put this in an envelope, sealed it, took a stamp from her bag, and on the envelope wrote: 'Mr Yeung Lee. To be called for.' She put a cross on the back, addressed the envelope to Hyde Post Office, and pushed it into her bodice. Then she went down the staff stairs into the main hall.

Every evening at six the page, who collected the morning and afternoon deliveries of mail, opened the locked mailbox in the hall, put letters to be posted in a bag and carried it to the Post Office. As Arabella dropped the envelope into the box, the clock began to chime six. She walked up the back staircase and passed the page whistling on his way down. She went on into the servants' dining room. A kettle simmered on a big black grate in one corner.

'You look tired, child,' said the housekeeper sympathetically.

'Yes, I am rather. I think I've a cold coming on.'

'Have a cup of tea.'

This was the housekeeper's antidote for all ills, the panacea for every trouble. She poured out a huge china cup of very strong black tea, added milk, and two spoonfuls of sugar, stirred vigorously.

'Here you are. It's all those figures and poring over books gives you a headache. Not natural work for a girl, I say.'

Arabella sipped the tea thankfully. Ten minutes later, the under-housekeeper came into the room, glanced at Arabella and then nodded her head to the housekeeper. They went out together, were back within two minutes.

'Are you sure nothing's happened, Arabella?' the housekeeper asked her.

'Nothing except that Master Orlando wants to get familiar.'

'That's nothing new. But her ladyship says she's missing a pair of earrings.'

'This is what happened with the Irish girl, isn't it? Only then it was a ring.'

'Apparently you've been seen in her ladyship's bedroom.'

'By Master Orlando?'

The housekeeper nodded.

'So history repeats itself. But I don't even know where Lady Rosael's bedroom is. My place is in the office with Mr Beaumont, not in any of the other rooms.'

'That's as maybe. But I've been asked to look through your box. If there's nothing there, you're in the clear.'

'I don't know how long I'll stay in the clear if Master Orlando's against me. He'll find a way of putting me out. But come up, by all means. Only, could I ask one thing? Can you get her ladyship there? I've a pair of earrings with bits of glass instead of diamonds. You might confuse those with Lady Rosael's.'

'Don't be so impertinent,' said the housekeeper sternly. 'Her ladyship won't be summoned to your quarters by me or anybody else.'

Arabella finished her tea, and they all walked in silence up the worn carpets to her bedroom. Arabella pulled out her box, opened it.

'There you are,' she said. 'Go through it. I've nothing to hide.'

The two women lifted out her clothes, shook out petticoats, towels, shirts, stockings, vests, knickers, two pairs of shoes, and then replaced them all carefully.

'There's nothing there, girl,' said the housekeeper thankfully. 'I didn't think there would be. Sometimes I think you're a hard little madam. But I always thought you honest as the day is long.'

'I'd like to tell her ladyship the earrings aren't here.'

'I will inform her, don't you worry.'

'I would still like to see her.'

'Very well. You come down and I'll ask if she'll see you. But I don't think she will.'

Down the stairs they went in silence, through the swing doors on the first landing. The butler was waiting.

'Well?' he asked the housekeeper.

'Nothing there, Sidney. We've both been through her box. Now she wants to see her ladyship.'

'What about?'

'Suspicion has been cast on me,' Arabella explained. 'I'd like to assure her ladyship that it was wrongly cast.'

'This is most irregular,' said the butler uneasily. 'Her ladyship is drinking a glass of sherry at the moment.'

'Please ask her, Sidney. It's important to the girl – and to all of us. This is the second time we've had accusations. Whose turn will it be next?'

The butler nodded, went away, then returned.

'Her ladyship will see you,' he said, trying not to sound surprised. 'Follow me.'

Arabella had not been into the main sitting room before. Apart from Orlando's dressing room, the only other rooms she had seen were staff rooms with threadbare carpets, worn curtains, chairs with horsehair stuffing bursting out of cracks in the leather. She was unprepared for a room where the Persian carpet seemed the size of a tennis court; for the sight of gold-edged furniture, of tapestries and huge oil paintings on the wall. A fire burned beneath the carved arch of a marble mantelpiece. An ormolu clock ticked loudly, confidently, on a side table. Standing with her back to the fire was Lady Rosael.

'You wish to see me?' she asked coldly.

'Yes, your ladyship,' said Arabella. 'I was told you thought I had stolen your earrings.'

'I did not think that, girl,' replied Lady Rosael carefully. 'But the maid who was here before you took a valuable ring. It was found in her possession.'

'Nothing of yours has been found in mine,' said Arabella.

'So I understand. I am very glad to hear it. So we will have to look elsewhere for the culprit.'

'That is so,' said Arabella. 'You may find her – or him – under your roof. In the meantime, I would like to give you my notice.'

'There is no stigma on you, child. None whatever. We are not accusing you of anything.'

'I know that, your ladyship. But I just have a feeling that perhaps something else not mine might be discovered one day in my belongings – as it was with that other girl.'

'But you're doing well. Mr Beaumont is delighted with your progress. Lord Rosael was talking to him only yesterday. He says you're a wizard with figures. His very words – though perhaps the feminine for wizard is witch?' Lady Rosael smiled uneasily, trying to be pleasant.

'Thank you. I have enjoyed the job very much. It has been a great privilege, and I have learned a lot.'

'Even in the short time you've been here?'

'Yes,' Arabella said. 'Even in that short time.'

'Well, if you want to go, that's up to you. You had better see Mr Beaumont. He engaged you.'

Lady Rosael turned away, poured herself another glass of sherry from a decanter on a side table, sipped it. The interview was at an end. Really, these little servant girls were getting above themselves. Yet there was something she had to admire in the child. She had courage; she stood up for herself, and she could have no savings to fall back on. If only Orlando had half her character. She shook her head sadly.

Beaumont tried to persuade Arabella to stay.

'No, I can't,' she replied. 'I don't believe that the other girl, Kathleen, tried to steal her ladyship's ring. She didn't like Master Orlando's advances any more than I do. Like her, I threatened to tell her ladyship. That frightened him. He got her out of the way, and he wanted me out of the way.'

'I am sorry you feel like that, but I can quite understand. But have you really learned anything here, as you told her ladyship?'

'A great deal,' she assured him. 'Probably more than either of us realise – specially about human nature.'

She went back to the Silent Witness; Jamie was disturbed

when he heard her story, and surprised that his sister seemed to show no concern whatever, although she was now without a job.

'You collect letters for the Chinaman, don't you?' she asked him.

'Yes, often,' he said. 'Sometimes they are addressed to him care of the railway station, sometimes at the Post Office.'

'There will be a letter waiting at the Post Office tomorrow addressed to him and marked "To be called for". On the back there is a cross, like a kiss, to mark it as something special. Bring it back here when you come.'

'I can't do that. I always take anything for him to his shop. It's his.'

'Not this time,' she replied. 'I wrote that envelope myself and just used his name. What's inside is not his. It's not mine, either. But now it's ours. I would have told you before, but I simply didn't have the chance.'

Jamie brought the letter back the next afternoon and stood watching while she opened it. Two diamond earrings dropped on to the kitchen table out of a print-smudged piece of newspaper.

'Where the devil did you get those? You didn't steal them, did you?'

'No. Someone put them in my box. Let's just leave it at that. But these stones will make us enough money to live on when we land in South Africa.'

'Are you going to pawn them?'

'No. But maybe we can borrow on them when we reach the Cape. They are what you might call collateral, and very easy to carry about. I will never sell them. Never. They are the first diamonds I have owned. I will write to the steamship company and ask when they next have two berths going south to the Cape. I'll also see if I can sell the third ticket to someone.'

'You're a sharp one, Bella. Is that what Mr Beaumont taught you?'

'No. Experience taught me. And from now on, I'm going to be very hard. If you're not, you're trodden on, treated like dirt.' Arabella paused, remembering words she had spoken to Snakesby's clerk. 'I'm going to be hard as a diamond,' she said. 'Diamond-hard.'

SIX

Diamond Dreams

Old man Rosen was dying.

He lay, propped up by pillows, in a bed in the little room behind the shop, gasping for breath, his head wearily on one side. For more than a year, after the death of his wife Rachel, many who regularly came to the shop to pawn or, more rarely, to redeem their belongings, had never seen him. He had been ill for so long that some only realised he was still there because they heard the rasping sound of his chronic cough through the wall.

His son Sammy, who had run the business for the last few years, sat on a hard wooden chair by the side of the narrow bed, watching his father die. The old man had been ailing ever since Sammy was a boy, and the approach of death was so long expected that now the hour was almost at hand, he felt little emotion. The doctor had called that morning and taken him on one side so his father would not hear, assuming the old man could still hear and understand.

'He's dying, Sammy,' the doctor told him gravely. 'There's nothing anyone can do for him now.'

'How long before the end?'

The doctor shrugged. Relatives invariably asked him this question, and usually there was no definite answer he could give. Only the Almighty knew for certain when we came into this world and when we had to leave it.

'I don't think he will last the night,' the doctor replied. 'At about three o'clock in the morning, every organ in the human body slows down, just before it wakes up again at dawn. When you are old and ill, everything can run down then and simply never start again. Three o'clock in the morning, Sammy, the worst hour of all the twenty-four. Napoleon used to say he wanted men around him with three-in-the-morning courage. If they could be brave then, they could be doubly brave at any other time.'

So Sammy sat in the little room, waiting for the end. A flame burned smokily in an oil lamp on a bedside table, making dim shadows dance on the walls. The light was reflected in the glass of pictures his father had hung from nails. They were all unredeemed pledges, mostly watercolours of country scenes, river banks, thatched cottages, totally alien to the harsh northern landscape surrounding the Rosens: terraced houses and mill chimneys.

Old Rosen had come to like his pictures. Sammy had often seen his father examine them through a magnifying glass. It was as though he drew comfort from their gentle colours and peace: they were painted windows on a world he would have liked to have experienced but never had, and now never would.

The old man's mind wandered. He could see the pictures from where he lay, but dimly and hazily, as though glimpsed through a deepening mist. Far more clearly, he could recall distant memories of places and people he had until now all but forgotten. He saw them not as they might be now, old and changed, but as they were when he was young. As he lay in the cramped room, heavy with the smell of paraffin from the lamp, his mind moved effortlessly through lost landscapes of his youth.

He had been born and brought up in Russia, and recalled with terrible clarity a morning when the Cossacks came riding down the Neva Prospekt in St Petersburg, twelve abreast, sabres drawn. A crowd of shabbily dressed Jews had gathered, and at first the approach of so many riders did not alarm them. Then, as they came nearer and the crowd could see sabres gleam gold in the December sun, they realised their danger – but some too late to escape.

The horses' hooves trampled into the snow those too old or infirm to escape, and others who had slipped. Down and up, down and up went the sabres in long practised drill movements. In seconds, so it seemed, the horsemen had gone and the wide street was littered with bodies, some writhing feebly, but more lying still, little humps of dark clothes in trodden snow, stained with blood and horse droppings. Rosen had escaped – but for how long would he be free?

That night, he decided to take his family away across the Polish border; Poles tolerated Jews, whereas in Russia they would never be assimilated. For the Rosens, it seemed they had either to escape or die. But wherever they settled, they feared they would always remain aliens, strangers, set apart from others by their clothes, their religion, their business acumen. And always they faced the risk endemic simply in being Jewish. They could be persecuted, beaten up, their homes set alight for no better reason than they did not conform.

'People are like birds,' Sammy's father used to say sadly. 'If birds in the forest see a strange bird with brighter feathers, they will peck it to death just because it is different. That is what happens to us, because we are strangers, without roots, without our own land.'

In Poland, he took over a small timber mill that had belonged to some relation who had died recently, and whose widow could not run it on her own. Here, in a forest clearing outside the town of Vilna, Sammy Rosen and his three brothers had grown up. There were no neighbours within miles, but somehow, as a family, they seemed complete, without any great need for neighbours or even for friends.

Their great and uniting interest had been horses; Sammy could ride when he was four. Circus trainers out of a job, or waiting for their circus to go on tour, would come to work in the mill for a few weeks or even months every year. They taught him and his brothers how to ride bareback, how to slide off a horse on one side, go underneath its belly and come up on the other side without losing balance, or making the horse falter in its stride.

The old man remembered the smell of hot horses, of well-oiled supple leather, the clean pine scent of newly cut logs, laid out in criss-cross formation for the winds to season.

Horses were important for another reason more rewarding than a willingness to learn circus tricks. When winter snow halted the felling of trees, the Rosens took their horses, bred and trained during the rest of the year, for the long trip across the frozen Vistula.

The relative who originally owned the mill had negotiated a contract with the German military authorities to provide an annual number of horses for the German cavalry. Each year the Rosens would deliver these animals to their new owners. At night, they would camp, with the horses tethered or hobbled near them. Often, the snow would stretch to infinity through the dark pillars of the forest pines – always silent, always empty.

The Rosens, father and sons, all looked forward to these annual treks. They liked the feeling of freedom, of contained excitement, and the achievement when they finally delivered the horses to the regiment. Usually, they would stay on for a few days, and before they returned would indulge in riding competitions with the cavalry. These traditionally ended on the eve of their departure with a boisterous party, when both sides tried to drink each other senseless – and sometimes succeeded. Then came the long walk back to the timber mill. As soon as they reached home, they immediately began to train new horses for the following year's requirements.

There was a satisfying, almost comforting, routine about this life that the family had never known since. Each boy had his own task, and in the evenings, by the light of a candle or an oil lamp, their mother would give the younger ones lessons in reading and mathematics – simple addition, subtraction, division. Then came a day when what seemed to be a secure and satisfying existence was shattered with the speed of a tall fir falling to the woodman's axe.

Old Rosen had been away for several days in Vilna. Sammy still remembered how, when he returned, his face was grave. He saw fear in his eyes.

'We must leave,' he said shortly.

'Leave?' asked his wife Rachel. 'Again? Why?'

'A pogrom. They are rounding up the Jews, driving them out.'

'But I thought we were safe here? Where can we go?' Her husband's fear had infected Rachel. To her sons, she suddenly seemed somehow smaller, infinitely more vulnerable than she had appeared only moments earlier.

'We must go west,' his father said. 'England is the nearest safe place. If I had more money I would try America, but the fares for so many of us will be too expensive. And we must go now.'

'What about the horses, the mill?'

'Someone approached me in Vilna. He had heard of our situation. He says he wants to buy the mill and the horses – at his price, of course. It is not a good price, not even a fair one. But either I take it or we will be killed or at best driven out with only what we can carry, and then it will be too late to sell anything.'

'But where can we live in England? We don't speak English.'

'We will learn,' Old Rosen assured his wife patiently. 'We are Jews. Because we have no country of our own, we must

114

learn the languages of other people's countries. There is no other way.'

Three weeks later, their belongings packed in wooden trunks bound with ropes, they landed at Tilbury Docks on the River Thames. What had seemed a large sum of money in Polish zlotys now seemed very little in pounds, shillings and pence. There was no work in any timber mill for a foreigner who could not speak a word of English; too many local workmen were eager for any vacant place.

They rented two rooms above a tailor's shop in Brick Lane in the East End of London. The tailor, Abraham Karnovski, was also a refugee from Russia. Sammy's parents used one room, and the brothers the other.

The old man sat up in bed now, imagining he was back in that tiny space, six people in two rooms, little bigger than cells, the air always heavy with the foul stench of blocked and crumbling drains elsewhere in the building. He remembered the bright emerald eyes of rats watching warily from holes in rotten floorboards; bugs that lived in the crumbling walls – Sammy and his brothers would prick them with pins – and an odorous outside lavatory, shared between four house-holds. They did not have space for a table in their rooms, but at mealtimes sat on the beds, balancing plates on their knees. Rachel kept a paraffin cooker in the bedroom. Old Rosen could still smell it – or was that the lamp burning low by his bedside?

Old Rosen suddenly sat up and spoke clearly. 'Two o'clock in the morning,' he said. 'Every morning, for years.'

Then he sank back with a sigh against the pillows.

Sammy thought his father meant three o'clock; he must have overheard the doctor. But he was wrong. The old man meant two; every morning at that hour he would get up to rake the embers of the fire, put on more coal and heat the tailor's iron. He never understood English well, and so he could not learn to be a cutter, but Karnovski, the tailor, paid him to press suits he made cheaply in his shop, to be sold for ten times as much from a bespoke tailor in Savile Row.

Apart from not speaking the language except for a few simple words and phrases, the old man had no trade, no profession. He had always been a dealer, living from one small transaction to another, just making sufficient profit each time to carry him on to the next. But now, he had nothing in which he could deal, only his own time.

'I can't put any of you through a training in one of the professions. A doctor, a lawyer,' he told Sammy. 'I wish I could. That would give you all standing. You never see a poor doctor or a starving lawyer, any more than you see a poor undertaker. They all work together, those three, in my view. But Abraham will teach you tailoring, Sammy. Then you'll never be out of work, boy. Never. Not be like me, getting up every morning at two to heat the iron, just to press some rich man's suit. That's no life. You can have a life. But first you need a trade.'

Sammy was formally apprenticed to Abraham Karnovski in the East End. He learned tailoring the hard way; cutting cloth, measuring, sewing, pressing – everything; and always in basements with indifferent light, but spurred on by the feeling he had to master the craft. He knew that this was important for his immediate survival, but deep down in his heart he had other plans, and it could be even more important in realising them.

He had the idea that if somehow he could establish a tailoring factory to produce good quality clothes at a cheap price – better material and better cut than the fustian stuff poor customers were offered from outfitters now – there could be an unlimited demand. Many sweatshops in the East End used Jewish, Chinese and Algerian labourers to produce ready-made suits to be sold by outfitters in provincial towns and villages, but the material was shoddy, usually manufactured with

116

reclaimed cloth from secondhand clothes. The cut was also so bad that suits barely fitted where they touched. Worst of all, they looked cheap. They were all plain grey or dark brown or blue; no stripes, no checks, no cheviots. Who, wearing such a suit, could ever feel confident? They covered people's bodies, but they gave neither pleasure nor assurance to the wearer.

Sammy would lie awake at night planning how he would produce the suits he had in mind. He did not want to farm them out around the East End, as other firms did, sending trousers to one man to make, jackets to another, waistcoats somewhere else. He wanted to work to a plan; to have one group of employees in a big room all cutting out. More, perhaps on the floor above, could sew; others would press and pack the suits for dispatch. But it was all a dream. He did not see how he could raise enough capital to start even the smallest factory.

Old Rosen regarded the East End as a staging post, not the family's eventual destination. He kept an eye out for any possible business venture he could undertake, despite the fact that he could not speak the language properly and had no money.

Eventually, he found a part-time job in the most prosperous shop in the area – the pawnbroker's. On Monday mornings, housewives would bring in little trinkets; a jacket, a watch, a clock. The pawnbroker would lend them one third of their value on the understanding that the item was redeemed, usually on pay day, the following Friday. The owner's brother owned a pawnbroker's shop in Hyde in the north of England. His chest was weak, made worse by the damp, sooty atmosphere. When he died prematurely from tuberculosis, the pawnbroker for whom Old Rosen worked inherited this shop and suggested he might care to buy it.

'How can I pay you for it?' Old Rosen asked, recognising the opportunity, but unsophisticated about finance.

'I know what the turnover is,' the pawnbroker replied. 'I can also guess what the profit should be. I suggest we split the profit for five years – and then the shop is yours.'

'You trust me?' Sammy's father asked him in surprise.

'I trust very few people,' the other man admitted. 'But you have an honest face, and you have risked all for freedom. If you do not keep your word, then I have made a mistake, which I do not often make in my business. I lend on the person, not just on what they can offer as security. Character is the best security. So if you cheat me, what have I lost except a little faith in my fellow men? The shop came to me for nothing. How can I lose what I never paid for?'

So the Rosens went north, and for the next twenty years Old Rosen ran the shop. One of Sammy's brothers went to America, one to Australia, one to South Africa. When the brothers parted, they wrote to each other fairly regularly at first and then less frequently. None of them were good correspondents, so Sammy only knew in the vaguest terms what they were doing. One was in the construction business in New Jersey, another managed to find work in a clothing store in Durban; the third, in Australia, was a cashier in a hotel. Sammy helped his father run the shop, but he never forgot his dreams of one day owning a clothing factory.

And then he heard of someone else who had also dreamed and turned his dream into reality. Sammy was walking through Whitechapel from Karnovski's cellar one day when he saw a splendid carriage, gleaming maroon varnish with crimson coachlines, drawn by four matched white horses with a liveried coachman and footman. The carriage door opened as he drew level with it, and a small alert-looking man stepped down. He didn't exactly step, he seemed to leap, and then walked on the balls of his feet like a boxer or a runner. He wore a dark suit, beautifully cut, a bow tie.

'Who's that?' Sammy asked a shopkeeper who had come out to see the carriage. No one so rich, so opulent, had come to Whitechapel in anyone's memory.

'Barney Barnato,' the man responded in awe.

'Who's he?'

'He was Barnett Isaacs. His parents still live round in Cobb's Court on the corner of Middlesex Street and Wentworth Street. He's a millionaire many times over. He's building a mansion up west in Park Lane.'

'I know the Isaacs. They are here, in London. The old man deals in secondhand clothes. Used to make caps. If that's their son, how is he so rich?'

'Diamonds,' said the shopkeeper importantly. 'He went out to South Africa with a few pounds in his pocket and some boxes of old cigars he'd picked up somewhere. He didn't do much in Cape Town, then he heard men were digging for diamonds up north in a place called New Rush. That's called Kimberley now, after Lord Kimberley, who was Secretary of State for the Colonies.

'Barney couldn't afford the fare there by ox wagon, which would cost him forty pounds, so he paid a fiver for the driver to carry his luggage on the cart and he walked by the side of it. Took him two months to cover six hundred miles on foot. When he finally got to Kimberley, he dug for diamonds.'

'How? With a spade? Where did he dig?'

'There's apparently a mine called the Big Hole. He bought claims in it from people, I don't know who, and he started to dig. The diggers go down it on ropes and so forth and bring out buckets of earth and gravel. They shake this out on a wire-netting sieve, and if they're lucky, they're left with diamonds. Some people say Barney was lucky, but I say he *earned* his fortune. He and his brother Harry worked like hell for two years in Kimberley, living rough, and didn't find any diamonds worth a toss. Barney gave boxing exhibitions to try and make a pound or two. He'd do music hall turns, stand on his head and recite "To be or not to be" from Hamlet, anything to make a few bob.

'Meanwhile, he taught himself all he could about diamonds, bought a watchmaker's magnifying glass, and started going round to buy diamonds from the diggers. They'd sell to him because Barney gave them a fair price. Other buyers would take advantage of the diggers because they knew they needed money badly, just to buy food, and neither the sellers nor the buyers really understood what the diamonds were worth. But Barney was straight. And he knew what each diamond was worth, whatever their size or colour or markings.

'Then, when all the yellow soil had been dug away in the mine, the diggers came to hard blue rock. Like iron, it was. They thought all the diamonds must have been dug out, so they quit, and sold up their claims for whatever they might get – which obviously wasn't much. Barney didn't accept that all the diamonds had gone. He'd read that diamonds were carbon, crystallised in the fiery centre of the earth and then spewed out in the form of little hard stones – diamonds – from erupting volcanoes and washed down mountain sides into rivers by centuries of rain.

'Barney and his brother bought all the claims they could afford between them and then dug as though their lives depended on it.'

The shopkeeper paused dramatically.

'They found a treasure house of diamonds. Soon, they were making two thousand pounds *a week*. That's the sort of money there is in diamonds. They decided to mine and sell the stones themselves, and cut out the middlemen. That's how Barney made his millions – and bloody good luck to him! I only wish I could do the same.'

Diamonds. Sammy looked in the windows of jewellers' shops with new interest. Behind metal grilles, even the smallest diamonds glittered like tiny unwinking stars in rings and brooches. How could these minute stones be worth so much? Who paid such sums for them? He didn't know the answer to either question, but he decided to find out. Following Barney Barnato's example, he set himself the task of reading everything he could about diamonds in the local free library. He asked his brother in Durban to send him copies of newspapers that contained articles on the finds in Kimberley. He made notes on what he read and kept all this information in a folder. He learned that the word 'diamond' had two sources. The Greek *adamas* meant literally 'what cannot be conquered or subdued'. The Latin *diamas* meant invincible. Because diamonds were so hard and so rare, kings, shahs, emperors and sultans all believed that their possession would confer on them the qualities of courage and hardness.

Originally, Sammy learned, most diamonds had come from the ancient mines of Golconda, a fortress city west of Hyderabad, in India. As the Indians steadily stripped the Golconda mines of diamonds, another source was fortuitously found in Brazil. And when it seemed that these Brazilian mines were also almost exhausted, diamonds were unexpectedly discovered in South Africa. This is what concerned Sammy Rosen; the other mines had all belonged to the past. To him, South Africa represented the present – and his future.

His imagination was fired. He longed to sail to the Cape and join the fortune hunters on their journey to the diamond mines. He could imagine the heat and the dust, the harsh extremes of burning sun by day, and freezing nights. He believed that if he could only join these diamond diggers, even if he did not make a fortune, he would surely make enough money to realise his dream of founding a unique tailoring factory.

But how could he possibly go? He could not leave his old, ill father to fend for himself. But now his father was dying.

The doctor's estimate proved too generous, by three hours. Old Rosen died at midnight.

Sammy had fallen asleep in the chair by his bed, and the distant chime of the town-hall clock wakened him as it marked the hour. Something felt different; the room was quiet – too quiet. His father's painful gasps for breath had been such a familiar background noise for so long that Sammy had come to take the sound for granted, as someone who lives on a stormy coast accepts and discounts the constant roar of ocean waves. Now, Sammy felt afraid.

He picked up the oil lamp and peered at his father's face.

'Are you awake?' he asked him quietly, almost nervously.

There was no answer, and even as Sammy spoke, he knew there would never be any answer. His father's dead eyes stared sightlessly at the ceiling; his face was the colour of candlewax.

Sammy leaned across the bed, closed his father's eyes, turned down the wick of the lamp. Then he tiptoed out of the room, as though leaving a sleeper whom he did not wish to waken. Oddly, he did not feel sad. Instead, he felt almost elated. At last he was free to do whatever he wanted, to go wherever he wished. At last he was on the way to realise his dream of discovering diamonds, and through them, he was certain, a life of achievement and wealth and influence beyond accounting.

SEVEN

The Cape Beckons

Lady Rosael was already seated at one end of the long mahogany breakfast table when her husband came into the room. He nodded a greeting. He was not a communicative man, and rarely spoke if he thought a grunt or a nod would serve as well as words.

Now, he walked over to the sideboard, lifted the lids from two silver chafing dishes; scrambled eggs in one, devilled kidneys in the other. He wrinkled his nose in distaste. He did not feel hungry this morning. He had an important decision to make, and the thought of deciding anything always took away his appetite.

Lord Rosael frequently considered himself fortunate to have so few resolutions to reach. He had inherited streets of shops and houses in several northern towns, two cotton mills, 50,000 acres, and trustees who ran everything for him. Lawyers and accountants added their views, and, of course, their fees. Lord Rosael's decisions simply meant rubber-stamping theirs: a nod, a shrug of his shoulders, a shake of his head. This was an expensive way to run his inheritance, so friends told him. But then he consoled himself that life was expensive, and using the skills of experts, trusting their judgement rather than his own, gave him peace of mind. Today, however, after several retreats and innumerable procrastinations, he faced a problem he had to resolve on his own.

He helped himself to some porridge, sprinkled it with

salt, sat down at the far end of the table, facing his wife.

'Have you seen Orlando yet?' she asked him ominously. 'You said you would.'

'I've been busy for the last couple of days,' Rosael replied defensively. 'Why?'

'You remember that Irish girl we had, Kathleen, who left?'

'The one who stole your ring and then killed herself?'

'Yes.'

'Well, what about her?'

'I wasn't entirely sure she ever stole it.'

'News to me. It was found in her box, wasn't it? What more proof do you want? Why have doubts now? She's dead – and you've got the ring back.'

'She seemed a nice child. I didn't think she was that kind at the time. Her priest gave her a very good record.'

'Damn these priests! All they think about are numbers. The more people they inveigle into their church, the likelier they think they will go to heaven. Numbers. Nothing else. Quantity. Never quality.'

'Maybe, maybe not. But anyhow, as you say, she's dead.'

'What are you getting at? Come to the point, woman.'

'Orlando told me my ring was missing and suggested we looked for it in that girl's room. So we did. Yesterday, Orlando asked me out of the blue – just like before – whether I had seen my diamond earrings recently. I told him they were in my jewel box. But when I opened it, they weren't. He then said he thought the new girl, Arabella Baird, who helps Mr Beaumont, had a devious nature, and he suggested I look in her box in her room.'

'And did you?'

'The housekeeper and the under-housekeeper did. They found nothing.'

'So she wasn't guilty?'

'It would appear not. Then she asked to see me and of course,

124

after that, I could hardly refuse. And although I assured her there was nothing against her character whatever, she gave her notice, and said she would leave at once. And she did.'

'What will Beaumont do without her, I wonder? He thought highly of her. Very highly. Amazing with figures, he told me,' said Lord Rosael, wondering how anyone – let alone a girl – could possibly master addition and subtraction and double-entry bookkeeping, whatever that was.

'I don't know. He'll miss her, I'm sure. But that's not what is worrying me.'

'What is worrying you? Come to the point, can't you?'

'Orlando is worrying me. First there was that business with the waitress at Oxford we had to buy off.'

'An expensive business, too. Luckily, it came out of one of the trusts. Five thousand flat,' said her husband grimly.

'Exactly. And then we sent him to Heidelberg for a year to learn German and try to behave in a more responsible way. And the university authorities sent him home after six months because he had an affair with a professor's wife – *and* the professor's daughter.'

'I'd forgotten that,' said Rosael. 'Yes, a very bad business – especially as the girl claimed she was pregnant. More money for lawyers and a generous settlement to keep things out of the courts.'

'And after Heidelberg we had that trouble with dud cheques, which Orlando claimed had been stolen and his name forged.'

'I remember. I always thought his excuse a bit thin. Anyway, I paid up. Gambling debts. Unsavoury business altogether.'

'Then this Irish maid, Kathleen. She was pregnant, you know.'

'I didn't know. No one told me. Who was the father – or would have been the father if the girl had lived? Not Orlando, surely?'

'That's what my maid thinks.'

125

'You discussed this matter with a servant? Our son and heir?'

'I asked her for her views. She is closer to these people than we are. And now this odd business of my earrings.'

'You think Orlando wanted to be rid of the Baird girl for some reason? She'd refused him? Something like that?'

'It is a possibility – and a very worrying one.'

'What's happened to these earrings is more important. Have you put them down somewhere?'

'No. I always keep them in my jewel box, Henry.'

'They'll turn up. The ring did.'

'Somehow, I don't think they will. I'm worried about that, but I'm much more worried about Orlando. He's the only common factor in all these incidents. What do you suggest? You're his father.'

'I've talked to the boy, but that's no good. He knows he'll inherit a fortune when he's twenty-five, more when I die. That sort of knowledge spoils you for getting down to do a job of work. I've been meaning to ask you to write to your cousin in the Cape, see if he can give Orlando a job on his farm. Something for a few months or even a year. Outdoor work would be good for him, healthy. Take his mind off gambling and women and wasting his life. I've been thinking about this for some time.'

Then why didn't you say so earlier? Why didn't you *do* something instead of just thinking about it? Lady Rosael thought, but she did not speak her thoughts. Like many weak men, always reluctant to give a lead on any matter involving the slightest controversy, or even its possibility, her husband had a very unsettled temper. Push him too far and he would retreat from the prospect of making any decision and do nothing.

'He hasn't even got his degree yet,' she pointed out.

'You know as well as I do, he'll never get his degree.'

'Very well,' said Lady Rosael. 'I'll write to my cousin today.'

Her husband nodded his head, breathing a silent sigh of

relief. The decision that had been worrying him was made. He knew his wife wanted him to decide about Orlando. There had been so many conversations about him, all fruitless, all inconclusive. And now she had prompted the decision.

When he finished his porridge, Lord Rosael began to hum under his breath. Maybe, he would try the scrambled egg after all. His appetite was coming back.

For the first few days after old Rosen died, Sammy found it difficult to accept the fact that, apart from an uncle living on the far side of Manchester, he was entirely on his own in the world.

The uncle was his father's younger brother, and had followed them to England. A gap of twelve years separated them; they had never been close. Sammy was not told exactly why this was so. Whenever he mentioned Uncle Jacob, his father would shake his head sadly. 'He is not one of us, Sammy boy. He has gone off the rails, as they say here. You don't want to become involved with him.'

'But why not?'

The old man never gave him a direct answer, but would shrug his shoulders, roll his eyes up to the ceiling, or draw his hand across his throat.

'He mixes with people you would not like. Bad people. Their money is dirty money. And dirty money brings no blessing.'

'Does clean money, whatever that is?'

The old man smiled wryly. 'I would like to have the chance, my boy, to find out for myself.'

Sammy had an address for his uncle, and sent him a postcard, explaining when the funeral would be. Uncle Jacob turned up at the shop half an hour early, driving a Benz motorcar. This was the first car that had stopped in their road. Little boys swarmed out of houses to examine it, to leave sticky fingerprints on its warm enamelled bonnet.

Sammy could see a strong family likeness in Uncle Jacob;

127

he might be looking at his father twelve years earlier.

'I never knew he was ill,' Uncle Jacob said sadly. 'You should have told me, Sammy.'

'I should,' Sammy agreed. 'But I didn't think you two were very close.'

'Blood is always thicker than wine. Much thicker, boy. He was a good, honest man, your father.'

'He was indeed,' Sammy agreed, looking at his uncle sharply.

Jacob smiled. 'I know he thought I wasn't,' he admitted. 'But I know what he went through. He had no money, and none of the muscle that money means. I didn't want to be like him. I didn't want to be pushed around always. If there was any pushing to be done, I wanted to be doing it. You understand me, boy?'

'I think so,' said Sammy.

After the service, Sammy invited his uncle back to the house. He was surprised how sad Jacob appeared. He did not seem to be at all the sort of man he had imagined, from the few times his father had mentioned him.

Sammy opened the kitchen cupboard, took out a bottle of whisky, poured two glasses, added water from the tap. Jacob Rosen finished his drink quickly, held out the glass to be refilled.

'Before you were born,' he said reflectively, 'when our father died, your father and I were the only mourners. There was only one more plot in the graveyard there, and two of us to follow him.

' "So who has the plot?" I asked him.

' "First come, first served," said your father, just like that. He had a nice turn of phrase. But I never thought, although he was older than me, I would come to see him buried first. Fact is, when you're young, Sammy, you don't think about such things at all. You feel you're going to live for ever. It's only other

128

people who die, who have fatal accidents. Not you. Never you.'

He sipped the second glass of whisky, shaking his head from time to time, as though he still could not believe that his elder brother was dead. They sat in silence for a few minutes. Outside, a lamplighter lit the lamps in the street, cycling past with a long pole to turn on the gas taps. Their pale, faintly green glow shone into the kitchen. Neither of the men wanted to draw the curtains, or to turn on the light. At such a time, it seemed somehow more apt to be sitting quietly in the half-darkness with their thoughts.

'What are you going to do now, Sammy boy?' asked his uncle at last.

'I'm going to emigrate. To the Cape. My brother Bernard is in Durban. I'm going up north to Kimberley, looking for diamonds.'

'Has Bernard done that?'

'I don't think so. At least, he never said he had. But we don't write often to each other. Anyway, that's where I'm going. I don't want to stay here dealing in the rubbish people want to pawn for a few shillings or even a few pennies – old clothes, shoes, anything. A lot of the old clothes stink. I don't want to spend my life down on this level.'

'You could get a job tailoring, Sammy. It would be steady work. Maybe open your own shop eventually.'

'I'll see, Uncle. But first, before I do anything else, I have to make some money.'

'When you told me my brother was dead, I didn't think he would leave much. He was a good man, and a good name is worth more than great riches. Although, speaking personally, I've always been more concerned with the riches.'

'So I heard from my father. You're right. He didn't leave much. This shop is leased. My father left two hundred in notes in an envelope under his mattress and the stock here. As you say, not a great deal for a life's hard work.'

Jacob nodded, slowly, reflectively, as though digesting this information.

'But then, as the rabbis tell us, there are other currencies than money. And remember, when you die, you can only carry with you things you've given away. Kind deeds. Helping people – even with just an encouraging word. The good often die poor, as I count poverty. But I don't think you will die poor, Sammy, and I will do something now to try to stop such a possibility, unlikely as I think it is.

'Your father and I were never close, as you say. We were separated not only by years but by our outlooks. He liked people, and I don't. He trusted people. I don't. He thought I sailed close to the wind. I didn't. I sailed right into it. Often. And still do. And I always come away with a profit.

'He would never foreclose on anyone who could not redeem their pledge. I know, because several of his clients have told me. As I say, he was a good man, and now I would like to pay you a small dividend on his goodness. I will give you a cheque today for five hundred pounds. I do this in your father's name and in his memory. I hope you will use it to achieve whatever it is you want to achieve. And as you go forward to whatever goal you set yourself, remember you are doing it for him as well as for yourself.

'So, my boy, when you sit sunning yourself in Italy or the South of France, or wherever you decide to go when you are rich, remember all the other Rosens who never had the chance, who lived and died in ghettos and jails. Forced to move on, to learn new languages, new sets of other people's rules that kept on changing. Think of all those who will never reach the sun, as you will reach it. And then too, my boy, maybe you can think of me.'

The room was almost dark now, the only sound the clop-clop of a horse's hooves pulling a trap outside. Jacob took out a cheque book, wrote out a cheque, signed it with a flourish, handed it to Sammy. He looked at it closely, not because he doubted the signature, but because he had never seen a cheque before for so much money.

'Thank you, Uncle. It is very kind of you. I really don't know what to say.'

'Then you've no problem. Don't say a word.' Uncle Jacob stood up. 'Must be off, boy. It's been twenty-odd years since I last saw you. Don't wait another twenty before we meet again, or that may be at my funeral. And I shouldn't think there will be too many other mourners.'

Sammy followed his uncle out to his car, watched him as he turned on the petrol, set the choke and gave two quick upward turns on the starting handle. The engine began to run, making the whole vehicle tremble. Jacob lit the acetylene headlights, the oil tail lamp with its polished ruby glass, and climbed behind the wheel. With a wave of his hand, he was gone. Sammy watched him out of sight, and then went back to the room.

He lit the gas lamp, poured himself another whisky and again examined the cheque. The room felt very still, totally silent save for the ticking of a grandfather clock on which his father had advanced the owner the sum of £5. For a moment, he could not understand why the room was so quiet. Then he remembered. He had grown so used to hearing his father cough and the sound of his painful breathing that silence now seemed almost sinister. He must get used to being on his own and stop remembering the past: tomorrow was where his future lay.

He went into the shop and pulled down the blinds. The smell of old clothes, secondhand boots was foul in his nostrils. He stood behind the counter, surrounded by imitation jewellery, cheap metal watches, a morning suit, a top hat, a cluster of bowlers, one fitted on top of another.

He heard a tap on the shop door. He opened the counter flap, crossed to the door, ran up the canvas curtain behind it. Jamie

Baird was standing outside. He opened the door for him.

'I've only just heard your father died,' said Jamie. 'I know what it's like to lose a father. I thought I'd call to say how sorry Arabella and I were to hear the news.'

'I've just come back from the funeral,' said Sammy.

'I didn't know it was today, or I would have come with you.'

'But you never knew him. You never saw him, as far as I know.'

'No, that's true, but I heard he helped lots of people here when he could have taken their possessions and sold them at a profit. Just as you helped me.'

'How?' asked Sammy, surprised.

'You introduced me to Yeung Lee. And now I'm leaving him. Arabella and I are going to emigrate to Cape Colony. My father had bought three tickets, and then, as you know, he was killed. But the tickets are still valid. I've saved a few pounds and so has Arabella, so now we're off at last.'

'Lucky you! If I were going there, I'd head straight for Kimberley where they've found diamonds. That's the place to be now.'

'Why don't you come too, then?'

'When are you going?'

'Tuesday week. Matter of fact, I wonder if you'd value something for me. Pair of earrings Arabella picked up.' Jamie produced them.

Sammy screwed a jeweller's glass into his right eye, turned the earrings over in his hands.

'They're genuine,' he announced. 'What did she give for them?'

'No idea. But what would you give for them?'

'Seventy quid. Cash. Now.'

'Thanks, but I'll hang on to them.'

Jamie took back the earrings, surprised at their value. If Sammy would offer £70, they must be worth at least three times as much. A pawnbroker's mark-up was never less than that.

'What are you doing with the third ticket?' Sammy asked him.

'Nothing. They won't give us cash for it. I'll have to keep it.'

Sammy Rosen made up his mind. He had to go now or he sensed he might never leave.

'I'll buy it from you,' he said recklessly. 'For whatever you paid.'

'You'll not be able to make a turn on it, then.'

'I don't intend to. I want to use it myself. I'm emigrating to the Cape, too.'

On Friday and Saturday evenings, Yeung Lee kept his shop open until nine o'clock, sometimes even to ten. He felt it was as easy to keep it open as to close it, for there was always the chance, the hope (not often realised) that a passer-by would pause at the window, see something they liked and come in to buy it. Alternatively, a sailor might be in town from his ship in Liverpool to visit his parents or his wife, and want to raise money quickly by selling some curio he had brought back from the East.

Yeung Lee was an optimist. In his business, he had to be, but on this particular evening, as he looked at Jamie Baird sweeping up the shop floor before closing, he felt uneasy. He sensed that the young man had something important to tell him; something was worrying him.

He was used to Jamie being cheerful and willing, but in the last few days his mood had been sombre as the clouds that hung constantly above the mill chimneys. Yeung Lee would not ask him what his problem was. People did not like to be questioned; if Jamie wished to inform Yeung Lee, no doubt he would do so.

Jamie told him after they had shut the shop. The two of them stood together by the counter with all the bric-a-brac of the store around them: a stuffed alligator, a swordfish blade, some

133

strange curved kudu horns brought from an African port. In the light of the unshaded electric bulb, Jamie's face looked pale and set.

'I wonder if I could have a private word with you?' he asked Yeung Lee nervously.

'Of course. Who is there to hear? The wind has no ears, my son.'

'I am going to leave you, Mr Yeung.'

'I am very sorry indeed to hear that. For some days I have noticed that you appeared grave. I thought something might be worrying you. Is this the reason for your gloom, that you are going?'

'In a sense, yes. I have been very happy here. You have helped me a lot, much more than you realised, teaching me martial arts, showing me the difference between buying and selling.'

'The difference, my son, is very simple. It is either a profit or a loss, and thanks to your efforts we have had more of the former than the latter. Are you unhappy here? You wish for more money?'

'No,' said Jamie. 'I am going to emigrate to the Cape.'

'That is a long way. South Africa is a wonderful country, quite different from this. The sun always seems to shine there. I remember being in a ship that used to call regularly at Cape Town, for coaling. They grow wine in the vineyards of Constantia nearby and it is far better than wine costing ten times as much over here. Much better, of course, than this English beer which makes for flatulence and gross swelling of the stomach. What are you going to do in the Cape?'

'Seek my fortune.'

The admission seemed so naive when put in such bald terms that Jamie half expected Yeung Lee to smile, but he simply nodded his head gravely, as though he completely understood Jamie's ambition.

'It is ever so with enterprising young men,' he agreed. 'But fortune is like a rainbow. You can see it shine in the sky – but always out of reach. You can see it ahead of you. But can you ever actually find where it ends?'

'I am going to find it,' Jamie declared confidently.

'I hope you will. I hope, also, that you realise that in making their fortune, people can lose something else which, as they grow older, they may consider to have been of equal value or even greater value.'

'I don't understand you,' said Jamie. 'I've been poor all my life. I would like to be rich for a change. I have heard sermons in church where the parsons say that wealth doesn't bring happiness. I would like the chance of proving that this is not true.'

Yeung Lee smiled. 'You may well have the chance of proving it. But remember, seeking a fortune is like fighting a battle. Of course, all life is a battle. We fight to come into the world, we fight against leaving it. But you, my son, are a person of direct approach. You face a problem, you fight it head on.

'When those ruffians came into my shop, you punched them. They outnumbered you, were stronger than you, more experienced than you. I did not attack them directly. I attacked them from the side. As the great master Sun Tzu declared in his treatise on the art of war: "Attack where the enemy is unprepared. Sally out when he does not expect you. Exhaust him by causing him continually to run about."

'You must regard those who hold or guard the fortune you seek – even the elements – as a general assesses an enemy in command of a great citadel. You must gauge the opposition and prepare appropriate measures. How in the Cape do you propose to achieve your ambition?'

'I have no real idea,' admitted Jamie, 'but Sammy Rosen up the road, who introduced me to you, is coming out, too. My father had three tickets. Sammy feels his future lies in diamonds. To sell one diamond could bring enough money

135

to enable a man to live his whole life without working again.'

'Very possibly. But diamonds of that size are few and the seekers after them are many, and the prospect of such wealth clouds all their other judgements. Be on your guard, my son, against avariciousness and also against the greed of your fellow men. I will miss you here. I have enjoyed your companionship. I have a little present I would like you to take with you.'

He opened a drawer in the back of the counter, pulled out a small book, handed it to Jamie.

'It is my own personal translation of Sun Tzu,' he said. 'He was one of the wisest men, not only of his age, but of any age. His maxims will help any soldier to victory. And now, my friend, you are a soldier.'

'Write something in it for me,' Jamie asked him.

'I will write it in Chinese characters,' Yeung Lee replied. He picked up a small paintbrush, dipped it in a well of ink and delineated the characters on the title page. Then he handed the book back to Jamie.

'What have you written?' Jamie asked him.

'Words for the wise. Again from Sun Tzu. "One who esteems life above all will be overcome with hesitance." Hesitancy in a general – and in your war to achieve riches, my friend – is a great calamity.'

'Thank you,' said Jamie. 'I will remember that.'

'When do you want to leave?' Yeung Lee asked him.

'The ship sails a week on Tuesday.'

'I wish you well. You want to go tonight?'

'No, I would like to work until the evening of my departure.'

'Well said. And when you do go, you must write to me. You must give me an address. It could be that in your enterprises you may need someone in the rear echelons. Not to give you advice, but perhaps to purchase something for you, or maybe to negotiate some sale of any goods you might send back. And your sister. Is she going with you?'

'Yes,' said Jamie. 'We're twins,' he added by way of explanation.

'To be one of a twin is very fortunate,' said Yeung Lee. 'Like a person with two heads, they can see both sides of any problem. But the Cape can be a harsh place for a young girl.' He turned to a cupboard behind the counter, took out several small glass pots with cork stoppers in wide necks, and wooden pill boxes. 'Before you go, I will give you some medicaments which may be useful.'

He held up one pot, removed the cork, showed Jamie the pale yellowish cream it contained. 'A Chinese antidote for snake bite,' he explained. He pointed to another pot. 'Wipe this cream on your hands and your face to repel mosquitoes and stinging flies and bees. If you ever go to China, you will see that the women all have very smooth skins, free of wrinkles, although they may be seventy or even eighty years old. This is because they regularly use this special cream.' He opened another pot. 'This also stops skin peeling in the sun.'

Jamie removed the stopper, sniffed at the thick whitish cream inside. 'What is it made of?'

'Almonds ground up very fine and powdered until they totally dissolve in their own oil. Various herbs – some grow wild here in the countryside. Others come from the East. And then an essence from the bark of evergreen trees. They do not shed their leaves, so they must contain something other trees lack.'

Yeung Lee opened another pot.

'This is to stop the sun drying and burning your face. It contains fat taken from the newly sheared wool of sheep. This has a most soothing effect on sore skin or burns caused by fire. But the real magic in all these preparations lies in the proportions of the ingredients. And that is *my* secret.'

'Thank you,' said Jamie appreciatively. 'You are very kind.' He looked at the pots, never imagining in what strange and unexpected way their possession would one day change his life and Arabella's.

'Wherever you go,' Yeung Lee told Jamie, 'wherever you are, however long your journey takes, my best wishes go with you. And may the spirits of our illustrious ancestors look upon you both with favour and guard you from all ill fortune.'

On the following evening, Yeung Lee sat in his room behind the shop, watching the dying fire, trying to read his future in the flames. He heard a faint knocking at the shop door and looked up, frowning. Since it was Sunday, his shop was shut, but sometimes small boys would run along the street knocking on front doors one after the other, in a kind of game. Yeung Lee waited, but when the knocking was repeated, he realised some-one genuinely wanted to see him.

He went through the darkened shop, unbolted the door. Arabella was standing on the pavement.

'I hope I am not disturbing you,' she said, 'but I felt I had to come and thank you for supplying us with these ointments and pills. Neither Jamie nor I have ever been abroad, and we had no idea we might need such things.'

'Your brother has already thanked me,' Yeung Lee replied. 'But do come into the shop. We need not stand out here in the cold. Would you like a cup of tea? I have Indian as well as China tea. I am not biased.' Yeung Lee allowed himself a smile at what he thought was a joke.

'No, thank you,' Arabella said. 'I have had supper. I just wanted to let you know how pleased I was with your gift. It was so unexpected.'

'The unexpected is twice welcome – if it brings good news,' replied Yeung Lee. 'Your brother has been telling me he feels the future may lie in finding diamonds. And you? What do you want to search for and, hopefully, find?'

Arabella looked at the old man for a moment before replying.

His face seemed infinitely wise, infinitely kind. She felt she could trust him; he would never use a confidence against her.

'I don't really know what I want,' she admitted, 'except to get out of this cold, damp town with its memories of my father and his terrible accident. I know what I *don't* want – and that is to spend my days helping in the pub, washing dishes, polishing glasses. At school, I found I had quite a gift for figures. I would like to use it, if I could.'

'I heard you were working with Mr Beaumont in his office. But that ended, yes?'

'Yes,' she said. 'There was an unpleasantness with the son of the house. I resigned.'

Yeung Lee shook his head disapprovingly. 'You should never resign,' he said gravely. 'Always wait until you are pushed out. That way you can exert your influence far longer. Just imagine, the Prime Minister of this country resigns. One moment, he is all-powerful. The next, he is simply a private person. His voice then is only a cry in the political wilderness – and few hear him. And those who do, they do not listen.'

'In this case, it was different,' said Arabella.

Yeung Lee shrugged as though he found the excuse difficult to accept. 'Let me look at your right hand,' he said. Arabella held it out. He put on a pair of thick glasses, peered closely at her palm.

'They say, Arabella, that our faces are maps of our past. Our faces show our triumphs, our defeats, happiness and tears. Our bad temper, or our readiness to smile are etched in lines that only death can erase. Our palms, however, mark paths we will take in the future.'

He pointed a thin, long-fingered nail at the various lines.

'This is your life line. You see, there are no breaks. You will also enjoy good health. Look, no breaks for illness. And this is your line of fortune. You will indeed become rich in terms of money – although perhaps not in the way you may imagine.'

'You mean we will not find diamonds?'

'I cannot say how you will find your wealth, but look at these small breaks in the line. They show a parting of the ways. The line joins up again, but not quite as it was. Your personal line is also confusing. Tell me, what would you like most of all in your life, apart from the wealth you say you seek?'

Arabella smiled awkwardly. She had never really considered the matter. No one had ever asked her this question, and she did not know the answer.

'Perhaps,' she said, only half serious, 'I would like to marry a handsome prince and live happily ever after – like in a fairy story.'

'How long is "ever after"? In your life, or for as long as you remain married? I can see here that you may indeed marry someone the world considers a prince, or at least the equal of a prince – maybe even, some would say, a man of superior birth. But thereafter I cannot see clearly. I suspect there may be arguments or discord. But I can only hint at these as a sailor senses the approach of a storm from the calmness of the sea, or a deepening of dark clouds.'

'But in the end?' Arabella asked him, now totally serious.

'In the end, who can say? The mists of distance grow thick and then become impenetrable. I can only tell you what I see in your hand now. Other clearer lines may well appear, giving other signs and signals, in the years ahead. You should ask me then.'

'I will,' she promised, not really meaning it. 'And thank you again.'

When Arabella had left the shop, Yeung Lee bolted the door behind her. For a moment, he stood in the darkness, wishing he was young again and about to seek his own fortune. Would it be simply wealth he strived for, if he was offered a second chance? Or something more estimable? Surely, the pursuit of wisdom would be a worthier aim. But who could ever teach a young person that? Truly it was written: 'If only youth knew . . . if only old age could.'

Yeung Lee went back into his room behind the shop and stood looking at the fire. Now he did not try to see his future, but his past: people and places he had known once and wondered whether he would ever know again.

EIGHT

Death at Sea

Aunt Hannah and Uncle Don stood on the platform at Exchange Station, Manchester, waiting for the train to leave. Aunt Hannah was trying not to cry, and kept dabbing her nose with a damp rolled-up ball of handkerchief. Her husband puffed furiously at his pipe in an attempt to conceal his feelings. Arabella and Jamie leaned out of the carriage window, only a few feet away but already, in their thoughts, in another country.

'You will write, now, won't you?' said Aunt Hannah, repeating the question she had already asked several times, largely because she could not think of anything else to say.

'Of course we'll write,' Jamie assured her. 'As soon as we have an address I'll send it to you. Why, you both might come out and join us.'

'We're getting old for such a journey,' said Uncle Don. 'But it's a nice idea.'

'Our father was older than you,' Jamie pointed out.

'By two years. But he was more adventurous.'

'We're doing what he wanted to do,' said Arabella.

'He'll be with you in spirit,' said Uncle Don confidently. 'And so will your aunt and I. Always remember that. If ever you're in any trouble, or if things don't work out – you've got a home here.'

The guard blew his whistle importantly, waved a green flag. The train gave a jerk and began to move forward slowly. Several people on the platform kept pace with it for the first few yards, waving, and shouting good wishes. Then, as it gathered speed, they dropped behind. Arabella's last view of Uncle Don and Aunt Hannah was of a homely middle-aged couple standing very close together, as though for comfort. They diminished with each turn of the wheels, waving until the smoke and steam that hung under the station roof obscured them, and Arabella and her brother were on their own.

Each had a small trunk packed with their clothes on the luggage rack above their heads. They sat in silence, facing each other, both wondering whether they were being wise, or just incredibly foolish, and yet unwilling to voice these thoughts. They were setting off to start a totally new life without any qualifications or training whatever. They had no real idea what South Africa would be like, or what it could offer, except a better climate and space. They had no clear plans for the future, beyond Sammy Rosen's suggestion that they should search for diamonds. But where – and how? Sammy had caught an earlier train; he said he wanted to visit a distant relation in Liverpool before joining the ship. He would meet them on board.

The train chugged past Manchester's dreary outskirts – slagheaps of clinkers, rows of identical houses, giant red-brick mills. Gradually, the houses fell away and they were trundling between fields, against a gentle swell of distant hills and isolated farms and cottages. Then a road, newly built, and a rash of factories outside Liverpool came into view. Over the roofs of more terraced houses, the masts and rigging and funnels of ships in the docks stood out sharply against the grey, northern sky.

The train stopped. They handed out their trunks to a porter who wheeled them on a trolley to the quay. Neither of the twins had ever seen an ocean-going ship close to, and the sight was impressive. Only feet away, held to the concrete quayside by ropes as thick as a man's thigh, soared a pitch-black cliff face.

They paused, looking up at the ship. High in the sky, so it seemed, they saw a white superstructure with rails and white lifeboats strung along the side. Some first-class passengers, who had already boarded, were up there looking down on the bustling scene beneath. Two gangways led into the heart of the ship. The porter started to go towards the nearest. A steward waiting at the bottom of the gangway examined the tickets.

'First-Class passengers only,' he said curtly. 'You're steerage.' He pointed to a door on a much lower level further down towards the ship's stern. 'That's for you.'

As the porter pushed their luggage on towards the steerage entrance, a crowd of passengers from the First-Class carriages of the train came out on to the quay. It was clear that they had been drinking heavily on the journey. Their laughter sounded unnaturally loud; the men raised their voices as though calling against a gale, guffawing at each other's remarks. All were smartly dressed; the women with fur muffs, the men in dark suits and polished top hats. One man walked towards the first-class gangway. The steward saluted him smartly. The man turned and kissed a woman, who flung her arms round him.

'Good luck!' cried one of his companions. 'We'll see you back again soon, I have no doubt.'

'Nor have I,' the man assured them. 'Meanwhile, put the champers on ice for that day. It won't be long.'

Arabella felt fingers of fear clutch her heart. She would recognise that voice anywhere, just as she recognised the soft weak face under the sleek hat, and the name. The Honourable Orlando Sutton was a fellow passenger.

For a moment, Arabella stood staring at him in horror and disbelief.

'What's the matter?' Jamie asked her. 'You've gone all white. Are you ill?'

'No,' she said. 'Just had a bad shock. Orlando Sutton is on the boat with us. He's going up the gangway now.'

'Well, he won't bother us,' Jamie assured her. 'He's travelling first class and we're down with the dead men. He's not likely to come there. Has he seen you?'

'I don't think so. He was busy with friends who've come to see him off. But won't there be a passenger list on board, which he can look through, and find us?'

'There may be for First- and Second-Class passengers, but not for us. And anyhow, if he hasn't seen you, why should he start searching for you among the steerage passengers?'

Steerage accommodation was more primitive than either of them had imagined. It consisted of two long galleries with wire netting tacked to metal rails to stop any child from falling down into the bowels of the ship. They looked down and saw the propeller shaft, thick as a telegraph pole, lying at a slight angle to the horizontal in a pool of slimy water, streaked with oil. On either side, resting on the rusty metal plates of the hull, two giant chains came from the centre of the ship to turn the rudder. The propeller shaft passed through two huge bearings. Yellow grease oozed like thick yellow snakes from their lubrication cups. The smell of rust, stale sea water and oil was almost overpowering.

This would be their home for the next few weeks.

'Rather you than me,' said the porter as he manhandled their trunks on to the gallery. There was no need to be polite to these people. They were of no account, barely able to give him a tip, he thought, as his hand closed over a sixpenny piece. A sailor approached them with a list of names clipped to a board.

'What are your numbers, then?'

Jamie handed him the tickets.

'Eleven and twelve, port side.'

'What are they, cabins?' asked Arabella.

'Cabins? You're joking! You get a cubicle each. The bunk folds up. You lie on it at night, and you can sit on it by day. This is steerage not staterooms, remember.'

'We're not likely to forget,' Jamie retorted.

The sailor led them along the gallery. Above the opening to each cubicle was a small number, white figures on a blue porcelain plate. He crossed their names off his list and went back to await the next arrivals.

The cubicles did not have portholes. The only ventilation was by way of a metal duct that ran the length of the gallery. Nozzles pointed down at the passengers; a faint metallic-tasting breeze blew down constantly on them. Light came from electric bulbs behind wire screens set high in a bulkhead. The filaments throbbed slightly with the beat of the ship's dynamos. Jamie lifted Arabella's trunk into her cubicle, went on to his own.

'Where do we wash?' Arabella asked him.

'I'll find out.'

The sailor had returned with a family of five; mother, father and three small children. The smallest was crying. Up a metal staircase, its diamond-patterned tread smoothed and scuffed by years of use, Jamie found half a dozen metal basins with cold water taps on either side of a washroom. The sailor followed him into the room.

'It's sea water,' he explained. 'No fresh water for washing in steerage. You can get fresh water for drinking from that tap in the corner, from seven till ten in the morning, seven till ten at night. You'll need sea-water soap to wash. Ordinary soap won't lather because of the salt.'

'Where do I get that?' Jamie asked him.

'From me. Two shillings a bar.'

'That's dear enough, isn't it?'

'I've got to make something out of it. Take it or leave it.'

'I'll take it,' Jamie told him, and gave him a florin.

The sailor threw a small bar of yellow soap into the nearest basin.

'I'll cut it in half,' said Arabella when Jamie told her, 'so we'll have a piece each.'

They sat on their bunks in their cubicles. Other passengers were now arriving, men who stank of sweat, unwashed women with crying children, one with a baby in arms who vomited on the floor.

'Never mind,' said Arabella consolingly as she saw distaste on her brother's face. 'When we come back, we'll travel first class. This is a once-only voyage. And you have to know what it's like to be poor before you can appreciate being rich.'

'I know what it's like to be poor,' retorted Jamie. 'So do you. It's galling to think that Orlando Sutton is in a cabin above our heads, no doubt drinking champagne, sending out for smoked-salmon sandwiches. He'll never know we're here.'

'And I hope he never finds out,' said Arabella fervently.

The sailor came down the companionway again. All the steerage passengers had arrived; every name was crossed off his list.

'Emigrating, are you?' he asked them, more conciliatory now.

'Yes. Can we go up on deck for a last look at England?'

'Sorry, no. You're locked in down here until we dock at Cape Town. No deck space for steerage.'

'How do we get air?'

'Plenty of air down here,' replied the sailor. 'When we reach the Bay of Biscay and it gets rather warm, this place stinks a bit, so we lower a canvas tube through the upper decks. The wind blows down that, keeps things a bit fresher.'

'So we don't get out of here at all until we dock?'

'That's what I said. Unless, of course, you can come to an arrangement.'

'With whom?'

'With me, for a start. Then with whoever is on duty here.'

'What sort of arrangement?'

'Cash or kind,' the sailor explained, eyeing Arabella lasciviously.

'How much?' Jamie asked him.

'Five shillings. I could unlock the door after dark for that. Then you can get up on to the promenade deck, take the air, even go on up further to the top deck, where the swells are. But remember, you shouldn't be out of here, and if any First- or Second-Class passengers complain, or any ship's officer sees you and suspects you're steerage, you're in trouble.'

'But you'll have given us the key.'

'I'm not likely to say that, am I? You'll have stolen the key more like. So that's how we stand. Take it or leave it.'

'How many times can we have the key?'

'Many as you like. But it's five bob a time, every time.'

'No discount for a lot of use?' Arabella asked him.

'Now, you're a smart one, aren't you, girlie, eh?'

'It seems very expensive.'

'Well, what's the alternative? Stink in here like hogs in a pen when the mercury is up in the nineties? You'll be crying to breathe even an hour of fresh air after we've been at sea for a week. Mark my words. Everyone's the same. They all want to get out, up on deck.'

'What if they have no money?' asked Jamie.

'They stay here. Or they can accommodate whoever has the key.'

'What do you mean, "accommodate"?' asked Arabella.

'You're a naive one. Or you're pretending to be. They let the keyholder get up them, that's what I mean, if you want it without frills. Man, woman or boy. We've all sorts in the crew, just as there are all sorts on shore.'

'Is this a common practice on every ship, hiring out a key?' Jamie asked him.

'No idea. But it's the rule here, matey. And has been, every voyage I've made. As I said, take it or leave it.'

Arabella and Jamie left it for five days. All through this time they breathed the increasingly foetid air, shared by a hundred others. Steerage stank with faeces, urine and vomit, overlaid by the smells of oil and filthy sea water from the bilge. Some passengers lay day after day, apparently comatose, in their own excrement, too wretched to move.

Jamie and Arabella were surprised and disappointed that Sammy Rosen had not joined them. At first, they thought he must have missed the sailing through staying too long with his relation in Liverpool. But then they asked the sailor to check his list and he told them that no one named Rosen was in steerage.

So had he never intended to join them? Had he bought their third ticket as an act of friendship, simply to help them with some money? They had no way of knowing; it would have to wait until they docked at Cape Town and they could write to Uncle Don and ask him whether Sammy was still in his shop.

Throughout each day and night, only feet from their ears, the propeller's huge blades slowly and heavily pounded the sea. One side of the shaft near a main bearing was scored by a deep scratch, and Jamie found himself mesmerised by this, watching it appear and disappear, counting the revolutions every minute. He had nothing to read, and in any case the light was too dim.

Every now and then the anchor chains shrieked against the metal hull and stirred the turgid bilge water that slopped to and fro. Several old men and young boys, unable to reach the primitive lavatories, would urinate directly into the bilge through the net safety screens. After five days, the water began to froth and the stench of ammonia overcame the smell of warm grease.

On the sixth day, the sailor who had shown them the cubicles was on duty.

'What about the key?' Jamie asked him.

'Coming round to it, are you, then? Five shillings. Like I said.'

Jamie produced two half-crowns.

'I'm off duty at ten,' the man went on, pocketing the coins. 'I've a spare key which I'll leave with you. But you'll be responsible for it. If there's any trouble, or it goes missing, I'll know who's got it. Make myself clear, do I?'

'Perfectly.'

'Then you'll be on your own. Keep out of the way of the First- and Second-Class passengers. Or if you can't, try to look as much like them as you can – though that's going to be difficult, coming from here. They don't take kindly to steerage folk mixing with them. Understandably, when you think what the voyage is costing them.'

'We have other clothes in our trunks,' Arabella told him.

'Then put them on. Ship's officers most likely won't trouble you. So many of the very rich always look shabby. We had a millionaire on the last trip up from the Cape and he wore rags, like a scarecrow. We had Cecil Rhodes once; worth millions, he was. He came aboard with so many tears in his trousers, the sailmaker had to mend them.

'The man to watch out for is the Sergeant-at-Arms. He's in charge of discipline and that. He might challenge you. Easiest is to keep out of everyone's way altogether and get back here before dawn. You'll have to go through the Second-Class lounge both ways. There'll be people there playing cards who'll think you've been in your cabin all the voyage and they may ask if you've been seasick or something. Don't get into conversation with them. That would be asking for trouble.'

The sailor spat on the key, handed it to Jamie.

That evening, they washed carefully and dressed in their best clothes. The key turned easily in the oiled lock. They went through and closed the watertight door behind them, pausing for a moment in the unfamiliar surroundings. The corridor floor and walls and ceiling were all painted battleship grey, and highly polished. A cluster of pipes and conduits carrying electric wires was clipped neatly to the ceiling. Every few yards a bulkhead light cast a shadowless glow. The air smelled strongly of hot engine oil, the walls warm to the touch. Under their feet, the floor trembled slightly with the pulse of the ship's engines.

They hurried along the corridor, opened a door at the end, then paused again. They were on a landing with rubber treads on stairs leading to a deck above them. As they climbed slowly, carefully, they heard faint sounds of music; the ship's orchestra was playing somewhere. At least they were going in the right direction. They passed two swing doors with glass panels, and looked through them. This was clearly the Second-Class lounge; as the sailor had told them, men and women were sitting at cane tables playing cards.

A steward passed them, expertly pushed open the door with his elbow. He was carrying a tray of drinks and a bowl of ice cubes and he did not give them a second glance. This gave them confidence. Their clothes might not be First Class, but at least they could pass as Second Class.

'Let's go up on deck,' said Arabella.

Jamie nodded. As they started to climb the stairs, the door opened suddenly and a man's voice shouted peremptorily:

'Where d'you think you're going?'

For a second their hearts seemed to cease beating. How could they have been discovered so quickly? What mistake had given them away? They turned towards the caller.

Sammy Rosen stood at the bottom of the stairs, a glass of port in one hand, a lighted cigar in the other.

'You!' cried Arabella in relief.

'Me,' agreed Sammy, grinning.

'What are you doing here?' asked Arabella. 'Out of your league – like us?'

151

'No. I felt rather mean actually, but a man in the shipping office at Liverpool told me steerage was worse than prison, and for a few pounds he could fiddle it for me to go Second Class. So I changed my ticket. He slipped a few pounds in his back pocket, and I slipped into a very nice single-berth cabin, port side – best side – and Bob's your uncle.'

'I wish he was ours, too!' retorted Arabella. 'We thought you'd missed the boat.'

'Not me. Too fly for that. But tell me, how did you get out?' He drew on his cigar, half closing his eyes as he exhaled expensive blue smoke.

For a moment they paused before replying, but there was no point in telling a lie.

'We bribed a sailor, who rented us a duplicate key. We're locked in down there like convicts – just as your man in the shipping office told you.'

'How much did you pay him?'

'Five shillings.'

'Let's see the key.'

Jamie produced it. Sammy turned it over in his hands, ran his fingertips over the tongue.

'I can get you another one cut for ten shillings,' he said.

'How? At sea?'

'Fellow down in the machine shop will do it for me.'

'We have to take this key back tonight.'

'You can take it back now. I'll make an impression on a piece of soap.'

'Are you *sure* you can get it done?' asked Arabella anxiously.

'Of course. He's one of us. The son of the relation I saw in Liverpool. Meanwhile, come in and sit down. Let me buy you a port each while I make the arrangements.'

As he went through the door, he added almost casually, 'That ten bob. It's cash in advance for my friend.'

'Good motto,' said Jamie.

'The only one,' Sammy agreed as he put Jamie's ten-shilling note in his pocket.

They sat sipping their drinks until he returned.

'We thought we'd take a stroll on the upper deck, First Class,' said Arabella. 'In for a lamb, in for a sheep is my motto. Will you join us?'

'No. I'll stay where I am.'

'You sure? The sea air will do you good.'

He shook his head. 'Don't push your luck too far,' he warned them. 'Only wants one passenger to doubt you're sailing First, and you're in trouble.'

Arabella and Jamie walked up to the First-Class deck. Here the saloon was more palatial, with fluted pillars and gilded cornices on the ceiling. Long red curtains concealed portholes. At the far end, on a stage as large as any theatre's, an orchestra in evening dress played a Strauss waltz. The only clue that this was not in the ballroom of some great hotel came from an occasional tremor beneath their feet as the liner hit an unusually big wave head on.

They walked out through the port-side door on to the deck. Here the air felt crisp and cool, slightly damp from spray as the ship ran into a cross current. They leaned against the white, still-warm wooden rail, while the vessel dipped and moved in a gentle, almost soporific roll. The moon had risen and stars hung like a necklace of jewels in the cloudless sky. Diamonds, thought Arabella. That must be a good omen. For the first time since they had left Hyde, they felt content.

On the following evening, the sailor with the key came to see them.

'Second-Class steward has given me a parcel to deliver from someone you know, apparently. A Mr Rosen. Same name as that man you were asking about.'

'Thank you,' said Jamie. He put the small brown paper

parcel, carefully sealed with red wax, in his pocket.

'You wanting the key again tonight?' the sailor asked him hopefully.

'No, thanks. Five bob's too expensive for us.'

'Well, that's the price. Take it or leave it.'

'We'll leave it.'

As soon as he was out of the way, Jamie tried the key in the door; it fitted perfectly.

They spent most of that night leaning on the upper-deck rail, feeling relaxed and far fitter because they were breathing fresh air after the foul smells of steerage.

The next evening they again joined Rosen for a drink in the lounge. He seemed unexpectedly pleased to see them.

'Funny thing happened this afternoon,' he said. 'I met my old landlord, face to face.'

'Who is he?'

'The Honourable Orlando Sutton. His father didn't just own my shop, he owned the whole street, and half a dozen more in the area. Plus goodness knows how much else. Sutton's travelling First-Class, of course.'

'Of course,' said Arabella. 'But I thought you didn't want to mix with them?'

'Well, I thought if you could take the risk, so could I. And if someone rumbled me, I could always say I didn't realise it was the First-Class part of the deck. He didn't seem a bad fellow, for an Honourable.'

'What did you talk about?'

'Nothing much, at first. I recognised him from a picture in the paper, introduced myself. He wasn't very forthcoming, until I told him my father had been his tenant for years. He asked me what he did. I told him we'd both been pawnbrokers. Then he became interested, asked me how I gauged the value of things people pledged, how many people could not afford to redeem their pledges and so on. Then he looked me straight in the eye and said, "Your shop must be near the public house, the Silent Witness."

'"That's right," I said. "End of the road."

'"How interesting," he said.

'"Why?" I asked him.

'"Nothing," he said, "nothing at all. But to meet you like this on the high sea is most strange. Coincidence or providence?"

'He stood for a minute, saying nothing at all but obviously turning something over in his mind, like a cow chewing the cud. And then he asked me: "Do you ever get anything really valuable?"

'"Yes," I said, putting it on a bit. Didn't want to appear too down-at-heel with the aristocracy, though, to be fair, he was talking just like you or me. No side, no looking down his nose at me.

'"What do you get?" he asked.

'"Gold watches, rings, jewellery," I told him.

'"Jewellery," he repeated. "Ever see any earrings, really valuable ones?"

'I was just going to say I had seen a really wonderful pair of diamond earrings – the ones you showed me, which I valued for you. Then I bit my lip. He looked at me as though he thought I was going to say more, but didn't want to.

'"Any other former tenants aboard?" he asked, joking, I thought.

'"I don't imagine so," I said, laughing. But I think he sensed I was lying, so I cleared off.'

'Where was he on the upper deck?' asked Arabella.

'On the port side, fairly far forward, between the first and second lifeboats which hang over the side. He goes there most nights, he said. I think he tries to sober up in the sea air. He'd certainly had a few before I saw him.'

'You're sure you didn't tell him we're here?'

155

'Of course I didn't. I wouldn't dream of it. But if I were you, I'd keep out of First Class. I know you worked in their Estate Office,' Sammy added pointedly.

They sat on for another ten minutes, making small talk, but so far as Arabella and Jamie were concerned, it was as though a dark cloud had suddenly obscured the moon. They did not go up on deck that night, but straight back to their cubicles.

'He'll find us,' said Arabella when they were once more on the far side of the watertight door. 'When you're rich and important like him, you can find anybody. It's not difficult to get the purser on your side, to check on the passengers, even the steerage ones. That sailor had a list. Then Orlando can see the captain or someone, and ask them to search our trunks.'

'You have the earrings with you?'

'Of course. I was going to put them into a bank in Cape Town.'

'You'll not do that if Orlando discovers you're on board. He'll try to find the earrings if he has to search the whole ship. And, knowing who he is, the captain will probably let him.'

Arabella put her head in her hands for a moment. 'I can't think in this heat and stench. Let me go out on deck. I'll fathom a way out.'

'Shall I come with you?' asked Jamie.

'No, I'll think better on my own.'

Arabella walked down the corridor, up the stairs. She came to the First-Class saloon, turned right on to the starboard deck. If Orlando kept to the port side, at least she would have the thickness of the ship separating her from him. She leaned on the rail, breathing the cool night air thankfully. Clouds were chasing each other across the moon. One moment everything was bathed in an ethereal silver light, and the next, all had darkened. Behind the ship stretched a wide phosphorescent wake.

Arabella leaned on the rail for probably half an hour, but still could not think of any way out of her dilemma. She decided to go down and fetch Jamie; two heads must be better than one. As she turned away from the rail, towards the door, a hand gripped her right arm tightly. A man stepped out from the shadow of a canvas sheet that shrouded some deck mechanism. At that moment, the clouds fled from the moon, and Arabella was looking into Orlando's face, only inches from her, so close she could smell rich brandy fumes on his breath.

'I thought you'd come up here,' he said triumphantly, his voice thick and slurred with alcohol. 'I told the Jew boy pawnbroker I always walked on the port side – just in case you or your brother were aboard. I guessed that if you had some way of coming up here, you'd choose this side – and I was right.

'That pawnbroker's attitude made me guess he was holding something back, so I checked with the purser. He confirmed that two Bairds, brother and sister, were travelling steerage. You get better pickings up in First Class, don't you? Earrings, diamond brooches, necklaces. I shouldn't doubt Rosen is in league with you.'

'You're talking rubbish.'

'We will see. I'm going down to visit the purser, and you, my girl, are coming with me. They have a gaol aboard ship, and that's where you'll spend the rest of the voyage, in irons, if I have anything to do with it. Your brother, too, I imagine. Accessory after the fact, as the lawyers say. Teach you both a lesson.'

Arabella saw hatred glitter in his eyes. She recoiled and, at that moment, realised her only hope of escape. She put one hand up to her eyes, and her shoulders began to heave. She sobbed.

'No good crying, you little bitch! Too late for tears. You're going to get what's been coming to you for too long.'

He opened the door, roughly pushed her through it.

'I have your mother's earrings,' Arabella admitted quickly.

157

'But take me to the purser and charge me, as you say you will, and you'll never see them again. My brother will throw them into the sea if I'm not back with him by half past eleven. But if you let me go, I'll give them to you.'

'I'll come down to steerage with you.'

'Not if you value your good looks. They're a tough bunch down there. One word about your accusations and they'll beat you up. They've no cause to like folk like you. Wait here. I'll be back. After all, I can't run away, can I?'

Reluctantly, Orlando released his hold.

'I'll wait here for ten minutes. If you're not back then, I'll see the purser, and the Sergeant-at-Arms will have you and your brother arrested.'

'Give me a quarter of an hour. It's a long way down to steerage.'

'All right,' he agreed. 'Fifteen minutes.' He checked his watch and lit a cigar.

Arabella walked down the stairs, along the corridor, let herself into steerage. She stood for a moment in the gallery, hearing the dull hammering of the propeller against the sea and the scrape of chains as the helmsman turned the ship's rudder against a running tide. Strangely, she felt totally calm; as calm as she had felt when she faced Lady Rosael.

Jamie was lying on his bed, trying to sleep. He had tied a handkerchief across his eyes to keep out the throbbing glare of the lamp. Arabella sat down beside him on the bunk.

'I've seen him.'

Jamie sat up. 'Who?' he asked, still fuddled with sleep.

'Orlando. He's guessed I've got the earrings with me. And he's going to have steerage searched if I'm not back in fifteen minutes. If he finds them – and he will – he says we'll both be put in irons.'

'My God!' Jamie cried, staring at her in horror.

'It's all right,' she said. 'You'll have to go up and see him in my place.'

'Me? Why? How can that possibly help us?'

'You can teach him a lesson. I've got two long dresses. One on, one in the trunk. Carry one up with you under your arm, like a bundle of old washing. Change in the Second-Class cloakroom, tuck your trousers into your socks, and go up to the promenade deck. There'll be no one else there but him. It's not a night for lovers to stroll on deck under the moon. The clouds are so thick, at times you'll hardly be able to see your way across the deck.'

'He'll hear my voice.'

'Pitch it higher.'

'I don't know what to say to him,' said Jamie.

'Listen,' she said. 'I'll tell you.'

As his sister outlined her proposal, Jamie cupped his chin in the palm of his hand. Her plan was risky, but it could be even riskier not to attempt it.

'All right,' he said reluctantly. 'Let's have the dress.'

She gave it to him. He rolled it up, took the key, went through the door, out and up to the Second-Class lounge. Outside it, across a narrow corridor, were two cloakrooms, marked Ladies and Gentlemen. He paused for a moment, until he was certain no one could see him. Then he went into the Ladies' room, locked himself in a cubicle. He hurriedly pulled the dress over his shoulders, tucked his trousers into his socks, tied Arabella's scarf round his head, and checked his appearance in the wall mirror. He waited for a moment until he was certain he was on his own. Then he went out and up to the First-Class promenade deck.

Several decks down in the steerage, Arabella was walking along the gallery. Two women and a man sat on upturned boxes playing cards, using a third box as a table. For a moment, she stood watching them.

'Care to join in?' the man asked her. 'Make a foursome?'

159

'Delighted,' said Arabella. 'But I must tell you, I'm not very good at cards.'

'You'll learn.'

The man brought another box out from his cubicle for her to sit on.

'We're playing for matchsticks,' he explained. 'We have no money.'

'I'll play for anything,' said Arabella, and sat down beside him.

From what Arabella had told him, Jamie calculated that Orlando would be standing against the ship's rail, facing the fitful light of the moon. Jamie wanted to approach him from the other side so that he would be in shadow. This gave him a faint chance that the deception would not immediately be recognised.

He came out of the swing door and saw a man leaning with his back against the rail. Every few moments he glanced at his watch. His face was in shadow. In the gloom, the red glow of his cigar shone like a warning light. Far away, through metal walls, the ship's orchestra played a polka.

Jamie walked along the deck towards Orlando, keeping close to the central structure, making use of every casing and ventilator that offered cover. He moved quietly, breathing carefully, and was within three feet of Orlando before he coughed to show he was there. He saw Orlando jerk nervously, take the cigar out of his mouth and peer towards the darkness.

'Who's that?' he asked gruffly.

'Me,' replied Jamie, raising his voice, speaking slowly, in falsetto tones. 'I said I'd come back.'

'Your voice sounds funny. Got a cold?'

'No.'

'What about the earrings, then? Let's have them.'

'I haven't got them.'

'*What?*'

160

Orlando seized Jamie roughly by the wrist, drew him towards him.

'Take your hand off me,' said Jamie warningly. In his annoyance, he forgot to raise his voice.

'Who the bloody hell are you?' asked Orlando, mystified. 'You're not Arabella. You're her bloody brother – in her clothes! My God! Wait until the captain hears of this. Stealing jewels, dressing in women's clothes, he'll have you in irons.'

Orlando took a step forward, seized Jamie's other wrist tightly. They were so close, Jamie could smell brandy on Orlando's breath.

Clouds scudded across the face of the moon. Jamie was not on the upper deck, where the pulsing beat of the ship's orchestra sounded faintly on the warm night air. He was back in the fairground ring under the naphtha lights, fighting against the clock. In an automatic reflex action, he dropped both his arms and then swept them up, hands clasped together, breaking Orlando's grip.

Orlando staggered against the rails, spat out his cigar and came at Jamie, both fists flying. Jamie stepped back, then to one side, dodging the blows. Orlando paused, realising he faced a shrewd and practised opponent. This was not going to be a simple matter of thrashing some cheeky servant girl.

'You bastard, whoever you are!' he said thickly.

He lunged at Jamie again. This time, Jamie dodged too late to avoid the blow. It hit his right ear. He saw a sudden fierce scattering of stars. Then as Yeung Lee had taught him, he bent forward, gripped Orlando's wrist. His arm was still over Jamie's shoulder, and Jamie put his weight beneath Orlando's chest and pivoted him up and over.

For a second, Orlando spun horizontally as Jamie turned – and then he was gone. Jamie stared almost disbelievingly over the rail. He heard a faint, frantic cry, the splash of a falling body, saw a sudden small turbulence of foam, and a man's hand raised despairingly from the darkness of the sea. Then the ship swept on.

Jamie turned away from the rail. Behind him was a voice pipe with a plug on a chain. He pulled out the plug, shouted down the pipe, which he guessed would be connected to the bridge.

'Man overboard!' he cried. 'Starboard! Man overboard!'

Bells clanged somewhere in the heart of the vessel. The propeller slowed, stopped. Jamie ran downstairs, then walked through the Second-Class lounge as quickly as he could without appearing to hurry. A few passengers glanced up incuriously as he went past. He kept his face turned away from them.

When at last he reached the corridor facing the watertight door of the steerage compartment, he ripped off his sister's dress, rolled it into a ball under his arm, pulled the turn-ups of his trousers from his socks. Then he unlocked the door, went through it, locked it carefully behind him.

Arabella was sitting at the far end of the gallery, still playing cards. The stern of the ship began to shudder and buck as the propeller reversed. No one paid any attention to Jamie. He walked to his cubicle, sat down thankfully on the bunk. His heart was pounding and he felt faintly sick. His ear still burned where Orlando had punched it. He looked at himself in a mirror. He could not see any traces of blood; a bruise might come later, but that would be all.

He sat for a minute with his head in his hands. He had not meant to throw Orlando overboard. He had only meant to teach him a sharp lesson, frighten him off, as Arabella had suggested. But the blow to his head had triggered all that Yeung Lee had taught him over so many sessions. In Sun Tzu's words, 'A skilled commander seeks victory from the situation.' That was what Jamie had done. And he had achieved victory, although not in the way he had imagined. Now Orlando was drowned; he

162

would never trouble them again. Arabella was safe, and so was her secret.

Bilge water slopped untidily, noisily, over the propeller shaft; rusty chain links rasped as the ship heeled over to starboard. She was turning in search of the man overboard. They would never find him, or if they did, he'd be dead, thought Jamie. He had read once that a vessel of this size would travel for at least a mile before she could stop, and then they would have to search the darkened heaving sea. Even with lights, they would be unlikely to see him. Jamie kicked off his shoes, lay back on his bunk.

He must have slept, overcome by reaction, because suddenly he was awake. The gallery seemed full of strangers: a ship's officer in uniform with gold braid on his sleeves; the sailor with the key; a tough burly man, like an army sergeant-major, who he guessed was the Sergeant-at-Arms. Two paunchy, middle-aged male passengers in evening dress were with them, smoking cigars self-consciously. The smell of their Havanas added a rare and unexpected scent of opulence to the squalid background. People came out of their cubicles, some half dressed, others wrapped in blankets, to stare at these visitors, as though they were creatures from another world; and in terms of wealth, they were.

Arabella sat with her back to the newcomers. She did not look at them as they began to walk round the gallery, peering at everyone intently. The older of the two passengers wrinkled his face with distaste at the sight of bodies still asleep with mouths wide open, at children snoring in makeshift cribs made from cardboard boxes. He took a few paces to the left, then to the right, looking around him, then stopped by Arabella's side.

'Here she is!' he called triumphantly. 'This is the woman I saw come down from the top deck moments after the man overboard call. She passed right by me in the lounge.'

'Stand up!' the Sergeant-at-Arms ordered Arabella roughly.

Arabella put her cards down on top of the box.

'Are you addressing me?' she asked him coolly, with a composure she did not feel.

'Of course I am. Think I'm talking to myself?'

'What do you want?'

'A First-Class passenger has been lost overboard,' the officer explained. 'What were you doing on the First-Class promenade deck?'

'I was not on the First-Class promenade deck.'

'This gentleman says he saw you after you came down.'

'This gentleman, as you describe him, is wrong. I can prove I was here all evening. And in any case, how could I possibly get out of steerage, much as I might wish to do so? We're locked in here like animals in a pen.' She turned to the sailor. 'Aren't we?' she appealed to him.

'That's right, sir,' he replied, speaking to the officer, carefully not looking at Arabella. 'I have the only key myself in my possession. No one else ever has it. You'll vouch for that, Sergeant-at-Arms?'

'I will indeed. But that doesn't mean to say someone couldn't have picked your pocket. There are some pretty sharp customers here, you know, sir.'

'Well, ask the sailor,' said Arabella. 'Has he still got the key or hasn't he?'

The sailor produced it triumphantly from his trouser pocket.

'Been in my possession all day, sir. Till I came down here now to unlock the door for you gentlemen.'

'She *was* coming down from the top deck,' said the passenger stubbornly. He did not like to be contradicted.

Arabella turned to the card players. 'Was I here or not?' she asked them.

'You've been here for the past hour and a bit,' said the man who had invited her to join their game.

'It's your word against his,' the Sergeant-at-Arms pointed out.

164

'But how could she get out? We're locked in like felons.' The man turned to address the crowd that had gathered round them. 'How long has Arabella been sitting with us?'

'More than an hour, like you said,' shouted someone. 'Who are these people coming in and waking us up? We've paid for our tickets, same as them. We don't go into their quarters – and we don't want them here, either, nosing around. Do we?'

'We certainly don't. Who do they think we are? This isn't a convict ship,' were some of the angry replies.

By now, nearly all the steerage passengers had left their cubicles. The men began to move slowly towards the visitors. Menace crackled like electricity in the foetid air.

'With the deepest respect, sir, I think you may be mistaken,' the officer said nervously to the passenger.

'No!'

'Well, you heard these people. And, as you can see, they are all locked in. So she must have been here all the time.'

'Damned odd,' said the other passenger. 'I could have sworn . . .'

'Then it's lucky you didn't have to,' said Arabella shortly. 'You would have been swearing to a lie.'

'Damned hussy!'

'There's no need for personal abuse,' said Arabella. 'You've made a mistake. If you're a gentleman, as this officer chooses to call you, you should at least apologise to a lady.'

The passenger snorted in disgust. 'I've had enough of this nonsense,' he declared. 'I know what I saw, and I've told you what I saw.'

'I think we had better leave, gentlemen,' said the officer. He looked around at faces now dark with anger.

The men began to stamp their feet, clap their hands as the little party went out of the watertight door. The sailor followed them, carefully not looking back. As Jamie heard the key turn in the lock, he sank back thankfully on his bunk. It was quite true. Arabella had not been on deck – but he had. The thought that his sister had very possibly visualised this ending of any argument he might have with Orlando, disturbed him. Her plan that he should pretend to be her had seemed absurd, but it had worked splendidly – from her point of view.

She had not thrown a man into the sea. He had. She would not have his death on her conscience. He would. She was hard, he knew, but until then, he had not realised just how ruthless she could be. And as he lay, he remembered her words after she'd shown him the earrings: 'I'm going to be hard – diamond-hard.'

Jamie undressed, pulled his blanket over him. But it was a long time before he fell asleep.

NINE

Cape Town

When the ship docked at Cape Town, the social and financial divisions of disembarking passengers became obvious to all.

First- and Second-Class passengers were solicitously shepherded down gangways to meet friends or relations on the quayside who drove them on to their hotels or homes. Third-Class passengers found their own way out of the ship down a smaller uncovered gangway. Steerage passengers, last on, were also last off, humping their bundles and bags and cheap cases and trunks as best they could through a narrow door that opened directly on to the quay.

After so long at sea, Arabella and Jamie felt slightly dizzy, almost off balance for a few moments, when they had to walk on firm ground. Everything seemed strange. But then, what had they expected – another Hyde or Manchester halfway round the world?

The sun was pitilessly bright and hot, far brighter and hotter than it had ever been on the warmest day in any summer they could recall. And colours glowed with a life of their own; all seemed to be vibrant primary colours, not pastel shades washed by rain. Also, in Hyde they might see one or two Indian or African seamen visiting Yeung Lee to sell him something. Here, there were hundreds of Africans, some in uniform and others in what appeared to be robes.

Behind the docks, they could see white buildings; no soot, no dirt, no fog. And behind these buildings stretched fields of a size neither had imagined in the confines of a small country. Behind the fields rose Table Mountain, wearing a tablecloth of cloud. To Arabella, deeply impressed by the size and space of everything, the mountain had the magnificence of a table being set for the gods.

Rosen had disembarked before them. He waited for them on the quay.

'Where are we going to stay?' he asked.

He wanted to get his feet under some solid table, a roof over his head, a wall behind his back. He did not feel at ease in this wide, unfenced land, near these strange black men with rolling eyes and thick lips and very white teeth. They were larger than he was. Were they also cleverer? He did not want to put that to the test.

'Our father made some arrangements with a Miss Pienaar,' said Jamie. 'I still have the address, but I haven't been in touch with her.'

They hailed a cab, bundled their trunks into it. The horse clip-clopped along the hard tarmac road. Some of the shops they passed had big glass windows; others, open unglazed fronts. They went through streets where sacks of nuts and beans stood outside small stores. Indians sat cross-legged on the pavement and spat red juice into the dust.

They saw tall Dutchmen riding by on fine horses. Six or even twelve oxen were yoked to carts, pulling vast loads wrapped in sackcloth. Half a dozen carriages, a truck, passed along the road. Everyone seemed busy. The air was electric with a pulsing urgency. People had come out here to make a fortune. Because of this, because they believed that whoever could travel lightest and alone also travelled fastest, they had left behind families and friends in other countries. This city was a bustling staging post on the road to riches.

Miss Pienaar lived in a neat house on a side street. It had a corrugated iron roof; two rooms in front downstairs, two behind, and a verandah with the balustrade palings painted alternately dark green and white. A bird in a cage whistled a welcome as the cab stopped outside. Miss Pienaar, a thin, tall woman of unknown age, with sharp eyes and a pointed nose, came to the front door, wiping her hands on a cloth. She looked at them all inquiringly.

'You were in contact with my father,' explained Arabella, 'Mr Hamish Baird. We've come to take up his rooms.'

'You have?' she said, surprised. 'That was a long time ago. Months, no, a year, at least. You were coming out – and then I never heard another word.'

'I am sorry. I should have written. Our father died, you see, and we were on our own. Anyway, here we are. I hope you can put us up. This is a friend of ours, Samuel Rosen, my brother Jamie, and I am Arabella.'

'It's lucky for you I have some rooms vacant,' said Miss Pienaar. 'A pity you didn't write and tell me you were coming.'

'Again, I'm sorry,' Arabella replied. 'We've not been abroad before.'

'Come in, then,' said Miss Pienaar, slightly mollified. These English people had not intended any discourtesy; they just didn't know any better. She must make allowances for their ignorance.

She led them through the house to a rear room which had been split into three by vertical wooden screens.

'Here you are. You decide who goes where,' she said, and left them on their own.

Their arrival seemed an anticlimax to what they had expected on their first day in South Africa. But what, Jamie wondered, had they expected? They knew no one here. Sammy Rosen was the best placed of the three. He had his uncle's £500, and some more money from the sale of his father's stock.

'I don't know what you plan,' he told the others, 'but I don't fancy staying any longer than I have to in these quarters. I'm for going north as soon as possible.'

'So are we,' replied Jamie. 'But first we have to raise money in order to live when we've bought a claim to dig for diamonds. You've got your money already, Sammy, so nothing need hold you back.'

Arabella and Jamie unpacked as few of their clothes as they thought they would need. They realised the wisdom of keeping their trunks locked and as few belongings visible as possible. Other lodgers were staying in the house, but none for more than a few days. Anything lost or stolen was unlikely to be recovered.

Sammy went off on his own to find the offices of the Inland Transport Company and book a passage to the diamond fields. After Manchester, the streets of Cape Town seemed strangely old-fashioned to him. The buildings were smaller, many made of wood and corrugated iron. People on the pavements wore what seemed to him outlandish clothes – rough serge jackets and trousers and wide-brimmed hats, and he thought he saw some smile at him. Did he appear to them as oddly dressed as they seemed to him? He had clearly just arrived; he did not quite fit in.

He found the offices in a side street. Several wagons with teams of oxen were drawn up outside, either waiting to leave or just arrived. A clerk was writing at a table inside the building.

'I want to book a seat north,' Sammy explained, not quite sure where exactly; the names of the places here all seemed so difficult to pronounce. He didn't wish to make a fool of himself.

'How far north? The diamond fields? Kimberley?'

'Yes.'

'They're all booked,' the clerk said shortly. 'You can't get a seat for another two months.'

'Two months! That's impossible. I can't believe it.'

'You don't have to. But it's the truth.'

'I've just arrived,' Sammy explained. 'All this is very new to me. Isn't there any way of getting there more quickly?'

'Sure there is. Find another passenger who has to cancel his trip. Make him an offer for his ticket.'

'How much is a ticket?'

'Forty pounds. Cash.'

'Where can I find any other passengers?'

'In the bars, round about.'

The clerk was non-committal, clearly not concerned about Sammy's problem. Sammy took a £1 note from his back pocket, folded it over and over to the size of a postage stamp, pushed it across the table.

'I told you I'm new here. What bars?'

'I'll take you round to one,' said the clerk, more civilly. He came out of the office, locked the door. They walked up the street together.

The saloon had a wooden floor, a scrubbed wooden counter. A lot of men, of the type Sammy had seen outside, rough-looking, unshaven, some with the watery eyes of seasoned drinkers, were lounging against the bar.

'What will you have?' Sammy asked the clerk.

'A Cape brandy. Try it. You'll like it. We call it Cape Smoke, it's so hot. Drives the bugs out.'

He nodded to one or two of the men. They nodded back. No one spoke. Then the clerk raised one finger of his right hand, beckoned towards a man at the far end of the bar.

The man brought a full glass of beer with him, dumped this so heavily on the counter that it spilled. He dipped a finger in the froth, licked it off his finger.

'Piet here is going north Thursday, but he's got wife trouble,' the clerk explained to Sammy. 'He could be delayed. He might sell you his ticket.' He turned to Piet. 'This gentleman has just come off the boat. Wants to go to the diamond fields.'

'That'll cost him sixty pounds,' said Piet immediately.

'I thought the fare was forty?' said Sammy.

'You thought right, it is forty. But as you can't get a ticket for months, it'll cost you more than an extra twenty pounds just living here. If you don't want it, don't buy it.'

'I'll buy it,' said Sammy. 'What about fifty pounds?'

'What about it?' replied Piet with the air of a man who had heard this proposal many times and always been able to turn it down. 'Sixty is the price.' He made as though to move away.

'All right,' said Sammy quickly. 'Sixty it is.'

'Come back to the office,' said the clerk. 'You don't want to flash money about here.'

Back in the company's office Sammy paid over six £10 notes. Piet stretched each one between his fingers, smoothed it, put it in a metal clip.

'I think you're mad, going,' he said.

'Why?'

'There's so many people up there already – and such a poor chance of finding anything. Last count there were said to be fifty thousand diggers. But who knows if there are fifty thousand diamonds? And even if there are, that would be only one each. Hardly pay your fare.'

'You got your money, now back to the bar,' said the clerk sharply. He did not want anyone to talk down the chances of finding a fortune in the fields. The more who tried, the more seats his company sold. Piet shrugged, shuffled out of the office.

As soon as he had gone, the clerk turned to Sammy. 'Don't pay any attention to him. He's just sore he's not got rich like so many others. He had a spell up there and picked up a few diamonds. But he drank all his profits away. Now he makes a living by buying tickets in advance and trying to sell them off at a profit – like to you. Tell me, you've heard of Barney Barnato?'

'Of course. I saw him once in London. Not to speak to, though.'

'Well, when Barney was on his way north, he had a drink with Piet and told him he was going to dig for diamonds. Piet said: "Don't waste your time. I've had a go up there, I didn't find anything worth a damn."

'Not so long afterwards, when Barney was a diamond millionaire, he ran into Piet again, and Piet asked him how had he been so lucky to find all those diamonds.

' "I'll tell you," said Barnato. "I did it by not taking your advice." '

When Jamie and Arabella heard how much Sammy had paid for a seat in a cart going north, they realised they would have to book two seats at the set price and wait for two months -- if they could not find any cheaper means of transport. This meant they would have to keep themselves in Cape Town for two months. And how could they do this in a strange city, when they both lacked any qualifications?

Miss Pienaar had nothing to suggest. 'It would have been different with your father,' she said gloomily, stating the obvious. 'I remember, in his letter he said he had been an estate carpenter. There's always work here for carpenters, making doors, furniture and so on for the new houses going up. But for you two, I don't know what to say. I wish I could help you.'

'I could keep your books,' said Arabella hopefully. 'I have a good head for figures.'

'Books!' snorted Miss Pienaar. 'I don't bother with those. People pay me so much a week. I pay out what I have to to run the place. The difference is my profit. I have no need for books.'

'Could you introduce me to anyone who might want a bookkeeper?'

'I would if I could, but I've never met anyone like that. You'd better ask at the bank. They deal in money.'

Arabella put on her best clothes and went to the main office of the Cape County Chartered Bank. She thought she would have a better chance of employment here than by going to a sub-branch where the local manager might not have the authority to engage staff. She carried the two diamond earrings in her handbag.

The bank entrance in St George's Street was flanked by impressive Doric columns. Huge bronze lanterns hung from the stone wall on either side of the front door. A tall native, dressed in khaki uniform, with a highly polished leather belt, waited on the pavement to open carriage doors and salute the occupants if they went up the steps to the bank.

Arabella momentarily and uncharacteristically lost her nerve when she saw the sheer size and importance of the building, and walked on to the next intersection. There, she stood for a moment, considering her best means of approach, and telling herself how absurd it was to feel so nervous about approaching a bank. She had seen equally impressive bank buildings in Manchester, and all marked by the same florid Byzantine style of architecture. Why was it that banks built their offices to look so imposing, so unyielding, so safe – when nearly every week the newspapers reported details of another bank that had failed?

This thought reassured her. She walked back resolutely to the bank, nodded briefly to the doorman who bowed respectfully and then bounded up the steps to open the door for her.

Arabella walked into a hall tiled in marble; busts of Roman emperors looked down from niches in the walls. Men were cashing cheques, drawing out money, paying it in from blue bags; she was the only woman. She crossed the tiles to the nearest free booth, her heels clicking on the hard polished surface. A clerk counting notes with a rubber thimble on his finger glanced up at her.

'I would like to see the manager,' she said.

'Have you an appointment, ma'am?'

'No. I would like you to make one for me.'

174

'He's very busy.'

'So am I.'

'Your name?'

'Miss Arabella Baird of England.'

'Could you tell me your business?'

'I would rather tell him.'

'Please wait a moment.'

The clerk went on counting the notes. He scribbled the total on a pad, left his stool without looking at her. A few moments later he returned.

'The manager is still busy, but one of his deputies, Mr Roosner, will see you.'

She came round to his side of the counter, through a door, into a room panelled in light pine. A high window had bars across it. To keep people out or in? she wondered absurdly. A small man, wearing a blue barathea suit with a round-edged stiff white collar, looked up from his desk.

'Miss Baird,' he said. 'How can I help you?'

'I would like to open an account, and lodge as security two items of jewellery.'

She opened her handbag, pushed the earrings across the table to Mr Roosner, and sat down facing him.

'We could place these in a safety-deposit box, Miss Baird, if you were a customer. But how do I know what they are worth? They are very pretty, but are they valuable?'

'I am new to this country, but from what I have read, Mr Roosner, South Africa is the home of diamonds. Have you no one here who could value them?'

'I will ask one of my colleagues.'

Mr Roosner punched a bell. A clerk came in. 'Mr Straaten, please.'

Mr Straaten was an older man, bald and gaunt-looking. He wore spectacles with lenses so thick they reminded Arabella of the bottoms of beer bottles at the Silent Witness.

'Can you put a value on these earrings?' Mr Roosner asked him.

'For the owner, or the bank?'

'The bank.'

'Is there a difference?' asked Arabella.

'Of course. We might be prepared to lend on our valuation, but not on yours which, naturally, would be higher.'

Mr Straaten produced a jeweller's glass from his pocket, pushed his spectacles up on to his forehead, placed the glass in his right eye and examined the earrings.

'They are good diamonds,' he said. 'Seventeen carats each, at a guess. I would think we could value these from the bank's point of view at one hundred and fifty pounds.'

'That's surely very low?' said Arabella.

'It's on the side of safety,' said Straaten.

'Would you lend me the amount of your valuation?'

'Without any other monies coming into the account?' asked Mr Roosner.

'For the time being. But later on, I hope there would be quite a lot of money coming in.'

'Can I ask from what source?'

'Business,' she replied shortly.

'Have you any guarantors?'

'My brother. My twin brother.'

'And how old are you, Miss Baird?'

'Seventeen.'

'I regret we cannot accept a guarantor under the age of twenty-one. Indeed, it is not usual for anyone below that age to have their own account.'

'I would like to make it more usual. Will you advance me one hundred pounds on these earrings?'

'I think that that would be rather much.' He paused uneasily. This girl disturbed him; she seemed so full of confidence.

'I see. Then I have something else to ask you,' said Arabella.

'I would like to have a job in your bank.'

'A *job*, Miss Baird? But you have only recently arrived in the Cape.'

'Does that affect my suitability to add up figures?'

'Not necessarily so. But you do not understand the ways of the country. Also, I must tell you that in this bank we do not employ any women.'

'Could you not employ one?'

'It would be against the policy of the board. They consider that women employees could prove a distraction for the male staff.'

'In England, women are already working in offices. They are called "typewriters" because they operate typing machines.'

'I am aware of that, but England is not the Cape. And how do I know you can add up figures?'

'Give me any sum, any set of figures, any percentage to be worked out, any profit ratio. Try me.'

'This is most unusual,' said Mr Roosner. 'But, purely as a matter of interest, I will.'

He opened a drawer, pulled out a balance sheet, held a piece of paper over the totals of the profit and loss accounts so that Arabella could not see them, turned the sheet towards her.

'Please add up the column on the left,' he said.

Arabella did so quickly.

'It comes to seven thousand, four hundred and thirteen pounds, six shillings and eight pence,' she said.

Mr Roosner checked the bottom line. 'You are wrong!' he said triumphantly. 'It is actually seven thousand, *nine* hundred and thirteen pounds, six shillings and eight pence. You are five hundred pounds out.'

'Not so,' replied Arabella. 'If you look at the bottom of the page, there's an additional sum of five hundred pounds cash paid out.'

'So there is. You are in the right, Miss Baird.'

'Do I also have the right to a job – *any* job?'

'I am sorry. It is beyond my power to give you one.'

'Is there any part-time work? Anything I could do at home?'

'I fear not, Miss Baird. However, I will open an account for you with a letter to the effect that you will guarantee the account to the value of fifty pounds. Having regard to your present situation, where you are seeking employment, and not, as you gave me to understand, actually engaged in business, I would not be prepared to advance any more.'

'It's very low, given the security. Your expert values the earrings at three times that amount, and they are obviously worth at least four or five times that figure.'

'One has to protect the interests of the shareholders.'

'You do that very efficiently, Mr Roosner. Well, if you will draw up the letter of guarantee, I will sign it.'

Arabella waited while a clerk wrote it out. She signed it and then went out, keeping her head averted, not looking Mr Roosner in the eye. She did not wish him to see she was near to tears – not of disappointment, but of frustration and rage.

Sometimes, years later, Arabella and Jamie would remember the next two months in Cape Town: not at all clearly, or with any pleasure, or even much pain, but wondering whether they had ever experienced them at all. There was something so unreal about those eight weeks that it seemed as though they had imagined them. Arabella went back from the bank to Miss Pienaar's house and explained that she had not been able to get a job working with figures.

'Is there anything I can do for you, Miss Pienaar, any work about the house, if you don't want your books kept?'

'There is nothing, child,' said Miss Pienaar. 'You see, we've got natives to do most of the work. I look after the place. There is nothing at all.'

'I'm sorry to have to keep on asking,' said Arabella, 'but

do you know anybody who would give me a job?'

'I don't,' Miss Pienaar replied. 'Look in the local papers, see what they advertise.'

Arabella did so. An English family, lately arrived, required an English nursemaid; an elderly man, wife recently deceased, desired a housekeeper. She applied for both jobs – and half a dozen like them. But someone had always beaten her to it – or she was too young or not quite right, or the widower really wanted a mistress, not a housekeeper. Each attempt seemed blocked.

Jamie fared similarly. He applied for jobs as a clerk, messenger boy, as general handyman, but the vacancies were ludicrously outnumbered by all manner of English or Afrikaners who apparently had seen the advertisement first. He despaired until one day, returning to Miss Pienaar's, and wondering how they could economise even more to preserve their dwindling capital until a seat became vacant, he heard the familiar trumpeting of a steam organ, and followed the sound. At the end of a narrow street, on a great stretch of wasteland where children played and some animals were tethered, men were setting up tents for a fair.

The organ was being tuned. Two men were working on the pipes while a third, cheroot in his mouth, played 'O, promise me' on the keys. As Jamie stood among the caravans and heavy trucks, a fat man in khaki trousers and a stained khaki shirt with a huge leather belt studded with brass ornaments came towards him.

'No vacancies, son,' he said. 'Nothing. Sorry.'

'What about someone for a side-show?' asked Jamie.

'What do you mean? What sort of side-show?'

'A fellow who takes on all comers for, say, a five-pound purse, maybe a ten-pound purse, I don't know. Free-for-all fighting. One five-minute round and the first time a man's thrown, his opponent's the winner.'

'We got a boxer already,' said the man doubtfully. 'Who have you got in mind for this?'

'Me,' said Jamie.

'You? Why, some of the blokes out here could eat you for breakfast.'

'Maybe,' said Jamie, 'but not for dinner. Anyhow, why not give me a try?'

'How can you fight anyone free-for-all? They'll kick you in the pills first thing out, then you're down. They're a tough lot here. You just out from England?'

'Yes.'

'What's your name?'

'Jamie Baird. And yours?'

'Bill Carter. I came out here ten years ago. In the merchant navy. Jumped ship, as a matter of fact. Went up north, dug for diamonds, found a few but thought this was a better way of making a living. My father used to be in it so I know something about it. I sold the diamonds and started. I own the whole show.'

'In Hyde, in the north of England,' said Jamie, 'I stood in for a fighter. The Mexican Typhoon, name of Monrova.'

'Ah, yes,' he said. 'Jed Mainwright was running him. That right?'

'I don't know. The manager just paid me.'

'What did he pay you?'

For a moment, Jamie did not answer. What he'd earned was none of this man's business. Then he changed his mind; he needed the job and the fee might be a useful bargaining lever.

'A pound a fight,' he said. 'Five fights a night, Monday to Saturday. Thirty pounds.'

'What happened then? You got beaten?'

'No. When I had enough money to pay my debts, I cleared off, came out here.'

'You waiting to go diamond digging, too?'

'Yes.'

'How are you so good, fighting? You look pretty slim-built to me.'

'Try me, see what I can do.'

'You could get hurt. Badly. I don't want to cripple a young bloke. But if you want a fight, I'll put you in against our boxer. He's twenty stone, used to be a heavyweight wrestler. He'll mix it, you know. If you can beat him, I'd say you could beat anyone.'

'If I can, do I get a job?'

Carter rubbed his jaw, still unsure of Jamie's capabilities.

'I need the money,' said Jamie. 'I am here with my sister. She's very good with figures, can add up any sort of columns, double-entry bookkeeping, you name it. But she can't get a job and we're waiting here for two months until we can get a cheap seat going north. I don't want to make a career of this.'

'Who did?' asked Carter. 'Not me. It just seemed a good thing at the time.'

'So does this to me. Give me a break. See if I can do it. If not, OK, I'm the loser, not you.'

'Right,' Carter agreed, making up his mind. 'Follow me.'

On the far side of the steam organ a tent larger than the rest was already set up. They went inside. A boxing ring had been erected on a small platform, with a set of wooden steps leading up to it. Two men were tightening the ropes. They looked up as Carter and Jamie came in. One was a thin man in shabby dungarees; the other was very much larger, with a bullet head totally shaven, menacing by his sheer size. He wore a dirty blue vest. His shoulders and arms were liberally tattooed: on the right, 'Death before dishonour'; on the left, 'Mother love'.

'Here he is,' said Carter.

Jamie held out his hand. The boxer shook it.

'What do you want, son?'

'A job.'

'Nothing doing here, Bill. The two of us work this booth. You know that.'

181

'He doesn't want a job setting up the booth or taking money. He wants a job fighting.'

'Who – me?'

'No, but I thought you could try and see if he's any good.'

'Go on! I don't want to kill the kid. I weigh in at twenty stone. He can't be more than eleven.'

'I'm not,' Jamie agreed, 'but I need a job. I'll take on all comers for an agreed price.'

'Is he serious?' the boxer asked Carter in amazement.

'Dead serious. We could do with another stunt – if he's any good. But don't kill him. He's only trying to make enough money to go and dig for diamonds.'

'He must be barmy, twice over. Once, to try it with me. Second, to think he's got a hope of finding diamonds. They've all been dug out long ago.'

'Maybe,' agreed Jamie. 'But let's start if we're going to.'

The boxer shrugged. 'You've asked for it,' he said. 'Don't cry if you get it.'

Jamie went up the steps, ducked under the top rope, took off his jacket, his tie and collar, put the studs in a side pocket, rolled up his sleeves.

'What's the spiel, exactly?' asked Carter. 'Imagine this is packed with punters. What do you tell them?'

'This,' said Jamie. 'I'll take on anybody, fight to win over one five-minute round. No fall, no win. No draws. There are no holds barred. Stress that people can get hurt, *badly* hurt. Every challenger comes into the ring entirely at his own risk and in full knowledge that this is a dangerous business. Play on that and you'll have to shoe-horn the punters in. The crowd hopes they'll be seeing someone getting hurt. They will be, too, if they get thrown out of the ring.'

'Or if you do.'

'Exactly,' agreed Jamie.

The boxer climbed into the ring with Jamie, spat on his hands, flexed his shoulders, his knees, did a bit of shadow boxing to show the speed of his reflexes.

'As you're the challenger, you'd better attack me,' Jamie told him.

The boxer nodded. He was basically a kindly man. He did not want to kill this kid, but he could not afford to look a fool or a cissy in front of the fair's owner. His own job wasn't all that safe or secure. He was old for this game, running to fat. And one day, some challenger would come in and beat him. If he was beaten once, he would be beaten a second time. And after that, he'd lose his nerve. This was a young man's game. He could not appear to be expendable.

He approached Jamie, his hands balled into fists, left arm out, right arm across his body as a guard. Suddenly, he jumped forward, hit Jamie a straight right to his jaw. Jamie had seen the boxer's eyes narrow momentarily before he punched. Jamie swerved. The boxer's huge fist went harmlessly over his shoulder, past his ear.

Instinctively, Jamie ducked, stepped forward, pivoted the boxer on his arm, swung him up, over – and out. The man landed on the top rope, teetered for a moment, then fell heavily on his back on the sawdust boards of the ring. He lay, half stunned, and then slowly stood up, struck himself on the side of the head with the flat of his left hand to clear his dizziness. He put out his right hand to hold the top rope.

'What happened?' he asked weakly.

'I threw you,' said Jamie.

'You certainly threw him,' said Carter admiringly. 'Never seen anything so quick in all my life.'

'If we were doing this for money,' said Jamie, 'I wouldn't make it so quick. I'd let him get a few blows in, but not too many, and not too hard – just enough to give the paying customers a bit of a show.'

'Right, son. If you can do that with him, you can do it with anyone. What do you want?'

'What are you offering?'

'You got a pound a fight in England. Five fights a night. What about that again?'

'What about that for the first week?' said Jamie. 'After that, maybe we go up, or if you don't like the show, we could go down. I'll take the risk on that. And one other thing. No, two.'

'What are they?'

'You provide me with proper gear to fight in. Vest and shorts. Canvas shoes. And my sister and I, after the last fight each night, get a good meal here, free. As much as we can eat.'

'Agreed,' said Carter. 'You're a strange bloke. But you've got pluck, and you may have an act.'

'I've got something more important,' said Jamie, smiling. 'A job.'

But when he told Arabella, she frowned at the deal he had arranged. 'You should have asked for more,' she said. 'You'll be the sensation of the fair. The man they can't beat. I'd have gone for double.'

'You're a hard girl, Bella.'

'Someone has to be out of us two, for you're not.'

TEN

Murder in Nice

As Noel Rudgers came into his suite at the Royale Hotel, overlooking the Promenade des Anglais in Nice, a man who had been sitting in an easy chair, facing the window, stood up to greet him.

'Who the hell are you?' Noel asked him roughly, and then he recognised the fellow; he had seen him on several occasions in the casino at Monte Carlo. He was a manager or some such thing, a person of little account, a hireling whose obsequious greetings Noel had always accepted with a curt nod or brief acknowledgement to show the extent of the gulf between their social classes.

'How did you get in here?' he asked now, less abrasively but still angrily. He had been frightened by seeing a stranger in his room. He owed a lot of money to a lot of people and not all were gentlemanly in their endeavours to reduce his indebtedness.

'Through the door,' the man replied coldly. 'Like you. I have friends on the staff.'

'Surely it isn't usual for a hotel of this calibre and quality to allow a complete stranger to wander into a guest's rooms without permission – even if he has friends on the staff?'

'That depends on the guest in question. I could ask you whether it is usual for someone staying in a hotel of what you describe as this calibre and quality to run up a month's

185

bills – as he has done with several other hotels along the coast? Perhaps there comes a time when the management feels concern as to the guest's ability to pay?'

'That is no business of yours. I have the money. I will pay when I want to. Now get out!'

'When I am ready, I will be pleased to leave. I am not here because I am concerned about your debts to hotels, Mr Rudgers, important though I know them to be, but because of your debt to the casino. Do you know how much you owe?'

'Nothing substantial, I would think.'

'That would depend on your definition of substantial. In pounds sterling, rounded to the nearest pound, it is ten thousand pounds. I have the exact figure here.'

The man took out a piece of paper, put it down on an ormolu table. Noel picked it up, glanced at the rows of figures and the dates beside them. The sum seemed unbelievable. How could a few evenings with a bottle or two of bubbly, a flutter here and there on the wheel, possibly amount to so much?

'You should have told me before it mounted up,' said Noel sulkily.

'I endeavoured to do so on several occasions, as you may recall. But you always said you were too busy to discuss the matter. You did not wish to be disturbed. Now, I think I am disturbing you. Your easiest course, Mr Rudgers, is to pay.'

'In all honesty, I haven't that amount of money with me,' Noel admitted. 'I will have to wire to London for it.'

'You have given me that excuse in the past. Frequently. I am reluctant to accept it again. Either you pay this money in full within a week, or we shall take other steps to collect it. And I do not necessarily mean the process of law. One week, Mr Rudgers. In the meantime, all credit at the casino is suspended. I will not visit you again. You know where my office is. You know the time limit. Now, goodbye.'

Noel watched the manager leave the room. He crossed to the

window and stood looking out across the wide street at the shingle beach and the sea. Ten thousand pounds. He had nothing like that amount of money in all the world. Well, he had, of course, but it was already bespoken to three or four other people who were dunning him mercilessly.

Debts increased hourly with compound interest payable to banks, to strange tiny men with pointed beards and thick middle-European accents, who, in the back pages of newspapers, advertised their willingness to lend large sums 'on note of hand' without security. Such advertisements did not include details of the interest this facility attracted; it could be as much as seventy per cent.

In one such transaction, which offered what the money-lender described as 'accommodation', the interest was agreeably low at ten per cent and Noel had borrowed heavily. Only when he had signed the agreement did he read some lines in minute print at the bottom of the page. The interest was indeed only ten per cent – but p.m. instead of p.a. He was paying ten per cent per month – 120 per cent annually.

There was only one way he could raise anything like this new amount now – from his wife Emily. But Emily had already helped him on too many occasions. He knew she would not be willing to advance him any more money to pay gambling debts. For one thing, she disapproved of gambling. For another, she was disappointed in him as a man and as a husband.

As Noel watched his uninvited visitor cross the road and walk along the promenade, he reached a decision which he admitted had been fermenting in his mind for some time. He must kill his wife. By such a simple and finite act he would release her fortune and soar above all these disagreeable creditors, for she had frequently told him he was the only beneficiary of her will.

For a moment, Noel leant against the cream and gold stripes of the wallpaper, wondering when and where and how he would do what he had finally decided must be done. Then he poured himself a treble measure of whisky and emptied the glass at a single draught. He poured himself another, and sat down in a silk brocaded armchair to ponder the problem.

The room was filled with flowers, their scent strong. He might already be in a funeral parlour, and he wished he was, with the deed done and a rich golden future stretching ahead.

Noel Rudgers was not his real name, of course, but as King Edward VII liked, for sound reasons of his own, to use the pseudonym of the Duke of Lancaster when he travelled on the Continent, so Rudgers concealed his true identity behind this humble name when he came to France to gamble.

He was twenty-five, standing six foot four in his monogrammed silk socks. Catching sight of himself in one of the mirror panels on the wall, Noel instinctively smoothed back his glossy black hair. He was handsome, damned handsome, he knew, and one day he would inherit from an uncle the title of Lord Doncaster, and miles and miles of Scottish moors, row upon row of terraced houses in south-east London that had been in the family for years.

They had been built to house workers at the armaments factories in Erith and Crayford in which his grandfather had held a majority share. But inheritance was still far away. His uncle was not old, although his habit of drinking a bottle of port a day was unlikely to prolong his life. Even so, Noel might have to wait for years before he could claim the estate. What he desperately needed was money now, within a week, before ruin and social ostracism overtook him.

He had gambled since boyhood, betting on the most unlikely things at Eton: that the Provost would be wearing a blue suit; that the three o'clock train from London to Windsor would be drawn by a Leviathan-class locomotive; that the next vehicle past the college gates would be a brougham, or one of the new Panhard motor cars.

At Oxford, he had accepted more sophisticated wagers. He had bet on the outcome of the Boat Race; on which college would be Head of the River; how many punts would pass within an hour beneath Magdalen Bridge on May Day. Sometimes he had won, but more often he had lost.

At first, his losses did not amount to much – a few shillings, then a few pounds; then, more seriously, a few hundred pounds. But everyone knew who he was, and what he was. In England, the foibles of the rich were treated with tolerance.

Initially, Noel had been able to raise money by surreptitiously selling a gold watch or diamond cufflinks someone had given him as a birthday present. Once or twice, he had helped himself to other small items of value, from either the family's London house in Hanover Square or their seat in Scotland. A silver cigar box, which no one seemed to miss, would disappear, or a couple of silver napkin rings in a plush-lined case that no one appeared to remember was kept in the back of a rarely opened cupboard.

Once or twice, spoons with the family crest had actually turned up in local shops and been recognised. Of course, an under-butler or a footman had been instantly dismissed for gross dishonesty. Noel viewed their misfortune with total equanimity, but he realised that it must only be a matter of time before the finger of suspicion must finally point at him. He was the common factor in all these disappearances.

As a gentleman, of course, he was expected to run up debts, and he knew he could not be sued for a gambling debt. The law had been carefully framed to champion the interests of the aristocracy who liked to gamble, but the obverse of this was that society demanded that a gentleman always paid his gambling debts.

He could owe his tailor, his shoemaker, his wine merchant; he could ruin a grocer through not paying his bills for years, but gambling was something special. Gamblers had their own strict rules of etiquette which no one could break and expect to remain a man of honour. Also, if he did not pay he would lose more than caste. He would lose the right to gamble, and this was the ultimate, unthinkable punishment.

The person who had just visited him knew these rules; he also knew Noel's real identity. A few discreet words from him could affect his uncle's opinion of him to the extent that he might alter his will.

To Noel, the sum he owed at Monte Carlo was only an impersonal matter of numbers and noughts on a piece of paper. What was important was the excitement he felt as soon as he entered the casino. Red-shaded lights cast a dim, warming glow over the room. Brighter pools of light illuminated the spinning roulette wheels and the gaunt faces of compulsive gamblers like Noel who sat around each table. Their faces appeared as grotesque as painted skulls. Above their stiff shirts, their eyes seemed hollow. Cigars glowed unnaturally red between white and bloodless lips. Like Noel, gambling was for them a disease without a cure. Their lives began when they entered the casino at dusk, and ended when they left in the early hours of the following morning, when dawn had touched the sky with gold, and cab drivers dozed and weary horses slept on their feet waiting for the rich to go home.

Noel had been gambling in the casino every night for the three weeks he had spent on the Riviera. He could not live – as he called living – without that feeling of rising excitement he looked forward to each day after dark when he was back in his special world of green baize tables, the red and the black, the croupiers' cry: '*Faites vos jeux. Rien ne va plus.*'

Earlier in the year, he had been forced to take his most serious step towards solvency. He had married. Emily was an American heiress. She had inherited a fortune from her father, whose father before him had patented a process for toasting grains of wheat, dusting them with sugar and selling them in packets by the million as a breakfast cereal.

Noel had never wished to marry Emily, but then he had never wished to marry anyone. He always felt uneasy in the company of girls, or indeed with women of any age. His love was for boys in their early teens, when their sexual responses were immediate, and their powers of attraction and recuperation at their peak.

Other men of Noel's class and position, but with more orthodox desires, could go regularly to houses in Jermyn Street, off the Haymarket, where girls, all claiming to be virgins just up from the country, would minister to their sexual inclinations. Noel preferred to travel to the safety of Paris, or – as now – to Nice, where the need of an English aristocratic male for the companionship of boys was viewed tolerantly, and whimsically called 'the English vice'.

In England, such associations could lead to imprisonment, ruin, and not infrequently to suicide, if the terrible facts ever became publicly known. In France, it was accepted without drama as being no more important than a difference of taste, just as in a restaurant one diner preferred boeuf en croûte to homard froid.

Did the casino manager suspect that he was a pederast? Worse, did he *know*?

Noel's uncle, Lord Doncaster, who had a sharp tongue and suspected Noel's weakness, was caustic about his marriage – as about so much else concerning his nephew, especially his gambling.

'You're a damned fool,' he told Noel gruffly, his voice hoarse from fifty years of smoking six five-inch Havanas a day.

'Just like your mother. She was French, of course. Continentals are different from us. No backbone. She could never resist a flutter, as she called it. Went through tens of thousands in the end. Must run in the blood.

'But remember this, Noel. With your wife's American money, you will just be a kept man, a gigolo, selling your flesh. And made to dance to her tune – if that worries you, which I doubt – so long as she pays your debts.'

'In all honesty, I love her,' Noel assured his uncle insincerely.

'Rubbish! You love her money, that's all. Well, she has enough of it. And my advice to you is, get your hands on it quickly – before she finds out that's all you want. She can't kid herself you fell for her good looks. She's as pretty as the back of a hansom cab. And as dull.'

This was true; Noel knew that quite well. He had been surprised, flattered, even slightly disgusted at Emily's almost pathetic pleasure when he asked for her hand in marriage. She seemed incredibly naive, innocent. The mind of an uninquiring and gentle child lived in the dumpy, plain suet-pudding body of a woman of thirty-five.

Emily knew nothing about men; she never had the chance to learn. Her mother died when she was five, and her father was always remote, gruff, uncommunicative. A succession of strict spinster nurses and governesses brought her up. They knew no more about men than she did, and so lacked knowledge or experience to pass on to her.

She was, of course, a virgin; she had no idea what a husband might ask of her sexually. She knew people did what she called 'something' to have a baby, but this almost incredible innocence pleased Noel. He felt a distaste for normal intercourse (unless it was absolutely essential in order to have his debts paid) but lying with Emily and keeping his eyes closed, he could almost imagine he was entering a boy from the rear instead of his wife.

This was not wholly satisfactory to either of them, but like their marriage as a whole, it was a compromise. Noel could endure this, and might even satisfy any other request she might make, as long as she remained generous to him.

At first, she appeared surprised to discover how what to her were relatively unimportant sums of money – five or six thousand pounds – could appear vital in the calculations of a man whose family had owned estates since the days when all England was a forest, and Normans were fighting Saxons on the shingle of a Sussex beach.

Emily remembered how her father would make her walk with him around his mills, where the air always seemed foggy with flour and drying wheat, and even as a child she noticed how workpeople deferred to him.

'You'll own all this one day,' he told Emily on these occasions, as though he was giving her news she did not already know. 'So you might as well see how everything works. Then you'll never be short-changed by anyone. Employees will try all sorts of fiddles, given half a chance. So don't give any of 'em – or anyone else – a quarter chance. If you suspect anyone, *anywhere*, is short-changing you, go for 'em. No excuses. No mercy. No second chances.'

Emily used to feel embarrassed at being virtually put on show, but she realised that her father talked sense, so she learned more about his business – now her business – than she would ever admit. If she wasn't good-looking or sophisticated, she need not also be foolish about matters involving money.

She had travelled to Nice for the last week of Noel's visit. He had not wanted her to arrive earlier, and had explained at length, but not altogether convincingly, how heavily he would be involved in business discussions which would simply be boring for her. For the last week, however, he would be relatively free and then they could enjoy themselves.

Noel had recently bought from a Russian archduke what he assured him was an absolutely foolproof system to win at roulette. Unfortunately, in practice, it did not prove to be infallible. If it had been, why would the archduke be willing to share such a valuable secret for a relatively small sum? But Noel thought of that too late; many thousands of francs too late.

Emily soon found that French food was too rich for her. She complained of indigestion, and she hated late nights, especially the hot, stuffy atmosphere in the casino to which her husband insisted on taking her. The air around the tables and the wheels was thick with blue and choking clouds of cigar smoke in which the gamblers' faces seemed to waft, disembodied, an effect exaggerated by lights above the tables which shone on their faces but left the rest of their bodies in darkness. To Emily, the gamblers seemed not real people, but pale ghouls, creatures of the night, spectres who only ventured out at an hour when honest hardworking folk were all in bed. What would her father have said about them?

Sometimes, Emily almost wished she was back at home in his house in Pittsburg. She knew that life; she understood it. She might not have liked it greatly when she was there, but it was infinitely to be preferred to this false and brittle sham of turning night into day, of spending the hours of darkness breathing cigar smoke and peering at cards or a slowly turning wheel.

Emily came into the hotel suite now, crossed the room, gave Noel a light kiss on his cheek. Instinctively, he turned away. He could not bear to kiss her, and also he did not wish her to smell whisky on his breath. Usually, he chewed a peppermint or a cashew when he had been drinking, but because of his visitor he had forgotten to put one in his mouth. Emily would never drink any alcoholic beverage. Her father had been an enthusiastic member of several temperance societies, and she had spoken to Noel on several occasions about the need to abandon his habit of drinking several whiskies every evening before he went out. It would shorten his life, she said.

In one of the wall mirrors that lined the room, he saw Emily's face muscles tighten. She was growing used by now to his coldness, but each instance of it still hurt. Noel felt vaguely surprised that such a dull woman could be hurt so easily, or even at all.

'You are late, darling,' he said brightly, not critically, simply for something to say.

'Yes,' Emily agreed. 'I took a cab and had it drive me along the coast to Cannes. It was wonderful, like fairyland. Lights were coming on in all the big hotels and the houses, and they were reflected in the water. I realised for the first time the charm and beauty of this coast. Take me out to dinner somewhere exciting,' she added unexpectedly. '*Please.*'

'Of course,' Noel replied mechanically.

This was the first time Emily had ever suggested going out to a restaurant; he was the one who liked to dine expensively and often. Now a tiny voice inside him whispered that if he did what he intended, this would be the last meal they took together. Surely, he owed it to her – and himself – to make certain this was an evening to remember? Certainly, it would be one he would never forget.

'Where would you like to go?' he asked dutifully. He had never felt less like eating a five-course meal in a restaurant, with each succeeding dish richer than the last, while a string orchestera played softly in the background. However, Emily would be paying; she always did. He need not stint himself over the bubbly. That would cheer him up.

'I don't know,' she admitted, giggling suddenly like a little girl. 'You choose.'

'Of course.'

He took her to the grill room of the Bristol Hotel where the head waiter knew him well. As far as Noel was concerned, the meal was not a total success. He felt tired, morose. His thoughts churned like a mill race gone mad. He could not put out of his mind what he had to do, and he hated the prospect. It made his flesh crawl, but he had convinced himself he had no alternative.

He could, of course, just ask his wife for more money to pay his debts, but she had already told him she would not give him any more. He had assured her, when he accepted £9,000 from her less than a month previously, that this would cover all his debts. But, as always, he had been lying. She would not easily forgive this. There had been too many earlier promises he had broken, and women shared one characteristic with elephants: they never forgot.

Emily prattled on inconsequentially, like one of the new clockwork gramophones that did not need rewinding for each record. She was trying to be cheerful and entertaining; the sort of woman she imagined Noel would appreciate. But Noel paid little attention to her beyond now and then nodding mechanically and saying 'Really?' or 'How extraordinary!'

He kept looking around the restaurant in case he saw someone he knew, who could join them and so dilute the boredom of Emily's chatter and dispel the horror of his plan. But he could see no one worth inviting. Their last evening would be spent alone together.

They were back in their suite by midnight. Emily undressed, went into the bathroom. In her dull yet inordinately expensive silk nightgown she bent over the marble wash basin, turned on the taps. Noel approached her from behind, placed his hands gently on her shoulders.

Emily looked at his reflection in the mirror, smiling and pleased at his attention; she had never known him so demonstrative before. Noel slowly raised his hands and pressed gently, then more fiercely, behind her ears. Emily straightened up. What was he doing?

In the mirror, Noel could see a fine white foam of toothpaste round her mouth. Then surprise, amazement, total disbelief, and finally the unbearable horror of realisation in her eyes. They seemed to swell to enormous size, accusing him, pleading silently with him. Then they grew hazy and dark.

Emily struggled and kicked, but in her bare feet she could

not hurt him. Suddenly, unexpectedly, her shoulders sagged. She would have fallen, but Noel supported her and carried her back to the bedroom. He laid her on her back on top of the silk coverlet, rearranged her nightgown modestly.

For a moment he thought he would wipe her face clean of toothpaste, but decided against it. This would bear out his story. While cleaning her teeth, she had suddenly felt unwell, and he had helped her back to the bedroom, where, as peacefully as she had lived, she had died.

Emily's face showed no sign of violence. But there had been no violence; Noel could not abide that sort of thing. The application of pressure to points in her neck where blood vessels came near the skin hindered the flow to the brain and assured a swift and painless passing. Emily had never made a fuss or hurt anyone in her life and she did neither at her death.

Noel stood looking down at her, trying to convince himself that he had not deliberately murdered his wife. In a sense, of course, it was her own fault. She had told him so often that, on her death, he would inherit all that was hers. If she had not said this, there would have been no need to kill her. He touched her forehead; it was not yet cold, but it was cooling. There was no doubt; she was dead, and he had killed her.

Noel felt mild regret that such a drastic and irrevocable act had been necessary, but he kept assuring himself there had simply been no other way of raising money it was imperative for him to secure. None. Now, he was free. Now, he could follow his own lusts, his own pleasures; but it would be unwise to do either too quickly with his wife so recently dead.

That young page boy with his eyes carefully and wickedly darkened by kohl, those full pink moistened lips, his rounded bottom so agonisingly and provocatively encased beneath tight trousers in a way infinitely more seductive than simple nakedness – he would investigate him. But later, not now. Now he had to act as the bereaved husband: bewildered, shocked, incredulous at what had happened, but always English, aristocratic, bravely containing his grief.

He pressed the bell at the bedside. Within seconds, a servant was knocking discreetly at the door. Noel opened it.

'Fetch a doctor quickly,' he said sharply. 'One who speaks English preferably. My wife has fainted.'

'*Mais oui, monsieur.*'

Within minutes, the servant was back with the hotel doctor, a stooping man in his late fifties, carrying the black bag of his calling.

'You speak English?' Noel asked him.

'I have an English wife.'

'Good. My wife was performing her ablutions – actually cleaning her teeth – when she complained of a headache and called to me. I ran into the bathroom – you can see I had not even started to undress – and caught her just as she began to faint. I managed to carry her back and put her on the bed here. I can't feel her heart beat. She doesn't seem to be breathing.'

The doctor felt Emily's pulse, took a mirror from his bag, held it in front of her mouth and nose. He raised her left eyelid, shone a torch into the eye. Then he turned to Noel.

'I am sorry to tell you, sir, your wife is dead.'

'*Dead*? What of?'

'That is impossible to say without a full examination. Was she subject to fainting fits? Did she complain of any chest pains?'

'No. This was the first time I have ever seen her faint.'

'Forgive me, sir, but was she *enceinte*?'

'Not as far as I am aware. No. Nothing like that. We had been out to dinner at the Bristol.'

'I will make arrangements with the hotel for you to have another suite. Where would you like your late wife to be taken?'

'I don't know. I have no idea.'

'There is a British consul in Nice. I suggest you see him and arrange the formalities.'

He handed Noel his card. He read it mechanically: Dr Artur Delauneville.

'I am at your service, sir. That is my private address. I have a surgery here in the hotel.'

'You are very kind,' said Noel.

They shook hands. Noel watched the doctor leave, then turned back to stare at his dead wife.

Emily had fluttered like a rich butterfly into his life. For a brief time, her money and generosity had financed his gambling. Now she had folded her wings and would not fly again. It had all been so absurdly easy. One moment she was alive, and the next she wasn't.

Noel poured himself four fingers of whisky. As he raised the glass to his lips, toasting the glorious future that would now be his, the telephone began to ring.

ELEVEN

Veldt and Desert

Jamie and Arabella went to see Sammy Rosen off on his journey by coach. He appeared nervous, ill at ease.

'I wish I was staying here and coming on with you,' he admitted.

'No,' said Arabella. 'You go ahead – the pioneer. Have a good look round Kimberley. Then, when we arrive, we can be all set to make our fortunes.'

'You make it sound so easy,' said Sammy.

'That's the only way to tackle it,' Arabella told him. 'Optimism. Confidence. Those must be our watchwords. I read the other day how a man went across Niagara Falls on a tightrope pushing a wheelbarrow with a barrel in it. He didn't think what was going to happen if he fell – he knew. So he said, "When I get to the other side, I'm going to sell my story to the newspapers." '

'And did he?' asked Sammy.

'He must have done,' said Jamie. 'I read it, too! Come on, cheer up!'

As Sammy was about to climb into the coach, he suddenly turned to them, handed Jamie an envelope.

'Something in it for you both,' he said. 'Don't open it until I've gone.'

'Rubbish! I'll open it now.' Jamie ripped open the envelope. Inside was a pound note.

'What's this?' he asked.

'I felt rather bad taking that ten shillings off you for the key on the boat. Here it is, with interest – one hundred per cent.'

'There's no need for that. But thank you very much.'

'I didn't mean to be sharp with you, taking money off you,' said Sammy. 'It's just that when all your life you've had to watch pennies and ha'pennies and try to turn everything into a profit, the habit dies hard.'

'I know how you feel,' Arabella agreed. She stood on tiptoe, kissed him on the cheek. 'Good luck!' she said. 'Good luck!'

Sammy looked at her for a moment with surprise, almost amazement, as though he had never really seen her before. Then he put up his right hand to his cheek where she had kissed him.

'Goodbye!' he said, and climbed up into the coach. They watched him out of sight, and then walked back to Miss Pienaar's house.

On the morning of their own departure, Jamie and Arabella took the train from Cape Town to Wellington, forty-five miles away. This left them with another seven hundred to cover before they reached the diamond fields. There was a choice of vehicles in which they could make the journey. Each had advantages and disadvantages.

The quickest, but at £40 a head the most expensive, was by mail cart, or post cart, which Sammy had chosen. Then came passenger carts or wagons drawn by teams of eight horses or mules and claiming to cover an average distance of a hundred miles a day. Lastly, there were ox wagons, slow but cheap at £12 a head, and because they were slow, less bruising to the body. Their pace was so leisurely that they gave newcomers to the country a better opportunity to become acclimatised to the heat and dust, and to primitive facilities. Jamie and Arabella took the middle choice – an eight-horse wagon, not as expensive as the cart, but quicker than the ox wagon.

It was one of the largest four-wheeled vehicles they had ever seen. It weighed four tons, had low wooden sides and back, and a canvas roof supported on four vertical iron poles. Canvas curtains could be lowered to cover the sides and the back in case of rain, or to give some shade from the pitiless sun.

The curtains were now neatly rolled up, furled like sails, and strapped into position against the roof. Underneath them hung pouches for tins of meat, cured hams, bottles of water, flasks of whisky and brandy, and metal and canvas buckets to collect water from any river or stream, for washing or drinking.

The wagon had three benches, each wide enough to sit three people. In the rear was a space where the guard travelled with one or two other passengers who cared to come to a private arrangement with him to share this slightly more comfortable accommodation. After £5 had changed hands, this was where Jamie and Arabella took their seats.

The driver of the wagon, a light-skinned half-caste, sat with another man, a black Hottentot, known as the leader, on a bench up front. Harnesses, straps, thongs, coils of rope, pegs and brake wedges for the wheels were stowed beneath their feet. Sometimes the two men squeezed in an extra passenger beside them, against company rules; they would pocket the money for the fare themselves. On this occasion they were on their own.

The driver wielded a long whip like a fishing rod. Its handle was about fifteen feet in length, cut from the stem of a pliant tree, like an English willow. Woven into its end was a twenty-foot-long lash of thin, plaited strips of bullock hide. At the end of the whip, the driver tied a small tuft of antelope skin which would flip the backs of the horses gently and not cut into them as raw hide would.

The driver was in charge of the wagon in that he told the leader when to restrain one horse, when to encourage another and so keep them all moving steadily as a team, never against each other. It was not an easy task.

The transport company did not provide food or refreshments of any kind for their clients. Passengers had to take with them what they could carry – or go without. Jamie and Arabella had packed tins of sardines and potted meat, loaves of bread which would soon be hard as rock, and a flagon each of brandy as a pick-me-up or for medicinal use. There was the hope that each night the wagon might stop near a town that contained an inn. If not, they would halt near a Boer home.

The Boers who farmed along the route were very poor, living a hand-to-mouth existence in a harsh countryside. They were extremely religious and looked upon it as a duty to the Lord to help wayfarers, even the disliked *Uitlanders* or foreigners, who came in search of diamonds. This did not mean, however, that they would refuse payment for any food or shelter they could provide.

Eleven passengers climbed aboard, all strangers to each other, and the three crew. The leader pulled the reins. The driver's whip cracked like a gun and slowly, almost reluctantly, the clumsy, unsprung vehicle began to lumber forward.

Arabella looked round in her seat at the town she was leaving; white houses, hedges of apricot trees, green-painted palings, each fencing in a small, well-kept garden. It was difficult to believe that she and her brother were really setting out on the last lap of a journey which she felt convinced would bring them fortune. The mathematical odds against this happening were prodigious, she knew. But she told herself that odds were only figures worked out on paper, based on other figures accumulated from past experience. They lacked life; they took no account of endeavour and perseverance, or faith, and most important of all, the totally unknown quantity essential in these equations: luck.

The driver shouted: 'Keep 'em going!' His whip flicked like a stinging insect above the backs of the eight horses, keeping them in line, curbing any inclination to pull at an individual angle.

As the wagon rumbled on, the passengers began to talk to each other. In the seat ahead of Arabella and Jamie sat three men. One was a chemist, hoping to open a shop in Kimberley. Next to him was a diamond digger. He said he had made a thousand pounds in less than a month – and then spent it all in three weeks in Cape Town. He was now on his way back to make another fortune – and, this time, keep it. The third man was a doctor hoping to set up in a practice in Kimberley. The only other woman was a Mrs Riley, on her way to rejoin her husband, the Kimberley postmaster.

Talking at any length was difficult against the sudden shouts from driver and leader, the creak of boards as the wagon jolted on the rough track, the constant rattle and clang of pans, pots and bottles slung from the roof. The passengers had to keep moving their heads to avoid being hit around their ears by the bundles of food and flasks of brandy.

Heat beat down on them constantly like a blast from an open oven door. The guard lowered the side curtains, and then everyone sat sweating in the shade, constantly swatting greedy flies that settled on their hands and faces, bracing their bodies against the jerk and lumbering movement of the vehicle. Its huge, wooden-spoked, iron-tyred wheels laboriously climbed out of each rut and over each stone, striking sparks from pieces of quartz. The motion was like the rocking of a small boat in a rough sea. Mrs Riley, up front, leaned over the side to be violently sick.

Suddenly, there was a despairing cry from the driver and a great cracking of his whip in the air. The wagon stopped. Driver and leader both jumped down.

'What's the matter?' the guard called out.

'Harness broken,' came the reply.

They removed the harness from the leading horse on the left, brought it back, laid it on a flat rock to use as a bench, and began to hammer metal staples into the leather where it had split. On the first day, the harnesses broke four times and the wagon was stuck in the burning veldt for hours. The driver, cursing constantly under his breath, sweat pouring from him, worked frantically to repair the straps.

Once, as the passengers waited, other groups of men, heading for the diamond fields on foot, came up, and as they passed the stationary wagon, called out ironically: 'On your way! Get moving! You're blocking up the road!'

They carried water bottles, with small packs and blankets rolled army style on their backs, each with an axe and a knife in his belt. They walked with long easy strides, not talking to each other, just marching on, heads down against the sun, until they disappeared into the shimmering distance.

Jamie and Arabella and the digger often walked by the side of the wagon. This relieved the cramp that gripped their muscles through sitting for hours in the same position, lacking room to stretch their legs. Passengers who declined to join them, saying they had paid good money to ride not to walk, soon began to complain. Their ankles and feet swelled so much that when they removed their shoes to ease the constriction, they could not put them on again. They had to wait until the wagon stopped for the night and they could lie down on a blanket spread out on the dry ground, their feet propped above their heads on a log or stone until the swelling subsided.

When Jamie walked, he kept one hand on the warm wood of the side of the wagon. There was no real need to do this; it did not help him physically, but it felt reassuring, a symbolic umbilical cord. The wagon represented other people, not just himself and his sister on their own. In England, he had never been conscious of great distances; you walked five miles from one town and you reached another town, and five miles seemed a long way. Here, fifty or five hundred miles seemed the equivalent of those five miles back home.

The emptiness all around them seemed total. Vast beyond imagination, the desert stretched, relentless, cruel; sometimes grey, sometimes brown with a curious greenish tinge to it. The sun bored its way through clouds which, in the distance, seemed to pile up like the frozen peaks of some ethereal mountain range. Sometimes, the sky seemed an unusually deep blue, and it was easy for Jamie to think he was not looking at the desert, but at a calm and peaceful sea only an hour's march ahead. But as he trudged on, the sea receded and then vanished. It was all imagined, all in the mind, a trick of light and heat and tired eyes. Only the desert was real, burning like an enormous fire brick.

Here and there, eruptions of chalky sand sprouted by the side of small hutments, square boxes of corrugated iron which served as homesteads for impoverished farmers. Occasionally, a few oxen could be seen tearing hungrily at the dry, short, sparse grass.

One evening, they stopped near such a Boer homestead. The owners had planted fields of corn on the cob to feed their animals and themselves. Other fields were filled with huge yellow sunflowers that opened their petals to the sun every day and closed them and bowed their heads when night came. The farmer ground the corn into maize, squeezed sunflower seeds to make cooking oil. This was subsistence farming. He – and others like him they met on the journey – made just enough money to buy the essentials to keep going, day to day.

Everyone, everything in this wide land had to work hard simply to stay alive; much harder if they wished to make progress. It was a life of drudgery, only redeemed by the warmth of a dry climate and the feeling of space.

Three men with an ox cart were already camped here. A spare horse stood dejectedly, head down, tied behind their cart; it had gone lame.

'Where are you heading?' the leader asked Jamie.

'Kimberley.'

'Diamonds?'

'We thought of having a look.'

'You and how many hundreds and thousands of others? We're just coming back. We've blued our savings. The lot. All three of us.'

'And what did you find?'

'Nothing. Nothing at all. You're wasting your time, mate. Don't waste your money, too. We sold everything we had between us to raise a couple of hundred pounds to stake claims and buy gear and have something left to live on while we dug.'

'We lost it all – and more,' said his colleague, lighting a long, black cheroot from the fire. 'We worked from sun up to sun down day after day, and we didn't get a sight or smell of a diamond – not even the hair of a diamond.'

'But some must have been luckier, otherwise so many wouldn't be up there.'

'Oh, sure. *Some*. But what percentage? One in a thousand, ten thousand? It's about that.'

The third man came up. 'They haven't told you the hardest thing we had to bear,' he said drily. 'We so nearly got rich, very rich.'

'The hell with that!' said the leader angrily. 'We didn't, and that's all that matters.'

'How near were you?' asked Jamie.

For a moment no one replied, then the third man spoke.

'Painfully close,' he said. 'We had to sell our last claim for twenty-five pounds. That was the highest offer we had. After our experience, I tell you, people weren't fighting to take it off our hands, and we'd have let it go for less if we hadn't had this offer. And if no one had bought it, we would have abandoned it. So twenty-five pounds was better than nothing to us – and the best bargain the buyer ever had. The day after we sold it, he put his pick in the ground and winkled out a diamond worth five hundred pounds. He kept on digging, and he found more – about ten thousand pounds' worth while we were still packing up!'

'That must make you pretty bitter,' said Jamie.

The leader shrugged. 'What's the use of feeling bitter?' he asked philosophically. 'We did our best. You can't do more than that. If the luck is with you, you find the diamonds. It wasn't with us. It was with the other man.'

Jamie went to meet Arabella coming up from the water hole carrying a canvas bucket of water. The canvas had dried and hardened in the sun; water seeped through the thick green side. He told her what he had just heard.

'Do you think we're mad?' he asked her.

'In what way mad?'

'Going up after diamonds. Those fellows have lost everything. And the day they left a new digger makes a fortune.'

'He wouldn't say it was mad, would he?' she replied. 'It will be like that for us, too, I tell you. We'll make a fortune.'

'How can you be so sure?'

'I believe,' she replied simply. 'And what else are we going to do? Hang around in Cape Town, you fighting in a fair, me maybe working in a house as a servant? We're going to get rich. I know it.'

Jamie said nothing, but Arabella could see his doubts by the look on his face, and squeezed his hand encouragingly.

'Yeung Lee read my palm,' she said. 'That's one reason why I feel so confident. He said he could see in it that I'd be rich. Do you remember that book I was given at school as a prize for being top of the class in arithmetic?'

Jamie nodded.

'It was about Christopher Columbus and his voyages. Every day on his voyage to America, he faced trouble with his crew. They feared they were going to sail off the end of the world,

208

that their ship would sink and terrible sea serpents would eat them all. They threatened to mutiny unless he turned back. Columbus had no truck with that fainthearted talk. Every night in his log, he simply wrote: "This day, I sailed on." We should do the same. After all, there's nothing for us to go back to, either in Cape Town or in England.'

Next morning, they set off again, starting early as always, before the sun grew hot. Here and there, out of an expanse of brownish earth, and patches of greenish weed or grass, they passed eucalyptus trees with long, thin trunks and branches twenty feet off the ground. The land around them lay flat, as though exhausted, defeated by heat like a constant fire. The air they breathed dried their nostrils and then their throats. There was no wind, and no water. Hour after hour, day after day, this was all they knew.

Each morning, Arabella rubbed some of Yeung Lee's ointment into her face to stop the skin becoming rough from the constant heat and dust. At first, Mrs Riley could not understand why she did this.

'Soap and water's good enough for me,' she said firmly.

But as her own skin hardened, and her lips cracked, she changed her mind. Arabella shared a pot of ointment with her. To Mrs Riley's surprise and delight, her skin lost its rough feel, and the cracks in her lips healed within hours.

'How many pots of this stuff have you got?' she asked Arabella. 'I'd like to buy one from you, if you have any to spare.'

'Unfortunately I haven't any more after this is finished. All sorts of other pills and potions for stomach upsets, and snake bite, but no face cream.'

'Where did you get it? Perhaps I could buy some for myself? This climate is very hard on our skin, you know. That's why you'll see most women wearing hats with wide brims to keep the sun off. But on a journey like this, that's impossible.'

'It was given to me by someone in England. He mixed it up to a Chinese formula. Chinese women all have very good complexions because they use it every day, so he said.'

'Then maybe we'll all have to go to China to get some more! But seriously, if you're writing to your friend, please ask him if he would send me several pots. I can either pay you or deal with him direct, whatever you prefer.'

Every day, the sky was cloudless, like a vast blue reflector, beating heat back on the wagon. Hawks sometimes hovered above them in the clear air; vultures circled around the remains of some animal. All the passengers now walked whenever they could. Otherwise, their legs and ankles swelled so grotesquely they feared they might lose the use of them. They walked silently, like people in a dream; slowly, beyond fatigue, beyond wondering how many miles they had still to cover before dusk. Then, hopefully, there would be water for the oxen and for themselves, before the merciful dark came down like a curtain from the sky. Sometimes they passed human skeletons, bleached bones unburied only yards off the track, the remains of travellers who had run short of water and finally died of thirst.

Each evening, they all became infinitely aware of the utter insignificance of a handful of disparate human beings in the chilly and enormous veldt. Trees stood out in sharp silhouette against a strange and translucent sky. Towards the horizon it was pink, merging first with light blue, and then dark blue. As they watched, the colours would melt away into a dark oblivion of their own. The only lights left were tiny pinpricks, like glow-worms, from lamps in farmhouse windows, or the friendly and reassuring flames of a camp fire.

On some days, the scenery changed so dramatically that it seemed they were not simply in another part of the country, but in another country altogether. One day, they came to an area of deep gullies with ferns and broom on either side, and a stream

210

at the bottom reminding the twins of burns in Scotland. Next day, through a pass in hills that ringed this unexpected scene, they were out on a plateau covered in round pebbles, each one hot to the touch. Dusty stretches of dried grass or scrub, scattered with burned-out bushes or dead shrubs, trembled under a burnished sky. Nothing lived here but serpents. At night, the driver told them, some animals did prowl this wasteland but most slept throughout the heat of each day.

There was something eerie in the total emptiness, the absence of any visible life. They might be the last people left alive in all the world. Jamie found himself glancing behind the wagon, feeling that perhaps they were being followed, that out of the hazy flat distance, from the left or the right, a band of horsemen would come riding in to attack them. But there was nothing, and nobody behind them. It was all imagination, illusion.

Now and then they passed pools of water, known as pans, the size of giant dew ponds. Some were fresh, others phosphorescent with decay, or bright orange with algae. One had been fouled by the body of an ox. Swollen with gas, it lay putrefying in the centre of what could have been drinking water.

The last part of their journey lay across the Karoo, a barren desert made of gritted reddish rocks, every one dry and angry. Now and then a tiny flash of light twinkled as sunlight reflected from a splinter of crystal in the dust. Nothing on any side stood more than six inches high out of the ground: no stone, no plant, no shrub. There were no shadows, for nothing grew tall enough to cast a shadow. Occasionally, the strange dead level of the Karoo was broken by a knot of dusty prickles, a tuft of camomile or sage, a tuber the size of a football, peeling and yellow, dried and hard as a stone in the heat. From time to time, a faint breeze – it could hardly be called a wind – stirred the dust and blew it around them like a hot gritty shroud. When the dust settled, they all could see ahead of them a shining lake, with an island of green palm trees, a waterfall. They blinked tired, aching eyes and shook their heads, and at once the mirage vanished.

Once, they overhauled a group of six men, marching two abreast, like an army column. They had one horse with them, laden with shovels, picks and sieves. They had run short of water, and hailed the wagon thankfully and drank greedily from their water bottles. When the wagon stopped, flies descended on it in thousands. The movement of the wagon had previously kept most of them away from their faces. Now, like a black cloud, the insects swarmed greedily around wrists, mouths, nostrils, eyes. One passenger fell off the end of his seat on to the desert, screaming, 'Get them away! Get them away! They'll eat me alive!'

The chemist and the doctor climbed down to him and between them hauled him back aboard. The wagon moved on.

They passed over a series of plains, still dusty, still burning hot, but slightly greener than the desert. They reached a river, and dragging the wagon out of the water at the far bank, the leading horses slipped. Two of them fell and the wagon began to roll back.

'Everyone out! To the wheels!' shouted the driver at once.

They all jumped down, gripped the wheels by their spokes and pushed or pulled on them while the driver cracked his whip above the horses' flanks. Slowly, they came up the other side.

They passed several shallow pools of water, all strangely coloured – bright green, bright blue, orange – from mineral deposits in the ground. On the banks of a vast river a crowd of Kaffirs, each carrying a rifle and a bandolier of ammunition, but otherwise naked except for loincloths, cheered them wildly as if they were welcoming friends.

The desert was now steadily falling behind them. Out of a

reddish earth, clumps of long grass, thick and spiky like pampas, waved and rattled in the wind. Trees had green leaves, and suddenly they were on a recognisable track, almost a road. It was still dusty, still unmade, but better by far than anything they had seen on their journey. And ahead of them were houses, shacks, tents. This was Kimberley – the end of their journey.

TWELVE

A Desert Fortune

All afternoon, wind had been blowing in from a sullen sea across the Namib desert in German South West Africa. The sand swirled up, faint at first, yellow against the sun, then deepening into a dark abrasive fog. It had the strength of a snowstorm, but was more dangerous. Landmarks vanished in the wake of this high, choking, whirling storm. Within minutes, the road from the sea was covered in eighteen inches of sand; only the tips of the marker posts, every few metres, showed where it had been.

The Germans who had settled here, possibly the most inhospitable colony in the world, claimed that when the wind blew, it blew for eight days every week, not seven. It made people irritable. Their clothes rasped continually against their bodies. They drank sand in their beer, ate it in their food. Sand lived between their toes, in their hair, in their beds.

Herr August Stauch sat in his corrugated iron hut by the side of the railway track and watched the storm swirl outside and deposit hundreds of tons of sand against the walls, darkening windows, spreading up towards the eaves.

He was writing a letter home to his wife, Ida, whom he had left behind in Neumark, Germany, with their two children. How different was his home there to this two-roomed hut in the hot, empty desert! What a contrast between the fields and the woods and this arid place, thousands of miles away, where he was celebrating – if that was the right word – his twenty-ninth birthday.

He wondered about his son Hans, aged three, and daughter Marianne, a year younger; what they were doing, how he could put his thoughts on paper. He was used to dealing with figures, commanding gangs of labourers; he did not have a similar gift with words. When he read what he had written, the letter seemed stilted. He found it impossible to describe his surroundings to his wife without making them appear melodramatic, grotesque, almost fictitious. If he had known what life here was like, would he ever have agreed to come out for a two-year period?

Stauch sat back, listening to the storm, watching amber sand steadily obliterate the windows as it piled higher and higher. As an inspector, his task was to keep free of sand a section of the newly laid railway track from Lüderitz up through Kolmanskop towards Windhoek, the capital of the colony. He was used to making decisions or accepting the decisions of his superiors without procrastination or quibble. He could write a formal report or memorandum with the best of them. But writing a letter to his wife was something altogether different.

Memories of the goose-liver pies Ida would make, of smoked eel and flounders, veal roasts served with cream sauce came tantalisingly to mind. She was an excellent cook, but even thinking of such rich dishes here in this metal oven he called a house made him sweat. How could he conceivably describe to someone who had never left a cool climate, who had only seen sand on the seashore, what the desert looked like?

Before Stauch had arrived here, he had thought that the desert was simply flat sand, like a foreshore when the tide is low. Instead, he had discovered that it was a living, moving, sometimes frightening presence that changed day by day, often hour by hour. Great winds from the sea would raise the sand, gently at first, and then like a vortex, roaring, whistling, sweeping everything in front of it with ferocious power. Within minutes, a sunny day could be changed into a fog of sand so thick it was impossible to see further than a few feet in any direction, as was happening now. Thousands of tons of hot burning sand would scour the whole area, rasp the faces and hands of anyone caught out in it, blast away paint from doors, eat through the bricks of houses.

Until Stauch had come to German South West Africa, he had often regretted that he had weak eyes and needed to wear glasses. Now he knew his spectacles had saved him from the chronic infection of the eyes which seemed to afflict so many of his compatriots, caused by grains of sand continually peppering their faces.

The Germans had built their little settlement on rock foundations, thinking they could overcome the desert and the strange winds and fogs and furious sandstorms, but they felt frequently that the elements were laughing at them. They were only biding their time, and within years, possibly within Stauch's own lifetime, this settlement would be swept away and become no more than a ghost town with the wind and sand blowing triumphantly through empty doorways into empty rooms.

Stauch picked up his pen again, and tried to write, but then found himself thinking of his boyhood on a farm in Ettenhausen, near Eisenach, the birthplace of Johann Sebastian Bach, on the edge of the vast Thuringian forest lands. When he was still a boy, a railway line was built along the edge of the village and Stauch met the works manager, who became a family friend.

When Stauch did his compulsory military service in the Pioneer Corps, his health began to fail and he suffered a serious attack of asthma. He blamed this on the fact that since he was attached to a bridge-building company, he had to stand for hours in water, often up to his thighs, and this brought on a series of chills and fevers and finally affected his breathing.

When his military service was over, the works manager remembered Stauch and offered him a job. His company was now building a railway line from Mecklenburg to East Prussia. Stauch found lodgings with a married couple and in due course married their youngest daughter, Ida. But single or married, the railway occupied most of August's waking hours: he was a dedicated employee.

As Stauch's responsibilities grew, so did the frequency of his asthma attacks. At last, the works manager, who had been promoted, suggested it might help Stauch's health if he went out to South West Africa. The company had won a contract to build a railway initially from Lüderitz to the village of Aus and on to Keetmanskop. The dry, hot climate might cure Stauch's asthma, but Kolmanskop, where he would be based, was still too primitive for a woman and two young children.

Stauch and his wife did not like the prospect of parting, but the opportunity to cure his asthma might not come again, nor would the chance of saving some money. He would be better paid than in Germany and, of course, would have little chance to spend money. In two years he could return healthy and much better off financially. So he agreed to go.

Lüderitz, where he disembarked, was a primitive colonial outpost. Buildings, roofed with red sheets of corrugated iron, hung on rocky slopes with the desert behind them. A small jetty poked its stone finger into the bay, ringed by harsh rocks and cliffs.

A railway company representative was on the quay to meet Stauch. They walked up the jetty to the hotel where he would stay the night until he moved a few miles inland to Kolmanskop. The street names, Bismarckstrasse, Bülowstrasse, Kirchestrasse, in white letters on familiar blue backgrounds reminded him of Germany and so of home; but nothing else did.

All around in thick sand that covered the streets, lay thousands of empty mineral water bottles, and beer bottles, green and blue and brown glass.

'Why isn't this cleared away?' Stauch asked; such untidiness offended his sense of order.

'No one to do the work,' the company man told him grimly. 'Drinking water here is very expensive because there's so little of it. Most comes by ship from the Cape, and although we have a condenser here to distil sea water, it's always going wrong. It's cheaper to drink beer or mineral water – and safer, too.'

The town was named after Adolf Lüderitz, a wealthy tobacco merchant from Bremen. In his business, he travelled to the States, where he met captains of sealers and whalers, who had sailed here.

Lüderitz realised that no other European country was particularly interested in colonising this desert, and rather like the Englishman, Cecil Rhodes, he had dreams of extending his country's empire. He could not interest the officials in Berlin to any great extent in investing enough money, so he arranged a deal with local Hottentots that he would buy the site of the town, its harbour and all land within a radius of five miles for a hundred pounds down and two hundred rifles. He then ran up the German flag and began to pour his own fortune into the place.

He believed there could be mineral deposits here, so he brought out geologists, mining engineers. He was also after diamonds, where the Orange River enters the sea. He knew that English settlers were making tremendous finds of diamonds on the upper reaches of that river and the Vaal River which joins it.

Lüderitz and a companion, a seaman of many years' experience, set off with two collapsible canvas boats to investigate the Orange River for themselves. On the way back, they reached Alexander Bay, and then faced a long overland journey across the desert. Instead, they decided to sail on in one of their boats. They were never seen again.

Since Adolf Lüderitz's deal with the Hottentots for rifles, other African chiefs had also offered concessions of land in exchange for rifles. And now, with thousands of rifles and sufficient ammunition to fire them indefinitely, they were threatening to drive the Germans from the colony. For this reason, 4000 German troops had been sent to safeguard German lives and property. The railway was being extended as a matter of great urgency because the only supply line was by carts pulled by 24 oxen, which took days to cover distances a train could cross in a matter of hours.

Next morning, Stauch went out by cart to his new posting in the desert. He put down his bags in the little hut only yards from the railway line and an inspector described his duties. He would be a *Bahnmeister*, a railway supervisor, and he had to supervise a stretch of the line between the posts marked Kilometre 18–27 to keep it free from sand so that trains could use it. This seemed a simple enough job to Stauch – until it was explained that the sand dunes in the area were the highest in the world. They could achieve a height of 350 metres and then, overnight, be wiped out completely.

'What's the name of this place?' Stauch asked.

'Grasplatz, a place of grass.'

This seemed ironic, but the name had been given because drivers of ox wagons, coming in from the desert towards Lüderitz, would drop off bales of dried grass at this point. They would then pick them up on their return journey because there was no grazing for oxen on the coast.

After his initial shock at the loneliness and harshness of his new life, Stauch, an ebullient character, made the best of matters and decided to learn everything he could, not only about the desert and its ways, but about the wildlife. He saw ostriches and springbok and oryx; birds whose perfectly camouflaged plumage made them look just like tiny lumps of sand until they took flight; crickets that resembled stones; sidewinders

219

and horned adders that wriggled through the sand, usually at night, making strange patterns, mysterious to those who did not know what had caused them.

In May, the wind dropped slightly, and he had time on his hands. He applied to the Deutsche Kolonialgesellschaft für Südwestafrika, the DKG, for licences to prospect for stones. There were all manner of mica, jasper, crystals, garnets and agates, and with official sanction he decided to search for these in his spare time.

By then he felt he had accepted – if not entirely overcome – the difficulties his company faced in building a railway and, almost as bad, in maintaining it through constantly shifting sands that could bury the line completely to a depth of six feet one day and blow it clear the next.

The local Hottentots were an unreliable work force – reporting for work at set hours was alien to their nomadic life – so the company had brought in two thousand half-castes from the Cape to work on the railway. These were the sons and grandsons of Dutch settlers who had married local native women. They worked hard, drank hard, were unambitious, loyal and, to Stauch's mind, very sad men.

They worked under the abrasive rasp of sandstorms with cloths tied round their noses and mouths as crude filters for the air. They did not seem to notice the heat by day or the cold at night or the winds that could rage for weeks.

Keeping the line clear of sand was an unending task which many might have found hopeless, but Stauch was an optimist. He relished the challenge, although he would have felt happier to have his family with him. But he could not ask his wife or children to endure the heat and isolation and general malaise, chronic indigestion or diarrhoea, that came from eating sand with every meal.

As he sat at his table, trying to compose his letter, the field telephone tinkled. He picked up the receiver. A superior in Lüderitz was on the line.

'Stauch,' he told him, 'bring an engine and a car down to the port immediately.'

'Is there trouble?' asked Stauch.

'Someone is seriously ill. We want to get him to the doctor in Kolmanskop.'

'Right, sir.'

Stauch put down his pen, glad of the excuse to postpone writing his letter. He went out of the hut and told his overseer he would be away for a couple of hours. An engine and another carriage, known as a car, was always kept ready to move on his orders. As he and the driver climbed in, a labourer, Zacharias Lewala, approached. He had been a coachman in the Cape and before that had worked in the diamond mines at Kimberley.

'I was wanting to see you, sir,' he said now. 'Something to tell you.'

'Later,' said Stauch. 'I have to go to Lüderitz urgently. I'll see you when I get back.'

The driver blew the whistle. The engine started. Wind blew sand against them; through their shirts, jackets, trousers, beneath their pith helmets. When Stauch wiped sweat from his forehead with his handkerchief, he felt as though he was sand-papering his skin. The engine chugged through Kolmanskop, past newly built houses, the casino and the hospital, on across the desert, over the points, to the jetty at Lüderitz. A colleague waved them to a stop.

'What's the matter?' Stauch asked him.

'A fellow's been nearly drowned. He's in a bad way.'

They crossed the jetty. Two sailors from a German ship that had just docked were already carrying a stretcher over the concrete quay. They placed it on top of the seat in the open rail car, lashed the handles firmly with ropes to the underside. Under a grey woollen army blanket, a man lay

221

with his eyes closed, his face ashen, as though already dead.

'Who is he?' Stauch asked. 'What happened?'

'There must have been a shipwreck,' one of the stretcher bearers explained. 'We passed by just afterwards. Lookout saw this body in the sea. Apparently, he's the only survivor.'

'What nationality?'

The man shrugged. 'He speaks German. I asked him who he was, but all he could say was "I don't know" in German. They'll look after him in the hospital. One of the officers will be up to have a word with him when he comes round.'

'If he comes round,' said Stauch.

The engine driver reversed his locomotive and car back to the sidings, turned, went north to Kolmanskop. Stauch sat with one hand on the stretcher to steady it. Now and then the man groaned slightly and tried to rise feebly under the straps that held the blanket tight. He lay with his mouth open, breathing heavily. Stauch covered the man's face with a handkerchief to try and protect him from gusts of sand that could choke him.

At the hospital, two nurses in long white dresses and caps were already waiting by the side of the railway track with four porters to carry in the new arrival. Stauch followed them into the ward. It was neat, with iron beds, red blankets, white sheets, a coloured picture of the Kaiser on the wall. Surgical instruments, red rubber tubes, kidney-shaped basins, nickel-plated scalpels and saws and forceps were laid out on a white cloth on a table.

A doctor Stauch knew slightly, named Braff, came over to him later as he waited in an anteroom.

'Interesting case,' Dr Braff said conversationally. 'We pumped out a mass of seawater, and now he's recovering. I hope.'

'Any idea who he is? A sailor said he spoke German.'

'He does, but not very well, though that may just be due to the shock he's had. No bones broken, luckily, but he's had a bad blow to his head. He's got a cigarette case in his jacket pocket and a signet ring on the little finger of his left hand. Any papers he was carrying have gone but one pocket had a button flap over it which protected the cigarette case. The cigarettes are no good, though.' The doctor laughed.

When Stauch got back to his hut, Zacharias Lewala was still waiting to see him. He came straight to the point.

'Sir, you remember some time ago you said that we should all look out for anything unusual we might see on the track?'

'I do,' said Stauch.

Lewala put his hand in his trouser pocket, took out a twist of paper, undid it. A tiny stone lay in the palm of his hand. 'I found this early today,' he said.

Stauch picked it up, turned it over and over, looked at it critically.

'I don't think it's anything,' he said at last. 'Probably crystal, or something like that.'

'No, sir,' said Lewala. He was wearing a watch and moved the stone across the glass dial. The stone left a deep scratch. 'It's a diamond.'

'All sorts of other stones can cut glass,' said Stauch. 'Where did you find it?'

'In the sand. By the side of the rails. I'm sure it's a diamond. I've worked for De Beers in Kimberley for years. I've seen enough of them.'

'All right,' said Stauch. 'I'll take it into town and see if anyone can identify it properly.'

Next morning, Stauch travelled in his engine and car to Aus, the nearest town to the north. Here, the railway hospital was under the authority of a Dr Peyer, whom Stauch had met on several occasions. He would get an honest, unbiased opinion from Peyer. He went to see him in his little laboratory.

'You are ill, August?' the doctor asked him.

'No. My asthma is much better now. In fact, it seems totally

223

cured. I want your opinion on something else, not medical. One of my men has found a stone on the railway. He thinks it's a diamond. I don't. But could you identify it?'

'If it is a diamond,' said Dr Peyer slowly, 'then it won't be the only one out there. There will be others. And we will have all manner of unwanted people here – prospectors, diggers, rogues. Fortunes will be made. What percentage do you offer me of any deal you may do with them?'

'What percentage do you want?' asked Stauch, surprised by this commercial approach.

'Five per cent,' said Dr Peyer shortly.

'Agreed,' said Stauch. 'Five per cent it is. Now, will you give me your verdict?'

'Only when we have drawn up a contract, August. It is better to be safe, both of us knowing what we have agreed, than to be arguing later what was agreed or otherwise.'

'As you say,' said Stauch, and scribbled out a short document. He signed it. The doctor read it and signed as well.

'Now let me see the stone.'

Stauch gave him the twist of paper, watched Peyer put the stone in a watchglass, pour acid on to it, brush it carefully with a toothbrush to remove the crust of sediment that tainted it.

Suddenly, the stone throbbed with brilliant colour as though it had a life of its own, as though it held imprisoned sunbeams within its glittering grasp. No other stone in all the world looked like this or had this gift, except a diamond.

'Well?' Stauch asked him, knowing the answer before he asked the question.

The doctor shook his hand warmly. 'My heartiest congratulations, August. Your man was right and you were wrong. This is indeed a diamond, a very valuable diamond, and the first of who knows how many. We are both going to be very, very rich.'

*   *   *

Stauch and two senior colleagues on the railway formed a company to extract and sell diamonds. They each held twenty per cent of shares; banks and other institutions – including the railway – held the rest.

The company, Koloniale Bergbau Gesellschaft, made fortunes for all involved. It paid dividends on an astonishingly high scale: as much as 3,800 per cent on each individual share. At first, the diamonds did not need to be dug out; they lay in the desert sand, waiting to be scooped up. Within a short time, all three men became prodigiously rich. They bought estates in Germany, built fine houses in the colony, invested heavily in other enterprises.

The prospect of what seemed like instant wealth brought fortune hunters by the hundred from all over South Africa and from Europe. They did not require capital in order to prospect. All they needed then was a shovel, a round sieve with a fine mesh, like a garden sieve, a washing tub, and a box to collect any diamonds they discovered.

They shovelled sand into the sieve, shook it steadily until only small stones and gravel were left. Then they filled the tub with seawater and dipped the sieve into it to clean the stones. Next, they shook out the stones into the box where they formed a set pattern according to their weight: diamonds in the centre, garnets round them.

The work seemed easy – until prospectors found that constantly shovelling sand in the desert under a pitiless sun was like working near an open furnace. They suffered terribly from sunburn, from skin blisters that swelled and burst and suppurated. The light-coloured sand and the sea reflected the sun and magnified its strength. Many suffered from sun blindness, which led to permanently damaged eyesight, or even to total loss of sight. To combat this, they wore spectacles with thick black lenses, and fixed pieces of gauze at each side to try and prevent light filtering in behind the glass.

Many did their prospecting on their hands and knees, sometimes running a tin through the sand to fill it and then emptying it into the sieve. Some would scrape the sand with the blade of a knife until the glitter of a stone shone up against the sharpened steel. Others, working on a bigger scale, would organise native labourers to lie in line, flat on their stomachs, hands outstretched, fingers touching. Then they would all edge forward, picking up every stone they saw.

Within a year, August Stauch, who had come out to the South West African colony an ill man in search of health and the opportunity to augment his savings, found with delight tinged with amazement that he was a millionaire.

THIRTEEN
Kimberley

On their journey from Cape Town to Kimberley, Jamie and
Arabella had seen very few other travellers. Now, the road
suddenly seemed crowded with wagons, carts, pedestrians.
The surface was soft with a layer of sand and lined on either
side by tents and canvas houses, built on metal frames, interspersed with shacks and shanties made from sheets of galva-
nised, corrugated iron. Some were painted green with red roofs
to simulate tiles, others were grey or still bright metal that
caught the sun like huge heliographs.

They passed diggers with shirt sleeves rolled up, others in
dark suits with stiff collars and formal ties, most with long
beards and butchers' knives or axes stuck into thick leather
belts. Africans simply wore a few ostrich feathers round their
middles, or cast-off suits from a white digger. None of them
paid any attention to another wagon arriving; this was an every-
day occurrence.

Some of the huts had been made into saloons, and shouts
and cheers and the sound of singing came through open doorways, magnified by the bare metal roofs and walls. Outside
several of them, men lay like corpses in the dust, on their faces
or on their backs, sleeping off the effects of too much raw Cape
brandy.

'We go to the Market Square,' said the driver, turning to

address his passengers. 'Everybody out there, and good luck to you all!'

The square was a wide, flat area cleared of shops and tents and buildings, by the side of the kopje from which Kimberley took its original name. What had once been a sizeable hill had been burrowed into by thousands of spades every day (except Sundays) for several years. First, they had levelled it. Then they had dug down deep into the ground. Now, what had been a hill was a vast, deep hole – a hill totally hollowed out. The roads through Kimberley wound round a huge pyramid of waste soil, called Mount Ararat, which had grown from wheel-barrows of earth dumped by early diggers.

As the wagon stopped, men came out of shops, counting houses and diamond buyers' offices to see whether anyone they knew was arriving. When they did not recognise any of the passengers, they went back inside. Heat beat down on the square like a drum; there was no shade, no shadow.

Jamie and Arabella unloaded their trunks and waited at the side of the road. All around them stood wagons: horses and oxen with heads down, apparently asleep on their feet. Some wagons were piled with produce to sell: dead springbok at a shilling each, wildebeest at half a crown. Other wagons were loaded with vegetables, planks, sheets of corrugated iron, canvas for tents. Diggers' wives and families were examining vegetables, feeling the haunch of a springbok, discussing prices, looking for the best bargain.

'It's no good standing about,' Arabella told Jamie briskly. 'We must find lodgings and then start work.'

As she spoke, they both heard a familiar voice behind them. Sammy Rosen was calling from across the square. He already gave the impression of having been here for years, wearing thick dark trousers, dark jacket, heavy boots, a shirt with a stiff collar.

'I've met every wagon coming in for the last five days,' he

told them. 'Thought you must have given up and gone home.'

'Looking about me,' said Jamie, 'I wonder if perhaps we should.'

'Nonsense,' Sammy replied. 'I've got you a house here, near mine. I've bought two digging licences – one for you two, one for me. I've staked out claims, and I'm ready to start just as soon as you like.'

He called to two Africans leaning against a wall, smoking thin cheroots. They picked up the trunks between them and followed Sammy Rosen across the square, down side streets near the mine.

'Here's my house, and I've rented this one for you for three months,' he said, and glanced rather apprehensively at his companions.

The houses were corrugated-iron shanties, painted brown. White-framed windows bound with coloured ribbons gave a touch of brightness to the drabness of the metal.

'It doesn't look much,' he agreed defensively, 'but it's all I could get. You've no idea the demand for these places. All the wood and iron and canvas used here has to be brought at least four hundred miles.'

'It will suit us fine,' Arabella assured him. 'Thank you for arranging it.'

She went inside. The house was simply a painted iron box, divided into four. The walls were lined with strips of calico and squares of brown cardboard to try and prevent the building becoming an oven by day, an icebox at night.

Two of the rooms were bedrooms, each with a single bed which stood on a hard earth floor. Animal skins were spread over this instead of carpets. By the side of each bed stood a wooden box which served as a table, with a large hurricane lamp. On a chest of drawers was a china bowl and soap dish, a ewer and pitcher for water.

Nails had been driven into the wooden framework of the

walls for hanging clothes. A few wooden coathangers hung from them. On one wall of the living room was a faded daguereotype of the kopje when it had still been a hill, with a poem underneath, written by a digger:

> Of course I thought that once on the field
> Every load a stone would yield.
> But I owned after many a weary day
> That gravel is gravel and clay is clay.

Beyond was a kitchen with a fireplace built into the wall. A copper kettle hung from a metal tripod; a cauldron from a chain. Behind the house was the privy. Its smell seeped through the open window.

'Sanitation is poor,' admitted Sammy. 'We use convict labour to dig latrine pits, but they also have to keep the roads clear, so it depends which job has priority.'

'Never mind,' said Arabella. 'This is a house. We'll now try to make it into a home. And when we are all rich, we will look back on it with affection. Now, let's unpack and see what a diamond mine looks like.'

Somehow, they had assumed that it would resemble a coal mine. There were several in Lancashire and on the Cheshire border, and they were accustomed to seeing the spidery winding wheel dark against the sky, with a cable over it to carry the cage that took miners down to the coal face. Jamie and Arabella were quite unprepared for the huge pit that faced them.

'There's only one deeper hole in all the world,' said Sammy, 'and as you might expect, that's in the United States – the copper mine in Bingham Canyon outside Salt Lake City.'

Arabella and Jamie stood staring at the gigantic excavation, nearly half a mile wide.

'How deep is it?' she asked.

'From the top down to hard rocks, about ninety metres,'

replied Sammy. 'Then down to water, one hundred and sixty-five metres. The water itself is two hundred and thirty metres deep. It seeps in all the time, and has to be pumped out. That's how Cecil Rhodes made some of his money in the early days. He ordered a steam pump from the coast, and then hired it out. He and his partner, Charles Rudd, were into all sorts of activities – making ice, for instance – until they struck it rich.'

'I'm beginning to have some doubts, now I'm here,' Jamie admitted, to his sister's surprise. 'So many people have been digging here for diamonds for so long, as we've heard already, that there can't be many left. Like the man said in Cape Town, if you have fifty thousand people digging and they find as many diamonds, it would still only be one each.'

'Rubbish!' retorted Arabella. 'You are assuming everyone finds *one*. Most find none worthwhile, but a few find the big ones. And we're going to find them for one very good reason – we have to. It's that or nothing.'

'Everybody who came here must have thought the same,' said Sammy.

They walked towards the edge of the hole, peered down into its depths. A fence had been set up round it to prevent drunks from falling in after dark. The sides showed formations of different strata. First, a brownish layer of grass dried by the sun, then a thick layer of dark sandstone, then at the bottom an even thicker layer of bluish-green stone.

'That's where Rhodes and Barnato found the big diamonds,' Sammy explained. 'They dug out a number in the sand, but when they came down to this blue ground, as they call it here, most of the other diggers gave up. It was so hard it snapped the heads off their picks. They did not believe there could be any diamonds in such a rocky base. They thought they had taken them all out, but Rhodes and Barnato thought otherwise. They'd studied the geological background. They didn't listen to theories and fainthearts. They learned facts.'

'In other words,' said Arabella, 'they didn't give up. An example to us. You're not losing heart, are you, Jamie?'

'No. Not yet. Not ever, I hope. But you must admit, standing here, peering down into this hole, it seems a lot less likely we're going to be rich finding stones the size of big pebbles than it did when we were back in England. Everything seemed possible then.'

'It still does,' retorted Arabella. 'Don't you agree, Sammy?'

'Whatever you say,' Sammy replied diplomatically. But glancing at Sammy's face, Arabella could see he also had his doubts. So, indeed, did she, but this was not the time to voice them. She recalled a phrase from a Bible story she had heard in Sunday School: 'If the trumpet give an uncertain sound, who shall prepare himself to the battle?' And here it was clear they all faced a hard fight.

At the bottom of the pit lay a pool of dark green water, a motionless lake. All around the rim of the hole, metal cables gleamed in the sun as they stretched down to different levels. These were to haul diggers up and down, and to bring up buckets filled with the earth and stones cut from the sides to be sieved. The ropes looked like the web of some gigantic spider. They looped over pulleys fixed in a huge overhead frame, made of wooden beams the size of railway sleepers.

The motive power to work the pulleys and the complex web of cables and buckets came from steam winches, or huge wooden windlasses, known as whims. These pivoted parallel to the ground. A horse or mule was harnessed to each one, and plodded round and round, to wind in the buckets.

Work had stopped briefly and diggers were sitting on chairs and stools outside their tin huts and tents. A handful of children played with tops or hoops in the dust. Dogs lay sleeping in what shade they could find, and a few wives stood in the doorways of houses talking to each other. Birds flew around the hole, diving deep down inside it, and then soaring up into the sky.

Shacks and huts had been erected round the rim of the hole, their hand-painted signs proclaiming their business: Rothschilds Auction Mart, Bromwich's Dispensary (Homoeopathic and Patent Medicines), Abraham and Co.'s Market Store (Wholesale and Retail Grocers), J. Baird & Co. (General Merchants), J. B. Bodley (Hairdresser).

'There was a scientist called James Gregory who came out here some years ago, when the first diamonds were found,' Sammy went on. 'I read about him back home. A Bond Street jeweller paid him to check whether there really was any new source of diamonds here.

'He was afraid that if diamonds were discovered on a big scale in South Africa, the value would drop and he would lose business. He wanted Gregory to pooh-pooh the idea. Gregory did so. He said he thought ostriches must be responsible for any diamonds that had been found. They swallow any bright stone or bead they see – but Gregory couldn't say where the ostriches might have found them, except round here. And when the diamond rush started, he was totally discredited. Anyone now who puts forward a ridiculous theory or point of view out here is told it's a Gregory.'

The diggers began to drift back to work. The steam engine started, pulleys began to turn and the cables and buckets and diggers went up and down the side of the chasm, the men toiling with axes, shovels and hammers. Each digger was initially allowed a maximum of two claims, each one 31 feet square. They swarmed like ants, some wearing shirts and long serge trousers, others stripped to their underpants; natives were naked except for loincloths. From the depths of the pit came shouts and cries, the constant crack of axes against rock, the boom of empty buckets hitting the hard sides like giant gongs.

To reach some parts of the mine, wooden ladders had been set up precariously against the rocks. Narrow tracks were left when digging claims were marked out, so that the soil could be carried to sorting places at the side of the mine. Men with wheelbarrows piled high with the dirt heaved it from one thin pathway to another.

'I've already seen several accidents,' said Sammy. 'You have a man with a barrow who meets a man with a cart. There's no room to pass. Neither gives way – and in the argument they both go over the side. And there's not much in the way of a hospital here to put them right if anything happens.'

'I'm surprised there's a hospital at all,' said Arabella.

'Oh yes, there is one. But conditions are primitive, for this is still a frontier town, remember – the frontier between poverty and wealth! A doctor told me that not long ago, after he came off duty, a patient died in the night. His body was taken out of the ward and put in a tent next to the hospital. Next morning when he went to the tent to examine the corpse he was horrified to see that all the limbs had been torn off by wild animals, and only the trunk remained. The moral is, not to have an accident, and never to fall ill.'

Sammy turned away and wiped sweat off his forehead. 'That story made me feel ill,' he admitted. 'I never imagined life would be so rough out here. I hate the idea of going down that hole. It makes me giddy just to look at it. There's so much noise and confusion down there. It's so hot and humid, for there's no breeze. Men climb up and down ropes, and on ladders and by toe-holds cut in the rock. It's Bedlam.'

'Have courage!' Arabella said firmly. 'It's our great, and only, chance, and we're going to stay here for just as long as it takes to find diamonds. No longer. Agreed? But the sooner we start, the sooner we'll finish. So no more doubts. Let's get down to the real business – digging.'

'I thought you'd cheer us up, Bella,' said Sammy. 'Let's go

back to my house now. I've saved a bottle of whisky to celebrate your arrival.'

They walked round the edge of the mine, past the shacks of the diamond buyers. Some had the flags of the buyers' nationalities flying outside them: Austrian, German, French. One of the biggest shacks was painted dark green. Inside, a double-sided partner's desk with a green leather top and wooden handles on each of the drawers seemed incongruous in such a place. On the desk was a letter rack and a tin box with small, square, different-sized compartments for holding diamonds. In the corner of the room, a set of scales, protected from the heat and dust by a glass case, stood on a table. Its weights were minute, all polished; there was a tiny shovel, the size of a small sugar spoon, to move the diamonds. In the wall facing the desk was a large brass safe with 'Patent Fire Resistant' stamped on its door in bold lettering.

The diamond buyer sat outside on a wooden stool, his wide-brimmed hat pulled down over his face against the sun. He gave the impression he was dozing, but he was actually wide awake and had already noticed the newcomers.

'Just arrived?' he asked Jamie.

'Today,' Jamie admitted.

'Well, Hirschmann's the name. Harry Hirschmann. I give a fair price always. That's how Barney Barnato got his good name, and that's how I'm making mine. I hope we can do business together.'

'I hope so, too,' Jamie agreed.

Every morning, soon after sunrise, Jamie and Sammy would set off to the mine, joining thousands of other men also heading for the big hole. They carried shovels and sieves. They took stools, they took magnifying glasses. Some diamonds were very small and after hours of peering at trays of dirt under a blazing sun, it was easy to miss them. All through the day the buckets went down to the men hacking at the ground several hundred feet below the surface of the earth. Then, with a squeal and winding of the cables, the buckets came up and the contents were tipped on to tables, sieved, and useless earth thrown away.

More sophisticated diggers used a pulsator to separate the diamonds from the gravel. This was a table smeared with grease and shaken constantly as the gravel was poured over it. The grease caught and held any diamonds while the gravel was washed away by a stream of water. No one could tell Arabella how the grease could select one type of stone from another, but it did.

Tired eyes played unkind tricks. Diggers would suddenly pounce on a piece of gravel, shouting excitedly that they had found a hundred-carat diamond, and then they'd blink and see they were gripping a pebble.

For the first few days, Sammy and Jamie set off in high spirits, telling each other that this would be their lucky day. But after a while, when they came back in the evening, to sit usually in Sammy's house while Arabella cooked a meal, with only a few diamonds worth £5 or £7 or none at all, their confidence began to wane.

Harry Hirschmann, the buyer, kept telling them that they had lucky faces. They were going to be rich. He knew it. Then they'd make him rich. They wanted to believe him, and Arabella always insisted she did believe him. They just had to keep at it. That was the thing. Perseverance.

Kimberley was a town of contrasts; someone who might be a pauper one day could be a millionaire the next. And the other way round. A single claim that was bought originally for ten or twenty pounds could change hands for thousands if diamonds were discovered and the digger wanted to clear out with a profit. The next month, when no more diamonds were discovered, the new owner, facing bankruptcy or with a loan to pay off at a high rate of interest, would be glad to take twenty pounds to clear out himself. Soda water manufactured in a local factory cost five shillings a bottle; an onion, half that amount. In the drought, a cabbage which cost ten shillings might be sold for thirty.

Lightning storms were frequent and diggers were struck down as they walked home, as they worked, or sitting in their tents. Most tents had a bottle inverted on the tent pole as a kind of insurance against being struck by lightning. Droughts could be followed by floods which swept away tents, houses, horses, oxen. The next day the sun would be shining, as bright as ever.

Whenever a digger found a worthwhile diamond, he would give a great shout and others would join in his triumph and celebration. The stone might be worth £1,000 or £5,000, and then crates of champagne would be ordered and drunk. If there weren't enough glasses or mugs, men would drink a toast out of the bucket that had carried up the diamond.

Oddly, when so much else was expensive, drink was cheap. A dozen quart bottles of champagne cost £3. Brandy was 7s.6d. a gallon, Cape sherry four shillings a gallon. At night there was heavy drinking in the pubs but none of the violence associated with the gold rushes in Australia and the United States. The men drank to share the triumph of lucky colleagues, to remember their own good fortune, or to forget their bad luck, the months they'd spent here, the money they'd wasted, with no dividend, no result at all. And as they staggered back to their huts or tents, tripping over guy ropes, cursing grazing mules that got in their way, they would pass the big hole, dark, empty, sombre under the moon. It was a constant and silent reminder of hope won, hope lost, of despair, frustration, elation.

The statistics of the big hole were daunting: more than one and a half kilometres round, five hundred metres across from north to south, rather less east to west. The whole area covered seventeen hectares. Surely, in all that space there must be more diamonds? They could not all have been picked out. Could they?

And all around this echoing pit, thousands of men, some with wives, children, and maybe a horse or a dog, lived in hope until their money ran out and they could borrow no more. They believed to the very last moment, when they had to sell their few belongings and go, that tomorrow, this afternoon, in ten minutes, they would make their fortune. Then everything – the privations, the heat, the hunger, the dust, the storms, the drought – all would have been worthwhile.

Frequently, Harry Hirschmann would call in to see Jamie or Sammy, and Arabella would make supper for them all. He would tell them stories of Kimberley characters past. One man, John Darbyshire, could not wait to come from the Knysna district because there were no carts to take him. He did not fancy walking, so he made himself a wooden tricycle with a sail. The machine was so heavy, he could barely push it along the ground. But with a fair wind behind him, it brought him into Kimberley.

Barney Barnato had what he called a boxing academy in the Pniel Road where aficionados could watch boxing matches which he promoted. Sometimes, he would go into the ring himself. When he won he was quite likely to stand on his head and in that position recite 'To be or not to be . . .' from *Hamlet*.

Cecil Rhodes was the opposite of Barney Barnato; tall where Barney was small, grave where Barney was a humorist. And while Barney's reading largely consisted of the racing papers, Rhodes always carried his Greek lexicon and the 'Meditations of Marcus Aurelius'. One phrase he found particularly apt – and so did Arabella: 'A man's life is what his thoughts make of it.'

Hirschmann told them how, in the early days, Rhodes had

signed an agreement to pump out flooded mines within a certain time. Ox wagons were totally bogged down because of unseasonal heavy rains and it was therefore impossible to bring in any heavy equipment from Cape Town or Port Elizabeth.

The miners were furious, and could have lynched Rhodes. He pacified them by promising to have a pump working within 30 days, as agreed, or he would forfeit £100.

Someone told him that a farmer in the Karoo owned a steam pump which brought up water from an underground stream. Rhodes set out in a Cape-cart to reach the farmer – a journey that took eight days – and explained he wished to buy his pump.

The farmer refused; the pump was far too useful to him. Day after day, Rhodes called on the farmer, increasing his offer at each visit. Finally, for £1000, a tremendous sum for a piece of rickety equipment, the farmer reluctantly agreed to sell. Neither man had a pen, but such was Rhodes' charm that the farmer accepted his cheque written in pencil – although he had never heard of Rhodes before. It then cost Rhodes a further £120 to bring the pump up to the mine.

'So to save one hundred pounds, he spent one thousand, one hundred and twenty pounds,' said Jamie doubtfully.

'Of course he did,' said Arabella. 'But you've missed the whole point. For that amount, he had also bought a monopoly for pumping out the mines, which was far more valuable.'

Then there was Joseph Benjamin Robinson, who had started in South Africa as an itinerant general trader. One day, crossing a river he noticed a number of glittering pebbles in the water. Out of curiosity, he picked a handful. That night, he rubbed each pebble carefully against a glass tumbler. Only one scratched the glass; it was a diamond.

Next morning, Robinson casually asked local natives whether any of them had seen any bright stones. One old man produced a stone which Robinson recognised instantly as a diamond. He offered £12 for it. The old man refused; he did not understand money. Robinson then offered him 20 goats, which only cost him 7s.6d. each – a total of £7.10.0d. The old man gladly accepted this offer, and Robinson had a new career – diamond buyer.

He bought diamonds; he sold them. He made millions quickly – and never spent a penny unless almost forced to do so. He was so mean he would not enter any bar until he was certain no one he knew was already there – in case he should be asked to buy a drink.

Arabella perceived that all these men shared one strong characteristic. They were utterly resolute. They never gave up, no matter what the cost to them, or to others around them, in terms of personal relationships or peace of mind. The end was all important; the means used to gain that end meant nothing to them.

Arabella could not bear to see the unsuccessful diggers and their families trekking out of town, going back to whatever job they could find. They were like a defeated army. I'm not one of them, she told herself. I never will be. I'd die rather than do that. She would pause outside the impressive gates of the Kimberley Club and watch the rich in their carriages and new motor cars. They were living proof that wealth could be made here, even if she and Jamie weren't making it yet. But they would. They must. There was nothing else for them if they didn't.

On the ground floor of the club, set into the tiles, was a long metal arrow, pointing north. Rhodes had had it put there so that he could always keep in his mind the fact that his destiny lay to the north: from the Cape to the country that would one day bear his name, then on to Cairo. This intensity of ambition was a constant source of inspiration to Arabella. Like him, she would follow her dream, no matter how rough the road, how painful to herself or to others on the way.

Days stretched into weeks and became months, and still they found only a few tiny diamonds, so small they looked like specks of glass, worth £5, £10, £20. They were not even breaking even; they were simply using up their capital.

Jamie came in after another day of profitless toil, sat down, closed his eyes. After hours in the heat, straining his eyes to catch the tiniest diamond glint in masses of gravel, he felt totally exhausted, with a throbbing headache.

'Harry Hirschmann was here just before you came back,' Arabella told him.

'What did he want?'

'There's a Boer ostrich hunter, Jan, in town. He suggested you might care to shoot with him.'

'Why?'

'Ostriches pick up anything that glints, like diamonds. Hirschmann thinks you could come to an arrangement with the hunter to slit open their gizzards, their guts, and see if they have swallowed any diamonds. It can't be harder than digging out in the sun all day.'

'I'll give it a try,' said Jamie wearily. 'Where is this hunter to be found?'

'He's got a tent somewhere. I said I thought you would be interested. He'll be here at seven in the morning.'

The Boer hunter came into their house, sat down at the table opposite Jamie. He was old, grizzled, his hair short, like grey steel wool.

'Things not good, yes,' he said, making the question into a statement.

Jamie shrugged. 'They could be better.'

'For all of us,' the hunter agreed. 'But if you want to make a few pounds, you could help me. Shooting ostriches. All the smart ladies in Holland and England and France and Germany love their feathers. They wear them in hats, on capes with

241

evening dress, anything. They dye them all colours. They go crazy for these feathers. Fellow in the general store had a head for figures and told me that last year more than a million pounds changed hands in London for Cape Colony feathers. I get thirty-six pounds cash in my hand for every pound weight of feathers. You come in with me for a few days. We might make a hundred between us.'

'I'm on,' said Jamie. 'When do we start?'

'Tomorrow. I've a spare rifle. But, remember, the cartridges are very expensive. So don't fire until I give the word. We can't afford to miss.'

In England, people laughed at the idea of the ostrich burying its head in the sand and thinking it was concealed, but this was not the folly Jamie had been led to believe. The ostrich did not bury its head, but extended its neck flat on the ground. From a distance the hump of its back would appear to any adversary simply as a brown boulder or a hillock. The ostrich was a bird to approach with caution, even when holding a shotgun. It could kill a large dog with a single kick.

They set off before dawn the following morning. Jamie saw his first ostriches three hours later. A group of the birds were tearing at the grass for food. Behind them stood a herd of zebras.

'They go together,' Jan explained. 'The ostrich has no brain, but the best eyes of any creature I've ever heard of. The zebra's eyes are not too sharp, but he can smell and hear a stranger from half a mile away. So they are useful to each other.'

They went downwind, moving slowly, cautiously, keeping their eyes on the grazing birds until they reached the cover of a clump of trees.

'I'll stay here,' said Jan. 'You go fifty yards further on. Ostriches run in circles when they're frightened. I'll take those that go to the left. You handle the others on the right.'

Jamie nodded.

'If anything goes wrong and they chase you,' Jan continued,

'don't try to run for it. The males are eight feet tall, a single pace to them is eight yards, and they're the fastest runners in the world. If you can't get a forked stick to thrust in his neck to keep him at bay until I can shoot him, lie flat on the ground, face down and pull your hat over the back of your neck. If you move, or if he sees those bright buttons on your shirt, he'll peck at you and put his claws in your guts. I've seen 'em do that to a native often. Not a nice way to go. Now, ever shot before?'

'Never.'

'Then here are the basic rules. Aim slightly ahead of a running target. Aim low – bullets tend to rise. Don't shut your eyes – so many do – when you *squeeze* the trigger – you never pull it. And don't let the gun jerk upwards as you fire. All simple rules. But all essential. Right?'

'I suppose so.'

'Then let's go.'

Jamie walked forward, counting fifty paces. He turned. Jan gave him the thumbs up, raised his rifle, took aim. At the movement, the ostriches lifted their heads as though on cue. They turned and looked in the hunter's direction, synchronised like a drill movement or the chorus in a musical.

Jan fired. Two ostriches fluttered their huge wings as their long, thin legs slid under them. The rest scattered. Jan fired the second barrel. Two more dropped. Now the ostriches began to run frantically in a wide circle, their huge, iron-hard claws sending up a thick cloud of dust.

Jamie heard Jan fire again twice and then took aim himself. His first barrel hit one ostrich, which fell, beating its head against the ground. He fired again. Nothing. Either a dud round, or a pin had jammed. He broke the gun. The cartridge did not eject.

To his left, he heard Jan shout warningly: '*Look out!*'

At that moment, Jamie saw a huge ostrich with the black and white feathers of an adult male racing towards him, wings

243

outstretched. Jamie snapped the gun together, pressed the trigger. Again, nothing. The bird was now less than thirty yards away, head lowered, long neck extended, straight as a lance. What the devil was Jan doing? Why didn't he shoot it?

Then Jamie realised Jan would not know his rifle had jammed. This was his shot and he couldn't take it. Forgetting Jan's advice, Jamie ran to one side, hoping to reach the shelter of a small clump of trees. The ostrich veered after him; there was no way he could escape this furious bird.

Jamie dropped flat on the ground, tugged his sweat-soaked felt hat over the back of his neck and lay face down in the dust, eyes closed, hands pressed against his ears to give some protection. He braced his muscles, his whole body, against the giant bird's attack. He imagined it would jump on him with all its weight and then tear at his flesh with its talon-like claws.

A cloud of dust blew around his head as the bird stopped a few feet away. Jamie breathed carefully through his mouth. If he breathed through his nose, he knew he would sneeze with the dust. He felt the bird's feet move round him, pushing insensitively at his body, a jab at his left wrist, another at his right. The bird had seen metal buttons on his shirt sleeves, bright with use, and was attracted by them. Blood beat in Jamie's brain like a hammer.

What was Jan doing? Had he been injured? How long would he have to lie like this? An hour? A day?

Slowly, very carefully, Jamie moved his head so that through one half-closed eye he could see if the bird was still near. It was, squatting down, barely a foot away, watching him. Jamie closed his eye. If the bird saw that his eye was open, it could attack him.

He heard a zebra whinny, and then nothing but the beat of his own terrified heart in his ears. He lay, muscles tensed, unable to mark the passage of time. Every so often he would half open one eye again. The ostrich was still by his side, waiting for a movement, waiting to trample him or kick him to death. He closed his eye and lay, sweating in the heat, body tensed. He must have dozed because when he looked again, he could not see the bird. He turned his head carefully. The ostrich had moved. It was sitting about a yard away, to his right, neck stretched out on the sand, huge liquid eyes watching him.

It had seen Jamie move his head. The great hump of ruffled feathers trembled as the ostrich made to stand upright. It reached its full height, towering over Jamie's body. This was the moment of death, thought Jamie despairingly, here in the heat and the sunlit dust. He could imagine the huge mass of oily, stinking feathers on him while the bird's claws tore him to pieces.

Then, as though from an immeasurable distance of time and space, he heard a crack like a dry branch breaking. The bird took one pace towards Jamie and then suddenly collapsed, falling across his legs. A great mass of bloodied feathers fluttered. Claws dug uselessly in the earth in death throes, and then the long neck sank and its head dropped.

Jamie waited for a moment, then crawled out from under the dead weight. Jan came towards him through the grass.

'I couldn't shoot when he was on your left side,' he explained. 'Lucky for you he moved. Otherwise you'd have been there all day.'

'Thanks for saving my life,' said Jamie shakily. 'I'd have been dead if you hadn't been there.'

'Well, I was. You'd have done the same for me. Now, give me a hand in cutting the feathers off. We must have made a few pounds today.'

He gave Jamie a sheath knife, showed him how to remove the quills, not to pull them roughly from the bird's flesh. The breeze tended to blow the feathers away before they could cram them into the sacks they had brought with them. They filled three sacks that day, and on the following day, two more. They seemed to weigh very little for an enormous bulk, because the feathers could not be pushed in too harshly or they would get damaged.

'There's a lot of meat on these birds,' said Jamie.

'I know,' said Jan. 'I've often made biltong, but it's just more weight to carry back. Hardly worth the effort of cutting it. But I'll show you how.'

He slit the breast of a hen ostrich. Steaming pink entrails cascaded out in a stinking mass on the dust. Jan's hands searched through them to find the stomach, cut it free, slit it open. It contained a sodden mass of grit and small stones the bird used to churn the food into tiny particles, chewed-up leaves, softened by bile, and then a few stones that glittered, reflecting the sunlight like tiny heliographs.

'What are they?' asked Jamie hopefully. 'Diamonds?'

'No,' said Jan dismissively.

'They look like diamonds,' said Jamie.

'That's what I thought, but they're not. I've taken dozens to Harry Hirschmann, but they were worthless. Take 'em and prove it for yourself.'

By afternoon, Jamie had slit the gizzards and guts of thirty ostriches. He felt sick at the sight of steaming viscera, the stench of half-digested food and oily feathers. He had extracted a dozen small stones that shone more brightly than the rest, kept them in a twist of paper.

'I hope they're all diamonds – for your sake,' said Jan. 'But myself, I don't think they're worth carrying back.'

They were in Kimberley by dusk. The storeman weighed the feathers in the sacks, carefully subtracted the weight of an empty sack. They had shot only one pound in weight, worth £36.

'That was last week's price,' said the buyer sourly. 'There's a glut on the market today. We're only paying thirty.'

He counted out the notes.

Jan took out £10 for his cartridges and gave Jamie £10 as his half share in the profits. He did not invite Jamie to join him on the next shoot, and Jamie did not invite himself.

He went back to his house, took out the stones, washed them in a cup, and wrapped them in a clean twist of paper.

Next morning, he tied his handkerchief round the paper, which looked pathetically small, and set off for Hirschmann's hut. Already, early as it was, kopje-wallopers – men who bought diamonds from diggers as intermediaries – were waiting in line. Harry was not working that day and the sorter was an old Scot who chewed tobacco and spat to right and left while his fingers fluttered over each new stone, expertly sifting any diamonds from garnets and moonstones and crystals.

One after the other, diggers emptied the previous day's haul on to the fine mesh of his screen. Jamie knew that stones a hard-up digger might sell for a few pounds could eventually fetch hundreds, or even thousands. But not the ones he poured out from his piece of paper.

'Sorry, son,' said the Scot, moving his quid of tobacco from his left to his right cheek. 'Just quartz and crystal. Where did you find 'em?'

'Inside ostriches when I went shooting with a Dutch hunter, Jan. Harry suggested it.'

The Scot spat expressively. 'He always does. Means to give newcomers a helping hand. Once, he got a five-hundred-pound diamond that way. Sometimes they find a few worth a tenner in an ostrich's guts, but not often. Maybe the ostriches don't like 'em. Too hard for them, eh? Give 'em indigestion!' He laughed at his own joke and swept the bright worthless stones into a bucket.

'Well, it was worth a try,' Arabella assured Jamie when he told her what had happened. 'So we'll try something else. I've had an idea how I can make some money.'

'I hope it's better than ostriches.'

'It is. Look out across the road and what do you see?'

Jamie looked. A middle-aged wife of one of the more successful diggers was walking along, holding her skirt up out of the dust. She wore a wide-brimmed hat to keep the heat and glare of the sun from her face.

'What about her?' he asked. 'Looks quite normal to me.'

'Look at her hat.'

'Are you going to make new hats or something, Bella?'

'No. But look at all the women you see out here in the sun. They all wear hats. I do. Everyone does, primarily to keep the sun off our heads, but as far as women are concerned, also to stop the sun ruining their complexions. Mrs Riley, on the wagon coming up from the Cape – her lips were cracking, her face was rough with the heat and the dust. I gave her some of Yeung Lee's cream and it smoothed her face within a day. I've been using it myself and my face is just as smooth as it was back in England. But all the other women here look old by the time they are forty. The sun has wrecked their skin. I'm running short of the cream, but I'm going to see the chemist we travelled up with on the wagon and ask him to analyse it.'

'And if he does,' asked Jamie, 'you'll get him to make some more?'

'No. I'll make some more. I'll mix it up myself, in the back room, and bottle it in jars or boxes, sell it at a shilling a time, maybe two shillings. I know it's good. So does Mrs Riley. I could give her some kind of an agency. Offer her sixpence on each pot she can sell. Everyone goes in and out of the Post Office. It's the busiest place in town.'

'If you start that, won't the chemist copy you?'

'I don't think so. He's not in this business. He doesn't want all that hassle. Besides, he's not a woman. Women like to buy from other women. In a draper's shop, you have women behind the counter, not men. I reckon all sorts of women, probably all the women in Kimberley, will try this at least

248

once. When they find it's good – which it is – they'll come back for more. I'll market it in small pots. Each will last only a fortnight. So they have to come back.'

Jamie stroked his chin. 'It's certainly got more potential than shooting ostriches to see what they've eaten for breakfast! But do you really think it is a viable proposition?'

'I don't *think*,' replied Arabella firmly. 'I *know*.'

FOURTEEN

Gray's Inn, London

Noel sat well back on the buttoned Bedford cord upholstery of his Rolls-Royce Silver Ghost. Ahead of him, in the open air, without either roof or side windows to shield them from the elements, were his chauffeur and footman. Both sat rigidly upright, wearing the family livery of dark red tunics, buttoned to the neck, with shining patent-leather peaks to their caps.

Ahead of them, the polished aluminium bonnet stretched to the Parthenon shape of the German silver radiator, crowned by a silver Spirit of Ecstasy mascot. Other lesser cars might sport mascots of brass, nickel, or even chromium plate, but for Noel now only the best could be good enough; and solid silver must be the best. After all, with his wife's money, what need was there to economise on anything? Now this was a mark of his money. Never again would he have to bend his will to the arguments of others. His wealth – or rather, his late wife's – would buy him the almost priceless gift that prodigious funds can confer: total independence.

The great car sighed discreetly through the early lunchtime traffic – trams, omnibuses, horses and carts – and turned beneath the stone archway that leads to Gray's Inn. As it stopped in the stone-flagged forecourt, the footman leapt down, opened the door, bowed deferentially when Noel stepped on to the paving. Ahead, he could see the new-mown lawns of the Inn. Ancient elms rustled their leaves reassuringly above his head. He thought whimsically that they sounded like £10 notes, hundreds, thousands, millions of them.

The footman opened the door of the solicitors' chambers and announced to the clerk: 'Lord Doncaster.'

The clerk bowed. 'The senior partner, Mr Jennings, is expecting you, my lord,' he intoned unctuously. He was used to a regular procession of aristocratic clients, but always had a feeling of occasion at the arrival of a lord, an earl, a duke. The partnership specialised in the foibles and follies of such aristocrats: the entailing of a great estate, a discreet divorce, the payment of cash for the return of some unfortunate letters, and not infrequently the circumspect committal of a member of a noble family to an asylum for the insane.

The clerk led Noel up a flight of worn oak stairs, knocked on the double, dark-stained doors that opened on to the senior partner's room. A middle-aged man, dark-suited as for a funeral, with a high, uncomfortable starched collar that pinched the loose flesh of his neck, came round the side of his wide partner's desk to shake Doncaster's hand.

'A very pleasant morning, is it not, Lord Doncaster? For this time of year, I mean. But no doubt we'll pay for it later.'

Noel nodded. He didn't care who paid for what then or later. As far as he was concerned, the morning would be a devil more pleasant when he knew the precise value of Emily's shares, her properties in Pittsburgh and New York. His own private estimate, from casual hints she had dropped, was that it must run into several million dollars. A fraction of the income would buy off those impudent creditors in the casinos and the Semitic moneylenders in North London. The worst of them – because he was the most tenacious – traded under the ridiculously pompous name of the North London Loan Accommodation Company.

'Would you care to join me in a glass of Madeira, sir?' Jennings asked him solicitously.

'No, thank you,' Noel replied. Why did the fellow want to waste time in this manner? Noel sat down in the leather chair, crossed his knees, folded his hands and waited for the man to begin.

Jennings slowly, almost reluctantly, untied a pink tape round a buff folder. 'I asked you to come here, Lord Doncaster,' the solicitor began, almost hesitantly, as an actor about to make a key speech on stage begins unhurriedly and then winds up to the heart of the matter, 'because, as you know, we were favoured with legal instructions by your late wife. May she rest in peace.'

'Amen,' said Noel gravely. 'She was a very dear person.'

For a moment, they sat in silence, each recalling different aspects of the dead. Jennings remembered her sitting, barely three months earlier, on a warm spring day, parasol in her hand, in the chair her husband now occupied.

Noel remembered Emily's lifeless face more recently, pale as the pillow beside her, and the sudden realisation that never again would he hear her boring, chattering, prattling voice. Never.

What an extraordinary night that had been! Only moments after the hotel doctor had left the suite, the telephone rang; an urgent telegraphed message awaited him at the reception desk. He told the clerk to send it up. A page – that same boy with the rounded bottom – delivered it personally.

The telegram was from his uncle's bailiff. The old man had died after a fall while riding; Noel was now Lord Doncaster. Not that any money came with the title; the reverse, in fact. His uncle had been a prodigious spender. When money in his bank account ran low, he had immediately borrowed more against the estate, or sold off a village or a row of cottages. The estate was burdened by huge debts at usurious interest, but Emily's money would instantly lift Noel clear of a generation of financial mismanagement. And he had a title. That in itself was almost as good as money in the bank. Not quite, but almost.

The lawyer's voice cut into his thoughts. 'Shall I read the will to you? Or would you prefer to peruse it yourself?'

'You read it.'

Jennings exchanged one pair of spectacles for another. Over his shoulder, a flutter of rooks flew out from the upper branches of an elm. Gardeners wearing green baize aprons were methodically brushing the lawns carefully with brooms of twigs. Jennings cleared his throat.

'The last will and testament . . . being of sound mind . . . revokes all and any previous will and testament . . .'

Come to the meat of it, thought Noel irritably. Get on with it, man. As soon as I come into the money, I will be rid of this bumbling fellow, get someone sharper, someone who knows his way around, not a pontificating bore. And then, suddenly, he was listening intently, unable to believe what he heard.

'I leave everything in trust for my dear nephew, Richard Ardmore, the son of my only and dearly loved sister, Kathleen, until he reaches the age of twenty-one . . . To each servant in my employ who has been with me over twelve months and is not under notice at the time of my death, I leave the sum of one hundred guineas . . .

'To my husband, Noel, I leave the contents of my cellar in my freehold property in Curzon Street, my father's gold cigarette case and my earnest good wishes that he may find lasting fulfilment for his undeniable talents, and peace and happiness in so doing . . .'

Jennings droned on, giving details of various other small legacies or gifts of furniture or jewellery to relations, but they were unimportant, they did not concern Noel. He stared disbelievingly at the lawyer, who at last lowered the will and looked over his glasses at him.

For a moment, neither man spoke. Then Noel cleared his

throat, and in a voice he hardly recognised as his own, asked: 'Is that all?'

'That is all, my lord, yes. Everything she owned – shares, properties, the mills in Pittsburgh, office buildings in New York – all that is in the Trust. I could give you the details if you so wish.'

'But what about me?' Noel asked him hoarsely, answering one question with another.

'Well, my lord, as you heard, she has left you a cellar of wine and this gold cigarette case which, as it belonged to her father, she valued very greatly.'

'But that's *nothing*,' said Noel, anger sharpening his voice. 'She promised to leave me everything – *everything*. We discussed it often enough. It was part of our arrangement.'

'Your arrangement, sir? I confess I do not quite follow you.'

Jennings' eyes were suddenly hard as polished pebbles behind the thick lenses of his spectacles.

'What I mean is that her father made millions out of some wheat breakfast cereal. She wanted a title. I had the title. That, basically, is why she married me.'

'Well, of course, sir, I cannot comment on that. I was not privy to anything that may have been discussed, or may not have been discussed, as the case may be. There was, I take it, no formal statement of this intent on your wife's part?'

'Of course there was no formal statement. We just agreed it between ourselves when we got married.'

'And even if there had been a formal statement of intent, I have to tell you that since this will is of a later date, it revokes all earlier testaments and any earlier documents of like kind.'

'Have you any idea why she has done this to me?'

'Since you ask me directly, I must admit I do have some idea, my lord. Your wife did favour me with her confidence on the matter.'

'Then tell me why, man.'

254

'I would prefer not to, sir, but she did give me permission to divulge her reasons, if you showed any surprise at her will. But these reasons may not make pleasant listening for you, sir.'

'Damn that! What were they?'

Jennings was often told he should have been an actor; preferably a tragedian, declaiming to an enthralled audience some great speech by Shakespeare or Marlowe or Kyd. He knew instinctively the value of silence, the power that a pause possesses. Now he moved papers about with his long, soft fingers and deliberately counted to ten before he replied.

'Lord Doncaster, I have here a note of your late wife's reasons. Since you insist I tell you them, I will do so. They are, sir, that she believed you had been consistently unfaithful, almost since your wedding, not with other women, but – I hardly like to say this – with people of your own sex. You continued to run up gambling and other debts, despite repeated promises and assurances you would not do so.

'Time and again, she paid large sums to bookmakers and the managers of casinos on the Continent to save you from shame, or sometimes – as you persuaded her – actual bodily harm for non-payment of monies outstanding.

'Time and again, she advanced monies to you which you claimed were needed for repairs in connection with her properties. I have a complete list of the sums involved and the relevant dates, should you wish to refresh your memory. Your lady wife had her father's habit of accuracy in all financial undertakings.

'The most superficial inquiries proved that these repairs and improvements were never carried out. You needed the money to pay other debts of your own. In brief and to be blunt, you lied to her. Some would even suggest that you obtained many, many thousands of pounds from her under totally false pretences.

'As a result of your unsatisfactory and, to her, very hurtful behaviour, she came to see me. She took my advice, and that of my partner who deals with trust matters. We were both strongly of the opinion that should you inherit everything – as you claim she promised, although no document whatever corroborating that protestation appears to exist – you would decimate even the huge fortune her father had built up.'

'That is an opinion,' retorted Noel. 'Not a fact.'

'It was a deduction based on my client's experience as your wife.'

'So now you and your partner will continue to draw fees from the Trust until this boy is twenty-one – and he is only three now?'

'That is so, sir. That was your wife's express desire. I have it in writing, of course.'

'Of course. You would have. But if she were here now, she would have a very different story to tell. She would not want her estate to be bled white by men of law doing what they would willingly send others to jail for even contemplating.'

'Those are strong words, sir, and I am sure you do not mean them.'

'I bloody well do! I have been fooled.'

'I would not say that, sir. Now, I assume that you wish to take possession of the wine at an early date?'

'Since it is in the cellars of the house we lived in, I already have possession of it.'

'Not entirely a correct assumption, Lord Doncaster. A codicil to the will states that the house – which you will recall is in your late wife's name – will be vacated within three months of the owner's death. I believe her sister and her husband wish to move in.'

'But then I have nowhere to put the wine.'

'That should not present any difficulty, sir. You must own other properties.'

Noel could not bring himself to admit to this creature that he was almost penniless. Mortgage interest and repayments ran to several times the income from the properties his uncle had left him.

'There is one other thing, Lord Doncaster,' said Jennings. 'The matter of an insurance policy taken out on your late wife's life.'

'What of it? I insured her for ten thousand pounds. It was a sort of joke between us. She was insuring me for the same amount. I don't know why exactly.'

'There is no record of such an insurance transaction in her papers. And she kept everything in perfect order. But be that as it may, I am informed that the insurance company will dispute payment to you of the ten thousand pounds.'

'Why? They have not told me this.'

'Then they will do so in the near future, I do not doubt. But they have advised us, as we handled her affairs.'

'What is their reason for this?'

'I understand that they are not satisfied with the circumstances of her death.'

'But this is outrageous.'

'They have been in touch with the doctor who examined her body in the hotel, Dr Artur Delauneville. He has, I understand, been most helpful. You will have to institute proceedings against the insurance company if you wish to press the matter.'

'You also act for them, I suppose?'

'In this particular instance, yes.'

Noel rose. 'Please send me a copy of the will by messenger today, to my house,' he told Jennings curtly. 'I will then inform you what I intend to do.'

Jennings pressed a handbell. The door opened. A clerk appeared so quickly, he must have been waiting outside, a silent listening witness. Noel trembled with revulsion, not only at the way Emily, the dull, dumb Emily, had fooled him, but at this smug, unctuous lawyer. And as he went down the stairs, he felt an equal revulsion for his own actions. He had killed his wife for nothing. He was a murderer, branded with the mark of Cain – for a few bottles of wine and a cigarette case he had

257

never liked. Why, he never smoked cigarettes, only cigars.

If the crime were discovered and his guilt proved, he could hang. Then his only consolation would be that instead of the hemp Bridport rope by which a commoner dangled above the open trap door, he would, as a peer, have the distinction of entering eternity at the end of a silken cord. The prospect was appalling – and all for nothing.

And then, as he was about to leave, passing his footman who held open the outer door of the chambers, he had an idea, a possible solution to his problem. He turned to the clerk, took a sovereign from his pocket, slipped it between his fingers under the pretence of shaking hands with the man. The clerk received the coin without any sign of acknowledgement.

'Can you give me the name of a reputable private investigator?' Noel asked him. 'On a personal matter, nothing to do with the law.'

'We always use Sergeant O'Malley, Red Lion Court, my lord. If you mention that Johnny sent you, I am sure he will be of service.'

'I am in your debt,' Noel assured him.

The man bowed, and pocketed the sovereign. Lord Doncaster was a real gentleman; anyone could see that.

FIFTEEN

Diamond-Hard

On Saturday mornings, Jamie and Arabella allowed themselves the luxury of a later start. At eight o'clock on this particular Saturday, Jamie was carrying the plates into the kitchen after breakfast to help Arabella wash up, when Sammy Rosen appeared. For a moment, Sammy stood hesitantly in the doorway, as though reluctant to come inside.

'There's a wagon going down to the Cape, Monday,' he said at last. 'There won't be another for ten days. I've made up my mind to go on it.'

He stared at them almost belligerently, as though expecting them to tell him he was a deserter. They both looked at him in surprise.

'You're leaving?' asked Arabella. 'But why? You'll never make a fortune down there.'

'I'll never make even a living here, let alone a fortune,' retorted Sammy. 'In Cape Town or Durban I can set up a shop of some kind – tailoring, if possible. And if I haven't enough money left to do that, then I can always work for some other tailor until I have saved some.

'My brother in Durban is doing quite well. He'll give me some introductions. That may not be riches, but it should be a living. Here, it's madness, crawling down a giant hole every morning, dragging up buckets of earth at the end of a rope, sieving dirt from dawn to dusk, risking falling down in the hole every working day – all in the hope of finding diamonds. There've been too many people after these diamonds already. That's what so many others have told us. We should have listened to them. We got here too late to find anything worth a damn now. There's nothing left.'

'Of course there is,' Jamie told him. 'Positive thinking, that's what we need, not this defeatism.'

'That's what I'm doing for the first time since I left Hyde. Thinking positively, sensibly. I have three hundred pounds left out of what my uncle gave me. When that's gone I'll be reduced to selling my sieve and shovel for a few pounds, as I've seen so many others do since I've been here.'

'Three hundred is three hundred more than we have,' Arabella replied. 'But we're not giving up. And I've got high hopes that my face creams will keep us going until we do find diamonds.'

'Well, I wish you both luck,' said Sammy. 'I'll drop you a line as soon as I get an address.'

They shook hands formally. Arabella kissed him. As she did so, Jamie noticed that Sammy looked at her in the same surprised, almost disbelieving way he had looked at her when she had kissed him on his departure from Cape Town.

'Are you sure we can't make you change your mind?' she asked.

Sammy shook his head. 'It's not been an easy decision. In fact, I've been thinking about it for weeks, trying to screw up my courage to tell you. But I'm living off my own cash now. Every day my capital gets smaller. It's like watching a block of ice melt away to nothing on a hot day. You know what the Good Book says? "Hope deferred maketh the heart sick." And I'm sick of hoping for diamonds.'

They followed him to the door, saddened to see him go. A wagon was coming slowly towards them along the dusty road. The driver jumped down, crossed over to them.

'Either of you Mr Baird?' he asked.

'Yes,' said Jamie.

'Mr J. Baird?'

'Yes.'

'We got your deliveries.'

'What deliveries?'

'Canvas tenting. Here's the paper.'

He handed Jamie an envelope, marked 'For attention: J. Baird & Co.' Jamie ripped it open. Inside was a bill for 500 yards of best quality, service standard white canvas in rolls two yards wide.

Jamie looked at the man, about to tell him he was talking to the wrong Baird. J. Baird & Co.'s office and warehouse were in another street. But Arabella suddenly gripped his arm so tightly he turned to look at her in surprise. She did not look at him, but spoke to the driver.

'That's right,' she told him calmly. 'But deliver it round the back of the house. It'll block the road if you leave it here.'

The driver nodded, walked back to his wagon, turned it down a track that led behind the house. Jamie and Sammy looked at Arabella in amazement.

'What are you doing?' Jamie asked her. 'That's not for us.'

'It is now. We're buying it.'

'What with?'

'Sammy's three hundred.'

'Are you out of your mind?' asked Sammy. 'I need that to start a business in Durban.'

'You need it to start one here,' Arabella told him. She turned to her brother. 'You should remember the words of that man you like to quote, Sun Tzu: "Weigh the situation, then move." That's what I'm doing.'

'How can we possibly make a profit on five hundred yards of canvas?' Sammy asked her, bewildered. 'We can't make tents. It's come to the wrong place, this canvas.'

'We're not going to make tents. You keep talking about tailoring. Now's your chance to be a tailor, making trousers.'

'Out of tenting canvas? I've never heard of such nonsense.'

'Nor has anyone else, no doubt, but it's going to work. Now, get that money out of the bank while Jamie and I see to the driver here. Quickly!'

Obediently, Sammy hurried away.

Natives unloaded the huge rolls of canvas, carried them into a corrugated iron shed behind the house. Arabella paid the driver with Sammy's money, added £2 as a tip on condition that the wagon left town immediately. She did not want anyone connected with J. Baird & Co. to know what had happened. Then she sat down at the table with Sammy and Jamie.

'Well,' said Sammy uneasily. 'How am I going to make trousers out of five hundred yards of canvas? And who will buy them?'

'You've always said how you wanted to start some new kind of clothing factory to produce trousers and jackets of a better quality than the shoddy stuff most stores stock,' said Arabella. 'And how if you found diamonds, you'd do just that. Right?'

'Right,' Sammy agreed, mystified.

'Well, this is your chance. Look at the diggers here in Kimberley. Look at Jamie – and yourself. Your trousers are worn through, your jackets are threadbare, rubbing elbows on rocks climbing in and out of diggings. Almost every man in Kimberley looks like a scarecrow, except on Sundays when they all put on their best suits. Their working clothes are literally falling apart, for the cloth and stitching aren't strong enough for the hard wear they get. I'm suggesting you make – and we all sell – trousers and jackets out of this canvas.'

'That's ridiculous,' said Sammy immediately. 'Just wash that canvas a couple of times and it will come out white as snow. People will look as though they're wearing shrouds. And white

262

shows every stain. In no time, they'll look shabbier than they do now. No one will buy them. They'd be laughing stocks.'

'Who said we have to keep the canvas white? We'll dye it. Your name is Rosen. So we'll dye it dark red and call the trousers Rosens. They will *never* wear through that canvas. They will sell like hot cakes.'

'You may be right,' said Sammy doubtfully. 'But even if you are, how am I going to make them? It takes time to cut out one pair of trousers and sew them, let alone a dozen. And to make this pay, you'd need hundreds. At the fastest rate I can go it would take months, years, to make enough just to sell in Kimberley.'

'Agreed,' said Arabella. 'But I'm not suggesting you cut them out and sew them up yourself, Sammy. There are an awful lot of women here in Kimberley who have nothing much to do during the day – wives, sisters, aunts, cousins. Most have their own sewing machines. If they haven't, we can supply them on rent. Not for sale. That way we have a hold on them. Give each woman paper patterns, and they can cut them out on their kitchen tables and sew them at so much a time.'

'Sail canvas will blunt any needle,' Sammy pointed out.

'Then give them more needles, tougher needles – sail-maker's needles.'

'That cloth can be rough as a knife edge. It can literally saw through thread.'

'Then use stronger thread,' said Jamie, taking up his sister's lead. 'And to strengthen the seams we can rivet them and the edges of the pockets where they take the most strain.'

'Maybe you do have a good idea,' admitted Sammy slowly.

'We have more than that,' Arabella told him confidently. 'We've a whole project here that simply can't go wrong. We have a new product, and a huge market on our doorstep. And this will only be the beginning. Think of all the workmen in the Cape – even back home – who would welcome these tough working clothes. Their wives will like them even more, for canvas is easy to wash and dry. Not like serge.'

Sammy sat for a moment, and then he suddenly stood up and walked to the front door.

'Where are you going?' Arabella asked him in surprise. 'Not still walking out on us, surely?'

'No. I'm going to tell the coach office I won't be taking up my seat. I'm staying here.'

That afternoon, using Jamie as a model, Sammy cut out a master set of paper patterns for a pair of canvas trousers. Then he pinned the pattern to another sheet of paper on the table, cut round that, and when he had copied half a dozen patterns, he rolled them up and with Arabella went in search of seamstresses.

The first woman he approached said she was too busy with her children. The next had broken her arm. She said she would help when the plaster came off, but she didn't really know when that would be. The third was enthusiastic. She already made most of her own clothes and knew short cuts for sewing seams. They agreed a price, and Sammy gave her a packet of sailmaker's needles he bought in the general store.

'The canvas is very rough,' she pointed out dubiously. 'When you put any strain on it, say a hand in a pocket, it will literally cut the thread – even if it's relatively thick – like a knife.'

'We've already thought of that,' Sammy told her. 'You do the sewing and I will rivet the pockets.'

'*Rivet* them? I've never heard of rivets being used to hold trousers together.'

'Maybe not, but you have now. And you'll see, it'll become fashionable.'

By evening, he had delivered the patterns to six women and worked out a price for every pair of trousers they made. Next morning, he and Jamie cut lengths from one of the rolls of canvas and took these round to the women he had persuaded to sew for them.

'One thing we insist on,' said Jamie. 'That is secrecy. Don't mention to *anyone* what you are doing.'

'Why? Is there something wrong in it?' asked one woman suspiciously.

'Nothing. But it's such a good idea that if others copied it, we could all lose out.'

That was, in fact, only part of the reason for Jamie's wish for secrecy. The other concerned J. Baird & Co. For that afternoon, in the bar of the London Inn, where diggers congregated to exchange news, he had overheard a conversation between two of J. Baird's employees.

'The old man was rather ratty this morning,' said one. 'We have a contract for a hundred tents – but no canvas. It was ordered weeks ago. Should have been delivered yesterday at the latest. He sent a telegraph to the makers and they say it was delivered.'

'Not to us,' said his colleague, shaking his head. 'They're lying in their teeth. You can't trust anyone these days, not anyone.'

On the day Arabella's advertisement appeared in the *Diamond Advertiser* offering special face creams to women to protect their skin against the sun and dust, she received a visit from Mrs Murphy, the wife of the keeper of the nearest inn, the Goat and Compasses.

'I saw your advertisement in the paper,' Mrs Murphy explained. 'Not met you before, but I thought I would like to try some of your cream. My friend Mrs Riley, who came up from Cape Town with you, told me some you let her use on the journey had miraculous effects on her skin. I have trouble with my hands. So much washing up to do, wiping glasses. I wonder if you have anything that could help me?'

'I think I have something for you,' said Arabella. 'Back in England, I worked in a pub, too. One's hands get so sore. Come into the kitchen.'

On the table against the wall, she had laid out a number of small pots and jars. Each one was neatly labelled in pen and ink; they had rubber or wooden stoppers. The chemist had analysed the face cream quickly enough, and Arabella had bought all the ingredients from Cape Town or Durban.

'This is my stock,' Arabella explained. 'If there is enough demand, I'll get pots in different sizes from very large right down to ones you could put in your handbag, if you're going out for the day, or something. But that all costs money and I want to see what people think about the products before I spend too much.'

'I understand,' said Mrs Murphy. 'I don't think any of us is doing too well. I know trade is down in the bar, which is always a pretty good barometer. But if your cream is anything like as good as Mrs Riley says, I think you'll have a lot of customers. Now, what do you recommend?'

Arabella looked closely at the woman's face. She was fair-haired, her skin was freckled and had started to peel in places.

'I think you should try this,' she said, and handed her a pot of yellowish cream. 'Rub some into your face and hands every night and a little in the morning. It has the effect of filtering the sun's rays, and it's cooling, too. That makes you feel better, and if you feel better, my philosophy is that you look better.'

'I'll let you know by the end of the week,' said Mrs Murphy. 'How much is it?'

'Two shillings.'

A coin changed hands. Five other women came to see Arabella that day. Three bought pots. One said she thought it was against the teachings in the Holy Scriptures for a woman to paint her face with anything. That was the work of the devil.

266

The fifth looked into all the pots, sniffed the creams, and went back home, saying she would have to ask her husband.

Within the week, Mrs Murphy was back. Her complexion had much improved.

'I'll have another pot,' she said.

And then Mrs Riley came to see Arabella. 'I ran into Colleen Murphy,' she explained. 'She tells me you've given her some wonderful cream. Well, I was first in the field, you know, Arabella. I'd like a pot of whatever it was you let me have on the way here. Two shillings is the price, isn't it?'

'Yes,' said Arabella. 'But let's see if we can't come to some arrangement. You have a lot of people in the Post Office every day, women as well as men, don't you?'

'I do indeed. Why?'

'Offer them some of this cream. I'll give you twenty-five per cent off. A two shilling pot will cost you one and sixpence.'

'And on the other creams you have?'

'You'll make a tanner on them all.'

'Good,' said Mrs Riley approvingly. 'I'll try that.'

The next week, six more women came in, and the following week, Arabella put a second advertisement in the local paper, worded more graphically than the first bald announcement.

'Just arrived,' it stated. 'First samples of a wonderful cream based on a centuries-old Chinese formula, made specially to protect your complexion. Why look old when you can stay young? It is the right – the duty – of every woman to make herself beautiful, not only for the pleasure of those around her, but for her own personal satisfaction.'

That week, Arabella sold twenty-one pots; the next week, fifty. Within a month, she was selling a hundred pots a week, not only to women in Kimberley, but for them to post to friends, relations, mothers, sisters, aunts, daughters, elsewhere in South Africa. The *Diamond Advertiser* sent a reporter to interview her. Arabella made certain that the reporter's story was picked up by other papers elsewhere, because she personally sent copies to their offices throughout the colony.

When letters from women wanting creams to help their complexions or ointments to cure spots or soothe insect bites began to arrive in such numbers that the postman brought them in a bag instead of just in his hand, Arabella realised that she would have to move.

Accordingly, she rented a small house a few hundred yards from the Kimberley Club. Jamie stayed on in the house they had shared. Sammy Rosen was now living on the other side of town, where he had built a corrugated iron shed for packing and dispatching his canvas trousers. For reasons of cost, it was totally unpainted outside, and when the sun struck it, the whole building glowed and glittered like a giant mirror.

Arabella's new house was also of corrugated iron, like most of the other houses in Kimberley, but the walls were green and the roof dark red. It was approached by a small path and a gate in a white paling fence with tiny flower beds on either side. The rooms were all on one floor, with a concrete passage going from the front right through to the back. On the left was a sitting room furnished in heavy Victorian style, with anti-macassars on the chairs; a sideboard with a clock, photogravure pictures of London scenes: Buckingham Palace, the Tower, Westminster Abbey. Opposite this was the main bedroom with fourposter bed and a canopy. Behind that, a second bedroom and then a kitchen.

Arabella redecorated the smaller bedroom, because here she intended to meet any clients who wished to discuss their special skin problems. She remembered that when she had landed at Cape Town what had struck her initially was the fierce brightness of the sun and the colours. She calculated she needed a cool room where women could come out of the heat and the dust and the wind and the scorching sun into an atmosphere of calmness and quiet. Here they could relax and explain their problems in a clinical and yet friendly atmosphere.

She had the room boarded inside to conceal the corrugations in the iron walls. It was then painted white with a pale blue ceiling, the colour of an English summer sky. She hung white curtains over the windows, laid a carpet on the floor, and bought a desk and three chairs. On the desk, she placed an adjustable electric lamp which she could focus on the face of a client if any close examination was asked for, or simply use it to light the room with a soft diffused radiance when women called in the evening to consult her.

Behind the house, she constructed another corrugated-iron building and here, on long trestle tables, set out drums of ointments and unguents and creams. She wrote to Yeung Lee and explained what she had in mind, offering him five per cent of all her profits, after necessary expenses were deducted, if he would provide her with a list of ingredients, and the proportions required, in any other ointments and specifics he could recommend. Yeung Lee gladly accepted the offer, and also supplied the names and addresses of shippers in Shanghai, Hong Kong and Singapore.

Arabella employed schoolgirls, and their elder sisters who might be waiting to find permanent work, in the evenings and at weekends to fill the tubs of cream with spatulas and spoons, and stick on printed labels.

Arabella felt it essential to establish a feeling of trust between clients and herself. She did not wish to appear like hucksters she had seen in Hyde market who would peddle pills and potions and then be off to another town's market on the following day. She realised that once women trusted her, when they discovered that her creams really suited their complexions, or if they genuinely prevented sunburn, they would come back for more.

There was nothing of the chemist's shop in her room, or the

269

doctor's surgery: that is why she called it a salon. Here, confidence could overcome any initial reticence, and when she established confidence, word of mouth would do the rest. Once clients trusted her, not in a buyer-to-seller relationship but as a confidante or a friend, she would be on her way to real success. And this success would not simply be in the heat and dust of Kimberley or even just in the Cape. She was determined that it would be worldwide.

One morning, Arabella was in her salon, working out the increase in profits if, instead of buying the basic ingredients in five-gallon drums, she increased the size of the drum to ten gallons. She was halfway through her calculations when Sammy came into the house.

He looked around appreciatively, sat down. 'I'm not interrupting you, I hope?' he asked almost nervously.

'You are,' Arabella replied, 'but I'm always glad of an interruption from you. Is this a business or a social call?'

'A bit of both, really. First of all, I've been having a bit of trouble with a solicitor here representing J. Baird and Co. You know how we took the first load of canvas which should have gone to them? Well, they say they lost business as a result of that, and because we're now buying far more canvas from the suppliers than they have ever done, their orders don't receive priority and so they're losing even more business. They're going to sue us.'

'There are more lawyers in Kimberley than any other breed of people,' said Arabella reflectively. 'I know. I've checked with the Town Hall. There are always lawsuits in progress here, people jumping each other's claims, one rope fouling another going down in the Big Hole. Anything that should be solved quite amicably with a talk and a handshake, or maybe an apology and a promise that it won't happen again, is stirred up until only the lawyers can solve it. My memories of the law, after my father was killed, are not the happiest. You are defending the case?'

'I wanted to talk it over with you and Jamie first.'

'Jamie's not here. He's in Johannesburg. But what do you feel about it?'

'There's no doubt we've cost J. Baird some business because we took their canvas. And now that they can't rely on their supply of canvas because we get priority, they're obviously in trouble. I can't deny any of that.'

'You don't have to. But if it goes on like this, they'll be out of business altogether.'

'I hope not. I bear them no animosity. We're not even in competition. They're making tents, we're making trousers.'

'There's a higher mark-up on trousers than tents,' said Arabella. 'More people are living in corrugated-iron houses or brick houses now instead of tents. And while a tent can last for several years, most men buy two pairs of trousers every twelvemonth. So I'll tell you what to do, Sammy. Go and see them. Say they've had a monopoly on tenting ever since digging started here, and good luck to them. You're not in competition with them, you wish them well, there's room for you both. But if they feel there's no hope for their business, then you can give them hope. You will buy their business. Buy them out. Now.'

'But I don't want to make tents.'

'You don't have to, but they've got bigger sheds and shacks than you have, Sammy. And their sheds are standing, already built. You could buy them today and be using them tomorrow. They are also nearer the railway station. When you get the mail-order business going through your brother in Durban, when people simply send in their measurements and you send them their trousers, you can just load the stuff direct from the sheds on to the railways trucks. Here, it's got to be put on carts or trucks and lorries and taken to the station.

'Also, if you can't fill all the buildings with your workers, I'll put my girls in any space you may have. I've got to move to somewhere larger soon, the demand for cosmetics is growing so

271

fast, and I might as well move in with you as with anyone else.'

'You've got a point,' said Sammy. 'Two points, in fact.'

'J. Baird will see that at once. But don't go in with a lawyer. Say it's just between you and them. They either take your offer or they don't.'

'And if they don't?'

'Then you drop the hint you'll be buying more and more canvas. And without canvas, they're finished. They know that. That's what's worrying them now.'

'What about the lawyers then?'

'What about them? Lawyers are like vultures. The way they like to dress in black even makes them look like vultures. And the way they act proves the similarity beyond any argument. When there's no meat left on the corpse, they'll leave it. They can't eat bones. So they'll advise J. Baird and Co. to accept – for a fee. Show me the books. I'll work out what you should offer them, on, say, a three-year-profit basis, which has been diminishing all the time. You won't have to pay them a lump sum down.'

'I can't,' said Sammy. 'Everything I've got is in the business.'

'Right. Then pay them in instalments. That means that while your business goes up, whatever you're paying out becomes less and less important to you. So that's the end of the business part of your visit. What's the social part?'

Sammy sat staring at her. 'There was something else,' he said hesitantly. 'I've enjoyed working with you, and if it hadn't been for you and the idea of the canvas, I'd have gone back to Cape Town with my tail between my legs. Now I'd probably be serving behind a counter in a men's outfitters there or in Durban, thinking I was doing well. I admire you, Arabella. More than that, I like you.'

'I like you, too, Sammy. You cheer me up – because you're always so pessimistic. I feel that if I can convince you that

272

something's worth doing, then I can convince anybody! And I always remember that if it hadn't been for you, Jamie would never have gone to Yeung Lee. And look where that led. You started us off, and we all get on together, the three of us. A trinity. Three for one, one for three.'

'As a matter of fact, Arabella, when I said I like you, I meant rather more than like you. I think I love you.'

'But you don't know me, really,' replied Arabella gently. 'I'm hard, you know, Sammy.'

'I know that. You keep saying you're diamond-hard. All right, a diamond is hard, but the rough edges can be polished until it becomes smooth and glows.'

'And you'd like to polish my rough edges?'

'I'd like to spend my whole life doing that,' Sammy said quietly.

'You'd get tired of it very soon, Sammy. You don't really know me. I'm never happy in one place. I like to keep moving. I'm restless. The grass is always greener just over the fence.'

'I know, and I'll tell you something. You're always running away from yourself. You can't sit down and say, I'm happy, I've worked hard, and let's face it, I have been lucky. Here, at the right time and the right place. You must always keep on the run, chasing after yourself. Then you catch up briefly, and off you have to go again.'

'I think that's rather fanciful, Sammy.'

'I think it's true. We've all known what it's like to be poor, and constantly worried about money. And you and Jamie especially, being left orphans so young. But now those days are behind us. We just have to keep our heads and our health and we're all going to be immensely rich. Money is no worry any more. But there are other worries.'

'I've none,' said Arabella quickly.

'You answered that so fast that I don't think you really care to consider the matter. You don't just want to go on making more and more money endlessly, taking on more and more business commitments.'

'How do you know what I want, Sammy?'

'Because, as I said, I love you. I feel I know you as well as you know yourself. You'll get rich with all those creams and so on, but that could take up all your time, maybe all your life. You'll have no time left for other things.'

'What things, Sammy?'

'Sounds odd to be discussing this here, in this white room, with the heat outside. I mean marriage, children.'

'Marriage is something I've never contemplated. It's like an insurance. You have to die to beat it.'

'That's not the way I see things, Arabella. Think about it.'

'I will,' she said. 'But in all fairness to you, I have to say I don't think I'll change my mind. I don't want to settle down – not yet, at least. I don't want to be tied. I want to be free. To go where I want, to live where I want, to be who I want to be, without asking anyone else's permission or their views on what I do. I couldn't make you happy, Sammy. You want someone who will settle down. You want a nice house, children, to be well regarded in the community. I don't want that.'

'Then what do you want?'

'I don't know. But I know what I don't want. Yeung Lee once asked me what I wanted in life. I told him I didn't know, but I knew what I *didn't* want – staying back in Hyde, washing up.'

'So this is your last word? You may think about it, but you won't change your views?'

'I'm sorry, dear Sammy, but that's the truth of the matter. I wouldn't be fair to you – or honest with myself – if I told you otherwise. But you'll find someone who'll make you happy in a way I never could. You deserve someone who is warm and friendly, who shares your views, your ambitions.'

'I think you're that person,' said Sammy.

Arabella shook her head. 'No. I wish I were. More than I can tell you, I wish I were. But I'm not. And I'm sorry, Sammy. Very sorry.'

'For that?'

'Yes. And because I like you.'

He stood up. 'Well, that's it, I suppose. I'm going down to Durban tomorrow,' he said. 'My brother Reuben and I are going to discuss business there. He has just got married himself and his wife has a sister, Rebecca. He wants to introduce me to her. Goodbye, then.'

'Goodbye, Sammy.'

This time, Arabella kissed him not on the cheek but on his mouth. For a moment they stood, locked in each other's arms. He felt the salt taste of tears on his tongue. He drew back. To his surprise, Arabella was crying. He did not know why and he knew too little about women to ask her. And if he had, she might not have told him the reason.

She was crying not for him, because he was unhappy, nor yet for herself, but because she liked him and wished desperately she could love him. She was crying because she wondered whether she had the ability to love anyone. She didn't want to end as she began, alone; by then much richer, maybe, but also much older and even more lonely.

Sammy went out of the house into the hard hot sunshine. For long after he had gone, Arabella stood looking at the open doorway, seeing and yet not seeing people pass by, cars, carts, cabs, and wishing she could have accepted Sammy's proposal.

But there was so much she wanted to do on her own, and it would be on her own, with no one except her brother to care whether she achieved her aims or whether she failed. An imperative force within her was pushing her on. To what end she still was not sure, but it would not be denied.

*   *   *

Within a couple of months, Arabella realised that her business was becoming too big to run from any house. Several of the girls who had been working in the evenings now decided to make a career with her and work full time. She had advertisements running in newspapers throughout the colony and it was clear she must take the next step forward and buy her own shop.

Between the Kimberley Club and the Town Hall stood several empty shops. The diamond trade was going through one of its minor recessions and the landlord of the largest shop was willing to redecorate it for Arabella to her specification, at no cost, if she would take it on a two-year lease.

'I want it painted white inside,' she said. 'I want a gold coping round the ceiling and I want my name, Arabella, painted in gold letters on a white background right across the front window. We'll keep the window – but either paint it white inside or cover it with a curtain so that people cannot see in. Then they will have to come in personally to see what is on offer.'

'Do you think they will?' asked the landlord.

'It's my problem if they don't,' she said. 'But yes, I do think so. People are inquisitive, and once they're inside, it's easier to sell them something.

'The front part of the shop will have a counter in it with a white marble or imitation-marble top. Something that looks rich and unusual. Foreign. Continental. Exotic. And I want several chairs here all painted white. Behind the shop, the back room, which is now used as a store room, I'll have that white, too, and a carpet on the floor. Dark, discreet, good taste.'

'I would think you'd want something like a chemist's shop,' said the landlord, 'with lots of cupboards, glass-fronted, so people can see what they're going to buy.'

'No,' she told him. 'This shop is going to sell something that has never been marketed before in this country. *Beauty.* I read that in Australia a young Polish girl, Helena Rubinstein, who emigrated there, is doing much the same thing.

'This shop is going to be especially for women. Men can come in and buy creams for their wives or sisters if they want, but this is a personal woman-to-woman business, and I want elegance. We're not selling creams like pats of butter over the counter. We're selling them elixirs that will improve the appearance of even the ugliest woman.'

'Well, there'll certainly be a call for that in Kimberley,' said the landlord drily. 'I daresay you know what you're doing, but this is going to cost me a lot of money. My terms are usually a month's rent in advance but here I want three months, in case you go down. To get marble up from the Cape will cost goodness knows what for a start.'

She wrote him a cheque but did not sign it, handed it over. He looked at it.

'This is useless without your signature.'

'And this shop is useless unless the work is carried out. I sign the day you finish.'

'You're a hard person,' he said.

'I've had to be,' she said. 'Diamond-hard, if you like.'

That gave her another idea. She'd register the name, Diamond-Hard. It was unusual. Women would ask her what it meant. She could give all kinds of explanations; that her cream, soft and gentle as it was, was actually as hard as a diamond in protecting their complexions from the harmful rays of the sun, the dust, the wind, the rain – anything. She saw a solicitor that afternoon and formed a company – two companies: Lady Arabella and Diamond-Hard.

'Why "lady"?' asked the solicitor.

She signed the final forms. 'Well, I'm not a man,' she said, 'and I think the word "lady" adds something to a name. One hears of Lady Godiva, Lady Macbeth. Just Godiva or Macbeth are nothing. And I'm dealing not just with women

277

and girls, grandmothers, but ladies. It's an uplifting word.'

'Well, you know what you're doing,' he said, and added to himself, 'I suppose.'

The first day Arabella moved in, she sat behind the counter expecting women to flock in to buy from her as they had come to her house day after day. But, to her surprise and disappointment, no one arrived. She could not understand why. Jamie gave her the reason.

'They're shy,' he said. 'Women will visit a private house, for then they could be guests coming to tea, or to pay a call. But when all the other shopkeepers see women going into your shop, they know they're going in for some special purpose connected with their beauty, which shows them as vain or, even worse, not quite sure of themselves.'

Arabella agreed: she should have thought of this herself. 'What we'll do then is give a party for them,' she said.

She had kept a record of everyone who bought any of her creams, even a single small pot, with details of their complexion, their age, what they thought of the cream, and whether it had helped them. Now she sent to every one of her customers a special hand-written invitation to Lady Arabella's opening party.

She also invited newspaper reporters from every paper in the colony. Most, of course, would not accept, or could not come because of the distances involved, but Arabella sent to each one a list of acceptances, what she intended to serve at the party, and full details of all the preparations she had on offer. The reporters had a mass of facts on which to base their articles, and gave great space to their reports. After all, the occasion was unique: the first time a young, good-looking single woman had set up shop in South Africa to sell beauty to other women.

The party was a total success. Women came with their husbands, their brothers, their uncles, their fathers. Within a week, Arabella's business had doubled. Within two weeks, she had to take on more staff.

Six months later, Arabella was sitting in a back room going through the books. Profit was running at five hundred pounds a week, rising every week. She had plans to open a salon in Cape Town, another in Durban, a third in Johannesburg. And then she'd go back to England and start there. Yeung Lee had told her that he felt there would be a great future in marketing Chinese medicines, especially their ancient treatments for arthritis and rheumatism, colds and asthma.

Jamie came into the room and sat down.

'You look shaky,' she told him. 'Are you sickening for something?'

He shook his head. 'The reverse,' he said. 'I've made it.'

'What?'

'I've found the biggest diamond I've ever seen.'

'How?'

'By digging. I was tapping away and suddenly, the pick struck something harder than the rest of the rock. It was so hard, I felt a tremor, like a minor electric shock from the handle of the pick, and I knew I had hit something unusual. I bent down, scratched away, and I dug out a diamond the size of a marble. Good colour, too. Bluish. Not a bad tint.'

'What did you do then?'

'I wrapped it in my handkerchief, put the handkerchief in my pocket and climbed up out of the hole. Then I put my hand in my pocket to hold the handkerchief in case somehow or other I dropped the stone.'

'You've taken it to Harry Hirschmann?'

Jamie nodded. Harry had been sitting, as was his custom, outside his shack.

'Got a one-carat for me, have you?' he asked, half joking.

'I've got a big one for you, Harry,' Jamie told him.

'Let's see it. It's probably quartz or crystal.'

Jamie followed Harry inside the shack, shut the door behind him, locked it.

'What's that about?' asked Harry, puzzled.

'When you see this stone, you'll know. People would murder for it.'

'Are you serious?'

'Never more so.'

Jamie took out his handkerchief, undid the knot. There, against the crumpled white square of linen, the stone glittered like a fallen star.

'My God!' said Harry softly. 'You're bloody right, boy!'

He picked up his tweezers, screwed his jeweller's glass into his eye, examined the diamond from every angle, weighed it, took it off the scales very carefully, laid it on the blotting pad on his desk.

'Do you know what this is worth?' he asked. His voice was hushed, as though he was speaking in a church, as though what he had to say was not for other ears.

'Tell me,' said Jamie.

'Fifty thousand pounds sterling.'

Actually, this was an understatement. When it was sold, it fetched £100,000.

SIXTEEN

The Difference Money Makes

On the morning after the sale of the diamond, Jamie, Arabella and Sammy Rosen sat down in the back room of her house to discuss their future.

They had several options. One, they could continue as they were – Sammy making Rosens, Arabella producing cosmetics and Jamie digging for more diamonds. Two, they could divide the profit from the diamond into three equal shares, and each go their own way. This would mean dissolving a partnership they had all enjoyed and found prosperous.

As a third alternative, they could remain in partnership, but not spend any more time digging for diamonds. They all knew of diggers who had found one valuable stone and then had frittered away their treasure and their time hoping, like compulsive gamblers, for the big find that would make them really rich and independent for the rest of their lives.

Then Arabella gave her opinion.

'I suggest we invest this money in Sammy's company and mine,' she said. 'Then we amalgamate them, each of us takes a third of the equity and we build a business empire of our own, adding any other companies we feel would fit in with ours.

'We know we can make profits, because we are making them already. With this sort of capital behind us, we would be free of any bank involvement and have no need of any outside investors who could weaken our control. Sammy could then start a worldwide marketing survey to sell Rosens to workmen in every country. He might establish factories in countries where the potential is very high – the United States, Canada, Australia – to make them on the spot, and save freight and carriage costs and hold-ups in Customs sheds. I would like to do the same with my cosmetics and creams.

'Searching for diamonds might be successful, or it might not. It seems really to be a matter of chance, and the casualness of the early days will soon belong to the past. Everything is more organised now, very much more competitive. If we take the course I propose, then we run our own affairs, and the future literally belongs to us. We will not be dependent on the vagaries of fashions in diamonds, or fluctuations in their prices. Workmen will always need hard-wearing clothes, and women of every age and class and country will always want to look their best. We have here a double-headed penny. Heads we win, tails we win. What do you say?'

'I agree,' said Jamie, 'but where exactly do I fit in if we are not going to dig for any more diamonds?'

'If it hadn't been for you finding that one, none of this could happen,' Arabella replied. 'You can be the first chairman of our holding company, Diamond-Hard. It would embrace Sammy's factories, Yeung Lee's Eastern medicines and my cosmetics. We started off on equal shares. I would like to go on that way. What do you both say?'

Jamie glanced inquiringly at Sammy, who nodded.

'We both say yes,' they told her.

'Good,' said Arabella. 'In the meantime, while this is being set up, I want to go to England and look into the cost of starting a salon in the West End of London, then one in Manchester, and possibly a third in Edinburgh. Also, I have a little unfinished business I would like to attend to.'

She turned to Jamie. 'I hope you can help me with that, Jamie.'

'In any way,' he assured her. 'Let's all go back to England – I still think of it as home.'

'Home now is where we want it to be,' replied Arabella thoughtfully. 'That's the difference money makes.'

'There's a company I know in Kent, making canvas,' said Sammy. 'We could possibly take it over. It's owned by an old widower, whose waster of a son does not want to go into the business. We might relieve him of that necessity – at a bargain price.'

So it was agreed. They would return to England for a brief visit. But to give them a stake in the country that had made all this possible, they each bought a house, with land, in the Colony, within a few miles of each other. All the properties faced the sea. There was something symbolic in the vast empty horizon; no houses in between, no fences. It seemed to sum up their ambitions: their future was infinite, boundless as the rolling, restless ocean, strong and tireless as the pounding waves on the beach.

They delegated their day-to-day duties to people they had initially engaged on a part-time basis. Arabella found that several young wives in Kimberley, not having children of their own, were delighted at a totally new opportunity to make careers for themselves with her. Sammy contacted his brother in Durban, and through him hired half a dozen young men with a knowledge of tailoring and a nose for business.

What had begun at a small level was suddenly almost overwhelmingly successful. For the first time since they had arrived in South Africa, Arabella, Jamie and Sammy felt totally confident about their future.

Arabella booked a passage from Cape Town on the next direct sailing to Southampton. As the ship came round the Cape, and Table Mountain sank behind in a haze of distance, Arabella watched the Namibian coastline grow like a faint flat darkness.

283

The purser joined her on deck. 'People say that's like Kimberley all over again,' he commented, indicating the desert. 'A German there, Herr August Stauch, discovered a diamond by chance, and within no time at all he was rich as Croesus.'

He handed a pair of binoculars to Arabella.

'If you look, ma'am, slightly to the right, you will see we are just passing Lüderitz. That used to be a very rough town. In the early days, a tremendous trade was done in guano from islands off the coast. Centuries of bird droppings were thirty feet thick on the rocks. Ships would come in and load the stuff, which was worth a fortune as fertiliser. Then other ships would arrive and want their share. Fights would break out between the crews, who used dead penguins as clubs! That's all changed, of course. Very respectable nowadays.'

Arabella could see roofs glint in the afternoon sun; the spire of a church, a lighthouse on a promontory, and then a house larger than the rest. She asked the purser whose that was.

'That's Diamantberg, the biggest house in the town. It was built specially for a visit by the German Crown Prince that never came off.'

'Anyone living there now?' Arabella asked him.

'I couldn't say, ma'am.'

The ship steamed on, and slowly the land fell away.

In fact, at that moment, two men were sitting in the main drawing room of Diamantberg, now used for accommodating important visitors and for meetings when one side or the other – and sometimes both – felt it expedient not to be seen talking together.

The senior surgeon at Lüderitz Hospital looked pensively at Dr Braff, from Kolmanskop, weighing him up. Dr Braff felt uncomfortable under the surgeon's gaze and glanced nervously through the window, as if looking for a way out. He could see the road winding down to the harbour; flocks of gulls circled round a crayfish boat coming into the bay.

'I called you here,' said the surgeon at last, 'because it is easier to have a personal, quiet talk in this house than in your hospital or mine. Some things are best discussed in private, *unter vier Augen* – between four eyes. No one else to see or hear. Only us.'

'There's no problem with my work, I hope, sir?' asked Braff uneasily. The senior surgeon was new; he did not know him well.

'None at all. Quite the reverse, in fact. I am most impressed with all I have seen and heard about the way you run things. No. I wanted to talk to you about this shipwrecked patient who was brought in some time ago. How is he doing?'

Braff relaxed a little. 'He is making fair progress, sir. He still suffers from amnesia. I would also say he has delusions. He speaks German, as I think you know, but he is not fluent in our language. He might have learned it as a student. I think he is English, because he lapses into rambling accounts of his child-hood, which seems to have been spent in England, and odd events since then.'

'What sort of odd events? What kind of childhood?'

'He appears to have been brought up in a very large house, with servants, on an estate. According to his rambling accounts, he had his own horses and groom. But there seems to be a very weak streak in him somewhere. He was sent down from Oxford – or so he claims. That was after some scandal with a waitress in the town.

'Then he claims that a maid, or a servant girl of some sort, stole his mother's earrings. What seems so odd is that he says he saw her again on the ship coming out to the Cape. She was a passenger – and somehow threw him into the sea. I can't under-stand why or how, for he is a big, strongly built fellow, but he keeps returning to this claim. And the details never vary.'

'So he was not the sole survivor of a shipwreck, as was origi-nally thought likely?'

'No, sir. We have checked all available maritime records and there was no shipwreck. Injuries to his head were actually consistent with having fallen overboard.'

'Or been thrown?'

'Yes, sir. Or been thrown.'

'Thank you, Braff. I am most interested to hear what you have to say. Now I will tell you what I have discovered, which fits in very closely with your observations.

'As you know, we photographed the signet ring he wears. In Berlin, they enlarged this photograph and checked it against all sorts of armorial bearings and crests. They found that the ring was engraved with the arms of Lord Rosael.

'We made discreet inquiries about him through our Embassy in London, and found that Lord Rosael had – or has – a son of the same age and physical description as your patient. He was reported as having fallen overboard from a steamship taking him to Cape Town. He had also been sent down from the university, and then studied briefly at Heidelberg, which he also left after some scandal.

'According to the ship's records, two male passengers travelling first class, claimed they had seen a young woman, one Arabella Baird, leaving the upper deck immediately after the alarm was raised that a man was overboard. However, most oddly, although the ship's officers checked this woman, who was travelling steerage, and these two men seemed positive they saw her, it was clear that she had not left steerage accommodation at the time in question.'

'So they were mistaken?'

'So it appears. But what is strange is that she had been employed by Lord Rosael. She worked in the office of his agent, a Mr Beaumont. She has a twin brother, who was travelling steerage with her. It could be that your patient is confused about what happened when he fell – or was thrown – into the sea. The brother might have been on deck with him – not the girl. A point to consider, if no more, Braff.'

The surgeon took a newspaper cutting from a file on his desk.

'Here are the brother and sister, photographed celebrating the discovery of a diamond sold for one hundred thousand pounds sterling in Kimberley. They are extremely prosperous through various business enterprises started by Arabella Baird.'

'Do you wish me to tell the patient this, sir?'

'No,' said the surgeon sharply. 'On no account. I wish you to keep the patient in total ignorance of everything I have told you, and you are not to pass on this information to anyone else.'

'He might discover it for himself, sir, if he sees any newspapers. And a shock like that could release his own memories. He might then know who he is – and want to leave.'

'Exactly. So I wish you to move him to more secure accommodation, where he can be watched over – guarded, if you like – so that there is no chance of such a situation ever arising.'

'For how long, sir?'

'Indefinitely. You can tell anyone who asks that he is having specialist treatment. If you can keep him in total ignorance of his real identity, possibly even under constant sedation, almost, you will say, a prisoner, or a strongly guarded guest, he may be able to render to the Fatherland a service of enormous importance.'

'Can I ask in what way, sir?'

The surgeon smiled. He had been young once, but never so naive and idealistic as this man half his age.

'You can ask, Dr Braff. But you can hardly expect me to tell you – yet.'

So far as Arabella was concerned, the only obvious similarities between the liner which now brought her back to Southampton and the primitive vessel that had carried Jamie and her out to Cape Town was that they both had a sharp bow at one end and a rounded stern at the other.

Passengers travelling steerage were no doubt cramped below decks in the bilge and bowels of the ship, just as they had been in the vessel that had taken her south, but that kind of travel was now of no concern or interest to her, and, please God, never would be again. Now Arabella had a large stateroom with a sitting room and private bathroom on the starboard side of the ship. This, the purser assured her, was the most comfortable side for homeward-bound travellers.

'Port out, starboard home,' he had explained. 'That's where the word "Posh" comes from!'

Certainly that adjective could describe everything about her voyage. At half past seven each evening, a gong would sound so that first-class passengers could change for dinner. At eight thirty they would take their places in the dining room under massive crystal chandeliers, surrounded by Corinthian pillars and banks of fresh flowers. Waiters would stand by each table, obsequiously ready to move chairs, proffer menus and wine lists, and to unfold crisply starched napkins as if the diners lacked the strength to do this themselves. The only suspicion of being at sea, rather than in the dining room of some magnificent hotel, was the sight through big picture windows of the sun setting across an indigo ocean, or the occasional, muted, hesitant tremor of the floor as thousands of tons of iron and mahogany crashed at 18 knots through an unusually big wave.

The purser had carefully checked the antecedents of all passengers who boarded at Cape Town; regular travellers on the Bombay run he knew well and counted as friends. As always on these vessels, where passengers were confined for days or weeks, shipboard flirtations would begin, often hesitantly, then flare to passionate heat, and die (usually more quickly on one side) as the chill winds of the English Channel dispersed romantic and impossible dreams. It was always the same, the purser thought. Tears and promises to write, insincere protestations of affection. But in the end the old adage of the sea still applied: first turn of the screw pays all debts.

The purser knew the cardsharpers, the personable seducers, the cashiered ex-officers on the look-out for rich pickings from a wealthy widow fool enough to delude herself they could be attracted by her looks rather than by her money.

He was a kindly man and felt it his duty to advise single ladies that male passengers travelling alone should be treated with circumspection. It was always easier to do this before these people had introduced themselves. Such was their charm – a gift on which, of course, their livelihoods depended – that single women of uncertain age did not all take kindly to his suggestion that men they imagined as serious suitors, were, in fact, simply bounty hunters.

Arabella was amused at the purser's careful, almost hesitant, approach to this matter, but she thanked him for it.

'You are very kind,' she said, touched by his embarrassment, 'but really, I think I can take care of myself.'

The purser nodded. He knew that Arabella was wealthy, but he did not know the circumstances of her birth. He never imagined she had once swept bar floors in the Silent Witness, washed glasses, cleaned away vomit from the lavatory. And Arabella did not feel it necessary to inform him.

On the voyage, she parried the advances of three men. One claimed to be a major returning from the North-West Frontier to be ADC to the sovereign. The second introduced himself as the younger son of an Irish peer. The third hinted at vast private means, a huge estate in the Shires and a house in Belgravia.

They all made themselves known delicately enough in the lounge. The first offered her the loan of his powerful binoculars to watch a passing naval vessel. The second asked whether she had finished with her copy of the *Illustrated London News*, because he understood it contained an article about his father's castle. The third apologised for intruding on her, but asked whether she was by any chance related to Lord Baird, whose estate marched with his in Leicestershire?

Arabella was amused by these approaches and rather flattered, but to proposals that she might join them after dinner she always pleaded some excuse. Despite these refusals, she would have liked to have dined with any man who had a cheerful face and twinkling eyes. It was lonely travelling on her own, exchanging a few words about the ship's speed or the weather with the older wives she encountered doggedly walking a dozen circuits on the promenade deck or sitting in deck chairs, wrapped in camelhair rugs, sipping cups of bouillon.

It would have been fun to be squired by a young man, to discuss more entertaining matters, to dance to one of the ship's three orchestras; maybe to walk on the moonlit afterdeck and see the ship's long white, phosphorescent wake trailing behind them under a summer sky. And who knew how such encounters might end?

One part of her wanted to discover just what that end might be. What would it really be like to be held in the arms of a man she loved and admired? Another part of Arabella's character urged her to hold back. She had not yet seen a sign and if she fell in love with someone, even married him, she felt she might lose – or at least seriously weaken – her own identity. Then would she still be her own person?

Also, there was the fear, totally new to her, but proved by the purser's warning, that men might be attracted more by her money than by her. How could she be certain this was not so? Until she felt sure, it seemed safer to be cautious.

The major London hotels sent representatives to Southampton to meet the liner and welcome regular and potential clients. They waited in splendid uniforms, with epaulettes, gold braid and tall top hats. Arabella had no idea where to stay in London and the thought of handling several cabin trunks was beyond her. It had been a simple matter when all her belongings could fit into a single trunk. The representative from Claridges politely offered his assistance, which she accepted.

She stayed for a week at Claridges, and then rented an apartment in a large house in Belgravia. It was fully furnished, including vases of fresh flowers, arranged each morning after the housekeeper and the cook had come to her bedroom to learn her wishes for the day. What would she like for luncheon – and for how many guests? Did she wish a car to be brought to the door for a shopping expedition?

At first, Arabella felt slightly embarrassed by these attentions, not quite certain whether the two older women were serious. Could they conceivably be making fun of her with this daily pantomime? She thought not, but she came to dread their arrival in white starched uniforms with skirts that brushed the carpet, their humourless, meticulous adherence to all her comments. But she soon realised that beneath their cool impersonal veneer they were just as insecure as she had once been, in need of a job, afraid of dismissal if they showed disrespect through over-familiarity.

After a couple of weeks, she travelled north to the Silent Witness. Instead of going third class, she booked a whole first-class compartment for herself. Porters bustled around her luggage, jostling each other for the privilege of carrying it. Idly, she watched them load it on a four-wheeled trolley – and for a moment felt almost physically sick. This was the same sort of trolley on which her father had been carried to the infirmary.

At Manchester the porter led her to the head of a line of taxis. Her bags were handed up to the top of the roof, coins changed hands and the porter saluted obsequiously.

'I see, ma'am, you are from the Cape,' he said, pointing to her luggage labels.

'Yes. You know it?'

'I was there in the Army, ma'am. A great place, if you

haven't got to fight. I was a corporal in the Buffs.'

'How interesting,' Arabella replied. But what was more interesting – and sobering – to her was that this man should fight his country's battles overseas and all he could find now was a job carrying bags for people like her who had only fought for their own interests.

She arrived at the Silent Witness to find another girl, about her own age, sweeping the floor of the private bar. She stood up sheepishly, and bowed.

'I am Arabella Baird. Is Aunt Hannah in, or Uncle Don?'

'Mrs Douglas is in Manchester and the master is checking levels in the cellar, ma'am,' the girl explained.

Uncle Don came up the stairs as they spoke. He looked older than Arabella had remembered, just as the bar seemed smaller and shabbier. The carpet, which she had once thought so smart, was threadbare in places; seat covers had holes in them; the curtains could do with changing.

'Why, Arabella!' Uncle Don exclaimed in delighted surprise. He was expecting her, of course, but not to come in such style, wearing such expensive clothes and with hand-stitched leather luggage. He kissed her, and then drew back to admire her pretty clothes. She was glad he had drawn back: he smelled of tobacco and beer. She didn't remember that when she was living here. Everything had changed so much, and she realised she had changed even more.

'You'll have your old room?'

'I would love to.'

He carried her luggage up the stairs, panting at the weight, pausing on the first half-landing to regain his breath. Her old room seemed pitifully small. The bed was narrow, the sheets thin with age. A china basin and a ewer of water stood, just as she remembered, with a soap dish and folded towel, on a marble-topped washstand. There was no running hot water, not even a cold-water tap, and the lavatory was at the end of a long corridor. A fire had to be stoked in the saloon bar to heat water for a bath; she had forgotten about that.

She only stayed for two days. The reunion had not been as she had imagined. She felt like a stranger; more, she was a stranger. A way of life now completely familiar to her in South Africa was totally alien to Aunt Hannah and Uncle Don, and seemingly beyond their comprehension or imagination. She was rich and they were not, and she sensed they thought she was patronising them. She offered to take them out to the Midland Hotel in Manchester for dinner. They declined. Aunt Hannah said she had nothing smart enough to wear. Arabella said she would like to buy her a new dress and a new coat, but the older woman shook her head.

'No! You're very kind and generous, Bella, but I don't want charity.'

'It's not charity, Aunt Hannah. It's something I want to do,' Arabella assured her.

'You keep your money for a rainy day,' advised Uncle Don philosophically. Neither could comprehend that, financially, Arabella need never face any more rainy days.

'Did you ever hear anything further from Mr Snakesby?' Arabella asked her uncle.

He shook his head. 'Nothing. But he's going up in the world. He has become a councillor. I hear he'll probably be the next mayor.'

'And the judge who came up with that extraordinary decision?'

'There has been a lot about him in the papers recently, praising him for his attacks on corruption and vice in Manchester. The police have been tightening up on prostitutes, who are apparently parading openly up and down the streets. The judge has a lot to say about that – been jailing a number of them. But to give him fair, he's been unexpectedly lenient to one or two of the younger ones. Said he would give them a last chance to go straight.'

Yeung Lee was delighted to see Arabella. He showed her lists of aromatic roots, herbs, spices and unusual ointments. He had already written to her suggesting she should market them, and Arabella accepted the reasoning behind the proposal.

'If a person is healthy, her complexion must respond more fully to your creams,' he said. 'If unhealthy, she will have spots and blemishes on the skin. She can cover them up for a time, but that does not cure the source. It is like painting over rotten wood or rusty metal.'

'We will start another company,' said Arabella. 'A subsidiary of Diamond-Hard. 'We will call it Diamond-Lee, shares to be split fifty-fifty between you on one side, and Jamie, Sammy and me on the other. Agreed?'

Yeung Lee held out his hands. 'Agreed. As a mighty oak grows from a tiny acorn, as a willow from a seed, so a whole new enterprise is developing for all of us because your brother earned a few shillings a week here.'

Arabella went back to Belgravia at the end of the week. There, she was delighted to see a card from Samuel Rosen; he had also arrived in London and proposed calling on her. He did not give his address, so she was pleased when he arrived unexpectedly after dinner that same evening. For the first time since Arabella had left the Cape, she felt relaxed and at ease.

They sat together in the library, in front of a log fire. The butler set out a tray of drinks and they raised glasses of iced Beaume Venise to each other.

'I am especially pleased to catch you on your own,' Sammy told her. 'I wanted to tell you something. You will be the first to know. I am getting married.'

'Congratulations!' said Arabella, but she could not bring herself to add, 'I am glad.' She felt a curious sense of loss, of diminishment at the news. Sammy had asked her to marry him, and she had turned him down: now the opportunity had gone for ever.

'Yes. She is the sister of my brother's wife. I told you I

was going to meet her in Durban. We got on from the start.'

'Wonderful!' said Arabella dutifully, and raised her glass to him. She kept it in front of her eyes for a moment, so he would not see how moist they were.

'We're getting married when I go back. I wanted to tell you before you heard the news from someone else.'

'Thank you,' she said. 'I hope you will both be very, very happy.'

Sammy reached for his cigar case. 'Mind if I smoke?'

She shook her head. He lit a Corona.

'It's funny to think that a few years ago I had only seen cigars through the windows of tobacconists' shops in Manchester. Now, I smoke two or three a day at a fiver each. It's incredible how easy it is to become used to money, to realise that you have so much you find it hard to spend it all.'

'I could try,' said Arabella, smiling.

'You always were a hard one,' said Rosen. 'Is your acceptance of being rich so different to mine?'

'In one way, yes,' she said. 'On the liner coming over, the purser warned me against fortune hunters. The result was that I had almost no one to speak to except old people coming back from India to die. And when I went up to Hyde, I found that I did not fit in. I just didn't belong any more. So I came back here, but the fact is, Sammy, I know no one in London. How can I get to know anyone? It seems impossible. I am a woman on my own and that is not a good thing to be if you want to meet people. Wives meet people through their husbands' jobs, or their children at school. Here, the only people I talk to are the housekeeper and the cook. And I'm the one who talks. They just listen. I've hardly heard them utter a word.'

'What you need is to be introduced to people,' Sammy told her, 'or rather to one person, high in the social scene. Once you are accepted by him or her, then all the others will follow meekly. You'll have more invitations to parties, to dinner and the theatre than there are days in the week. It is not what you are in this country that matters so much as who you are. We've all made a lot of money, but that's not enough. Now, if our grandfathers or great-grandfathers had made the money, and we were just spending what they had left us in their wills, that would be altogether different. Someone would have bought a title on the way.'

'I wouldn't waste money like that.'

'It's not altogether a waste. If you have a family, it's something to hand on, and people somehow look up to you. But that's an academic point. What I must do now is arrange a meeting with someone who can help you. Give me a cheque for five hundred guineas, made out to Bearer. I will put it in the hand of the person I have in mind, who has titles as long as your arm, but no money to go with them.'

'But will the person I meet know that the introduction has been arranged?'

'Of course not. I work discreetly. Leave it to me. This money will buy the key to open the doors of the greatest houses in the land to you. Whether you want to go through those doors and whether you'll like the people you meet who live behind them remains to be seen.'

Arabella wrote out the cheque and did not hear from Rosen for a week. Then he telephoned her.

'I have arranged for you to meet Lady Belsize at the Connaught Hotel at eight thirty tomorrow night.'

'Who is she?'

'I don't think she's in Debrett,' he replied. 'Some of these older families like to keep their name out of reference books – they think that sort of thing is rather common, but Lady Belsize is the doyenne of society in London. After Queen Alexandra, of course. And several royal mistresses.'

'You must have a jibe, always,' said Arabella.

'Of course,' Rosen replied cheerfully. 'I supply the sauce.

Others, the meat. I will meet you at the Connaught tomorrow night, eight thirty, and conduct you to her ladyship's private room, where the three of us will dine. Evening dress, of course.'

'Do you know her?' asked Arabella, surprised.

'I know everyone,' replied Samuel Rosen enigmatically. 'Or, rather, I should say everyone knows me.'

'How is that?' asked Arabella. 'You knew no one in London when we sailed for the Cape.'

'My dear Arabella,' said Sammy. 'You are still naive about some things, which surprises me. None of us knew anyone in London when we left – because we weren't worth knowing, or so they thought. Now we are rich, very rich. I could buy any estate I want in the country, any house in London. It amuses me to have people with pedigrees as long as your leg inviting me to their homes, to their parties.

'They want something from me of course, a sub for a charity, a job for a useless son or brother, or just simply to see what kind of person was running a pawnshop in Manchester, and now owns a mansion in Park Lane, within such a short time.'

'I quite understand that,' said Arabella, 'but how do they know about you?'

'Word of mouth. I put a notice in *The Times* and *The Enquirer* to say that Mr Samuel Rosen, the financier and industrialist, was staying at his house in Belgrave Square.'

'But you didn't have a house in Belgrave Square.'

'I rented one. I then gave a reception for the gentlemen of the Press, explaining that having made a fortune – I multiplied it a few times, Bella, I must admit – I was now looking for other enterprises or projects to invest in. You didn't see their reports?'

'I did not,' she said. 'Maybe I was still at sea.'

'Maybe you still are about some things. You leave this to me, Bella. We will have you in society, if that's where you really want to be.'

On Friday evening, rain began to fall, slowly at first, and then steadily. By eight o'clock, the roads were awash, and cabs and cars splashed waves of water across the pavements. Under the new electric street lamps, they glittered like rivers of shining gold.

As Arabella's hired Panhard limousine approached the Connaught, the rain stopped unexpectedly. People, waiting under the porch for taxis, lowered their umbrellas. At exactly eight thirty, her limousine stopped. The hotel doorman was occupied opening the door of a car in front, so Arabella's chauffeur jumped from his seat and held open the rear door for her.

Arabella stepped out, pausing for a moment in the clear, fresh, rain-washed dusk. She felt nervous, unsure of herself. Was this really the way to get on in society – to write out an open cheque to be cashed by someone you had never met?

She took a step towards the doorway, and at that moment, two men jumped from the shadows. They wore dark fustian suits with jacket collars turned up, black cloth caps pulled low over their faces. Their clothes steamed with rain. They looked poor, desperate – and frightened.

'Give us your rings, lady!' shouted one of them hoarsely, and seized her right hand. Arabella struck him across the face with her handbag. It burst open. The contents scattered into the gutter. The chauffeur stared uselessly in amazement. The doorman was still ushering another couple into the hotel and had not seen the incident. Someone shouted. A whistle blew.

A man jumped from an approaching car, behind Arabella's Panhard, raced across the pavement, hit one of the two men on the jaw. He fell back, slipped on the wet pavement as his companion put up his fists to fight. The stranger struck him twice, once in his stomach, then in his face. The man gave a cry of agony and ran. His companion picked himself up and followed, limping.

The whole incident had taken only seconds. Most of the

people sheltering in the porch had no clear idea what had happened.

'Are you all right, ma'am?' Arabella's chauffeur asked her nervously.

'No thanks to you,' retorted Arabella angrily. 'If it had not been for this gentleman here, it could have been a very different story.'

'But this story,' the stranger assured her, 'has a happy ending. You are, I hope, quite unhurt? You have not lost any jewels? I will look for the contents of your handbag.' He bent down to search in the streaming gutter.

'Please,' Arabella said. 'There's nothing of value. Only a book of powder leaves, a silk handkerchief, a few coins.'

'Allow me.' The handsome stranger took her arm and escorted her into the hotel. People on the steps parted to let them through. The hotel foyer felt reassuringly warm, dry and friendly after the unexpected violence in the wet street outside.

'For this to have a truly happy ending, ma'am,' said the young man, 'we really should dine together.'

'You are too kind,' Arabella replied. 'But I have an engagement.'

'Most unfortunately, so have I,' he said. 'A regimental dinner – the Golds.'

'I must thank you very warmly,' said Arabella, 'but I don't know who you are.'

'Lord Doncaster. Known more familiarly as Noel. And you, ma'am?'

'Arabella Baird.'

'An interesting Scottish name. And your address? I appreciate that it is not strict etiquette for a gentleman to ask a lady for her address at their first meeting, but then, as I am sure you will agree, our meeting was not altogether a formal one. I would like to inquire tomorrow whether you have suffered any ill effects from this unfortunate incident – and without your address, how could I do so?'

'It is Fifteen Belgravia Square. But who do you think those men were? Why attack me?'

'They envied you your money – and your good looks. It's a thieving climate these days, ma'am. A single one of the diamonds round your neck could keep those two ruffians in comfort for a whole year. And their families, too. But I see you are expected.'

Sammy stepped forward. Arabella introduced them. The two men bowed stiffly to each other. Then Noel went on upstairs. Arabella looked inquiringly at Sammy.

'A bit of bad news,' he said gloomily as they waited for the elevator. 'The old lady has gout and begs to be excused tonight. She will arrange another date.'

'Is that a genuine excuse? Do you think it's true?'

'My dear Arabella, remember the question Pontius Pilate asked: "What is truth?" He didn't know then, so how can we know now? I suggest that while we ponder the problem you dine with me in the private room I reserved for Lady Belsize.'

On the third floor, Noel waited until the elevator indicating light showed that it had gone up and down several times, to make sure Arabella was out of the way. Then he walked downstairs and out of the hotel. After the summer rain, the night felt warm, somehow in tune with his feelings. As he walked along briskly, he began to hum a cheerful music-hall song to himself. His luck was turning.

SEVENTEEN

A Debt Is Paid

The Unic taxi spluttered and groaned its way out of Manchester
along the Hyde Road. It was already dusk, and through the
steamy windows Jamie, who had followed Arabella to England,
could just make out dark contours of distant hills and long stone
walls that stretched across them like sooty serpents. The walls
were innocent of all cement or any adhesive; the stones had been
placed one on the other in a seemingly haphazard way, and yet
they had lasted for hundreds of years. He found something
reassuring in their strength and simplicity. How wonderful the
world would be if life could be as straightforward – and as
enduring.

The contact sat next to him, moving about on the hard
leather seat and smelling unpleasantly of nervous sweat. He
was a small man with narrow shoulders. He wore a Homburg
hat, one size too large, so that it rested on his ears. Jamie
regarded him with distaste. He always considered contacts,
go-betweens, men who introduced principals to each other, as
people of little account. Frequently, there was something
despicable about them. They fawned on the powerful, like
panders. They willingly followed anyone who agreed to their
price, and in the end what happened to them? Before Jamie
could dwell further on this, the contact cleared his throat.

'You are certain, sir, you want to meet Mr Lotto?'

'I do,' said Jamie. 'I would not have come this far from South Africa if I didn't.'

'He is a hard man, Mr Lotto, sir.'

'I have heard he has that reputation. It is one of which I am sure he is proud.' ·

'He has two brothers and there is also a fourth man involved. A Mr Rosen.'

'Of the Jewish faith?'

'Yes. He is known usually simply as the Jew. A very clever man, sir. Not young by any means. He really is the brain behind the brothers who, up here – behind their backs, of course – we call the Maltese Brothers. For Valetta is where they came from.'

'So I have heard. And tonight we are meeting them all?'

'Yes, sir. But I have to make my position quite plain. I will introduce you, but I cannot vouch for them, just as I hope you will understand I cannot vouch for you.'

'Of course not. I do not need anyone to vouch for me,' said Jamie. 'I am my own ambassador. I represent myself.'

'Of course, of course. No offence meant, I hope, sir?'

'None taken,' Jamie assured him.

The driver slowed, changed gear, missed a cog. Whirring wheels in the gear box screamed protest as toothed wheels bit. He turned sideways towards his passengers.

'It must be along here, sir. If you will just tell me where you think the house is. Difficult to see the numbers in this light.'

'There are no numbers,' the contact explained. 'You don't have numbers on this type of house. We are looking for names. Acacia, Beechwood, that sort of thing.'

'Well, tell me when we're there.'

The contact shone a light through the window. 'Here,' he said. 'Turn in.'

The driver turned into a wide driveway that led to a modern

house of yellow brick. Jamie noticed that lights burned all around it, not illuminating the house but the garden. Anyone who attempted to approach the house uninvited would be seen within fifty yards of the building.

The taxi stopped. The driver switched on the inside light. Jamie could see his companion's face now. Under the feeble 20-watt bulb, his flesh shone with sweat as though varnished. The driver climbed down, opened the door. In the darkness, Jamie heard a baying of dogs from the rear of the house.

'Please wait for me,' Jamie told the driver.

'But sit in your cab,' the contact warned. 'They've got guard dogs here.'

'I can hear them,' said the driver. 'Well, they won't get a meal off me.'

The front door opened. A manservant stood in the porch; he was big and muscular.

'You have business here?' he asked Jamie.

'With Mr Lotto. My name is Baird.'

The servant bowed, instantly respectful. 'He is expecting you, sir. Will you please come this way?'

Jamie and the contact followed him into the house. It felt very warm. Heavy curtains concealed the windows. A huge aspidistra sprouted from a giant Ali Baba pot. The walls were hung with brightly coloured prints of Maltese scenes.

The butler opened a door. Jamie went in. The contact stayed in the hall. 'You will want to be private, I expect, sir,' he said.

The door closed silently behind Jamie.

Four men stood in a row in front of the fireplace, holding up the backs of their jackets, warming themselves against the fire. Flames spat and flared from scented wooden logs.

'Mr Baird?' said the man on the left. He was small, with very broad shoulders, his black beard flecked with grey.

'The same, sir. Mr Lotto?'

'Juan Lotto.'

He held out his hand. Jamie felt the sharp impress of rings, the harshness of large cut stones.

'My younger brother here, Luis. My other brother, Manuel, and, shall I say, our religious adviser, Mr Rosen. Although we are not of the same faith, we all seek an entrance into paradise.'

Jamie shook hands with them all. The other two brothers were taller than Juan, but all three had the same hard cold eyes, like stones. Mr Rosen was rather different. He wore the skull cap of the orthodox Jew; he had a greyish beard which he stroked with his left hand constantly as though combing it. He had dark, sad eyes. Jamie didn't trust any of them, but Mr Rosen he could respect. The contact could have been right. He was probably the brain behind the other three.

'You come with an introduction from my nephew, Sammy Rosen?' he said now.

'I do. He sends you his best regards. And asked me to tell you that the sum you gave him before he left for the Cape he has put to good use.'

'So I understand. I hear he is opening a clothes factory outside Hyde in the near future. I hope to see him then. We are not a very close family, Mr Baird, but we do keep in touch.'

'And how can we help you, Mr Baird?' asked Juan Lotto.

'In rather an unusual way. I have a request to make of you gentlemen – not for nothing, of course. Everyone demands a price, and some deserve one.'

'What is your request?'

'I have a woman friend who is obsessed by a wild idea. She wants to be a writer – a poetess, no less.'

'Has she published anything?' asked Luis Lotto quickly.

'As yet, sir, no. But she is attempting to write what she calls a narrative poem – a very long one, I understand – about a great city after dark. She is especially interested in the feelings of women who offer their bodies for sale. In a word, whores.'

'And what makes you think we can help you, Mr Baird? We

are all married men. We have families. Mr Rosen has three grandchildren.'

'Of course. That is the natural order of things, but even so, I am led to believe from my friend, Sammy, that you may have some involvement – at a distance, of course – with these ladies of the night.'

'Go on,' said Juan Lotto. His voice was cold now; hard, menacing.

'My good friend wishes to walk the streets for one night, maybe two, maybe three, maybe for a week. For the purposes of research for her poem, simply to see for herself how these women operate. And how the police treat them when they are arrested. I am, of course, prepared to pay for this privilege, because I would not wish to encroach on what may be someone else's business territory.'

'How much would you pay for a week?' asked Luis bluntly.

'What do you want for a week?'

'I want a drink,' said Manuel. 'This is a most unusual request.' He walked to a cabinet, flipped up the lid. A dozen bottles glowed in the sudden amber light reflected by a mirror.

'A brandy,' said Jamie. 'Cape, if you have it.'

'I regret we haven't, but we have Portuguese, Spanish, French.'

'Portuguese, then. There are large Portuguese colonies in Africa. It will remind me of home.'

Manuel poured a Fundador. The others chose whisky, rum, gin. They drank a silent toast to each other, no one trusting anyone else, each man watching the others warily.

'I have, of course, gone into your background,' admitted Juan. 'Sammy gives you – as the doctor would say – a clean bill of health. Otherwise I might have wondered whether you are a police spy, an informer, or some person of that kind.'

'I have nothing to hide,' replied Jamie. 'Make any investigations you wish. And remember, I do not haggle over money. I will pay whatever you ask if you can help me to help my friend.'

'Well, then. Within these four walls, and with four of us to deny it should others ever learn this secret, we do have some influence over prostitutes in Manchester and in other cities in the north. Bradford, York, Sheffield, Leeds. We are like fathers to the poor creatures. They rely on us. We give them protection – even pay their fines. In turn, they pay us a small amount every week as a kind of insurance, if you like. And they know that no pimp or ponce or runagate can come between them and their clients.

'It would be difficult for the friend you mention to walk the streets without our permission. She could have an accident. Her face might be accidentally slashed. She might even be branded with a hot iron or a flame. These women are jealous of their rights. Some have extremely fiery temperaments. Life has not been easy for them. Can one blame them if they resent people to whom life has been more generous? So, you see, we would have to come to some accommodation with them. They might lose trade, and that would affect their earnings – and ours.'

'I have told you, I will pay whatever is required. And in return perhaps one or more of the prostitutes could protect my friend. She does not wish to follow their calling, only to observe it. I do not wish her to be in any danger.'

'That is always a risk, of course, in their profession. We had a girl, married, two little children, who died most disgustingly only last week. A man approached her, they agreed a price, they went to her room. Apparently, he was endowed with a penis of enormous size which he inserted, not in the orifice designed to receive it, but in her mouth. He pressed it with all his strength against the back of her throat and literally choked her, killed her.'

'What happened to him?'

'Her lover, who lived in the back of the flat, rushed out and seized him, but the fellow got away. He was a powerful swine. The police are looking for him now. But not, I imagine, with much enthusiasm or with any hope of finding him. So, there are risks.'

'I heard about that case from a person I met,' said Jamie casually. 'He was of the opinion – quite wrongly, I'm sure – that people you might know had been involved in some way. He thought that the woman had fallen behind in what you call her insurance premiums.'

The three brothers looked at each other.

Jamie smiled ingenuously and sipped his drink.

Rosen broke the silence. 'To business,' he said briskly. 'For one week, we shall require a hundred sovereigns paid in advance, in gold. Nothing in writing, no cheques, no notes of hand. Cash.'

'You have a deal,' said Jamie. 'When do you want the money?'

'The day before your friend goes on the streets. We will speak to two of our girls so she can walk with them. They will look after her as far as they can – once they know she is not a poacher on their preserve.'

'I give you my word, gentlemen, that she is not.'

'Where does she want to walk, then?'

'Where she is most likely to be picked up by the police. Then she can see these poor wretched outcasts of society when they come to court.'

'Piccadilly,' said Manuel instantly. 'By the gardens. The police pick them up there every night. The more they can pull in, the greater their chances of promotion. A sad thing, but there is corruption, even in the force. Even in the judiciary, I fear.'

'It is everywhere,' agreed Jamie, shaking his head at the thought. 'She would like to go out on Monday night.'

'A bad night. People are recuperating from the weekend.

Many husbands are still at home in the country. They have not yet come back to Manchester. Wednesday, Thursday and Friday are the best. Saturday, you get drunks, people who try without paying. There is violence, unfortunately, sometimes. There are knife fights, beatings. It is a very volatile area, Mr Baird. And a dangerous trade.'

'Tuesday, then.'

'Come here Monday, with the money. Same time as tonight.'

'I will,' said Jamie. He finished his brandy. 'One last thing,' he said, as though the thought had just occurred to him. 'You have, I assume, influence with the police?'

'To what extent?' asked Rosen quickly.

'To make sure that this friend of mine is taken in and appears at court? From all our points of view, the sooner, the better. I do not wish to interfere with the normal patterns of trade for these women. You follow me?'

'Totally.'

'Good. Now – another drink?'

The oldest of the three whores on the Manchester beat was known locally as Red-haired Rita for the good reason that she had red hair and her Christian name was Rita. She never mentioned her surname. Rita was Irish, and admitted to being over forty, but not how much over forty. She would never loiter under street lights, which could be very unflattering to a tired and middle-aged woman. Only the young girls, new to the game, did that.

Rita wore a dark overcoat with a belt, a wide-brimmed hat and sensible low-heeled shoes. At this time of year, there was more walking to do than working, and nothing was worse than having to walk miles in high heels with soles too thin and genteel to keep out the damp.

Next to Rita walked a slightly younger woman, Janine. She had dark hair, eyes heavily ringed with kohl, and reddened lips.

She carried a handbag over her left shoulder and usually walked a small terrier on a long lead. Her defence, if she should be picked up by the police on charges of importuning, was always that she was only walking the dog. Tonight, she had left the dog at home.

Between them walked a much younger woman, more slightly built. Her clothes were obviously of better quality than those of her companions. Her shoes had higher heels and their bright buckles might have been silver, not just silver plate. She walked with her hands pushed deeply into the big pockets of her tweed overcoat. Red-haired Rita glanced across at her enviously from time to time, trying to weigh her up, to discover exactly why she was there.

The Maltese Brothers had only told Rita and Janine that she was not competing on their beat, and she would be with them for just a night or two. Rita and Janine were unenthusiastic, but no one argued with the Maltese Brothers. Arguments and aggravation meant that people could get their faces slashed by a razor; silence was always safer. One of the Brothers used to quote what he claimed was a Maltese proverb: 'He who sees nothing, says nothing, hears nothing, lives for a hundred years in peace.' The women he controlled agreed there was something in that.

The newcomer said her name was Mary O'Hara, but her accent was not Irish; Rita wasn't quite sure what it was. It could just possibly be north country or even colonial, but certainly not Irish. Hints as to why she was on the game so briefly had not produced any answers beyond the bare fact that the Maltese Brothers had agreed she should be there. Maybe, thought Rita, she was hoping to pick up a few tricks and then latch on to a rich man who'd keep her. These new young girls had a lot more sense than she had had at their age, that was for sure.

Now Janine tried her hand at conversation.

'What do you specialise in, love?' she asked her conversationally.

Mary O'Hara shrugged. 'I'm new to the game,' she admitted. 'Depends what they want.'

'They want it everywhere,' Janine said bitterly. 'In your mouth, up your back end, under your armpit, anywhere but where it's meant to go. You want to specialise in one thing, love. That gives you less chance of being hurt.'

'How do you mean exactly, hurt?'

'I mean set about, beaten up. Some of the men only want to rough you up because they can't do anything with you or with anyone else, probably not even with a boy. So they try to take it out on you. You've got to watch for that.'

'How do you tell?'

'Experience,' Red-haired Rita replied. 'Which you haven't got. You look young for this game.'

'How old were you when you started?' Mary asked her.

' 'Bout your age, I reckon. I was a maid in service, in a big house. The son of the house got his hand up my skirt and I made him pay, because he had money. He didn't mind that. Soon, I was making more from him and his friends than his mother was paying me to work from six in the morning to seven at night. So I threw up the job and went on the game.'

'Do you regret it?'

'Yes and no. You make more money like this, but it's cold and tiring, just walking up and down. And you never know what sort of men you're going to get, but you can be sure they're not going to be the pick. And then you've got the coppers on your back. Some of them want a bunk up, a quick rub or cash. The cash ones are the worst. The other doesn't hurt you. But it hurts when you've got to pay ten bob or a quid rather than be nicked. That can be a lot out of a poor night's earnings this time of the year.'

They walked slowly and carefully out of step along the pave-

310

ment. Shop windows glittered bright with electric and gas lights. Street lanterns threw a pale amber glow over tram lines; strips of cobble shone with dampness in the centre of the roads. A few cars and carts, and here and there a cab trundled along slowly, lamps flickering.

The three women came to the edge of Piccadilly, stood for a moment looking across the Central Gardens. Then they turned slowly, and sauntered back the way they had come, pausing now and then to look in at the windows. They were in no hurry. They weren't going anywhere, and it was early yet for clients; the pubs and the music halls were still full.

'Prices are terrible,' said Red-haired Rita. 'Look at that overcoat. Three guineas. But it will be sold to someone. Amazing, the money that's about.'

'It's not about us,' retorted Janine bitterly.

A man walked slowly towards them, pausing every now and then to look closely at shop windows as though searching for something he could not see.

'We tossed for it, remember?' Red-haired Rita reminded her companions. 'I'll have first go.'

Janine and Mary O'Hara stood looking at rows of dresses in another window while Rita walked on towards the man, drew level with him. He turned slightly, looked at her inquiringly.

'A cold night,' she said quietly. Always start the spiel with a remark no one can object to. Even if a copper reads it from his notebook in court, it still sounds innocent.

'Yes,' the man agreed, looking her up and down, his eyes hanging prices on her clothes, mentally undressing her. Rita's face seemed clean and her shoes were polished.

'Not so cold if there's two,' said Rita more confidently. 'Looking in the window for something, are you then? For a naughty girl, eh?'

'Depends how naughty,' said the man carefully. 'I'm a stranger here. From Birmingham.'

'Big city, Birmingham,' said Red-haired Rita, resisting the temptation to stamp her feet and clap her hands together. She felt cold and weary. How much better to be in a warm house by a fire, reading a book, perhaps with a cat on her lap instead of talking to a noncommittal stranger. Birmingham. Brum. Couldn't be worse than here, she thought.

'Yes,' he said, pleased, as though she had paid him a compliment. 'Very large. Very go-ahead.'

'Bet you have a lot of fun there, eh?' she said roguishly.

'I'm married there.'

'Well,' she said, 'your wife's not here, then, is she? Or you wouldn't be out on your own. What would you like to warm you up on a night like this?'

He looked at her, came closer. 'How much?'

'Everything, clothes off, two quid,' she said. 'In my place. Fire blazing. Warm room, clean bed. Much better than out here.'

'It's a lot of money,' said the man slowly.

In the light from the shop window she could see his face, pasty, with mean, cautious features, eyes too close together, a small mouth; like a rosebud, she thought – or an arsehole. He licked his lips with his tongue, working out what he should offer her.

'Thirty bob,' he said.

Red-haired Rita shrugged. 'All right,' she said. 'Thirty bob it is.'

It was better than nothing, and by the looks of him it shouldn't take long.

'Take my arm,' she told him. They linked arms. Now they could be man and wife, window-shopping, walking home from the theatre.

After dark, the Salford Road police station smelled strongly of leaking gas from the mantles and carbolic soap used to scrub out the cells beneath the street. The desk sergeant, within a year of retirement age, slightly bald, a wisp of hair trained into a heavily

312

greased curl on his forehead, was reading the daily record book. A constable came out of the rest room, flexed his knees to make himself more comfortable in his thick serge trousers, picked up his helmet from its peg.

'You on Piccadilly?' the sergeant asked him.

'Yes. Till midnight.'

'I hear three tarts been causing a bit of bother up there,' said the sergeant.

'Who are they?'

'Two are the usual old lags. Red-haired Rita and the tart she hangs around with, Janine. Apparently there's a new recruit with them. A sort of makee learnee. Young Irish girl. At least an Irish name – Mary O'Hara.'

'Well?' asked the constable.

'I think we should bring them in. Specially the kid,' said the sergeant.

'Had a complaint, have we?'

'Not from the public. But some of our good friends think this is what should be done. If you see what I mean.'

'I see,' replied the constable, nodding. He knew who were their good friends: the Maltese Brothers, who ran the whores. A five-pound note here; six bottles of whisky there; ten shillings in a brown envelope slipped into a uniform pocket elsewhere. Such favours meant that officers usually followed their advice. The constable felt vaguely aggrieved that bribes he only heard about didn't come down to him – not yet, anyhow. But they would, if he got promotion. And once this old bastard sergeant finally cleared out he would be next in line for it. In the meantime, he might take five bob each off these tarts if he promised to speak up for them. He'd do nothing, of course, but they didn't know that. Or even if they did, they were in no position to argue, for if they refused to pay, then he could say in court that they had given him a lot of trouble, resisting arrest, using foul language, causing a breach of the peace. He could throw a lot of charges at them; two or more would usually stick.

'You want 'em in here, then?' he asked the desk sergeant.

'That's right.'

'Not paying their dues, then, are they?'

'I don't know anything about that, but you heard what I said. It shouldn't be hard to find them accosting.'

'I'll find them.'

'The sooner, the better. It's a bloody cold night. You could be doing them a good turn. It's warmer in the cells than on the hoof out there, this weather.'

The constable went out through the swing door, down stone steps into the cold, foggy, acrid darkness. He passed various whores decked up to attract men of special tastes: one wore the habit of a nun, another was in school uniform. They all wished him good night respectfully and were thankful when he passed them by.

He saw Red-haired Rita and a man in a Homburg hat and heavy overcoat saying hello or goodbye on the pavement near a side turning. He knew she had a room there; it was cheaper and safer than going to an hotel. Rita saw him and smiled. The copper wouldn't touch her when she was with a man, surely? The man might object. This had happened once – and then it came out that he was a Manchester city councillor. There had been a lot of coming and going over that; hadn't done the copper's chances of promotion any good, either.

The constable walked slowly along Piccadilly, big hotels on one side, gardens on the other. More people were about here than on the Stockport Road. Public houses were just emptying, and the Ardwick Empire and the Hippodrome had finished their second shows. It was a good time to pick up clients.

Janine noticed the policeman. 'There's a copper following us,' she warned Mary O'Hara. 'Don't speak to anyone, even if they give you the glad eye, till I give you the say-so. Otherwise we'll be nicked for importuning.'

They walked on past shop windows, the policeman keeping a few paces behind them. It was only a matter of time before he took them in, because even if they did not speak to strange men, someone was bound to speak to them.

A man, waiting in a shop doorway, came out, raised his eyebrows inquiringly at Janine. The women walked past him quickly.

'Don't you know me, then?' he called after her.

'No,' she said. But she recognised him. He came in from Stalybridge once a week on some business matter, spent a couple of hours drinking. Sometimes she saw him afterwards. He wasn't a regular, but going on that way. She couldn't afford to be rude to him. He fell into step with them.

'Who's your lady friend?' he asked.

'Go away,' said Janine urgently. 'Copper's behind us.'

The man paused, turned round.

The policeman asked him very politely, 'Are these ladies annoying you, sir?'

'No, no. Just asking them the time of day.'

'Time of night, you mean, sir. I can oblige. Twenty to eleven.'

'Thanks, officer.'

'I saw them accost you, sir.'

'No, no, you saw nothing like that, officer,' said the man hastily. He was married, with three children, one an invalid, and a nagging wife. He wanted no more trouble; he had enough already. 'You've got it wrong, officer,' he said earnestly.

'I don't think I did, sir. I been watching these ladies for some time. Their behaviour's been, as you might say, a bit suspicious.'

'How d'you mean suspicious?' Janine asked him.

'I'll tell you at the proper time, in the proper place,' the constable replied primly.

The man put his hand in his pocket; his fingers closed around two half-crowns. 'You got a family, officer?'

'A little girl, sir. Just rising five.'

315

'Then buy her a present,' said the man. He gave him the five shillings. The officer put the coins in his back pocket.

'You are very generous, sir. You don't wish to prefer charges?'

'I wish nothing of the kind,' he said. 'Nothing at all.' He melted away down the alleyway.

'Well, you heard what the gentleman said,' said the policeman. 'On the other hand, I know what I saw. I've got to take you two ladies in.'

'On what charge?'

'Accosting, importuning for an immoral purpose.'

'You can't prove that.'

'You've got a record,' he said. 'Who's your lady friend?'

'Mary O'Hara. Come in from the country.'

'Then we'd better show her Manchester. From the police station.'

'This is ridiculous,' said Mary O'Hara. 'We're doing nothing but walking along.'

'That's what you say, girlie, but I saw you talking to three or four men back there.'

'Then why didn't you stop us?'

'I was preparing my case. Once could be genuine, twice a coincidence, but three means you're on the game.'

'I've got a ten-bob note in my pocket,' said Janine bitterly. 'It could have your name on it.'

'I can't let you off with this, ladies, much as I appreciate your kindness. On the other hand, if you gave me ten bob I'd put it in the police charity box, and I'd do my best to speak up for you, of course.'

'Of course,' said Janine bitterly. 'Here's your blood money.'

She gave him a crumpled note. He put it in his trouser pocket.

'Now, I'll ask you ladies to accompany me back to the station. And no trouble, please. It would be embarrassing to have a chase with all your friends about on the street.'

'Embarrassing for who?' asked Mary O'Hara.

He looked at her. She was young and pretty. There was a certain piquancy about her face, quite unusual in a whore. She looked fresh, clean, and somehow sharp, alert. Strange to see them on the game so young but, of course, they only needed a few rich regulars and they could be off the streets and living in a big house with servants and a motor car. He had seen it happen before. They could even marry into the aristocracy. There was no justice nowadays. But then had there ever been?

Judge Percival Donovan was robing in a large room behind the court; a small fat man with a pustuled face, sandy hairs bristling out of his nostrils. His clerk had already poured out a whisky and soda for him. He drank greedily and noisily.

'A busy morning, sir?' the clerk asked him obsequiously.

'Every bloody morning's busy,' the judge retorted grumpily. It was the usual petty rubbish. Some driver of one of these new motor cars had run into a tram car on the Ashton Old Road and killed the conductor. There were a number of whores, drunks, a handful of petty thieves and one GBH. He would never get a knighthood when he was stuck with this rubbish. He should be at the Bailey, dealing with the big stuff. But that would never happen, not now. He was in a rut and the only way out was to resign or die. He nodded to his clerk, banged the empty glass down on the table, and went out into the court.

He sat, splendid in his wig and robes, beneath the royal arms. He listened to the prosecution, the defence, heard or did not hear evidence and witnesses, and would then nod to show he was about to speak. The sentences he awarded were always harsh.

'Two years in the first division.'

'Six months hard labour.'

'Three months in the second division.'

The last to appear before him, as usual, were prostitutes who had been arrested the previous evening or during the night. In the harsh morning light, they looked grotesque, faces sometimes ravished with disease. Scabs and weeping sores and chancres were carefully, but never totally, covered by rouge and powder; in some cases, by beauty spots. It was amazing to think that these women earned a living by attracting men.

Janine Fowler of no fixed address, and Mary O'Hara, ditto, came up last. He looked at them. Janine, in the morning light, not having had a wash and lacking the benefit of a mirror in the cells, looked seedy and bedraggled. She had slept in her clothes, which were creased and crumpled.

Mary O'Hara was quite different. Even after a night in a police cell, she appeared young and fresh. She had a glow of health in her cheeks, not the pallor of nightwalkers who slept or drank by day and only came out when the sun went down.

If he had a daughter, the judge thought, she could have been the same age, probably in her early twenties. If. It was difficult to tell with girls nowadays, specially ones who looked smart. Her clothes were of good quality, no doubt about it. She was clean. He imagined her naked, stripped of those clothes, seeing in his mind's eye the firm breasts, the large nipples, the invitingly dark triangle of hair. She fingered two heavy necklaces of gold-plated chain links. He wondered what it would be like to be bound by her in chains like that, naked, to be assaulted by her and humiliated, always an exciting prospect to him, ever since his days at boarding school when he had been bullied, first by older and bigger boys, and then by masters.

Every day he dealt sentences of all kinds on all manner of people, but at night he lived with his own fantasies – bondage, degradation. He had never dared tell his wife; she would not have understood. Anyway, she was miles away today.

The constable who had arrested the two women was

mumbling away, reading from his crude notes. The charge was importuning for an immoral purpose.

'Have you anything to say?' the judge asked the women curtly.

Janine shook her head. There was no point in arguing against the police. She had no one to stand up for her. And who would believe the word of a common whore?

'And you?' The judge nodded towards Mary O'Hara.

'Not guilty, my lord,' she replied.

'The police think you are.'

'That is the constable's impression, sir. But I am not guilty.'

The judge grunted. She had a pleasant voice, a wide sensual mouth. He could imagine those lips gripping his phallus, soothing it, stroking its burning purple head with her tongue.

'Anything known?' he asked the policeman.

'Janine Fowler has a record, my lord. She was arrested in June and before that in April, previously in February and last Christmas Eve. A fine each time of two guineas and told to keep the peace.'

'O'Hara?'

'Nothing known in this court, my lord.'

'I see.' The judge smoothed his spatulate fingers over the papers on his desk. 'Five guineas or three months for Fowler. And as for O'Hara . . .'

He paused, looking at her. She met his gaze with frank, untroubled blue eyes. Her calm features gave no clue of the storm of emotion raging within her. It grew so strong, so compelling that she feared her feelings would show in her gaze. She lowered her eyes demurely, modestly. The judge cleared his throat, reaching his own decision.

'I see in you, O'Hara, a young girl, not conscious of original sin, possibly just come to the city from the peace of the country, and fallen into wicked ways with hardened evil women of the streets. I could send you to gaol. I could fine you heavily. Or I could do both. But in gaol you would only meet others of the same calibre as those who have brought you to this present sad situation. And if I fine you, no doubt one of those criminals who, I understand, play a great part in paying fines for prostitutes, will pay yours on the understanding you will work for them again.

'Therefore, in the hope, nay, the belief that you still have the basic elements of goodness and Christianity in you, and would benefit from a chance to go, as we say in court, straight, I will discharge you. But let me add that if ever I find you again before me, you will be punished with the utmost severity of the law. Next case.'

As Mary O'Hara came out of the side door of the court, an official approached her.

'Miss O'Hara?' he asked.

'Yes.'

'A letter for you.'

She took it, surprised. Who could be writing to her, care of the law court? She stood on the porch just outside the door, ripped open the envelope. Inside was a sheet of paper stamped with the arms of the court.

'Miss O'Hara,' she read. 'I would like to take a personal interest in your case and your future. Please call on me at the judge's lodgings tonight at 9.30 p.m. You will be expected. Percival Donovan.'

She folded up the letter, replaced it in the envelope. Her plan was working better than she'd expected. She hurried along the crowded pavement and then turned down a side street, walked slowly past a row of shabby shops all with peeling paint and fly-blown windows. One sold pies. In a butcher's shop, black puddings and trays of tripe, displayed unappetisingly on marble slabs, wore garlands of stale parsley sprigs. She passed a pawnbroker's shop where secondhand suits hung on hangers. Then she saw an ironmonger and went into his shop.

'I want to buy thirty feet of good quality, reasonably strong chain,' she told the man behind the counter.

'Can I ask for what purpose, madam? We do this in several strengths and sizes. A task that might be suitable for an iron chain would not be suitable for a brass one.'

'Brass would do me,' she said. 'Something light but strong.'

The man nodded. He measured up the length of chain against a yard rule nailed to the counter, told her the price. She counted it out exactly from her purse, picked up the brown paper parcel and went back into the street. Her heart was beating faster now; there was no going back.

On one side of the oak door to the judge's lodgings, a gas lamp flickered in an ornate shade; on the other, a chain hung down with a wrought-iron handle at its end.

Mary O'Hara stood for a moment, trying to compose herself, wondering how the judge would receive her. She ran one hand reflectively over the door, studied the huge octagonal boltheads with which it was decorated. Were they real or purely for ornament? Something about their pretentiousness irritated her. It seemed to represent the legal system: much for effect, little for justice. She pulled the chain hard. A bell pealed in the deep dark recesses of the building. She heard footsteps, a creak of dry shoe leather. The door opened. A flunkey looked at her inquiringly.

'Mr Justice Donovan,' she said. 'He is expecting me.'

'And your name, madam?' The flunkey had not intended to address her so politely, but something in her demeanour, in the cut of her clothes, told him that she was not a mendicant, nor a girl seeking a job as a maidservant.

'Mary O'Hara. I saw him in court today.'

'You are expected, madam. Would you please come in?' He opened the door into a wide hall; polished black tiles on the floor, several thick Persian carpets. Gas lamps burned around the walls. The place had a not disagreeable smell of beeswax polish.

'This way, madam.'

The flunkey led her down the corridor into a side room lined with books bound in red or green leather with titles picked out in gold. She pulled one from the shelf, opened it; Halsbury's *Laws of England*. She glanced at the turgid prose, the careful phrasing, put the book back with a grimace of distaste.

'Not to your liking, then, Miss O'Hara?' said a man from behind her. She turned. The judge had entered by another door. He stood now wearing black trousers, a bow tie, his blue velvet smoking jacket tied with a tasselled belt. On his feet he wore satin slippers with the heads of foxes picked out in gold thread. Apt, she thought; he was foxy, all right.

'You asked to see me, Mr Donovan?' she said demurely. She deliberately did not call him Your Honour or My Lord or by any other title. To her, he was only a man who had a proposition to make.

'Yes,' he said. 'Do come into a more comfortable room than this. It reeks of those learned in the law, and as one who has spent his whole adult life involved with law in its many forms, I can tell you there is never much comfort in what the law lays down.'

'I would agree with that, Mr Donovan.'

'You have had experience of it, apart from in my court this morning?' the judge asked her, surprised at her reply. 'I thought that had almost a happy ending?'

'That had,' she agreed. 'Yes.'

The room to which he led her opened off the study and was furnished in a more mellow style. Three brass oil lamps burned in frosted glass globes. A chaise-longue covered in green watered silk stood against one wall. There were two leather armchairs, side tables for magazines and cut-glass decanters of whisky, port, sherry, a cheval glass on the wall. In the mirror she saw the judge watching her, his small eyes hard as diamonds.

'Please sit down,' he said. He closed the door behind them, turned the gilt key in the lock. Then he went to a sideboard, selected a cigar from a humidifier, cut the end expertly, lit it and sat down opposite her.

'Please take your coat off. I would like you to feel comfortable here,' he said. 'What have you in that parcel? Your food? Shopping?'

'Something I thought might come in useful.'

'I see. You seem rather tense, Miss O'Hara.'

'I'm not used to meeting judges.'

'Not in the plural, just the singular.'

His face was flushed, unhealthy. She could see a pulse beating in his left temple, and yellow flecks of matter in the corners of his eyes. She hated him; more, she despised him.

He stood up, came behind her chair, took her coat from her, folded it on a gilt chair.

'Sherry? Or a port and lemon, perhaps?' he asked her solicitously.

'No, thank you,' she said.

'Have something soft. Pineapple juice. Or maybe passion fruit juice might perhaps be more in your line, eh? We have a long discussion ahead of us. I want to help you back on to the right path.'

'Thank you. But I'll not drink, if you don't mind, Mr Donovan.'

Silence hung like an invisible shroud between them. Whatever either of them said now could be crucial; both realised this, if for totally different reasons.

The judge sat down across from her, leaned back in his chair, crossed his legs, drew heavily on his cigar, almost closing his eyes against the blue smoke he exhaled from his mouth.

'As you wish. I let you off today when I could quite easily have sent you to gaol, as I sent your companion. I wanted to help you. I sensed you were not like her.'

'She was doing nothing wrong, Mr Donovan. She was simply walking with me.'

'That is a matter of opinion. Women who walk the streets are called street-walkers in preference to an older, cruder name. Naturally, I would expect you to help your friend. But the police constable, in whose word I place the utmost trust, said differently.'

'I still say what I say, Mr Donovan. She was innocent.'

'Innocence is, like truth, difficult to define. A matter of degree or opinion. Two men, it is said in the fable, looked out from prison bars. One saw mud. The other, stars. Both men accurately described what they personally saw – as did the constable this morning.

'But I digress. As I say, you could now be in prison. Not a very pleasant house of correction for women. You would be wearing a sackcloth shift, wooden clogs, and you would feel very cold. You might be attacked, have your eyes scratched and your hair pulled out by other women who thought you put on airs. Or just because they resent the fact that you are young and good-looking and they are old and ugly. Some of them would remember they were like you once, until things went wrong. I want to help you avoid such a situation – now and in the years ahead.'

He paused, drew on his cigar. Mary O'Hara said nothing. The judge cleared his throat.

'I do not wish to keep you here unnecessarily, but I have a proposition to make to you. I have helped you. I can help you more and in many ways. But in return, I ask that you help me.'

'How can I do that, Mr Donovan?'

'I am a lonely man, and one who by reason of his profession – if you like, his success in that profession – is placed above

324

and apart from other men. But my passions, my feelings, my physical needs are just the same as others less successful. I have saved you from prison today. In return, I ask a small service, a small favour. Do I make myself clear?'

'You want to go to bed with me?' she asked bluntly.

'Not exactly as you describe it. I saw you in the dock fingering that gilt chain which I see you still wear round your neck. I thought how pleasant it would be to be bound in chains by you. You understand what I mean?'

'I understand,' said Mary O'Hara. 'You wish to be degraded. You, who have degraded so many others. I understand perfectly.'

'Then you have understanding beyond your years, my dear. I commend you for it. Now, if you are sure you will not have a drink, let us to business.'

'In this room?' she asked in surprise.

'Where else? I would not expect you to come to my bedroom.'

'I would much rather be there with you, Mr Donovan. It would be so much more intimate, warmer. Friendly, if you like. I can show my feelings for you better in such surroundings than here in this sitting room, elegant as it is.'

'If you wish,' said the judge, surprised and pleased.

He led the way back into the hall, up a staircase. On the landing, an empty suit of armour reflected a metallic glitter from wall sconces. He opened a door into a room where pink-shaded lights were already burning; sheets and coverlet were turned down on a double bed. Beyond, Mary O'Hara could see a bathroom. There were several books on a bedside table, a suit of silk pyjamas neatly folded on the bed; the silken rope of a bell pull near its head.

'This is better,' she said. 'Now, do you wish me to undress you?'

'Yes,' he said. 'Now.'

'And you will undress me?'

'Later,' he said. 'Later. But first, I want to feel your hands on me.'

'Where shall I put your clothes?'

'Throw them on the floor,' he said. 'I have a valet. He can pick them up in the morning.'

He had already taken off his jacket, his cummerbund. Now he ripped open the top of his shirt. Gold studs scattered across the pink carpet. Mary O'Hara undid his cufflinks, helped him pull his shirt, his silk vest, over his head. He was strongly built, with a hairy chest, but his muscles were flaccid and his flesh pale, like the skin of a creature that never saw the sun. She thought he looked like an enormous slug the size of a man.

The judge was staring at her.

'What's wrong?' she asked, unbuttoning his flies and then his braces. Slowly she coaxed his trousers down round his ankles.

'You're wearing gloves.'

'I always wear gloves,' Mary O'Hara replied. 'Silk gloves. They are softer, smoother. Judge for yourself.'

She pulled down his underpants, stroked his phallus. It rose tentatively to her touch.

'I like that,' he said. 'Keep them on. You are quite right. Silk is smoother.'

'I think you'll like what I brought as a present for you in the parcel.'

'For me? A present?'

He sounded surprised but flattered. His greedy eyes glinted with pleasurable anticipation. She opened the parcel, took out the chain. Then she folded up the brown paper, put it in her handbag. She smelled cigar and whisky and port on the judge's breath as he picked up the chain and then let it fall with a rattle of shining links.

'How did you know I liked chains?'

'It is my business to know what men like,' she replied.

'You're a clever young woman.'

'I've been called other things,' she said drily. 'Now, the chains. I shall bind your feet and tie your hands behind you, then take the chain right round your body to your neck. And then when you lie bound, in my power, I will show you how soft my gloved hands can be.'

The judge's phallus jerked slightly with each beat of his ageing heart as she expertly wound the chain round his ankles and up to his thighs, under the crotch, round the small of his back. Then she tied his wrists, keeping hold of the last yard of chain.

'Now,' she said, 'you're my prisoner. Come to bed.' She flicked the chain. 'You're a dirty, filthy old man, aren't you?'

'I wasn't always,' the judge replied, hobbling towards the bed, pleased she had understood so well what was required. 'I was young once, and clean. Like you, my dear.'

'But now you're foul as a dog's turd, an evil creature, yet a man of great power. Look at that! Standing up for himself nicely now.'

She pulled back the skin of his penis. The end glowed in the warm room like a polished purple plum.

'Now,' she said, 'tell me about your job on the bench. Do you ever – like this – come to arrangements with people who appear before you? Prisoners?'

'Sometimes,' he said. 'Sometimes I do. I have the power.'

'Do you remember all your cases?'

'Of course not. There are so many. Every day, every week. Sometimes people beat on the front door here and shout abuse, but I have two trusty ex-warders in the house. They send them on their way.'

'Lie down,' she told him.

'You take off your clothes now,' he pleaded. 'Please. I want to see you.'

'You'll see me,' she promised him. 'In good time.'

He was lying on the bed now, trussed like a long white naked

327

thing, fired by his strange and base perversion. Not a man, she thought, a creature. Carefully, she pulled the chain round his neck, down his back, wound it loosely round his wrists.

'Do you remember *any* cases?' she asked him gently.

'Only a few that stand out for some reason or other.'

'I wonder,' she said, stroking him with one hand, pulling the chain with the other, 'do you remember a case you tried some years ago? It involved the death of a man on a platform in Exchange Station.'

'No, I don't think so. Who was he? A friend of yours? Give me some details.' The judge wriggled slightly in sudden discomfort. 'Hold on,' he said sharply. 'This chain's a little tight round the neck.'

'I'll loosen it,' she said and pulled it one notch tighter.

'I said loosen it. It's difficult to breathe now.'

'That heightens the pleasure,' she told him, and squeezed his throbbing phallus.

'My God, you're right. It does. Oh, those gloves! Harder!'

She paused in her manipulation.

'That case,' she continued. 'Someone in the train opened a carriage door as the train was coming in. It hit the man, and knocked him right off the platform. He fell under the wheels and died later that day. This could not have happened if the ticket collector had obeyed the railway company's rules and kept the gate to the platform closed. But he didn't. He was negligent. He left the gate open, and a crowd of half-drunk young men rushed in. The man tried to get out of their way – and was struck by the door. Do you remember the case now, Mr Donovan?'

'I remember that case, vaguely – yes,' he agreed slowly.

'But, to use the legal phrase, you found for the railway company. A note was passed up to you that influenced you.'

'Ah yes, now I remember. A point of law. What a good memory you've got. This happened years ago.'

328

'There is no point of law that should alter what was natural justice.' She ceased stroking him.

'Go on!' he cried, trembling with pleasure, thrusting his body up towards her gloved hand. 'Go on! Don't stop.'

She pulled the chain another notch tighter. Veins began to stick out slightly from the judge's forehead, up his neck, across his bald head. He was sweating. With lust or lack of air? she wondered.

'Why are you so interested in this particular case?' he asked her. 'It was long ago. And quite unimportant.'

'To you, perhaps, but not to me. That man was my father.'

'He wasn't an Irishman, O'Hara, though, as I recall?'

'No,' she said. 'He was Scottish. Name of Baird.'

'That's right. There was a boy there, too, I seem to recall. Your brother, I suppose? You married and took the name O'Hara?'

'No. I simply made up that name. What was in the note you were handed, my brother and I have been at pains to discover. Now I can tell you we know that it offered you the prospect of a sinecure with the railway company on your retirement. If you found for them, of course.

'The company did not want to pay us any compensation, for that could have given the lead to others to pursue similar claims against them. So you sacrificed our future for yours. You – and they – knew we had no money to appeal, to go to the House of Lords if necessary. So we lost – or rather the other side won. You let them win. You made them win.'

'You've got it all wrong,' the judge said earnestly. 'All wrong. That note referred to a point of law, as I've just told you.'

'I've got it right,' she corrected him, and pulled the chain more roughly now. He began to choke, to gasp for air like a fish on the river bank. His eyes stood out like onions; in his extremity, saliva gathered at his lips; his tongue was a red, encrusted serpent.

'The chain's too tight. Let me go. Help!'

But instead of a shout, he could only croak. She stood and watched him as he thrashed about on the bed. Its springs creaked; the flames in the lamps on the bedside tables trembled.

'All our father's life savings were used in that fight, which we should have won. Afterwards, my brother and I went abroad. When we set sail I made up my mind I would return and deal with you – one day. I found that your custom of not sentencing all street-walkers who come up before you is well known. And then I discovered the real reason for these acts of mercy. You will die tonight, now. Not by anyone else's hand – though no doubt many would wish to see you dead – but through your own lusts. Through your fear of discovery and public humiliation. I will not kill you, Donovan, but I will wait here until the end.'

'You'll hang for this!' the judge gasped. 'You'll hang!'

He writhed within the chain, arching his body, bunching his flabby muscles to try and force a link, but they all held firm. He strained with all his strength, sobbing for breath. Veins stood out on his forehead like blue knotted cords. Then suddenly his body sagged. He gave a choking rattle in his throat. Yellowish bile spewed out of his mouth on to the white sheet. He arched his back once more in a final paroxysm, and then rolled over on his side, lay still. His phallus sank and drooped, dribbling pearly essence.

Arabella bent over the body, listening for his breathing. She felt his pulse through the thin stuff of her gloves. It was feeble and erratic. Then the beat faded and stopped. Judge Donovan was dead. Now, at last, Arabella felt that her father's dying had been avenged. A death for a death; the debt was paid. She had carried within her the seeds of revenge for so long that instead of release, all she felt now was a curious sense of anticlimax, almost apathy. It had all been so easy.

She regarded the body without any feelings whatever; the corpse could have been a sack of potatoes for all the emotion it aroused in her.

Arabella crossed the room, pulled the curtains, took a small torch from her handbag and flashed its beam outside as she had previously agreed with Jamie. Then, opening the window, she shouted: 'Help! Help!'

She saw Jamie running along the pavement, heard the peal of a bell in the heart of the building as she pulled the rope by the bed. The flunkey came running up the stairs.

'You called, Miss O'Hara?' he asked her.

'Yes, I called,' she said. 'The judge has had an attack of some kind. A fit. He's fainted.'

The man approached the body on the bed but recoiled from touching it.

'What's happened to him? He's in chains. Is it a heart attack, madam?'

'I have no idea.'

'How could he tie himself up with all these chains?'

'Perhaps the police or the coroner will tell you.'

The flunkey stared at her and then at the body. He did not feel any loss at the judge's death; he had not been well liked. He knew of Donovan's habit of asking women to his rooms – usually shabby middle-aged drabs, not like Miss O'Hara – but that was nothing to do with him. All that concerned the flunkey now was the possibility that his own job could conceivably be affected.

Arabella heard hammering on the front door, and the urgent pealing of a bell, and then her brother's voice.

'My sister's upstairs. Make way there, man.'

Jamie and another manservant came into the room.

Jamie took a piece of paper and an envelope from his jacket pocket, scribbled a few lines, sealed the envelope, handed it to the flunkey. 'Deliver this at once to the Chief Constable at his home. You have his address, of course?'

'Yes, sir.'

'Then make haste.'

331

The man left the room, thankful to escape the sight of his former master, chained and naked, lying dead in his own vomit.

When they were alone, Jamie turned to his sister. 'Well, that worked all right. But I thought you'd never shine the torch.'

'It took longer than I imagined – him dying, I mean.'

'*You* didn't kill him, did you?' Jamie asked Arabella anxiously.

'Of course not. He killed himself. Got too excited and tried to free himself from the chains. Of course I could have loosened them, but I didn't.' As she spoke, she took off her silk gloves, pushed them into her handbag.

'Well, that's a debt paid,' said Jamie. 'Do you feel that now?'

'I suppose I should. But actually I feel nothing at all.'

'The next stage will be the tricky one, even for you,' said Jamie.

'I'll pull through it. The last thing anyone in authority wants is the weakening of that authority. They'll put out that the judge had a heart attack and died. There will not be any mention of a prostitute or the chains, of course. And the servants will not talk about it. If they did, they would never work again. It will all be very discreetly handled.'

'I can imagine the obsequious obituaries,' said Jamie. ' "With the death of Judge Percival Donovan, yet another link with a long line of legal luminaries is broken. His great and selfless work, trying to reclaim women of the streets, when others might despair, is too well known to need elaboration here, etcetera, etcetera." '

'One odd thing,' said Arabella. 'You spoke just now of a debt being paid. That has given me words to live by, for people who help or hinder us. When I get a family crest – and I have asked the College of Arms in London to design one for me – I am told I need a motto to go with it. You've given me exactly what I want. *I pay all debts*. What do you think?'

'I think it's very apt. But I'll feel happier when I know the Chief Constable believes your story.'

'He will. I've checked on him, too, just in case we needed to persuade him where his own best interest lies.'

'And what did you find?'

'That he is involved with the Maltese Brothers. Has been for years. Sammy Rosen's uncle was very helpful here. If necessary, he will have a word with him. The Chief Constable won't make any trouble.'

'I hope you're right,' said Jamie doubtfully.

She was. He didn't.

EIGHTEEN

Private Matters

Sergeant O'Malley was a tall, thin man who appeared taller and thinner than he actually was because he favoured a dark blue narrow-waisted overcoat, which extended almost to his ankles.

He stood now, a gaunt scarecrow figure, in front of the wide mahogany desk in Jamie Baird's study, shifting his weight uneasily from one foot to the other as he watched Jamie reading the folder of papers he had brought to him.

This assignment meant a lot to Sergeant O'Malley as a private investigator. There hadn't been too many recently that carried even a reasonable retainer, and none with unquestioned expenses such as this. He had a wife to keep in Deptford in South London, and an ailing son in constant need of expensive medicines.

Sergeant O'Malley knew many secrets about the rich and well connected, and privately disliked his clients because he felt contempt for them. If he had been favoured with even a fraction of their opportunities and privileges, what could he not have achieved? Instead, as a retired constable from the City of London police – his rank was totally fictitious – he was dependent on these people for his livelihood.

He knew where the bodies were buried, as he liked to describe secrets he was sometimes paid to unearth – or to keep concealed. Sometimes there was an actual body; someone who should have inherited, or someone else who, before an unexpectedly sudden death, had inexplicably changed a will in favour of a stranger. There were repossessions of mortgaged estates; stolen family paintings to be recovered, or copies substituted without informing the insurers; cases of bankruptcy, depravity, insanity. He wondered now about Jamie Baird's background. Was there a dark shadow – or possibly several – in it, just as there had been in the past of the man he had been investigating?

Jamie looked up at him from the sheets of paper on his desk, bit his lower lip in his concern.

'You've checked all this thoroughly?' he asked O'Malley.

'I have, sir.'

'You make some very grave allegations about the subject. Are you certain they're accurate?'

'As certain as I can be, sir. I acquired the habit of accuracy with the City of London police. In each of the incidents I describe, sir, I have noted accounts from three and sometimes four people. There is no doubt that events took place as I describe here, sir.'

'I see,' said Jamie slowly. 'I suppose I suspected this all along, but it is never pleasant to have one's worst fears realised.'

'No, sir.'

'Well, you have done your part,' said Jamie. 'The balance of your fee is now due.'

'If you would be so kind, sir. I have the invoice in my pocket.'

'Forget the invoice. Throw it away,' Jamie told him. 'I will pay in notes. No cheques in these matters, eh?'

He stood up, crossed the room, spun the combination lock of the wall safe behind a Gainsborough, took out a black metal cash box. He unlocked this with a key from his watch chain. O'Malley saw with envy and amazement that the box was packed to the lid with £50 notes. Jamie counted out five, handed them to him, locked the box, replaced it in the safe, spun the combination again, swung back the painting on its hinge.

'I have your address,' he said. 'If I need any further investigations, I will be in touch. I would like to thank you for the very discreet and efficient way in which you carried out this task.'

'My pleasure, sir,' said the man.

'Hardly that, I think,' replied Jamie, 'but it is a job you have done quickly and methodically, and I appreciate it.'

'Thank you very much, sir. I wish all gentlemen paid as promptly.'

'The rich,' Jamie admitted, 'are slow payers. I like to think I am different. I was poor once, you know.'

'I didn't know that, sir.' O'Malley laughed; he imagined the remark was intended as a joke. This man, with his huge house in Grosvenor Square, a butler, liveried footmen, how could he ever have been poor? Why, he was still only young, and already rich as Croesus. Who did he think he was fooling?

'Would you have a drink?' asked Jamie suddenly. He was depressed by what O'Malley had told him, and he felt lonely, on his own. He wanted a friend, or, if this was asking too much, at least someone to talk to.

'You are very kind, sir,' said O'Malley. 'I'll have a whisky neat, if I may.'

Jamie poured out two whiskies. They raised their glasses.

'You're married, I suppose?' Jamie asked him.

'Yes, sir. Been married twelve years. Got one nipper.'

'A boy?'

'Yes. Unfortunately, sir, he's not very well. It's his chest, I think. And the fog. We live down by the river at Deptford. To be quite honest with you, things have been a bit hard since I came out of the force.'

'You mean short of money?' said Jamie.

'Yes, sir, short of money. Jobs like yours aren't too frequent, and often you have to do them at your own expense. Travel about the country, entertain people in public houses for information, sometimes give disbursements to people to get the facts. That's why I appreciate your generosity.'

'Well,' said Jamie, 'as I said, I was poor myself once, though I see from your face you don't believe me. One of the benefits of being rich is that you can sometimes help other people.'

Jamie took out his wallet, opened it, removed two £50 notes.

'These are for you, Sergeant. They are not a fee. They're not charity. Regard them as a present. None of us is in this world for long, and those who have been more fortunate than others should spread their good fortune about a bit. I say that's why coins are circular. Money should go round.'

'I don't know what to say, sir,' said O'Malley. 'If I can ever help you in any way, sir . . .'

'Thank you. I will certainly be in touch with you if I need you again. In the meantime, get some good food for your little boy. If he needs medicines, write to me here. I'll arrange for him to see a specialist. At my cost, not yours.'

Jamie turned away from O'Malley. He did not want to see the tears in the older man's eyes. But who was getting the most out of this transaction? he wondered. The boy would be helped, the sergeant's position would be eased, but Jamie also profited. He had enjoyed giving at least as much as O'Malley had appreciated his generosity.

After the sergeant had gone, Jamie stood, hands behind his back, gazing out of the great window that overlooked the garden in the centre of the square. It was that hour of evening when London trembled on the frontier between day and darkness. Gas lights were coming on one by one as the lamplighter cycled past them with his long pole over his shoulder, to turn on the tap in each of the lantern globes.

Faintly, filtered by the thick glass of the window, Jamie heard newsboys calling the latest editions of the evening papers, and in the background the muted hum of the great dynamo of London's traffic. He never tired of this view, but tonight there seemed something melancholy in it which he could not quite understand.

He tried to analyse his feelings. Not very difficult, he told himself brusquely. He was lonely. Nearly all the cars and cabs going round Grosvenor Square had two people in the passenger seats – a man and a woman. They were either going home or they were going out. Wherever they were going, they were going together.

He had probably more money than any half-dozen of those couples put together, perhaps more than all of them, yet he was here on his own. He had no one with whom he could share his success.

He wondered what it would be like now to be going out to the theatre with a pretty woman, on to supper, to Kettners or Rules and back here for the night. He could do that quite easily as often as he wished. He was continually being invited, as one of London's most eligible bachelors, to all manner of smart dinner parties where the hostess had an unmarried friend or a widow or even, sometimes, a divorcee. But although Jamie had been mildly attracted by several of them, he had always held back. He distrusted giving anyone his confidence. As with all lonely people, he felt vulnerable.

He was a watcher now, he told himself, a looker-on, rather than a participant. He envied these people, driving or being driven to or from their homes. He assumed they still had dreams, ambitions, aims, while he felt he had none. He was not an actor in life's drama any more; he was one of the audience, because he had achieved his ambition too soon.

You can climb a mountain, maybe even Everest, he thought, but no one can live for long up on the mountain peak. You had to come down, and what he really missed was the excitement of the climb. Robert Louis Stevenson had been quite right; it was better to travel hopefully than to arrive; much better. For when you had reached your destination, where could you go from there? Jamie gave a sigh at the perversity of life, turned back into the room, glanced at his watch. He had an hour to spare before he was due to meet Arabella for dinner. He put O'Malley's folder in a drawer in his desk, turned its double lock, and rang to order his bath to be drawn.

Arabella alighted from her Panhard and embraced Jamie who stood, waiting for her, cigar in hand, at the top of the steps of the Connaught entrance.

'What a surprise to hear from you,' she said delightedly. 'I didn't know you were back here in England. I feel rather guilty because I have been in London for nearly a year and enjoying it.'

'After our trip to Manchester, I felt I wanted to get out of towns and cramped little streets. I longed to be in South Africa. So I went back. Then I found I was really doing nothing. The managers are very competent, so I decided to come over here and see how my pretty sister was getting along.'

'When did you arrive?'

'A couple of weeks ago. Why?'

'I wondered. I sent you a telegram in the Cape, and you didn't answer.'

'What was in the cable?'

'Only that it was the anniversary of Father's death.'

'I had forgotten,' he said sadly. 'Not his death, but exactly when he died.'

He guided her to his favourite table. A waiter hovered attentively, handed them two menus. They both ordered the same dishes – smoked salmon with chablis and then boeuf Wellington with claret.

'Rather different from supper in the Silent Witness,' commented Jamie.

'Yes. But if it hadn't been for Uncle Don and Aunt Hannah then, we would not be sitting here now. I went to see them before we met in Manchester. They looked much older, and they are so proud. They wouldn't take *anything* from me, not even a gift. I suppose I wouldn't either, in their situation. But I felt dreadful about it, all the same. I mean, we have so much and, relatively speaking, they have so little.'

'Materially speaking, yes, perhaps so. But . . .' Jamie's voice tailed away.

'But what?' his sister asked. 'What else is there?'

'A lot of things, I've come to realise. Love. Companionship. Uncle Don and Aunt Hannah have each other. They're a team.'

'But so are we.'

'Yes,' he agreed. 'Yes.'

'You don't sound too convinced. Is something wrong? Something the matter?' Arabella looked at him quizzically.

Jamie shook his head, anxious to bring the conversation round to the real reason he had invited his sister to dinner, and not too sure how to guide it on to such a delicate, potentially hazardous course. At last, he took a long drink of wine and came to the point.

'I hear you are seeing a lot of a young nobleman.'

Arabella nodded. Jamie saw that her face had flushed; he had never seen his sister blush before.

'Yes,' she admitted. 'He's charming. We met in the oddest way, outside this hotel. I was coming here to have dinner with Sammy, and just as I stepped from my car, two ruffians tried to seize my handbag – right here in the middle of Mayfair. Amazing effrontery! And they would have succeeded, but for Noel. He happened to be getting out of his car right behind me at the same time, and saw what was happening. I didn't know him from Adam, but he pitched right into these two men and knocked one out. If my driver had been half a man, he'd have helped Noel, and they would have caught them. As it was, they both got away, of course.'

'Of course.'

'What do you mean – "of course"?' asked Arabella sharply. There was a hint of sarcasm in her brother's voice she had never heard before. It irritated her; it also disturbed her, although she did not know why.

'I mean,' Jamie replied, not totally truthfully, 'that with so few policemen around these days, robbers have it too much their own way. But tell me about Noel. Do you know anything about his background?'

'Only that his wife died very tragically when they were on holiday on the Riviera. They had only been married about a year.'

'How did she die?'

'I think a heart attack. She collapsed after going out to dinner. He found her literally dying in the bathroom.'

'What a terrible discovery.'

Again, Arabella looked at Jamie sharply. 'Are you being sarcastic?' she asked him coldly.

'Not at all,' he replied. 'It must have been a terrible discovery. But at least he was alive to make it. His wife wasn't.'

'What are you getting at?'

'Something that is very difficult for me to say, but I feel I have to say it. My concern for you, Arabella, is that you are my only close relation. I love you and admire you more than anyone else in the world. I just hope that this Noel is all you seem to think he is.'

'Why shouldn't he be? His uncle died quite recently and he has a huge estate up in the north. He isn't after my money, if that's what you're thinking.'

'Are you sure?'

'Of course I'm sure. I've seen photographs of his house, and several of the farms on his estate and so on. And he's so generous. Why, every day he sends me a present. Flowers. Three dozen long-stemmed red roses. A box of Swiss chocolates. He takes me out to the theatre every week – always the best seats, or a box – and we dine here or at Kettners. He couldn't be more considerate.'

'And what do you give him?' asked Jamie.

'Nothing, except my company. Oh, I know, once or twice, when he's left his cheque book at home, or his wallet in another suit – he's awfully careless about such things – I've lent him a little money to help pay the bill. Nothing, really.'

'And he always pays you back?'

'Well, there have been occasions when he hasn't. But the sums are trifling, and he says – rather wisely, I think – he is going to let them all add up to a reasonable sum and then he'll repay me in one lot.'

Jamie pushed away his plate. He had somehow lost his appetite. 'I hear rumours that you are even thinking of marrying him,' he said.

'Odd, isn't it? I chose the name Lady Arabella for my beauty preparations, and if I did marry Noel, then I'd be a real proper lady. When Yeung Lee read my palm before we went to the Cape, we joked about me wanting a handsome prince to come along, like in a fairy tale, to marry me. He said I might marry someone who was the equal of a prince. Maybe he meant a lord?'

'Did Yeung Lee say that if you did you'd live happily ever after – like they always do in fairy tales?'

'No. He said he couldn't see the future clearly after that point.'

'Perhaps that's just as well.'

'What do you mean?' Arabella asked him, sipping her wine, watching him warily across the table.

'Are you going to marry him?'

'He's asked me several times, as a matter of fact, and I think I will.'

'But you hardly know him.'

'I know him well enough to realise he is someone I have been looking for since Father died. I'm tired of being on my own, being warned about men who may be after my fortune. Noel isn't like that.'

'Did he tell you he wasn't?'

'Of course not. The matter never came up. You sound doubtful, Jamie. What are you hinting at?'

'I can't bear to think of you being hurt, Arabella.'

'But why should I be hurt? Noel's charming. You'd get on extraordinarily well together. In fact, you must meet. I think he's in the country at the moment, but he'll be back in London later this week. He sends me a letter every day. Amazing! I've never had letters from anyone every day. All the letters I receive seem to refer to my business. They want so many more tons of face cream or sun oil or powder or some such thing. It's rather nice to have letters written from the heart. Love letters.'

'I can imagine,' said Jamie. 'I've never had one. Never sent one. But getting married to someone is quite a serious step to take. We've always been close, always been together. Old Yeung Lee used to say twins are like someone with two heads: they can see both sides of a problem.'

'But I'll still be your twin. We'll still be together in business, in every way,' said Arabella.

She spoke so earnestly that Jamie guessed she was also trying to convince herself. He nodded, but without any conviction.

'I worry,' he said. 'Do you really know anything much about Noel – apart from the fact he's a lord?'

'Oh yes. He was at Eton, Christ Church, and then in the Hussars.'

'Why didn't he stay in the Hussars? With his background, he should have gained promotion very quickly.'

'He knew that, and he was most reluctant to leave. He resigned his commission because he wished to devote more time to helping his uncle run the estate. His uncle was old, and Noel was very close to him. His only relation.'

'He resigned his commission because he had to,' Jamie said drily. 'If he hadn't, he would have been cashiered for conduct unbecoming an officer and a gentleman.'

Arabella stared at him in amazed disbelief. 'You're making this up.'

'Unfortunately, I am not. It's quite true. He'd given a number of cheques for quite large sums to his tailor, his bootmaker, all sorts of tradespeople. The cheques weren't honoured.'

'How do you know this?'

'Someone told me.'

'I don't believe you.'

'That's your prerogative, Arabella, but facts are facts. He has a reputation as a gambler. He has already gambled away one inheritance he came into when he was twenty-one. He then borrowed on his expectations when his uncle died. At this moment, he is paying exorbitant interest to moneylenders. He is bankrupt, morally and actually. No wonder he is charming to you and generous. He hopes that once he marries you, you will pay his debts.'

'This is utterly ridiculous,' Arabella said angrily. 'How can you, my twin brother, say such disgusting things about a dear sweet man whom you've never even met?'

'Because what I am telling you is true. All of it. That estate that has impressed you so much is mortgaged over and over again. His uncle was a drunk. A bottle of port a day, at the very least. Sometimes two. He had a touch of gambling fever, too, and lived wildly above his means. When the moneylenders came knocking on his door, he sold off a row of shops or houses or a farm or five hundred acres to pay them off. That estate is a mess. Just to get it straight will cost a fortune when you consider the interest being paid on the mortgages. Did you know that?'

'No. And I don't believe a single of word of it. Noel would have told me if he was in any trouble at all.'

344

'Why? And see you sail away? Not a bit of it. He wanted to impress you. The landed gentleman. Eton, Oxford, the Hussars. Different from our background – village school in Burrelton, and then living in a pub in a mill town in Cheshire.'

'That's all in the past,' said Arabella shortly. 'We wanted to get out of that situation and we succeeded.'

'If you marry this man, you might land yourself back in it. He'll bleed you to death with his bills, his gambling, his debts. Can't you see that?'

Arabella stared at Jamie, her face white. 'No. I cannot see that. You're telling lies. I think you're jealous of him. How could you possibly know all this?'

'It wasn't very difficult to find out. He leaves a trail of bad debts wherever he goes.'

'Rubbish! He may owe a bit here or there, but so does everyone. You should meet him face to face before you spread such accusations. If you spoke to him just once, you'd know instantly what a straight fellow he is.'

'I think not,' said Jamie. 'There is also the mystery of his wife's death. Did you know he had insured her for ten thousand pounds only weeks before she died? But when he claimed on the policy, the company would not pay.'

'Why ever not?'

'The circumstances of her death were suspicious. He would have had to prove she had died naturally. It would not have been easy. A healthy, extremely wealthy woman of twenty-eight suddenly dead from no apparent cause? No post mortem, a cremation in Cannes and the ashes scattered at sea?'

'How can you possibly say all this?'

'Because, I repeat, it's true. On his insurance application, he had to state that his wife accepted he was insuring her life – not his – and was happy with this. But people who knew her well said she would never *ever* have agreed to be insured. Her father had drummed into her that insurance companies could not be

345

trusted. Because, once, some insurers welshed on a claim he made, he hated them all, and he brought his daughter round totally to his way of thinking.'

'I don't believe a single word of what you're telling me,' said Arabella firmly. 'I think you're just jealous. You must meet Noel. You will revise your views immediately. In the meantime, I am going to pretend this conversation has not taken place.'

'Arabella, listen to me,' Jamie pleaded. 'I hired a private investigator. He has sworn statements from all kinds of people testifying to Lord Doncaster's character.'

'You mean you actually had the man I hope I'm going to marry followed and trailed by some fearful little snooper?'

'If you put it like that, yes, I did. He wasn't particularly little, though I agree he could seem fearful from the noble lord's point of view – if he ever discovered it.'

'This isn't a matter to joke about, Jamie. It is quite the most disgusting thing I have ever heard. To think that my own brother has been paying someone to spy on the one man who has been genuinely kind to his sister!'

'Kindness is as kindness does. In being kind to you, he is being far kinder to himself. He had – and has – his own interests at heart, far more than yours.'

'You keep making these accusations, saying these awful things, without the slightest grounds for any of them. I've heard enough. I'm going home. I simply cannot sit here while you go on in this loathesome, vile way.' Arabella stood up.

'Wait,' said Jamie. 'One last point – just in case anyone else might appear to attack you in the street, and your hero isn't conveniently at hand to help. This investigator discovered that Noel had arranged the touching little scene which so impressed you outside this hotel, when he pretended to rescue you from two robbers.'

'*Pretended*? What *can* you mean? He knocked one down,

chased away the other. There was nothing *pretend* about that. I saw it.'

'What you saw was play-acting. He had you investigated just as I have investigated him. The fact is, your gentleman friend wanted to meet an heiress – indeed *had* to meet one to get him out of his money troubles. He hired the same man I engaged to find one for him. You happened to be the richest, the youngest and the prettiest.'

'This is absolute rubbish.'

'Unfortunately, it's true. When Noel discovered how rich you were, he worked out this little play to meet you, and hired two out-of-works as actors. It was not coincidence that he arrived just as it was happening. He organised everything so that he appeared on cue. I don't like telling you all this, Arabella, believe me. But I am doing it for your own good.'

'Damn my own good! I don't believe a word of any of it.'

'Nevertheless, it's all true. I don't like repeating this, because I can see how drawn to him you are. If I were cruel, I would say you're infatuated.'

'You *are* cruel. I am not infatuated by him. I *love* him. That's a word that has never been in your vocabulary.'

'I've not had a lot of time to put it there,' said Jamie.

'Nor have I,' retorted Arabella, 'but now I have, I want to keep it there. When we were young in the Silent Witness, I used to envy Uncle Don and Aunt Hannah. You made the point yourself just now – they're a team. They'd little money; no hope for betterment or preferment. They just got on with their job, and they liked each other, they *loved* each other. There was warmth in that little house. A lot of hard work, but something very precious, too. Something I have missed and wanted to find again, for myself. And now I think I've found it. If Noel asks me again to marry him, I'll say yes, on one condition.'

'Which is?'

'That we are married at once, before you can dig up any more lies about him. I love him. That is enough for me – and, I imagine, for him. Now, I really am going. I've heard enough from you. I can't bear to hear another word. Goodbye!'

She walked out of the restaurant without a backward glance. Jamie followed her to the hotel door. Her Panhard was parked outside the entrance. He saw her climb in and be driven away.

For a moment, Jamie stood on the steps, watching the tail light of Arabella's car dwindle like a tiny ruby. His eyes filled with tears. He loved Arabella more than anyone or anything in the world, and now he knew that despite all his efforts, he was losing her. He should have known from long experience that when she decided upon something, the more anyone tried to deflect her, the more determined she became to do what she wished. He stood for a moment, irresolute, then went back into the hotel.

He had not told Arabella what to him was the most important and damning fact he had discovered about the man she claimed to love. He simply had not been able to bring himself to tell her. If she did not believe what he had already said about Noel, then she would never accept there could be anything more serious in his past.

Jamie sat down in the lounge, ordered a brandy, went over in his mind what Sergeant O'Malley had told him.

Noel Rudgers, now Lord Doncaster, had been married for a second time, a fact not widely known. His second wife was a widow of forty-five when they married and already had two children. She appeared to have been a relatively rich and rather lonely woman. She lived in a country house in Norfolk where she kept a number of cats.

Jamie did not know how Noel had met her, but the date of their marriage was about a year after Emily's death on the Riviera. The wedding had been very quiet, in a register office; not even her children were invited. Almost immediately, Noel had begun to spend money again on a considerable scale. Then his wife died after a meal which they'd eaten in a London restaurant. She had returned to their hotel complaining of feeling ill, and died within the hour. Food poisoning was the cause stated on the death certificate.

Again, there had been no post mortem. Noel had explained that his wife belonged to a religious sect which could not bear any surgical operation on the body. It was the temple of the Lord; an operation would desecrate it. She had made a will leaving everything to Noel, and requested that her body should be buried within two days of dying in a churchyard at the edge of the Thames by Marlow.

Her two children were astonished at the death of their mother. When they had seen her a week earlier she seemed in perfect health. She had never suffered from food poisoning. They could not understand the business of a hasty funeral in Marlow. She had never been there as far as they knew but, of course, Noel, as her husband, had the last word.

When Jamie had read O'Malley's notes, he had looked up at the private investigator inquiringly.

'What's the reason for that, in your opinion?' he asked him.

'That particular graveyard, sir, has been used before when people leaving large sums of money – or who are believed to have large sums of money – have died suddenly, almost invariably after a heavy meal, from food poisoning.'

'I don't understand you.'

'I'll make it clearer, sir, if you'll pardon what I have to say.'

'Of course.'

'When an apparently healthy person dies suddenly in this country – especially when they are not old, and do not have a history of heart trouble, when they are not being treated for any disease – it is usual for a post mortem to be held before they can be cremated.'

'I know that,' said Jamie.

'They are, however, allowed to be buried without a post mortem first, because if a case is later made out that there could have been foul play, the body can always be exhumed.'

'So what is different about this cemetery by the side of the river?'

'The river, sir, is tidal. It rises and falls. Every day, twice every twenty-four hours, that churchyard, where Lord Doncaster's second wife is buried, is virtually under water. Within a week, any trace of poison – and I do not say there *was* any trace, sir, but *should* there have been – would be washed away. They could exhume the body, carry out any examination they like, and they would find nothing.'

'You think she was murdered?'

'I have not conducted any further investigations into that line of thought, sir. I was not asked to. But I have found that she was by no means as rich a woman as her husband had been led to believe. She lived quietly, and she had a number of very valuable Chinese ornaments which her father had brought back from Shanghai and Peking. From time to time, after she met Lord Doncaster, these were sold – discreetly – by auction. Her son and daughter told me that now there is virtually nothing left.'

'So he milked them?'

'That is one interpretation of the situation, sir.'

'I see. So here are two women, one very rich, who changes her will just before she dies, and one thought to be rich who dies perhaps because Doncaster thought she was rich. Or maybe he just wanted to sell up everything she had, and go on, as they say, to pastures new.'

'That is the interpretation I would put upon it, sir. But of course, in law, it would be very difficult to prove.'

'In law, Mr O'Malley, truth is always difficult to prove.'

* * *

Sergeant O'Malley let himself into his terraced house in a back street near the Thames. It had been washing day, and the narrow hall reeked with the strong scent of carbolic soap. His wife came out of the kitchen, wiping her hands on a towel.

'Supper's ready,' she told him briefly.

He nodded to her, hung his long coat and his black Homburg hat on a hook behind the front door, walked down the hall with its cheap, cracked linoleum.

'What's the matter?' she asked as he sat down at the kitchen table. 'You're looking thoughtful.'

'I'm feeling thoughtful. An odd thing has happened to me, first time in all my experience. Some time ago, a young and rather disagreeable aristocrat, short of cash, hired me to find out all I could about a rich young woman he hoped to marry. For her money, I didn't doubt. He never paid me – or rather he did – but his cheque bounced. And then, blow me, if this young woman's brother didn't ask me to check on the aristocrat!'

'So you lost one fee?'

'Yes and no. I added it on the brother's bill. And then the brother gave me a hundred quid on top of my fee. I felt a bit mean then, actually. But you've got to look after yourself.'

'I'm sure you do that very well,' said Mrs O'Malley with wifely pride, as she began to ladle out the Irish stew she had prepared for supper.

NINETEEN

Lies and Promises

When Noel walked into the entrance hall of the Connaught Hotel, a man who had been sitting in one of the easy chairs near an indoor palm tree, reading the *Morning Post*, stood up and walked towards him.

He was tall and wore a dark suit. His Guards tie was knotted very tightly and his stiff white collar made a sharp contrast to his blue striped shirt. To the casual glance, he seemed a well-to-do man about town, a boulevardier. But, close to, he seemed more like an actor playing the part of a gentleman than a genuine Guards officer. His trousers had been pressed too often; their turn-ups were frayed; the knot on his neck-tie was shiny.

'Excuse me, Lord Doncaster,' he said gravely. 'I wonder if I could have a private word with you?'

'Who are you?' Noel asked him bluntly.

'I will introduce myself in your room.'

'Like hell you will! What do you want?'

'I have something to say to you privately, sir, to discuss a matter that is not for other ears. There are several people here who might overhear our conversation. In your own interest, I suggest we talk quietly and elsewhere. I wish to save you any embarrassment. But if you do not mind whether a confidential conversation may be heard by other ears, then that is your decision.'

'What the devil are you talking about? Say whatever you have to say here and be done with it.'

'Very well, sir. I represent the North London Loan Accommodation Company. You owe them eleven thousand pounds. Now, I know you originally only borrowed nine thousand, but the interest rate is high, and I would remind you that your debt is being added to every minute of every hour of every day. My principal requires to know your proposals for repaying this loan.'

'The hell they do! I thought you were a gentleman at first, not a damn moneylender's nark sent by Jew boys who are too fat and cowardly to come themselves.'

'Since you wish to become personal, I must tell you that I do not claim to be a gentleman, any more than I imagine you would sincerely claim to be a man of honour. I am informed you also owe money to bookmakers and to casinos abroad. Our inquiries nearer home show that your tailor made you six suits last year and has not been paid for any. It is the same with your shoemaker, your shirtmaker. I know the aristocracy and the rich like to pay late. But you don't appear to pay at all.'

'Well, now you know,' said Noel angrily. 'What are you going to do about it?'

'Tomorrow morning,' the man replied, 'at your wedding, when you pose with your bride on the steps of St Margaret's, Westminster – so that you can be photographed as man and wife – a processor will approach and tap you on the shoulder with a writ.

'I can promise you that this picture will appear in every newspaper the following morning. Each newspaper will, of course, be informed in advance of the photographic and headline possibilities. A peer being pressed to pay a long overdue debt at his wedding to one of the country's richest women. I have come here now in an attempt to save you this embarrassment.

'The North London Loan Accommodation Company does not wish to distress you. But then, sir, as I am sure you will appreciate, neither do they wish to have you as a debtor. If you settle your debt now, you will be spared this humiliation. I cannot accept a cheque, of course. The company has already accepted three from you for earlier debts and none were honoured. You could, however, advise the all-night bank in Bishopsgate, and have a cheque paid by special clearance. The choice, as they say, sir, is yours.'

'You'd never do that tomorrow. You'd make a fool of me. And my wife. She could buy up your whole piddling little company and charge it to petty cash.'

'Perhaps that is so, sir. If it is, that only increases the irony in the situation – a point which doubtless the newspapers will not ignore. I repeat, it is not the company's wish to harm or distress you, or your wife. It is their wish simply to collect that which is owing.'

'I haven't got the money tonight. But I can get it after my honeymoon.'

'That is too late. My principals cannot allow this debt to extend indefinitely. I understand you are going abroad – I hear to Jamaica, which should be very pleasant at this time of year. But you might not come back. You might decide to stay there. Who knows? I am sorry, but the choice is simple and not negotiable in any way. Money tonight or a dunning tomorrow.'

Noel stroked his chin. He had the unhappy, uneasy feeling that events were about to repeat themselves. The matter of the casino manager from Monte Carlo was still vivid in his mind. As a result of that visit, he had murdered his wife – and taken a further loan on the strength of his expectations from her will.

How seriously could this imitation Guardee diminish his chance of marrying another rich woman? Very considerably, he thought – but only if Arabella discovered his desperate financial predicament and what had caused it. This she must never

354

do; at least, not until she was his wife. Of course, £11,000 was nothing to Arabella, barely small change, but it could be vital to him. Once he was married, though, life would be totally different.

He still had the wine Emily left him. He could sell that for several hundred pounds, no doubt. But where, on the eve of his marriage, could he find a buyer for a cellar of wine? It was in store, anyhow, and the store would be shut at this hour.

'Well?' asked the man shortly. 'What do you choose to do?'

'Wait here,' Noel told him, making up his mind. 'I will endeavour to raise the money now.'

'I will wait for one hour,' the man replied, checking the time with his watch, a cheap German silver timepiece. 'In the meantime, sir, you might care to order a drink for me.'

'Like hell!' retorted Noel. 'Pay for your own bloody drink!'

He stormed out of the door, walked round the corner into Grosvenor Square, pressed the bell of Arabella's new house. Her butler opened the door.

'Good evening, my lord. Have you left something behind?'

'No, I just want to see Miss Baird about a matter I had forgotten. That's all, Stevens. Nothing important. I will let myself out.'

He walked upstairs to the first-floor sitting room. Arabella was seated at the piano, extemporising, as she liked to do. When she played old music-hall songs, or military marches, she was always reminded of Kimberley and the pianos hammered by diggers in the public houses while others joined noisily in the homely choruses. There was something robust, honest, and unpretentious about those songs that appealed to her. These were qualities she admired.

Noel paused at the doorway, surveying the furniture and ornaments in the room; a Gobelin tapestry on one wall, Louis XIV chairs, an Aubusson carpet, Afghan rugs, Ming vases. Why, a vanload of these treasures would see him on Easy Street for the rest of his life, and they were nothing to her, nothing at all. It was so damned unfair. Through the wide windows, he could see cabs and taxis and private cars going round the square. To most of the people riding in them the amount of money he owed would be of no importance either; a small financial matter that a clerk would deal with on their behalf. Soon, please God, he would be in the same situation. It all depended how he handled the matter now.

Arabella looked up in pleased surprise as Noel came into the room.

'Darling,' she said happily. 'What brings you back again so soon?'

'To see you, my love,' Noel replied, and kissed her gently on her cheek.

'But you saw me barely ten minutes ago.'

'Ten minutes when you're in love can be a lifetime. And even one minute without you is like a day without sunshine.'

'You say the sweetest things.'

Suddenly (and quite irrationally, she assured herself) Arabella wondered whether Noel had paid similar compliments to his first wife. But what did that matter now? She was dead, poor soul. How tragic to be married to a man so charming, and then to die so young, and without bearing him a child.

'Actually, I have two requests to make,' Noel admitted shyly, like a small boy asking an indulgent aunt for a toy.

'What are they?'

'First, kiss me.'

Noel took her in his arms, kissed her gently, then more fiercely, seeking out her tongue with his. He drew apart, still holding her arms as though he could not bear to let her go. He hated to kiss her mouth, recoiled from the touch of her tongue. What hell it was to have to go through this nauseating procedure with a woman, not a boy. But he had to; there was no other way.

Noel smiled at Arabella, hoping that his eyes did not reveal his inner agony of concern and disgust at such intimate contact. To be so near to such wealth and to lose it was unthinkable.

'The second request is one I hesitate to ask,' he said, doing his best to appear reluctant. 'I find, quite unbelievably, my darling one, that – foolish me – I am short of ready cash. All my money is tied up in stocks and shares and trusts and so forth. I was speaking to my broker about this, but he says it takes time to release anything more than a few pounds. These people never hurry. I know nothing about financial matters and I thought they could all be cashed immediately, on demand. Wrongly, of course.'

'When were you speaking to your broker?'

'Well, in all honesty, I telephoned him as soon as I got back to the hotel. I have his home number. He said he could, in the circumstances, send a messenger to me with a banker's draft tomorrow morning, or even come to the church and give it to me there. But I don't want to be messing about with such boring things then, as you can imagine. I might, I suppose, invite the broker to the reception , and he could bring me funds then, but frankly, I don't want to become involved with the fellow socially.'

'How much money do you need?'

'Everything is so expensive now, as you know, my sweetheart, and I do not want to do anything on the cheap, or in any sort of dreary economical way, where you are involved. We only have one life and I have only one Arabella. And for all the days of my life I want to treasure you, and make your honeymoon – *our* honeymoon – a time to remember.'

Arabella smiled at him. 'How very pleasantly you put these things, Noel. Can I help you out?'

'I hardly like to ask, my dearest one, but I have to admit in all honesty that it would assist me greatly if you could. It would only be a temporary loan, of course. For a matter of days, or at the most until we come back from honeymoon. We won't want to be bothered by business things then, will we, dear heart?'

'Of course not. I'll do anything I can to help you. After all, when we're married, we'll not be two separate people any more, we'll be two parts of one. What's yours then will be mine, and what's mine will be yours. You know that. How much do you need now?'

She had in mind a few hundred pounds.

'I would think fifteen thousand pounds would fit the bill,' said Noel quickly.

'Fifteen *thousand* pounds,' Arabella repeated in amazement. 'That's an enormous sum. We won't conceivably spend that just on our honeymoon, will we?'

'Of course we won't, my dear. But the fact that we've got it, that it's *there*, means that I – who worry constantly about looking after you – will have nothing to worry about. Whatever happens, we will not have to concern ourselves about ready money. If we want to go on somewhere else from Jamaica, to Nassau in the Bahamas, say, or to New York, even to South America, anywhere, we can do it at once without all the boring business of sending cables to banks in London and waiting for them to telegraph us our own money.'

Arabella paused for a moment before she replied. She always kept a few hundred pounds in cash in the safe of her house, and she also had several blank bank drafts in her desk. But this seemed a huge sum to seek on the eve of their wedding. How could Noel have suddenly thought he needed it? How long had he known he was short of money? Could she really believe that he had only discovered this that evening?

Just for a moment, a slight feeling of unease darkened her happiness, but it was gone almost instantly, as a cloud passing on the wind can momentarily dim the sun on even the brightest day.

After all, Noel was being absolutely frank with her. That

phrase of his, 'in all honesty', showed his total integrity. It seemed somehow typical of his moral code, his refusal to compromise; always, and at whatever personal cost, to follow the path of honour. How wrong Jamie had been in his assessment of him! Men so often seemed to form the most idiotic opinions about other men; a woman had intuition in these matters. Too often jealousy seemed to influence men's opinions of other men. It must be acutely embarrassing for any man of his honour and breeding to have to admit to his bride-to-be that he lacked money to pay for their honeymoon. Perhaps it augured well for their future relationship. From this beginning, they would always be honest with each other. Looked at like that, it was a splendid start.

'I'll give you a draft for that amount,' Arabella told him, making up her mind. 'But it is rather a lot. You see, Noel, I still tend to remember my childhood, when we hadn't any money. I can't bear to see it wasted.'

'I entirely agree, dear heart. But this will not be wasted. Of that, I can assure you.' Noel kissed her gently on the cheek.

Arabella pressed the bell for the butler to bring in the locked leather case in which she kept her bank statements and securities. She opened the case, selected a blank draft, wrote the sum of '£15,000, cash, payable to bearer', signed it, and waved the heavy paper to let the ink dry. Then she handed the draft to Noel.

'I love you,' he said hoarsely. 'I love you.'

At that moment, he almost did. Her trust and her prodigal generosity had touched him.

'And I love you,' Arabella assured him.

They kissed again. This time, when Noel kissed her lips, he kept his mouth tightly closed.

'We must save something for tomorrow,' he said, half joking, in case she wondered at his lack of ardour.

'Of course.'

He went downstairs, let himself out, walked round to the Connaught. The man with the Guards tie was sitting in his chair, still reading his newspaper.

'Come up to my room,' Noel told him brusquely.

The fellow had been right. He couldn't argue in front of people coming and going. Their transaction must be carried out in private.

They went up in the elevator, standing well apart, not looking at each other. Noel led the way along the corridor, opened the door of his suite, went inside. His visitor followed him in. The bed had been neatly turned down. Fresh flowers bloomed in cut-glass vases in the sitting room; bottles of whisky, gin and seltzer waters, a bowl of ice cubes, were laid out tantalisingly on a side table. Noel turned to the man.

'Here's a draft for fifteen thousand pounds, payable to bearer.'

The man examined it closely, held it up to the light to check the watermark. 'My principal is only asking for eleven,' he pointed out cautiously.

'I know he is, but this is going into my bank account tomorrow. I'll give you a cheque for eleven now, dated tomorrow.'

'I cannot accept a cheque, sir, I have already told you that. My orders are to collect cash or a draft. No cheques.'

'Then you'll have to give yourself new orders. It is my cheque now or nothing. And if you send a bailiff to the church, I will make sure that the Press all know exactly how the North London Loan Accommodation Company does business. When a client wishes to repay a loan, you will not accept it.'

'I will have to speak to my principal.'

'Telephone him, then, but be quick about it.'

The man asked the operator for a number and held the mouthpiece up to his lips. A whispered conversation began. Noel crossed the room, poured himself a whisky and seltzer. The man finished his call.

'All right,' he said. 'We will make an exception this time. But I have to make certain you understand that if the cheque is not honoured before your marriage, we will dun you on the church steps. No more warnings, no further chances.'

Noel crossed to the desk, took out his cheque book, wrote a cheque for £11,000.

'Take your bloody money!' he said angrily. 'I hope you rot in hell!'

'Thank you, sir. And I hope, for your sake, that this cheque is not referred to drawer.'

'It won't be.'

'Then I will wish you good night.'

The man looked longingly at the bottles on the table, but Noel didn't offer him a drink, so he went out and closed the door quietly behind him.

Noel sat down. His heart was beating very quickly; his hands trembled, and he felt sweat dampen his back. He poured himself another whisky, drank it greedily. That had been a damned close-run thing. He must pay in the draft tomorrow or this bastard would ruin him. He'd send the draft round with a pageboy to the bank first thing in the morning, as soon as it opened.

Even so, he would be uneasy throughout the wedding ceremony in case there was some unexpected hold-up in clearing it and that swine actually had a bailiff at the church. What a humiliation that would be! How could he possibly explain it to Arabella – or to anyone? He couldn't, of course. If that happened, he was finished. The deaths of two wives, the courtship of another against all his unnatural instincts would have been totally in vain.

He poured himself a third whisky, larger than the first two together, and sat looking at the draft until the figures on the paper and the scrolled writing became blurred and fuzzy.

Noel shook himself awake. He had work to do, his clothes to

pack. By noon tomorrow he would have a rich wife and a valet to pack for him. And then, if he played his cards well, he would never know what lack of money could mean.

Just for a moment, as he pondered on this infinitely agreeable prospect, he thought of Arabella. But the face that swam mistily before his eyes was not her face. To his horror, it was the face of another woman, reflected in the mirror of a Monte Carlo hotel room.

TWENTY

Jamaica by Banana Boat

Arabella had decided to go to Jamaica for her honeymoon not so much for the obvious attractions of an island in almost perpetual sunshine, surrounded by a warm ocean, but for a business reason. She used considerable quantities of pineapple juice and coconut oil from Jamaica in several of her beauty preparations, and in dealing with the suppliers, she had learned something about the banana trade, with which several of them were also involved.

In the sixteenth century, Spanish colonists brought banana plants to the Caribbean from the Canary Islands. For the next three hundred and fifty years or so, bananas were grown in Jamaica largely as animal fodder. Then, in the year that diamonds were discovered in South Africa, the captain of an American merchant ship found that he could turn a useful profit on every cargo of bananas he carried from Port Antonio, on the north coast of Jamaica, to Boston.

Captain Lorenzo Dow Baker made this discovery largely by chance. He was returning to the United States out of ballast, and filled his ship's empty holds with bunches of green bananas, bought very cheaply, and only useful to him because of their weight.

On the voyage north, the bananas ripened – and he sold them for $2,000 profit. What he had done once, he knew he could do again, and he did, many times. The demand for ripe bananas soon increased so dramatically that in order to meet it, he had to reorganise Jamaica's rather haphazard attitude towards growing and collecting the fruit.

Soon he needed more ships to carry bananas to Boston, but did not like to see them return empty and unprofitably. To remedy this, the captain advertised cheap fares for passengers to go to Jamaica for holidays or for health reasons, or both. Then he found he had to acquire suitable accommodation for the travellers – and the Jamaican tourist business had begun.

Arabella admired his enterprise and had the intention of investing in this trade herself, and possibly expanding it. A natural progression would be to build hotels in Jamaica where tourists from the States could be accommodated at preferential rates – as long as they travelled by certain ships. And if these visitors liked the island, would it not also be possible to sell or rent plots of land to them so that they could build houses for themselves, either for holidays or retirement? Or, even better, Arabella could build the houses, and then sell them to the visitors.

This would mean establishing a property and building company. And once that was in operation, why not add a large convalescent home where patients recovering from operations or illnesses could be looked after – for a price – in the sun, on the edge of the sea?

The possibilities, like the permutations, seemed endless, and because Arabella wanted to examine Jamaica's potential personally, and not trust to the judgement of locals she did not know, and with whose conclusions she might not agree, she had booked passages for Noel and herself aboard a banana boat.

The captain was waiting for them as they came up the gangway. He bowed obsequiously. He knew the continually growing extent of Arabella's wealth, and had received a special directive from the directors of the line to do everything in his power to make the voyage enjoyable for her and her new husband.

'Warmest congratulations, my lord,' the captain said to Noel, who nodded briefly. His eyes roamed the deck as though looking for someone.

'It's not often we have a bridal couple aboard,' the captain went on sonorously. 'A great honour, and a very lucky happening for the ship, if I may say so.'

'You may,' Noel replied shortly. He had been drinking too much champagne; this always made him sharp in his responses. Why couldn't this bloody old fool shut up?

The captain led them along the deck to their cabin. The ship had limited accommodation for passengers, and they had the best, on the top deck.

A middle-aged stewardess was waiting outside the door. She curtseyed to Arabella, opened the door wide. Two cabins, extending across the ship, one portside, the other starboard, had been thrown into one by opening communicating doors. One cabin was made into a stateroom, with chairs; the other cabin would be their bedroom. The stateroom, facing them, was banked with flowers: red roses, carnations, daffodils and, in the centre, a vast bouquet of orchids.

'With the compliments of the directors,' said the captain brightly.

'I am overwhelmed,' said Arabella. 'Thank you – and them – so much. I never expected anything like this.'

'It is our pleasure, your ladyship. If you require anything at all, please see the stewardess. And now, if you will excuse me.' He bowed, clicked his heels and went up to the bridge.

The cabin walls were elegantly panelled with mahogany. Brass fittings around the portholes, and the taps in the bathroom, had been polished until they gleamed like melting gold.

Porters carried up their luggage. On Noel's cases, his initials were surmounted by a tiny gold coronet. Arabella smiled to herself. She had come a long way since the Silent Witness and Kimberley; hopefully, the best part of the journey still lay ahead.

In one corner of the stateroom stood a table, with a bottle of champagne in a silver ice bucket.

'Let's drink to the future,' said Noel. He advanced on the bottle, expertly removed the gold foil.

'I think you've had enough to drink already,' said Arabella. 'I know I have.'

'A day without wine is like a day without sunshine,' retorted Noel. 'And you can't ever have too much champagne. It is the wine of the gods.'

Noel withdrew the cork, poured out two glasses, offered one to Arabella.

She shook her head. 'I have had all I want.'

'Then I'll drink yours, too.' He did so.

'You are replacing the cork?' Arabella asked him.

'Why? Once a bottle of bubbly has been opened, it must be drunk.'

'Not the whole bottle, surely?'

'Why ever not? I think I can manage that quite easily. But if I can't, I'll chuck it over the side.'

'Why not give it to the stewardess? Let her have a treat.'

'Why should I? She's paid, isn't she? Why do you keep on needling me like this?'

'I'm not needling you. I'm simply saying that rather than waste more than half a bottle of champagne, you might as well give it to someone who'd appreciate it.'

'How do you know she would? She may be a teetotaller, signed the pledge. I'd forgotten . . .' he said, and paused.

'What have you forgotten?' Arabella asked him.

'That you and she must have so much in common. She's cleaning out our cabins and you used to clean out a public house – or so you told me.'

'What about it? There's nothing to be ashamed of in that. Do you know what George Herbert said?'

'I don't give a damn what he said, whoever he was.'

'I was given a book of his verses once as a prize at school. He was a religious poet. He wrote, "Who sweeps a room as for Thy laws, makes that and the action fine." '

'Some penny-a-liner hack, I suppose.'

'You suppose wrongly. He was the younger brother of Lord Herbert of Cherbury. Perhaps that makes him more acceptable to you?'

'It makes me think you are a little prig, quoting stuff like that.'

Arabella shrugged her shoulders. It was foolish to argue like this; he didn't mean to hurt her. It was just his way.

'Anyhow, it's wrong to throw away something someone else would be glad – and grateful – to have.'

'Wrong? What can possibly be wrong about chucking out half a bottle of flat bubbly?'

'Well, wasteful, then.'

Noel looked at her coolly for a moment, then crossed the room, opened the far porthole and flung the bottle out into the sea. He smiled at her triumphantly, almost cruelly, as though he enjoyed going against her wishes.

'Waste is relative, my dear Arabella. Always remember, there's plenty more champagne where that came from. Whole vineyards of grapes just waiting to be pressed.'

Arabella looked at Noel, surprised, and momentarily thought of asking him who would pay for this. Was it coming out of the £15,000 she had lent him? But she said nothing. It seemed petty and ridiculous to argue over the cost of a bottle of champagne at the start of their life together. Noel was probably tense and tired after the wedding and the reception. Perhaps she was, too. She forced from her mind the unworthy thought that perhaps Jamie was right, or at least might have some right on his side, when he had told her why he did not like Noel. She could not face such questions now, let alone dare to answer them.

She went into the bedroom, took off her hat, shook out her hair. Noel followed her as far as the doorway and stood watching her, a glass of champagne in one hand. The pose seemed somehow familiar. Who else had she ever seen who stood in this vaguely insolent and somehow menacing way? Then she remembered. The young men going to the wedding at Exchange Station; Orlando. They were from the same class; she hoped they were not also the same type.

'I thought the bridegroom carried his bride over the threshold of their new home,' she said, half joking, trying to ease what had suddenly become a moment of tension. Watching Noel's reflection in the dressing-table mirror for his reaction, she saw his facial muscles tighten. His eyes darkened briefly and then he was smiling again, ready with an instant and plausible explanation.

'I wouldn't call this our home, darling,' he said, almost chidingly.

'It is, temporarily.'

Why was he so cold, so aloof, so strange, when before they were married he had been so attentive? Noel sat down heavily in one of the two chairs in the stateroom. Champagne slopped from his glass into his lap. He put down the glass on the floor with the exaggerated care of someone slightly fuddled by drink. He brushed the spilled champagne from his trousers with his fingers, then licked them. Arabella looked away.

Bells clanged importantly, a siren blew. The little ship began to tremble as her propeller started to revolve. Noel and Arabella felt the floor dip slightly beneath their feet as the banana boat turned to meet the tide. They were on their way.

Arabella looked out through the porthole and saw the sheds and warehouses of Southampton docks slide slowly past. Men were walking along the quayside; a child stood on a bollard to wave to them. Those people might all live by the sea, she thought, and to them ships were so commonplace they took them for granted. Yet none were likely to have the chance of sailing to Jamaica, as she was doing. And from Jamaica, as Noel had said, they could go anywhere. The whole world could be their playground. Nowhere was too remote or too exotic. Her money was the key to a world of enchantment.

Again, she remembered the money she had advanced to her husband. Such a sum could take them round the globe several times; it was far in excess of what they could ever conceivably spend on any honeymoon, however protracted, however extravagant. Why, then, had Noel asked for so much? The reason he had given – that he would not wish to be involved with transferring money during their trip, because he wanted to devote every moment to her – had seemed intensely flattering in London. Now, Arabella was not quite so sure. When did a loan become a gift? And could such a gift, extracted on a false premise, become a point of contention between them?

Noel stood up, crossed the room shakily, banged the empty glass down on the table with such force that the stem shattered.

'Damn!' he said crossly. 'Could have cut myself badly, then. For the price I'm paying, they should give us proper glasses.'

Arabella bit back a correction: he was not paying for anything; she was paying for everything. 'You have had too much to drink,' she said instead. 'Why don't you have a seltzer water and lie down for a bit?'

'No. I'll go out on deck and say goodbye to England.'

'I'll join you,' said Arabella, trying to be pleasant.

'No,' he told her sharply. 'You stay here.'

'Why? I want to come with you.'

'I want you to stay here. Have a rest. You've been doing too much.'

Noel lurched out of the door, clumsily pulled it shut behind him. He could not tell his wife how, as he came up the gangway, he had seen a young steward look out of a porthole, perhaps sizing up the arriving passengers, to calculate what tips they might give.

Their eyes had met. Instantly, each recognised the other's potential. Noel recalled with admiration and growing lust, fuelled by champagne, the steward's full moist lips, his soft cheeks, blond hair, the way he modestly lowered his long-lashed eyes rather than meet Noel's bold, demanding gaze.

He would find the lad – which should present little problem, for the ship was small. He would exchange a few words with the fellow; size him up, but discreetly, of course. Very discreetly. Oscar Wilde had put their feelings brilliantly, poor devil: the love that dare not speak its name.

As far as Noel was concerned, his feelings could never be dignified by the name of love. He wanted boys and and pretty young men just as he wanted champagne: to satisfy a continuing need. When he had drunk a magnum, he would not keep the bottle. There was no reason to do so. He had exhausted the experience; it was time to move on to the next magnum, the next wager, the next conquest. When a compliant male companion had fulfilled his purpose, then, like the empty bottle, he was instantly expendable.

Noel walked slowly along the bleached and scrubbed deck planks with the narrow strips of black pitch between each one, and stood as close to the bows as he could reach. Ahead of him, railed off, were winches, neat coils of rope, and then the bow rail, rising and falling slightly as the banana boat met the incoming tide. The salty smell of the sea was very strong.

'Excuse me, my lord, but I think the view is possibly better from the other side.'

Noel turned. The young steward he had seen at the porthole was standing just behind him. He must have followed him along the deck. The implication behind this made Noel's heart leap and his throat contract with lust. The steward was beautifully slim, his hands soft and tapering, his face slightly flushed, as though not quite sure how this aristocratic passenger would react to being addressed by someone so obviously his social inferior.

Noel smiled, relishing his power, the authority and confidence his wife's wealth gave him.

'How kind,' he said, and his voice sounded thick with longing. 'Are you looking after me on this voyage?'

'I regret I am not, sir. It would have been my pleasure.'

'And mine,' Noel assured him truthfully.

They both smiled knowingly. But still nothing had been said, nothing had passed between them except a few impersonal remarks exchanged on a windy deck. Each could now draw back, and that would be the end of the matter. But Noel wanted this to be the beginning. The voyage would last for at least a week. This lovely creature could make it seven days he would remember and treasure, and relive time and again with pleasure.

Noel opened his wallet, selected a £5 note with infinite care, rubbing it between his finger and thumb, as though one note was somehow superior to another. Then he folded it neatly into the size of a postage stamp. The steward stood, watching him, almost at attention, his hands by his side.

He did not move when Noel offered him the note, so Noel pressed it gently but firmly – oh, the delicate language of that thrusting movement! – into his right hand. In doing so, he brushed the back of his own hand against the front of the steward's trousers. The steward would not have made such an obvious gesture towards Noel, but then he could not afford to do so. If he had read the signs wrongly, such a movement could easily cost him his job, if nothing worse. Noel had no such consideration in his mind.

'Thank you, my lord,' said the steward, and now his voice

also seemed thick and strange. 'You are most generous.'

As he spoke, he took a fraction of a step forward so that Noel's hand was now pressing more closely against his body. Beneath the thin cloth of the man's trousers, Noel could feel the beat of his phallus, a steady tell-tale hardening against his hand.

They stood thus for a moment. Then the steward, realising his value, and having no intention of debasing the currency – it was always folly to give too much too soon for too little, and especially to such a rich client – took a step back.

'If you will excuse me, my lord, I have to check my cabins. I am on B deck, the one below this. I saw you standing here and thought you might like to know what the various landmarks are.'

'Actually, I know what they are,' Noel assured him.

He smiled and the steward smiled back. Then the man turned and walked away. Noel watched his slightly swinging hips until he was out of sight. Then he also walked back along the deck, out of the freshening breeze.

While Arabella sat in the stateroom, the stewardess unpacked her luggage, hung up her dresses expertly in the wardrobe, put lavender sachets between her silk underclothes in the chest of drawers. Finally, she placed Arabella's black leather jewel case, gold-edged with a gold lock, on her dressing table, bowed, and withdrew.

What should she wear tonight for dinner? Arabella wondered. She decided on a black dress which would show off her diamond necklace and her diamond earrings. She had, of course, the choice of several necklaces, all diamond. Not quite certain which one she should select, she crossed the room, took a gold key from her handbag, opened the case.

Her jewels were neatly arranged in padded trays, each lined with red velvet. She lifted out the first tray and the second, and suddenly realised that, almost unconsciously, she was searching for something she could not see. She was looking for the diamond earrings.

She always kept them in a special little box which she had had made for them, which fitted inside the jewel case. Now the box was empty. She shook it in case, absurdly, incredibly, the earrings could somehow have slipped behind the red plush lining. They had not; they were missing. Someone must have stolen them – but deliberately, not casually, because they had left the box behind. A casual thief would not have been able to unlock this box without her key, or at least a duplicate. He would have taken the whole box, forced it open, extracted the contents and then thrown the box into the sea.

Arabella looked up and caught sight of her face in the mirror. She was drawn and pale; a terrible thought had just crossed her mind. She could guess who might have taken the earrings. But she could not think why.

Noel walked slowly along B deck, glancing with deliberate casualness through windows and portholes on his right, into cabins not nearly as luxurious as those on the top deck, and of course nothing like as opulent as his suite. He walked to the stern, paused for a moment, and then retraced his steps.

As he passed one cabin door, he saw a face framed in the porthole. The steward. He was smiling at him.

'A good way of getting some exercise, walking on deck, my lord. Gets up an appetite, I always say.'

The cabin door was open now.

'I've not seen this class of cabin before,' said Noel, as though this was why he had stopped.

'Of course, it's not nearly so nice as yours, my lord, not so luxurious, but they're very well done. Would you like to come inside and see round it?'

Noel went in. There were two single beds; a table between

373

them, with reading lights; chintz curtains on a brass rail at each side of the round portholes.

'If I pull the curtains, sir, like this, it makes it seem much more cosy, don't you think? Some people like to lie in bed asleep in the afternoon. And they can't do that with the light in their eyes, can they?'

'Are you one of them?' Noel asked him gently.

The steward smiled. He was an impudent devil, thought Noel. Why was it that these low-class people were so confoundedly attractive to him? But then why did other men go for blousy tarts and whores with dyed hair and blood-red rouge on chancred lips? It was the roughness, the dirt, that drew them like flies to a pot of poisoned honey.

Both men knew exactly what was going to happen, but the steward was surprised that a lord had come after him so quickly. Usually, his special passengers, as he called them, managed to stay away from him for at least a couple of days, and then, in mid-Atlantic, when their wives were seasick, they would seek him out. This man was different. Clearly, he wanted it badly. He would therefore make him pay the highest price he could for what he wanted.

'Can I get anything for you, my lord?' the steward asked solicitously, no echo of his thoughts in his voice, faintly hesitant, obsequious, anxious to please.

'No,' said Noel. He glanced down at his trousers. He could plainly see the slight bulge of his own rising, hardening phallus. The steward followed his gaze.

'Oh!' he said appreciatively. 'You *are* a naughty man. I didn't know lords felt like that.'

'Not about ladies,' retorted Noel, and smiled. Such was his need that the smile was more like a grimace, a faint baring of his teeth.

He held out his hand in a gesture of imperative command. The steward bowed as he undid Noel's flies. Noel performed the same service for him, all in silence, without apparent haste, yet with the speed of long practice.

They stood in the room, a faint breeze ruffling the curtains, holding each other's phalluses in splendid erection. Noel felt faint with lust, and pressed his cheek against the steward's forehead and then kissed him on the lips. The same pulse now beat like a warning drum in their swollen throbbing veins. Noel stood for a further moment, while the flesh on his body prickled with desire, as though pierced by a mass of sharp needle points or electric shocks. Then he was tearing off his clothes, and so was the steward, as though time was running against them both in a roaring, raging tide which they must overcome at once or die.

The steward flung himself down naked on the bed, then, as Noel came behind to mount him, the man turned to face him.

'How much are you paying me for this?' he asked coolly.

The question shocked Noel. He had imagined that their attraction was mutual. He was so vain he had never considered that to the steward this coupling could simply be a commercial transaction, the trade of a harlot, and as such, worthy of a harlot's price. Noel felt his penis begin to droop. This fellow was too mercenary. He must not become involved; all the signals warned of danger ahead.

'I don't mean money,' the steward said quickly, sensing Noel's reaction. He had been unwise to mention the subject of payment at such a tense moment, but the passenger would either pay or he wouldn't. It was all right for these rich people to carry on as they did without any thought for those who ministered to their needs.

'I meant something else altogether. Something *personal*, just between us. So I can keep it and remember you. Perhaps a wristwatch, cuff links.'

'No,' said Noel sharply. He could not possibly give him his cuff links or his watch. They could be traced back to him so easily. And there would be only one reason why a lord, recently married to a millionairess, would give a ship's steward so expensive a gift only hours after his wedding. Then he remembered the earrings.

He had removed them from the box in Arabella's jewel case, not with this in mind, but simply to keep as security, evidence that he was not without funds, should he need credit in a hurry for a bet or to settle up a bill in a bar. But why did he need such evidence? Who could doubt his wealth now?

He had been able to fool Emily about his sexual inclinations because her innocence had been his protection. But Arabella would not be so innocent; few women with her looks could be. She would make demands of him, and he did not want to meet them. The thought of coupling with her, of feeling soft breasts, hardening nipples, wiry pubic hair and that warm, wet, waiting mouth that never closed; all this repulsed him. He had to have someone; he knew that, and her earrings could buy him the person he needed. He felt in his jacket pocket, pulled them out.

'What about these?' he asked.

'Oh, they *are* lovely,' said the steward. 'Put them in my pocket, dearie, and then put whatever you've got in your hand into the place it should go.' He put out his own hand, stroked Noel slowly, expertly. His phallus began to rise, to harden.

'Now,' the steward commanded. 'Now. Quickly. *Hard*. I love it that way.'

As he spoke, he drew his knees up under him so that he seemed like a runner straining at the mark.

Then Noel was on him with the strength of a wild beast. Animal fashion, Adam his guide, he thrust with all the despair of a lonely man who had at last found a friend, as though by his sheer exertions he could discover the secret that others had for so long denied him.

* * *

Noel went into the bar, ordered a bottle of champagne, drank two glasses quickly, greedily, one after the other. He examined his face in the engraved mirror behind the bar. There was nothing in the reflection that showed what he had done, he told himself thankfully. Nothing at all. He might be slightly tired, but then he had just got married and was facing all the responsibilities of matrimony. That was surely enough to weary any man.

Suddenly, Noel pushed the bottle from him. The champagne repeated in his stomach; he felt bile, bitter as wormwood, on his tongue. The barman polished glasses, set them out neatly in rows, upside down, in front of the bottles with their cheerful, brightly coloured labels for rum, whisky, anise. All the time, he watched Noel without appearing to do so. He had seen too many like him; one sniff of the barman's apron, and they got obstreperous and wanted to fight everyone.

'Shall I keep it on ice for you, my lord?' he asked Noel deferentially.

'No, drink it yourself, if you want. My wife says it's wrong to waste the stuff.'

'How right she is, my lord. And thank you, indeed.'

As he watched Noel go out of the bar, the barman wondered about him, what it would be like to be rich, to be a lord. Still, he reflected, there were quite a few perks in being a ship's barman in a first-class lounge. Most of his customers had no idea whether they were being served full measure or short measure or, indeed, any measure at all. It was absurdly easy to fake the strength of a gin and Indian tonic water by freezing the tonic water. Like many barmen aboard passenger ships, he had brought his own bottles, which he kept hidden beneath the counter. Using them, he need not make money for his employers every time he served a drink, but for himself. Lord Doncaster's champagne would bring him a quid or two. He never drank himself: that was for suckers, not wise men. He began to hum cheerfully as he polished his glasses.

Noel went along the deck, tried the door of his cabin. It was locked.

He called: 'Open up!'

He heard a key turn in the lock, lurched into the room.

'Where have you been?' Arabella asked him.

'Just walking. Looking at things.'

'You've been quite a time.'

'Not really. A matter of moments.'

'A matter of three quarters of an hour.'

'Well, in a lifetime, darling, what is that? Nothing. A fraction of a second against a whole life.'

'Yes, maybe, but we are married.'

'Just married.'

'You might have come back and asked if I wanted to walk with you.'

'You were busy unpacking your things.'

'The stewardess did that for me. And I have just made a terrible discovery.'

'You have? What is that, my dearest heart?'

Concern showed on Noel's face. He hoped his voice carried the right amount of interest. He shook his head sadly, put out his hands, took her bare arms as tenderly as he was able. How soft and small her muscles felt after the arms of the steward.

'Now tell me,' he said gently. 'We must share everything.'

'Of course,' Arabella replied, instantly mollified. How she loved this man! He had the astonishing gift of soothing her apprehensions, of making her feel warm towards him and therefore generous towards the whole world. And surely, for this to happen, he must feel the same way about her? It was absurd to have doubts about him. Such thoughts were not only disloyal to her husband, they were totally unfounded, utterly ridiculous.

'It's my earrings,' she said.

'Your earrings? What about them?'

378

'They were in my box, in my jewel case, but they've gone.'

'*Gone*? How could they have gone? I mean, that case is locked, isn't it?'

'Yes. But the key was in the drawer here.'

'Even so, it's most unlikely anyone could get in here and take it. You've been here ever since we came aboard. I was here with you myself, until I went out. So who could it have been? The stewardess, do you think?'

'Oh, no. She is a most honest person. I can see that in her face.'

'You're certain you've not put them somewhere else?'

'Absolutely certain.'

'Well, it must have been *someone*.'

'That's what I am going to tell the purser and then the captain.'

'What good will that do?'

'Possibly none. On the other hand, it might just result in their being returned. They should know if they've any member of the crew who's been lightfingered before. And what else can I do – except sit here and do nothing?

'When I sailed to Cape Town, someone aboard that ship accused me of stealing these earrings. That was a lie, of course, but he threatened to tell the captain, and have the whole ship searched before whoever had them was able to throw them overboard. I had no money or power then to order such a search myself, but I have now. And I will.'

'Of course. But tell me, how were the earrings discovered then?'

'Oh,' Arabella replied enigmatically, 'they turned up.'

'Perhaps they will now?'

'I intend to make sure they do, have no fear.'

Arabella reached out to press a bell button for the stewardess. Noel gently but firmly gripped her hand before she reached it.

379

'Don't,' he said gently. 'I think it's unwise.'

'Unwise? Whatever do you mean? What other suggestion have you got?'

'Let me think a moment,' said Noel. His mind, fogged by alcohol, was churning like a demented mill race. If they found the earrings on the steward – and they could easily do so, for he had them in his pocket – the man might turn nasty. To save himself, he might say why he had them, even, heaven forbid, why Lord Doncaster had given them to him. Noel would deny it strenuously, of course, but for all he knew, the steward could have an accomplice as a witness, perhaps in the bathroom, listening. Someone might even have been under the bed; it was not the first time for the steward, and he had been very quick – much too quick – to ask for a fee. Fear tore at Noel's heart with claws of terror; sweat beaded his forehead.

'Are you all right?' Arabella asked him anxiously.

'Yes,' he assured her. 'Just terribly concerned. And I've got a better idea than telling the captain. I saw a young fellow walk past our cabin, very slowly, just after I went out.'

'You did? Did he come in?'

'I can't say. But I looked again and he wasn't there. I thought he must have gone into a cabin further up. But it could have been ours.'

'Well? Who was this fellow?'

'Oh, one of the crew. A steward, a sailor, someone in uniform. But I had a good view of his face. I'd know him again, all right. Before you make a fuss – which will obviously cause very bad feeling among those of the crew who are innocent, and I don't know what resentment among other passengers – just let me see if I can find this man and ask him if he saw anyone coming in.'

'You think he stole them?'

'I don't think anything – yet. I'll tell you what I think if I can find him – and that shouldn't be too difficult, should it? Then

I might at least be able to eliminate him from inquiries, as the police say. He may have seen someone.'

'All right,' she said, not wholly convinced by this argument. 'Do that. Then, if he can't help, I'll get on to the captain.'

Noel went out of the room, along the deck. A cool breeze blew off the open, heavy sea, and the banana boat was beginning to roll. He felt the wind chill on his wet forehead, and wondered whether he would be sick. The champagne still felt sour in his belly. He went down the stairs to B deck, walked slowly along, looking into all the cabin windows. The steward was making a bed in another cabin. Noel went in to see him.

'We can't do it again, my lord,' said the steward quickly. 'Not here. I have to go down to the lounge. I'm on duty. I can't . . . I *want* to . . . Oh, my God, I *want* to. Just looking at you makes me hard as a brick, but I can't.'

'Listen,' said Noel urgently, ignoring these remarks, not believing them, knowing his whole future could hinge on how this creature reacted. 'Those earrings. Give them back.'

'But they were a present. You *gave* them to me. They're our special thing, just between us.'

'Give them back, or I'll take them back.'

Fear sharpened Noel's voice. The man looked him up and down, his eyes cold and hostile as a serpent's. Noel stood six foot four against the steward's five foot six.

'If I do, then we won't have *anything* between us now, my lord. Nothing. You give and you take away. When I was living in Portsmouth a friend told me a story about a sailor who took a girl up the hill. On the way up, she saw a pretty bonnet in a shop. She said, "I'd love that." He said, "You'll have it – afterwards." But when they came down the hill, after he'd had his way with her, he wouldn't give it to her. And she asked, "Why? You promised." And he said: "I'll tell you something, dearie. When I'm hard, I'm soft, and when I'm soft, I'm hard."

You're like that, are you then? Well, take your bloody earrings, my lord!'

'I'll give you ten pounds,' said Noel.

'Ten pounds? How *generous*, your lordship! Those earrings are worth at least a hundred nicker, probably two hundred. Why the rush to get them back? Does the owner want them? Maybe your *wife* wants them, does she?'

The spasm of pain and horror that crossed Noel's face showed the steward he was on the right course. He had this weak, randy bastard now, and he'd never let him go.

'Twenty,' said Noel flatly. 'It's all I have on me.'

'For a start that'll do, dearie,' said the steward, suddenly smiling. 'For a start.'

He took out the earrings, threw them on the bed. Noel scooped them up, put them in his pocket, gave the steward two £10 notes. The steward turned.

'Charley!' he called softly.

Another steward came out of the bathroom. He had been washing his hands in the basin, and he was smiling as he wiped them dry on a white towel.

'Charley knows about us,' the steward explained to Noel. The second steward stood, his head on one side, regarding Noel. He pursed his lips, patted them with his hand and made a kissing sound.

Noel said nothing; there was nothing to say.

'Actually, my lord, Charley was in the bathroom in the other cabin. You see, my lord, we know our rights. We know how far we can go – and how far our clients can go. And I would say, with the greatest respect, my lord, we both regard this twenty pounds as just a down payment for much, much more.'

Noel almost ran back to the relative safety of his cabin. Blackmail! And so early in the voyage, on the very first day of his honeymoon. Those two fellows had done this before. He wasn't the first, that was all too clear. He wondered how much they'd want to keep their mouths shut. What an idiot he had been not to check the steward was alone when he first accosted him in the cabin. But he had thought the fellow was genuinely attracted to him. He was a bloody fool! A quick look in the bathroom and he'd have never gone on with it.

It would be two against one in court, but it must never come near any court. He would buy them off, threaten them, do anything to be free of them. It would cost a bit of money, of course, but money was nothing to him now. And if he did not pay their price, the cost would be ruinous. But what would the price be? Was there ever a last price for a blackmailer?

He went into the cabin.

'Did you find the fellow?' Arabella asked him.

'Yes.'

'Did he see anyone come into our cabin?'

'No,' Noel replied, 'but he did come in here himself.'

'Why?'

'Oh, a general check-up, I suppose. He's a young steward. This is very nearly his first voyage.'

'What's that got to do with it?'

'He thought it was dangerous your leaving the earrings lying about. He took them to give to the stewardess later.'

'Rubbish! You mean he stole them. Anyhow, they weren't lying about as he says. They were locked up.'

'Well, you've got them back.'

'Thanks to you. But I'm not going to let it rest there. We'll see what the captain has to say.'

'Listen, my darling,' said Noel, forcing the words out of his mouth with an urgency and sincerity he did not know he could command. 'You think – and I agree – that this young man may have taken those earrings not entirely as he claims. We might not be able to prove that in a court of law, but then we don't need to. He says he did it for the best of reasons. I don't know if this is so or not. What matters is that you have the earrings back. And, in addition, we have so much in our lives for which we should be thankful. We have love, we have money, we have trust.

'The steward, on the other hand, tells me he is an orphan with an ill grandmother to support, a sister who is in an insane asylum. I have more experience with servants and those of the servant class than you, Arabella. I think I know how these people act – and react. I think that probably he was tempted. It was not premeditated, possibly just an act of supreme folly that could have cost him not only his job, but his whole livelihood.

'I know what temptation is, my dear one. I was tempted when I first saw you outside the Connaught. Remember that moment? I was tempted then to take you in my arms, to smother you with kisses, to say I loved you – because I did – and I do. But it would have been wrong then.'

'It wouldn't,' said Arabella fiercely. 'It would have been *right*.'

'Well, I have my whole life to say that now. And let us not start our married life, our love together, with an attack, an accusation, on some poor wretched person who probably earns less in a year than we can spend in an hour. Let us show mercy, now and always, to others who are less fortunate. You quoted some poet to me a little while ago. Let me quote the greatest poet of them all. Remember what the Bard said? "The quality of mercy is not strain'd; it droppeth as the gentle rain from heaven upon the place beneath—" '

'All right,' Arabella interrupted him. 'I will do nothing more about this matter. I agree, it would be wrong to start our marriage on a bad note, but I must say, Noel, you are the only person in all the world who could ever make me take this view over such an obvious act of theft. You know something?'

'About what, dear heart?'

'About you. Because of your nobleness of spirit, you have changed my whole attitude towards money and people and possessions. Your love has quickened my whole life. I feel I am not worthy of you.'

'My dear heart, how absurd that is. It is I who do not deserve you, and the sheer happiness of just being close to you, loving you.'

Noel took her in his arms. Closing his eyes, and swallowing hard against his total animal revulsion, but sweating with relief that he had extricated himself from a potentially ruinous situation, he kissed Arabella gently on her lips.

TWENTY-ONE

A Spy in the Making

For the Germans in Lüderitz, the third week in July, 1908, had been the most impressive, if exhausting week they could remember. No less a person than His Excellency the State Secretary, Bernhard Dernburg, a director of the illustrious Darmstadter Bank, had been making a tour of inspection of the diamond fields.

The German government in Berlin had for some time been concerned about the cost of subsidising their South West African colony. Thousands of troops had to be paid for, provisioned and garrisoned; the railway line from Aus to Lüderitz had been unexpectedly expensive to build, continual sand storms made it difficult to maintain; and all with apparently little prospect of immediate and sustained return.

The government felt that if a man already successful in business, and now appointed State Secretary, paid the colony a personal visit, he might be able to propose ways of reducing the constant expenditure and even to suggest plans that would enable it to be run on a profitable basis. The sooner the colony could be made self-sufficient, the better for all concerned. That, in essence, was the reason for the State Secretary's visit.

News of his imminent arrival spurred the citizens of Lüderitz to present the area in the best possible light. The streets were cleaned. Tens of thousands of discarded beer and mineral-water bottles were collected and buried in the desert outside the town. A special train, decorated with laurels and imperial flags, took the State Secretary and his colleagues from Lüderitz up north to Keetmanshoop for a banquet, and to meet local dignitaries. All Germans living there were requested to wear white suits in honour of the visit.

Everyone was presented to him in strict order of seniority and importance. Officials formed a line up on one side, German settlers and farmers on the other. The State Secretary's carriage stopped exactly in the centre so that neither group could claim the other had received more favoured treatment.

Herr Stauch, as the moving figure behind diamond exploration and exploitation, decided to commemorate this auspicious occasion by presenting two gold caskets of diamonds to the visitor, with the request that he take them back to Berlin and present them to the Kaiser. Stauch had prudently found out by telegraph to the Kaiser's secretary whether His Imperial Majesty would accept such a gift. The Kaiser had been pleased to intimate that he would.

Now, glasses were raised, toasts drunk, as the State Secretary accepted the caskets, made of South African gold. The lid of the larger one had the Kaiser's imperial crown engraved on it. Inside was a second golden case, with the date engraved on its lid and the Southern Cross, marked out in seven diamonds. In this smaller box, Stauch had placed twenty diamonds from Kolmanskop, all exactly the same size, to mark twenty years of the Kaiser's reign.

Curiously enough, despite this impressive evidence of diamonds and their high quality, Herr Dernburg – not a man of great imagination – did not appear to accept Stauch's assurance that they could offer an important contribution towards the cost of the German outpost, or that a handful of them represented wealth on a prodigious scale. Dernburg was accustomed to financing deals involving such visibly solid investments as steel mills, textile factories, locomotive works. He found it difficult to realise that even greater profits could accrue so very much more easily from selling stones, some of which looked no larger than the head of a match.

While the State Secretary was meeting local dignitaries, speaking at *bierfeste* given in his honour, dutifully drinking glasses of water condensed from the sea, one of his colleagues, a Colonel Frischauer, was engaged in different and totally unpublicised activities.

He was a senior officer in the German Intelligence Service, and wished to make use of this official visit to recruit potential part-time agents, and to carry out his own assessment of the colony's chances of survival should any attempt be made by South Africa – or, more likely, by Britain through South Africa – to annex it in time of war.

Earlier, the German authorities in Windhoek had circularised all officials of a certain rank with a discreet and cautiously worded memorandum to the effect that Colonel Frischauer would be available to meet young men of good family and education, who were proficient in English, French and German, and who might wish to discuss secondment to a diplomatic mission.

There was apparently no one of this calibre in Kolmanskop or Lüderitz, but Colonel Frischauer had an appointment with the senior surgeon at Lüderitz Hospital. He knew the surgeon by reputation through a mutual friend in Berlin. After initial social pleasantries, the surgeon came to the heart of the matter.

'I understand, sir, that you are looking for people here who are at least bilingual, who might be able to render service – shall I say possibly of a secret nature – to His Imperial Majesty.'

Frischauer nodded.

'There is a male patient I have been keeping in a private house in Kolmanskop because I think, in certain circumstances, he could render a unique service to the Fatherland.'

'Indeed? Who is that?'

'An Englishman. The heir to a peerage and a fortune in property and estates in England.'

'So what is he doing out here? What is the nature of this man's illness?'

'He was emigrating to the Cape, Colonel, and became involved in some kind of argument aboard ship. As a result, he was either thrown or fell overboard – I think the former. He suffered a head injury in his fall from the top deck of the liner, which caused him – in layman's terms – to lose his memory. Fortunately for him, he was picked up shortly afterwards by one of our vessels on the way here, and has been under medical care ever since. He speaks a little German, and rambles on about his past in England, but generally appears to have no real knowledge of who he is. We have made our own inquiries, however, and know exactly who he is.'

'So how could he help us? He appears to be permanently incapacitated mentally, if I am following you correctly.'

'You are, Colonel. But my opinion is that his brain has not suffered irreversible damage.'

'How long has he been here?'

'A matter of some years.'

'Years?' The colonel's amazement showed in his voice. 'And he is still not showing any improvement in that time?'

'He is being kept heavily sedated. Largely, I must admit, in our own imperial interests, rather than the interests of his swift recovery.'

This reply puzzled Colonel Frischauer. What was the surgeon hinting at? How could keeping a shipwrecked English aristocrat in a kind of coma for so long help Germany? The colonel's bewilderment showed in his face.

'Let me elucidate, Colonel,' said the surgeon. 'In the event, which let us pray God does not come to pass, that a state of war

389

could ever be declared between our country and England, our position in this remote colony, in a continent largely under British suzerainty, could come under very serious threat.'

'I know that,' said the colonel testily.

'If there is such a war, then the South Africans, or the British, would doubtless seize this colony.'

'What can this man do to prevent that happening?'

'Nothing, sir. None of us here could do much with our present military resources to prevent that situation. But while this colony may appear bleak and inhospitable and largely desert to the visitor, under these shifting, feckless sands lies probably the world's largest source of diamonds. We have already removed a huge quantity, Colonel. Some have gone to Germany, but because it is important not to flood the market and so bring down the value of diamonds, more are kept stored here.

'In the event of war, we would attempt to get these out of the colony, perhaps to a neutral port, where they could be put to a more warlike purpose than decorating the necklaces of rich old women. I am sure that the South Africans know this, and so would attempt to commandeer the stones, worth millions of pounds sterling, before we could move them to a safe place. In the unhappy event of war or invasion on any other pretext, it might be possible for this patient – who is, remember, a British subject, son of a noble English family – to go to the Cape, suddenly and almost miraculously cured. There he would be welcomed, as in the Bible the father welcomed home his prodigal son. No one would imagine he was actually working for us – even if unknowingly. Or that on our instructions and under our direction, he was actually taking out with him diamonds worth millions of pounds.

'The Fatherland could use that money in sterling accounts in South Africa or elsewhere in the British Empire, even in London. You may recall, Colonel Frischauer, that Napoleon once said that a good spy was worth twenty thousand men in the field. I would suggest that in these circumstances, this Englishman, awoken like Rip Van Winkle from his long sleep, would be worth a hundred thousand men.'

'But how could he possibly do this if he has lost his memory?'

'Let me explain my plan, sir. Agreed, our treatment has obliterated his memories of his own country. But gradually we prescribed different drugs, and carefully fed into his brain a totally new set of associations. The end result is that while obviously British by birth, he will be German in outlook and allegiance.'

'Ah,' said Frischauer, beaming in admiration. 'A brilliant scheme.'

TWENTY-TWO

St Petersburg

The diamond buyer in Kimberley, the cutter in Amsterdam and the Russian émigré who dealt in diamonds in Hatton Garden had all given Jamie the same advice: go to Russia.

Now that Arabella had married, despite his opposition, and without even inviting him to her wedding – he had only read about it afterwards in *The Enquirer* – he decided that a journey to a new country, away from the familiar backgrounds of England and South Africa, would enable him to come to terms with the situation. Many brothers feel a sense of loss when a sister marries, but for a twin this can be traumatic. So it seemed to Jamie.

'In Russia you will find some of the greatest diamonds in the world decorating the necks and ears of the grand duchesses,' the dealer explained. 'Their value is prodigious. The Tsar's wife, the Tsarina Alexandra, had a German father, but her mother is Queen Victoria's daughter. The Tsarina naturally has the pick of the diamonds from the mines in German South West Africa. All the ladies of the Russian court are so rich themselves – or have rich husbands or lovers, often both – that expense has no meaning whatever. And they all love diamonds, because diamonds are the ultimate badge of wealth. They vie with each other to persuade their husbands or lovers to buy the largest, and the most expensive.

'And this sort of expenditure is not limited to women of noble birth. I know of half a dozen ballet dancers who own diamonds worth half a million pounds. Mathilde Kschessinska was the Tsar's mistress before he came to the throne. To mark twenty years as prima ballerina, her admirers gave her a phenomenal collection of jewels. She had a mahogany chest, bound with gold bands, totally packed with yellow diamonds – a diamond watch, a diamond and platinum chain. Diamonds, diamonds, everywhere. Why, the Tsar gave her an outstretched diamond eagle mounted in platinum with platinum chain. Under the eagle, just to show he had diamonds to spare, he ordered the court jewellers to set a rose sapphire surrounded with more diamonds.

'Her present lover, the Grand Duke Andrei, did not care to be outdone, so he commissioned Peter Carl Fabergé to make her a diadem of diamonds and sapphires. This was so valuable that when she dined at the Savoy Hotel in London, the management insisted two plainclothes policemen sat at the next table in case some gentleman prankster literally seized it from her as she ate! The best dinner those policemen ever had, I expect – and the most valuable diamonds they had ever seen.

'Money is so plentiful in Russia, Mr Baird, that whenever I go there, I think they must sell diamonds by the pound weight like tea or coffee. To see how these stones have been cut and set is an education. If you have time on your hands, it could not be spent more profitably anywhere. I know what I am talking about. Remember, I was brought up in St Petersburg. I don't speak from hearsay, but from experience.'

When Jamie still appeared doubtful, the dealer explained how Fabergé employed seven hundred full-time craftsmen to manufacture all manner of diamond-studded toys for the very rich. He maintained one showroom in Moscow, the country's focus of trade and manufacturing industries, for these had brought prodigious wealth to their owners; another in Odessa;

but his main establishment was in the capital, St Petersburg.

Fabergé was especially well known for the jewelled and exquisitely finished Imperial Easter eggs which contained one egg inside another, right down to a final minute golden egg in the centre. Through his London branch, Fabergé made an icon of jewels for the Duchess of Norfolk. Queen Alexandra commissioned him to carve precious stones from the Ural Mountains into the likenesses of cows and horses and ducks and geese on the royal Sandringham farms. The King of Siam, not to be outdone, ordered a nephrite buddha. Heavily jewelled cigarette cases, inlaid bell pushes and picture frames, diamond-studded handles worth thousands of pounds for ladies' parasols; there seemed no limit to his ingenuity – or to the price of his handiwork.

The more Jamie heard about Russia, the more intrigued he became and the more he wanted to visit the country. It seemed a long journey to undertake simply for curiosity, so he convinced himself that it might also be profitable – not that there was any real reason why it should be. He had the time, he had the money, and a visit to Russia seemed an excellent way to spend them both.

Jamie sailed from Hull aboard a liner of the Wilson Line, which ran a regular service to St Petersburg. He found the voyage unexpectedly dull. The only moments of real interest came when the ship passed the German fleet lying at anchor in the Kiel Canal, and then, in the Baltic, passengers saw warships of the Russian fleet.

After dinner one evening, a Russian industrialist, who spoke perfect English, enthused about the popularity of the Tsar and his country's economic achievements under the Tsar's rule. He expressed his confidence that soon Russian factories would overtake factories in North America and become the most productive and profitable in the world.

'What about your labour? Do they have a share in this prosperity?' Jamie asked him.

'Of course. Labourers have a firm roof over their heads, and they have food – which is more than most of them have ever had before. It is only a few years ago, remember, that land-owners bought and sold peasants as casually as they would deal in hogs or cows. There is a parliament now, the Duma, where the people's representatives can raise any grievances. And working people are very content with their lives. Of that I can assure you.'

The Russian kept early hours, and after he had gone to his cabin, a middle-aged Englishman sat down beside Jamie. A steward was passing and Jamie asked the newcomer if he would join him in a brandy.

'You are very kind,' he replied. 'But if I may suggest it, since this will be your first visit to Russia, let us try a Russian drink – kwass.'

The drink was dark brown with a froth on the top, not unlike stout. It tasted sweet and pleasant.

'Any bad effects?' asked Jamie, half joking.

'None. It's not intoxicating, you see. This is fermented only by yeast, made from bread. They brew another type from apples, which is amber in colour, and a third from berries which make it red like wine.'

'I thought vodka was the staple drink in Russia.'

'For the rich, yes. I could not but help overhear your conversation with that Russian gentleman. He painted a very rosy picture of his country's situation. One with which I must say I would not agree. However, he would obviously drink vodka himself, and so would his friends; probably Monopolnaïa No. 1, which is the best. However, those who cannot afford to follow his example run into tens of millions, while those who can are counted only by the thousand.'

'What do you mean exactly?'

'You saw, sir, the Russian fleet at anchor?'

'I did. Very fine vessels, they looked to me. As impressive as the German warships.'

'Agreed. They are well made, but very old-fashioned – on a par with Russian naval strategy. You may remember that in 1905, Russia went to war with Japan. They sailed their then enormous fleet halfway round the world – and lost most of it off Port Arthur before war was declared. They were convinced they could trounce the Japanese, but instead they were humiliated. The crafty Nipponese simply sailed torpedo boats through them at night as they lay at anchor. *Then* the Japs declared war.'

'What caused that conflict?'

'The old Roman maxim of organising bread and circuses to turn the thoughts of the poor away from miseries and problems at home. The intention was to have a great victory, to cheer everyone up – and so take their minds off their poverty. There are a number of revolutionary parties in Russia, but I do not think the peasants would necessarily be drawn to them if their living conditions were better. And despite what our fellow passenger said, they live in misery and destitution.

'Whole families, perhaps seven or eight people of all ages, fathers, mothers, children, grandparents, have to share one room. Others make do under a strip of tent canvas slung between two poles or trees. Sanitation does not exist. Typhoid and typhus are as common as influenza is with us.

'In winter, snow is so deep you can't walk through it. In summer, heat and dust can be stupefying – and then rivers run dry and there is no water, and the crops fail. The country is so huge and communications so poor, that the west of Russia does not know what is happening in the east, several thousand miles away. And all the while agitators constantly whip up resentment against the ruling classes.'

'Do you know Russia well?' Jamie asked him.

'I have been visiting St Petersburg and Moscow regularly for several years now. My company manufactures bicycles in Coventry, and an enormous market exists in Russia for this inexpensive means of transport. Bicycles are much quicker than walking. And cheap to use, of course. No petrol, no coal, no expenses at all, once you pay for the machine. But I cannot get permission from the Russian authorities to import more than a handful at a time – when I could sell thousands. Madness! Bureaucracy in Russia stifles all enterprise, just as the Okhrana, the secret police, stifles free speech. So be circumspect in any comments you may make about Russia unless they are adulatory. You follow me?'

'Totally,' replied Jamie. 'Thank you.'

The Englishman finished his kwass, stood up. 'I hope you will forgive my introducing myself in this way, but I felt it would be unwise for you to arrive with too rosy a view of Mother Russia. Wise is the man who expects nothing. Then he is rarely disappointed.'

Two days later, Jamie saw stone fortifications on either side of the River Neva, and then the gilded spires and minarets and domes of the city that took the name of Russia's most famous tsar, Peter the Great. Forty thousand workmen, recruited from all parts of his empire, had drained marshes on each bank of the river, sunk piles into the reclaimed earth and on them built this capital city in his honour.

As the ship docked, Jamie went up on deck. Byzantine temples, shining pinnacles, domes and spires crowned the streets. The impression was much more of the East than the West. This was accentuated by hieroglyphics on walls and signs, the bright crude colours of people's clothes, and the exterior decorations of the buildings. The Admiralty Quays were thick with well-dressed men taking the air. Coachmen or chauffeurs drove pretty ladies in beautifully turned out carriages or motor cars.

Steamers and ferries puffed importantly up and down the Neva, carrying passengers and produce. A feeling of immense vitality trembled in the air like a high electric charge – or could it be a hidden, seething resentment, as of a great and dangerous beast now sleeping fitfully but ready to be roused?

Jamie felt suddenly uneasy. This country was so large, cold and hot in violent extremes of temperature. But then so was South Africa, yet the Cape lacked this strange pulsing undercurrent of menace. The diggers might be rough and rowdy and ready for a fight, but they were relatively few against a huge empty landscape. Here, Jamie sensed that resentment was widespread.

Jamie left the ship, ordered a porter to handle his bags and hired a troika, a vehicle drawn by three horses. He had booked a suite at the Hotel d'Angleterre opposite St Isaak's Cathedral, whose golden spire, gilded by Dutch ducats given to Peter the Great, reflected the afternoon sunshine like a giant mirror. The main cupola and its lantern and cross, overlaid by two hundred pounds' weight of gold leaf, glowed like a second sun.

The price for a suite in the five-star hotel was ludicrously cheap – less than three pounds a day for a bedroom, a bathroom, a sitting room, a dressing room. That was in itself a mark of the value of English money, backed by the prodigious resources of history's greatest empire, protected by ships of the world's largest navy.

A servant unpacked his bags, and Jamie decided to waste no time, but to meet his contacts immediately. He already had the name of a buyer in Fabergé and of an under-director in Denisov-Uralski's, a rival concern which claimed to be the most exclusive store specialising in immensely valuable trinkets encrusted with diamonds, and tiny animals carved from jade.

Jamie spoke no Russian, but that did not seem to be any impediment. Hotel managers, waiters, even some of the room servants, all spoke English, at least to a limited extent. He telephoned for appointments with both men, and arranged to meet them on the following morning.

The contact in Fabergé professed himself flattered to meet a

398

visitor who, as he put it, had actually found raw diamonds. He had never met anyone so closely involved with their discovery, but he made it clear that the company's contracts and agreements with other concerns selling diamonds were many and complex, and the visitor would appreciate that they could not be broken.

'Can you introduce me to any potential buyers?' Jamie asked him, wondering how to break the deadlock. He was not at all concerned about selling diamonds, but he did not wish to appear simply as a voyeur, someone who wanted to see all manner of rings and brooches but without the intention of buying one.

The director frowned and shook his head. 'That would be most improper, sir. All our dealings are confidential. Understandably, we must keep them that way. We would be doing ourselves a grave disservice if we introduced a competitor to our customers. They, in turn, would think this a strange way of doing business – and possibly decide to do no more with us. I am very happy to show you our craftsmen at work, or to provide a guide to introduce you to our city. But I cannot buy diamonds from you.'

When Jamie saw the under-director at Denisov-Uralski, he did not even raise the question; it was simply a courtesy visit by a former diamond digger interested to see the diamond necklaces and earrings the company produced.

Jamie returned to his hotel, took a bath, ordered a bottle of French champagne, a bowl of Beluga caviar and some toast, and sat down to consider the matter. He had to admit that he was foolish to make himself out to be a salesman, like commercial travellers who used to call at the Silent Witness before Christmas, hoping to interest Uncle Don in their merchandise, paper chains and coloured candles. He remembered how cursorily Uncle Don had treated them. They were people of no consequence, and here in this city, he was not only a stranger but an uninvited stranger; and until proved otherwise, the people he met would regard him in the same unflattering way.

Possibly the sheer size of the place made him feel unusually nervous, unsure of himself.

Everything in this strange capital seemed built on a gigantic scale. The main promenade in the centre of St Petersburg, the Nevsky Prospekt, ran in a straight line for two and three-quarter miles from the Admiralty at one end to the Alexander Nevsky monastery at the other. And for all its length, the road seemed as wide as Trafalgar Square in London.

On one side, backing on to the river, stood great government buildings with cupolas and flagposts, separated from the road by a thick hedge. On the other side of the Prospekt were rows of expensive shops, and five-storey buildings with carriages parked outside. In the centre, two sets of lines carried single-decker horse trams. Carriages and troikas, their coachmen splendidly apparelled in scarlet capes, and wearing brightly coloured three-cornered caps trimmed with fur and gold braid, bowled up and down the vast thoroughfare. At night, the scene was lit like a gigantic stage, and to reinforce this illusion, he heard sounds of music from orchestras playing for private parties in palaces that faced the river.

It was a city of magnificent distances, wide straight roads; of open squares, parks, cathedrals, palaces. Peter the Great had called it a window through which he might look out on Europe. Equally, thought Jamie, it was a window on which, from Europe, he could look out on Russia.

Cheered by this thought, on the following day he presented himself at the British Embassy to leave his card.

The Ambassador was in the Crimea, so Jamie saw a Fourth Secretary. He was tall, languid, and obviously bored. He turned Jamie's card over and over in his hands, running the tips of his fingers over the print to assess the depth of the embossing and hence calculate its cost. This visitor was only a tradesman, he felt sure. He need not waste time with such a person, one of those parvenus who had made a fortune – or who would no doubt claim he had – from diamond digging in Cape Colony. Indeed, he was rather surprised the fellow had bothered to call at the Embassy.

'I really don't think I can help you very much,' he told Jamie. 'This is specifically a matter of trade. We are here as diplomats, trade does not concern us primarily.'

'I thought it would.'

'Well, in the broad sense of helping to promote British goods, we do what we can, naturally. But what you seek apparently are introductions to sell South African diamonds to rich Russian ladies. Is that right?'

'Not entirely,' Jamie replied, making up a reason for his trip. 'I simply want to discover the kind and colour of diamonds that are most sought after. For my own interest, really. But naturally I would tell my agents in London of my conclusions.'

'I cannot see how we can help you, Mr Baird, but if I can, I will. I have your address.'

'Thank you,' said Jamie. They shook hands.

Because the day was warm and sunny, Jamie walked back to his hotel instead of taking a troika or ordering a cab. As he was approaching the entrance, he heard footsteps quicken behind him and turned. A man in his mid-forties, with a sallow face, a slightly greying beard, was running after him. Jamie paused until he caught up with him and then looked at the runner enquiringly.

'You must forgive me, sir,' the man began in English, 'but I was informed by a friend at the British Embassy that you sought certain introductions, possibly with a view to trade?'

'Possibly. And who are you?'

'My name, sir, is Serov. Mikhail Serov.'

'And you are employed by the Embassy?'

'Not employed as such, sir. Not *directly*, if you understand me. But sometimes my services are called for discreetly, and then I am always delighted to be of any use, in whatever capacity, however humble, to any subject of His Britannic Majesty King George. I am, sir, at your total service.'

'In what way do you think you can help me?'

'I am informed, sir, that you are concerned with diamonds, and seek introductions to ladies of society.'

'You are well informed,' Jamie told him. 'Let us talk about this inside.'

Serov followed him up the stairs to his suite. His little eyes, dark as sloe berries, darted around the room, noting Jamie's hand-stitched leather suitcases, his neatly pressed Savile Row suit which the valet had laid out on the bed; the silk shirt and underwear he would wear that evening. Jamie poured two vodkas, raised his glass in a toast.

'Now, Mr Serov, what is your proposition?'

'Simply this, sir. You tell me who you want to meet and I will endeavour to introduce you. For a fee.'

'I don't know who I want to meet,' Jamie admitted. 'I suppose rich women, or their husbands. I want to find out what their favourite diamonds are. I am not a salesman. This is simply for my own interest. I have been involved with producing diamonds.'

'In the Caucasus?' Serov sounded surprised.

'No. In Cape Colony in South Africa.'

'You have an agent here?'

'No, but I might appoint one.'

'You might appoint me, sir?' suggested Serov boldly.

'I might indeed, but first, I would need to have positive evidence of your ability as a salesman.'

'I do not know how well you are versed in matters pertaining to Russian society, sir, but as you would say in English, this is a difficult nut to crack. First, you have to be introduced. Then, you have to be accepted. Since great wealth here is commonplace, it is rank that really counts, not money.'

'Can you help me with any introductions?' Jamie asked him.

'It will be my pleasure, sir. But there are certain disbursements I have to make, and for this reason I have to be put in funds, as your English lawyers say. I am sure you understand.'

'How much do you want?'

'A hundred sovereigns now, and as much again if you get whatever you want as a result.'

'How will you know whether I have or not?'

'As you can imagine, sir, I do have my sources of information. Supplying information, intelligence if you like, is part of the profession by which I live. But apart from that, I would trust you as an English gentleman.'

'Scottish,' Jamie corrected.

'You know what I mean, sir. A native of the British Isles.'

'Right. I will give you a hundred sovereigns.'

The sum was trifling, and if he lost it, then at least he would have a story to tell against himself, to show he could still make a mistake. Jamie had made arrangements with his bank in London that the Azov-Don Commercial Bank in St Petersburg would honour his cheques and drafts on sight. He wrote out a cheque, handed it to Serov.

'That's my part of the bargain,' he said. 'Now, what about yours?'

'I will explain, sir. This is the summer season. The Tsar and his wife are at their country palace in Tsarskoe-Selo, which literally means the "Tsar's village". Actually, it is quite a large town, with twenty thousand inhabitants. The court is there, of course, for wherever the Tsar goes, the archdukes and duchesses follow and gather. I suggest we go there. I have been invited to a picnic. My host will be honoured to meet you. We do not see many Englishmen – or Scotsmen – here, I am sad to say.'

'I am in your hands, Mr Serov.'

'Then we will leave tomorrow morning,' said Serov. 'I will await you here at eleven o'clock precisely.'

Jamie and Serov caught the noon train from the Baltic Station in St Petersburg. The platform was crowded, and a bell tolled to inform passengers when the train was fifteen minutes away. It rang twice more to advise them that it would arrive within five minutes – and then three times to warn that it was about to leave.

Their compartment in the blue First-Class carriage had only two spare seats; Serov sent a porter ahead to keep them both until they boarded. The journey lasted for barely three quarters of an hour, and during this time Serov explained the extent of the possessions of the very wealthy.

'This is a huge country, Mr Baird, and the appetites and expectations of the aristocracy are on that scale – prodigious. They demand the best, the biggest, the most expensive – and they always have done. Nothing must stand in the way of any whim they, or especially their wives, may wish to gratify.

'One of the most influential young men in the empire will be at our picnic – Prince Yussoupov. His estates are so great and so many that he actually forgot he owned one at Spaskoie Selo, and consequently never visited it. At length, his agent discovered this and I accompanied them when they went to see it for the first time. The walls had fallen completely in, the roof had disappeared. Great Doric pillars had toppled over, all doors and window frames had been looted, but the Prince only shrugged. "I have so many palaces," he said. "What is one out of such a number?" You follow the scale of these people's possessions, sir?'

'I am beginning to.'

'The Prince owns another estate in the Caucasus that stretches for one hundred and twenty-five miles along the edge

404

of the Caspian Sea. The soil there contains such enormous quantities of petroleum just waiting to be pumped out, that the earth is literally soaking with oil, a huge marsh of liquid gold. Peasants will scoop up a handful of soil to grease the axles of their carts. The Prince has only to put in pumping machinery, a filtering plant, and he will make another fortune, supplying petrol spirit to the motor cars that now throng our streets. He owns sawmills for his forests, sugar mills to process cane from his plantations. He is married to one of the most beautiful women in Russia, Princess Irina, the Tsar's niece. They were deluged with presents at their wedding. Diamonds, sapphires, jewels of every kind.

'However, the Lord gives and the Lord taketh away. No one on this earth enjoys complete happiness. Always, as in an old jig-saw, one piece is missing. There is a dark side to the Prince's character, which, I assume, came as a shock to his beautiful bride. He is, shall I say, of strongly effeminate tendencies. His mother wanted a baby girl, not a boy, and so brought him up as a daughter. He even had a pink basinette. Imagine!'

As Serov prattled on, Baird looked out of the window at the fields. Horses, heads down, pulled heavy carts piled high with corn. Women, wearing black serge dresses, with black scarves round their heads, and hump-backed from carrying heavy loads, briefly turned wrinkled leathery faces towards the train. He saw a brief glitter of silver teeth as some of the younger ones smiled. In one village, a black bull stood tethered on a patch of grass; ducks waddled around a dirty pool. The houses were not houses in his understanding of the word. They were hovels, huts, shacks, barely fit for pigs. He drew Serov's attention to them.

'What do those poor peasants feel about wealth such as you describe?'

'My dear sir, most don't even know about it. They cannot read, so they have no newspapers. They are lucky to get their food. They are like animals, beasts of burden, asking for very little. They are content.'

'If they lose their jobs on these farms, what happens to them? Can they survive?'

'Only by the grace of God. Otherwise, they will starve. There are only so many employers, you know, and peasants breed like mice. So they take care not to lose their jobs.'

'There was a revolution here, though, so I have read, back in 1905?'

'Ah, yes, of course. Not a revolution as I would describe it. More riots and an uprising. After our war against Japan, which did not go in our favour, wounded soldiers returned, and their accounts belied earlier newspaper talk of heroism and glory. A great crowd of peasants marched on the Tsar's palace at St Petersburg to express their feelings. They were quite peaceable, but starving. They had no bread, no meat, nothing. They became agitated when they learned the Tsar was not in residence.

'The military fired at them – a foolish act, but understandable when a relatively small number of troops are faced by a crowd of thousands and fear for their lives. At the time, there was great anger, but it all blew over. As I say, this is a big country. Its population of many, many millions is not greatly diminished by the deaths of a few hundred. One must see these things in perspective, Mr Baird.'

The train drew into Tsarskoe-Selo Station with a great clanging of bells. A huge Mors landaulette, engine running, stood waiting in the station yard. The driver, in olive-green uniform, with a polished patent-leather peak to his cap, saluted smartly when he saw Serov. He held open the door. Jamie and Serov climbed inside; the interior smelled of oiled leather and cigar smoke.

'Usually,' Serov explained, as they started off, 'the hostess arranges for a fleet of cars to take guests to the picnic, but the others must have arrived on an earlier train.'

As they drove along the rough road, with fields on either side that seemed to stretch to the horizon, Jamie remembered another unmade road under an umber sky, that had taken him to Kimberley and fortune in another life, another world. It seemed incredible that in a relatively short time he could be transported from washing the outside lavatory of a Cheshire public house to being a guest at a picnic given by a member of the Tsar of Russia's court. What would Yeung Lee make of this incongruous, almost miraculous transformation?

The car turned off the road between two huge stone gate posts, and its rough surface gave way to a wide drive of washed gravel. Twenty men holding long metal rakes were busily obliterating tyre marks left by a previous arrival. They all stood smartly to attention and bowed deeply as the car passed. An ornamental lake with an artificial island lay on the left, a river on the right. Lawns stretched away on either side. On these lawns, Jamie counted twenty-five more men, spread out in a long line, each one sweeping the grass with a broom.

'How many gardeners are there here, would you say?' Jamie asked.

'About two hundred,' replied Serov at once. 'Probably more. Labour is cheap.'

'It must be. And their employer very rich?'

'Very,' agreed Serov soberly. 'But I have already attempted to explain to you the extent of these people's possessions.'

'The way you describe them as "these people" makes me feel that you do not include yourself in their number.'

'Quite correct, sir. If I did, I would hardly be offering my services to you for a hundred English sovereigns. I class myself as an observer of the social scene. On the outside, as you say, always looking in through the window. Never inside. But, perhaps one day . . .'

Serov's voice tailed away. Jamie saw a shadow flit across his face; a narrowing of his eyes, a tightening of his lips. Envy? Dislike? Or simply regret?

'How do they become so wealthy, when there must also be great poverty in the country?'

'From factories and properties and investments their ancestors made. They own houses in the country, the town, on the coast. Do you know, the Tsar has one hundred and thirty-eight palaces? And each one is maintained with a full staff of hundreds of men and women, inside and outside, the year round! Just in case he might decide to spend a night there – or even an afternoon.'

'Does he ever visit them?'

'I would think he has set foot in only four or five, if that. The one here is his favourite. He probably can't remember where the others are – if he even knows.'

The car approached a house the colour of Cotswold stone, big as an army barracks. Byzantine cupolas, minarets and towers sprouted from the roof in a prodigal array of architectural exuberance. The driver stopped outside the front door. Immediately, two footmen in red livery came forward in step, bowed and opened the rear door of the car.

'Follow me,' Serov told Jamie.

Stone angels watched them climb a wide flight of steps. In the main hall, a minstrels' gallery ran under the roof. The vast room was furnished in French Renaissance style with gilded chairs and chaise-longues. Tapestries covered the walls. Crystal chandeliers, each holding one hundred gold candles, hung like frozen waterfalls from the tessellated ceiling. Across the mosaic floor, Persian and Kouba rugs were scattered in carefully planned casualness. The air was delicately scented by bowls of pot-pourri.

At the far end of the hall, high French doors opened on to a terrace. On a tennis court beyond it, four girls in long white dresses were playing a languid game, to the accompaniment of gusts of laughter from spectators sprawled in canvas chairs.

The lawn stretched to the lake where young men in immaculate white trousers and dark blazers, wearing straw hats with bright ribbons, expertly wielded punt poles. The little flat-bottomed boats, each bright in a different colour – blue, red, white – darted like huge dragonflies across the placid surface of the water. By the side of the lake, an immense marquee had been erected. Its canvas walls were striped in the Imperial colours of maroon and white, and as they approached, Jamie could see that it was lined inside with striped silk in the same design.

They walked across the stone-flagged terrace. Everything seemed built on a vast scale. On a balustrade two hundred yards long stood larger-than-life statues of figures from Greek and Roman history and mythology. Nymphs and dryads and satyrs supported fountains that sprayed water into half a dozen orna-mental ponds, each a hundred feet across. Beneath the shade of a grove of tall trees, a military band, wearing white ceremonial uniforms, played a Strauss waltz. Men in court dress were walking past the band towards the marquee, escorting wives and daughters and other companions.

'As I expected, I see some familiar faces,' said Serov, scanning the scene. 'I will introduce you.'

After the sunshine outside, the light in the marquee was much softer, vaguely pink, filtered through silk and canvas. An old lady, her face powdered like a baker's loaf, stood watching the guests arrive. Her fingers were encrusted with glittering jewels, blue, red, amber. Diamonds drooped in clusters from her ears, and ropes more were strung round her neck, thin as a turkey's gizzard. She smiled mechanically as she saw Serov.

'The Grand Duchess Victoria,' said Serov, and bowed. 'May I introduce an English – or rather, a Scottish – visitor, Mr Jamie Baird?'

'Delighted to meet you, Mr Baird,' said the Grand Duchess in English. 'And what brings you to Russia? I trust not busi-ness, but pleasure? There is so little pleasure these days, so much business. It does one good to escape from city life to a simple picnic like this – even if only for a few hours.'

'I entirely agree, ma'am,' replied Jamie. He would have said more, but the Grand Duchess turned away to greet someone behind him. A liveried servant hovered with a silver tray of crystal goblets of red and white wine, and pink champagne.

'All from Russian vineyards,' Serov explained. 'I recommend the red. The Crimean grapes are especially good this year.'

Jamie took a glass, raised it in a toast to his companion. 'To our future,' he said.

'May it not be worse than the past – or the present,' replied Serov seriously. 'Now, we shall have a light luncheon and I will introduce you to Prince Feliks Yussoupov and one or two other people who may help you in your search for whatever it is you seek. Eternal life, I suppose, in the end. Like all of us.'

'I'm more immediately concerned with this life,' replied Jamie.

'Of course you are. It is us Russians who believe so strongly in life after death. The West is losing faith in that comforting belief. A sad thing. However. Come with me. First, we have *zakuska*, what you in the West call hors d'oeuvres.'

A long refectory table covered with a starched linen cloth was laid out with platters of smoked raw salmon, pickled mushrooms, a paste of Camembert and Swiss cheese beaten into a rich cream with port wine, to be eaten on silvers of black bread with Finland butter. There were liqueurs made from caraway and bayberry and a row of bottles of Monopolnaïa No. 1 vodka.

Cucumber soup was served with sour cream, and then sterlet, a rare fish. Chefs carved slices from a whole pig baked in milk. Others offered breast of smoked goose, grouse, dried fish. Plates heaped with black salted caviar and fresh grey caviar stood in bowls of ice.

Women servants, wearing bright dresses with strings of

410

heavy beads and hats like starched linen coronets, hovered around the guests. They carried dishes of ham smoked over burning beech leaves and plates of minced meat, rice and egg baked with a crusty pastry. The hospitality seemed as overpowering as the opulence of its setting. For possibly a hundred guests, Jamie counted nearly as many servants, and these were only the ones he could see, not cooks and other kitchen staff.

Jamie left Serov in the marquee engaged in earnest conversation with a middle-aged man in the gold-edged frockcoat of the nobility, and wandered out on to the lawn and down towards the lake. He wanted to be on his own, in fresh air, for a few moments. He found it difficult, almost impossible, to equate this overpowering luxury, almost gluttony, in his view, with the lined weary faces of peasants he had seen from the railway train. There was poverty in England, too, and poverty in every country; that was the way of the world. But here in this gigantic land the gulf between the wealthy and the starving yawned wide as an abyss. What would happen if the poor ever attempted to cross the gap – or even do away with it?

He came to the edge of the lake and stood for a moment watching tiny waves lap the shore through beds of different kinds of reeds, all cunningly arranged to give the impression they were natural, not artificial. The water was so clear, he could see tiny silver fish dart like penknife blades just beneath its surface.

Jamie walked slowly along the bank. The trunks of the trees had been specially planed to remove any roughness. Some trees had even been varnished and then polished. He stood staring at one of them in surprise and a voice behind him asked, 'What's wrong? Have you lost something?'

He turned. A girl of about his own age was standing smiling at him. She wore a long white dress that reached to the ground, and carried a rolled-up silk parasol. Under a wide-brimmed straw hat decorated with flowers, her face was fresh and smiling.

'You are English?' he asked her.

'No, Russian. But I had an English governess. My grand-mama, the Grand Duchess Victoria, told me Mikhail Serov had brought an English guest. Or rather, a Scottish one. She said there was a difference.'

'A great difference,' Jamie agreed with a smile.

'I hope you don't think me forward in introducing myself? I wouldn't do that to a Russian, you know, or to a Frenchman. But I want to try out my English. Do I speak it well?'

'Perfectly.'

'I get little chance to practise it, but Grandmama and my mama are taking me to England next spring, and I will have lots of opportunities then. First, we are going to the Riviera in southern France. It's a long way to travel from here, and they have never been able to arrange it before. They have so many engagements with relations. But now Grandmama put her foot down and insisted we all went. Otherwise, it could be too late.' She paused.

'Too late? In what way?' Jamie asked her.

'Well, Grandmama says she will be too old to travel very soon. I tell her that this is simply not so. More important, I think, is the political situation in Europe.'

'What do you mean?'

Jamie had not seen a newspaper for some time and, in any case, had never been interested in politics, whether local, national or international.

'The heir to the Austrian throne, Archduke Franz Ferdinand, has been assassinated.'

'Where? In Austria?'

'No, in Sarajevo, in Serbia, the south of the Austro-Hungarian empire. He and his wife were on a state visit. An assassin shot them both as they drove in their car.'

'A terrible tragedy. But how can that possibly affect your trip to Europe?'

'Because the German Kaiser wants to attack Serbia. To teach

412

them a lesson, he says. If he does, Grandmama says that Russia will come in on Serbia's side, however reluctantly. There is an agreement between their government and ours. Then France has a treaty to help us, as your country has one with France. So soon all these countries can be involved. It is very serious. Two bullets could start a war.'

'But that's not very likely, surely?'

'We all hope not. And me especially, because after our stay in France, Grandmama and my mama have promised we will go to London for Christmas. Do you live in London?'

'Well, I do have a house there, yes,' Jamie admitted. 'But my main house is in South Africa.'

'Are you a hunter, something like that?'

'Something like that,' he agreed. 'In the broadest sense, I could say I hunt for diamonds, or rather I did. I'd better introduce myself. Jamie Baird.'

'Katharina Sokolov.'

They shook hands formally.

'Can you steer a punt?' she asked him.

'I've never tried,' Jamie admitted. 'But I'm willing to.'

'There's one moored to the bank. The pole's in it. I can teach you.'

Katharina ran along the bank, untied the rope, which was wound round a tree.

'You get in first,' she told him. 'I'll push off.'

'I feel I should be doing that.'

'You can do it next time.'

Jamie climbed gingerly into the boat, stood at the far end with his feet braced against its rocking movement, carefully picked up the pole. Katharina pushed the punt out into the lake and jumped in when it was about a yard from the bank. She sat down quickly as it rocked wildly from side to side.

'Now,' she said. 'You grip that pole and push it right down into the bottom of the lake. Keep it vertical, not at an angle, or

413

it will stick in the mud. Then, when you try to pull it out, if you're not very careful, you'll either overbalance or be left hanging on the pole. Now, *slowly*. That's it.'

Jamie soon got the knack, and between strokes steered the punt with the end of the pole. Katharina sat on a cushion, leaning back against the varnished wood of the seat, her long legs stretched out over wooden slats on the floor. She trailed one hand in the clear water. As she lifted her fingers, drops fell from them, glittering in the sun like diamonds.

'I shouldn't be doing this,' she said suddenly. 'It's not strict etiquette.'

'So who should I apply to before you are allowed to come in a punt with me?'

'Well, my mama is here and of course Grandmama, and there's a relation by marriage, Prince Yussoupov. You could ask any of them.'

'Please introduce me to the Prince, and I will ask his formal permission,' said Jamie gravely. He knew so little about girls that he did not know whether she was making fun of him or was genuinely concerned. Did she realise his shyness was not assumed? Overwhelmingly, he wanted her to like him, not as someone to amuse her, because he had strange European ways and spoke no Russian, but as a friend. He punted back to the bank, helped Katharina out on to the grass, tied up the little boat.

'Now I will introduce you to the Prince,' she promised him.

She led the way through a crowd of people drinking wine or champagne, up to a small group of men who puffed on cigars and held their glasses up to the light. They turned as she approached.

'My dear Katharina,' said one, 'I was hoping you would be here.' He had a soft, almost feminine voice.

'Cousin Feliks,' she replied, 'I would like to introduce you to a friend. Jamie Baird, from England – I mean, Scotland.'

414

'How long have you known Mr Baird?' the Prince asked her, ignoring Jamie.

'About fifteen minutes. I saw him by the lake. He took me out in a punt.'

Prince Yussoupov turned to Jamie, bowed, extended his hand.

'My pleasure, sir,' he said formally. His grip was soft and damp and cold.

'You see,' Katharina explained quickly, observing displeasure on the faces of the others, 'I am going to England with Mama and Grandmama. I thought it would help my English to talk to Mr Baird.'

'I am sure you are quite right, my dear,' said the Prince. He turned to Jamie. 'Are you over here on business, or as a tourist?'

'Largely as a tourist, but I am interested in diamonds. I like to see the beautiful jewel settings so many Russian ladies like.'

'You are in the business of trading in diamonds?' asked one of the Prince's companions, a short fat man with a red face and sandy moustache. He introduced himself as Dr Lazovert, an army surgeon.

'I prospected for them in South Africa. To that extent I suppose I have been a trader.'

'I do not know about English society, sir,' said Dr Lazovert, 'but here, we have four estates. The nobility, the merchants, the peasants and the burghers. Here, we do not esteem trading as highly as you do in England. After all, Napoleon called you a nation of shopkeepers.'

'That's unfair, and unkind to a visitor,' cried Katharina. 'You may remember last summer in Moscow, when the Tsar was celebrating the three hundredth birthday of the Imperial House, representatives of all four estates were presented to him.'

She turned to Jamie.

'It was arranged that the nobility would be received in the main room of the Kremlin palace, and the merchants were told to gather in a much smaller room. They refused this indignity, and quite right, too. They said that if they could not meet His Majesty on equal terms with those who had simply inherited their wealth instead of creating it, they meant no disloyalty, but they would not meet him at all.'

'I remember the incident well,' said Prince Yussoupov, nodding. 'A most unhappy moment.'

'What did the Tsar say?' asked Jamie.

'He agreed,' said Katharina. 'Very quickly.'

Suddenly Jamie noticed that all conversation had stopped; so had the music. He look across the lawn, bright in the summer sun. A man of immense size and presence was striding down the terrace steps, towards the marquee. He disregarded everyone, as though they were not even there. Everything about him seemed somehow overblown. He had long black hair, a thick unkempt beard, and wore a blood-red robe. A huge gold crucifix dangled from a heavy golden chain round his neck.

A servant approached him with a silver tray of wine and champagne, bowed. The man waved him away, but the tray was so close, his hand knocked over several glasses. They splintered on the grass in a pool of wine, red as new-spilled blood. The man walked on without a backward glance, without an apology; the incident might never have happened. The waiter bent down to pick up the broken pieces of glass. Two women servants with brushes and dustpan ran to help him.

'My God!' said the Prince. 'How does that swine have the nerve to come here?'

'Probably the Tsar invited him,' suggested Katharina.

'Or the Tsarina,' said someone else.

'Considering he has pleasured most of the lady guests here and doubtless all the female staff in his time, I would think he feels he has every right to be here,' said the doctor.

'Please do not talk in that way in Katharina's presence,' said the Prince sharply.

He turned to Jamie, who was still watching the man stride through groups that parted instantly to let him pass into the marquee. Outside, there was an audible sigh of relief. Immediately, people started to talk again, but Jamie noticed that now their voices seemed pitched higher. They chattered like birds, talking for the sake of hearing voices. They had been frightened, and now, at least for the time being, the object of their fear had left them. The bandmaster picked up his baton and led his musicians into a lively polka.

'You must wonder at our remarks about a fellow guest,' Prince Yussoupov said to Jamie.

'I am sure you have just cause to make them.'

'More cause, sir, than you could conceivably imagine,' said the doctor gravely.

'But who is that rough-looking fellow? Is he a priest?'

'A *strannick*, rather. The name we give to someone who can work miracles – or at least who persuades people he can,' Katharina explained. 'The Tsar and the Tsarina claim he is a holy man, and no one would publicly disagree – whatever we may think or say privately. They met him first of all about nine years ago.'

'It was a terrible time,' the doctor explained. 'After the war with Japan, we had an economic depression here in Russia. Workers went on strike for more money. There was violence.'

'I have heard about that,' said Jamie.

'We feared for our country,' Dr Lazovert continued.

'And for our possessions,' added Yussoupov drily. 'Revolution seemed so close that the shops in Petersburg boarded up their windows. A crowd of people, led by a priest, paraded outside the Winter Palace, begging the Tsar to help them. But the Tsar was not in the palace, he was here. When the crowd realised this there was some shouting, and the troops became alarmed and opened fire.

'Sailors in the battleship *Potemkin*, the pride of the Baltic fleet, declared that meat they were offered was rotten, and impossible to eat. Their officers ordered the ringleaders to be shot, but the firing party refused. Instead, they threw the officers into the sea, and hoisted the red flag of rebellion. Then they sailed the ship to Odessa and fired on the city with the *Potemkin*'s guns, the murderous swine. All the time they were shouting slogans: "Death to the bloodsuckers!" "Hurrah for freedom!" "Crew of the squadron flagship, *Potemkin*, one for all, all for one!" and other revolutionary slogans like that.

'I will always remember those words,' Yussoupov went on gravely. 'We realised then we were at a time of deep crisis. The Tsar was advised that he had only one way of stopping this revolutionary fervour from spreading across the land, which would mean that rivers of blood would flow. He had to give the people some civil rights at once – freedom of speech and newspapers – and to have all laws confirmed by a state Duma or parliament.'

'Did that end the trouble?'

'For the moment, yes. But when the Tsar was beset by all these worries, and the fact that his only son and heir, the Tsarevich, was sickly and indeed slowly dying of a disease no doctor could cure, he met this *strannick*. The man prayed for the boy apparently – and he recovered. At least, that is the story. Peasants actually believe he is Christ come down to earth again. They kneel in the street when he passes by and kiss the hem of his robe, crying: "Our Christ, our Saviour, pray for us poor sinners!" And the fellow does seem to have unusual powers of some sort, whether from God or from the devil, I know not. He can apparently cure people of all sorts of ailments. My own view is that he hypnotises them, actually forces them to think they are better – and so they appear cured – for a time, at least until the spell wears off.'

418

'How did he meet the Tsar in the first place?'

'Grand Duke Nicholas, the Tsar's uncle, heard about this man and introduced him to the palace. When the boy bruised himself and began to bleed internally, this man appeared to have a steadying influence on him. The Tsar and his wife – especially his wife – were convinced that the *strannick* had saved his life.

'The Tsar wrote in his diary: "We have got to know a man of God." The Rector of St Petersburg's Theological College told the Tsar that God had called this man to be one of his chosen.

'I would not agree with that, sir. He uses his enormous influence with the Tsarina to promote totally unworthy people. To be blunt, in the opinion of every gentleman here, Mr Baird, he is simply the most dangerous and unprincipled man in Russia. His name is Gregori Efimovich. But he does not use that humble name any more. He boasts of his licentious life and proudly calls himself "The Dissolute".

'In Russian, the word for that is Rasputin.'

TWENTY-THREE

A New Life

Arabella lay alone in bed in the house she had rented for her honeymoon with Noel, near the village of Montego Bay on the north coast of Jamaica. From the window, which overlooked a beach smooth and white as bone, she could see the moon make a wide silver path, rippled and dappled by tiny waves, on the shining face of the sea.

She glanced at her diamond-studded wristwatch: a quarter to three in the morning. Noel had been out all evening, seeing an old friend from university days, he said, but somehow – unreasonably, she told herself – she doubted this. She had an uneasy feeling he was otherwise engaged, and she hated herself for even suspecting he could not be all he seemed.

To her surprise and initial disbelief, early on during their stay she had seen Noel smile at young Jamaican boys who would dive for coins thrown into the water. They would then salute him and grin cheerfully, showing their perfect white teeth. She had seen how her husband watched them, his eyes concentrating on their buttocks, on the bulge of firm genitals beneath their thin shorts soaking from the sea, tight against their flesh as a second skin. Could this interest in young boys be why he had been so disappointing a lover?

Arabella had expected to be taken in his arms, kissed, aroused and then to be entered, to be brought to a climax as exciting as fireworks exploding in an evening sky. Instead, there had only been a furtive and ineffectual and unsatisfactory groping, a kiss on the cheek or an ear, a vague suggestion that later, when he was rested and she had recovered from the voyage, they could make love properly.

'But there is no question of recovering from the voyage. I enjoyed it,' Arabella told her husband.

This was not entirely true. Noel had been absent from the cabin on a number of occasions. She had not liked to ask the stewardess whether she had seen him on the deck or in the lounge or the bar. When he returned, always with some excuse of walking more times round the deck than he had contemplated, or of falling asleep in a deck chair, or even becoming so involved in a discussion with some person in the lounge that he had not noticed how time was passing, Arabella noticed how the stewardess looked at him with contempt in her eyes.

Now, as Arabella lay, listening to the faint movement of the waves on the beach, she wondered what her husband would say when she told him she was pregnant. She had not expected to become pregnant so early in their marriage, and she sensed that Noel had certainly no wish to become a father. The ironical – almost unbelievable – fact was that Noel had only attempted intercourse once – a hurried, jerking business she preferred not to recall. But this single time had apparently been enough. Yet what a depressing way to regard the fact that now the seed of a new generation was growing in her body! Within months, her husband would have an heir or an heiress.

Arabella realised she should have been filled with pleasure, joy, pride at the prospect. Instead, she felt depression, a feeling of hopelessness, as though somehow she had become caught in a net from which she could not extricate herself. She had everything except the gift she wished for most; she had longed to be loved, longed for a child, but not now, not in this way when her marriage already seemed so strange and sterile. She had wanted a child at some future time, when she and her husband had come to know each other, when they had travelled the world together, when they had built the firm foundations of a life together. Not now, not so soon, and not like this.

Perhaps Jamie had been right about Noel, after all. Arabella could not bear to think she had made so grave a mistake about such a supremely important decision as choosing a husband. Mistakes had always been for other people to make. But now, lying there, she had to admit, if only to herself, that she wished she was single again, that she had never met Noel or, in meeting him, at least had recognised his faults instead of being so willingly seduced by his charm, his honeyed words.

She heard voices, the clatter of a door closing outside. A car accelerated away. A key turned in the front door. Arabella heard laboured breathing outside the bedroom door, stumbling, a muttered curse, and then the door was flung open. The light in the ceiling came on, making her blink with its unexpected glare.

'Oh, sorry!' said Noel, his voice thick and slurred by alcohol. 'Didn't mean to wake you.'

'I was awake,' Arabella told him.

'Oh. Anything the matter?'

'Nothing,' she said. 'Where have you been?'

'Well, first, I went down into Montego Bay. There's a fine little bar down by the shore near a beach they call Doctor's Cove – apparently after some doctor who uses it. I had a few rums and then a few more.'

'But you've been away for nearly nine hours. You left at six. You said you were going to have a sherry with someone you'd known at Christ Church. You couldn't take me because he was so shy in the presence of women. Did you meet him?'

'Him?'

For a moment, Noel's face puckered as he dredged for excuses. He had forgotten that story. Had he given the man

422

a name? He wasn't sure, so he'd better go carefully.

'Oh, no. At the last moment, he couldn't make it.'

'Why couldn't he make it – when you'd only just arranged to meet? How did you know that?'

'Because he didn't turn up. In all honesty, that's how I knew it.'

'So who did you see?'

'Oh, other people. What's all this cross-examination about, anyway? I'm not in the witness box or the condemned cell, though, damn me, it sometimes feels like it. You always ask where I am, what I'm doing, who I'm seeing, why I'm not here.'

'I'm only asking,' Arabella replied as calmly as she could, 'because we are on our honeymoon, and it seems that we are missing so much by not being together.'

'Well, it doesn't seem like that to me. Absence makes the heart grow fonder, that's what the poet said, and it's true. I love you. You can see that, can't you?'

Noel sat down clumsily on the edge of the bed. The springs creaked beneath his weight, and she smelled sweet sugary rum on his breath. His eyes were bloodshot, and his hands trembled slightly. Had there been boys in the bar?

'I was hoping you would come back earlier,' she said. 'I've got something to tell you.'

'Yes? What?'

'You don't sound very receptive to what should be good news, even great news.'

'I'm a little tired,' he explained, not following what she said. 'Don't tell me now. Wait till tomorrow. Tomorrow morning at breakfast. We'll have it on the terrace. Guavas, hot rolls. Blue Mountain coffee. Honey. I'll be ready, all ears then, for your news. Be a shame to waste it on me now. That'll be something for me to look forward to.'

'Are you coming to bed?' Arabella asked him.

'Of course. Rather, *going* to bed, not coming. I wouldn't want to disturb you tonight. I mean, I've woken you up. It'll be difficult for you to go to sleep if I'm around. I'll use the room next door, I think. But I'll be out there on the terrace when the maids come at eight tomorrow. Ready to hear all you've got to tell me. Until then, my dear.'

He leaned towards her. The smell on his breath was overpowering. She turned away from it. He kissed her clumsily, wetly, on an ear and then lurched unsteadily towards the door and was gone. Arabella turned out the light, but it was a long time before she fell asleep.

A table had been laid for breakfast on the wooden terrace, surrounded by frangipani and bougainvillaea, overlooking white sands and an empty glittering sea.

Arabella sat, without any appetite, toying with a roll, sipping black coffee. She had been there at eight o'clock and it was now nine. She waited for another half-hour before her husband arrived. Noel was unshaven. His face looked puffy, sweaty, unhealthy. He sat down. On a side table stood jugs of various fruit juices, bowls of guavas, prunes, pineapple slices. Noel looked at the selection and grimaced.

'Can't face that,' he said. 'Black coffee and a cigar will do me. The best breakfast a man can have.' He poured himself a coffee, sipped it appreciatively. 'Been up long?'

'You said you would be here at eight. I was here at eight.'

'Oh, don't start finding fault. Can't one sleep in on one's honeymoon? What is this, an inquisition? You can't wonder there are so many jokes about marriage on the music halls, can you? Last one I heard was that marriage was an institution. But who wants to live in an institution, eh?'

'I said I had some good news to tell you.'

Noel's face puckered and creased as his memory backtracked desperately. When had she said that? Good news about what?

424

What could the good news possibly be? Then he remembered last night. She had been lying in bed, awake. He had come in, a bit tiddly. That had obviously set her off.

'Oh, yes,' he agreed. 'I'm ready to hear it now. As I said, I'm all ears.'

'I'm going to have a baby,' Arabella told him.

'*A baby?*'

Noel repeated the words as though he had never heard them before this. For a moment he stared at her in horror, then hostility.

'You've been having an affair? Who with?'

'Don't be silly! It's *your* baby. You're the father.'

'Me?' Incredulity cracked his voice. He had done nothing to make her pregnant. Then he corrected himself. He had – once. He remembered that humiliating occasion. Surely a union so swift and fleeting could not produce a child?

'Are you sure?' he asked her hopefully.

'Certain. I saw the doctor yesterday. There's no doubt about it.'

'Well, when is it -- he – she due?'

'In about seven months' time.'

'Oh.' Noel took a cigar out of a case, clipped the end, lit it, drew heavily, blowing blue smoke in her face. 'Well, that *is* quick.'

She thought, sharply, she could reply, '*You* were very quick, too, but not quick enough, not good enough.' But she bit back the words and shrugged. 'It only wants one time, you know.'

'So it appears.'

He looked at her through the drifting smoke of his cigar. The last thing he wanted was a child. But then again, maybe a child was just what he did want. He had noticed what he considered Arabella's sharpness of tongue towards him when he had drunk too much or stayed out too late. It had occurred to him that she might even leave him if she had a mind to do so, but she would never allow a divorce, let alone seek one from him, if a son or daughter were involved. What had seemed an encumbrance appeared, on second thought, as an insurance.

He finished his coffee, stood up. His hangover had gone. He felt remarkably sprightly. Arabella watched him. Surely he was going to congratulate her, tell her how pleased and proud he was, even if really he was neither of these things? Even if she knew he was lying, she would still like to hear the words.

'I think I'll take a walk on the beach,' he said shortly.

Arabella smiled at him, not letting her disappointment show in her face. Only the hurt in her eyes revealed what she felt. 'I'll come with you,' she said loyally.

'No, *no*. I want to get used to the idea of parenthood on my own. It is a serious matter, Arabella. An immense responsibility. And so unexpected.'

Noel strolled down the path to the beach and walked along the sand. Arabella watched him out of sight. Then she rang the handbell for the maid to come and clear the table.

Arabella did not, in fact, do anything about her idea of involving herself in Jamaica with the export of bananas, and possibly the tourist trade, as she had thought she might. At first, this had seemed a novel and entertaining idea. She liked the sun, she liked bathing in a warm sea, and she was certain that thousands of others from colder climates would also enjoy these two great benefits of the Jamaican coast. Even so, she decided against any involvement. She had simply lost her zest for such enterprises.

Before, she had been the driving force of the twins; now, she felt that her force was spent. She had always believed a saying of Confucius which Jamie had heard from Yeung Lee: 'The road to success is filled with wives pushing their husbands along.' She had pushed her brother: it was impossible to push her husband. There was something lacking in his character, some backbone had either gone soft or had never been there. He was beautiful to look at, but devious and disappointing to know.

They cut short their stay in Montego Bay and went back to England where she had bought a house in Belgravia. In London, Arabella had made friends she could visit or entertain and so not be alone with her husband. In Jamaica, they were together for too much of the time with almost nothing in common. Their conversation was limited to safe remarks about the weather or some local dish the cook had prepared. Instinctively, they both avoided any topic that the other might consider controversial.

On several occasions after their return, she missed small items of jewellery but, not wishing to start an argument, had said nothing to Noel. A maid could have been responsible, or a butler whom she had once seen the worse for drink, but secretly she did not think either of them were guilty. She issued a description of the jewels to the police and a pendant was found in a junk shop in Camden Town, full of elephants' feet designed to be used as wastepaper baskets, old oil lamps, photogravures of riverside scenes and country churches. The proprietor strenuously denied he had bought stolen property, but then, of course, he would. Arabella went to the shop herself and asked him who had sold it to him.

'That was my pendant,' she told him, 'but I will give you what you paid for it and a profit into the bargain.'

'You are very kind, ma'am,' said the man. 'This is the first time this has ever happened to me. I try to make an honest living. I am approached by all kinds of people with things to sell, but if I have any doubts, I never touch them.'

'I'm sure you don't,' said Arabella. 'But what about this one? Who sold it to you?'

'A very tall man. About mid-thirties, I suppose. He wore a

muffler right up round his face, and a hat pulled down. Well-spoken bloke.'

'Recently?'

'About two weeks ago.'

'But that was midsummer.'

'I know. He didn't want to be recognised.'

'Why, if he was genuinely selling something that belonged to him?'

'Well, it turned out he wasn't, ma'am, didn't it? He was, so you tell me, selling what belonged to you.'

'Would you recognise him again?'

'Oh, I don't know about that. He had a funny sort of voice. I think it was put on. I only saw his eyes. He had glasses as well.'

'I see.' Arabella took a photograph from her handbag. 'Is that the man?'

'He isn't wearing glasses,' said the shopkeeper.

Arabella took out a pencil, ringed in the eyes with spectacles.

'Yes, that's him, I'm fairly sure. There's something about the eyes that gives away anyone. You can disguise your voice, your walk, your looks, but not your eyes. I know some people change the colour by putting dye in them, but for this sort of transaction, it wouldn't be worth it.'

'Had you ever seen him before?'

'Never.'

'Since?'

'No, ma'am.'

Arabella opened her wallet, took out a bundle of £5 notes, counted out several for the man and put Noel's photograph back in her handbag.

Rather than submit to this constant petty thieving – and not so petty, because some of the jewels were worth several hundred pounds – she decided to pay Noel an allowance of £5,000 a year.

* * *

Arabella had her baby in a private nursing home and engaged a day nurse and a night nurse to look after him when she brought him home. The day after the boy was born, Noel came to see her. In a small bassinet by the side of her bed lay the son she wanted to call Charles. There had been a cheerful king of that name, she remembered from school history lessons; a man with curly hair and a roguish eye and ready wit. She admired those sort of looks, that sort of man. Noel glanced at the child, wrinkled his face dubiously.

'He looks very ugly,' he said, almost disbelieving that the boy could be his.

'They change,' Arabella assured him. 'The doctor said he'll be the most handsome man in England when he grows up.'

'Then he'll take after me,' said Noel, only half joking.

'Are you pleased?' she asked him.

'Of course I am. Of course I am.'

He bent and kissed her on the cheek and although he held in his breath, she could smell whisky on it, and the faint aroma of stale cigar smoke, like a smoking room on the morning after a party.

'In all honesty,' he said, 'I've been a bit worried recently.'

'Over what – not me?'

Arabella desperately hoped that her husband would nod, admitting at least some feeling for her. But Noel simply shook his head.

'Oh, no. It's about some damned fellow who says I owe him money.'

Arabella tried to keep the disappointment out of her voice. 'What sort of damned fellow?'

'Oh, a nothing person, really.'

'You mean a gambling person?'

'Yes. He runs a private gambling club.'

'I thought you were giving up gambling?'

'This was different. It was difficult to refuse his invitation.

Lord Robey and the Duke of Ansty were there *and* a prince of the blood. It was very hard not to get drawn in without causing great offence.'

'How much does he say you owe him?'

'Rather more than my allowance.'

'I allow you five thousand pounds. Have you lost *all* that?'

'Hmm . . . and the rest,' Noel admitted sheepishly.

'Well,' she said coldly, 'how you resolve your dispute is up to you. It is nothing whatever to do with me. You have a generous allowance, and you have spent it. I cannot become involved in this matter.'

Noel stared at Arabella in disbelief, leaned over her, shook her roughly by the shoulders.

'Listen,' he said hoarsely. 'If I go under, you go under. I need the money now.'

'How much money?'

'Eight thousand. They'll beat me up. He's threatened he'll put ruffians on me.'

'I haven't got eight thousand.'

'You've got ten, a hundred times that,' he retorted.

'Not here,' she said, 'and not for you, anyhow. I've given you enough.'

'You're all the same, you rich women! It's like tearing flesh off your body to give a pound note to anyone.'

'In that case, you can imagine what it feels like when we've given away thousands and thousands of pound notes. I am not giving you any more. Perhaps I have already given you too much, but always you promised this was the last time you would go gambling, or you needed the money for some other worthwhile purpose. Remember the fifteen thousand pounds I advanced you to spend on our honeymoon? A loan, you said. But it was only the first gift of too many more. Maybe if I had not advanced you anything, you would have been forced to put your affairs in order and stand on your own feet.'

'I'll kill myself,' Noel said angrily.

'I don't believe you,' she said.

'I will. I have a revolver.'

He put his hand in his pocket, took out a small pearl-handled .38 with a snub barrel. Because of its size, it could fit snugly in the side pocket of his jacket without causing a bulge.

'What on earth have you got that for?' As Arabella asked the question, she saw fear in his face, and she knew the answer. 'Because you are afraid some of these gambling friends of yours to whom you owe money may come after you, to beat you up – as you tell me? Is that the reason?'

'It's for self-defence,' he admitted sulkily, 'purely self-defence. But I tell you this. If you don't pay me this money, I *will* kill myself.'

Arabella put her hand down the side of the bed, pressed a button. A nurse came in.

'You rang, your ladyship?'

'Yes. My husband here is threatening to kill himself.'

'What on earth for, my lord? You have so much to live for. A pretty wife, a handsome son and heir. No, your ladyship, he must be joking.'

'I'm not!' shouted Noel. '*I will kill myself!*'

He ran from the room. The two women looked at each other.

'Becoming a father takes some men in an odd way, your ladyship,' the nurse told Arabella, trying to make light of a situation outside her experience. 'They can't accept the responsibility at first. It is one thing doing what they have to do to get a child. It's quite another facing up to the fact they've brought someone into the world who is going to outlive them, who'll be young and healthy long after they are dead. They've started a dynasty. A sobering thought, your ladyship.'

'I think it's rather a nice thought,' said Arabella.

She heard Noel outside the window.

'I'll give you three!' he shouted. 'Then I'll shoot myself. If you don't say you're going to pay, you will be responsible for my death. You will have murdered me!'

'You're talking nonsense,' said Arabella, with more assurance than she felt. Perhaps she was being too harsh. Perhaps she was relying too much on her own upbringing, when money had always been tight and no unnecessary frivolous expense could ever be tolerated. The sum was trifling, after all, nothing to her.

Noel shouted: 'One!'

The nurse looked nervously at Arabella, not quite sure whether this was some elaborate upper-class joke, a jape, a conceit they found amusing, but about which she could not see anything funny.

'Two!'

The nurse now looked inquiringly at Arabella, who shook her head.

'*Three!*'

Both women held their breath. The baby moved slightly in his cot as they heard a crack like the whip of the driver of the wagon that had taken Arabella and Jamie to Kimberley. Then came a second crack, then silence.

'He's killed himself!' shouted Arabella. 'He *has* killed himself!'

'No, your ladyship,' said the nurse calmly. 'It would not need two shots to do that.' She bent over the sleeping child. 'All I can say, your ladyship, is that I am thankful his lordship's antics have not woken the baby.'

TWENTY-FOUR

The Winter Palace

Katharina sat well back on the quilted seat of the troika. Her grandmother, the Grand Duchess Victoria, regarded her with quizzical eyes. It was a long time since she was seventeen, but she still remembered that surge of the spirit, that quickening of the blood when she met a handsome young man. She wondered sometimes what had happened to all those dashing young men in their uniforms of the Cavalry and the Guards. They were either old now, stooped, pot-bellied, grey-haired, bald, or they were dead. There was a naval officer of whom she had especially warm memories, but he had died in the war against Japan nine years earlier. Nothing for her had been quite the same since then; but she could not expect her granddaughter to understand that. The old were allowed no pasts, only memories.

'Who was that Englishman?' she asked Katharina, not looking at her, staring ahead through the glass, seeing the sleek backs of the horses perfectly matched, perfectly groomed.

'He is not an Englishman. He's a Scotsman.'

'Is there a difference?'

'Oh, yes, Grandmama. It's like saying someone here in Russia comes from Georgia or the Ukraine. You can't mix them up.'

'The distances are rather greater here, child. I would have thought on a tiny island like Britain it would not have mattered.'

'I have been reading about it. It does matter.'

'Oh well, it matters. Now tell me, who is he? Is he well connected?'

'I don't know. He is rich, though.'

'Did he tell you that?'

'No, but I saw his gold watch. His suit was superb, his shoes obviously hand-made.'

'He may be a charlatan, my dear, coming amongst us to try and cloud the judgements of pretty girls like you. If you married him, or rather he married you, you would have to make over your family fortune to him.'

'You know I haven't got any fortune, Grandmama. We've only these houses and the estate which Papa has borrowed on and then borrowed on the borrowings. Mr Baird couldn't hope to get money from me. Anyhow, I have only just met him. There is no talk of marriage. That is an absurd idea.'

'But if you do not talk about it, you think about it. Am I right, child?'

Katharina did not reply.

'How is he so rich?' her grandmother went on.

'He was in South Africa, the British colony. They discovered diamonds, or rather he discovered diamonds.'

'He's not married, I suppose?'

'Oh, no. Nothing like that. He said he's had no time.'

'But you'd like to give him time?'

'I don't know, Grandmama. I can't discuss this with Mama. You know what she's like. Always with her own young men of the moment.'

'I know,' said the Grand Duchess grimly. 'Especially that very disagreeable Gregori Rasputin.'

She turned to her granddaughter. 'How long is this Englishman – Scotsman – staying in Petersburg?'

'I don't know. Not very long. The news from Serbia is so bad.'

'News from Serbia always is. I would pay no attention to that.

It has always been my experience, as the mother of several sons and daughters, that when one of them became, shall I say, enamoured of a person who perhaps did not seem to have much in common with us, we would ask him or her to one of our houses. We could then see if they knew how to behave. I could ask your friend to the ball in the Winter Palace.'

'Would that be possible?' asked Katharina.

'Certainly. And very probably he'll come, too. Shall I do that?'

'Oh, please, Grandmama. *Please*.'

The old woman squeezed Katharina's hand. 'Delighted,' she said, and looked out at the crowded streets, wishing she were young again.

The troika dropped Jamie outside the Winter Palace. He paused for a moment to admire the enormous red stucco building, which could house six thousand people – and had frequently done so on great state occasions.

When he had received the gold-embossed invitation to the ball, he asked the Fourth Secretary at the British Embassy about the procedure. He had, of course, no court dress and was advised to buy a ready-made suit of tails. The fit was good, and he felt comfortable.

But now, as he stood in the enormous entry hall, he was impressed, almost cudgelled, by the sheer magnificence that surrounded him. Thousands of palm trees and cacti and summer plants had been specially imported from the Crimea to decorate the palace. The Tsar's huge hothouses at Tsarskoe-Selo had been emptied to supply lilac branches, roses, tulips. On each step of the wide marble stairway which led up to the White Salon, where the ball was to be held, stood Cossack Life Guards in crimson and blue uniforms. Negro footmen, dressed in scarlet, moved among the guests, and in the vast salon itself an orchestra of a hundred musicians played a waltz.

Men wearing court dress and the stars of honours and medals, and coloured silk sashes, danced with partners in evening dress. The women's hair glittered with tiaras. Diamonds by the thousand reflected the light from huge candelabras suspended on gilded ropes from the gilded ceiling. This was not a ball, this was part of fairyland, Jamie thought in amazement.

A footman approached, bowed. 'May you forgive me, sir,' he said in English. 'You are Mr Baird?'

Jamie nodded.

'Her Highness, the Grand Duchess Victoria, requests the pleasure of your company, sir. If you will kindly follow me.'

He threaded his way round the edge of the dancers. Under vast oil paintings of Tsars and their relations, the Grand Duchess was sitting on a gold chair, fanning herself with an ivory fan, pricked by diamonds. By her side sat Katharina, apparently studying her programme of dances. She did not look up as Jamie bowed to them both.

'I am very honoured, ma'am, that you should have invited me to this ball. And I must admit, I am overwhelmed with the splendour of everything.'

'Russia, Mr Baird, is a large country. We like to do things, as the Americans say, on a big scale. I hope you will enjoy your evening. Tomorrow my granddaughter and I leave for the Crimea for a week or ten days. So this is our last outing here.'

She indicated a gold chair by her side. Jamie sat down, turned to Katharina.

'I don't know the etiquette here,' he said, 'but in England, it is usual for the man to ask a girl to dance.'

'That is the custom here, too,' agreed Katharina, looking up at him for the first time.

'It would give me great pleasure if I could have the next waltz with you.'

Katharina wrote his name in her programme.

Looking back years later, as Jamie often did, that night

passed with the speed of a gadfly's gossamer wings. Katharina, of course, had to dance with other partners but not with many, and without enthusiasm.

As dawn began to tint the sky, Jamie took her out on to the balustrade, decorated with wide swathes of red and blue silk. Beneath them, the River Neva reflected the dawn. The city was just stirring into wakefulness; a few trucks and carts were already crossing the bridges.

'I feel like Cinderella,' said Jamie. 'Except I am male.'

'Who is Cinderella?'

'A beautiful girl in a children's story. She had two elder ugly sisters who were envious of her. When they went to a ball, Cinderella had to stay at home to clear out the fire grate in the kitchen. A good fairy appeared to her, turned a pumpkin into a coach, and her rags into a wonderful dress – and she was the belle of the ball, and fell in love with a handsome prince . . .'

'And then?'

Jamie told her the rest of story.

'And they lived happily ever after?' Katharina asked finally.

'I like to think so. But then, who knows? Ever after is a very long time.'

'Perhaps it might not seem so long – or even long enough to someone who shared Cinderella's good fortune.'

Lights outside the Palace reflected in Katharina's eyes. She looked unbelievably young and attractive, and something else: vulnerable. Jamie had an almost overpowering wish to endow her with all his money, to shield and shelter her from any possible harm or hurt. For ever would not be too long, if he could achieve this, if she would allow him to attempt to do so.

He felt he could not bear to leave her, to return on his own to London or to the Cape. Both places had once seemed so attractive, but now seemed dull and empty.

He heard himself speak, as if it was someone else talking.

'I know this is probably against all Russian etiquette, or I expect it is,' he said. 'But I am asking you to marry me.'

He could hardly believe what he was saying. He, who had shared Cecil Rhodes' views about women; who had criticised what they spent on useless things, wasting money a man had to earn. But somehow these views no longer made any sense; they had been held by someone else, surely? Was this how his sister had felt about Noel, a man he considered to be a total waster, the sort of person Rhodes unequivocally condemned as 'a loafer'? If so, for the first time, Jamie understood Arabella's feelings.

'But you don't know me,' Katharina said slowly. 'And I don't know you. We have only just met.'

'If we had a whole lifetime together, we could get to know each other,' Jamie said stubbornly. 'I will ask your father's permission – that is to say, if you want me to.'

'I don't know,' she admitted frankly, ingenuously. 'I want time to think, to be quite certain.'

She stood on tiptoe and kissed him. For a moment, Jamie held her close to him. Beyond her, he could see the sky lightening as the great city awoke.

And he thought, this is a moment I will always keep, between darkness and the day. Whenever I see dawn breaking, whenever I see the sun shine on any river, I will remember.

When Jamie returned to the hotel in the early hours, the reception clerk handed him a telegram from Arabella in London: 'INTERNATIONAL SITUATION VERY SERIOUS STOP WAR WITH GERMANY SEEMS IMMINENT STOP SUGGEST YOU RETURN SOONEST BEFORE TRAVEL BECOMES IMPOSSIBLE STOP'

Jamie had had no idea that war could be a real possibility. At the picnic, Katharina had warned him that it might, but the likelihood seemed far-fetched and absurd.

Next morning, he consulted a Secretary at the Embassy. Were things really as bad as this?

'Worse, Mr Baird. A state of war with Germany could mean

that it might be extremely difficult for British nationals to reach England from Russia. In consequence, the Embassy is advising all British subjects to leave while they can.'

'I would like to stay on for a few more days at least,' said Jamie.

'That is your prerogative, Mr Baird. But I must tell you that the Embassy cannot offer protection on the journey to anyone not of diplomatic status. I most strongly advise you to leave as soon as your business is concluded.'

Jamie telephoned Katharina; an English-speaking servant answered. No, the Archduchess was not at home. She and her grandmother had left for the Crimea. No, she could not give their address to callers not known personally to her. She was sorry, but those were her instructions. She was sure the Englishman would understand.

Jamie had no means of contacting Katharina in the Crimea; no postal or telegraphic address, no telephone number. There had seemed no need to ask for them; she intended to return within a week or ten days. But if war was declared, all such arrangements could change. For his part, he felt he should join up; in these circumstances, he did not wish to delay his departure home. But where was home now, when he had houses in England and South Africa?

Jamie decided to write to Katharina at Tsarkoe-Selo, explaining that in this new and, as far as he was concerned, unexpected situation, he must leave Petersburg at once. If there was no war – and he tried to convince himself there would not be – he would return as soon as he could.

He decided to go back to South Africa. He owed his fortune to that country; that was where his future lay.

He asked the reception clerk to book him a rail ticket to Helsinki in Finland. From here, he took passage on a Danish cargo vessel bound for Cape Town and Bombay.

When he reached Cape Town, he wrote another long letter to

Katharina. He did not receive a reply. Communications must be difficult, he told himself. He wrote again, and for a third time, and telegraphed each week for the next few months, in each cable giving her his address in South Africa. He did not receive a reply, or even an acknowledgement.

He read dispatches in the newspapers describing military advances and retreats, and growing disaffection with the progress of the war in Russian cities and factories. There seemed to be immense difficulties in supplying food and military equipment to armies across incredible distances, with very poor railways and roads. He could understand that in this chaotic situation, mail deliveries – especially from overseas, written in English – would be delayed. They would probably be censored, too, and this could only add to the delays.

He regretted that he had left Russia without even saying goodbye to Katharina. But this was not goodbye, he kept telling himself. He had gone away temporarily, not permanently. He would return as soon as he could. For he was determined that wherever he went from then on, Katharina would go with him. He would not leave her a second time.

When Arabella returned from London to the house she had bought in Kleinmond, overlooking the sea some miles along the coast from Cape Town, Jamie drove over to see her.

He had heard rumours of Noel's extravagance and his increasing debts, and he guessed Arabella would be too proud to contact him. Of course, she might not even know about her husband's improvidence, but as soon as Jamie saw her he realised from the pain in her eyes that she did know. Her son, Charles, seemed to look remarkably like his father. Jamie felt a small twinge of disappointment that the boy did not appear to have inherited any of his sister's features. Arabella must have sensed what he was thinking.

'Perhaps he will have my character,' she said brightly.

'Perhaps he'll have his father's,' he replied shortly. He saw her mouth tighten.

'Where is Noel, by the way? Over here with you?'

'No. He stayed in London. He's going to join up in some Staff job apparently.'

'On the Staff right away?'

'I think so. He seems to be related to half the generals. That helps.'

'What about you? Are you staying out here?'

'I think it's better for Charles if we do. The climate is good and there is all sorts of talk of Zeppelin raids and gas bombs and I don't know what other horrors.'

'I'm joining up,' Jamie told her. 'Not on the Staff though. The recruiting people in Cape Town say the infantry will have me if I pass the medical. I am due for that next week.'

'It's ironic,' said Arabella reflectively, 'that a war which may cost the lives of millions and ruin whole nations, may be very profitable for our companies. Sammy already has had orders for literally thousands of yards of cloth for tents, uniforms, all sorts of things. I'm turning over half of the laboratories to manufacture medicaments, antiseptic creams, anything the government wants. I have also made arrangements to start up in Canada. If the United States should ever get embroiled in the war, we would then be well placed for supplying their forces.'

'You think of everything,' said Jamie admiringly.

'Not always the most important things,' Arabella admitted. 'You were right about Noel.'

'I'm sorry I was right,' said Jamie, 'but at least you have a fine son.'

Arabella smiled gently at the little boy.

'Yes,' she agreed. 'Having Charles makes everything else worthwhile.'

TWENTY-FIVE

Kolmanskop

In the army recruiting centre, above a tailoring shop in St George's Street, Cape Town, the medical officer faced Jamie across a trestle table covered by an army blanket.

He was beyond retiring age, with thinning grey hair and half-glasses, over which he regarded Jamie with all the compassion of a kindly family physician who has had to break bad news to generations of patients, and knows how to do this gently.

'I am sorry, Mr Baird, but my colleague and I have, as you know, examined you very thoroughly, and we regret we cannot pass you fit for active military service.'

'What exactly is the trouble? I feel fit, I look fit, I *am* fit – except for something I've never heard of that you say will not allow me to become a soldier.'

'Unfortunately, Mr Baird, it is not just me saying this, or my colleague. Independent tests of your circulatory system show you have a slight constriction in one of the arteries close to your heart. There is no risk whatever of this preventing you from leading a normal life, but it does prevent you from becoming a soldier of the King.'

'Is there any cure?'

'Not as yet, Mr Baird. But no doubt one day there will be.'

'Could I not enlist for something other than the infantry,

maybe even some lowly clerical post? Surely there must be military tasks that do not require everyone to be A1 in the Army medical definition?'

'Unfortunately, there are no more vacancies in those branches of the services. I have checked.'

'I am willing to give you written assurance that I would not make any claim whatever for a pension or anything of that kind, should this disability get worse.'

'I am sorry, Mr Baird, but that could not be arranged.'

Jamie nodded, stood up, walked slowly out of the room, past lines of other young men waiting for their medicals. He walked on to the Civil Service Club in Church Square, went up the stairs into the bar. A strong drink was what he needed after this unexpected rebuff. Maybe he could find some way round the refusal.

At that hour, the bar was empty; a barman polished glasses. Jamie ordered a whisky and soda and sat down at a table in the far corner. He noticed that another man, middle-aged, wearing a light grey suit, had followed him up the stairs, and Jamie vaguely remembered seeing him outside in the street. This man ordered a drink and then crossed to Jamie's table.

'Mind if I join you?' he asked.

Jamie looked up with irritation. Every other table in the room was empty. Why should this stranger wish to sit with him? He wanted to be alone with this thoughts.

'Delighted,' he said insincerely, and hoped the newcomer was not a bore. The man sat down.

'But not as delighted, Mr Baird, I assume, as if the medicos had passed you fit and you were now Private Baird?'

'How the devil do you know that?'

The man produced a card and pushed it across the table. Jamie read 'Colonel Dugdale' and an address in Muizenberg, a seaside resort on the Cape coast. Curiously, he thought, that was where Cecil Rhodes had died, in a tiny cottage overlooking the ocean.

'I am attached to a branch of military affairs,' Dugdale

explained vaguely. 'I asked the recruiting officer to let me know if anyone was turned down for normal service who might be fit for clandestine operations. I saw a couple of possibles yesterday, as a matter of fact. But one was too old and the other had such bad eyesight he could scarcely read a poster across the street. Not much use to me, I'm sorry to say. But you are young, Mr Baird, and you do not wear glasses. Could I ask you – in the broadest terms – whether you would be willing to put your abilities to the service of our country in a very specialised way, in the first instance for a single extremely important and delicate operation?'

'That depends,' said Jamie cautiously. 'What is this operation? And what do you know about my abilities?'

'To answer your second question first, I know that you have made a fortune. I also know that you can defend yourself in a tight corner. I assume you are patriotic, or you would not have wished to enlist. All these are significant qualifications for what I have in mind. Come back to my office and I can tell you more about this project. It is never safe to talk about private matters in a public place.'

Colonel Dugdale's office was a small room on the upstairs floor of a house overlooking a vast expanse of empty beach. Huge Atlantic rollers pounded the sand in a thick white mist of spray. Downstairs in the house, various clerks and orderlies were busy filing documents or typing letters. The colonel's room was sparsely furnished: two wooden chairs, a desk, a metal filing cabinet with padlocks for each drawer. A large map of southern African covered one entire wall.

'I am speaking to you in strict confidence,' he said, as they stood before this map. 'I would ask you, for obvious reasons, not to repeat to anyone what I say.'

'How do you know you can trust me?' Jamie asked him.

'The recruiting people gave me some details yesterday, after

444

the doctors finally reached their decision. So I had time to make a few inquiries. In the light of the answers, I believe I can trust you. Within a week to ten days it will not matter who hears about this, for the operation will be over and done with – or not done at all. We haven't a lot of time, hence my eagerness to recruit you.'

The colonel offered a cigar to Jamie, then lit one himself.

'First, the background. German South West Africa, which occupies a good part of this map, is Germany's richest source of diamonds. They are especially useful to Germany – as, of course, to us. Because diamonds are so small, they can be easily transported anywhere in the world, and they have an agreed and very high value in every country.

'There are no complications with exchange rates, no banking nonsense of that kind. If Germany suddenly needs quantities of a certain expensive commodity, such as oil or nickel, for example, or even information, this could be difficult to acquire in a hurry. Money would have to be transferred, perhaps even governments might need to be informed. And so what was initially a secret transaction can very easily become public knowledge. A few diamonds changing hands, however, can instantly secure the deal. The seller may not even declare there has been a deal. It can be invoiced to a neutral country, and then, in mid-ocean, the destination is suddenly changed. The seller can even list it as a loss, a debt never paid, and so claim tax relief. While, all the time, diamonds have been sold, and money is in a foreign bank under another name.

'It is therefore imperative we do all we can to prevent the enormous quantity of diamonds the Germans have dug out of the Namib desert from reaching the fatherland. The German governor of the colony, Dr Theodor Seitz, denies that any diamonds remain in the territory. But then, in his position, we would no doubt say the same. We know that they have already hidden quantities of diamonds in the foundations of buildings, in newly dug graves. Some of these caches we have been able to sequester.'

'How did you find them?' asked Jamie.

'You would not really expect me to give you the source of our information, Mr Baird? However, shall I say that we always pay natives for any information about people burying things – other than genuine corpses in coffins, of course.

'Up in the north of the colony, at Grootfontein, we heard that the Germans had marched a number of native convicts and Bushmen to the cemetery to dig a grave, although no burial had been announced. Afterwards, they marched them all out into the desert and shot them, rather as the Egyptians killed the slaves who buried the Pharaohs in their tombs – in case they gave away their location.

'One Bushman escaped and told our people. We sent a party over the border. They dug up the grave and found a box containing a mass of silver plate, engraved with the Hohenzollern arms. This had been specially ordered from Germany because the Crown Prince was supposed to be paying the colony a special visit. We also found diamonds, a lot of them.

'The same Bushman reported digging at night in a government experimental farm, also outside Grootfontein. This is a very large area, and he was not exactly certain where the digging had taken place, except that it was in an orchard. Our people examined every tree. When they found a withered apple tree, they dug beneath it and again found diamonds.

'Our information – and we cannot corroborate it because it comes from a single source – is that some of the largest and most valuable diamonds are still in the colony. Either in the port, Lüderitz, or in the actual mining headquarters, a little town called Kolmanskop, about eight miles north of Lüderitz.

'We suspect that as many as fifty thousand carats of diamonds will be loaded aboard a ship of the Woermann Line, which regularly carries diamonds back to Germany. This is the

Gertrud Woermann now in Lüderitz harbour, and bound for Santos, south of Rio de Janeiro in Brazil, which is still neutral. In an ideal world, we would seize this vessel and her cargo of diamonds, but this is not an ideal world, Mr Baird.

'My own belief is that some really big diamonds are still in Kolmanskop. I am inviting you to find those diamonds and bring them out.'

'On what you tell me, I would like to accept your invitation,' replied Jamie. 'But do you know exactly where they are in Kolmanskop?'

'I have the location of a house. Our information is that some diamonds have been packed in tissue paper in a nondescript bag in that house.'

'Are you certain?'

'No. Nothing is certain in this world, Mr Baird, except that one day we shall all have to leave it. But so far our information has been accurate. I have no reason to doubt it on this occasion.'

'How would I get into the colony and, more important, how would I get out if I undertook this assignment?'

'To take you there, we could provide a fishing boat from Angola, or Mozambique, flying a neutral Portuguese flag, with half a dozen Portuguese crew. All would have a strong link with England. They have married English girls, or their parents work for the English owners of vineyards in Oporto. Something like that. Their loyalty would be unquestioned.

'As neutrals, on the pretext of repairs, the vessel could put into Lüderitz and drop you off. Then you could make your own way across the desert to Kolmanskop and back. No frontier to cross, because you would already be on German soil.'

'You make it sound so simple,' said Jamie drily. 'Going in should present no great problems, but if these diamonds are as valuable as you say, even if I find them – which might be difficult enough – I would never be allowed to trek back across the desert with them. The Germans must have camel patrols out

447

there around Lüderitz. They might stop me, find I spoke neither Portuguese nor German – and then what?'

'Then you would be in trouble, Mr Baird.'

'And even if I evade the guards and patrols, they are almost certain to search everyone going aboard ship, neutral or not, just in case any are trying to smuggle diamonds out. That won't work, Colonel.'

'Well, have you a better way?' Dugdale pointed at the map. 'You will see that Kolmanskop is only a few miles from the coast, but the current is so strong, the sea so cold and the waves so high that no one has ever been known to survive for more than a few minutes in the water. And for only a few days of the year is it safe to navigate close to the shore. No ship could come in to pick you up, or even just take off the diamonds.

'The beach is empty and totally deserted. Sand dunes, wreathed in mist worse than a London pea-souper, stretch for nearly a hundred miles. The coastline is so flat that lookouts on many merchant ships in the past could see nothing and therefore thought, quite wrongly, they were heading for the open sea – until they ran aground. There are no distinguishing features to show where land begins. So many wrecks are still stuck in the sand that this is known as the "Skeleton Coast". You have no hope whatever of getting out to sea there. And anyone seen on the beach would almost certainly be interrogated. My proposal is not brilliant, but it is the only one that could work.'

Jamie stood for a moment in silence, remembering accounts he had heard in Kimberley about diamond smugglers who had ferried stolen stones into the Orange Free State. One of the most successful ways had been for an accomplice to bring homing pigeons to the mining area. The diamonds were taped to the legs of the birds, which would fly home across the border.

But who could train pigeons to fly out to a boat they had never seen before? Equally impossible was the idea of persuading an ostrich to eat the diamonds and then cross the border into Cape Colony where the bird could be shot or captured. But somehow moving the diamonds on their own seemed far more likely to succeed than transporting them personally across the desert.

Suddenly, Jamie remembered the Human Cannon Ball, the man in the red silk turban at the fair in Hyde. If Colonel Dugdale knew the approximate weight of the diamonds, then surely it could be calculated how much explosive would be required to blow a small shell case, or some similar canister, from a gun or a mortar to travel for a set distance?

But to fire this across the border from the German colony to the Cape would mean carrying the canister containing the diamonds and the mortar back across the desert – far more risky than simply carrying the diamonds. If it was fired out to sea, however, perhaps some kind of buoy or balloon could keep the canister afloat until a ship picked it up. That meant he would only need to carry the diamonds from Kolmanskop a very short distance to the shore. This seemed altogether more promising.

'Could this Portuguese fishing boat lie offshore from Kolmanskop, say half a mile out to sea, for an hour or so after dark on the night I collect the diamonds – if I can?'

'Provided the Germans have no patrol boats there, yes, I should think so. Why?'

'The fishing boat could then pick up a small rubber buoy?'

'In theory, yes, again. But what's behind these questions?'

'In Kimberley, diamond smugglers would tie the stones to the leg of a homing pigeon that would fly back to the Orange Free State. My idea is to use a gun or a mortar of some kind instead of a pigeon. You would have to supply me with a strong metal canister in which I can put the diamonds – if I find them. The canister fits into, say, a two-inch infantry mortar, in place of the usual mortar bomb or projectile. It is attached by a line to a rubber balloon, the size of a football bladder. Perhaps several, in case one burst. When the canister is fired out to sea at an agreed time, set to an agreed range, say five to six hundred yards, the fishing boat is waiting for it and hauls it in. We might even coat the balloons with phosphorescent paint so that they can be seen more easily at night.'

'Then how would you get back?'

'The way I came in. If I am searched, the Germans would find nothing on me except perhaps a Portuguese passport. I could carry papers that confirm I am deaf and dumb – which would save me from discovery, because I can't speak Portuguese or German.

'I could also have a few ten-pound notes in my pocket which I could have got in the Cape. German officials wouldn't bother too much about a deaf and dumb Portuguese seaman returning to his ship – especially if they lifted, say, fifty or a hundred pounds from him. The best thing would be to get him back aboard as quickly as possible, in case he started complaining.'

Dugdale stood for a moment, drawing on his cigar.

'Your plan is like the curate's egg – good in parts,' he said. 'But no one ever heard whether the curate ate both the good and the bad parts. Here, we have to take the whole thing. On the good parts, are you serious?'

'Yes.'

'Then can I assume you will undertake this assignment?'

'If you have no one better qualified. But on one condition.'

'And what is that?'

'That I can discuss this plan with my twin sister. She may have some better ideas.'

'You mean Lady Doncaster?'

'Yes. She is over here with her young son.'

'I see.' The colonel looked thoughtful. 'When will you let me know your answer? Remember, time isn't on our side.'

'By five o'clock this afternoon.'

By four, Jamie was speaking to Dugdale on the telephone, careful not to mention anything specific.

'We would like to accept your invitation to go on a fishing trip,' Jamie told him.

'*We?*'

'Yes. My sister and I.'

The Portuguese captain of the fishing vessel *San Miguel* spoke perfect English, as indeed he should do. Although he held Portuguese nationality, his grandfather had been English, one of many emigrants who married into wealthy Portuguese families, and whose descendants now controlled thousands of hectares of vineyards north of Oporto.

Jamie and Arabella were in the bridgehouse with him as they approached the rocky cliffs around Lüderitz. Gulls swooped and dipped above their catch, like pale parentheses against the darkening sky.

'Just to run through the arrangements, Mr Baird,' the captain said. 'We will dock here and take on fuel. According to the weather reports, there will be a thick mist this evening, which is fairly common here. When you and Lady Doncaster have gone ashore, we will wait for a further four hours, on the pretext of engine trouble. Then we sail south, keeping just out of sight of land all the way. Finally, we will come inshore off Kolmanskop, and watch for your signal, a red light over green over red.

'We will not acknowledge this visually in case a shore patrol reports it, but by a single blast on our siren. If we do not acknowledge, you will repeat your signal three times, at fifteen-minute intervals. If we do not reply, we both withdraw until twenty-three hundred hours on the following night and repeat the procedure. If we still do not make contact, we sail back to Cape Town. Is that your understanding, too, sir?'

'Absolutely,' said Jamie. He indicated Kolmanskop on the map. 'We hope to be here, on the beach. After we acknowledge each other's signals, watch for this yellow buoy.' He picked up a deflated rubber bladder from the chart table.

'And if there is no buoy after the signals?' the captain asked him.

'It should be there, floating somewhere. I hope the tide doesn't wash it ashore. Look for it as soon as there's enough light. Check which way the current flows. Throw a piece of wood into the water to see which direction it takes. If you can't find it, then return. Our trip will have been a failure. Head off back to the Cape.'

The captain peered through the glass front of the bridge-house. 'We will be coming alongside in under half an hour.'

'Right,' said Jamie to Arabella, 'let's dress for the part.'

With a team of army gunners and engineers, Jamie had experimented with several different sizes of charge and canister and balloon on the empty beach at Muizenberg, beyond Colonel Dugdale's house. A small motor boat, with the Portuguese captain aboard, had spotted the balloons as they were fired and checked meticulously on the distances that lesser and greater amounts of explosive would propel the canister.

Jamie finally decided to use an ordinary two-inch mortar, cut down from the military version to make it easier and lighter to carry; he only needed to use it once.

In his cabin he pulled on a pair of khaki-coloured Rosens, an army shirt without epaulettes, with a khaki sweater against the cold. He had a belt with a water bottle, a pistol in his back pocket with three clips of ammunition, a small compass, and £100 in Portuguese money. In a button-down pocket on his shirt he had a Portuguese passport with his photograph, in the name of Jose Gomez, shipwright, and a letter in Portuguese, with the address of a hospital in Luanda, describing him as deaf and dumb. To balance the water bottle on his belt, he had a small canvas bag of hard biscuits, strips of biltong and a handful of raisins.

He went into Arabella's cabin. She also wore Rosens and a

sweater. Her long hair was tucked up under a dark green beret. She handed him a khaki silk scarf which he put round his neck. This could be useful tied round the lower part of his face, as camouflage and also as a filter for the sand. They had been warned that sand could be far more dangerous than the thickest fog.

'Ready?' Arabella asked.

'As soon as we get the word,' replied Jamie.

High up on a rocky promontory to the left of the port, under the lighthouse, two German naval watchers peered through night glasses into the gathering gloom.

'One small fishing vessel coming alongside the jetty,' reported one of the sailors. 'Flying the Portuguese flag. There's a green and red stripe all round her gunwales – the Portuguese national colours. I can just make out her name on the bow – *San Miguel.*'

The other sailor consulted a list of names on a pad clipped to a piece of plywood.

'It's all right, we're expecting her. She's neutral.'

The *San Miguel* came alongside the deserted jetty, under the overhead gantries of cranes that could travel on rails to lift larger cargoes. Through the porthole in his cabin, Jamie saw a few fishing boats and rusty freighters moored fore and aft against the stone sides of the jetty. He heard the captain shout orders into the speaking tube. The engines stopped, and the *San Miguel* wallowed in a slight evening swell. Ropes were thrown overboard and made fast to bollards. They had arrived in German territory, enemy country.

The deck dipped slightly as three German officers came aboard. Because they spoke no Portuguese, and the Portuguese claimed no German, they conducted their business in English. They all went into the deckhouse where the captain spread out the ship's papers on a table for the officers to examine. Through the boards of the deck, Jamie and Arabella could follow the conversation.

'Care for a beer? We have a crate of Sagres aboard.'

'Thank you, Captain.'

Jamie heard a clink of bottles, a faint clatter of glasses.

'Crew of seven,' the captain reported. 'Including one woman, married to the shipwright. We are carrying a cargo of tunny fish. We've had a poor trip, made just enough to pay for fuel to get us back north to Benguela.'

'How do you account for that?' asked one German. 'Our people do a lot of cray fishing here, and the catches are good.'

'That's closer inshore, by the rocks. Maybe there's a storm coming, maybe the water's too cold, anything. Tunny are very susceptible to all sorts of odd things.'

'How long are you staying here?'

'No longer than we have to. But we have trouble with the engine. It is old and the water jacket is leaking. It could be dangerous if that cracked out at sea, for we have no sails. I would like to get it welded here if I can.'

'Have you equipment on board?'

'For a simple weld, yes.'

'There is a good man here in Lüderitz, if you need help. I will give you his name.'

'Thank you. We will get in touch if we have to, but I hope we won't. We have to cut expenses down as much as possible, as I am sure you can understand.'

'Perfectly, Captain. Perfectly.'

The captain put down the passports for the official to examine.

'This shipwright,' said another German. 'Deaf and dumb, according to these papers. How does he communicate, then?'

An almost imperceptible pause, then the captain explained.

'He doesn't – now. He got hit on the head a month or so

back. Sea cook went berserk and attacked him. Doctors say they can't do anything for him. He's really supernumerary, but the owners don't want to pay him off. He was very good at his job. They hope he may recover by doing the job he's always done.'

'I see. Kindly employers, yes?'

'Yes. Very good.'

There was the thump of a stamp being applied to the captain's papers and passports.

'There. You are all right here for twenty-four hours. Is that long enough for your repairs?'

'If not, I can come back to you?'

'Yes. My office is at the head of the quay here.'

Jamie and Arabella heard steps cross the deck. The vessel rocked very slightly as the officers jumped down on to the jetty. Jamie drew the curtain across the porthole.

The captain waited for several minutes, then came to see him.

'You're all right,' he said, relieved. 'A bit near the bone, a question about the shipwright.'

'I heard,' said Jamie.

'Now, stay here until it's dark. They probably have naval shore patrols in the town, and it cuts down your risk if you don't run into them. Then head out through the town. You'll see a building on the left, Kapps Hotel, with a painted tower, like a steeple. That's the Spitz Bar. Keep that on your left. Go straight up the hill and you'll reach the desert road. It's very straight. Then just keep on until you see the houses of Kolmanskop. It should take you under two hours. The road is patrolled by police on camels by day, and in cars at night. You'll see their lights if the mist hasn't reached that far inland, so you can get off the road into the sand in good time. And if there is mist, you won't need to. Good luck. Look forward to seeing you soon.'

The captain shook hands.

After he had left, Jamie and Arabella sat in their cabin for another hour, then came up on deck. A few lights were burning in the port, and a regular beam from the lighthouse swept out across the sea. In its spasmodic glare they could see mist running in towards the shore, thick, white, moving quickly. It felt cold and clammy to their skin, their hair. They waited until the mist completely engulfed the buildings ashore and the lights grew dim and diffused in the water vapour. Then they climbed out on the deck, went down the gangway.

Jamie carried the small canvas case containing the mortar, two explosive charges, the canister and a trowel. They walked into the town, past the bar at Kapps Hotel. Sounds of laughter, singing, an accordion playing, filtered through heavy, closed doors. At the top of the hill, the houses thinned and then fell away. Soon they were out on a hard, surfaced road.

The mist had still not reached here, although it was coming in fast. Under a half-moon the desert stretched like a silvery sea on either side. There were no sounds up here, except the faint, restless moaning of the wind and the furtive rustle of sand moving under eddying currents of air.

Half an hour along the road they saw the yellow acetylene lights of a car coming towards them. At once, Jamie went to the left of the road, Arabella to the right. They rolled across the sand, hastily scratched together a small barrier of it between them and the road. The car approached, passed without slackening speed. Its rear red light diminished as it sped away, leaving only the smell of exhaust. They stood up, dusted the sand off their clothes and kept on marching.

Two hours later they approached the outskirts of Kolmanskop. It appeared to be built on the slope of a deep valley of sand. A railway line ran through the centre: the rails shone like two silvery serpents laid side by side under the moon. Against the sky stood a reservoir and the mine manager's house, largest of the private houses. On the other side was the casino, a bowling alley, shops, a school.

Jamie knew what each building was; he had studied every map Colonel Dugdale could provide, as well as photographs taken of the town before the war.

The house where the colonel believed the diamonds were stored stood on the far side of Kolmanskop, some distance from the others, a small, single-storey building. Jamie and Arabella began to move carefully round the perimeter of the town, keeping out in the desert, well away from the houses. They could hear music coming from the casino; a brass band appeared to be rehearsing. Some houses had front doors and windows open, to let in cool air during a brief respite from the wind and the drifting sand.

From several houses they could hear music from gramophone records. A dog barked a warning, and another echoed his bark. They stood still until the barking ceased, then moved on again, more cautiously. There was still no mist here and no wind; they wished fervently for both to provide some cover for them.

They reached the house and, higher up the hill behind it, lay down in the sand. They could not hear any voices or sounds of anyone inside, and the shuttered windows were all dark. It could be deserted.

The windows were protected by thick wooden shutters; the front and back doors were of stout wood, with several locks. The Germans were not a race to surrender possessions easily to any uninvited nightcomer.

The longer Jamie and Arabella stayed, the greater their chance of discovery. Their best hope lay in a quick entry to the house, a search, and then rapid departure. Jamie stood up.

'We'll try the back window,' he whispered to his sister.

Arabella nodded. She covered his mortar case with sand and stuck in two twigs from a bush to mark the spot. As she did so, they both sensed rather than saw someone, or something, moving behind them. They turned quickly, hands going instinctively to their pistols. But there was only sand, wraiths of it starting to move under a welcome wind that began to whistle beneath the dry eaves of the house.

They were jumpy; that was all. No one was behind them. They moved more quickly, eager to be in and out and away. Jamie checked the metal hasp of the nearest shutter. The screws in the hinges were loose; the wood had dried. He prised them out easily enough, lifted off the shutter, put it down carefully in the sand against the wall.

The window behind was closed. He wrapped his handkerchief round his right hand, punched in a pane of glass, then paused, in case the tinkling of breaking glass had aroused anyone. But there was no sound apart from the wind and the other shutter creaking slightly on its salt-caked, rusting hinges.

Jamie put a hand carefully through the shattered pane, opened the catch, climbed inside. Arabella followed him. They stood for a moment in a sparsely furnished room, breathing slowly, trying to accustom their eyes to the dimness.

Arabella pulled the curtain across the window, while Jamie shone his torch around the room, shielding the beam with one hand. They were in the kitchen. Against one wall was a heavy porcelain sink with a single brass tap, a wooden draining board, cupboards. In the centre stood a wooden table, covered with a patterned oilcloth, and two chairs. Arabella opened each cupboard. They were empty.

The tap dripped slowly like a metronome. In a cupboard under the sink they saw some pans, a packet of washing soda, another of scouring powder, but no diamonds.

They went into the living room, peered under the settee, lifted cushions from easy chairs, felt behind a handful of German books and a family Bible on a shelf. They took out each book and riffled through its pages, in case a hollow hiding place had been cut out.

A cuckoo clock ticked on the mantelpiece. Suddenly, its door flew open, the cuckoo popped its head out as the clock struck the hour – two o'clock in the morning. Someone must have been here within the past day or so to wind the clock. Had the diamonds already gone? Were they too late?

There was only one room left – the bedroom. This had a strip of carpet on a wood floor, an iron bedstead, the bed neatly made, a table by its head with a Swiss-made alarm clock. The hands showed faintly luminous in the light of the torch. The clothes cupboard was empty; a chest of drawers contained a few shirts and socks, but nothing else.

A rough wooden door with a latch opened off the bedroom into a privy. Sheets torn from a newspaper were threaded on a spike behind the door. At the far end, under a six-inch square window, was a scrubbed wooden plank with a single hole cut in the middle. The plank was hinged. Jamie raised it, shone his torch into the white enamel bucket beneath the hole. It was perfectly clean.

Jamie looked more closely, saw there were two buckets, one inside the other. He pulled them both out and lifted them apart. Between them was a small waterproof bag, the size of a quarter-pound of sweets. He took it out, opened it. In the torchlight, uncut stones glittered hazily in a twist of tissue paper. He nodded to Arabella.

Jamie put the bag in the pouch on his belt, replaced the buckets, lowered the seat. They went back through the house and waited for a moment by the kitchen window, listening. The wind was rising, and above the rustling of the sand they could hear surf thunder on the shore. They had found what they had come for, but somehow it was all too easy.

If the house had been furnished, the diamonds could have been hidden in a hundred different places. But it was virtually unfurnished, and that left very few. Perhaps whoever had been there had packed all his belongings and left in a hurry, and the last thing he had time to take would be diamonds. That was possible – but was it likely? Surely, these stones would be the first thing anyone would remove?

They climbed out of the window, refixed the shutter, holding it in place until they could push the loose screws back into their holes. The wind was rising now, blowing the sand against their faces, their necks, their hands. Arabella was thankful she had marked the hiding place of the mortar. As it was, only the tips of the twigs were visible above the rising level of sand. They took a step towards them – and at that moment the ground ahead exploded into light.

A man who had been hiding behind a hillock of sand stood up, facing them triumphantly. He held a powerful torch in one hand, a double-barrelled shotgun in the crook of his other arm. At that range, a blind man couldn't miss. The distance was less than six feet.

'Stay where you are! Hands up high!' he shouted in German.

Slowly, Jamie and Arabella raised their hands. The man switched off his torch, let it fall on to the soft sand. He could see well enough by moonlight.

'Who are you?' he asked in English.

'We are from the Portuguese ship, the *San Miguel*, in Lüderitz,' Jamie explained. This was not the time to maintain the fiction of being deaf and dumb.

'And you speak English?' said the man.

'Many Portuguese do. We are a neutral country, remember.'

'So what are you doing breaking into this house? Far from the port, too – for neutral sailors.'

The man took a step closer to them. The two muzzles of his shotgun were now barely a yard away. If he fired, they would die at once. If he called out, they could be captured. Clouds which had been drifting like shredded silk across the face of the moon suddenly parted. The light lit up the man's face which until that moment had been hidden in shadow.

'*Orlando!*' cried Arabella in amazement.

For a second, the shotgun wavered in Orlando's hands, then he gripped it more strongly. They could see his face contorted with conflicting emotions: astonishment, disbelief, naked hate. They were watching a man wake from a long nightmare to face people he had forgotten ever existed. He had travelled back into time and a long-buried memory was coming to life. He peered disbelievingly into Arabella's face.

'You *bitch*!' he said slowly. 'You stole my mother's earrings. You threw me into the sea. You tried to kill me.'

'I did that,' said Jamie. 'But not intentionally.'

'No? You are her brother then. You bastard! You thought you *had* killed me, but you were wrong. Did you find in the house what I left for you?'

'You mean the diamonds?'

'I mean a bag of stones in a lavatory pail.'

'I found them,' said Jamie.

'We thought you would.'

Orlando came closer to them. The shotgun barrels loomed like the gaping nostrils of some deadly beast.

'The Germans aren't fools, you know. As soon as they realised war was coming, they started to move some diamonds north. Others went out to Brazil. We thought your people would think the big diamonds had not all gone, that they were still here. So they laid a trap for whoever came calling. They thought it would be a professional. Not a cheap jewel thief and her brother. Now you are prisoners. Not prisoners of war, because you are not military, but civilians. Spies. And spies are shot.'

'You are wrong about the diamonds,' said Jamie easily. 'They are not worthless. Quite the reverse. They will fetch millions. Can I show you how I know?'

'Don't try anything clever, or you both die. Which would give me great pleasure.'

'Am I likely to take that risk?' Jamie opened his pouch,

took out the bag of diamonds, tipped them into his two hands.

'They're glass,' said Orlando. 'Old bottle tops, washed up by the sea. All the gloss is taken off by the sand. Diggers wanting to salt a dud mine often use these things. We salted a trap for you.'

'I know most are glass,' agreed Jamie. 'But not this one. This is an amazing one-hundred-carat diamond, the best colour. But don't take my word. Look for yourself.'

He held out his cupped hands towards Orlando who instinctively bent forward slightly.

At that moment, Jamie threw the stones in Orlando's face, kicked him with all his force on his right shin and forced the gun up into the air. Orlando pressed both triggers. The two shots boomed like thunder. Orlando jumped back a pace, reloaded expertly, took aim.

'You bastard!' he said angrily.

Jamie and Arabella could see his finger tighten on the first trigger, his eyes narrow. Then, suddenly, inexplicably, he collapsed at their feet.

Jamie seized his gun as he fell. From Orlando's back, the long feathered shaft of an arrow trembled in the moonlight. Jamie knelt down by Orlando's side, felt his pulse. There was no beat. He was dead. Jamie stood up.

Arabella was already uncovering the case she had buried. Between them, like a wraith rising from the whirling sand, a small, dark figure appeared. He was naked except for a pair of shorts. He carried a bow and held five more arrows in his hand.

'Who are you?' asked Jamie hoarsely.

'Bushman tracker,' replied the stranger.

'You just saved our lives,' said Jamie thankfully.

The man did not reply. He stood, still as a statue, and clicked his teeth in the way of his race.

'Why are you here?' Arabella asked him.

'I followed you across the desert. I saw where he was hiding. I waited.'

462

'How did you know we were coming here?'

'Your friends told me.'

What friends? Jamie wondered. Colonel Dugdale? The Portuguese captain?

'I saw this man kill my people after they had dug a grave to hide the diamonds at Grootfontein. He tried to kill me, too, but I escaped.'

'Those stones were all fakes,' said Jamie. 'But good fakes. By people who knew what they were about.'

'Are there any real diamonds left down here?' Arabella asked the Bushman.

'Yes,' said the Bushman. He indicated Orlando, lying face down on the sand. 'He has them.'

'Where?'

'In his belly. He swallowed them. He was to take them out, over the border, to the Cape. He was not German, so I heard. He was English.'

'So we have lost them?'

'No. You have found them.'

As he spoke, the Bushman bent down, rolled Orlando over on to his back, ripped open his skirt. He dug a curved knife into his stomach and pulled up with all his strength towards his chest.

Arabella turned away in horror as Orlando's bowels gushed out, steaming and shining under the moon. Jamie watched, fascinated, as he had watched Yeung Lee search the stomachs of birds for odd items they had eaten; as he, Jamie, had also cut open ostrich stomachs.

The Bushman's agile fingers worked through the viscera. He cut away again. The stench of warm, half-digested food made Jamie choke. Then the Bushman held out both hands towards him, slippery with blood and slime. Six diamonds, one the largest Jamie had ever seen, glittered weakly in the dim light.

'Take them,' said the Bushman. 'This is what you came for.'

463

Jamie shook his head. He felt sickened with violence and death. 'You take them,' he told the Bushman. 'You have earned them.'

'No. I will take the gun. That is my prize.'

He stood up suddenly, turned his head into the wind, listening.

'Hurry!' he said sharply. 'People are coming here. They have heard the shots.'

Jamie scooped up the diamonds, rammed them into his pouch, seized Arabella's hand. He pulled the case with the mortar out of its hiding place, and together they set off through the clogging, choking sand towards the sea.

The wind was blowing strongly now. All around them, as well as under their feet, they felt the desert move. Against the roar of the wind, they could hear voices shouting. A whistle blew, a dog began to bark.

By now, whoever was out there might have discovered Orlando's body, but in the storm this was by no means certain. Jamie heard two shots. They sounded too heavy for an ordinary rifle. Perhaps the Bushman was firing the shotgun? Then he heard a single shot from a smaller-calibre weapon. The shouts died away as the storm increased – or maybe their pursuers were going in the opposite direction.

The dunes were changing shape as they ran. One step would be firm; the next, they would sink up to their knees in soft warm sand which prickled their eyes, their throats, their nostrils. They wrapped Arabella's scarves round their faces, but such was the force of the wind that these could not filter more than a small amount of the driven sand.

Finally, gasping for breath, they reached the beach. The whirling sand had totally obscured the moon. They only knew where the sea lay from the thunder of its waves and the damp salty smell of seaweed ripped from its roots by the angry tide.

Jamie checked the direction with his compass, pointed his

torch towards the waves. He slid the coloured lenses across it, pressed the switch: red over green over red. They listened, straining their ears for the sound of a ship's hooter, but there was nothing. Were they too soon? Too late? In the wrong place?

Perhaps the *San Miguel* had been delayed, or in the mist had overshot the meeting point? Whatever had happened, they must be rid of the diamonds. Without them, they might stand a chance, even if they were arrested. With them, they had none.

Although the diamonds were larger than Jamie expected, there were fewer of them; he wondered whether the charge would blow the canister too far out to sea. He inflated the orange bladder, checked that its cord was loose. He screwed on the canister's brass top, tied the end of the cord to it. Then he set up the mortar in the sand at a 45-degree angle, slid the charge carefully down the barrel.

The charge was in the form of a small cylinder of explosive tightly wrapped in tin foil. When he dropped the canister on this, a small sharp spike in the canister's base would pierce the foil and detonate the charge. He held the canister up in the mouth of the mortar, checking the buoy was hanging free, waiting for the signal to fire.

For a second time, Arabella flashed the signal. Now a faint moaning, as from a foghorn, came from the darkened sea; message received and understood. Standing well back from the mouth of the mortar, Jamie let the canister drop down inside it.

The explosion boomed like a giant gong. Trailing its balloon, the canister soared up through the driving sand and sea mist, into the opaque sky, and was gone.

Whatever happened to the diamonds now, they had kept their part of the agreement. The rest was up to others. Jamie picked up the mortar, replaced it in its case, and used the trowel to dig a hole in the sand. Then he buried the case with the trowel on top.

As he stood up, sweating with exertion, sand sticking to his damp flesh, the shifting dunes moved across the hiding place. Soon it would have totally disappeared beneath a new hillock – until the wind changed again. But by then they should be safe aboard ship.

Jamie and Arabella stood for a moment, backs against the wind, and rinsed their mouths out with water from their bottles. Jamie checked direction with his compass. Then, heads down against driving sand and roaring wind, they set out slowly along the edge of the sea, back towards Lüderitz and the *San Miguel*.

Jamie faced Colonel Dugdale in his room overlooking the sea at Muizenburg. The diamonds he and Arabella had brought out from Lüderitz lay on a small square of white lint on Dugdale's desk between them.

'Mission successful,' said the colonel approvingly. 'Pity about that Englishman being killed, however. Actually, he wasn't the Honourable Orlando Sutton, but Lord Rosael. I checked. His father died last year. The title is now extinct, I suppose. Wouldn't do to let too many people know how we actually acquired these diamonds. Some people get squeamish about that sort of thing. Can't think why.'

'Since only you, my sister and I know, that secret should be easy to keep,' Jamie replied.

'Lady Doncaster, I suppose, would not mention it to anyone?'

'Of course not,' replied Jamie. 'We're twins. We act alike, we think alike.'

'I hear that her laboratories have gone over to producing medical supplies full time for the duration. She is certainly doing an amazing job.'

'She is an amazing person,' said Jamie. 'But I am not so concerned about what she is doing as about what I am not doing. Couldn't my case for joining the Army be reconsidered now?'

The colonel shook his head. 'Sorry,' he said, 'but that's really out of my hands. We can only go on what the medical people say.'

'Then I might as well go back to England and try my luck there.'

'That's a good idea,' said the colonel. 'I've one or two contacts there. I'll tell them you're on your way.'

Dugdale opened a drawer in his desk, took out a small narrow leather box, like a pencil case, and handed it to Jamie.

'I nearly forgot,' he said. 'A memento for you and Lady Doncaster. We can't pay you a fee, but I thought you might like this.'

Jamie opened the case. Inside were two wrist watches, for a man and a woman. Their dials were encrusted with tiny diamonds.

'A present from the desert,' Dugdale explained. 'Some of the diamonds our people dug out up north seemed too small to put on the market, so I got a jeweller to decorate these watches with them. A bit unusual, eh? I hope you will both find them useful.'

TWENTY-SIX

In Defence of the Realm

Jamie Baird was sitting in the first-class lounge with Sammy Rosen when the liner docked at Southampton. For the first time since they had left Cape Town, the ship fell silent with that peculiar, almost unexpected stillness aboard a liner when the engines stop at the end of a voyage.

A half-empty bottle of champagne stood on the table between them. Jamie refilled their glasses and they drank a silent toast to each other. In South Africa, away from all parameters of remembered poverty, it had been very easy to become used to wealth. But each time Jamie returned to England, under a sky of forgotten greyness, the reality seemed more difficult to accept.

Sammy planned to give presents to everyone in the street where he had lived with his father. He did this every time he came back to England. His hero, Barney Barnato, had been equally generous when he returned, and Sammy was never a man to be outclassed.

He intended to take a suite at the Savoy, and to see every play in London. He loved the theatre, and especially the theatricality of each performance. Dressing up, pretending to be someone else had a peculiar fascination for him, and amateur dramatics in Kimberley, even the touring companies that visited Johannesburg and Cape Town, were a poor substitute for the Gaiety or the Alhambra in London.

Jamie had no specific plans. He had not been back to England since the outbreak of the war over two years earlier, and he hoped vaguely there might be some positive work he could do to help his country. He did not consider his trip to Lüderitz and Kolmanskop as being much more than an adventure. Holding his glass of champagne up to his eye, he saw, through the rising bubbles, a man of his own age approaching him with a steward. He had thick black hair and a moustache, and wore Army uniform, with a captain's stars on his sleeve. I might be like that fellow, holding the King's commission, Jamie thought enviously – if only the doctors had passed me as fit. Which, of course, I am.

As he drained his glass, the two men stopped at his table.

'Excuse me, Mr Baird, sir,' said the steward. 'But this gentleman has come aboard expressly to see you.'

The officer clicked his heels and bowed. 'Captain Drake,' he said.

Sammy looked at him quizzically, his tailor's eyes hanging a price tag on his superbly cut uniform.

'How can I help you?' Jamie asked him. Presumably he wanted something; people who arrived unannounced invariably did. The officer glanced at Sammy Rosen.

'I wonder if I could have a word in private, sir? A confidential matter.'

'Really?' Jamie's surprise sounded in his voice. He had never seen the man before. He could not imagine what confidential matter he could now wish to discuss. And how did the fellow know who he was?

'Take a seat,' said Jamie. 'You will join us in a drink?'

'No, sir, I am on duty.'

'I don't think we have met before.'

'That is true, sir. I was first on board when the liner docked. I have a letter to deliver to you.'

'From whom?'

469

'You had better read it, sir.' Drake looked pointedly at Sammy. 'It's a personal matter,' he explained.

Sammy stood up. 'Then I will leave you gentlemen. I would not wish to intrude.' He walked across the lounge, sat down on a settee in the far corner, picked up a magazine.

Jamie slit open the letter, which was sealed with red wax with a signature written beneath the seal. It was from someone of whom he had never heard – Major General Kirby Brookes, CIE, DSO, MC. The address was of a country house, Leinster Grange, outside Marlborough in Wiltshire. Under this were typed two words in red: 'Most Secret'. He read the typewritten note carefully.

Dear Mr Baird, I would be most grateful if you could arrange with the bearer of this note, my ADC, Captain Drake, to visit me at the above address as soon as may be convenient to you.

I wish to discuss a matter of the highest importance and greatest secrecy, which concerns the Defence of the Realm, so I ask you not to question Captain Drake about it or about my present responsibilities.

I apologise for this brusque request, but your name has been given to me by a colleague, Colonel Dugdale, in the Cape, who holds you in the highest regard. I ask you to treat this communication as confidential, and I look forward to meeting you.

Jamie folded the letter, replaced it in the envelope, put it in his pocket.

'I will take that back, sir, if you don't mind,' said Drake. 'It might fall into the wrong hands.'

'This seems very melodramatic,' said Jamie, handing over the letter and the envelope. 'Who is General Kirby Brookes?' Even as he spoke, he realised he was asking a question Brookes had specifically requested him not to ask.

'He is involved with a branch of the War Office, sir. I can tell you no more. Would it be convenient for you to consult your diary and tell me when you could see the general?'

'As far as my engagements in England are concerned, my diary is empty. How did you come here? By motor?'

'Yes, sir.'

'I will send my cases on to Claridges – they are bound to have a representative on the quay. Then, if you so wish, I can accompany you immediately. Are you certain you won't join me in a glass of champagne now that your mission in delivering this letter has been successful?'

'I would like to, sir. But, as I said, I am on duty.'

'Well, I'm not – yet,' Jamie replied and emptied the bottle into his glass. 'Where is your motor?'

'On the quay, sir. A green Silver Ghost. With a Service Corps driver.'

'I'll meet you by it in half an hour.'

Drake stood up, bowed smartly and left the lounge. Jamie waited until he had gone, then crossed the lounge and sat down by Sammy's side.

'Anything wrong?' Sammy asked him, putting aside the magazine. 'He didn't bring bad news, I hope?'

'No,' said Jamie slowly, wondering whether he should tell Sammy anything about the letter. He had been asked not to, of course, but he had known Sammy for so many years, and trusted him.

'If I may tell you in confidence, it's from a general who lives near Marlborough. He wants to see me about some matter he won't divulge. Goodness knows what it is. But I'll see him. The unknown always intrigues me.'

'Well, I wish you luck. You'll be at Claridges – eventually?'

'Yes. If I'm delayed or change my plans, I'll ask them to hold my mail. I will be in touch as soon as I can.'

Drake's Rolls had an ornate roof rack where the chauffeur,

an Army corporal, strapped Jamie's overnight bag. As he climbed into the back with Drake, Jamie glanced up at the ship. Sammy was leaning over the rail on the promenade deck to wave him goodbye.

The road from Southampton to Marlborough was dusty and unmade for several stretches; frequently, it seemed more like a country lane than a main thoroughfare. The only traffic they saw were farm carts, a motor omnibus and several army lorries. They stopped for lunch at the Red Lion in Salisbury. The driver stayed outside in the courtyard with the car; a waiter took out sandwiches and a pint of beer to him on a tray.

They reached Leinster Grange in the early afternoon. It was a large house, built of Chilmark stone, in the centre of a wood. One of the stone gateposts had been hit by a truck, and leaned over at an angle. The iron gates were green with moss and mildew, the drive covered by brown leaves, still damp from autumn rain, and rutted by the tyres of many vehicles. Several cars were parked outside the house, which had an unkempt appearance. A gutter was broken and rain had streaked the stone wall beneath it with green slime.

'It's only temporary accommodation,' explained Drake. 'We tend to move addresses fairly regularly.'

'To avoid creditors?' Jamie asked him, in an attempt at humour.

'Oh no, sir!' The young man appeared shocked at such a suggestion. 'It's just that we do not like to draw too much attention to our presence with motors arriving day and night. That's why the general likes old country houses, tucked away from villages and roads.'

The hall was sparsely furnished: a suit of armour gathered dust near an oak staircase; the grandfather clock was ten minutes slow. A manservant opened the front door, stood to one side respectfully as they entered. Baird saw that under his green baize apron he wore khaki shirt and trousers.

On a gold-panelled door, Jamie read a freshly varnished notice: General Kirby Brookes. Drake tapped discreetly on the panel.

'Captain Drake, sir,' he called out.

'Come!' said a voice within. Drake brushed down the sides of his tunic, smoothed his hair, obviously in awe of the general. Then he opened the door and led Jamie into the room.

A fire burned low in a black-leaded grate. On the walls, covered with deep red silk, less faded squares marked where paintings had hung. In one corner of the room, out of line with the window, stood a large desk with two telephones, one with a hand crank of Army design. In front of the fire was a brass fender with a red leather seat. There were several red leather chairs, a settee, a table thick with buff-coloured files tied in pink tape. The walls were bare of pictures except for a text embroidered on a sheet of linen, in a Victorian frame.

I returned, and saw under the sun, that the race is not to the swift nor the battle to the strong, neither yet bread to the wise, nor yet riches to men of understanding, nor yet favour to men of skill; but time and chance happeneth to them all.

For man also knoweth not his time: as the fishes that are taken in an evil net, and as the birds that are caught in the snare; so are the sons of men snared in an evil time, when it falleth suddenly upon them.

This wisdom have I seen also under the sun, and it seemed great unto me.

—Ecclesiastes, Chapter 9,
Verses 11–13.

A man wearing a general's uniform with red tabs, his tunic unbuttoned, stood behind the desk. He had greyish hair, smoked a pipe. He crossed the room, held out his hand in welcome.

'Mr Baird, sir. How kind of you to come at such short

notice. Would you like a coffee, or perhaps a whisky?'

'A coffee, I think. Black, without sugar.'

'Of course.'

The general nodded to Captain Drake, who went out and shortly returned with an orderly who carried in a tray with a percolator and a single cup and saucer. Jamie drank one cup of coffee. The general pressed a bell on his desk. The orderly reappeared, removed the tray.

'Now, to business,' said the general briskly. 'You will be wondering, sir, why I invited you here, and why I am so pleased that you could come at once.'

'The question has crossed my mind, yes.'

Kirby Brookes turned to Drake. 'Put a guard on the door,' he told him brusquely. 'We are not to be disturbed until I ring.'

'Very good, sir.' Drake clicked his heels and left the room.

Jamie looked at the general expectantly. Brookes sat down behind the desk. The swivel chair, also upholstered in red leather, creaked under his weight.

'I must apologise for what may seem a rather melodramatic introduction,' he said, 'but I wanted to see you, if at all possible, before you made other plans. I understand you volunteered for Army service in the Cape?'

'I was told I was medically unfit.'

'That would apply to many of the world's greatest leaders. It's a mark of the absurd bureaucratic thinking of our time. Why, Napoleon suffered from dyspepsia and piles – and was an epileptic. So, curiously enough, was Julius Caesar. Nelson had only one eye. So there's hope, Mr Baird.'

'For whom? To do what?'

'For you, sir, to strike a blow, not only for your country, but for our allies. For the cause of victory, of good over evil.'

'How, exactly?'

'Before I tell you, sir, I must ask you to sign a form under the Official Secrets Act, to put on record the fact that you realise

474

you must not divulge anything you learn, hear or see in this office to any other party.'

'Is that necessary?'

'Not as far as I am concerned, Mr Baird, but those are the orders.'

He came round the desk, handed Baird a typewritten form. Jamie signed it, then sat back. He glanced up at the framed text.

'Ecclesiastes, Mr Baird,' said the general. 'A wonderful book, the Bible. No illusions there about life – or death. My father was a rural dean,' he continued. 'His sister – a maiden lady – embroidered that text. I think it is apt. The rain falls on the just and the unjust alike, Mr Baird. A point that one continually proves all through life.'

'You didn't ask me here to tell me that, surely, General?'

'No. To ask you some questions, actually. I hear you are an expert in diamonds?'

'I've been called other things,' replied Jamie with a smile. 'I do know something about diamonds. But not nearly as much as a dozen other men I could name.'

'Quite possibly. But you have one inestimable advantage over them. You are here and they are not. Can you recognise a real diamond from a fake – quickly?'

'I think so,' Jamie said modestly.

The general unlocked a drawer in his desk, took out a silver cigarette case, opened it. Half a dozen stones glittered in the firelight.

'Could you tell me which of these are counterfeit – if any are?'

Jamie crossed the room, stirred the stones with his forefinger. 'These three are false, the others are genuine, but only three carats. They are much as one might find in an inexpensive engagement ring. Do you want me to say how I know?'

Brookes shook his head. 'No,' he said. 'It is immaterial to me

475

how you know. The important fact is that you do. If I consult a physician for some complaint, I do not need to be told the processes of elimination he goes through in his mind before he diagnoses the ailment. You are right about the three good diamonds. That is all that matters.'

He put the case and the stones back in the drawer, locked it with a key on a gold chain, and sat back in his chair, puffing his pipe for a moment, as though not quite certain how to proceed. Then he tapped out his pipe in an ashtray, laid it down on one side and began to speak.

'I don't know whether you are familiar with the current political situation in Russia?' he asked abruptly.

'I know nothing about that country,' said Jamie. 'I have been concerned with South Africa. I did visit St Petersburg before the war, though, and left days before it broke out.'

'So I understand. Well, Russia has been, as you may know, our very good ally. She could, of course, have done infinitely more had her troops been better provisioned and equipped – and led. The Tsar of Russia has personally taken charge of military strategy with predictably unfortunate results. He is, by all accounts, an amiable man, but totally without experience in the arts of war, or the even more difficult art of handling people.

'I am told that his dearest wish is to live peacefully like an English country gentleman on an estate, removed from all violence and the memory of assassinations and revolution. A wish I would think unlikely to be granted to him – judging from past experience, at least. All his life he has lived in the shadow of revolution and sudden death. And that shadow grows darker every day.

'As a little boy still in a sailor suit, the Tsar saw his grandfather, Emperor Alexander II, bleed to death on the marble stairs of the Winter Palace in St Petersburg. A terrorist bomb had broken his legs, torn open his stomach, blown away his

476

whole face. Such a sight is not easily forgotten, Mr Baird.

'The Tsar loves military ceremonial and ritual, and wearing fancy uniforms – incidentally, he is Colonel-in-Chief of the Scots Greys. More importantly, he is the ruler of one hundred and thirty million people, in a country occupying one-sixth of the earth's surface, so large that when it's evening on Russia's western frontier, the sun is rising on its eastern border.

'He never wished to be Tsar, but that was his destiny. Whenever possible, he has retreated from the great responsibilities involved. All the portents for his reign were wrong from the start. At the coronation ceremony, for instance, when the Chain of Office was put around the Tsar's chest, it fell to the ground. Everyone who saw this was sworn to secrecy, but, of course, this evil omen was soon known across the nation. Then, next day, hundreds of people were killed and thousands more crushed with fearful injuries when tiers of seats collapsed at an open-air feast to mark the coronation.

'The Tsar understandably wanted to call off all further celebrations as a mark of respect to the dead, but his German wife, Alexandra, convinced him that the junketings should go on. The people expected it, she said. They didn't, of course. They resented it, bitterly.

'Curiously enough, Mr Baird, the same mob who shouted against him then, shouted for him equally loudly when, in 1914, on the balcony of the Winter Palace, he repeated Alexander I's pledge in the face of Napoleon's invasion that he would never make peace until all enemies had been driven from his country.

'Grand Duke Nicholas commanded the army at that time and was a tolerably good commander, but Alexandra disliked him and persuaded her husband to sack him, and run the country and the war.

'At this, the cabinet resigned virtually en masse, but the Tsar ignored this and left for the front, where chaos and catastrophe have since beggared description. Four million Russian soldiers have already died, and thousands more die every day – needlessly. They lack boots, bullets, food and, most of all, leadership.

'Most haven't even rifles. They have to wait until a soldier with a rifle is killed, and then take his. The artillery is so short of shells that if a battery fires more than three shells a day, their officers face court martial. One general told me that so chaotic are the railways, a draft of reinforcements took twenty-three days – more than three *weeks* – to reach the front. And when they got there, the front had moved and everyone was in retreat.

'At home, the cost of living is up three hundred per cent. Hundreds of thousands are idle in the cities. Factories have closed because they cannot get supplies. Queues a mile long wait at dawn each morning for the bakeries to open – and then have to go away hungry because there isn't enough bread for them. And all the while, the astonishing social life enjoyed by the very rich goes on unabated. Russia is ripe for revolution.

'The blame for all this is laid at the door of the Tsarina, because of her German background, and Rasputin, who has an extraordinary influence over her. Most know him as a drunken, lecherous degenerate.

'To the Tsarina Rasputin is a *strannick*, a holy man, a worker of miracles. Her only son – Alexei, the Tsarevitch – is a haemophiliac, and what Rasputin possesses, in the view of our experts, is a great, perhaps unparalleled gift of personal hypnotism. As far as haemophiliacs are concerned, medical thinking is that a haemorrhage may be in some way linked to stress in the patient. When Rasputin superimposes his stronger will on the boy's mind, he makes him feel better. His condition stabilises. He becomes relaxed, his fever falls. Not a cure, of course, but a remission. There is no permanent cure, but because the Tsarina believes Rasputin literally holds the power of life or death over her son, she thinks that his gifts in other directions must be equally rare. When he speaks to her about political or military matters, about which, as a peasant, he knows nothing at all, she heeds his advice, however ridiculous or dangerous it may be.

'He is knowledgeable about drugs, and it has been suggested that in some way he has drugged the Tsar, to weaken his will. Certainly, the Tsar never goes against his wife. He says frequently that if he did so, and Rasputin left him and the boy died, he would then feel personally responsible for killing his own son.

'The Tsar has the highest motives, but lacks common sense. For example, to try and minimise criticism of his wife that she secretly sides with Germany, he changed the name of the capital from Petersburg to Petrograd, which he believes sounds more Russian.

'All this brings me to the reason I asked you here. We expect two things will happen in Russia before the year is out. First, feeling against Rasputin will rise to such an extent that he will be assassinated. Then, as a result, anger against the appalling and needless casualties at the front, the hunger and misery at home – compared with the life of luxury the rich still manage to enjoy – will erupt. There will be a revolution. Russia will leave the Allies. At best, she will be neutral. At worst, she may actually take up arms against us.'

The general paused, picked up his pipe, tapped its empty bowl on the desk.

'Is any of this fomented by the Germans?' Jamie asked him.

'Much of it, yes. They have put forty million roubles in the bank accounts of all manner of malcontents. Agitators flit in and out like will-o'-the-wisps. The most dangerous, because he's easily the most intelligent, is one Vladimir Ilyich Ulyanov, who has taken his present name, Lenin, from the Lena River.

'His father was a school inspector, his mother a doctor's

daughter. His whole outlook changed when his elder brother Alexander was hanged for an attempt on the life of Tsar Alexander III. This made Lenin a revolutionary. He qualified as a lawyer, was exiled to Siberia for years for revolutionary activity and on his release came to London and worked on his theories in the British Museum.

'In Austria in 1914 the police arrested him as a Russian spy, but he was released, and now moves between Switzerland and Russia, sometimes in disguise as a locomotive engineer or driver. Somehow, the Tsar's police always just miss catching him – or maybe they see the way things are going and don't try too hard. There is a Russian saying, Mr Baird: "Unless the wood is dry, the tinder sparks in vain." Now the wood is very dry and ready to blaze instantly.'

'So what specifically do you wish to discuss with me, General?'

'We know that the Tsar, on the prudent advice of loyal ministers, has been moving huge sums of money out of Russia into accounts in London and Geneva, in case of political emergencies that might demand his abdication. We also know that the Tsarina and her daughters, and others in the royal family, have one of the largest and most valuable collections of personal and court diamonds in the world. If disaster comes, they may not have time – or the opportunity – to remove a single stone.

'It has been proposed from the highest sources – and more than that I cannot say, as you will understand, Mr Baird – that paste copies of the more valuable of their diamonds could be substituted for the real stones, which it would be prudent to bring out as soon as possible. Then the heirlooms would be safe, whenever or wherever the owners choose to travel. In the worst possible case, the diamonds could be sold for cash.'

'Do they know of this proposal?'

'Not yet. They may be discreetly informed, when the time is

right. But that is a political decision, not mine. It would be most unwise to suggest such a substitution before it was absolutely necessary. And by then, arguably, it could be too late. I am asking you to undertake to substitute false diamonds for real ones – now. You will then bring the real diamonds back to England.'

'*Me?*' said Jamie in astonishment. 'But why me?'

'Because, sir, you have shown yourself a man of enterprise in the Cape, loyal to his country, and ready to rise to a challenge.'

'That may be, General, but I have never in all my life heard a more absurd proposition. Or one less likely to succeed.'

'Then, Mr Baird, you have led a very sheltered life. I hear far more unlikely propositions every day, and a surprising number of them are totally successful. After all, we must have more successes than failures in our business or we wouldn't be in business.'

'What exactly is your business, General?'

'In the loosest sense, Mr Baird, we call it Intelligence – with a big I. That covers a multitude of things; some say, a multitude of sins. We try to influence neutral countries, such as the United States, in favour of the Allies, especially towards the policies of this country. We sometimes arrange for an unfriendly neutral to have problems of one kind or another. Individuals, or countries.'

'And this idea would come into your category of helping this country?'

'It would indeed. The Tsar knows that Britain wants to help him in any positive way it can. If, partly as a result of his being our ally, events go against him, this could stiffen his back, harden his muscle. We would be helping him to help himself.'

Jamie stood up. 'General,' he said, 'I am flattered that you should have considered me as being worthy to undertake such an assignment. But I must say, right here and now, that it appears to be totally beyond my capabilities.'

'I am sorry to hear you say that, Mr Baird. My friends in the Cape had given me good reason to believe that this enterprise would interest you.'

'This task is for a professional agent, General, not for me. I had best bid you good-day now, sir, and hope that you find someone more suitable. I feel we are simply wasting time discussing it further. I trust I can have the use of Captain Drake's car to take me to the nearest railway station?'

'Indeed,' said the general, 'but before you go, there is something else I would like to say.'

'About this?'

'In a sense about this, Mr Baird, but also about another matter.'

'Well?'

'I understand that when you and your sister, who has prospered to a remarkable degree with her cosmetics and allied interests, were sailing to South Africa years ago, you took passage, steerage class, in the Royal Mail ship *Vanessa* from Liverpool?'

'And?'

'On the way out, a most regrettable accident occurred. The son and heir of Lord Rosael, the Honorable Orlando Sutton, fell from the ship into the sea.'

'Well?'

'Two passengers claimed that they saw your sister – or someone looking like your sister, possibly dressed especially to look like your sister – come down from the top deck shortly afterwards. They informed the purser and ship's officers, and visited the steerage accommodation to interview her.'

'And?'

'One of them – in fact, I think, both of them – picked out your sister. Several witnesses there insisted she had not left her quarters. But no one said that you hadn't, Mr Baird. The captain ordered that secret tests should be made for fingerprints on the ship's rail near where the fall occurred. He found several. Mr Sutton's. And someone else's.'

The general pressed a bellpush. An orderly came in holding an enlarged photographic negative two feet square, dripping with water. It had just been developed.

'Here, Mr Baird, is a magnified photograph of your fingerprint, taken as we sit here. From your coffee cup.' He opened a file. 'In this folder is a photograph of the print discovered on the ship's rail. You will see they are identical. It would seem, therefore, Mr Baird, you were present when Mr Sutton fell into the sea.'

Jamie said nothing; he sat watching the general's face.

'What do you say to that, sir?' General Brookes asked him.

'I've nothing to say to that at all. You show me a photograph of a fingerprint which you tell me is mine. You compare it with another photograph which you claim came from the deck of a ship. I was right in my first assumption in saying that to travel to Russia on your assignment would be absurd. I think this claim you now make is even more extraordinary.'

'Extraordinary, yes, Mr Baird. Absurd, no.'

'What exactly is the object of all this?'

'The object, Mr Baird, is that we need you to undertake an assignment for which you have unusual gifts. Agreed, you are not a professional agent, but possibly that is a good qualification in this instance. We need a diamond expert. A man who can look after himself. And someone with money of his own.'

'In other words,' said Jamie, 'someone who won't be a charge on the state if anything goes wrong. Who will bear his own expenses.'

The general bowed his assent. 'You understand my approach perfectly.'

'I still want nothing to do with it.'

'In that case, I think that the late Mr Sutton's mother, the

Dowager Lady Rosael, might be advised to take proceedings against you and your sister.'

'On what grounds? My sister wasn't there. That has already been proved.'

'But you were. Your fingerprints prove that conclusively. What do you say, Mr Baird?'

'I say, General, that I think you are not acting like an officer and a gentleman, but like a bastard.'

'I never claim to be a gentleman, Mr Baird. But I am a professional, and I want the best man for the job. That man is you. Fair or foul, I have to use any means whatever to persuade you.'

'And if you succeed?'

'Then, first, we will destroy all evidence of the fingerprints.'

'Blackmail?'

'No. Persuasion. There is another inducement, too. On your last visit to St Petersburg, I believe you met a young lady, the Archduchess Katharina Sokolov?'

'You believe a lot of things, sir.'

'I hear a lot of things. One of them is that this young lady would like to see you again.'

'Do you hear this from her?'

'Of course not. Young ladies are not so forward in their approach.'

'From whom, then? A Mr Serov?'

'I cannot reveal my sources, but since you do not query what I have heard, I assume it is accurate.'

'You like the whip and the carrot, General.'

'Both have their uses, Mr Baird. Well?'

'I will go to St Petersburg – Petrograd. But I am not at all optimistic I will achieve anything. I mean, how can I conceivably effect such a substitution? Have you a plan worked out?'

General Brookes shook his head. 'Unfortunately, no. I like to trust the man on the spot. I leave the mechanics of the matter to you, Mr Baird.'

'What backing will I have? Who do I have to help me?'

'Regrettably, our establishment in Russia is depleted.'

'You mean I will be on my own?'

General Brookes inclined his head gravely. 'You will be provided with twelve imitation diamonds, of course, to take the place of any genuine stones you remove. You will go by way of Sweden, then to Finland, and on to Petrograd.'

'How am I expected to bring the diamonds out? In a shoebox – where so many of the early diamond magnates in the Cape kept their diamonds?'

'You will be provided with a soft leather bag of the sort used for carrying overnight requirements – razor, slippers, pyjamas, and so on. This will have a false bottom with the two parts separated by sheets of sorbo rubber. Small holes will be cut in the sheets to accept the diamonds.'

'Won't Customs examine the bag at the frontier?'

'Possibly. But even if they use the new X-ray machines – which it is unlikely that the Russians possess – the diamonds will not be revealed. Only uncut diamonds show on an X-ray screen.'

'Won't they strip the case and find the false bottom?'

'Why should they? To them you will simply be an English visitor, not someone likely to smuggle anything out. Instead, you might find it worthwhile to have a few hundred-rouble notes in your wallet, or maybe some chocolate bars in your bag for the Customs officers' children, in case they become inquisitive.'

'It sounds a pretty amateur arrangement to me. Anything else I should know?'

'We will give you an emergency commission in the Army with the honorary rank of major, and you will receive the pay and emoluments of that rank. That is simply a form of insurance for you, a safeguard. You have a military rank, so if anything went wrong, you would not be arrested as a spy, which could have most serious consequences for you. A spy, Mr Baird, has no friends – on either side. An officer is – despite our mutual doubts – always considered to be a gentleman.'

'You make this assignment sound so alluring I cannot wait to go on it – or to be back safely.'

Brookes smiled slightly. 'I cannot offer you a fee, but I may say, in the privacy of this room, that the King would personally regard your acceptance of this assignment very favourably. The Tsar, after all, is his cousin.'

'When do you want me to start?'

'As soon as possible. In fact, since I took the liberty of anticipating your acceptance, a cabin has already been reserved for you, in the name of Provost, an officer in the Dental Corps, for next Tuesday's sailing of the *Gothenburg Princess* from Harwich.'

'Why Provost? Why a dentist?'

'Someone might see your real name on a passenger list and wonder how and why, in the middle of the war, a rich man like you was making this trip. I have a high-spirited nephew, an undergraduate at Oxford, who has recently been in some trouble with the provost of his college. I liked the name, and will give it to you.

'Your cover as a dentist will explain a case of tweezers and pincers and probes you will take in case you have to extract the diamonds from their settings. We do not need the settings, only the stones.'

General Brookes stood up to show that the meeting was at an end. The two men shook hands.

Captain Drake drove Jamie to the railway station; they did not exchange a word on the journey.

TWENTY-SEVEN

Petrograd

Jamie travelled to Petrograd by way of Finland, as General Brookes had proposed. The railway carriage for the last part of his journey was dirty and unheated, and the train made a number of unscheduled stops. At each of them, thinking he might already have reached his destination, Jamie lowered the window and peered out, trying to find where he was. This was impossible; all he knew for certain was that he was not in Petrograd. When the train stopped at a country station, he could not read the Cyrillic writing on the board, giving the station's name, and when it stopped in open country, he could see nothing but a snowy wasteland stretching to infinity.

Sometimes, the stops lasted for only a few minutes; at others, they stretched to an hour or more. Passengers walked up and down the platform, grateful for a chance to stretch their legs, flapping their arms to keep warm. Before the war, all snow on railway platforms had been shovelled away every day. Now it lay a foot thick, frozen underneath to ice. At these stops, some passengers went into the town or village in search of a meal or food of any kind. But they always returned within minutes, shaking their heads at the poverty they encountered. No one had any food to spare to sell to travellers; the locals were themselves nearly starving.

As the express trundled on at its top speed of 40 miles an

hour, gaunt, black trunks of leafless trees stood like marker posts by the side of the line. Here and there, Jamie saw a curl of smoke from some mud-walled hut with a foot of thick snow on its roof. A few peasants, their legs wrapped in rags, and wearing blankets or animal skins, moved slowly, carrying on their backs unknown loads, like grotesque humps. Cows stood patiently near patches of steaming, dung-trodden straw.

Jamie sensed the change of feeling in Petrograd the moment he stepped down on to the platform. A horse-drawn sledge conveyed him to the Hotel d'Angleterre where he had stayed during his previous visit, but instead of the cheerful waves and salutations he had noticed then, the driver sat slumped dejectedly on his wooden seat, his face sunk with hunger and cold. The bones of his horses showed against the thin flesh on their flanks.

Snow lay thick and uncleared in the streets. The ice, which covered most of the River Neva, was so thick that it blocked entry to small ships. A handful of surly men, dressed in rags and holding long pointed staves, stood at the edge of the ice, picking at it half-heartedly to make a passage for the boats.

In Jamie's hotel, pages and porters hung about the entrance hall, gaunt-faced and hungry. Jamie had seen hungry people in the north of England before he went to the Cape, but they did not give the appearance of having lost all zest for life. These men already seemed defeated, not only in a war which, he guessed, could still have years to run, but in the battle for life and their own self-respect.

He ordered toast and caviare, still plentiful enough for those who could afford it. The Caspian Sea was filled with sturgeon and their eggs did not have the cachet they had assumed in the West. In the eighteenth century, after all, only the poor in England ate oysters. Jamie supervised the unpacking of his clothes by a listless, hollow-eyed valet, and then ordered a sledge to take him to Serov's house.

Jamie had the address, but he had never visited Serov at home. He had not written to advise him of his arrival, and he was not even certain whether he still lived there. But he felt he must sound out someone as to his best approach.

As the sledge's iron runners glided across the shining, hard-packed snow, the only sounds were a tinkling of its tiny bells and the blowing of the horses. There was something eerie in the silence and emptiness of this capital city. Jamie noted landmarks – a church here, an emporium there, a palace on the other side of the road – in case he had to walk back to his hotel. He would not keep the sledge waiting. It might attract attention, and as the wide avenues became narrower streets, and finally no more than alleyways rutted with frozen snow, he realised he probably would have to walk.

The horses' pace grew slower, and the bells ceased to tinkle as the sledge stopped. The driver nodded towards a wooden door, studded with bolt heads, in a high building. Snow lay thickly on each window sill. Not one window was open. Indeed, the building seemed deserted. Hesitantly, Jamie climbed down. The door had neither knocker nor bell pull. He beat on it with his fist. The driver hawked and spat in the snow. One of the horses made water; the yellow puddle steamed on the frozen road.

The door opened a few inches. An old man peered out and raised his eyebrows inquiringly.

'Mr Serov?' said Jamie hopefully.

The man shrugged his shoulders, shook his head. The sledge driver spoke to him in Russian. The man nodded, opened the door and held his right hand at shoulder height, four fingers extended. Jamie nodded his thanks to the driver, paid him off, and went into the building.

The hall stank of drains and stale cabbage water: the smell of defeat and decay. There was no elevator. He walked up flights of stone steps, carefully keeping away from the greasy wall on one side, the unpolished brass banister on the other, until he reached the fourth floor. A single door faced him. He beat on it, heard movement within, and someone calling out inquiringly in Russian. Then the door opened on a chain. Serov stared at him in amazement.

'*You?*' he said. 'What are you doing here?' He undid the chain, opened the door.

'To seek your advice,' Jamie explained.

'You had better come in.'

As he spoke, Serov glanced down over the edge of the banister into the stairwell. The old man who had let Jamie in was standing there, looking up at him. Serov shouted something in Russian and threw down a coin. It tinkled on the flagstones. The man made no movement to pick it up. Serov muttered under his breath and threw down a second coin. This time the man made a vague gesture of acceptance, and stooped to pick up both coins.

Serov took Jamie into his apartment, shut the door, bolted it, replaced the chain. They were in a small hall. Overcoats and fur hats hung from pegs on one wall; two pairs of rubber galoshes were on the floor beneath them. Serov led the way into a larger room. All its windows were shut and fly-blown. The air felt stale, used up. The room was over-furnished with brocaded chairs, a heavy table, a settee. Colour prints and sepia photographs were framed on the walls. In one corner, plants sprouted from earthenware pots, standing in plates of water. Somehow they added to the impression of squalor; their soft, fleshy leaves had all the attraction of fungus.

'Sit down,' said Serov. 'You have caught me unawares. I would rather have met you at your hotel than here.'

'Why?'

'Because you are a foreigner, and the secret police are everywhere. That old fool who let you in is their informant. It does not do me any good to be seen talking to foreigners.'

'But when I was here last, that was your job,' Jamie reminded him.

'Before the war, yes, that was my job,' Serov agreed. 'And I still work for the British from time to time. I translate for them. I help them as and how I can, but times have changed, Mr Baird. There has been mutiny in the Army.'

'What happened?'

'Accounts differ, but there is no doubt it was serious. A few ringleaders have been shot, but with the slaughter every day at the front, that is really nothing. The war news is terrible. Every day the casualty lists are so great the newspapers no longer print them. They dare not. They say we have lost at least four million young men. What for? Why? Crowds in the streets shout "Down with the German woman," meaning the Tsarina. Such behaviour would never have been tolerated in the past. But now, who can stop them?

'The police are hated and dare not risk confrontation with such large numbers of people. They fear being lynched, torn apart, burned alive. And the Cossacks are reluctant to charge the crowds – even when they are given direct orders to do so. Instead, they just meander through them. The people know they hold the power now. And when they learn – or are told by the agitators – how to use it, then, my friend, it is the end.'

'I did not realise this,' said Jamie. 'We have privations in England and terrible casualties on the Western Front but, thank God, not the feeling of resignation and defeat I sense here. But your influential friends – aren't they above all this? Cannot they bring their influence to bear in a constructive way?'

'No to both questions. They live lives totally remote from the rest of us. They are cushioned by their wealth, their myriads of servants, their all-consuming social round, from what is actually happening. Theirs is a dream world, Mr Baird. I speak of the real world, the nightmare world. But, tell me, what brings you to Russia now?'

491

'When I was here last,' replied Jamie, 'you helped me very considerably. Now, as I said outside, I want your advice, discreet but honest. Do not tell me what you think I may want to hear.' He paused.

Serov said nothing, but sat looking at him. His face was thin, the flesh drawn tight as a drumskin over his cheekbones. He was also hungry.

'I will pay you in sovereigns for your advice,' Jamie assured him. 'I do not seek something for nothing.'

'It is as well,' said Serov bitterly. 'Nothing for nothing is the law these days. That said, what can I do for you?'

Jamie stroked his nose between his thumb and forefinger. He had worked out several possible ways of seeking Serov's help. Now he selected the one he believed most suitable for Serov's changed circumstances. He took a deep breath and began to speak.

'As you will remember,' he said. 'I have been a diamond digger, a diamond seller. I am what you might call a diamond man. It is in this capacity that I seek your advice.

'We in England have no real idea of the seriousness of conditions here, which I am shocked and most disturbed to learn. But in the City of London it is known that many distinguished Russian people, not excluding your ruler and his relations, have moved considerable sums of money from Russian banks into what they feel may be safer custody in London, Paris and Geneva.'

'You mean they think there will be more trouble here, and they are making contingency plans in case they have to leave?' asked Serov nervously.

'I am not privy to their thoughts,' said Jamie. 'But that seems to me a reasonable assumption. You must draw your own conclusions. Since Russia is such a stout ally of ours in this war, naturally our government wishes to help her and her rulers in every possible way. If – and I stress the *if* – there is a revolution and the Tsar is overthrown, the first thing the revolutionaries would do would be to make a separate peace with Germany. There is always the possibility that instead of being neutral in this war, they would actually side with the Central Powers, in exchange for wheat or whatever they need most. It is therefore imperative from the Allies' point of view that this does not happen.

'As one conversant with diamonds, I have been asked to come here on a most delicate mission. I wish, if possible, to have at least a sight of some of the royal family's jewels, so that on my valuation they can be adequately insured by Lloyd's of London.'

'Why?' asked Serov, his eyes narrowing. 'How can that help your country or mine?'

'Should the political situation deteriorate here, and these people wish to get out – or are forced to get out – they might have to leave jewels worth millions of roubles behind them, simply because they could not carry them away. They would, in such unhappy circumstances, lose their jewels and also find themselves refugee beggars in a foreign country. But if the jewels are insured against such a risk, at least they would have some comfort in knowing they would receive their equivalent value in money.'

For a few moments, Serov said nothing. A clock in the corner chimed the hour. Then he spoke.

'You say you were asked to come here. Who asked you?'

'I cannot be specific,' replied Jamie cautiously. 'I can, however, say that the request came from a very high authority indeed, someone with the warmest admiration for your ruler. Someone I can trust – as I hope you can trust me.'

'What you seek is for these jewels to be laid out somewhere so you can perhaps weigh them, or whatever you need to do, to assess their value?'

'Exactly. That would be ideal, but is that possible?'

493

'It will be extremely difficult. The jewels are worth a king's ransom. They are not lying about on a boudoir table, but kept under the strictest possible guard in the Winter Palace. There is a safe with walls of solid steel, a door with ten separate tongues; a safe said to be totally bombproof, fireproof, thiefproof. This safe is in turn bolted into another room with walls of reinforced concrete – the Diamond Room.

'Only two men, apart from the Tsar, are ever allowed into this room. One is the Keeper of His Majesty's Wardrobe. The other is Chamberlain to Her Majesty the Tsarina. If they have occasion to go into this room, they first have to present to the High Keeper of the Imperial Cabinet a letter signed by the Tsar, written in his own hand and bearing His Majesty's official seal. Only then will they be allowed inside.

'The room contains more than twenty-five thousand, three hundred carats of diamonds, six thousand carats of pearls, about half that amount of emeralds, plus enormous quantities of rubies and sapphires, so these safeguards are necessary. Anyone – of whatever rank or aristocratic family, and no matter on whose authority – attempting to enter the Diamond Room without the High Keeper's permission is liable to be shot.'

Serov paused and then, becoming more confidential, put a hand on Jamie's sleeve.

'And even assuming you obtain these permissions, which in itself would be a miracle, you would not find everything in the Diamond Room, a fact that is not well known, of course. On the outbreak of war, nine iron strong-boxes were filled with jewels and moved by special train to Moscow. That city is further from the western frontier than Petrograd and consequently less likely to be captured by the Germans, if they advance.

'The jewels are now under constant guard in a specially constructed vault in the Armoury Hall of the Kremlin. But for every poison there is fortunately an antidote, for every lock there is a key. I feel it is Providence who sent you to me today, Mr Baird.

'I have friends at many levels in the palace. Quite recently, one told me that some jewels – the Empress's diamond tiara, her personal necklaces, diamond bracelets, and possibly forty or fifty diamond rings and some Fabergé eggs the Tsar gave to her – are not at this moment in the Diamond Room, or in Moscow.'

'Where are they?'

'They have been removed under guard to a jeweller's workshop for their annual cleaning and checking.'

'At Fabergé?'

'No. They are in the workshop of another jeweller who carries out such work for many ladies of the court. In these times, it is not wise for any public display to be made of people's possessions – a far cry, indeed, Mr Baird, from when you were last here.'

'Can you arrange for me to see them?'

'I will try – on the absolute assurance you do not explain the reason for your inspection. I will introduce you as a diamond expert from South Africa. I may need some money to defray my expenses. You understand me?'

'Perfectly. How much do you want?'

'Fifty sovereigns should suffice. Initially, at least. And now, a point I hesitate to mention, but I must – *my* recompense.'

'Of course. What do you wish for this service?'

'On this occasion not money, but something in difficult times like these worth more than almost any amount of money – a British passport.'

'For yourself? You anticipate leaving?'

'I would go if I could, but I feel my duty lies with my country. I would just say that whoever has need of this would only make use of it in the utmost extremity of danger.'

'Who is he – or she? And why should they wish to leave?'

'I cannot answer your first question, for the same reason you did not tell me who asked you to come here. These are dangerous matters involving life and death – perhaps our own lives and deaths. What is whispered in private can sometimes be published, with disastrous consequences.'

'Could this person not apply to the British Embassy?'

'Absolutely impossible. Questions would be asked and could not be answered – yet. But you have a passport?'

'Of course.'

'Then why could you not lose it? It is stolen from your locked case in your hotel bedroom. No lock is proof against thieving fingers in this city today. You can easily get a second passport. By then, this man would be out of the country – if he needs to go. Then he could destroy your old passport, or even deliver it to you in London – or to your Embassy here should events have a happier conclusion, and he can stay.'

'But my passport has my photograph.'

'That is the least of our problems. He would alter his appearance to look as like the photograph as possible. No questions would be asked.'

'I can't do it,' said Jamie firmly. 'I would like to help you, but this I cannot do.'

'You asked my price,' said Serov coldly. 'I have told you. This is not a matter on which we can bargain.'

Jamie walked across the room, looked out through the dirty window at the street beneath. He held two passports; he could, if it was absolutely necessary, give up the one in Provost's name. Then he remembered that an immigration official on the frontier had stamped it. He needed that passport himself to leave, otherwise the officials would want to know how he had entered the country without an entry stamp.

Jamie made up his mind. It was essential that he saw the jewels, and Serov was the only person he knew who could arrange this. He would have to pay the price.

'I will do what I can,' Jamie told him. 'When will you need the passport?'

'As soon as you can give it to me. It is a key to freedom. For this person, the only key.'

Jamie did not like the proposal, but he was not in a position to argue. He nodded his head. 'I will do it,' he said. 'You can have my passport. Give me your hand on the deal.'

They shook hands. It was the first time he had shaken Serov's hand. Afterwards, Jamie rubbed his palm on the side of his trousers. Serov's flesh felt distastefully damp and cold and clammy, like the scales of a dead fish.

The jeweller's house was two blocks away. His workshop was in the cellar, a bare room, with white-washed walls lit by naked electric bulbs. They throbbed and flickered with each pulse of the dynamo; shadows from tools on the workbench danced on the walls like living things.

The jeweller was a small, bald man, with a pointed, waxed beard. He wore a brown overall with a large breast pocket to accommodate several eyepieces of different sizes. He employed a younger assistant, with hair the colour of straw. He was adjusting the flame on a blow-lamp as Serov and Jamie came down the staircase.

Serov translated, explaining that the visitor was one of the most respected experts in diamonds in the British colony of South Africa. He would be honoured if he could see the stones in the Tsarina's diamond tiara, because he had been told they had been cut and set in a special way, totally unknown to Western European jewellers.

The jeweller nodded slowly, as though he quite understood the visitor's interest. He crossed to a wall safe, opened one lock with a key, indicated to his colleague to use a second key, which he kept chained to his belt, to undo another lock. The heavy door swung open on oiled hinges. Inside lay several black leather boxes. The jeweller spoke to Serov, who translated.

'Since I assume you are only concerned with diamonds, he

497

does not think you wish to examine the contents of other boxes, which contain rubies and sapphires.'

'That is correct,' Jamie told him.

'Here is a royal tiara,' Serov explained in English. 'Not the one worn on State occasions, but a lighter one – in the jeweller's opinion a more beautiful work of art, which the Empress, may God bless and keep her always, wears at formal balls and banquets.

'Also, Her Royal Highness's diamond necklace, and these diamond rings and bracelets. He regrets that some diamond earrings have already been returned to the Winter Palace. Otherwise, it would have been an honour to show them all to you.'

'It is most kind of him to help me in this matter. I am deeply appreciative.'

The old man lifted out the biggest of the boxes. It was locked by a golden clasp. He fitted another key, opened the lid. The box was lined with scarlet velvet, quilted so that the cascade of jewels glittered like a frozen waterfall, reflecting the harsh glare from the bulbs in a thousand trembling stars on walls and ceiling.

'May I touch the jewels?' asked Jamie. More translation.

'Only with these gloves on. You will understand, I am sure.'

Serov handed to Jamie a pair of loose chamois-leather gloves. Jamie took his own magnifying glass from his pocket, screwed it into his right eye, lifted up a necklace, examined the stones critically from every angle. Then, carefully, almost reverently, he replaced the necklace on its velvet pad. He did the same with the tiara and the rings and bracelets, bowed his thanks to the jeweller. They shook hands.

'I am greatly in your debt for showing me these beautiful things,' Jamie said.

The jeweller and his assistant bowed appreciatively as Serov translated.

Serov led Jamie up the wooden stairs, through the hall, dark now with dusk, out into the freezing street. Downstairs, the old jeweller locked up the box, replaced it in the safe. He and his colleague then locked the double locks, and stood for a moment, looking at each other.

'You were not impressed by the visitor?' the young man asked the jeweller.

The old man shook his head. 'How can he possibly claim to be a diamond expert,' he replied dismissively, 'when he cannot even recognise worthless fakes?'

The Tsarina, pale-faced and miserable, sat in an armchair covered in cretonne in two shades of mauve, and tried to hold back her tears. Her son was ill again, and each time he sickened, he grew weaker. Every attack seriously diminished his already puny strength.

Purple and mauve were the Tsarina's favourite colours. Her room had a purple carpet, purple curtains and chair covers; purple lilies filled the flower vases. Today, the Tsarina's mood matched these sombre colours.

The Tsarevitch's life so far had consisted of alternating relapses and remissions, and ultimately, possibly within a very few years, he would face an early and agonising death.

The Tsarina's loneliness and helplessness were accentuated by the size and luxury of the palace. She felt alone and bereft in the midst of priceless treasures.

The palace was set in the centre of 800 acres of clósely mown lawns. Wide paths, spreading out like spokes in a wheel, led to hothouses for exotic plants, to greenhouses, groups of stone statues, summer pavilions, pagodas.

The palace was heated by wood-burning stoves covered in coloured porcelain tiles. Relays of crimson-liveried footmen carried bronze pots of burning incense from room to room to counter the smell of burning wood. On the Tsarina's explicit instructions all rooms were also always rich with flowers: lilies, violets, hyacinths, cascades of colour, in china and crystal vases. During the winter, when the palace greenhouses could not supply purple blooms in sufficient quantity, special trains from the Tsar's Crimean estates brought in new supplies every day.

On parquet floors, polished with scented wax, lay a rich profusion of rugs and carpets woven in different parts of the Russian empire. To keep this palace in a state of total perfection every day and every night of every year, demanded the skills of 2,000 servants. In addition, 5,000 troops guarded it from their own barracks nearby. Thirty armed sentries were also stationed at strategic points inside the palace. In cellars; on landings; in niches originally intended for marble statues; outside the double sets of double doors that opened on to the Royal Family's private apartments, they stood rigidly to attention, looking neither to right nor left.

When the Tsar was in his study, four Negroes, each six foot six inches tall, and wearing jackets edged in gold, crimson trousers and white turbans, and shoes with curved points in the ancient Turkish style, stood guard outside his door.

But what did all this matter when her only son had not known a single day without pain or illness all his life?

Everyone having any close association with the Royal Family had to swear on the Bible never to reveal the name of the boy's incurable illness. It was allowed to be known publicly – because this simply could not be concealed – that the Tsarevitch suffered from delicate health. But his sudden absences from official functions – or the fact that even if he did attend, he invariably had to be carried by a giant sailor because he was too weak to walk, or transported in a metal carrier above the front wheel of a cycle – were said to be due to a bad cold, or influenza.

The fact that an attack could strike at any moment had reduced the Tsarina to a state of constant concern and nervousness. Because she refused to admit publicly the real cause of her tense expression, and her consuming concern for her son, people assumed she was arrogant, aloof, a hard aristocrat, an *inostranka*, a foreigner who did not conform to Russian ideals.

Two days previously the Tsarevitch had fallen against a table, bruising his knee. Immediately, his leg began to swell. The flesh around the bruise grew hard and distended, swollen with blood beneath the skin. This swelling stretched steadily from his knee to his groin, his body gross and puffy from leaking blood. The pain became excruciating, and no drug could bring relief.

So far as the Tsarina was concerned, only one person in all the world could conceivably help her son over this crisis as he had helped him survive others – Rasputin.

She sat alone in her room, mouthing a prayer for God's help, knowing that Rasputin was in the sickroom two doors along the corridor. Here, on an iron bed under crisply laundered white sheets, her son lay, eyes closed in utter exhaustion, his face pale as his pillow, while Rasputin knelt by the bed, his strangely luminous eyes fixed on the boy's pale face.

Maybe he was only a hypnotist, as his critics said. Maybe he was hypnotising her son, calming him, assuring him he would beat this otherwise unbeatable illness. But did this matter? The end was all important; whatever means were needed to achieve that end must be totally irrelevant.

She looked up inquiringly now as she heard Rasputin come through the secret door into her boudoir.

'He will live,' he assured her. 'The little one will live.'

She stood up and took Rasputin's hands. She did not see the dirt and pieces of egg in his beard, or smell the sour goatlike stench of his unwashed body. Others could not bear to be in the same room with Rasputin, because of his filthy appearance and his foul smell of sweat and faeces. But to the Tsarina, Mother of All the Russias, he was more than a man, more than a saint;

Rasputin was the personal emissary of the Almighty holding the power of resurrection, life over death.

'I don't know how to thank you,' she said, choking back tears of relief.

'It is my duty. With God's help, the boy will live. But as I have told Your Majesty, I cannot guarantee his life after mine. Only today, when the Tsar asked me to bless him, I told him: "Now it is *your* turn to bless me." '

'You have no reason to think you are going to die soon, surely? You are healthy. I would to God my son was half as healthy.'

'And I would to God your son never has enemies like mine,' replied Rasputin grimly. 'Now, I must leave you.'

'I would like to give you something before you go,' the Tsarina said hesitantly.

'You are very kind, Majesty, but I do not wish for money. Whenever anyone gives me money, I give it away, as you know. I have enough for my needs, and the accumulation of wealth is a barren exercise.'

The Tsarina opened a small cardboard box. Rasputin looked at the diamonds it contained, set out on padded velvet.

'I could not accept these, Majesty,' Rasputin told her. 'What I have done, I do through the power and help and the will of God. I do not heal for reward, and you offer me a reward worth the ransom of a king.'

'You have ransomed a king-to-be,' replied the Tsarina simply. 'Deal with these as you wish. Give them away if you will. But, take them. It is more than my wish you should do so. It is my command.'

Rasputin bowed.

'In that case, Majesty, I bow to your command. You are far more generous than I have words to thank you.'

The lady's maid in the next room, who had watched all this through a tiny spyhole bored with an awl in a corner of one of the gilded panels, tiptoed away. She had seen something which could be of great value to the man who paid her a regular retainer for any information about the Royal Household.

For a moment, she felt a tiny spasm of guilt at what she did, and what she was about to do, but it passed quickly. These were difficult times, and as Serov had so often told her, whenever she seemed reluctant to pass on news, if you did not look after your own interests, who else would?

Jamie sat alone in the cold and cheerless sitting room of his suite at the Hotel d'Angleterre. Coal was not available in Petrograd for hotel furnaces, and they did not burn wood. The windows were opaque with ice, and he sat wearing his heavy overcoat, sipping vodka. His breath hung like fog in the freezing air.

He stood up, poured more vodka into his glass. On a side table stood a huge bowl of goldfish. The water had not been changed recently and they swam in a mist, round and round, above an inch of sand and small stones in which thin feathery wisps of green weed had taken root. Their eyes, hugely magnified by the thick glass, stared vacantly at him.

They aren't going anywhere, Jamie thought; but they still swam ceaselessly, as though their journey was of vital importance. He felt something in common with these shimmering fish: he was trying to progress and not succeeding. Questions chased answers through his mind, but never found them.

Why had the court jeweller shown him imitation gems instead of real ones? Who, with access to the Diamond Room in the Winter Palace, could – or would – have ordered nearly perfect copies to be made of some of the most valuable stones? Had whoever did this then abstracted the genuine stones? If they were missed, whoever was responsible could alleviate any immediate alarm by explaining that they had gone to the court jeweller for their annual cleaning. According to Serov only the two high court officials had access to the jewels – apart from the Tsar and Tsarina – and their access depended on written authority from the Tsar.

Jamie could not see any reason for the Tsar, one of the half-dozen richest men in the world, to undertake such a deception. He was far too heavily engaged at Army Headquarters.

That left the Tsarina as a possible suspect. But surely it was as out of character for the German-born Tsarina to send replicas of her jewels to be cleaned as for the German-born Queen Mary in England to do the same thing?

Suppose, however, that the Tsarina knew someone to whom, for whatever reason, she wished to give a present worth millions, whether for love, or gratitude, or even for both, but felt it prudent to conceal the gift from her husband and his ministers? That provided a better reason. There was only one person Jamie could think of who might possibly have been that recipient; the man the Tsarina believed had saved the life of her son on whom she doted: Rasputin.

Jamie finished his drink, went down to the reception desk to order a sledge. As he did as, he saw Serov coming through the main door. Serov paused, then beckoned to Jamie, drew him to one side.

'You need my help,' he said bluntly, in a low voice. 'And I need yours. You speak of helping my country and so your own. I have a far more positive way of doing this than by insuring some diamonds. Come with me to the Duma and you will see exactly what I mean.'

'Now?'

'Now.'

Serov led Jamie into the front hall of the Tauride Palace, a vast white room furnished in ornate Louis XVI style. Jamie could hear the hum of animated conversation, like a giant swarm of bees, from the even larger room beyond, the debating chamber of the Duma, the Russian parliament, which the Tsar had been forced to form after the aborted uprising just over ten years previously.

Serov stood in the huge doorway for a moment, trying to find someone he knew among the crowd of deputies milling about inside. He never came here without remembering that day in the Winter Palace when the Tsar had finally been obliged to inaugurate Russia's first elected parliament. That decision had struck fear into those who regarded the Tsar as the chosen instrument of God, and to whom it was tantamount to blasphemy to invite discussion or even criticism of his edicts. Afterwards, the Tsar's mother, the Dowager Empress Marie Feodorovna, was in tears.

'I could not stop myself looking at certain of the faces,' she told Serov miserably. 'So much did they seem to reflect an incomprehensible *hatred* for us all.'

Count Vladimir Fredericks, the Minister of the Court, the master of royal ceremonies, was more specific.

'The deputies give me the impression of a gang of criminals only waiting for the signal to throw themselves upon the ministers and cut their throats. What wicked faces they have!'

Now, Serov thought much the same. The deputies who crowded the great hall seemed a strange and motley crowd, talking excitedly, as though at some kind of public entertainment. They did not appear interested in the desperately serious business of agreeing policy towards a war steadily dividing the country and leading it into starvation and economic ruin.

Some wore full court dress. Others, to show their independence and to demonstrate publicly that such an important assembly did not impress them, deliberately appeared in cotton shirts and workers' blouses. Jamie, accustomed to the more sombre dress of politicians in the South African parliament, was surprised to see peasants wearing national dress and clergymen in black robes.

Deputies with highly polished soft leather boots reaching to their knees were talking to labourers who had come here in working clothes, boots caked with mud and dung. As they walked up and down, most of them smoked cigarettes, tapping the ash on to the marble floor. Sometimes they ground the burning ends of cigarettes in with their heels, as if to show their total lack of respect for the palatial surroundings.

Serov led Jamie upstairs to find seats in the gallery. An important statement was expected that day, and he wished to hear it personally, not to rely on hearsay. Also, he wished a foreigner to hear it, so that afterwards there could be no doubt or argument over what had been said.

On each of the chairs below them lay a white card bearing the name of a deputy. One by one, they took their places, still chattering, smoking, an extraordinary diversity of people and costumes. Jamie found it difficult to believe that this could be a serious parliament; looked down on from the gallery, the people seemed more like a grotesque gathering of theatricals wearing fancy dress. Only when the president took his place beneath the blue and white portrait of the Tsar did conversation fade and finally die. The session began.

Jamie glanced at the other visitors in the gallery. At the far end, he recognised the pale, composed face of Prince Yussoupov.

After some routine business was transacted, a deputy in his middle fifties, Vladimir Purishkevich, stood up to speak. He was a highly strung man (so Serov whispered to Jamie), given to making long perorations rather than reasoned speeches. He enjoyed a caustic turn of phrase and had published a number of satirical poems about Petrograd society. Of all deputies in the Duma, he was the most devoted to the Tsar and to the monarchy as an institution.

Purishkevich's personal patriotism was practical. Too old for active service in the war, he had worked as close to the front as he was allowed, helping to evacuate the wounded. Now, he spoke about the sad state of the country, for which he blamed one man – Rasputin.

'Dark forces are destroying the dynasty,' he cried. 'One man is their leader – Rasputin! It only requires the recommendation of Rasputin – no one else – to raise the most abject citizen to high office.'

Deputies nodded their agreement.

Then, addressing himself to the ministers who sat in front of the president, Purishkevich continued in a grave voice. 'If you are truly loyal, if the glory of Russia and her mighty future, which is closely bound up with the brightness of the name of the Tsar, means anything to you, then *on your feet*, you ministers! Go to the Tsar! Have the courage to tell him that the multitude is threatening in its wrath! Tell him that revolution threatens and an obscure peasant shall govern Russia no longer!'

The deputies began to cheer. Then, row upon row, they stood up, roaring their approval, clapping their hands, turning to each other, nodding vigorously in their enthusiasm for these stirring words. Purishkevich had given voice to the thoughts of them all. The roof echoed with their shouts: 'Bravo! I agree!'

Purishkevich's attack and this response was what Serov had brought Jamie to hear. Both men glanced across at Feliks Yussoupov to see his reaction. The Prince's naturally pale face was now white. As he stroked his chin, his hand trembled.

Afterwards, Serov walked with Jamie to his hotel, excusing himself from coming in for a vodka. He had some business of his own to transact. He would call for him later that night, or in the morning, and explain how and why he needed Jamie's help.

A woman Serov had been expecting to see for some days was waiting for him in the downstairs hall of his apartment building. She was a maid in the service of the Tsarina. She only visited Serov when she had information for which she felt he would pay a good price. Her husband was a private soldier at the front. She had not heard from him for months; he might even be dead. She had a small daughter to support and any extra money, however little, she regarded as a gift from heaven.

'I saw the Empress give Rasputin six huge diamonds for his help in treating the little boy,' she explained now in a whisper. 'The boy has been very ill again, almost to the death. He could not accompany his father to review the troops. They announced he had caught a cold.'

'You are absolutely certain what you saw?'

'Absolutely,' she said. 'They were in a small white cardboard box. The sort that could have held face powder or tooth powder.'

'You have been very observant. Here is your fee.'

Serov gave her five ten-rouble notes.

'Don't come here again,' he told her. 'The concierge watches everyone who calls.'

Through the stained window, he watched her walk away, then went up the stairs to his room. As he did so, he heard the faint click of a door closing on the ground floor. So the concierge had seen them. Well, what did that matter now? He had far more important matters to consider.

He unlocked the cupboard where he kept his last bottle of vodka. It had become expensive in Petrograd, and extremely scarce. The woman who cleaned for him liked a nip, so now he kept it locked away. He poured himself half a glass, drank it quickly, then another, while he pondered how he could best turn to his own advantage the information the maid had just given to him.

Serov finished his vodka, locked up the bottle and went out of the building. He hurried through the trodden snow. As he did so, feeling the chilly slush seep through his worn galoshes, he consoled himself that if his plan succeeded, soon he would be riding in his own Rolls-Royce.

TWENTY-EIGHT

On the Brink

A liveried servant showed Serov into Purishkevich's study. The two men knew each other on a professional level, if not socially. Serov's services were useful to politicians in passing messages to people it might not be politic for them to meet, in sounding out foreign diplomats for their views. Now Purishkevich guessed that Serov might suspect – or had heard from one of his many secret sources – that definite action was being planned against Rasputin. The deputy greeted Serov warmly; it was safer to keep him as an ally than an adversary.

Purishkevich always knew who was sleeping with whom; who was about to be demoted, promoted, rewarded, exiled, but he could never keep such sometimes invaluable information to himself. Serov knew he had to tell others, to seek their opinion as to its importance.

'I wished to come and congratulate you personally, sir,' Serov now said sonorously. 'I was in the gallery and heard you speak. I am in full agreement with every word you uttered. So is everyone I have met since.'

'I am glad to hear that. But what would you think reaction among our Allies would be if Rasputin were to be – eliminated?'

'It is impossible to say. Foreigners with whom I have spoken simply tend to regard him as what their newspapers call a mad monk.'

'He's neither mad nor a monk. If he were either, or both, the solution would be easier. He could be contained in an asylum or a monastery.'

'Agreed. I am telling you what foreigners think. Not what I think.'

'Quite so. I am meeting Prince Yussoupov tomorrow evening in the Moika Palace. I suggest you come with me. You will then know why I ask you this question. It may be a meeting of great historical importance. I know you have many contacts with diplomats and gentlemen of the foreign Press. Your view and comments on our meeting could be of the greatest value in presenting events to them in the most favourable light. Not only of value to our country, but to us personally. You understand me?'

'I think I do, sir. And I am honoured by your confidence.'

The Moika Palace was one of four palaces Prince Yussoupov owned in Petrograd. He owned three more of equal size in Moscow and a further 37 estates, most of which he had never visited, in different parts of the country. His family had accumulated their stupendous wealth by shrewdly keeping close to the Tsar of the time, through each generation. They did whatever he might ask of them, however distasteful or unpleasant. As a direct result, the Yussoupov estates embraced enormous areas of land, hundreds, sometimes thousands of square miles in extent. At Archangelskoe outside Moscow, for example, in addition to vast parks, with tropical gardens, heated greenhouses the size of Kew Gardens and a private zoo, the estate contained factories producing porcelain and glass, and entire townships built to house their workers. It had its own private theatre where Prince Nicholas Yussoupov, one of Catherine the Great's many lovers, had maintained his own private companies of musicians, dancers, actors and actresses, to provide ballet, concerts, plays. Everything in his life was on this grandiose scale. The palace gallery contained three hundred portraits, each painted from life, of his more important mistresses. At the age of 81, he died, as he had spent so much of his life, in the arms of a lovely woman; in this last encounter, one just 18 years old.

Feliks Yussoupov had been born here, surrounded by rare antiquities of prodigious value. As a child, he had eaten off golden plates served by Arab, Tartar and Ethiopian servants. In powdered wigs and Yussoupov livery, they stood silently behind the chair of each guest. No matter how much Prince Yussoupov spent as he grew older – and he spent money on an unprecedented scale – it seemed impossible to diminish in any serious way the family cascade of rents, fees, royalties, profits.

But there was another, darker, side to all this. Beneath one of the Yussoupov palaces, the Prince, as a boy, had discovered an underground passage that stretched literally for miles. At intervals, he noticed locked doors sealed with cement round their edges. Through idle curiosity, he broke one down, went inside the room behind it. In the dim light of his oil lamp, he saw the bare walls of a sealed cell, streaming with damp. Hanging in chains from them, were skeletons still clothed in rotting rags. What palace, what jewels or paintings or estates had been the price his ancestors received for these prisoners' lives?

The almost incalculable extent of Yussoupov's wealth did not greatly concern him. It was impossible to imagine life without it, so he did not attempt to do so. What he needed now was the courage to carry through an act of decision that he believed would make him the saviour of his country.

With this in mind, he sat in his study with four other men. The room was furnished after the manner of a gentlemen's club in St James's, with green leather chairs, books round the walls, pictures of hunting scenes, bronze sculptures.

On his right sat Grand Duke Dmitri Pavlovich. He was three years younger than Yussoupov, and held a commission in the

Army. He showed no enthusiasm whatever for the rigours of a military life, and instead spent so much time in Petrograd, drinking heavily and squiring beautiful women to restaurants and private parties, that the Tsarina had asked the Tsar to order him back to his regiment. So far, the Grand Duke had been able to postpone his departure from the capital.

Next to him sat Purishkevich, and then the Army physician, Dr Lazovert, invited because he had access to drugs unavailable to laymen. Serov sat slightly apart from the others. He was, he told himself, as much an observer as a conspirator. He did not really have the interests of his country at heart; he was solely concerned with his own.

Yussoupov stood up and walked to the door, opened it quickly, in case any servant should be on duty outside and could overhear their conversation. The corridor was empty. He shut the door, locked it, came back to his seat.

'Just a precaution, gentlemen,' he explained. 'You know why I have asked you here, so there is no need to speak further on the reason for this meeting. Naturally, we must feel concern at what we plan, and in particular whether any repercussions could affect us. My view is that none will, unless through our own mishandling of the matter, we invite comment and suspicion.

'If we maintain our counsel, if we rehearse fully what each of us has to do, nothing can go wrong. Then we will have successfully carried out an act which will at one stroke release our country from the thrall of an evil and malignant person.'

'What exactly is your plan?' Dmitri asked him; he had a dinner engagement with a general's daughter. He had no intention of being late.

'This. Rasputin knows that my wife, Irina, suffers from severe headaches. I will ask him to come here late tomorrow night and see if he can soothe her pain.'

'But she's in the Crimea,' Dmitri pointed out.

'I know that,' Yussoupov agreed. 'But Rasputin does not. He will believe me. He will accept my invitation. Reluctantly, maybe, if the hour is late, but he will come.

'You, Dr Lazovert, will have meanwhile prepared a poison that you can mix with wine, and also spread some on the little sweet cakes he likes so much. We will therefore kill him twice over, by food and by drink, in order, as the English playwright Shakespeare wrote, "to make assurance double sure". Rasputin is a strong man, but no human being can survive that amount of poison.'

'Will you be alone here?' asked the doctor.

'With Rasputin, yes. I suggest you gentlemen stay in an upper room, just above this one. There is a staircase outside. You will play a record on the gramophone so that it appears that my wife is actually upstairs in that room, entertaining friends, trying to forget her pain.'

'What do we do with the body?' asked Serov.

'Dr Lazovert tells me the poison will take effect almost immediately,' replied Yussoupov. 'He may have a brief paroxysm of pain, but then – nothing. We'll wrap him up in a carpet or a blanket, and carry him out to a car and take him to the River Neva.'

'It's frozen over.'

'Exactly. Which is why we'll go there. Several holes have been made in the ice for fishing or some such purpose. We will push him into one of the holes and under the ice. By the time the river melts, no one will know the body was Rasputin's. A number of bodies are always found in the river in the spring. Suicides, people who have accidentally fallen in. When four million Russians have already died on the Western Front, there are not going to be many inquiries about one more body.'

'There will be inquiries about Rasputin,' warned Purishkevich.

'Of course. But he often goes away for days on end, sometimes weeks, drinking with gypsies, carousing, fornicating. This time, he will go away for ever. That is my plan, gentlemen.'

The others sat in silence, turning the proposal over in their minds. It sounded so easy to discuss Rasputin's death, sitting amidst this elegance: a fire burning in the grate, delicately shaded lights casting gentle shadows on the leatherbound books, on polished furniture, great vases, statues. But out there on the banks of the river, in the freezing night, so many things could go wrong. The car might not start. It could skid. Some nightwalker might see them.

But there were risks in every important enterprise, and these were acceptable. The plan seemed sound. They glanced at each other inquiringly.

'We'll do it,' they agreed.

'Let's drink to that,' said Yussoupov.

He poured out five glasses of vodka. They clinked glasses, paused for a moment, wondering whether they had forgotten or overlooked some apparently trifling detail that could ruin the whole enterprise. Then they nodded, raised their glasses and drank to the success of their plan.

Rasputin's two young daughters, Maria and Varya, were asleep in his house on Gorokhovaya Ulitsa Street when Maria woke up suddenly. She had heard a car stop outside the house. Usually, people came to see her father on foot, and very few called so late, around midnight.

She went to the window, pulled the curtain. A tall man climbed out of the back of the car. The collar of his fur coat was turned up, the flaps on his fur cap pulled down over his ears so tightly that she could not see his face. He went round the house to the back door, so Maria knew he must be expected. This was the entrance used by important visitors. She moved away from the window – and so did not see a second man leave the front seat beside the driver.

The house was in darkness. Serov and Yussoupov had to feel their way along the wall to reach the door. Yussoupov rang the bell; it clanged somewhere in the deep recesses of the building.

Rasputin called out, 'Who is that?'

Yussoupov replied: 'It is me. I have come to take you to my house. I told you, Princess Irina is unwell. One of her worst headaches.'

A pause, the rattle of a chain being freed. A key turned in the lock. The door opened. Yussoupov went inside, followed Rasputin upstairs. He did not close the door behind him. Serov waited until they had reached Rasputin's bedroom, then carefully moved the safety lever on the lock. The door would close, but could still be opened from outside. Then he returned to the car.

An oil lamp burned dimly behind a row of icons in Rasputin's room. The only other light came from a candle by his bed. The flame flickered and swayed in the draught from the open door. Yussoupov noted with distaste that the bed had been slept in or at least lain on; bedclothes lay in a tousled heap.

Rasputin dressed quickly. He put on a silk blouse, with a pattern of cornflowers embroidered into it, threaded a red cord into the belt loops of blue velvet breeches. His boots were highly polished. He seemed smarter than usual; he even smelled of a sharply scented soap. Usually, he was unwashed and dirty, smelling strongly of stale sweat. Obviously, he wished to make a good impression on Princess Irina.

He pulled on a heavy beaver greatcoat, a gift from a gratified banker whose niece he had treated for an ailment that had confounded her doctors, and pronounced himself ready to leave.

Maria came into the room to ask her father where he was going at such a late hour.

'Princess Irina is suffering from a very bad headache,' he explained. 'I will return as soon as I can. You go back to bed. Do not stay awake for me.'

515

Maria remembered how only that morning the Minister of the Interior, Aleksandr Protopopov – who owed his promotion to Rasputin – had warned her father against leaving the house on his own. Protopopov explained that after Purishkevich's speech in the Duma, he had heard rumours of a plot to assassinate Rasputin.

'I will be all right, my dear,' Rasputin assured his daughter. 'If it is God's will, no harm can come to me.' He turned to Yussoupov. 'You are certain the Princess wishes to see me now? It is very late.' He glanced at his watch: 12.30 a.m.

'She insisted I bring you,' Yussoupov replied.

Rasputin shrugged. Maria watched the two men go down to the car.

Rasputin and the Prince sat in the back; in front, Dr Lazovert wore a chauffeur's peaked cap. By his side sat Serov, like a footman, his cap pulled down, his coat collar turned up. He was ready to help seize Rasputin if he became suspicious and tried to escape. But Rasputin sat well back against the buttoned cushions, eyes closed. Neither he nor Yussoupov spoke on the journey through freezing empty streets.

Dr Lazovert drove into the rear courtyard of the palace, stopped outside a small side entrance.

The Prince and Rasputin went upstairs. Serov and the doctor waited until they were out of sight. Then, removing their caps, they followed them in, went on up the stairs to the room above the study. As they entered, Dmitri Pavlovich wound up the clockwork gramophone, lowered the pick-up arm. The needle grated in the groove and the gramophone began to play in a thin, reedy tone, 'Yankee Doodle Went to Town'.

Inside the study, Rasputin took off his overcoat, threw it on a chair. He was surprised at the sound of the music. Was somebody giving a party? He thought he was coming to a house of sickness.

'My wife has been trying to cheer herself up with a few friends,'

Yussoupov explained. 'They are just leaving. Meanwhile, let us take some tea.'

The Prince poured out two cups, handed a plate of biscuits to Rasputin. He waved them away. Yussoupov offered him a plate of small, rum-flavoured cakes. He shook his head.

'They are too sweet,' he said and then suddenly changed his mind. 'No. I will have one. They look extremely tasty.'

Rasputin took a cake, swallowed it, nodded appreciatively, reached out to select another. The Prince watched him. Dr Lazovert had sprinkled all the cakes with a layer of cyanide powder, then covered this with hard sugar icing. The poison had been so concentrated that the doctor wore thick protective rubber gloves while he measured it out. A few grains would be enough to kill a man – and already Rasputin must have swallowed a teaspoonful. Within seconds, he should be dead. But, astonishingly, unbelievably, he showed no ill effects whatever. Instead, he appeared more alert and cheerful.

'I would like a glass of wine rather than tea,' he said.

'We have some from our vineyards in the Crimea,' Yussoupov told him. Poison had not been added to this wine, because Rasputin was known to prefer Madeira, which had been heavily laced with cyanide. Yussoupov filled two glasses, handed one to Rasputin, and sipped the second himself.

'I'd really rather have some Madeira, if you have it,' Rasputin said, wrinkling his nose. 'But don't bother with another glass.'

'You can't mix two kinds of wines,' said Yussoupov, shaking his head; he could not risk diluting the poison. He poured the Madeira into a large goblet of clouded glass. If the poison affected the wine's colour, this would prevent Rasputin from noticing it. The Prince watched Rasputin closely, ready to catch him if he fell. The dose was lethal; it could have killed a horse.

'Another glass, if you please,' said Rasputin, smacking his lips.

. The Prince filled a second goblet and the two men sat by the fire, sipping wine, one glass poisoned, one glass free. Now and then Rasputin held up his goblet to the lamp by his chair and regarded it appreciatively.

Yussoupov tried not to stare at his visitor. Surely he must be imagining this entire grotesque, macabre scene? He had poisoned the man three times – with a cake and two goblets of wine – and the poison had no effect whatever on him. By now Rasputin should be lying dead at his feet. Instead, he sat, apparently delighted with the Madeira. Yussoupov felt sick, faint with worry and apprehension. What sort of man could this be? Was he really a devil, as some declared?

'Play me something cheerful on your guitar,' said Rasputin suddenly.

The Prince had considerable skill on this instrument. He picked it up reluctantly, began to pluck abstractedly at the strings. He had no idea what he played; he felt like a man in a dream, locked into a nightmare. As soon as Yussoupov finished one sad Russian lament, Rasputin asked for another. The minutes ticked past. Why hadn't Rasputin asked when he could see the Princess? Did he guess this was simply an excuse to bring him here?

Rasputin now lolled back in his chair, apparently half asleep. Could he be dying at last? He put up one hand and stroked his throat.

'Is anything the matter?' Yussoupov asked him hopefully.

'No. Just a little tickling in my throat.'

Yussoupov handed him a third glass of poisoned wine. Rasputin drank it at a draught. Then he leaned forward and stared intently at Yussoupov. His eyes seemed to swell, to grow luminous and pulse like two green, glowing hearts. Yussoupov forced himself to look away: he felt he was being hypnotised. He knew he had to break this strange spell – or it would break him.

Upstairs, the gramophone record slowed, then speeded up as the doctor rewound the motor. Had they only one record up

518

there? Couldn't they find something more melodious than this scratchy song?

'Excuse me,' he said hoarsely at last. 'I will see what is happening with the Princess. I do not want to keep you waiting any longer.'

He ran up the stairs, two at a time. The other conspirators met him in the doorway, their faces tense.

'Is it over?' Dmitri Pavlovich asked him.

'It hasn't even started! The poison isn't working!'

'It *must* be. The dose was enormous,' said Dr Lazovert in astonishment.

'So is his resistance.'

'No human being could survive that amount of cyanide. It just isn't possible.'

'It is,' said Yussoupov grimly. 'He'll never die like this. I'll have to shoot him.'

He held out his hand. Dmitri passed him his Army pistol. Yussoupov went downstairs, holding it behind his back. Rasputin was standing in front of an ebony cabinet that contained a crystal crucifix. As Yussoupov came into the room, Rasputin bent forward to examine the glittering cross more closely.

'You'd better look at the crucifix – and say a prayer,' Yussoupov told him in a voice he did not recognise as his own.

As he raised the pistol, he prayed silently: 'Oh, Lord, give me the strength to finish it.'

He fired at Rasputin's back as he bent over the crucifix, aiming where he believed his heart would be. Rasputin fell backwards. His hands clenched and unclenched; blood spread across his blouse. The others came downstairs at the sound of the shot. They ran in so quickly, so excitedly, that one of them brushed against the main switch by the side of the door. Instantly, the light went out. The room was dark.

'Don't move!' Serov cried. 'You'll trip over the body!'

Everyone stood still while he carefully stepped across Rasputin, felt his way to the door, and turned on the light. Rasputin lay on his back on a bearskin rug, eyes closed. Dr Lazovert bent over him.

'He is dead,' he said with satisfaction.

After the strain of the previous two hours, the thought that their enemy had finally died brought an immense reaction of relief. For a moment they simply stood in silence, staring at his body, drained of all emotion and energy. Yussoupov felt he would faint. Then Dmitri, realising that time was running against them, took back his pistol and motioned to Purishkevich to help him lift Rasputin's body. They moved it from the rug, already soaked and clotted with blood, and put it down again on flagstones which would be easier to clean.

Now they began the second phase of their plan. Serov put on Rasputin's heavy coat. He was roughly the same size and build, and if the secret police were watching the palace and had seen Rasputin arrive, they could report he had also left in the same car that had brought him. This meant that no suspicion would fall upon Yussoupov, whose hostility to Rasputin was widely known. Serov set off with Dmitri in the car. The others went upstairs until the car returned. They would then put the body in the back and drive with it to the river.

After a few minutes, Yussoupov, for some reason he never could explain, went downstairs and felt Rasputin's pulse. It was still; the man was quite dead. *Or was he?*

On an impulse, Yussoupov gripped one of Rasputin's arms, and as he did so, he saw his eyelids open. Rasputin stared up at the Prince with eyes that seemed to glow venomously like those of a deadly serpent. Yussoupov stood mesmerised, unable to run. Then Rasputin leaped up from the flagstones. Foam and blood bubbled at his mouth. He gripped the Prince by the shoulder, tried to seize him by the throat and throttle him.

The two men struggled desperately together, swaying this

way and that, cursing, gasping for breath. Finally, Yussoupov managed to shake Rasputin away. He fell heavily, still gripping an epaulette he had torn from the Prince's jacket.

Yussoupov staggered upstairs, calling for Purishkevich. He knew that, like Dmitri, the deputy had brought a pistol with him.

'Quick!' the Prince shouted. 'Come down! *He's still alive!*'

Halfway down the stairs, they met Rasputin crawling up towards them on his hands and knees, like a beast. When he saw the two men facing him, one holding a pistol, he paused. And then with a speed that astounded both men, Rasputin jumped up and opened a side door.

They followed him as he ran across the courtyard, shouting back at them: 'I will tell the Empress *everything!*'

Purishkevich fired at him, missed, fired twice more.

At the third shot, Rasputin staggered and fell on to the hard-packed snow. At that moment, two servants came out of the palace to see what was happening. A policeman, who had been on guard at the front of the palace, also ran into the courtyard to discover who was firing shots at that early hour.

'It's all right,' the Prince told him reassuringly, trying to keep his voice calm. 'There's nothing to worry about. We've had a party. One of my guests drank a bit too much and fired his pistol in the air. Everything is all right, I assure you.'

He headed the policeman off back to the palace gate. If he had taken another half-dozen paces, the man would have seen Rasputin, arguably the most powerful man in Russia, lying in his own blood.

Then Yussoupov was astonished to see that Rasputin was still alive. His body was moving on the snow. As they stood, staring at this in shock and disbelief, footsteps crunched towards them. The policeman had returned. He explained apologetically that the shots had been heard in the local police station; his superiors had ordered him to make a written report, not simply a verbal one.

521

Then he saw Rasputin's body on the ground and backed away in astonishment.

The servants had also seen it, but they knew better than to admit who the victim was. Purishkevich gripped the policeman's arm with the strength of despair. Everything was going wrong; their careful plan had totally disintegrated.

'You know who I am?' he asked the policeman gruffly. 'I am a member of the Duma. The shots you heard killed Rasputin. If you love your country and your Tsar, *keep your mouth shut!*'

Yussoupov and Lazovert stared in horror at the deputy as he openly admitted to a policeman the crime they had all agreed must be kept an absolute secret. The policeman looked stupidly from one to the other, not certain whether this was some absurd aristocratic farce, a piece of complicated play-acting he could not understand.

Then he glanced again at the body in the snow. The blood was real. Whatever the truth of the matter, this was clearly something for his superiors to handle. He would placate these gentlemen as best he could, and report back to the station.

'You did right,' he said unconvincingly. 'I'll not say a word unless the judge puts me on oath. Then I would have to tell the truth. It would be wrong to tell a lie.'

Purishkevich led him to the gates of the palace. The others bent over Rasputin's body, wrapped it in a blue curtain, tied it round with ropes. As they finished, the car returned. They all manhandled the body into the back, then drove in silence through the awakening city, along the bank of the frozen river.

Dr Lazovert stopped the car near one of the holes in the ice. They checked that the street was empty, and then carried their heavy burden over the thick ice. They pushed it down into the nearest hole, prodded it as far as they could beneath the ice. Then they drove back to the palace.

When Serov heard of Purishkevich's blunder, he told them he would circulate a different version of events. He would claim that Purishkevich was drunk: they had been discussing his speech. The deputy must have imagined he was still addressing the Duma. At that hour of the morning, this seemed a plausible enough explanation. And feeble as they all realised it could sound in a court of law, no one had anything more convincing to suggest.

Serov walked back through the snow to Rasputin's house. It was in complete darkness. He waited in the shadows for a quarter of an hour in case any light appeared. Perhaps the police would telephone to check whether Rasputin was at home, and that the officer had made a mistake. But the house stayed dark and silent. Serov went round to the back door which he had left unlocked, went inside. Then he cautiously made his way to Rasputin's study.

He stood briefly outside each closed door, in case anyone might be in the room beyond, but all the downstairs rooms seemed empty, smelling slightly of cigar smoke and beeswax polish. Inside the study, he closed and locked the door behind him, opened a window slightly. If he was disturbed, he could leave that way quickly.

Rasputin had a huge table which he used as a desk, and on this he had piled all manner of unusual gifts that people gave to him. He was careless of his possessions, Serov was certain that the cardboard box he sought would be somewhere on this table. He just had to be patient and painstaking, and fight down an almost overwhelming temptation to abandon his search before someone heard him and he was arrested. What possible explanation could he give for his presence here? The Okhrana had their own harsh methods of extracting truth from any body-guard of lies.

Serov struck a match, lit a candle and stood looking about him to get his bearings, and to check on the positions of any obstacles – a chair, a table, a footstool – if he had to escape in a hurry. Then he began to sort very slowly and methodically through the bric-a-brac on the desk. After about ten minutes, he found a small box that fitted the maid's description, opened it. Six diamonds were inside it, just as she had described.

He took them out of the box, put them in his pockets, spreading them around his suit and his trousers. Then he replaced the empty box where he found it, blew out the candle and tiptoed from the house.

When Jamie gave the key of his suite to the reception clerk in his hotel, the man handed him a note. He read: 'Mr Provost. Please contact the undersigned, Fourth Secretary, British Embassy, urgently.' Jamie put the note in his pocket. When he had visited the Embassy just before war broke out, the Fourth Secretary had not been particularly helpful. To him, Jamie was simply a business man, of no particular consequence. Why was the Secretary keen to see him now? Had he heard from General Brookes?

Jamie walked towards the main door, looked out on the wide street. It was totally empty. There were no pedestrians or sledges, no horse trams, no cars, no carts.

As he stood, he heard a distant sound of shouting, then cheers, and then the thunder of big guns. Windows rattled in their frames. The noise was coming from the direction of the River Neva. Warships anchored there must be firing. Was this some royal salute, or target practice? Surely not the latter in a crowded capital city?

A single taxi stood outside the hotel, where usually there was a line of cabs, another of troikas, a third of sledges. Had they all been booked? He could not see any porters with their distinctive blouses and baggy blue trousers. He climbed into the cab.

'British Embassy, please,' he told the driver. The man understood that much English, and cranked up his engine. Five minutes later, after a run through deserted streets, cleared as though by some catastrophe, Jamie was sitting opposite Thomas Clarke, the Fourth Secretary, in his office. Maybe he was a little plumper, but otherwise he did not appear to have changed.

'How did you know I was here?' Jamie asked him. 'I didn't come to sign the book.'

'There is a very strong police presence here. Very strong. The Okhrana are said to have files on every citizen in the entire Russian empire. They make lists of all foreigners visiting the capital. As a matter of course, they send details to the relevant embassies. But it is no use making lists of malcontents and agitators and revolutionaries – if you allow them to get on with their activities.

'If the Tsar would only agree to have twenty, or even ten, ringleaders incarcerated, the whole situation might still be contained. If he does not, there will be far worse rioting than there was here in 1905.'

'So why does he not do as you say?'

'Because he is a weak man, relying on his wife, and she relied on Rasputin.'

'Relied?' Jamie noted the past tense.

'Yes. He is dead. His body has been discovered this morning under the ice in the Neva. The Minister of the Interior telephoned his home for some reason. Rasputin's daughter told him she had seen her father go out with Prince Yussoupov about half past midnight. A police agent later reported that Rasputin had returned about three o'clock this morning. But he made a mistake – or else he had gone off duty early and pretended he hadn't. Whoever he saw was not Rasputin.

'The Minister informed the Royal House – they wished to see Rasputin urgently – probably the Tsarevitch was ill again. Anyhow, the Tsarina became very concerned and ordered an immediate search for Rasputin. Then some policeman who had been on guard outside Yussoupov's palace came forward and made the astonishing claim that Vladimir Purishkevich had confessed to him *he* had personally killed Rasputin!

'The policeman said this confession was made in the early hours of this morning in the courtyard of the Moika Palace. It sounded absurd, but they checked – and it was true. Prince Yussoupov, Grand Duke Dmitri Pavlovich, some army doctor and Vladimir Purishkevich have all been arrested. Apparently someone else was also involved, but no one is saying who – yet.'

'How did he die?' asked Jamie.

'He had been shot. His hands were raw and bleeding and cut to the bone. He had struggled to be free from a curtain, into which he had been wrapped. Then he'd attempted to claw his way out from under ice inches thick. Amazing strength, the man had. Superhuman, in my view. There has been an autopsy, and his lungs were found full of water, so ironically he didn't die at the hands of his enemies, but by drowning.

'Now, I asked you to come here in your own interests. Russia is poised on the edge of revolution. Yesterday, ninety thousand workers in the textile mills in the Vyborg district went on strike. That has never happened before. They took to the streets, shouting for bread. There have been bread lines in every town and city for months. The whole country is a shambles.

'People are sick of being hungry and cold, sick of military defeats and reverses – and most of all sick of seeing how the rich seem to live as well as ever. They want a share of the cake – and Rasputin's death accelerates the situation. Now the Tsar's position is immeasurably weakened.

'This morning, factories all around the capital reported that their workforce arrived as usual on time, but none of them did any work. Instead, they stood about in groups, listening to fiery orators who whipped them up against their managers, their representatives in the Duma and, most significantly, against the Tsar. There was nothing the managers and owners of the factories could do. They were totally outnumbered.'

'What about the police?'

'They arrived, and the workers at once picked up stones, even pieces of ice, and pelted them and their horses. They cleared off. Next, they sent the troops in to try to grab the ringleaders, but instead of doing that, the soldiers fraternised with the strikers. When the Army does not support the government, that can only mark the beginning of the end.

'I advise you most strongly to leave Petrograd and Russia as soon as possible. The Embassy cannot give all British citizens protection if the entire machinery of government breaks down. If you delay, it could be too late to leave.'

Jamie stood up.

'Thanks for the warning,' he said. 'I will bear it in mind. But there are two things for which I would appreciate your help. First, when I was here before the war, I met a young lady, Katharina Sokolov, the granddaughter of the Grand Duchess Victoria. I have found her telephone number through my hotel, but it is unobtainable. Is she at her country residence?'

'I cannot be sure. She is either at Tsarskoe-Selo, or in the Crimea, where the weather is rather better at this time of year. But the telephone exchanges are not always manned these days. And her house may be closed, all the servants gone. Things are not as they were, you know. The servants could even have taken the place over. I would not advise you to pay a visit. You could be killed just for the coat on your back.'

'I see. Now, to my second matter. Also on my last visit, I met a man called Serov who was helpful. I have seen him again on this trip. He appears rather less ebullient than he was. Is he trustworthy?'

The Fourth Secretary shrugged his shoulders. 'Is anyone in his position? For years, Serov has cultivated archdukes and duchesses and royal chamberlains. He has also been helpful to several embassies, including ours. But how can he possibly make a living if all the aristocracy slip away?'

'You really think it is as bad as that?'

'Dear sir, it is worse. Much worse.'

Serov let himself into his apartment, locked the door on its double locks and sat down at the kitchen table to examine the diamonds he had taken from Rasputin's house. He had begun that day a poor man, totally reliant for his livelihood on the compliance, curiosity and generosity of others. Now he was rich as a king.

But how could he transport himself and his treasure to safety, to enjoy the luxurious life that fate had always denied him?

He had also heard that Rasputin's body had been found, but what disturbed him even more was that, having been fed enough poison to kill half a dozen men, having been shot once by the Prince and then by Purishkevich, Rasputin still had lived long enough to attempt to escape from the ice. Only the freezing water had prevented him.

Had he been a man – or a devil? And if the latter, could he from beyond the grave still avenge himself on those who had sought to bring him down? The other conspirators had already been arrested. It would not be long before his own identity was revealed. He must conceal the diamonds – but how?

As Serov sat, turning the stones over in his hands, he thought of a scheme that seemed so ingenious, so audacious, he sensed it might just succeed.

As he considered the implications and the risks, both equally fearful, he heard a fierce knocking on the door, and the concierge's voice, at first angry and then suddenly servile and obsequious. The police must already be here. Within moments, they would be in his room.

Serov knew he had to act now – or die.

TWENTY-NINE

Revolution

Most of the telephone lines in Petrograd were down and the exchanges deserted, so when the telephone rang in Jamie's hotel room, he was so surprised that he spilled his glass of vodka. He picked up the receiver quickly, before it could stop ringing. Serov was on the line.

'I must see you urgently,' he said in a hoarse whisper. 'I can't say why now.'

'Can you come here?'

'No. I will be outside the Winter Palace in an hour. That will be better.'

Better for whom? Jamie wondered as he put on his overcoat. The elevator was still out of order, so he walked downstairs to the front hall. No troikas or sledges waited at the hotel entrance; he would have to walk.

'It's not safe for you to go outside today in those fine clothes, sir,' the reception clerk told him nervously. The man went to a cupboard behind his desk, took out a shabby overcoat with a strip of moth-eaten fur round the collar.

'Take this, sir,' he said. 'You will be less conspicuous – less of a target for people who dislike foreigners, or the rich.'

'Thank you,' said Jamie. He exchanged overcoats, gave the man 20 roubles for his thoughtfulness, went out into the freezing street.

Men wearing shabby dungarees, women with scarves and shawls tied round their heads were pouring across the Troitskii Bridge from factories on the far bank of the river. They seemed to be fairly good-humoured, shouting slogans Jamie did not understand, waving to friends with fists clenched. But when they reached the plate-glass windows of the expensive shops and saw the soft leather belts, jewelled handbags and opulent furs in the windows, their attitude changed violently.

The nearest window shattered as a heavy log went through it. A hundred people poured in through the broken glass, seized goods on display, then surged on into storerooms, rushing out again carrying fur capes, shoes, coats, anything they could bear away. Those going in fought angrily with those coming out, enraged that they had not been first, fearful that by the time they reached the storerooms all the loot might have gone.

Around the front of the parliament building, soldiers stood on guard with bayonets fixed. They offered no resistance as the crowd propelled Jamie past them, up the steps and into the main entrance hall. He had come here with Serov only a short time previously, but that might have been in another world, another age. The hall was crowded now with workers wearing red armbands, and soldiers.

Some stood around, chatting idly. Others had stacked their rifles and squatted on the floor, eating rye bread and chopped-up herrings and noisily drinking mugs of tea. More were asleep, lying huddled in their greatcoats on the marble floor, oblivious of the chaos and confusion and chatter around them.

No one challenged Jamie. He walked from room to room, opened one door and saw members of the Duma, almost unbelievably, in the middle of a debate – as though anyone now cared what decisions they reached. He walked down a long, clammy corridor – once hung with tapestries, which had been stripped from the walls and now lay on the floor like rugs – and out of a side door towards the Winter Palace.

By his waving of his right hand above his head, fist clenched, the crowd accepted him as one of them. When people nearest him shouted questions or grinned at him, he nodded or grinned back. Like flotsam carried on a swiftly moving tide, the crowd bore him on towards the gates of the palace. The only people near it were groups of soldiers, hatless, with uniforms unbuttoned, rifles slung over their shoulders or being dragged along the pavement by their muzzles. At one street corner, Jamie passed a field gun abandoned, lying on its side, with a pyramid of shells yet to be fired.

Every window of the Winter Palace appeared to be lit. Light poured out across the wide street, but he could not see anyone standing at any of the windows. Had the whole palace been abandoned, deserted? And where was Serov? Could he be inside the building? Through an open door, Jamie wandered into a huge room, piled with packing cases. Soldiers were attacking them furiously with hammers, chisels, crowbars, tearing open wooden chests filled with linen sheets, curtains, carpets, and then a porcelain dinner service, bearing the royal arms in gold.

They threw some of the plates on the ground, thinking them of no value, went on burrowing inside each crate in the hope of finding silver plate, gold ornaments, jewels. More soldiers pushed through into other rooms, along corridors, up staircases. Their uniforms bulged with whatever they had been able to seize: gold-handled swords, china vases, bronze statuettes, even bottles of ink that leaked long red and blue stains down their trousers.

Still no sign of Serov. Puzzled, Jamie went into another room. A key was in the lock of a further door. Ahead lay a vault, lined with metal plates. Dome-shaped bolts secured these to the stone walls. The grey-painted metal reflected the pulsing of electric lights in protective shields. This must be the Diamond Room. No one had followed him here; the room was quite empty, with nothing left to loot.

Down the stairs, along corridors, he went, out into the street again, where the crowds were greater now. Hundreds of people were trying to surge into the palace. Those inside beat them off with rifle butts. But where was Serov? Had Jamie misunderstood his instructions? His own sense of direction seemed temporarily to have deserted him. He struck out, away from the palace, hoping to reach some higher point from which he could scan the whole area for Serov. In a few minutes, it would be impossible to move at all.

He put his head down, doggedly forced his way through the crowd, using his knees, boots, elbows. And suddenly, as though in a dream, he heard a distant braying of bugles. Was the Army coming through the streets at last to clear the rabble?

Then Jamie saw the huge Parthenon radiator of a Rolls-Royce flanked by two Zeiss headlamps and surmounted by the mascot, the Spirit of Ecstasy. Behind the long polished aluminium bonnet, studded with steel rivets, two men sat in the front seat. Both wore identical blue uniforms with fur collars and blue caps with shiny peaks.

The car came on through the crowd, regardless of the furious shouts and screams and people who flung snowballs at it, spat on the radiator, beat the doors and mudguards with sticks and rifle butts. What Jamie had heard were not bugles but two huge trumpet horns fitted on either side of the car's bonnet.

A rear side window was wound down. Framed in this, Jamie saw the face of the woman he had hoped above all others to see: Katharina.

'You!' he cried in delighted amazement. 'What are *you* doing here?'

'I live here,' she replied, smiling. 'But don't just stand there. Get in. *Quickly!*'

Katharina opened the door as she spoke. Jamie climbed in over the running board, sank down on the brocade cushions beside her. Katharina spoke to the driver through an ivory speaking tube. The car accelerated away, down the wide road.

The crowds fell back on either side, still shouting hatred and abuse at this supreme symbol of wealth and privilege, an English Rolls-Royce, the king of cars, the car of kings. Soon, the vehicle outdistanced the fastest runner, and they were out in the country, travelling silently on the packed snow, with empty fields, white and bare of animals and people, stretching in a frozen landscape on either side as far as they could see. In the distance, pale mists of evening began to roll in over the freezing wastes. Jamie turned to Katharina.

'If you hadn't shown up then, I don't know what would have happened to me. I had gone to the Winter Palace, to meet Serov.' He explained. 'He telephoned me to meet him there, but I couldn't find him. I was going back to my hotel. But I doubt if I'd have reached it.'

'I heard you were here,' she said. 'You had been asking about me?' Katharina blushed slightly as she spoke, lowered her eyes.

'Who told you that?'

'Oh, a mutual friend. We have only one. Sometimes I am not sure if he is a friend, but Mikhail Serov is certainly useful. I came out to see if I could find you. I knew you would never find me.'

'Why not?' asked Jamie. 'These disturbances can't go on for ever, can they?'

'Possibly they can. Or at least until they achieve their objective.'

'You don't mean that?'

'I do. It's revolution. Haven't you heard the news? The Tsar has been forced to abdicate. He was at Army Headquarters, five hundred miles away from here. His ministers informed him there were what they called "street disorders" in the capital, but the Empress managed to get a message through to him that things were much, much worse. The Tsar ordered a special train to come back and see for himself, but revolutionary soldiers blocked the track and set up machine guns, so he had to go back.

'They went up and down country lines aimlessly. The telegraphs are out of order. There was no means of communication. He stopped finally at a station called Pskov, where the headquarters of the northern group of armies is. They'd always been loyal to the Tsar. Then he heard that his own Imperial Guard, the whole garrison, Cossack escort, everything, led by Grand Duke Cyril, the Tsar's own cousin, had gone over to the Bolsheviks. The only hope of saving the country was for him to abdicate. He is now on his way back to Tsarskoe-Selo under escort – a prisoner.'

'Is this *really* true?' asked Jamie in amazement. He had failed totally in his assignment; events had overtaken him.

'All of it, unfortunately.'

'Where are we going now?'

'To my palace. My mother is in France. My grandmother is in residence, but for how long, I don't know.'

'Do your driver and footman speak English?'

'Not a word.'

'Are they loyal?'

She shrugged. 'The Tsar had fifteen hundred troops around the palace, every one picked for their loyalty to him. They have all been decorated in goodness knows how many campaigns. But as we drive past tonight, you'll see they all wear white handkerchiefs on their wrists.'

'What does that mean? Surrender?'

'In a sense. It is to show the Bolsheviks that while they are still technically guarding the Tsar, they won't offer any resistance to anyone who cares to come and take over the palace.'

They drove on in silence. The car was so cold that their breath froze on the windows. Katharina pulled a rug from a pocket behind the front seat underneath the glass partition, handed one side to Jamie and tucked it round their knees. As she smoothed the rug, their fingers touched briefly beneath it. Jamie gripped her hand. Their fingers entwined and they sat, not looking at each other, glad to be together, side by side, warmed and comforted by their nearness, as the great car sighed on into the freezing dark. Its big yellow headlights cast an amber flood on the snow ahead. Despite the fact that the tyres were fitted with metal studs for these conditions, the Rolls slithered and slid on the corners and in drifts of snow, and the rear wheels spun before they regained traction.

'What are your plans?' asked Jamie at last.

'I don't know,' Katharina admitted. 'We have a saying in Russia, man proposes, but God disposes. Now the Bolsheviks have the last word, the only word, I can't really have plans. None of us can. But you are different. What are your plans? Why did you come here?'

Jamie hesitated a second. There seemed no reason for secrecy now.

'I came on a special mission,' he explained. 'It was intended to help the Imperial family but was left too late. I shall have to return to England.'

'If you can get back.'

He shrugged. 'I will try. And you?'

'This is my home,' she replied. 'My family has lived here for as long as the Romanovs. We have suffered all kinds of troubles – pestilences, plagues, famines, revolts. And we've always come through.' Katharina paused.

'But this time?' he asked her gently.

'This time is different. But whatever happens, I cannot abandon what is our heritage – our duty, if you like. Great possessions bring great responsibilities. From those to whom much has been given, much is expected. We have thousands of people totally dependent on us. In farms, factories, on estates. I can't just go and leave them. How are they going to make a living?'

535

'They may take over the factories and estates.'

'They probably will, but they can't run them. That takes years of skill and experience. You can't suddenly start doing it when you have been pushing a plough for years.'

'Maybe they'll learn.'

'Maybe. But my family took years to learn. You can't know overnight. I feel I must stay, whatever happens.'

'This may all blow over,' said Jamie hopefully.

She shook her head. 'No. Not now the Tsar has gone. He was a sort of lynchpin for the whole country.'

Jamie said suddenly, remembering their first meeting: 'Did you ever get to the Riviera?'

'Of course not,' she said. 'My mother did. Then the war started and I couldn't.'

'I wrote to you,' he said. 'I sent telegraphs every week for months.'

Katharina looked at him, pleased and surprised. 'I didn't get any of them, or any letters.'

He gripped her hand more tightly and they looked at each other intently, as though trying to memorise each other's faces.

'Why did you come looking for me?' Jamie asked her, hoping he knew the answer.

'I thought you could be in trouble. I knew you didn't speak a word of Russian – or you didn't when we last met. And the English are so bad at foreign languages. And in your expensive clothes – despite that fearful overcoat – the mob would hate you. They could kill you.'

'But how are you still allowed to drive a car like this in a revolution?'

'Because no one has stopped me – yet. It's the only car we have left, anyway. We had a Ford, a Pierce-Arrow and an English Daimler. They have all been taken. This was in a local garage, being serviced. The revolutionaries didn't know that. Anyhow, the railway is very spasmodic now. There is no timetable, and you can't be sure you will reach the next station, let alone your destination. Mutineers, deserters come into the compartments, demanding money, threatening people.'

'I still have to get back to Petrograd, somehow.'

'I'll take you – if we have enough petrol.'

The car slowed, turned off the road between two stone gateposts, stopped. A crowd of fifty or sixty men was gathered around a bonfire, burning doors, window shutters and furniture from one of the lodges. Some held bottles in their hands. Others staggered around, clearly drunk. They looked up, saw the car, and ran towards it. They seized logs and planks that blazed like firebrands. Their faces contorted with hatred, fuming with vodka, they thrust at the car with their burning stakes.

The footman had wound down his window. Now he quickly closed it again, but not before the car filled with smoke and hot ash. The men outside began to shout and beat on the doors with sticks. Katharina tapped smartly on the glass partition, called a command to the chauffeur. He let in the clutch; the car moved forward. Some men ran alongside, waving fists and burning poles. Others pelted the car with stones and bottles and lumps of frozen snow.

'They've killed the lodgekeeper,' Katharina said tonelessly. 'They're burning his goods.'

'But he was only a peasant like them, surely?'

'Makes no difference. He worked for us. He represented something they hate.'

'You mean, *you*?'

'I mean three hundred years of living here, of owning everything in sight. And everyone. Their fathers, grandfathers, great-grandfathers. Now it is their turn.'

'You seem very philosophical about all this.'

'What else can I be? Your English king, Canute, so I was told at school, once sat on the beach to try and turn back the tide. He

537

failed. This is another tide. We cannot turn it back either. Not now, at least. One day, maybe. But not now.'

The car stopped outside the palace Jamie had last seen on a summer day before the war. Now it was in total darkness. No light glimmered in any window, yet Jamie could see that the curtains were not drawn. The footman stepped down, bowed politely, opened the car door. Katharina climbed out. She walked up the steps to the house, then paused.

'Grandmama!' she called out. Her voice echoed from the high stone building.

There was no answer. Jamie felt uneasy.

'Don't go inside,' he told her urgently.

'But I must. It is my home.'

'I'll go,' he said. 'You wait here.'

'I'll come with you.'

Together, they walked up the steps to the huge double doors. From the centre of gold-edged panels, polished bronze likenesses of lions and leopards stared out sightlessly across the snow. In the distance, thinned by the wind, Jamie could hear a crackle of flames at the lodge, drunken shouts and cheers. He turned the handle of one of the doors, opened it. They smelled burning ash inside as though a log had fallen from an open fireplace. He flicked the switches. No lights came on.

'There are candles on a shelf on the left, and a box of matches,' Katharina told him.

Jamie felt his way through the hall to a marble shelf, ran his fingers along it. He found a box of matches in a little silver case, struck one, lit a row of candles. The hall had already been looted. He had half expected that, but to see it made him feel physically sick. Mirrors on the walls had been smashed, books ripped from shelves, flung on the ground, their binding torn off. Ornaments had been hammered against the walls until they broke. Ming vases lay in pieces on the carpet.

He picked up a candle, shielding the flame against the wind

which blew from broken windows at the back of the house. He walked down the long corridor to the kitchen quarters. Here, cupboards had been opened with needless violence, doors torn from hinges. The contents of drawers were emptied on the floor: bags of sugar and flour had been spilled in the eagerness of looters to grab handfuls and stuff them in their pockets. It was a scene of total and pointless devastation.

Carrying the candle, he went into a downstairs sitting room. An old woman lay in a chair by an empty fireplace, her head lolling against its back. He stood looking at the dead face of the Grand Duchess Victoria. He had last seen her three years earlier at the picnic in the grounds of this palace.

She had been clubbed on the head; blood matted her hair. A necklace had been torn from her throat and hung broken, some jewels still stuck to the thread. Books had been pulled from their cases, to be flung on the ground, or ripped apart. In one corner, someone had defecated on a pile of family photographs in silver frames. He saw pools of urine on the polished floor. Ornaments were smashed, oil paintings on the wall cut into pieces so that strips of canvas hung down, revealing silk wallpaper behind them.

Jamie went back to Katharina.

'Don't go in there,' he warned her. 'Your grandmother has been killed.'

The colour drained from Katharina's face. 'Grandmama . . . ?'

Jamie held her, tried to comfort her. Then he put his hands on her shoulders. 'Listen to me, Katharina.' She raised her tear-streaked face to his. 'We've got to get away. It's not safe here.'

'I've nowhere to go,' Katharina replied, her voice rising with fear. 'I cannot just run away. There must be *some* loyal servants still. They have worked for us twenty, thirty years, remember. Often, their mothers and fathers before them. They can't all have deserted me, surely?'

She picked up a handbell from the floor. The handle had been bent in an attempt to break it, but the metal had proved too strong. Katharina shook it vigorously. The tinkling of the silver clapper echoed through the empty house. No one replied.

'Listen,' Jamie said gently. 'Come away with me. You can't stay here. Come back to Petrograd.'

'Then what?' she asked him. 'I can't live there. I've no money, for one thing. And everything my family's ever owned is in this house, on this estate.'

'If you stay here, and the mob come back, they'll kill you as they killed your grandmother. Pack what you can, while you can. The most valuable things, and the easiest to carry. We'll take them in your car.'

'There may not be enough gasoline,' she said.

'The driver will know.'

They ran out into the courtyard. The Rolls stood where it had been left. The front doors were still open, swinging slightly in the night wind. Katharina called to the chauffeur and the footman. There was no reply. They had abandoned the vehicle so hurriedly, they had not even bothered to shut the doors. Jamie walked round the car. It did not appear to be damaged, but the bonnet was unfastened. He raised it. The carburettor had been smashed with a sledgehammer. He lowered the bonnet. Katharina looked at him inquiringly. He shook his head.

'How can we reach Petrograd?' she asked him tearfully. 'We can't walk back. The Tsar's palace is just up the road. Maybe they'll lend us a car.'

'But he's abdicated.'

'He's still living there. He can help us, surely, if anyone can?'

'He probably can't even help himself,' said Jamie. 'He's a prisoner, you said.'

'It's our only hope. Come with me.'

'No,' Jamie insisted. 'Pack everything you want to take in a bag. We may not have the chance of coming back here.'

'I don't know what to pack,' she said, distraught and frightened. 'I've always had someone to pack for me. What do I take, what do I leave?'

'Take what you can carry. The things that are the most valuable. Jewels, a painting.'

'In its frame?'

'No. I can cut it out with a knife, roll it up. Anything. Diamonds. Deeds. Have you any money of your own?'

She shook her head. 'Very little. I never needed any. Someone always paid for me.'

'Then take this.'

He undid his watchstrap, handed her the watch inlaid with diamonds that Colonel Dugdale had given him in Muizenberg. Before he came to Russia, he had painted the diamonds black to conceal them in case a Customs officer showed any interest. Now he explained how Katharina could sell it or barter it against a steamship ticket, a visa, a passport.

'But they'll see me wearing a watch. It's the first thing they'll steal from me.'

'No, it will be the last thing,' he assured her. 'Do you have a medical chest upstairs?'

'Yes. In my bathroom.'

'Then put on the watch and wrap a bandage round it. Say you've damaged your wrist. Pack a spare bandage. And don't wind the watch up, then it won't tick. Just keep it under that bandage. It's worth hundreds, maybe thousands of English pounds, so don't let it go too cheaply. Now, where do you keep your bags?'

'In my dressing room.'

They went upstairs. He optimistically flicked the switches on each landing but all the electric lights were dead. He lit an oil lamp. By its gentle glow, Katharina found two leather suitcases with straps and big polished brass buckles, began rooting vaguely in drawers and cupboards.

'Take a couple of changes of clothes,' Jamie advised. 'I'll go round and find what silver is small enough to carry.'

He lit another lamp from the first and carried this through empty, echoing rooms. Outside, in the park, through the windows with their undrawn curtains, he could see flickering lamps and lights like glowworms move through the darkness. People were coming towards the house.

Could they see him? Were they just waiting for them to come out – and then kill them? He forced himself to keep calm. He had no idea what he should take, but going from one oil painting to another with his clasp knife, he cut out the canvas, rolled up each one.

He picked up little silver objects, tiny carvings, minute statuary, Fabergé eggs; the bric-a-brac of a life of wealth and elegance and peace. Soon, they had two suitcases packed. He carried them downstairs. Katharina went ahead with the lamps.

They started to go out of the front door. Suddenly, he pulled her back.

'No,' he said. 'They may be waiting for us there. Bolt the front door.'

Katharina slammed huge, polished bolts into place, then levers that locked into the walls and fitted neatly into dovetails between the double doors.

'The back door,' Jamie told her briefly.

She led him through a labyrinth of passages where groups of bells hung on springs with markers underneath to show which room demanded the attentions of a servant. Jamie had a feeling he was already living in the past. This was no longer a palace, nor even a home; it was a stage set for a terrible tragedy.

'I've just remembered, there was a car kept in a garage beyond a private chapel in the Tsar's grounds. The Bolsheviks may not know it's there.'

'All right, we'll go and see. But is there a hiding place where we can put these cases while we go and look?'

'There's a trap door in the kitchen, under the floor, to a cellar.'

They opened it, carried the cases down wooden stairs into a cellar. Jamie heard a faint rustling of rats in the darkness, and left one light burning. The risk of fire was slight and he wanted to know exactly where he had left the cases in case they had to return in a hurry. He pulled a carpet over the trap door.

They left the house and hurried down gravel paths neatly laid between rows and rows of vegetables covered with snow, past glass greenhouses where oil lamps and heaters still glowed. Somehow, in the midst of change so cataclysmic that Jamie could hardly credit it, he did not feel uneasy or even sad. He felt curiously elated, almost cheerful, and looking at Katharina's face, eyes bright in the frosty air, he knew that she was the reason.

They came to a side gate set in a row of high metal palings. They let themselves out, walked half a mile down the deserted track in snow unsullied by wheels or animal hoof prints. In the distance, they heard a faint jeering. They walked more slowly, more carefully.

Round a bend in the road, they came across a crowd of people holding up flaming torches made of wood dipped in tar. They crowded round a section of railings in the glare of the flickering torches. The railings were all newly painted black, with gold spears on top and, here and there, a crown; this was the perimeter fence of the royal palace park.

Katharina threw a scarf round her head and face, pulled it over her eyes in case she should be recognised.

'Stay close to me,' she whispered. 'But don't speak, don't ask me anything. Just watch. And when I go, come with me.'

They were now within yards of the crowd. A number were soldiers, some with rifles, others with stakes or bayonets. On the other side of the fence was a small man, a pickaxe in his hand. He wore Russian uniform, the peaked cap of a soldier, and soft black boots reaching to his knees. He was tapping with a pick at a section of ice on a narrow canal. The crowd jeered at him and shouted. Some of the men exposed themselves to him, urinating in his direction. He looked up at them gravely, as though oblivious of their insults. He had a pointed beard, sad spaniel eyes, and yet a curiously placid face. This was the Tsar, the fallen king. A couple of men outside the fence picked up horse droppings, threw them over the railings at him.. They spattered his uniform. He shrugged and went on chopping ice.

Katharina turned towards Jamie. He could see she was crying. She pulled his hand and they retreated down the road. Then she led him down a side path through a narrow open gate. Beyond a line of trees, he could see a dark building with a cross on one end of the roof.

'This is the chapel where Rasputin was buried,' she explained. As they came nearer, they could hear grunts and curses from people inside the chapel. Jamie looked at Katharina questioningly. They could not be worshippers, surely? Then he heard the crack of wood breaking.

'Don't go in,' he warned her. 'They are looting the place.'

'There is nothing to loot,' she said. 'It's very simple – an altar, candles, an icon, and his tomb.'

They came to the side of the chapel, looked through the blue and red and amber panes of a stained-glass window. Flickering hurricane lamps had been set up on the pews, on the altar itself. Men with crowbars were levering furiously at the lid of a tomb. As Jamie and Katharina watched, it crashed in pieces to the floor. Stone dust rose in the freezing air. Then the men jammed their crowbars into the coffin inside it, heaved it out.

Some had bottles of vodka or wine; every so often, they stopped to drink. They swallowed so greedily from the necks of the bottles that the liquid ran down their chins, on to their uniforms. When they had prised off the lid, they staggered back. Horror at the stench and appearance of the decomposing corpse showed on their crude, vicious faces. They hurriedly dug spikes and prongs into the body, lifted it over the edge of the coffin. Then they carried it to the door, like a trophy, shouting triumphantly, not wanting to touch the cadaver, crawling with worms and putrefaction, but still eager to possess it.

Jamie and Katharina went round the other side of the chapel, stood in the shadow of the trees, watching them. The men pushed the car out from its garage, unstrapped spare cans of gasoline from the running board. They emptied them on the body, set light to it. The corpse took fire with a roar and a crackle. As its sagging, rotting muscles tightened in the heat, the body began to move as though about to sit up. The men cheered wildly and began to dance drunkenly round it.

One of the soldiers gave a shout, and triumphantly held something up for the others to see. In the light of the burning torches the face of the Virgin Mary looked out from a small picture. The men kept on shouting excitedly, cheering.

Katharina whispered, 'They can see the signatures on the back of that image: Alexandra, Olga, Tatiana, Maria, Anastasia and Anna – the Tsar's wife and daughters. They all loved him. Maybe, in his own way, Rasputin also loved them.'

'Come away,' Jamie said urgently. 'While we can.'

He led Katharina silently back to the garden of her family home.

'They're like animals,' she said. 'And yet, we have just seen a prophecy Rasputin made come true. He said that when he died all the elements would be involved. Water – that was the River Neva. Earth – that's where he's buried. Fire – we've just seen, and Air. His ashes will now be scattered on the wind.'

She was trembling and Jamie took her in his arms.

'Listen,' he said. 'You're coming back with me now to England.'

'I can't leave here. I can't do that. My grandmother is dead and not even buried.'

'Let the dead bury the dead,' said Jamie, 'so the Bible told me when I was a boy, and it makes sense. We're concerned with the living. We can't stay here. You know that. By morning, if not before, the mob will be here, and then it will be too late.'

Katharina nodded. The thought was too painful, too horrible, to put into words.

'And there's another thing,' he said, almost as an afterthought. 'I love you.'

She did not move.

'I love you,' he repeated.

'I heard you,' she said. 'But I can't believe it. We don't know each other. We've only met a few times and danced once.'

'That has nothing whatever to do with it. You instantly know whether someone is right for you – or you have doubts. And I knew when I first saw you. I had no doubts. I asked you to marry me then. Remember?'

'Of course. But I had to go away. And then the war came.'

'Now we're together again. And this time we'll go away together.'

'You're not just saying that because you're sorry for me because of what is happening here?'

'Of course not. Come back with me to Petrograd. We'll go to the British Embassy and get married at once, so you can have a British passport. Then, if you don't like me, you can divorce me! Is that agreed?'

Katharina smiled and nodded.

'Do you mean that?' asked Jamie, his tone serious. 'You will marry me?'

'I do, and I will,' Katharina said simply. 'I love you, too. I think I did before. I know I do now.'

Jamie's spirits soared. He folded her into his arms and held her as if he would never let her go. Katharina's voice brought him back to earth.

'We must go,' she said:

They went into the palace and through to the kitchen door. A faint smell of hot fat still hung above the huge ranges. He could imagine armies of servants working here: cooks, kitchen maids, scullery boys, all gone now, and, he guessed, never to return, no matter who lived here.

'You go into the hall,' Jamie told Katharina. 'Don't go outside. I'll bring the cases up. Then we'll leave.'

He lifted the trap door, went down the stairs. The cellar now smelled strongly of paraffin; the lamp was running low and the wick was dim and red. It had lasted just long enough. He picked up the two cases, came up the stairs, closed the trap door. He started to carry the cases through to the hall when something made him stop. He heard voices, a man speaking, his voice slurred, drunk, all the syllables running together. Jamie went forward into the hall, keeping out of the light of the other oil lamp.

Katharina was standing in the centre, arguing with a soldier in uniform. He had epaulettes, a leather belt and was shouting as he kicked angrily at the base of a sideboard. An ornament on it rattled, tipped over and fell to the floor, crashed and splintered into pieces. It was Sèvres china.

Katharina stamped her foot furiously, shouted back at the man. Suddenly, he seized her, ripped open her jacket and her blouse, pressed his mouth on hers. She screamed and kicked and struggled, but he forced her back against the wall. Jamie came out from the shadows.

'Let her go!' he shouted. The man did not understand him, but he understood the menace in Jamie's voice. His hands dropped and he turned. Jamie saw the soldier's right hand go to the pocket of his uniform. Jamie leapt forward, drove his knuckles into the soldier's eyes. He screamed with shock and pain. Jamie spun him over his shoulder and dropped him heavily. He heard the soldier's skull crack as it hit the stone-flagged floor.

'Are you all right?' Jamie asked Katharina.

She nodded, holding up her hand modestly to her torn blouse.

'He's dead,' she said tonelessly. 'You've killed him.'

'He would have killed me otherwise, and then raped you.'

Now Jamie could hear the shouts and rumble of the crowd outside. In the cold darkness, the sounds seemed much clearer, much nearer. Within minutes they would be here. Would they stay out on the palace steps or come inside?

Jamie stood for a moment as though cast in stone, desperately trying to think of a way to escape. It was probably impossible for a grand duchess or a foreigner to travel on a train alone without being assaulted or arrested, robbed and probably killed. But if they travelled together, if they travelled in a certain way, they had a chance. He turned to her.

'Go in that room and get your clothes off! I am going to dress you in this soldier's uniform.'

'You must be mad!'

'So is everyone else out there. But this is our only chance of escape. You will be my Army escort, I'll be your prisoner. You speak Russian. I don't.'

'They'll know I'm a girl.'

'Lower your voice. They'll think you're a boy, a young recruit. I'll bind my wrist to yours, get through that way.'

'It will never work.'

'There's nothing else,' he said desperately. 'It *has* to work. Now get in there – and hurry! I'll throw you his uniform.'

Jamie bent over the man, unbuttoned his jacket, his trousers, unlaced his boots, slipped them off. The man stank; he had not washed for days. But he was not very tall so his uniform should fit Katharina. Jamie pulled off the soldier's hat, carried him into a side room, leaving him dead in his shirt and underpants.

'The boots are too big,' said Katharina practically.

'Haven't you got any walking shoes? The stoutest ones you can find. Riding boots, anything. But nothing with high heels.'

He carried the light through to her. She was almost dressed. She tucked her long hair under the military cap. With her bandaged wrist, she could possibly pass as a wounded soldier. Jamie turned up the cuff of the uniform jacket so the bandage would show more clearly. He felt in the soldier's pockets. There were some official-looking papers. He could not read Russian, but handed them to Katharina. They might be the man's pay book or identity card.

He went into the kitchen, opened and shut drawers until he came across a coil of twine, the sort used to tie hay bales or the necks of sacks of kitchen waste. He cut off a yard with a knife, brought it back, tied his own wrist to Katharina's. Then, each carrying a suitcase, they went out through the back door, avoiding the rabble at the front, down the long path, past the silent greenhouses, and out into the road towards the station.

A train was waiting at the platform, steam hissing from the locomotive's boiler. Some of the carriages were dark, others had oil lamps; a few, broken electric bulbs. They went into one with an oil lamp. They did not want to be in total darkness or yet in too bright a light. This seemed a safe, halfway house. An official came along, said something to Katharina. She shook her head, pointed at Jamie, spoke strongly to the man, spat to show her feelings. The official nodded and moved on to the next compartment.

'What was that about?' Jamie asked her.

'I said you were my prisoner, a foreign spy.'

'Let's hope he doesn't pass that information on to anyone else,' said Jamie with feeling.

A whistle blew. There was a lot of shouting on the platform, a great banging of carriage doors, a drumming of iron-shod heels on hard-packed snow. The train gave a jerk and they were off.

As it started to move, the compartment door swung open and three men came in, closed it noisily behind them. They glanced at Jamie and Katharina. One spat on the floor and asked a question. Katharina answered. The man stood up, stared at Jamie closely, face to face – then spat at him. He had mean eyes, close together, flecked with matter, reddened by alcohol. He had not shaved for several days.

He made as though to draw back his fist and hit Jamie, but Katharina held up her hand and spoke to him sharply. The man grumbled, sat down. He took out some tobacco, a cigarette paper, rolled a cigarette and smoked it.

The cold compartment was soon filled with acrid smoke, the sour smell of unwashed bodies, bad breath. Jamie recalled the first time he had travelled with Serov from the Baltic Station in St Petersburg to Tsarskoe-Selo. Then all had been elegance; a car to meet them at the end of their journey. Now all was disaster, revolution, a world in chaos, crumbling away. But at least he and Katharina were still alive, at least they were still free – and together. He leaned back thankfully against the rough padding of the third-class seat and closed his eyes.

He must have slept, exhausted with reaction, because he was jolted into wakefulness as the train shuddered to a standstill. Doors burst open all around them. They had arrived.

Katharina waited until the three men left. Then she climbed down on the platform, pulling Jamie with her. There was no ticket collector at the end of the platform. People were wandering about as though lost, dazedly looking for other people or places or guidance of some kind, any kind. Soldiers dragged their rifles by the muzzles. Others sat, leaning back against the station wall, obviously drunk, uniform tunics unbuttoned, boots unlaced. Some urinated openly in the concourse of the station.

Katharina and Jamie came out into the main street. They could not see any sledges or troikas, nothing but snowy streets, unswept. Here and there, Jamie saw the carcass of a horse. They had dropped dead from starvation in the shafts of a cart, then been cut free and abandoned.

They walked through the streets to Jamie's hotel, their breath fanning out before them in the bitingly cold air. A clerk at the reception desk looked up at them without interest.

Jamie said in English: 'I have a soldier friend here. He will be sharing my room.'

The man shrugged. He was unshaven; Jamie had never seen him before.

The elevator was still not working. They walked up the stairs to Jamie's room. He locked the door behind them, flicked the light switch up and down. It did not work. He ran the tap in his bath; hot water trickled out, brown and spattered with flakes of rust from ancient pipes, but still hot water. He dumped the cases, pulled off Katharina's Army cap, threw it away, and kissed her.

For a moment, she stood, passive, accepting his kiss. And then she kissed him back.

'The first time I've ever kissed a soldier,' said Jamie as they drew apart.

Katharina smiled. 'And I've never kissed a prisoner. You are now released through good conduct.'

'We'd better prepare for a stay here.'

'In this room – together?' Katharina sounded surprised.

'Of course. It's safer if we are together.'

'And that's the only reason?'

'No. But it's one your mother would approve.'

She laughed then. 'Poor Mama. She would never forgive me if she knew – or you for that matter.'

'Then she must never know. Now, let's get you out of that uniform. Have a bath and put on some other clothes while I see if there is any food left in the hotel.'

551

The dining room was locked, but a porter took him through to the kitchen. Here, all the shelves and cupboards were bare except for half a loaf of dry bread and a scrape of butter on a plate. He took a knife and two plates from a drawer, carried them back to his room.

Katharina wore a long dress, her hair combed out down her back. The dress seemed vaguely familiar to Jamie; he remarked on this. She looked pleased.

'I thought you'd notice,' she said. 'I wore it at the ball, just before the war started. Remember?'

'I will never forget,' he assured her.

He kissed her again, and they stood close together in the chilly room, not feeling the cold, ignoring the turmoil outside, secure and safe in each other's arms.

'Where are we going to sleep?' she asked him at last.

'Here. There's nowhere else.'

'I'm glad.'

'Even if your mama would not be?'

Katharina giggled. 'She's not here. I am. Lucky me!'

Katharina and Jamie sat down at the table to eat the bread and butter he had brought up from the kitchen.

'Different from the food we had at the picnic the first time we met,' he said. He felt embarrassed that this was all he could offer as host, when in almost any other country he could have commanded a banquet.

'The real difference is that then we ate as a social duty. Now, because we're hungry.'

Afterwards, they opened the curtains and stood at the window in the dark looking out over the city. Most other windows were also dark. Jamie wondered how many more silent, hidden watchers were also wondering, some fearfully, others hopefully, what the future held for them.

The streets were thronged with groups of people knocking on doors, breaking downstairs windows. Open cars drove about, each carrying ten or a dozen passengers, sitting on bonnets and running boards, every car with a pole waving the red flag of revolution.

At last, Jamie drew the curtains, lit an oil lamp. Katharina went into the bathroom, undressed and, modestly not meeting his eyes, climbed into one side of the bed. Jamie undressed and climbed into the other side – suddenly reminded of sleeping with Arabella in the upper room of the Silent Witness.

They lay for a moment, still and rigid, and then, as on a mutual signal sent, received and understood, they rolled gently towards each other. Katharina was trembling slightly.

'I've never done this before,' she whispered. 'It will be all right, won't it?'

For answer, Jamie folded her in his arms, kissed her gently on her nose, her mouth, and then moved down to her breasts. She snuggled up against him happily, contented, body to warm naked body. Soon what had been two became one, and the chill bleakness of the world beyond the frozen windows melted away in the warmth and ecstasy of love.

THIRTY

Lenin's Trade

Next morning, early, Jamie tried to telephone the British Embassy. This proved impossible; no one was on duty on the hotel switchboard through which all calls were routed. Leaving Katharina still in bed, he set out for the Embassy on foot, walking through slush and snow against a tide of people who all seemed to be going in the opposite direction.

Now and then, under a pewter sky, church bells tolled. They had a peculiarly gloomy sound – a knell for a world that had all but disappeared. The Embassy gates were closed. Jamie rang the bell, but without result. He guessed that, like so much else in the city now, the bell was out of order. He waited for an hour, then gave up and walked back to the hotel.

He decided to contact Serov; he was the only person who might be able to help him. And then, suddenly, he remembered his abortive visit to the Winter Palace; other more agreeable events had driven it from his mind. Why had Serov not kept that appointment?

Jamie stamped the snow off his galoshes on the hotel steps, which he saw had not been swept, and walked into the lobby. The reception desk was empty. He pressed the plunger on an ornate brass bell to summon a clerk or a messenger, anyone. There was no response.

He went behind the desk, opened a wall cupboard that concealed keys on their hooks. Fortunately, they were numbered with Roman numerals. He took his key, crossed to the elevator; still not working. He flicked the light switch up and down, but there was no current.

He walked up the stairs, a vague feeling of unease increasing with every step he took. On each landing he paused, looking along wide corridors with red carpets, marble busts on plinths. He reached his floor and opened the door of his room.

At once he smelled the thin acrid scent of Russian cigarettes. As he went in the sitting room, three men stood up. They were wearing overcoats, fur hats with ear muffs.

'Mr Provost?' asked one in English. He looked younger than the others. His face had the flattened features of the Slav, not the heavy brutishness and sullen appearance of his companions.

'Who are you?' asked Jamie. More important, where was Katharina?

'We are from the Immigration Department,' the young man explained unconvincingly.

'Is it usual for Immigration officials to enter a foreign visitor's hotel room without his permission?'

'Is it usual, Mr Provost, for a foreign visitor to travel with two passports?'

'I have a reason for that,' said Jamie.

'We would be interested to hear it.'

'I am a businessman,' Jamie explained, 'with companies in England and South Africa. If I travel abroad under my own name, newspapers might ask whether my journey was simply as a tourist, or to engage in business in that country. Such discussions in the Press could cause very serious fluctuations in the value of my shares. I therefore travel under another name. Does that answer your question?'

'An ingenious answer, Mr Provost. But not, I fear, the truth. The Press, I am sure, is more concerned with the war than with the value of your shares.'

555

Jamie shrugged. 'Then I can't help you further.'

'Not here, perhaps,' the young man agreed. 'But you will please accompany us to headquarters, where we will endeavour to reach the heart of the matter.'

'There's nothing more to reach,' said Jamie, trying desperately to sound convincing.

'Then you will not be detained for long. Now please pack your belongings.'

'Am I taking them with me?'

'No. But it will be easier if they are already packed.'

'Easier for whom?'

'For you. If you come back to collect them.'

'And if I don't?'

'Then, Mr Provost, you will not need your belongings. I hope I make myself clear?'

'Too clear,' agreed Jamie, trying not to show his concern.

He went into the bedroom; the bed had not been made. His clothes still hung over the back of a chair – but there was no sign of Katharina or her clothes.

He turned to the young man. 'Where is the young lady who was here?'

'The Archduchess, you mean? She has gone.'

'What do you mean "gone"?'

'For questioning.'

'About what? On whose authority?'

'The people's authority, Mr Provost.'

'When is she coming back?'

The man shrugged, tapped out his cigarette on the carpet. 'Please hurry, Mr Provost. You have already kept us waiting here an hour.'

Jamie packed quickly, his mind in turmoil. He should never have left Katharina on her own. He should have taken her with him to the Embassy. But then what would that have achieved?

He came out into the main room and automatically looked

round it, checking that he had left nothing unpacked. The tank of goldfish caught his attention. The water was very cloudy; he could scarcely see the fish. In his absence, someone had stirred up the sand at the bottom of the tank. But who – and why?

He was taken down back stairs to a service entrance, pushed into the rear of a windowless van, driven away. After a ten-minute journey, the van stopped in a courtyard ringed by high buildings.

The young man led Jamie down a stone corridor without any windows. Dim lights pulsed behind wire screens in the ceiling. The man tapped on a door. Someone inside answered. The door opened.

Jamie found himself in a small room with two chairs, one on each side of a plain wooden desk. In the far chair sat a middle-aged man wearing a shoddy grey suit. He indicated that Jamie should sit in the other chair. The door closed. Locks clicked into place. They were alone.

'We have been watching you, Mr Provost,' the man said. 'Your conduct gives rise to some suspicion. First, we understand you are a confederate of one Serov, known to us as a pander to the ruling class, a strong enemy of the revolution. With him, you recently paid a secret visit to a court jeweller, where you examined some of the former Tsarina's jewellery. We understand you were also in this city shortly before the war, travelling as Mr Baird. Why should you come back now as Mr Provost?'

Jamie repeated his previous explanation.

'We wish the truth, Mr Provost, or Mr Baird, whichever name you prefer. Not some easy fabrication.'

'That is the truth.'

'It is in your own interest to accede to our request. In the end, most people do.'

'But why am I here? Am I being charged with anything?'

'Not yet. But you may be.'

'Then I wish to consult the British Ambassador.'

'To make a wish is not always to have it granted. No one knows you are here, and you do not even know what this building is, or where it is. Let us confine ourselves to facts, Mr Provost, not fantasies. Now, why are you in Petrograd, and why do you need two passports?'

In the airless room, concern that no one knew he was there, increasing worry about Katharina's fate and the constant staccato repetition of the same queries combined to fuddle Jamie's brain as the interview dragged on, hour after hour. His interrogator's face seemed to loom large as Jamie wavered between wakefulness and sleep. He had no idea of time, of when the man stopped talking, or when he left the room.

Then suddenly, the light was brighter and the young official who had brought him here was in the room with him. He lit a cigarette and blew smoke into the air.

'I am sorry that you will not cooperate, Mr Provost. We have given you every opportunity to explain your presence in our city and our country under most dubious circumstances. You prefer, however, to stick to your obvious fabrication. You will spend the rest of the night here, and tomorrow morning at seven o'clock you will be brought before a People's Tribunal.'

'This is ridiculous. I am a visitor to your country. I am not an enemy of the revolution, or of anyone else. What charges do I face?'

'Illegal entry. Lies as to the true purpose of your visit. Consorting with those hostile to the people. I have to tell you that it is unlikely that the Tribunal will believe your story any more than we do.'

'Who are you, exactly?'

The man shrugged. 'What does that matter? It is who you are that concerns us.'

'And if, as you say, this charade of a trial decides I am guilty, what then?'

'Exile to a rehabilitation camp in Siberia for several years. Or death. It depends who is on the Tribunal. In our experience, women in these circumstances generally demand harsher sentences than men. Many have suffered at the hands of men and like to take what revenge they can.'

As he tapped out his cigarette, the door opened. An orderly came in, clicked his heels, bowed, handed a note to him. He read this with obvious surprise, and turned to Jamie.

'Comrade Lenin wishes to see you,' he said brusquely.

The last time Jamie had heard that name was from General Brookes in the country house outside Marlborough. Now, two guards fell in on either side of Jamie, marched him along the corridor, through the courtyard, into an Army staff car. Here and there along the streets, he saw buildings blazing furiously while soldiers and civilians fought firemen who were trying desperately to quench the flames. These had once been the homes of the rich and influential. The Bolsheviks preferred to see them burn.

The car stopped outside a large house. Soldiers carrying rifles, bayonets fixed, stood guard at the entrance. Wire netting stretched across ground-floor windows as a protection against hand grenades.

Inside, they climbed a wide marble staircase. Its red carpet was stained and fouled by muddy boots and melting snow. Soldiers lounged on landings which smelled of blocked drains, of too many unwashed bodies wearing unwashed clothes. Gilded doors had been torn from their hinges. A grand piano in a first-floor drawing room had been smashed, ink thrown on Regency-striped wallpaper.

On the second floor, across the landing, two soldiers, smarter than the rest, came to attention as they approached. Jamie was beckoned into an anteroom. An old sour-faced woman with a hump back was bent over a typewriter. She looked at him incuriously and then stood up to open an inner door. Jamie went in. She closed it silently behind him.

A very small man wearing a dark blue suit, with a scruffy collar, a necktie so loose it showed the collar stud, was seated behind a desk. A reading lamp cast a glow on its green leather top. Jamie's first impression was of an unusually large, bald head like a pale bladder, hard eyes, a wispy dark beard. Yet this insignificant-looking person, by his own magnetism, his own vitriolic hatred of established society, had overthrown a dynasty that had lasted for three hundred years, with all its protective panoply of guards, special regiments, uniformed police, secret police, paid informers and spies. This tiny man, looking so out of place in the large elegant room, had outwitted them all, coming and going unrecognised across frontiers. He had experienced imprisonment, release, exile, and had overcome all his opponents. Jamie regarded him with a mixture of distaste and respect.

'Mr Provost?' asked Lenin.

'Yes, sir.'

'You must forgive me if my English is not as good as my German. I lived longer on the Continent than in England, but I know London. Especially the inside of your British Museum. Do you know it?'

'I have never been there,' admitted Jamie.

'Ah! People surrounded by treasure houses of learning often take them for granted. I must admit that until quite recently I had not visited the Winter Palace here. And when I did visit it some days ago, the Tsar was not in residence.'

Lenin smiled with his mouth. His eyes remained pale and cold and hard as Kalahari diamonds.

'You may wonder why I wish to see you, Mr Provost – or Mr Baird. Usually, we deal swiftly with foreign spies and agents provocateurs. This was about to happen in your case, but then I learned something that made me wish to talk to you. The people who arrested you in your hotel made an imperfect job of searching your room. I sent a more sophisticated operator to see whether they had missed anything. They had missed two things. Here is the first.'

Lenin opened a drawer in his desk. The light from the reading lamp caught the polished faces of six of the twelve fake diamonds Jamie had brought from England.

'What was the second thing?'

'The false bottom in your suitcase. I was amused by this obvious subterfuge because, when I used to come and go, in and out of Russia, illegally under another name and with a false passport – just like you – I carried papers, lists, orders, in the false bottom of my suitcase. I wanted to see what sort of man still relied on such an ancient subterfuge.'

'Each stone had its special place in a sheet of rubber,' Jamie explained.

'And then you decided to hide them in a goldfish bowl, yes?' Lenin picked up one of the stones, looked at it closely.

'They are only copies,' Jamie told him. He had no idea what Lenin meant about the goldfish bowl, and this was not the moment to ask him. 'I can show you now just how worthless they are if you can give me a small hammer and a hard piece of wood.'

A hammer and block of firewood were brought into the room. Jamie wrapped one stone in his handkerchief and placed it on the block.

'If this was a diamond, sir, this hammer would never harm it.'

He gave the stone a sharp tap with the hammer, unfolded his handkerchief. The blow had shattered the stone.

'You see, it is rubbish.'

Lenin sat back, looked at Jamie, a puzzled expression on his face. 'Why bring such trifles to Russia, Mr Provost? What was your reason? To delude people they were real?'

'I have rich women clients in England who envy the diamonds of titled people – especially the diamonds of your

561

former Empress. It was my intention to examine the real stones, if I could, and check personally whether these copies would stand close scrutiny.'

'I can never understand the fascination of such baubles for any woman. Do you know who owned this house, for example?'

'I have no idea.'

'The prima ballerina, Mathilde Kschessinska. Every Sunday and Wednesday evening, from September to the beginning of Lent, she danced at the Maryinsky Theatre. She was actually dancing *Giselle* just before the Tsar abdicated. The theatre was always full; she had been the Tsar's mistress for many years before he married. I have heard it said she even loved him. She certainly loved the diamonds he gave her, worth millions of roubles.

'The candelabra, furniture, the chandeliers, curtains, even the door handles, were all specially designed for her in Paris. When the mob heard she had left Petrograd, they attempted to destroy these treasures. They would have succeeded totally if we had not prevented them.'

'I saw some of the damage coming upstairs.'

'Yes. She lacked the good sense of a more astute neighbour, Countess Kleinmichel, who guessed the mob would loot her house. She, clever woman, put up a notice on a piece of cardboard in the front window: "No trespassing. This house is the property of the Petrograd Soviet." So they passed her by, as in your Bible story the troops of Herod passed by Jewish houses marked with a cross. But, to return to your situation, Mr Provost, I still can see no reason why you should not stand trial at a Court of the People and let them decide on the evidence. Have you anything to say to that proposition?'

'I have indeed, sir. You mentioned the shrewdness of Countess Kleinmichel in a way which I think shows that you admired her sense of self-preservation. You also mentioned, without admiration, how the mob had smashed up all the furniture of this lovely house. I fear that the latter story, possibly repeated thousands of times, will be what Europe and the United States believe is happening all over Russia.' Jamie paused.

'Go on,' said Lenin slowly.

'If they have not already done so, these countries will stop all financial credit to Russia. They will maintain a blockade of your ports, especially if – as some fear – you come to a separate accommodation with Germany. I have heard that the Kaiser put forty million roubles at the disposal of Russian dissidents for the revolution.'

'You heard wrongly, Mr Provost. The sum was nearly eighty million – twice as much.'

'Which, sir, will make the Allies feel at least twice as hostile to your new regime. Russia can't survive in chaos for long. In this city alone, there is little electricity, my hotel is deserted, the streets are filled with people shouting slogans, riding in trucks, waving red flags. These are not scenes of stability likely to inspire cautious foreign bankers to invest here.

'You can, of course, send me to stand trial before your Tribunal. I may be found guilty of God knows what, although you and I know I have done nothing whatever against your country or your revolution.

'That could be the end of the matter as far as I personally am concerned. But I am a man of some wealth and influence, and if I do not return to England next week, as was my intention, my colleagues will use my money – millions of pounds sterling – to discover what happened to me, and why. If, however, I do return, I could use my money as surety to companies that normally trade with you but, for reasons of business prudence, will not do so in present conditions because they feel they might not be paid.'

'Why would you do such a thing, Mr Provost?'

'For several reasons. First, I would obviously rather be free than in a Soviet prison – or dead. Second, when I was in Russia before the war, I could not help but note the vast difference between the rich, of whom there were relatively few, and the poor, of whom there were millions. It may be that your Communist ideas can improve their living standards, although, after the initial euphoria, that is open to doubt. Since there can be no going back, you can only go forward. And if you succeed in your aims, there might be a place for my companies to share in your prosperity.'

'Thirdly, I wish to marry the Archduchess Katharina Sokolov who, like me, has been taken from the Hotel d'Angleterre by your officers.'

'Your proposal is unusual, Mr Provost. But once you are back in London, what will prevent you from forgetting all about any agreement we might reach?'

'I have always stood by my word,' Jamie replied. 'If I say something, I will do it. I will give you my assurances in writing.'

'Words, Mr Provost, are not deeds. Promises are never equal to performance. I might be disposed to come to some arrangement with you, but I would need a stronger assurance that you would do as you say. A hostage to fortune – your fortune and ours.'

'That, I regret, I cannot provide, sir.' Jamie felt a sudden weariness with this entire charade. He had no other proposition to make; nothing else to offer.

'We would not ask you to provide your hostage,' said Lenin, smiling thinly. 'We have already taken one.'

'I don't understand you.'

'I will make myself clear, Mr Provost. We need grain above all else. Without grain, the people will starve and the revolution will fail. We can pay for it with paintings, and other art treasures taken from the homes of the wealthy, such as this house, from people who have no further use for them. They have fled or . . .' He shrugged his narrow shoulders dismissively. 'We will let you go, but we will hold in protective custody, until the first shipments of grain are within our boundaries, the person who, you tell me, you wish to marry – Archduchess Katharina Sokolov.'

The train from Harwich was filled with soldiers returning on leave. When it steamed into the crowded platform at Liverpool Street Station, wives, mothers, sisters, girl friends shouted greetings and waved little Union Jack flags frantically to attract their attention.

As Jamie stepped down from the carriage, Captain Drake came forward through the crowd, saluted.

'I heard you were on this train, sir.'

'You have long ears,' Jamie replied.

'I must admit we sometimes use other people's ears,' the captain said, with a smile. 'Could I take you to meet the general? He is most anxious to see you.'

'Not down in Wiltshire,' Jamie told him. 'I am going to my sister's house in Belgravia.' He had turned over his own house to the Red Cross.

'The general is actually in London, sir.'

'So you have moved again?'

'Yes, sir. We are now in South Kensington – for the time being.'

Jamie handed the captain a card. 'Here's where I am staying. I will be available there if the general wishes to see me.'

'Immediately, sir?'

'If he so wishes.'

'I will inform him.'

The captain hailed a porter to carry Jamie's bags. A crowd was already waiting in line for taxis with suitcases, wicker baskets, kit bags piled on the pavement, but the porter bored his way to the head of the line. He recognised wealth when he

565

saw it, and Jamie's astrakhan coat must have cost several hundred guineas; a man wearing a coat like that could be worth a huge tip.

Arabella's butler opened the door of her house.

'Mr Baird, sir!' he exclaimed. 'Welcome home! Lady Doncaster will be so pleased to see you.'

'I'm glad she is in.'

'She is in the drawing room, sir. I will take your bags.'

Jamie followed him up the marble staircase to the great room overlooking the square.

'Why, Jamie!' said Arabella, obviously delighted to see her brother. 'How was Russia? The papers are full of the revolution. Chaos and shooting and riots everywhere. Was it really as bad as that?'

He shrugged. 'I will tell you all about it later. In the meantime, I am expecting a visit from the man who asked me to go there, General Kirby Brookes. He sent an aide to meet me at the station. I hope you don't mind, but I've asked him to see me here. It saves me going to his house. I feel I've had enough travelling for the moment.'

'Will he stay to dinner?'

'I think that will depend on how our meeting goes.'

Arabella regarding him with a sister's critical eye. 'You look somehow different, Jamie.'

'I feel, as you say, somehow different. I was arrested and then released, but more important, I renewed the acquaintance of a wonderful girl in Russia. I'd met her briefly in St Petersburg just before the war. I asked her to marry me then.'

'You never told me.'

'There was no need. She refused.'

'And now? You asked her again?'

'Yes. And this time she accepted.'

'Wonderful! But where is she?'

'I had to leave her behind.'

'In Russia? In the midst of a revolution? Why?'

'Because that was the condition on which I got out myself.'

'Are you serious?'

'Unfortunately, yes.'

'But how will she get out?'

'I came to an arrangement with Lenin, who seems to be running things there – at least for the time being. He promised he would allow her to leave later, on certain conditions.'

'You haven't got yourself into trouble?'

Jamie shrugged. 'Don't concern yourself about me. It's what happens to Katharina that worries me. I am pinning my hopes on the general, I have kept my side of the bargain with him. I hope he will help me here.'

The butler came into the room. 'General Brookes, your ladyship. To see Mr Baird.'

'I would like to see him privately, on my own,' said Jamie. 'Can I use your library?'

'Of course.'

The walls of the library were dark with rows of leather-bound books. He often wondered where his sister had found them, whether she ever read them. The butler showed General Brookes into the room.

'Delighted to see you back,' said Brookes briskly. 'I hear you had a bit of a tussle with our friend Ulyanov, otherwise Mr Lenin?'

'Yes. He got on to me pretty quickly. Things looked a little bleak at first. But we came to an accommodation – I think.'

'You must have done, or you wouldn't be here. Now, the matter of the diamonds. Can I have a look at them?'

'I fear I have to report failure.'

The general's face creased in disappointment. 'What went wrong? I know the Tsar and the Tsarina were arrested, so that rather ruled out the point of our exercise, but how have you failed?'

'I went to the Tsarina's jeweller, who showed me various items of jewellery which he claimed had been sent out to be cleaned. They were all fakes. Then a go-between I used, a man called Serov, apparently decided to act for the other side as well. That's when I was arrested.'

'So you took fake stones from London to Petrograd and brought them all the way back?'

'I am sorry to say that is so.'

'Well, as they were all paid for by public funds, I had better collect them. Where are they?'

'Still in my case, I suppose. I haven't even looked.'

Jamie pressed a bell-push. The butler appeared. He asked him to fetch his overnight case.

Jamie set it on the desk, opened it, removed his silk dressing gown, pyjamas, shaving gear, slippers. Then he lifted up the false bottom, carefully raised the layer of grey sorbo rubber. Stones glistened in their compartments like tiny eggs in minute nests. He removed one.

It was a perfect copy of one of the stones he had been shown by the Court jeweller, and worth very little. He passed it to Brookes. The general looked at it closely, turned it over and over, put it down on the table.

'I remember that one,' he said. 'A touch of blue in it.' He paused. 'I don't think, after all, it's worth taking these back. The minister who proposed the scheme has been promoted. He won't want to be reminded of failures – politicians never do. If I take them, I'll only have to write a report, get involved with something we'd all rather forget. You keep them. Or give them away.'

'Thanks,' said Jamie. 'I will. Now, there is something else, General. Lenin allowed me to come out on the understanding I would arrange for a shipload of grain to be sent to a Russian port to help the starving – of whom there are probably millions.'

'That is their problem,' the general replied sharply. 'They didn't have to join the Bolsheviks.'

'Probably they didn't want to, either. But I wouldn't think they had much option. I will pay for the grain, of course.'

'That could be very expensive. The price of grain is high. Chartering a ship as well would cost a lot of money.'

'I have a lot of money.'

'So you want to honour what you feel is your bond? A very worthy intention, Mr Baird.'

'There's another reason. Before I left London, you told me that the Archduchess Katharina Sokolov wanted to see me. Well, I saw her. More, I intend to marry her. But she will not be allowed out of Russia until that grain arrives. Then Lenin will let her travel.'

'Do you trust Lenin?'

Jamie shrugged. 'I have to. He trusted me. He let me out. If I honour my side of the bargain, I see no reason why he shouldn't keep his word. It's in his own interest to do so. A shipload of grain is a fair exchange, in his view, for one young woman.'

'Leave it with me,' said the general. 'I will organise this for you. But don't blame me if nothing happens. I personally wouldn't trust a man Jack of those Bolsheviks as far as I could throw him. But thank you for what you have done – or tried to do – Mr Baird. We will not forget it.'

'Nor will I,' said Jamie with feeling.

Arabella came into the room as the general was leaving. He politely declined her invitation to have a drink or to stay for dinner. Jamie saw him out of the front door, into an Army staff car. Captain Drake rode with him.

When they had gone, Arabella put her hand on her brother's arm. She followed him into the library. His case still stood on the desk. Idly, Jamie prised the stones from their holes. He counted five, all false, and was about to shut the case when a tiny glint of reflected light from one of the other six cavities made him pause. Tiny pieces of sorbo rubber had been torn from the main rubber block and pushed down into these holes to plug them. He lifted out the plugs, and stared in astonishment.

Six huge diamonds glowed like stars. He picked them out, one by one, laid them on the desk in a row.

'My mission was successful, after all,' he said, softly.

'They're beautiful,' exclaimed Arabella. 'They can't be copies, surely?'

'They're not,' Jamie replied. 'They're real. And they're mine. The general told me to keep the stones – or give them away. I said I would – and I will.'

'Is that strictly straight?'

'In love and war, my dear Bella, all is justified. This is both. And these are as much mine as those earrings you were given in equally strange circumstances, aren't they?'

Arabella laughed. 'Touché!'

As soon as the banks opened in the morning, Jamie decided he would open an account in Katharina's name and lodge the diamonds as security. They must be worth a fortune. Then, when she came to London, even if she had to leave behind all her possessions, she need never be poor. But who could have taken out the false diamonds and replaced them with these stones? He could think of only one person – Serov.

Somehow, Serov must have found – or stolen – the diamonds, but had no safe place to conceal them, and perhaps little time to find one. The only quick solution would be to get rid of them, and what better place than in the case of a foreigner whom he knew was secretly carrying imitation diamonds? He must have removed six of these and put the real stones in their place, intending then to lead the police to Jamie's room, arrest him and produce the stones from the goldfish bowl as evidence of his honesty and worth. This would account for the cloudiness of the water; he had hidden the stones in the sand at the bottom of the bowl. And it explained why he had asked Jamie to go to the Winter Palace, simply to get him out of the hotel, so he could go to his room.

But something had gone wrong; time and chance had not worked in his favour. He felt almost sorry for Serov; almost, but not quite.

The general sank back thankfully on the buttoned leather upholstery of his car.

'Did he get the diamonds back, sir?' Drake asked him.

'No,' said the general. 'He didn't.' He told the captain what had happened.

'Do you want me to make inquiries about shipping the grain, sir?'

'Don't be a bloody fool!' replied the general. 'We're at war with the Bolsheviks. British troops have landed at Archangel to try to restore stability. We can't possibly charter a ship full of grain to feed the Bolsheviks. That would be helping the King's enemies – treason. We could face a firing squad for that.'

'Perhaps the grain would not go to the revolutionaries, sir?'

'They are in control, Drake. They will use it as they think fit, not as we wish.'

'So what will you do, sir?'

'Do? Nothing. Nothing at all.'

'But Mr Baird gave his word.'

'That's his problem. I will tell him we've sent a ship. It doesn't arrive? Maybe it was torpedoed by the Germans. Maybe it was looted on arrival. Who knows? You don't expect a man like Lenin to keep his promises, do you?'

'He might, sir, if only to keep a trade line open.'

'Pigs might fly – if only they had wings.'

As soon as Jamie had seen General Brookes, he wrote two letters, one to Lenin and the other to Katharina. He put his address on the back of both envelopes in case they should be returned. Neither was returned, nor did he receive any reply.

He wrote again. And again. And again. He sent regular telegrams, he tried to telephone to Russia, but the numbers were always unobtainable. He had no replies to his telegrams, or to the equally regular letters he sent, using all the addresses he could find: the Parliament House in Petrograd, the Winter Palace, the Kremlin in Moscow, Katharina's house in Tsarskoe-Selo. Jamie made an appointment to visit the Foreign Secretary personally.

'His Majesty's Government is fully aware of the tragic situation of so many people in Soviet Russia who have lost everything,' he said at their meeting.

'Is the Archduchess Katharina Sokolov among them?'

'We know the Tsarina organised the exile of Prince Yussoupov, who was involved with the murder of Rasputin. He had to leave behind his fortune, and is now living very frugally in France. I can assure you, sir, that the Foreign Office is doing all in its power to establish lines of communication with the Soviet Union – on an unofficial level, at present, of course – until we can restore diplomatic relations. When – if – we have anything concrete to report, you have my word, sir, we will be in touch with you immediately.'

'In the meantime, could I get a visa or whatever papers are needed to go back and try and find her myself?'

'In view of what I know about the circumstances in which you left Russia on your last visit, that is not a course I could advise. As like as not, you would simply not return here at all. Visitors are not welcome in Soviet Russia, Mr Baird.'

THIRTY-ONE

Flight from France

In the early nineteen-twenties, Maître Duval, the shrewdest lawyer on the French Riviera, had his office in a house over-looking the old port of Antibes. Next to this house was a café with tables laid outside on the pavement. Sun glinted on polished glasses and a harbour breeze ruffled stiff white table-cloths; they reminded Arabella of a yacht's sails filling with wind, eager to be away.

Beyond the smells of garlic and newly baked croissants, beyond the houses, the cobbles and the wall of the enclosed har-bour where the yachts were moored, she could see her own 200-foot yacht, *Hyde Lady*, in the livery she chose for her cars and her servants – dark blue, dark red, the colours of Kimberley.

Opposite her, his back to the wide picture window, sat Maître Duval, a young man with the sharp face of a rodent. He regarded his client quizzically. He knew Arabella was rich but not how rich; he sensed she was unhappy, but not how unhappy. Poor people could not afford his services and happy people were rarely in need of them.

'I am sorry, your ladyship,' he began, 'but I have looked into the facts closely, and I regret I have little to tell you for your comfort.'

'I suspected as much,' Arabella replied drily, forcing a smile. 'What is the worst?'

'According to French law, your husband, as one born in France of a French mother, has jurisdiction over any children of his marriage.'

'What exactly does that mean, jurisdiction?'

'It means that they are in his total control until, of course, they come of age. He can say where they will live, where and how they will be educated, who can bring them up. Everything, in fact, appertaining to them.'

'If I were French, would I then have that control?' she asked.

'No. It is exercised in the male line only.'

'So if I decided to leave my husband, he could claim our son, *my* son?'

'If you decided to leave him in France, yes. If this took place in another country, there would doubtless be protracted and expensive lawsuits before the matter could be resolved.'

'Doubtless,' Arabella said bitterly. 'Everything to do with the law seems protracted and expensive.'

'And often unsatisfactory,' agreed Maître Duval. 'But you are not, I trust, anticipating doing anything precipitate?'

'I want to leave my husband, or rather, I don't *want* to leave him, but I must. He is gambling away thousands of francs every night in Monte Carlo. He is openly consorting with homosexuals – boys, sailors, servants. When I face him with these matters, he becomes hysterical. He carries a revolver about with him and spins the chamber and puts the muzzle to his head, saying he will shoot himself unless I agree with whatever he wants.'

'But I would assume that this is simply an empty threat, to attract attention – or your sympathy? Surely, the revolver is not always loaded?'

'I don't know. He says it is – another sort of gamble, maybe. I have kept quiet about these weaknesses,' Arabella continued. 'You are the first person I have ever told of them. I have supported him financially and publicly, because I loved him.

But there comes an end to everything, even to love. I must leave my husband. But I do not wish to leave my son.'

'If you leave your husband in France, you may not simply take your son with you.'

'How could he stop my son coming with me?'

'Very easily. He would apply for an order. This would mean you'd be stopped at the frontier, and, if need be, parted from your son.'

'I could sail away in my yacht.'

'Your yacht, Lady Doncaster, has had engine trouble for the last two weeks. I was talking to the captain in the café bar next door only last night. He tells me he is still waiting for Customs to release parts from the United States.'

'I could charter an aeroplane.'

'That would be the most foolish way to go because the pilot of a chartered plane would have to file a flight plan with the authorities. Your name would have to be listed as a passenger, just as it would if you flew by a commercial airline from Paris or Le Touquet to Croydon in England. Your best chance of success would be for you, your husband and your son to return to England and consult lawyers there.'

'I suppose it would,' Arabella said, unconvinced. 'Perhaps we will. Now, how much do I owe you? I would rather pay now. If we do leave, I may not be back in France again for some time.'

'I will send the bill to your London address, your ladyship. Don't worry about that now. And if I may say so, the very best of luck with – or even without – the law.'

Arabella drove back along the coast road to her house, the Château de la Mer. It was set in a pine and fir forest near the Garoupe, the lighthouse, on a gentle hill overlooking the sea. She parked her car outside the front door, went up the steps thoughtfully. She must take Charles now. If she delayed, her plan might leak out. If Maître Duval knew the captain of her yacht, then it was just possible that unintentionally he might mention what she had in mind. This was unlikely, she realised, and she trusted the man, but she was unwilling to take the slightest unnecessary risk of losing her son.

Arabella walked through the house on to the back terrace, sat down out of the sun under a red and blue striped awning. The butler had seen her arrive and followed her.

'His lordship has been on the telephone,' he told her.

'Where did you say I was?'

'I said you were out driving, your ladyship.'

'Did he leave a message?'

'He said he would ring again.'

'Thank you.'

'Would you like a drink, your ladyship?'

'Something soft, yes, Jules. A citron pressé, with lots of ice.'

Arabella sat looking over the splendid formal garden. The grass glowed green under a constant spray from sprinklers, and beyond the lawns lay beds full of flowers planted so close together that their petals were a blaze of pink and blue and yellow and red, like a riot of wildly coloured paints on the palette of a giant artist.

She sat here in the midst of beauty, surrounded by evidence of wealth: a Corot on this wall, a Monet on that. A full staff of servants administered the house, the garden, to bring her anything she wanted, to eat, to drink, to wear, and yet . . . and yet. The one thing she wanted, needed, yearned for more than anything – to love and be loved, to trust and be trusted; to have a man in whom she could put the total faith and belief he would feel for her – this was lacking. Without it, all her other possessions appeared dull and empty, like an expensive frame without the picture.

She would have to abandon this house, and unless she was very careful or very fortunate, she would also lose her son. She would willingly give up the house, although she had bought it and everything it contained, if she could keep Charles. But her

576

husband would never agree to this. Arabella sat for a long time, considering the problem, sipping her drink so slowly that the ice melted. Then she made up her mind, rang for the butler.

'I'm going out with Master Charles,' she told him.

'You will be having luncheon here, your ladyship?'

'Possibly. But if my husband comes back before then, or rings again, say I will be here by the early afternoon at the latest. I am just going to Cannes.'

'Shall I ask Pierre to bring the Delage to the door?'

'No, a taxi will do. I can hire another when I want to come home. No need for Pierre to sit about waiting for me.'

'Very good, your ladyship.'

Arabella walked upstairs, put her jewels in a strongbox, packed this in a small suitcase with a few clothes, a towel, a soap dish, a flannel cloth, a pair of slippers. She felt like a little girl going on a camp outing; she wasn't sure what she needed. It had been a long time since she had packed for herself, but whatever she left behind she could buy on the way.

She went into the nursery. The day nurse stood up politely.

'I was just about to take Master Charles for a walk, your ladyship.'

'Don't bother,' said Arabella, speaking as casually as she could. 'I am going to Cannes. I'll take him.'

'He would like that, I'm sure, your ladyship.'

'Good. You go off now, for the rest of the day if you like.'

There was a night nurse who came at five o'clock.

'You're sure that will be all right, your ladyship?'

'Of course. Take the Citroën if you want to go anywhere. Tell Pierre you have my permission.'

'You're very kind, your ladyship.'

Arabella waited until the nurse was out of sight and then sat down on the floor next to her son. He was playing with an electric train. The engine was not working. He banged it angrily on the floor until the wheels came off.

'We're going to have an adventure,' she told him, taking the toy out of his hands. 'We're going on a real train. A steam train.'

'With Daddy?' Charles asked, frowning. He wanted to go on the beach; Nanny had promised him that. He was expecting it.

'Daddy's not here,' Arabella explained gently. 'So for the time being, it's just you and me. You will have to look after Mummy.'

The boy nodded. He picked up a brightly painted toy tanker, began to spin the wheels with the palm of his hand. Arabella walked around the nursery, opening cupboards and drawers. She had never dressed Charles and was not even sure what he wore or where she could find his clothes. She dug out an odd assortment of vests and pants and shirts and socks and buttoned shoes, a sun hat, put them all in a bag, zipped it shut.

'Come on,' she said.

Charles tucked the tanker under his arm, and held out his hand. She gripped it and held it tightly. Together, they went downstairs and out to the waiting taxi.

The manager of the casino, usually so pleasant, so urbane, with a joke for this client, a smile for the next, a shrug of the shoulders and a warm handshake for a third, had another darker and less jovial side to his character. Noel was seeing this now in his office high up in the building. 'I asked you up here because despite repeated requests that you attempt to pay off at least a part of what you owe, you have studiously avoided me,' he said bluntly.

'I tried to see you once,' Noel replied lamely, 'But you were out.'

'No one told me you wished to see me,' said the manager, his voice harsh with disbelief. 'You owe us a great deal of money, and my principals are not prepared to allow this state of affairs to continue.'

'How much is a great deal?' asked Noel, playing for time.

The manager opened a small leather-bound notebook, looked up at Noel.

'At this moment, you owe us exactly seven thousand, four hundred and thirty-two pounds, seven and eightpence.'

'You will have the money,' said Noel stubbornly. 'I have always paid in the past.'

'Only after a long time. My principals cannot have such a large sum outstanding.'

'How long have I got?'

'One week.'

'I haven't got that amount of money out here,' said Noel.

'You have a very rich wife, who owns a large house along the coast. If she will not help you, I suggest that within the week you find someone else who will. That is all I have to say. One week. This time, next Tuesday. Here. In my office.'

How many years ago had another manager of another casino come to see him in his hotel in Nice, also about a debt? That meeting had resulted in him killing his own wife – for nothing at all. How could he pay off this new fellow?

Noel stepped out into the sunshine. The morning seemed unusually, almost unnaturally, hot and bright after the dimness of the casino. He breathed deeply, feeling welcome warmth through the silk of his shirt. He climbed into his Alfa Romeo, drove back along the coast road to his house. Or rather, he thought bitterly, to his wife's house. He just lived there, a lodger with a contract to his landlady; a contract of marriage.

He walked up the steps, through the main room, out on to the verandah, called for the butler to bring him a bottle of champagne, a plate of smoked-salmon sandwiches, cut very thin. He felt peckish.

'Where is her ladyship?' he asked.

'She has gone out, my lord.'

579

Noel looked surprised. 'You told her I rang?'

'Yes, my lord. She said she was going to Cannes. With Master Charles.'

'Cannes? At this time of day? It's almost lunchtime.'

'She said she would be back, if not for luncheon, then this afternoon.'

'Did she have Pierre drive her?'

'No, my lord. She had been driving herself in the morning. She specifically asked me to ring for a taxi.'

'Who did you ring?'

'Jean.'

'Well, get on to him and find out exactly where she went.'

'Now, my lord?'

'Yes. Before you bring the champagne. Now.'

Noel paced up and down the terrace until the butler returned with a tray, a bottle of champagne in an ice bucket, a single long-stemmed glass.

'Well?' Noel asked him irritably.

'Jean has just come back, my lord,' he said.

'Well, where's he been?'

'He took her ladyship to St Raphael railway station.'

'The *station*?'

'Yes. They arrived just before the Paris Express, the Blue Train. She got on the train with Master Charles.'

'On the train?'

Suddenly all the pieces fell into place like snowflakes in a toy kaleidoscope he had been given once as a birthday present when he was a child. Arabella was going to Paris. She was taking their son – his son. His only source of money was leaving him, indeed had already left him.

Without her backing, he was a pauper, facing total ruin; he owed money to many people who would hound him without mercy if they sensed his rich wife had gone. But if he held Charles, he had a weapon against her, a lever he would use to force Arabella to help him, lend him money he could never repay; better, give him money. But if she had Charles, he was finished.

He ran into the house, dialled his lawyer's number. The man was in conference, so his secretary explained. Noel poured out his fears and his orders to some subordinate who did not speak English well. He hoped he understood. Then, he went back to the terrace.

The butler had not moved. He stood, passive as a stone statue. What did he know or suspect? What had he heard? Whose side was he on? He's like a bloody automaton, Noel thought, as he motioned the man to pour him a glass of champagne; a second, a third, a fourth. Then he sat down and waited uneasily for the lawyer to ring him back.

Arabella sat in the corner of the First-Class compartment. Charles sat opposite her, watching her worried, set face, not understanding why she looked so unhappy, why they were travelling by train without his father, why they had ridden in a taxi, not a car. This wasn't the beach. He'd rather be on the beach than here. Something was wrong. He searched for clues in his mother's face and failed.

'You look very pretty, Mummy,' he said at last.

Arabella smiled at him. 'You think so? There are not too many who think that.'

'I think that. So does Daddy.'

'Good. That's very reassuring. Both the men in my life can't be wrong, can they?'

'*And* I love you very much,' said Charles, still shrewdly watching his mother's face. Her eyes grew moist with tears.

'I love you, too,' she said. 'More than anyone, or anything in all the world.'

'More than Daddy?' he asked. She nodded, not trusting herself to speak. When the train pulled in to the Gare de Lyon station in Paris, Arabella called a porter to carry their bags to a hotel across the road. She told the receptionist she was thinking of staying there, but in the meantime asked her to put through a long-distance telephone call to her house in the south. She distrusted French telephones; they took so long to connect, there was so much wheezing and repeating ' 'allo, 'allo, 'allo' on the line. It was easier and less fraught to let someone else do that for her.

'In number one cabine, madame,' said the clerk.

Arabella went into the booth, closed the door; a light in the roof came on as the door handle locked. She was certain no one could hear her outside. She picked up the telephone, heard the butler, Jules, say: 'Lord Doncaster's residence.'

'Jules, this is Lady Doncaster. Don't let on I am ringing, but just tell me three things. First, are you on your own? Can anyone overhear you?'

'Yes, your ladyship, on my own. There's no one in the staff room.'

'Are any of the extensions on?'

'No, your ladyship. This is the only line. Can I help you?'

'Yes,' she said, 'you can. Has my husband come back?'

'Yes, your ladyship. He came back shortly after you left.'

'Did he ask where I was?'

'I said you had gone off to Cannes, your ladyship, with Master Charles.'

'What did he say?'

'He asked me to telephone Jean at the taxi firm.'

'And?'

'Jean told me the taxi had taken you to St Raphael station. I had to inform his lordship.'

'What did he do then?'

'He appeared distraught, your ladyship. He made a telephone call. I heard him ask the operator for a number in Nice – 6300414.'

'His lawyer,' Arabella said, speaking aloud.

'Is that so, your ladyship?'

'Where is he now?'

'I do not know, your ladyship. He is not in the house. He has taken Pierre and the Rolls.'

'With any luggage?'

'No. Nothing, your ladyship.'

'I see.'

'Where are you speaking from, your ladyship?'

'Nowhere in particular,' she said miserably. 'I'll be in touch.' Arabella replaced the telephone.

If Noel had already got through to his lawyer, and the lawyer had acted with the speed with which lawyers can act when their clients are extremely wealthy and will not query absurdly inflated bills, the ports would all be watched. She had her own passport, but Charles was on her husband's passport. She had thought nothing about that when he had suggested it years ago. Now, she thought a lot. How could she get past any police or immigration check? Their description would already be circulating.

She pushed a hundred-franc note towards the clerk. 'Take the phone call out of that,' she said. 'And take ten francs for yourself.'

'Will you be staying the night, madame?' he asked.

'I'm not quite sure yet what I'm going to do.'

'I am,' said a voice behind her.

She turned. She had been looking down at the floor and she saw a pair of polished brogues, then well-pressed flannel trousers, a tweed jacket and finally, with amazement, the face of her brother, Jamie.

'What are *you* doing here?' she asked him in astonishment.

'Looking at you,' he replied. 'And looking after you – I hope.'

'But how did you get here?'

'Train, if you want to know. But I've been in Paris for some days.'

'On holiday?'

'In a sense. Waiting for things to happen.'

'What things?'

'For you to leave that husband of yours.'

'Well, I'm here now with Charles.'

'So I see.'

'But how did you know?'

'Money, my dear Arabella, is the universal key that can open the door of the most difficult prison. If you must have all the physical details, I have a contact in Antibes who made the acquaintance of your solicitor and then your butler, Jules. When you hired a taxi, Jules told this intermediary the name of the driver, who explained you had caught the Blue Train. I knew then I only had to wait at the station. And here you are, here *we* are.'

'Thank God for that. But even you can't get me out of France,' she said flatly. 'I'm sure of that. I've just phoned home and Jules tells me that Noel has been on to his lawyer. He was born in France, you know. French mother. He can stop me taking Charles away – for ever. Charles is on his passport.'

'And even if he wasn't, they'd be looking for you, and it wouldn't be much good.'

'Right,' she said. 'So what do we do now?'

Jamie had never heard his sister ask for advice. She had always been the one who gave it. He was about to reply when he saw two men come through the entrance of the hotel. They wore dark blue suits, dark hats. Even their faces seemed dark, as though they had shaved an hour ago and would need to shave again in less than an hour's time.

'Leave this to me,' Jamie told his sister sharply. 'And don't let the boy say a word.'

Arabella turned, saw the two men. They were clearly plain-

584

clothes police or officials of some kind. They had that semi-subservient look about them of men willing to bully the weak and pander to the wealthy. Her mouth dried with fear. Could she be arrested? Could her son be taken away from her here?

They approached her. One doffed his hat politely, addressed her in English.

'You are Lady Doncaster?' he asked Arabella.

She could not speak. Her throat was suddenly constricted; she could scarcely breathe. She did not even nod. As in a dream, she heard Jamie answer.

'No,' he said. 'You have made a mistake. This is my wife, Clara, and my son, Charles.'

'And you, sir?'

'I am James Jeans. Can we help you in any way?'

'We have reason to believe, sir, that an English lady, a young mother, Lady Doncaster, has just come off the Blue Train and is about to attempt to take her young son out of France illegally. Her husband does not wish this.'

'A very sad story,' said Jamie, shaking his head. 'I regret I cannot help you to resolve it.'

Jamie looked at Charles. If he spoke now, they'd all be lost. Jamie winked at him, trying to appear both friendly and con-spiratorial. Charles gave him a small smile. He liked his Uncle Jamie.

'Do you have a passport, madame?' the second man asked Arabella.

Her shoulders drooped in defeat. This was the end; she was beaten. Nothing Jamie could say or do could conceal the fact that her real name was on her passport. Arabella fumbled with the catch on her handbag. Jamie covered her hand with his.

'You forget, darling,' he said gently, 'I've got them this time.'

He took three passports out of his pocket, handed them over. The first one was for a boy of seven, Charles Jeans. The next

585

was in the name of James Jeans. The third was for his wife, Clara. Arabella recognised the photograph of herself; it had been taken the previous Christmas.

'Does that convince you?' Jamie asked pleasantly enough, but with just an edge of hardness to his voice. The two men looked at each other, then at Jamie's expensive clothes, his hand-made shoes, Arabella's supple leather suitcases. It could be unproductive to tangle with English visitors so obviously wealthy and doubtless equally influential. Also, they were looking for a woman and a boy on the run, not a whole family quietly waiting in an hotel. One gave an almost imperceptible nod to his companion.

'I am sorry if we have inconvenienced you,' he replied.

'Think nothing of it,' Jamie told him magnanimously. 'You have your job to do. I hope you find who you are seeking.'

The two men watched them as they walked out into the street, hailed a taxi. When the taxi was out of sight of the hotel, Arabella gave a great sigh of relief, and leaned back wearily against the rexine seat.

'How did you get those passports?' she asked at last.

'How does one get anything?' Jamie replied. 'Money. As I said, the universal key. Everything has its price – just like everyone. Now we'll go to the Gare du Nord and catch the Channel ferry from Calais to Dover. It would be quicker to fly from Le Touquet to Croydon, of course, but so few people do fly that you are almost bound to be searched. They might find some letters addressed to you in your real name, or a visiting card or something. If you go out on the boat second class with these passports, you're as good as home.'

'I just don't know how to thank you, Jamie.'

Jamie shrugged away his sister's gratitude; somehow, it did not seem in keeping with her character.

'Now,' he said briskly. 'Just as soon as you get home, no matter what time, get right on to a lawyer. Wake him up, if necessary. Fork him out of his bed and move to have Charles made a ward of court, as quickly as he can. Then no one can ever take Charles away from you until . . .'

'Until what?' she asked nervously.

'Until he grows up, and he wants to go.'

The boy looked up at Jamie now. 'I didn't give it away, did I?' he said.

'No, you were very good,' said Arabella gratefully and gave him a hug.

Charles looked at Jamie reproachfully. 'But you told a lie, Uncle Jamie.'

'I fear it was necessary not to tell the whole truth on that occasion.'

'Nanny says I mustn't ever tell lies. I would have spoiled it if I'd told the truth then, though, wouldn't I?'

'You'd have spoiled everything,' said his mother. 'More than you can possibly imagine.' She turned to her brother. 'I've been so concerned with my own problems, I haven't asked about yours. Any news of Katharina?'

'Still none, I'm sorry to say.'

'But you're still hopeful, even after all this time? It's been years.'

'I know. But it seems that is all I can do – hope.'

Jamie looked out of the window so his sister would not see the sadness in his eyes.

THIRTY-TWO

Russian Roulette

Arabella's English butler coughed discreetly as he stood in the doorway of her study in her London house. It was unusual for him to come to see her at that hour of the morning unless she summoned her. Arabella looked up inquiringly.

'Anything the matter?' she asked him.

'I thought, your ladyship, I should tell you that while I was taking Master Charles to Trumpers to have his hair cut this morning, as you instructed, it was such a sunny day that we walked back through the Park.'

He paused, as though unwilling to continue. Arabella waited.

'Well?' she asked at last.

'As we were walking, your ladyship, I saw a gentleman just behind us. He seemed to keep his distance, but when we came to Constitution Hill, he caught up with us.'

'Who was he?'

'Lord Doncaster, your ladyship. He made himself known to Master Charles.'

'What did he say?'

'He told him he hoped to have the pleasure of seeing his mother shortly. You, your ladyship. Knowing the difficulties you had in France with his lordship when you wished to leave, I thought it my duty to inform you of this at once.'

'Thank you. I am most grateful. In the meantime, please make sure that you, or one of the footmen, accompany Master Charles on all his walks and visits to the shops, indeed whenever he goes out of this house. Do not let him go out just with his nanny, or on his own.

'If Lord Doncaster is able to seize him, to carry him off, doubtless he would like to take him back to France. Then, through the French courts, he might never allow Master Charles to come back here. In the meantime, I will consider the whole matter and take advice. I cannot live indefinitely under this strain. None of us can.'

As the butler bowed and withdrew, Arabella ordered her car and went to see Jamie.

'I had no idea Noel would come over here like this,' she told Jamie. 'Looking back, I suppose it was pretty obvious he would, if he *really* wants Charles. But I never thought he cared for him. He has never showed the slightest interest in him or any affection whatever for him. But there you are. He is his father, after all. I should have taken your advice and made Charles a ward of court. But I thought that when I escaped from Antibes with him I had left Noel behind for ever.'

'You can never escape from any problem,' her brother replied. 'Running away is simply running in a circle. You then meet the same problem elsewhere, only now it's coming towards you. As you say, maybe he does genuinely care for the boy. He will be Lord Doncaster one day.'

'I have never told you what really disgusted me about Noel. You were quite right in everything you said about his character, and I was an idiot not to believe you. But I think you know – or must guess – the reason. I was lonely. I felt flattered. I'd made a lot of money and had a high opinion of myself, but somehow it all seemed empty. I wanted someone to share it with. I wanted to mean something to them. And I refused to see any faults at all in the man who persuaded me that he felt the same way about me. But you didn't go far enough in your criticism – as I very soon discovered.'

'What do you mean?'

'I mean that Noel is a pederast, a homosexual. We had intercourse once only, and that was enough for both of us. Charles must have been conceived then. Ironic, isn't it, how so many couples wish desperately for children and can never have them. And this creature, who wishes for nothing except nubile and compliant young men, can sire an heir instantly.

'Do you know,' Arabella went on, 'Noel has actually gone to the extraordinary length of taking out insurance on Charles because the rates are much lower for what companies call "a young life".'

'How do you know?'

'I received a letter from the company involved, advising me. Not that I could do anything to stop it. I'm only Charles's mother. A father can do what he likes apparently with his own son.'

'That's serious news, Bella, remembering how he insured his first wife.'

'That's why I came to see you. I used to be able to handle all my problems on my own, but not this one. My son is too close. I just want Noel out of the way. No harm to him, nothing like that. I've paid thousands of pounds to settle his debts, simply to keep details of his profligate gambling out of the newspapers. And I'd willingly pay thousands more to buy him off.'

'You'll never do that. He'll always come back for more.'

'I know. But I can't go on, Jamie, with the threat that one day he could kidnap my son. If he takes Charles back to France, I'll never see him again.'

'Do you love Charles very much?'

'More than anyone. Even you, Jamie, if I have to admit it. I adore him. He is my life, my whole reason for living. Sometimes, I think, the only one. I want him to have all the things we never had and missed. I don't want him to lack for anything. He must have the sort of childhood we'd have liked.'

'If we'd had that, Bella, we'd never have achieved anything at all. There wouldn't have been any need to.'

'Is that such a bad thing?'

'In theory, maybe not. In practice, it can be fatal.'

'That's your view. I'm not arguing with it, but I want to mould Charles into the sort of man I would have liked to marry. If Noel takes him, he'll be ruined.'

'And you want me to help get you out of this situation?'

'I don't know if you can. Frankly, I don't know if anyone can. But I had to tell you – the only person I have told.'

Jamie was about to reply, when the telephone rang on his desk. His secretary was on the line.

'I apologise for disturbing you,' she said. 'But there's a call for Lady Doncaster. The caller says it is personal and most urgent.'

Jamie handed the receiver to his sister. Her face went white as she took the call.

'Who is it?' he asked her.

Arabella did not reply, but when she replaced the receiver on its stand, her hand was trembling.

'Noel,' she said. 'He's actually in my house. He's ringing from there now. He looked in to see me, so he says.'

'Is Charles at home?'

'He was when I left to come here. Noel didn't mention him, so with any luck he's out with his nanny now. Noel says he wants to discuss everything in an amicable way, but I don't trust anything he says anymore. Oh God, I've made a mess of everything, Jamie. Please help me.'

Arabella leant forward, put her head in her hands and, for the first time since their father's death, Jamie saw his sister weep.

When Arabella had gone, Jamie sat in silence, considering

the problem. Then he opened a locked drawer in his desk, checked a number in his address book, and picked up his direct telephone to make a private call.

Noel lolled back in a silk-covered armchair in Arabella's drawing room. He did not stand up when she entered, but sat, glass in hand, smiling at her. He had ordered the butler to bring him a bottle of Taittinger and one glass as soon as he arrived.

'What do you want?' she asked him coldly.

'I have come to take my son back to France.' He spoke slowly and distinctly; he had been drinking heavily. 'You will be aware that under French law, a minor of French blood can be made a French subject, and I intend that Charles shall be brought up as a Frenchman. Your retreat from Antibes may have won a battle for you, but it has not won the war. I shall win that.'

'Must there be a battle, or a war?' she asked him.

'Of course not. If you agree to my terms, which are very reasonable, all will be resolved in the friendliest fashion. I take the boy back to France, where he stays with me. I also have the house in Antibes.'

'Which I paid for,' Arabella interrupted.

'Which you paid for,' Noel agreed. 'But which I now require to bring up my son as a gentleman in France should be brought up. Also, I will need an income, after tax, of, say, fifty thousand American dollars a year for its upkeep and maintenance, and for the education of my son. Plus, of course, a commensurate allowance for myself. I would not wish to let the boy down by not living up to a style appropriate to your wealth.'

'For how many years?'

'Until I die.'

'And what would I get out of this proposition?'

'I will allow you access to my son three times a year, for not more than one week at a time. In France, of course. Nowhere else. Certainly not here.'

'That is a hard bargain, Noel.'

'I learnt from you to be a hard bargainer, Arabella. You used to say you are hard as a diamond – hence the name of your company, Diamond-Hard. My terms are not negotiable, and my offer stands for three days, no more. I have an engagement back in France.'

'At the casino, I suppose?'

Noel shrugged.

'I will not meet your terms,' Arabella said firmly. 'I will fight them all the way. Even if I have to take Charles into hiding, go to another country, change his name. I am his mother and I will keep him.'

'Very nobly spoken. But from a woman's heart, not her head – especially not your head. Wherever you go, I will find you. You can't just disappear like that nowadays – not someone with your commercial responsibilities. And when I find you and my son, I will take him back by force if need be. The harder you struggle and fight me, the greater will be my determination to beat you. And, as I say, the offer I make now lapses after three days. Any new agreement we might come to after that will be much more expensive.'

'You are all talk,' retorted Arabella with a confidence she did not feel. 'You and your toy revolver, trying to frighten me you would kill yourself with it. It's typical of you. Your life and your mind are as empty as the chamber of that gun. You are a nothing person.'

Noel jumped up so quickly he upset his glass. Champagne poured in an effervescent tide across the white carpet.

'You think I'm joking, do you?' he cried furiously. 'Take me on – ten to one the gun's loaded.'

'I don't gamble,' Arabella replied, her voice hard with disgust.

Noel took the revolver from his pocket, spun the chamber, put the muzzle to his forehead, squeezed the trigger.

For a second, Arabella's heart contracted. She expected to see her husband's brains splattered across the wallpaper, the room to fill with the smell of cordite. Instead, there was only a feeble metallic click as the hammer struck the empty chamber. Noel smiled at her.

'Get out!' she shouted at him. She pressed the bell. The butler appeared. Behind him stood two burly footmen.

'Lord Doncaster wishes to leave,' Arabella told the butler.

Noel also saw the footmen.

'I will not say goodbye, my dear, but au revoir. Three days, I said. And then I'll be off to France for good. With Charles.'

He walked unsteadily through the door.

When Noel had gone, Arabella sat down, poured herself a glass of champagne, and drank it, her hand trembling. If there was any justice in the world, her husband would have blown his head off. But that was just an empty threat, one he had made before to her, and probably to many other people as well. And there was no justice in the world, none at all. Hadn't that been proved beyond all doubt when her father died?

As she sat drinking, Charles came into the room.

'I've just seen Daddy,' he said excitedly.

'Did he say anything to you?'

'No. He just went out. I saw him in the Park, too. Are we all going back to France together?'

'Sit down,' said Arabella gently. 'I'll try to explain. Your father is very fond of you, and I am very fond of you, as you know. But just as you find at school there are some people you like a lot at first, and then you don't like so much, the same happens when you grow up.'

She paused, not quite certain how to continue.

'Is that what's happening with you and Daddy?'

She nodded.

'Yes. I'm sorry to say, I think it is. But always remember, he is your father. You belong to both of us, until you grow up.'

'I really belong to you,' said Charles, and kissed her. 'I always will.'

Jamie sat in his favourite easy chair, cigar in one hand, brandy in the other. Arabella sat opposite him, her face drawn with worry. She had just told him what had happened in her house, and about Noel's ultimatum. She sipped nervously at her sherry.

'Can you help me, Jamie? Have you any suggestions to make?'

'Where is Noel staying at the moment?'

'In a hotel in Albemarle Street.'

'Then I suggest you make an appointment to see him in your house, or rather in the garden of your house, on the last evening of his three days' notice. Today is Tuesday, so that makes it Friday evening.'

'And what do I say when I see him – that I give in to his demands?'

'No. You tell him you have considered them very closely, and I have a proposition to make.'

'*You?*'

'Yes. I will be there and I will suggest that you leave Noel and me together in the garden to talk the matter through. Our discussion will then be totally private. And you must appear friendly, willing to be reasonable for everyone's sake. No sharp words, no barbed remarks. As much sweetness and light as you can manage. I cannot promise success – you must accept that – but we have not always been unfortunate in our lives. Let us pray luck will be with us on Friday. Oh, and it might be best if you made sure Charles is out of the house, just in case Noel tries anything.'

'You're not going to agree to something behind my back, Jamie?'

'Of course not. Confucius said, according to Yeung Lee, that the road to success is filled with wives pushing their husbands along. I have never had a wife, so I can't vouch for that. But you, as my sister, have pushed me along from my earliest days. Now, our positions are reversed. Or perhaps we are pushing each other along, together.'

'I sometimes wish I hadn't been so ambitious,' said Arabella sadly. 'I wanted to prove something to myself, perhaps to the world. And now I wonder whether the journey we've both made is worthwhile.'

'It's a lot better than being back in the Silent Witness,' Jamie retorted. 'And just how much better we will discover on Friday evening.'

He raised his glass in a silent toast.

Arabella's garden was surprisingly large for a London house; nearly two acres, with fir trees and silver birches that shielded the lawn from houses on either side. In the early morning and evening, when the traffic was silent, Arabella could almost imagine she was in the middle of the country, with the sound of birds and the smell of many flowers.

She sat now in a basket chair beneath the trees and sipped champagne, watching bubbles rise in her glass. Would her spirits rise with them after Jamie's arrival? Three other chairs were grouped around a table. On this stood two silver ice buckets, a bottle of champagne in each one.

The butler came across the lawn, bowed to her.

'Lord Doncaster, your ladyship.'

'Please show him out here.'

Noel was wearing a light-coloured suit, unsuitable for London in the evening, Arabella thought, especially with his garish tie. He looked like a tout or a bookmaker. He should have been one. At least then he might have made his gambling pay, she thought contemptuously.

'Let me pour you a drink,' she said, forcing a smile, doing her best to appear relaxed, at ease. She filled a large glass with

Taittinger. Noel sat down, drank it, held out his glass to be refilled. He lit a Turkish cigarette, tossed the spent match over his shoulder on to the lawn.

'Well?' he asked. 'What have you decided?'

'I have discussed the whole thing with my brother,' said Arabella, keeping to the form of words she had agreed with Jamie; not admitting anything, neither confirming nor denying her decision.

'And what does he say?'

'That there must be a friendly solution. No acrimony, no lawyers. But I think you'd better hear his views from him direct.' She poured Noel a third glass of champagne. 'Here he is now.'

Jamie crossed the lawn, sat down. His sister poured him a glass of champagne. He raised it in Noel's direction, then sipped it.

'Well, what is your proposal?' Noel asked him. 'May as well hear what you have to say, though it won't make any difference to what I have already told your sister. As far as my proposition is concerned, it's a matter of take it or leave it. No compromises whatever. None.'

'She told me.' Jamie turned to Arabella. 'I think Noel and I had better discuss this on our own,' he said. 'We'll join you in the drawing room afterwards. It's better, I think, man to man.'

'If you wish, Jamie.' Arabella stood up, walked across the lawn already damp with dew, entered the house.

'Good-looking woman, that,' said Noel appreciatively.

Jamie smiled. 'I agree. But I'm surprised you find any beauty in a woman – knowing your inclinations.'

'What the hell do you mean?'

'What I say. Surely I need not elaborate?'

Noel undid the foil from the second bottle, then the wire, withdrew the cork expertly, poured himself another glass.

'I won't argue the point,' he said easily. 'I have come to hear Arabella's decision on my offer regarding my son, not to discuss anything else. Is it yes or no?'

'I can give you the answer right away,' replied Jamie. 'We have discussed the matter at length. We both feel it is in Charles's best interests that we do not argue and quibble over money. Fortunately, we have quite a lot, and your demands do not seem to me to be excessive. To be brief, Arabella is prepared to agree to everything you request.'

Noel choked on his drink in surprise. Champagne dribbled down his chin. He wiped it away with the back of his hand.

'*Everything?*'

'Yes. On my advice. But there's one condition. A small one that I think will amuse you.'

'And what's that?'

'As a gambler, I hope it appeals to you. If you accept the condition, which is in the nature of a wager, not only will she pay you what you ask, but I will pay you the same amount on top, because I would like my nephew to be brought up in a way I myself would have liked to have been reared.'

Noel watched him closely, his eyes narrowed.

'That's very generous of you,' he said suspiciously, refilling his glass. He took a drink and came to a decision. 'All right. We have a deal. What is this wager?'

'A rather bizarre one. Arabella tells me you carry a revolver?'

'Purely for my protection.'

'Of course. She also tells me that on the last occasion you both met this week, you offered her a bet – ten to one your revolver was loaded. Is that right?'

'Absolutely correct,' said Noel.

'But women are not so attracted by gambling or games of chance as we men are. Certainly not Arabella. When you are born with little money, you tend to feel you shouldn't risk any of it. Life was different for you, of course.'

'Of course,' Noel agreed at once. 'Quite different. But get on with this bet.'

'Two to one your gun's loaded.'

'Two to one *what*?' asked Noel sharply. His eyes were wary slits in his puffy face.

'Twice what you have been promised. Two hundred thousand dollars a year – for the rest of your life.'

'You're bloody mad!' cried Noel in disbelief.

'No, just bloody rich.' Jamie grinned at him.

'You're on,' said Noel instantly. 'Two to one it is.'

He took the revolver from his pocket, spun the chamber three times.

'Two hundred thousand dollars,' said Jamie slowly.

Noel smiled. This man was an idiot, but a rich idiot. It would be a pleasure to take his money off him. Noel raised the revolver, winked confidently at Jamie, pressed the muzzle to his forehead.

'Your terms,' he said thickly. 'You can't back out now.'

Then he squeezed the trigger.

The bullet blew the back of Noel's head across the lawn. His trunk fell forward, spouting blood. One hand crashed down on the champagne bottle, breaking the champagne glass. Blood mixed with bubbly streaming over the darkening grass.

'Jackpot!' said Jamie quietly to himself.

He rang the bell. The butler appeared.

'You rang, sir?' he asked. Then he saw Noel's body, and started back in horror.

'Call a doctor urgently, and telephone the police,' Jamie instructed him. 'Lord Doncaster has just shot himself, right in front of me. Do not allow Lady Doncaster to come out here on any pretext. She must not see this. And do not inform her of this tragedy. I will.'

'Very good, sir.'

Jamie walked across the lawn to the house. It had all been so easy, almost too easy. Noel had not meant to kill himself, of course. His revolver was never loaded. Jamie had killed him in all but the act of murder. And, incredibly, he had no feelings whatever about it; no elation, no relief, no sorrow. He had been presented with a problem and he had solved it – with Sergeant O'Malley's help.

Arabella was waiting for him in the drawing room.

'What have you agreed?' she asked curiously.

'The matter is at an end,' Jamie told her quietly.

'At an end? How? What do you mean?'

'I mean, your husband has taken his own life.'

'Taken his own life? *Noel?* Are you making this up?'

'No. Didn't you hear a revolver shot just now?'

'I heard nothing.'

'Well, I offered to double the fifty thousand dollars you were to give him to one hundred thousand. And to double that if he would go through his little game of Russian roulette.'

'But his revolver was never loaded. He was a complete bluffer.'

'This time, his bluff was called. That's why I suggested you met him in the garden rather than in the house.'

'You *knew* this was going to happen?'

'I thought it might,' Jamie replied. 'If he had taken my offer, he would have had one hundred thousand dollars a year for life, but greed got the better of him.'

'I just don't know what to say.'

Jamie looked at Arabella closely. She was pale and obviously in some shock, but there was no sign of sorrow or even regret. Would that come later? Her next words reassured him.

'I feel free for the first time in years. But tell me, Jamie, who loaded his revolver? Not you, surely?'

'Certainly not me, Bella.'

'Who then?' Arabella insisted. 'And why?'

'He is, I believe, a former policeman with the City of London

Constabulary. He did it to repay a good turn someone did him. Someone who paid for medical attention so that his son, who had been sickly since birth, could be totally restored to health.

'Odd to think that this was in the nature of a gamble, if you like. A young boy's life for a worthless man's death. Strange, how things turn out. Now I will wait until the police arrive and then compose an obituary on the lines that Lord Doncaster died as he lived, a gentleman gambler. Unfortunately for him, he lost the last wager. But then, in the end, so do we all . . .'

THIRTY-THREE

The Price of a Wager

From behind the imitation leaded mullioned window of his study, the headmaster of Abbey Glade Preparatory School in Sussex watched Arabella's Rolls-Royce arrive. A liveried footman sprang down from beside the chauffeur and opened the rear door.

The headmaster left the window, sat down in his swivel chair behind the big leather-topped desk, like an actor waiting for the curtain to go up. Large framed photographs of groups of schoolboys looked down on him from the walls. Sometimes, one or two came back to see him.

But most now would never come back. They belonged to what writers in newspapers were already calling The Lost Generation. They had been blown to pieces at Mons; died on the wire in Flanders; drowned at sea; missing, believed killed.

Most of the boys he had now as pupils were the sons of parents made rich by the war. But Lady Doncaster was not one of them; she had been rich before the war. Diamonds, he thought vaguely – and all those cosmetics his wife swore by.

A maid knocked timidly on the door, opened it.

'Lady Doncaster, sir,' she announced respectfully.

The headmaster stood up, came round the side of his desk.

'My dear Lady Doncaster, how kind of you to come to see me so quickly.'

'I had your letter this morning,' Arabella replied shortly. 'You said there was a matter of urgency to discuss, so I thought I would come at once. Nothing has happened to Charles, I hope? He is not ill? Not had an accident playing games, or something like that?'

'Nothing like that at all, I am glad to say, Lady Doncaster. Please do be seated. Would you like a cup of tea or coffee?'

'No, thank you,' she said. 'What do you wish to discuss?'

In the headmaster's experience, this was always the most difficult moment. How he responded would invariably affect the parent's reaction.

'First of all, Lady Doncaster, let me assure you that your son has settled in well here. He has his own little coterie of friends. He is an individual, rather more than some of the boys we have, who conform in all their attitudes.'

The headmaster cleared his throat, adjusted his tie.

'I wanted to see you, Lady Doncaster, because – as is often the case with boys of strong character, perhaps one might also add, with artistic temperament – there have been difficulties with which I feel I should acquaint you personally.

'There have been two unfortunate incidents in which, I am sorry to say, your son has been involved.'

'What sort of incidents?'

'Oddly for a boy from such a wealthy background, they have concerned money.'

'I give him what you say he should have for pocket-money. What other money do you refer to?'

'You may not know, Lady Doncaster, but, regrettably, gardeners and servants sometimes have private arrangements with bookmakers to place bets – quite illegally of course – on their own behalf, or sometimes on behalf of others.

'There was a sum of five pounds owed, apparently, by your son. The publican in question threatened to make trouble. This sum was taken from a boy's locker. Charles admits he took it.

There was another similar incident. He admitted this quite readily and saw nothing wrong in what he had done. I told him it was stealing.'

'What did he say then?'

'Nothing. He just shrugged his shoulders.'

'An unusual reaction in a boy of his age, surely, Headmaster?'

'Most unusual. And very worrying.'

'For you? Or for me?'

'For all of us, Lady Doncaster. We accepted him here at Abbey Glade in good faith as a pupil. You told me he had been at two other preparatory schools, but had left them because he was unhappy. Since these unfortunate events, I have contacted their headmasters, and they have both told me that similar things had happened there. They had asked for him to be removed.'

'Is that what you are asking me to do now?'

'I am giving you the facts of the situation, Lady Doncaster. We have to consider the interests of the other boys. And, of course, the school.'

'Having considered all these interests, Headmaster, you wish me to remove my son from Abbey Glade?'

'It grieves me to have to tell you, Lady Doncaster, but in view of Charles's past history, I feel, with the utmost regret, that it would be best if he were removed at the end of term.'

'In that case,' said Arabella, 'I will take him away now. Please give instructions for his belongings to be packed. Have bills made out for whatever is owing and I will settle them at once.'

Arabella stood up.

'I will wait for my son outside in my car.'

'You are welcome to wait for him here, Lady Doncaster.'

'Headmaster, if my son is unwelcome here, I feel unwelcome, too.'

*　　*　　*

Jamie and Arabella were sitting on each side of the fireplace in his study. She had just told him what had happened.

'Well,' said Jamie, 'at least we didn't have such problems when we were at school. But it's no good looking back. Let me have a talk to Charles. He probably misses not having a father.'

'Then it must be all he does miss. I give him everything else he wants.'

'Then what he also misses is a more sensible mother. I have no children so far as I know, but I have seen something of other people's, and remembering my own boyhood, I know that a boy wants something to fight against. If you supply him with everything he wants, or thinks he wants, there's no incentive for him to make any effort to achieve anything. It's all there already. So what has he got to work for? If we'd both been rich at his age, we'd have never done a stroke. There would not have been any need to make the effort.'

'I suppose you're right,' his sister admitted grudgingly. 'I just wanted Charles to have a better start than we did.'

'The start doesn't matter a damn,' said Jamie. 'It's the finish that counts.'

He stood up.

'I'll drive him myself to his new school, and we can have a talk on the way. See if we can't get to the bottom of this – and find a way ahead.'

As Jamie's Phantom I sighed past Stonehenge, and Salisbury Plain stretched ahead to infinity, he glanced at his watch.

'Less than an hour, and we'll be there,' he told Charles.

The boy nodded, looking straight ahead, his face impassive.

'Looking forward to being a new boy at Erithian School?'

'Would you be, Uncle? This will be my fourth school in two years. I get used to a new place, start making friends and then . . .'

He shrugged.

'Then what, exactly?' asked Jamie. 'I've heard only the vaguest outline from your mother of what happened at Abbey Glade.'

'They said I stole money from another boy,' Charles explained.

'And did you?'

'Not really stealing.'

'So what gave them that idea?'

'I did take some money from a boy in the next bed in the dormitory, and I admitted it at once. He kept the money in a biscuit tin in his locker. There was a cert running at Newbury. Twenty to one. One of the gardeners handled bets and a lot of boys used him. So did the masters. I hadn't got any ready cash, so I borrowed this money from the boy. He was sick, in the san. I would have told him, asked him for a loan if he'd been in the dorm, but he wasn't.'

'Did the cert lose, as they so often seem to?'

'Oh, no,' said Charles. 'I follow form. It won. I knew it would. But *I* lost because the gardener hadn't put the money on. He thought the horse didn't have a chance, so he simply pocketed it. Then said he'd never had it. I couldn't prove otherwise. I would have paid the boy back, of course, out of my winnings, but as it was I couldn't. I told him what had happened and said I'd give him back the money out of my allowance in the following week. He got angry and told a master, and that was it.'

'And the second time?'

'Much the same thing. This time I gave an indoor servant money, then he denied I had asked him to put it on the winning horse. Said I'd wanted it to go on a horse that wasn't even placed. I believe he put it on himself.'

'You seem to have been rather trusting,' said Jamie musingly.

'Yes. I was. I didn't think they would cheat me like that.'

'Many people are dishonest when money is involved.'

'But it wasn't a lot of money, Uncle. That's what makes it so difficult for me to understand.'

'It was a lot to them. Remember, you are rich and they are not. You're talking about several weeks' wages.'

'I'd never thought about it like that.'

'Well, I'd start now if I were you. What about the other schools?'

'Some boys ganged up on me. They were jealous, I think, of Mother's Rolls when she came down to see me. Their parents only had Austins and Morrises. They told a lot of lies about me. Their parents believed them and wrote to the headmaster. Said they were thinking of taking their sons away if I stayed. I was a bad influence. It was easier for the school to lose one pupil and one set of fees, than several.'

'I see. Well, this time Charles, we've really got to show this new school that this is all in the past – and it's staying there.'

'*We*, Uncle?'

Charles looked sharply at Jamie.

'Yes, *we*, because I'll be backing you. You won't be on your own. But don't tell your mother. This is a male thing, just between the two of us – against all the rest.'

'Do you mean that, Uncle?'

'Of course I mean it,' Jamie answered him. 'What you must do is prove yourself better than the others at something. And not just making bets. I know that gambling is in your blood. Your father and apparently his uncle gambled on a prodigious scale. It's like an illness if you can't stop it. You either suffer from it or you don't. I don't. You do. I'm too cautious, I suppose. But we're going to beat it together – *now*.

'When I was a bit older than you, an old Chinaman taught me how to defend myself in almost any attack. This gave me enormous confidence and the chance to prove myself. I even fought in a fair against all comers. They thought they could

607

beat me because they didn't know I had practised ways of fighting they never knew existed.'

'I didn't know that, Uncle.'

'You mother doesn't always like to be reminded of our early days, Charles. But if you are better than anyone else in your school at *something*, you will become someone in your own right. Then you won't have to put up with jealousy. You'll have proved yourself.'

'What do you think I should choose, Uncle?'

'You'll have to decide that for yourself, but I suggest something individual, one against one, not in a team. I don't think as a family we're very good at team work. We like to be out there on our own. Now, I was looking at this school's prospectus and saw they are keen on archery.'

'I never knew *you* were keen on archery, Uncle.'

'I'm not, but your mother and I owe our lives to the fact that someone else was – a Bushman in what used to be German South West Africa. Someone was holding us up with a gun, and about to use it. The Bushman shot him with an arrow. Since then, I have had a soft spot for archery. Why not become a bowman of England – or at least of Erithian?'

Charles stood facing the housemaster in his study.

'I hear that you and Penthorpe Major are through to the finals in the school archery contest and you do battle together next week,' said the master.

'Yes, sir.'

The housemaster looked at Charles for a moment. The boy was pleasant enough, no arguing about that, but he was not in any way sycophantic and this independence did not commend itself to him. Of course, he was so damned rich he didn't need to be; and as a peer, you wouldn't expect him to be. He would never have to slave away half the night marking exam papers, taking evening classes at a technical college to make a little extra money. Charles would have no idea of that, he thought, and resented him for who and what he was.

Charles was thinking that the housemaster could have no conception of the amount of practice he had been putting in with his bow and arrows. Every day of the previous Easter holidays he had spent his entire allowance on fees at an archery school in West London. He had shot until his arms and eyes ached, for he was determined to win. At school, he had deliberately played down his ability. He did not want to appear as good as he was; that, he intended, would be the surprise of the tournament.

'I think you're pretty evenly matched,' the housemaster continued. 'But actually, if all things were equal I have to tell you that, if I were a betting man, I'd put my money on Penthorpe. But . . .'

He stopped.

'But what, sir?'

'Well, to be absolutely honest, if we assume that you and Penthorpe *are* of roughly the same standard, I think you'll agree that you do have the advantage in equipment. Your bow must have cost many times what Penthorpe's father paid for this. And your arrows – I've seen them – they're all beautifully made and weighted. Not the sort of off-the-peg arrows he'll be firing. So, I wish you both luck, but if you do win, don't get too swollen a head about your ability.'

'Despite what you say, sir, I think I'm the better archer.'

The housemaster shrugged. He did not wish to be drawn into a discussion that could become acrimonious.

'In fact,' Charles went on, 'to prove this I'll give Penthorpe my bow and arrows, and I'll take his.'

'He may not accept them. He wouldn't want charity, you know.'

'This isn't charity, sir. It's a chance for him to prove he really *is* the better shot.'

The master nodded. This was an unusual proposal, but the boy seemed sincere in making it.

'All right,' he said. 'You see him. But don't tell anyone else what you're doing. They could get the wrong impression, think you're being patronising. Just get on with the contest. And may the best shot win.'

The archery tournament was being held as one of the events of Sports Day a week later. Arabella could not be there because she was due to open a new salon in Los Angeles, so Jamie drove down to the school for the day.

When the two finalists came out on the field, he raised his binoculars, focused them on Charles's face. The boy looked tense, but confident. Jamie saw the groundsman set up the marks against the safety screens. Each competitor was to loose ten arrows, moving back twenty paces after each round. All the other contestants had already been eliminated; the contest was now between Charles and Penthorpe Major.

Penthorpe's first arrow secured an inner. Charles's first made gold. They moved back. Each time, Charles beat his opponent, sometimes narrowly; but it was still a victory. For the last flight at seventy paces, Penthorpe's shaft struck the outer rim of the target. Charles pierced the inner. He had won.

Jamie joined in the clapping. He was genuinely delighted at the result. Clearly, Charles had taken his advice to heart.

'Congratulations,' said Jamie, as they walked towards the tea marquee. 'But what happened to that wonderful bow your mother gave you? The one you were using looked a pretty ordinary sort of thing.'

'It was, Uncle. I let the other fellow have my bow – only a loan, of course. I wanted to prove I could beat him, even when he had better equipment than mine. That I was simply the better archer.'

'You took a big risk, didn't you?'

'No, Uncle. Not really. I'd been practising solidly for weeks, and every day during the Easter holidays.'

'I had no idea,' said Jamie, impressed.

'Well, I didn't spread it about. I *knew* I could win and I did. I'm sorry about one thing, though. For the last shot I was at the limit of the bow. Now if I'd been using my bow I know I could have gone back several more paces and cleaned up. They would have given me tremendous odds on that.'

'They? You didn't gamble on the result, did you?'

'Not a gamble, Uncle, no. An investment, really. I knew I could win so I put on a tenner with the local bookie at twenty to one. He knew the housemaster, who told him Penthorpe would win. I made two hundred pounds.'

'In that case, said Jamie gravely, 'you can treat me to tea.'

Extract from the City columns of *The Enquirer*, Saturday, March 15, 1929:

New York, Friday.

Wall Street bankers, Rubenovitch & Son Inc., reported last night one of the biggest financial coups of the decade. They have bought for $100,000,000, the entire voting shares of the London quoted company, Diamond-Hard. This values its shares at $100 each.

Since its flotation in the early 1920s, controlling shares in the Diamond-Hard Group have been held by Lady Doncaster, her twin brother, Mr Jamie Baird, her son, Lord Doncaster, Mr S. Rosen and Mr Y. Lee.

The company started some 30 years ago when Lady Doncaster – then Miss Arabella Baird – imported into South Africa, where she was living, a formula devised by Mr Lee for a face cream to mitigate the effects of sunburn on delicate skins.

From this small start has grown the Lady Arabella Cosmetics Group, Diamond-Lee Pharmaceuticals and the universally popular canvas jackets and trousers known as Rosens, from their colour and the name of their inventor, Mr Rosen.

The Group's founders have always shunned publicity. It is known that Lady Doncaster and her brother, who were orphaned in their teens, and Mr Rosen, have homes in England and South Africa. Mr Lee has homes in London and Singapore.

Originally, Lady Doncaster and her brother and Mr Rosen prospected for diamonds in Kimberley, South Africa. It is believed that they discovered only one diamond of any value and consequently decided to concentrate their endeavours on other commercial ventures. The name Diamond-Hard recalls these early days. No one seems to know how the Hard came to be incorporated in the name of this company.

Some say it refers to the tough and difficult times they experienced when digging for diamonds, but a more likely explanation is that it refers to Lady Doncaster's strong character – said by her colleagues to be hard as a diamond.

Lady Doncaster is the widow of Lord Doncaster, who died tragically in a shooting accident some years ago. Her son, Charles, the present Lord Doncaster, is 21 and a frequent visitor to Monte Carlo, where he has an apartment and a motor yacht. He is well known for his motor-racing activities at Brooklands Motor Racing Course, outside London.

None of the founders was immediately available for comment last night, but this deal puts them all firmly into the multimillionaire class.

When Arabella was in England, it was her custom to visit one or other of her salons very early in the morning, before they opened to the general public.

She would walk round to Bond Street from her home in London, let herself into the building with her own pass key and go from room to room, noting which of her executives had tidy desks and who left confidential papers scattered about carelessly for anyone to read.

She would open store cupboards, check inventories, and usually had gone before her staff arrived. On another day she would do the same in Manchester and Edinburgh. No one knew for certain where she was and where she was staying, because all the hotels she used were instructed never to disclose whether or not she was in residence.

On the desks of executives of whose activities she disapproved, she would leave her visiting-card, with the time she called, but no comment on what she found. If they did not take the hint, and left their desks untidy when she made a subsequent visit, they were automatically dismissed at the end of the month.

Thus, on an October morning in 1929, eight months after Rubenovitch & Son, the New York bankers, bought Diamond-Hard for $100,000,000, she was in the private office of her London manager. The financial columns of all newspapers had been carrying alarming reports of the fearful financial crash on Wall Street. Stockbrokers and other dealers in shares and securities, who had left their offices one evening as rich men, returned next morning to find that their wealth had vanished. It was not real money, of course, only paper; and, like a paper house in a storm, it had simply collapsed.

Brokers committed suicide rather than face up to the unspeakable reality of financial failure, utter destruction. Others begged friends, relations, colleagues, anyone to buy stock from them at almost any price. Overnight, it seemed that the entire Western world had plunged from the heights of prosperity into the abyss of total depression.

None of this worried Arabella. Shares in the companies were to her only bits of printed paper. Their value, she knew, was totally arbitrary, depending on how some financial commentator – possibly bribed – would praise or criticise their performance, and advise their acquisition or damn them as being too highly priced.

As she stood, looking through the papers on the manager's desk, the telephone rang. She picked it up.

Jamie was on the line. He had a teleprinter in his house and Arabella heard it chatter away mechanically in the background as he spoke.

'Thought I would catch you, Bella,' her brother said. 'There's a message on the tape from Rubenovitch.'

'What about?'

'Our stock has hit bottom.'

'What is bottom?' she asked, not really caring. The question and the answer were equally academic to her, although possibly of importance to investors who had bought the shares.

'Well, they paid us $100 a share. Now they are down to five dollars.'

As Jamie spoke, the teleprinter in the corner of the manager's office also began to chunter. A long strip of printed paper rolled jerkily out of its slot and then stopped. Arabella tore it off, read it. There was a long list of shares quoted on the New York Stock Exchange that had dropped even further. Then she saw the only share that interested her. Diamond-Hard was down to $4.51.

She heard a movement behind her, turned. Charles was reading the tape over her shoulder.

'I'll ring you back,' Arabella told her brother and replaced the receiver.

'I didn't hear you come in,' she said to Charles. 'Don't usually see you in the office. What brings you in this morning?'

'A certainty,' Charles replied.

'Not some gambling thing, surely?'

'No,' he said. 'I've been watching our shares fall. Do you think they'll go any lower?'

'Possibly. There's this tape in from New York. Everything there is going through the floor. It doesn't affect us, though.'

'You're wrong, Mother. It could affect us greatly.'

'How?'

'I suggest we buy the company back when we think Diamond-Hard shares have hit bottom.'

'A great idea,' said Arabella delightedly. 'I was coming round to that myself.'

'But I beat you,' said Charles, equally pleased. 'Some would say it's a gamble. That's what I like about it.'

'No,' Arabella replied. 'It's not a gamble at all. Anything but. As you said, it's a certainty.'

'You see, I'm becoming quite hard – like you,' said Charles, and kissed her.

Earlier in the year they had sold the company for a hundred million dollars. That morning they bought it back for four million. The newspapers later called this the deal of the decade. Arabella disagreed; to her it was only common sense.

As Arabella and Charles were about to leave the office, she noticed a full waste-paper basket by a secretary's desk. A shorthand pencil had been thrown away only half used. She frowned, made a mental note to speak to the manager about this. Arabella could never abide waste.

A manservant opened the door of Charles's Chelsea house to Jamie at nine o'clock on the following Saturday morning.

'I regret he is not at home, sir,' he explained. 'His lordship has gone to Brooklands for the day.'

'Racing?'

'I believe so, sir. He has taken two cars. His Bentley six and a half litre and his new Delage.'

'Will he be coming back tonight?'

'He did not acquaint me with his movements, sir. Shall I tell him you called?'

'You could,' said Jamie. 'But in the meantime, I'll go to Brooklands myself. There is something rather important I would like to see him about.'

Jamie preferred being driven to driving, and as he sat by the side of the chauffeur in his Phantom coupe, he pondered on the attraction Brooklands held for young men and women with money and a yearning for speed.

Brooklands Motor Course was originally built as an act of patriotism by a motoring enthusiast, Hugh Fortescue Locke-King, on his estate in Surrey, in the year August Stauch found diamonds in the desert. British motorists at that time were restricted by a 20 mph speed limit, while motorists on the Continent could drive their cars along wide, straight roads at any speed their cars could reach. As a result, continental cars were better designed, faster, safer and more reliable than cars made in Britain.

Locke-King decided to alter this ridiculous situation and build a track where cars of all makes and from any country could be tested and raced against each other, free of all speed restrictions. He did not seek government help or financial aid from anyone; he was a rich man and he used his own money for a purpose closest to his heart.

He engaged 2,000 workmen to build in his own grounds a concrete track, three and a quarter miles round and 100 feet wide with a banking 30 feet high. This decision was not welcomed by his neighbours, who complained that he was lowering the tone of the locality. Local doctors went so far as to claim that the noise of the cars would cause pregnant women to abort, and cows to produce curdled milk. Others said that the human body could not conceivably survive speeds of a mile a minute.

Despite this hostility, Locke-King pressed ahead with his plan. His workmen, living in huts of fir logs and corrugated iron, which reminded Jamie of Kimberley, took three months, having only Saturday and Sunday evenings free, to construct this track. It had seating for 5,000 people, and standing room for six times as many. Sentry boxes were set up every three hundred yards around the perimeter, connected by electric bells and telephones, so that in a crash or other emergency, help could quickly be available.

In the centre was the first aerodrome to be made in Britain, and here Vickers built the Vickers Vimy aircraft, in which two pilots flew the Atlantic for the first time non-stop.

The track, which covered three hundred and forty acres, soon became a social venue, like Ascot, Wimbledon, Cowes. Races were held every Saturday, except in the winter months. British, French, Italian, German and American cars and drivers competed against each other.

At first, Brooklands adopted the etiquette of horse racing. The owners of the cars did not always drive them, just as racehorse owners employed jockeys rather than ride themselves. Drivers, like jockeys, wore coloured silks; bookmakers flourished on the course; prize money was paid in sovereigns.

Before racing, the cars were inspected in an area called the Paddock, and a former Jockey Club official started each race. Throughout the week, the track was available for private races between friends and for road tests of prototypes or new models.

Jamie knew that Charles was a regular competitor in races, always with a side bet of his own. He would challenge a professional racing motor cyclist, or pit his car against an aircraft, or take part with friends the newspaper reports referred to as Bright Young Things, in more bizarre contests.

After a champagne party, the course would be opened late at night – money, Charles soon discovered was a universal key – and then the revellers might race for five laps without headlights. One lap could be driven in reverse, and one with the driver blindfolded, guided by the passenger.

Jamie had little sympathy for such wagers, which he considered pointless, but he realised that because this generation had missed a war, young people with too much money sought excitement in such ways.

A race was in progress as Jamie arrived. Half a dozen cars, glittering in the sun like brilliant blue, red, green and white beads, each buzzing like an angry wasp, followed each other round the track. They looked absurdly small and slow against the vast saucer-shaped expanse of white concrete, but he guessed that the leader was probably travelling at around 120 mph on tyres no thicker than those fitted to a motor cycle, and without any protection whatever if the car crashed or burst into flames.

Jamie told his driver to park his Rolls, and went through the tunnel beneath the track into the Paddock. Here, drivers, some in shirt sleeves, flannel trousers tucked neatly into the tops of their socks, others wearing white or coloured overalls, sat in their cars, warming up their engines. The blip and crackle of exhausts drowned all other sounds; the air felt heavy with the syrupy scent of petrol and castor-based racing oil.

Most drivers had a friend, or a professional mechanic, to help check and tune the engines of their cars. Charles had four mechanics, all wearing light blue overalls to match the paint of his Delage. On the back of these overalls was a large 'D', for Doncaster, surmounted by a coronet.

'I'm in the next race,' he explained. 'There's a lot hanging on it for me. I've a side bet with old Jacko Jackson over there. Two thousand if I win.'

'And if *he* wins?'

'He hasn't a chance. It's taking money from a blind beggar – only Jacko isn't a beggar. He's just come into a fortune from some old spinster aunt who owned her own oil well in the States.'

Jamie watched the cars leave the Paddock, heard the

crescendo of their exhausts, the faint howl of superchargers, the crackle of the commentator's voice through several loud-speakers. Within minutes, they were back.

'I've won,' said Charles simply.

'You get a cup for that?' Jamie asked him.

'And the money. Two thou. Not bad for ten minutes behind the wheel. Beat that if you can.'

'I can't,' said Jamie. 'Any more races?'

'Not today, but I've got a higher bet with him on Wednesday. You pay a fee and you can have your own private race, if you want.'

'What's the betting then?'

'Double today. He thinks he's got a chance. I know differently.'

'Is there somewhere we can talk?' Jamie asked him. 'I can hardly think here for all the noise.'

'The club house.'

Charles jumped out of his car, pulled off his overalls, took Jamie through the side entrance to another building. They sat down at a table on the verandah. Charles ordered a bottle of champagne.

'So what do you want to talk about, Uncle?' he asked.

'Money,' said Jamie. 'Your mother tells me you are handling all her affairs now.'

'That's right.'

'That's her business and yours,' said Jamie. 'But I wouldn't like to think that this money could be lost.'

'Why should it be?'

'The Rubenovitchs lost a fortune through no fault of their own when the crash came in the States.'

'I'm not a Rubenovitch. And the crash is over.'

'Financially, maybe, although things are still pretty bleak everywhere. But what if *you* crash, physically.'

'That's unlikely. I don't take risks.'

619

'All motor racing is risky.'

'So what do you want me to do?'

'Give it up. I thought you had already stopped gambling, but now you're putting your money – and your life – on the line. For what? What do you have to prove?'

'I simply don't know. I hate to hear people say I'm just a rich woman's son. I want to prove I am my own man. They bet me I can't do this or that – and I say to myself, I'll show them. And I go out and do that – like today. I race most Saturdays in the summer. And, touch wood, I've not had a crash yet.'

'If you or the fellow you bet against had one, then what?'

'Depends how bad it was.'

'My father,' said Jamie, 'used to say that all through life we were presented with signs, pointing this way or that, indicating what decisions we should make. Would a crash be a sign, make you see sense, Charles?'

'Could be. But let's keep our fingers crossed and hope that doesn't happen.'

THIRTY-FOUR

A Hard Lesson

Jamie Baird's butler opened the door to his study.

'Mr O'Malley, sir,' he announced.

Jamie crossed the carpet to meet his visitor.

'The last time we met,' he said, 'you were a Sergeant. I see you are Mister now. I hope that is promotion?'

'In a sense, sir, yes. My agency has prospered. You will see from my card, it is now O'Malley Investigations Ltd.'

'Congratulations,' said Jamie. 'But you deserve success. You did a very good job for me, I remember.'

'I thank you, sir. We endeavour to give satisfaction.'

'A drink?'

'Yes, if you please, sir. I am not technically on duty.'

Jamie poured a whisky for O'Malley, a mineral water for himself.

'Now, to business,' he said. 'Am I right in assuming that in your profession you are able to draw upon people – men and women – with special skills?'

O'Malley nodded.

'Have you on your books – or even in your firm – anyone who is an accurate rifle shot, perhaps a sharpshooter retired from the army – maybe a winner at Bisley?

'I don't mind who he or she may be, so long as they can hit a moving target from a distance of maybe one hundred and fifty yards. And, equally important, they must know how to keep a still tongue in their head.'

'I think I know such a person, sir. A corporal lately retired from the Buffs. Twenty-five years with the colours, largely in India, the North West Frontier, where accuracy with a rifle is vital. Won the inter-regimental trophy for sharpshooting three times. A record, I believe.'

'How old is he?'

'In his forties, sir.'

'I would like to see him in action before I say more about the assignment. I will, of course, pay whatever fee you, or he, require for this. Perhaps we could go to a rifle range, or a shooting club?'

'I will arrange it, sir.'

'How long will that take?'

'Today is Tuesday. Would tomorrow, Wednesday, be convenient, sir?'

'Meet me here at six o'clock.'

'Very good, sir. I take it there's not anything untoward involved? It is not an act of violence?'

'Mr O'Malley, I give you my word there is no violence or harm intended to any person. In fact, as I will explain if we go ahead, quite the reverse. I am trying to save a young man from his own folly.'

At six o'clock on Wednesday evening, Jamie sat outside his house in a taxi. He watched O'Malley and a smaller broad-shouldered man cross the gardens in the centre of Grosvenor Square. Jamie opened the door. The two men climbed in, sat side by side on the jump seats.

'I have made a booking at a shooting club in South East London,' O'Malley explained. He gave the address to the driver. The taxi took them down Piccadilly, along the Strand and Fleet Street, over Blackfriars Bridge, into an anonymous wasteland of terraced houses and corner shops. It stopped in a

622

side street opposite a corrugated-iron building, probably a war-time drill hall. The faded paint on the metal roof and walls reminded Jamie of Kimberley and Lüderitz.

'Here we are, sir,' said O'Malley.

They went into the hut. At the far end, against a thick concrete wall, stood various plywood cut-outs of men and animals and target cards. The air smelt slightly of cordite and rifle oil.

A man in his shirt sleeves, with tattooed forearms and heavy rings on all his fingers, shuffled towards them.

'I understand you want a moving target?' he said without any preamble.

'Yes,' O'Malley agreed.

The man began to turn a handle connected by a cord round pulleys to the outline of a German soldier against the wall.

'A leftover from the last struggle, sir,' he explained to Jamie. As he wound, the figure moved jerkily from left to right.

'Is that the sort of thing you had in mind?'

'No,' said Jamie. 'It's far too slow.'

'A matter of changing the gearing, sir,' the man replied. 'Give me a moment.'

He picked up a large metal wheel, toothed all round its edge, fitted this to a smaller cog wheel, and began to turn. Now the target leapt across the wall.

Jamie nodded. The proprietor handed the sharpshooter a rifle. He slipped a bullet into the breech, raised the rifle to his right shoulder.

'When you're ready, Bert,' he said.

The tattooed man spun the wheel. The rifle cracked like a circus whip. As the sharpshooter lowered it, a pale wisp of smoke drifted out of the muzzle.

'A perfect hit,' said O'Malley triumphantly. 'Have a look for yourself, sir.'

He handed Jamie a pair of opera glasses. O'Malley was right.

The marksman had hit the cut-out between the second and third fingers.

'Do it again, twice, to show this isn't a fluke,' Jamie told him. 'Then we will talk business.'

He wanted to be certain that this was not a chance success which he could not repeat.

The ex-corporal fired two more rounds. Each hit the target in exactly the same place.

'Excellent,' said Jamie approvingly. He led the way out to the taxi.

'Do you know a public house, a snug, where we can talk?'

'I do indeed, sir,' said O'Malley and gave the driver instructions.

They went in through the public bar, where music-hall play-bills decorated the walls, into a small bar with four chairs and a table; it reminded Jamie of the private bar in the Silent Witness. He sat down at the table, ordered whisky for his two guests, a mineral water for himself.

'Right,' said Jamie. 'I want you both to understand that what I am about to say is totally in confidence. Is that fully and absolutely understood?'

The two men nodded.

'Right,' said Jamie. 'Now, this is what I want you to do . . .'

The sharpshooter left the Southern Electric train from Waterloo at Byfleet Station, walked past the sign on the platform: *Alight here for Brooklands Motor Racing Course.*

He wore a tweed jacket and trousers and heavy boots, carried a fishing-rod case with a brown canvas bag slung over his shoulder.

Only two other people left the train with him. There was no racing at Brooklands mid-week, and Wednesday was early closing in Byfleet. He reached the edge of the banking near the railway line. The banked track high above his head was supported on a high ridge of earth by a mass of beams and girders, like the underside of a huge fairground switchback. Trees and thick bushes shielded this from the road.

The sharpshooter pulled on his gloves to protect his hands from splinters, and also to prevent him leaving fingerprints. Then, he climbed up the bank of earth. On top, he crouched in a clump of trees on the rim of the track. By some trick of acoustics he could hear the faint, angry growl of exhausts as mechanics in tuning sheds in the centre of the track worked on clients' engines. A train on the main line rumbled past behind him, its engine trailing a blue frond of smoke.

His instructions were to hit the right-hand front tyre of a black Duesenberg car racing against a green Bentley. No other cars would be on the track that afternoon, so there was no chance of making a mistake.

A distant roar of engines rose to a crescendo; the cars must have started early. He picked up his rifle, watched the two cars come into focus through his telescopic sight. He could see the white linen helmets and dark green goggles of the drivers, crouched behind their steering wheels. The cars drew level with him, raced past, almost side by side. They seemed fairly evenly matched. He estimated their speed at between 80 and 90 mph. He would aim one length ahead for the first shot, and if he missed, try two lengths ahead for a second.

Charles came down off the banking into the straight by the pits, pulled over to the side, cut his engine. The heavy Bentley coasted to a standstill.

He was the better driver; he knew that. Jackson might be as quick on the straight, but lacked courage on the curves. Jackson now pulled in ahead of Charles, stopped his engine.

'How's that for a warm-up?' he shouted, pushing his goggles up on his forehead.

Charles smiled. The Duesenberg engine displaced nearly

seven litres to the Bentley's six and a half, had eight cylinders to the Bentley's six, but it was heavy and clumsy. This fellow *could* beat him, and he could not afford to be beaten, not this time. Too much depended on the outcome of this race.

'Idea,' he said brightly. 'Double the bet – if I drive your car and you drive mine.'

Jackson looked puzzled.

'We are already playing for pretty high stakes,' he said cautiously.

Jackson eased himself out of the cockpit, as he pondered the proposition. This kid was an idiot; no question of it. He had taken large sums off many a rich young driver in the past, and now he was determined to take Charles for even more. This fellow had too high an opinion of himself, he thought. These young people who had not made the money themselves were all the same.

'Right,' said Jackson shortly. 'Double it is. You're on.'

At that moment, Jamie arrived. He climbed out of his car, walked across the hot, oil-stained concrete to the pits.

'Why, Uncle!' said Charles, pleased to see him. 'You're not putting money on me?'

'I'm not,' Jamie replied. 'I'm just interested in hoping you don't lose.'

'I won't,' Charles, assured him. 'Anyway, I've not seen any sign yet that I should give up – win or lose.'

'How many times did your father tell moneylenders that? How many times did he tell *himself* that? And every time he was proved wrong.'

'My father was a fine man,' said Charles defensively. 'He had bad luck.'

'There's no such thing as good luck or bad luck. We make our own good luck. He didn't make enough. I don't want to see you do the same.'

'Why should I?'

'You let these professional gamblers niggle you, push you over the brink. You're their living. Do you imagine this will be a fair race?'

'Why shouldn't it be?'

'Because too much is at stake, that's why. You stand to inherit a huge company. I'm asking you, Charles. Back out of this race. Pay the man off if you have to, but *don't do it*.'

After this race, Charles told himself, he should stop. He knew that, admitted it to himself. But – could he? Anyway, he couldn't conceivably back out now. But he recognised the truth in Jamie's concern for him.

'I *have* to,' he said. 'I've given my word.'

Jackson called to him from across the track.

'Ready when you are.'

'Wish me luck, Uncle,' said Charles.

He climbed into the black car.

'You're not driving that!' Jamie cried.

'But I am. We've just agreed.'

'You can't drive it. It's ... it's ...' Jamie dredged for words. 'It's unlucky!'

'You're joking, Uncle. It was lucky for me that I changed bows at school in the archery contest. Remember?'

'Of course I remember. But that was totally different. So much more hangs on this.'

Jamie could not tell Charles that his life could hang on it. Somewhere, hidden in the bushes high on the edge of the curved banking, between the green of the trees and the blue of the sky, the sharpshooter was watching – and waiting. It was impossible to warn him there had been a change of drivers, to tell him not to shoot at the black car, not to shoot at all.

'I beg you, don't drive that car!' Jamie cried in anguish.

'Why not? It's a damned good car. A bit heavy, but I just want to show Jackson I can beat him in either car. That an American car can trounce a British one.'

'There's more to it than that. I can't tell you now.'

Jamie could see mechanics looking at him, surprised at the urgency in his voice. He went up to Charles.

'Keep out of that bloody car!'

'Never seen you so rattled, Uncle. But there's always a first time, I suppose. Anyhow, I've given my word. I'd like to make you happy, Uncle, but I can't back down now. You must see that.'

He climbed in behind the wheel, adjusted the chinstrap on his leather helmet, pulled down the tinted goggles over his eyes.

Jamie stared at him, mesmerised. He could be looking at a man blindfolded before he faced a firing squad. He felt he was looking at a man about to die.

'Don't go!' he shouted. 'That car . . . !'

The rest of his desperate last warning was lost in the crackle of the Duesenberg's exhaust.

Charles began to drive slowly towards the starting line. Gouts of smoke blew out of the metal fish tail at the end of the exhaust pipe. A mechanic, neat in immaculate overalls, was walking beside the car. Jamie ran behind them, beat with the back of his hand on the hot black metal.

'Get out!' he shouted, 'Get *out!*'

But Charles, helmet flaps over his ears, could only shake his head. He did not hear. He did not want to hear. The race was the thing.

The two cars lined up side by side, front wheels on a white line painted across the track. An official held a stopwatch in one hand, a flag in the other above his head.

The flag dropped, wheels spun, streaming gouts of smoke and hot rubber. Then the tyres bit and the cars were away. The roar of their exhausts rose to a crescendo, died as the drivers changed gear, rose again in a shimmering haze of blue smoke as the cars began to climb the banking.

Jamie turned away. He felt physically sick. His heart was beating like a maddened drum. Instead of trying to ensure that Charles would win the race, he had practically guaranteed that he would lose it. It seemed unbelievable that an attempt to help his nephew could go so terribly wrong.

He stood for a moment, wondering whether he should rush out on to the track and try to stop the race on any pretext. But as he considered whether he could do that the cars came round, drivers crouched low behind their tiny aero screens, and were gone, on their second lap. Jamie could not bear to stay a moment longer. He walked slowly towards his own car, not really seeing anyone, scarcely knowing where he was, even who he was. He climbed into the back of the car, sank thankfully into the cushions. He felt defeated, totally deflated.

He should wait; he knew that. But for some reason, he could not. He should have stopped Charles by any means whatever; he had not. And now it was too late. He must get away before the crash occurred. If he stayed a moment longer, he might admit everything in the heat of his anguish. He had to go now.

'Home,' Jamie told the chauffeur. He closed his eyes as the great car glided forward towards the main road.

High up on the edge of the track, the marksman heard the drone of exhausts as the cars approached. He took aim, followed the black car out of sight. It seemed faster now, was leading by at least a length. Then the Bentley overtook it – and stayed in front. The driver held his line on the track, while the other man seemed to weave up and down the banking, as though he was not used to the car, as though its weight and power were really in control, not him.

The sharpshooter waited for the cars to pass him a second time. On the third lap, they were almost level, wheel to wheel. He drew a bead on the black car's front tyre as it came into his line of sight. He followed it round, then gently squeezed the trigger.

629

The noise of the shot was no louder than a small dry twig breaking. Instantly, the black car slowed, suddenly veered down the banking. The metal rim of its front wheel scored a stream of sparks from the concrete. The sharpshooter could see the driver wrestle frantically with the steering wheel. The two cars had been racing only feet apart. Now as the Duesenberg swung to the left, the driver of the Bentley pulled over to avoid it – but too late. The two vehicles touched briefly at 100 miles an hour with a great clanging of metal. Then the Bentley slithered down the track, a rear tyre torn off. The black car slewed away to the right, pivoting on the wheel rim, and shot up towards the top of the banking. Its three good tyres smoked, laying streaks of black rubber on the track as the driver braked frantically, trying desperately to control two tons of metal gone mad.

The punctured tyre hung in threads, ribbons of rubber flailing the track with each turn of the wheel. Then its rim caught the edge of the banking. In what seemed like slow motion the car rolled forward, over the top. For a second it reared up, nose in the air. The driver was flung out backwards on to the track. Then the car dipped down, plunged forward and was gone.

All around him, the marksman heard the crash of branches breaking as the Duesenberg catapulted through the trees.

Methodically, the marksman dismantled his rifle, put it in the case, climbed down on to the road. This was still deserted. He felt certain that no one had seen him arrive or leave. There was no need even to reverse his jacket. He walked back to the station, caught the next train, not back to London, but down the line to Woking. There he got out, let the next train to London pass, and jumped on the second one.

As Arabella's Rolls drew up outside her London home, reporters who had been sitting in their own little cars, awaiting her arrival, jumped out to greet her. She looked at them in surprise. What could they possibly want? Her footman opened the front door of her house as they crowded around her.

'We are very sorry to hear the news, Lady Doncaster,' said one gravely.

'Our deepest sympathy from the editor of *The Globe*,' said another. 'And could we please have your exclusive views on speed and the young, and the price they pay for excitement?'

'Did you know what the wager was?' asked a third.

'I don't know what you are talking about,' said Arabella, bewildered by these questions. 'Why should any editor extend his sympathy to me? What is happening?'

The Enquirer reporter, older than the others, coughed deprecatingly.

'You may not have heard, Lady Doncaster, but your son has been involved in a motoring accident.'

'Charles? When? Where? Is he badly hurt? What happened? Is he . . . ?' – she could not bring herself to pronounce the word 'dead'.

As she spoke, the reporters moved back, so that although she appeared surrounded by them, they were suddenly at a distance, and she stood in the centre of a circle of silent, watchful men, a strangely forlorn lonely figure. They had assumed she already knew about the accident.

'Have you heard anything about this?' Arabella asked her footman.

'In an edition of the evening paper, your ladyship, there was a Stop Press paragraph to the effect that Lord Doncaster had been injured in a motor race at Brooklands.'

'But there's no racing today at Brooklands. It's Wednesday.'

'The track can be hired by private people for testing cars – or racing them,' another reporter explained.

'I see. So where is he? In hospital? Do you know?'

She turned to the reporters now, seeking their help, heedless

631

of the fact that next day their accounts would dwell in detail on her questions, each one putting his own interpretation on the scene. ('Bravely fighting back tears from her astonishingly beautiful face, the multimillionairess Lady Arabella Doncaster, one of the world's most successful women, heard the tragic news yesterday . . .')

Arabella went up the steps into her house, not looking at any of the reporters. Jamie was waiting for her in the hall. She glanced at him questioningly, not wishing to put into words a request for details she desperately wanted to know.

'Where is he?' she asked him.

'In hospital.'

'Haven't they moved him?'

'Not yet,' Jamie replied, smiling. 'There's no reason to. He's comfortable where he is.'

'You mean he's all right? He isn't dead?'

'Charles has broken both legs and has a couple of black eyes, but he is not in any danger. If I know him, he's already sitting up in bed, chatting up the nurses, offering them champagne. He's very much alive!'

'He can't be,' said Arabella hoarsely, desperately wanting to believe, yet afraid to do so.

'It *is* so. My car is in the mews at the back of the house, away from all the reporters. Let's go and see him right away. Then maybe you'll believe me.'

Charles was sitting up in bed, as Jamie had guessed, but he was not drinking champagne. His face was purple with bruises, both eyes puffed up, so that he could scarcely see. A metal cage kept the weight of the sheets and blankets from his legs. The air in the room felt heavy with the scent of flowers. They cascaded in a blaze of colour from vases, bowls, sprays, on tables, windowsills, even on the floor.

'If you receive this number of bouquets from your friends

when you've only had an accident,' said Jamie, 'just imagine your funeral!'

'I don't want to think about it. That was a close-run thing this afternoon,' said Charles, trying to smile. 'As near as I ever want to go.'

Arabella kissed him, sat down by the side of the bed.

'You had me very worried,' she said.

'I had myself very worried,' Charles admitted. 'A tyre burst – and I wasn't used to the car. It felt heavy as lead. All I remember is trying to hold her in a straight line, but I failed. Worse still, I lost the bet. I'd doubled the stakes and switched cars. I was an idiot. You warned me against it, Uncle, and you were right. I was a bloody fool. The irony is the other fellow didn't want to up the ante. But I suppose he thought I'd consider him yellow if he didn't. Now he must be laughing his head off.'

'I think that's rather an exaggeration, Charles,' said Jamie.

'Why? I challenged him. First car home after five laps is the winner. That was the wager. And I lost it.'

'But he didn't win it, either. He never crossed the line.'

'What d'you mean?'

'What I say. When your tyre burst, and centrifugal force pulled your car up the banking, you fought it, turned the steering wheel full lock the other way – and your car hit his.'

'*He* isn't dead, is he?'

'No. Not hurt at all, except possibly in his expectations. You caught his rear wheel, burst the tyre. The tread wound itself round his rear axle and the car stopped. So no one won. Honours even.'

'You mean that?'

'Absolutely. I didn't come all the way here simply to make it up.'

Charles gave a sigh of relief, lay back against the pillows, eyes closed.

A sister came into the room.

'I don't think you should stay any longer,' she said disapprovingly. 'You are tiring him. He's had a very bad shock.'

'You're wrong,' reported Charles, opening his eyes. 'I've just had a very good one.'

'D'you remember how I once told you that your grandfather used to say that all through life we see signs that can point us along one course or another?' Jamie asked him.

'I remember.'

'Seems to me that your accident is the clearest possible sign that you should give up racing and gambling. If you don't, the next sign could be pointing towards the graveyard.'

Charles nodded.

'I follow your reasoning,' he said. 'Both points taken. No more gambling.'

He smiled and tried to wink at his mother.

'Except, of course, on certainties.'

THIRTY-FIVE

Echoes From the Past

When General Brookes retired, he received a knighthood for what the *London Gazette* described cautiously as 'political and public services'.

How political, how public – or, indeed, how private – many of these services had been, the general never divulged, and steadfastly refused all offers from publishers and newspapers to tell the story of his remarkable life.

In retirement, the general and his wife lived between a large flat in South Kensington and a small manor house in Dorset. When his wife died, and without any children who might make use of a country house, the general sold up and retreated to his flat.

From then on, his life tended to follow a set pattern. His housekeeper would bring him breakfast in bed (black coffee, porridge, a soft-boiled egg). He would then read *The Times* and *The Enquirer*, have a bath and, according to the weather, either walk or take a taxi to his club. Here, he would drink two large gin and limes, without ice, and hope that some contemporary would join him for lunch.

In the afternoon he would fall asleep in front of the fire until a club waiter woke him with Earl Grey tea and buttered toast and Patum Peperium.

More and more, General Brookes found names of friends and colleagues, with whom he had served in the Army or the Intelligence Service, appearing in the Deaths columns each morning, and each time he read a familiar name he did so with genuine surprise. He had never imagined So-and-so must have been very ill for years, but had bravely managed to conceal this. He wished he had been kinder to someone else when he had the chance, for now all thoughts and regrets of that kind came too late.

On this particular morning, the general scanned the Deaths columns and thankfully found no one whose name meant anything to him. He then turned to the Personal columns. One name immediately caught his attention.

'Provost,' he read. 'Will anyone having knowledge of the whereabouts of Mr Jamie Provost, who was in Petrograd, now Leningrad, Russia, before and during the Great War, please contact the undersigned where they may hear something to their advantage.' There was no name, only an address in South London.

The general put down the paper, pushed his glasses up on his forehead. Provost. The name rang a distant bell, long silenced by other more recent involvements. Then he remembered Provost had been the name he had chosen for the false passport he had given to Jamie Baird, when he went to Russia, just before the revolution. Baird had been arrested, and in those feverish days could well have been summarily executed as a spy. Many had been. But Baird had managed to buy his release with the promise of a shipment of grain.

Brookes recalled how he had agreed to help Baird keep his promise. But the British Army was in Russia, fighting the Bolsheviks. Brookes could not possibly send food to the enemy, and he had done nothing. He didn't expect Baird ever knew this, or if he did, that he would understand his delicate situation. You couldn't expect these business chappies to appreciate military matters; making money was the only thing that counted with them.

Could someone be wanting to contact Baird now? Who else besides himself knew Provost's real identity? There could not be too many left alive who remembered the affair. Captain Drake had come into a fortune unexpectedly and had drunk himself to death. The Army clerks were goodness knew where; dead, as like as not. The message somehow sounded false to the general. It could even be a trap, a hook to catch someone – but who? And why?

Were the Communists trying to draw Provost back, as they had lured other former British agents to Russia by claiming to be White Russians, opposed to the Bolsheviks, when in fact the reverse was the case? Well, that was not his affair now, thank goodness. The matter was no concern of his.

But, at the club that morning, the general had second thoughts. He must be one of the few, if not the only person, who knew why Baird had gone to Russia – except for Baird himself, of course. A few others might still be around who knew he had gone, but not the reason why. That made it all the more interesting to discover who now was advertising for information. What information did they want? What could anyone now learn to their advantage about this episode of long ago?

He went into the library, took down the latest issue of *Who's Who*, copied out Jamie's address and read a line beneath the entry: 'See also Lady Doncaster.' Underneath her entry was a private address near Kleinmond, South Africa.

He looked up Jamie Baird's number in the London telephone book and, on the impulse, rang him. A manservant answered, explained courteously that Mr Baird was out of the country. He had left no forwarding address, and there was no means of contacting him. All mail was being held for him to peruse on his return. His staff had no date when they expected him back.

General Brookes thought that Lady Doncaster might have some more definite news of her brother. A spokesman at her headquarters told him that she was at present in South Africa. Kleinmond, he thought, meaning 'little world'. The world was indeed a small place; often too small.

He had met Lady Doncaster only briefly, and he had almost forgotten about Jamie Baird, but now that he had been reminded, the memory would not go away.

The general did nothing more about the advertisement that day, but next morning he put on an old tweed suit and took a stick – a legacy of the past when every British agent was issued with an innocuous-seeming walking stick or umbrella, actually a swordstick.

Years of training persuaded him against arriving at a humble address in South London by taxi. This could only arouse interest and curiosity in an area where taxis would rarely be used, and after a lifetime in the shadows he knew what folly this could be.

Accordingly, General Brookes travelled by bus, making two changes which were largely unnecessary, but which, again, his training had taught him could be advisable, to shake off any possible follower. No one, however, walked along the seedy street – either behind him or, as professionals followed a suspect, on the other side of the road – to the address in the newspaper.

The houses appeared virtually identical, except for their curtains. Each had a bay window in the front room, facing a tiny patch of sooty garden, guarded by metal railings. A speculative builder had built them years before, to be bought by clerks and under-managers. Gradually, the area had sunk socially, and now the houses were split up into single rooms, bedsitters, to be rented by people either on their way up in the world, or, more frequently, on their way down.

On one side of the front door of the house he sought, bellpushes had names pinned on pieces of cardboard beneath them. They meant nothing to him: Mulrooney, Soames, Black, Jones. He pressed each one in turn. There was no answer from any of them. He banged on the knocker.

A woman, curlers still in her hair, an inch of dirty petticoat showing under a stained skirt, stockingless feet in faded, floppy slippers, opened the door to him, looked at him in silent inquiry. She carried an over-fed cat in her arms; an unlighted cigarette hung damp and brown between her lips. A faint and disagreeable smell of cat urine seeped out from the narrow hall.

'I've come in response to an advertisement in *The Enquirer*,' General Brookes explained. He didn't know the advertiser's name because the advertiser hadn't given it.

'Top floor,' the woman said at once. 'Mr Soames.'

'How do you know?'

'Because he told me he was putting the advert in. That's how. He's up there now. He almost never goes out.'

The general pushed past her, climbing stairs with worn lino treads, greasy wallpaper on one side where too many dirty coats had rubbed away the flock, a banister sticky with handprints on the other. He reached the top landing, knocked on the only door. He could hear breathing behind it, soft and laboured. No one answered. He called out.

'Your advertisement in *The Enquirer*,' he said. 'About Mr Provost. Petrograd.'

'Come in,' said a voice.

The general entered the room. It was very dark inside, with newspapers pasted across the windows. There were no curtains. A sash cord had broken and the windows were jammed shut with wooden wedges. The air smelt sour and stale. On a narrow bed a man lay under a mass of blankets and rugs. He was unshaven and old. He peered up at Brookes shortsightedly, as though hoping to see someone he knew. His disappointment showed when he did not recognise the general.

'Who are you?' he asked flatly.

'Name of Brookes. A friend of Mr Provost.'

'How do I know that?'

'I was involved with a government department. I asked him to go to Russia years ago,' said Brookes carefully. 'And who are you, sir?'

639

The man reached under his bed, pulled out an attaché case, opened it, handed Brookes a letter. It was well thumbed. Too many people had read it, fingered it over too many years, and handed it back again.

Brookes read the salient points '. . . will introduce Mr Mikhail Serov. I can personally recommend him as an accurate and swift translator.' It was signed by a Fourth Secretary in the British Embassy in Russia in 1913. A long time ago, thought Brookes. That man went on to become an ambassador and was now retired.

Brookes handed the letter back to Serov. He folded it up carefully, replaced it in the case, sank back on his soiled pillow, as though the effort had exhausted him.

'How well do you know Mr Provost?' he asked.

'I haven't seen him for years,' Brookes admitted. 'But I could get in contact with him.'

'Provost was not his real name,' said Serov.

'Why did you advertise for Provost, when you knew that?'

'Provost was the name on his passport, that's why. His real name was Baird.'

Serov leaned out of the bed again, searched through other papers in the attaché case, this time came up with an envelope. There was a signature across the flap. The general could make out only one word – Katharina. This name echoed faintly down the long aisles of his memory. Baird had told him he wanted to bring out a girl of that name, a grand duchess or something, and marry her. But of course they were all archdukes or grand duchesses then. And what were they now? Where were they now, if they survived? Driving taxicabs in Paris, or working in restaurants.

'I have not been well,' Serov explained. 'I got out of Russia at last, after a long long time, and was allowed into Britain. I used to do a lot of work for the British Embassy in the old days. That counted when I wanted to come here.

'I wanted to give this note to Mr Provost personally, but I don't know where he lives. He may even be dead now. So many people I knew then are, from natural causes or not. The Communists have long arms, and even longer memories. They don't forget easily. And they never forgive.'

'Am I to give this letter to Mr Provost – if I can find him?' asked Brookes. It was odd how both of them still used the false name. That came from living in the shadows for too long; deception and illusion became a way of life.

He felt suddenly anxious to be away. As his eyes had become accustomed to the gloom, he saw Serov's face more clearly. His cheeks had sunk in. The bones were like a framework on which the flesh stretched, tight as skin on a drum. He was clearly very ill; Brooke guessed he was dying.

He wanted to escape into the fresh air, away from the old memories of a dying man in a rented room, away from archdukes and archduchesses, and his own betrayal. Baird had kept his side of the bargain; Brookes knew he had not.

He took out his wallet. 'Here's a present,' he said. 'Buy yourself a few bottles.' He gave Serov a £10 note.

'Thank you,' said Serov gratefully, feeling the note between his thumb and forefinger. 'Will you let me know when you see Mr Provost? It is very important. For him, more than for me.'

'Yes. Do you know what is in the letter?'

'I can guess. You know where I live. What is your address, Mr Brookes?'

The general gave him a card. Serov peered at it in the dim light. His face lit up as he read it.

'Why – a general and a *knight*,' he said, impressed. 'I am honoured!' He held out his hand. It felt thin as a handful of brittle bones.

'Goodbye, then,' said Brookes.

He went down the stairs thankfully. He thought wryly of the text he used to have in his office: 'The race is not to the swift, nor the battle to the strong, neither yet bread to the wise, nor yet riches to men of understanding, nor yet favour to men of skill; but time and chance happeneth to them all.'

Time and chance. Good luck or bad. You were in the right place – or the wrong one – at the right or the wrong time. On such permutations of time and chance, empires fell and fortunes were founded.

The woman with the cat was waiting for him in the hall.

'You're not a doctor, are you?' she asked Brookes.

'No. Why?'

'He needs a doctor, does Mr Soames. He's got cancer.'

'How do you know?'

'Because my doctor came and had a look at him. Said he should go into hospital, have it seen to. But he won't budge. Of course, he's got no money.'

'How is he with the rent? Behind?'

'He owes me a month. Ten pounds.'

The general took out his wallet, gave her two £10 notes.

'My name's Brookes,' he said, and gave her the address of his club. 'Write to me when you need some more.'

'You're very kind, sir,' said the woman, suddenly respectful at the sight of money. 'A friend of his, are you?'

'Friend of a friend, actually. From the old days,' he added vaguely. 'Tell me, where has he got cancer?'

'In the stomach. It gives him gyp from time to time, I can tell you. There's no cure, of course. Funny thing, he says he got it through swallowing diamonds in Russia during the revolution. Had them in his stomach for some time apparently. So he says. He'd pass them out and wash them and swallow them again.'

She paused, as though suddenly unwilling to continue. Brookes recognised the signs, took another note from his wallet, handed it to her.

'What else does he say?' he asked casually.

'Oh, odd things. I think he's a bit gone really. One screw loose, if you understand me. About these diamonds, for instance. He said he'd got word somehow from some contact in the secret police – imagine! – that a foreign visitor had a false bottom in his suitcase for smuggling jewels. He got into this man's hotel room – another contact, if you can believe it – and found these stones all right, but they were fakes, worthless.'

Again she paused.

'So what did he do then?'

'He took them out and put the real diamonds in their place.'

'What did he do with the fakes?'

'Stuck 'em in a goldfish bowl and then called the police to say he'd found them and they were worth a fortune. He hoped to do a deal with them, with Lenin or something – I don't know all the ins and outs of it – so he could be allowed to leave Russia. Then he would go with the foreigner, and once over the frontier he'd remove the real diamonds and Bob's your uncle – he's rich.'

'But it didn't work out like that?'

' 'Course it didn't. It's all in his mind, if you ask me. He claims some maid working for the Tsar's wife shopped him. Sounds rubbish to me. Can you believe it, Mr Brookes?'

'Sometimes I don't know what to believe. But one thing I have learned in life, truth is often so fantastic that no one would ever believe it.'

'You've got something there, all right,' the woman agreed, and watched the general go down the street. There was a lot in what he said, she thought. Perhaps there was everything. Then she went to feed her cat; she thought he was looking a bit peaky.

General Brookes sat in his club, reading the letter Serov had given to him. As he read, he felt transported back in time to the revolution, to nightmare years of hatred, treachery, murder, imprisonment without reason, without hope. The writer described a loneliness and loss so desolate and so prolonged that Brookes felt ashamed at his own part in these events.

A lifetime in the shadowy half-world of espionage had long ago suppressed his own assessment of what was right or wrong. In the end, these considerations had virtually ceased to exist. Too often, he had chosen the expedient course, regardless of any moral argument, because it was easiest, or might cause less trouble if something went wrong; or perhaps because he thought that truth or honour could be temporarily ignored in what he felt then were his country's interests.

It had been impossible for him to become involved in sending grain to Russia during the revolution, but he need not have promised to do so and then reneged on his word. He could easily have helped Serov to leave Russia when he so desperately wanted to escape – all manner of secret exchanges were arranged for agents of either side – but he had done nothing. Yet Serov had, in his day, been very useful to the British Embassy. When his usefulness was over, and the Bolsheviks moved in, Brookes abandoned him; he was expendable. The more Brookes thought about the matter, the more uneasy he became.

That afternoon he went to see the club secretary in his office.

'You have teleprinter facilities here, I believe?' he asked him.

'We do, sir. Just been installed. Remarkably efficient.'

'If I pay for whatever the transmission costs, can I send a message to someone in South Africa?'

'If they have a machine at the other end, most certainly, sir.'

'I am sure they have. I would like this message to go as soon as possible to Lady Arabella Doncaster, Kleinmond, near Cape Town.'

He gave the man her full address. The secretary glanced at his watch.

'There's a two-hour time difference. Would you like it to go now?'

'That would mean she will receive it around six this evening? Good. She'll probably be at home then. Cocktail time out there, as I recall.'

THIRTY-SIX

Lost and Found

Arabella's Rolls stopped outside her house in Kleinmond. She climbed out, walked through the side door that led directly on to a shaded terrace overlooking the ocean. She poured herself an iced orange juice, and sat down in a cane chair, looking at the pounding waves.

The butler appeared in the doorway.

'I have put the guest in the blue room as you asked, your ladyship. First, she wished to go back to Cape Town, where she had left her case as security at the hotel where she was staying. Following your instructions, your ladyship, the under chauffeur drove her in the small car.'

'Good. When is she coming back?'

'As a matter of fact, she returned about half an hour ago. She is in her room.'

'Please ask her to join me for a drink.'

The butler bowed his acknowledgement. 'There is one other thing, your ladyship. A teleprinter message has just arrived.'

'Who from?'

'A General Brookes in London.'

'Oh, yes. I met him once. When Mr Baird came back from Russia, the general came to my house in London. I don't know his job, exactly!'

'If I may say so, your ladyship, I was in a field security

section during the war. The general was involved then at a high level with intelligence matters.'

He handed her the teleprinted message. Arabella put on her reading glasses.

From General Sir Kirby Brookes. Personal for Mr Jamie Baird, by way of Lady Doncaster. Begins: In *The Enquirer*, an advertisement has appeared seeking news of Mr Provost, in Russia during the revolution. Knowing Mr Provost's identity, I contacted the advertiser, a Russian refugee, one Mikhail Serov, now in reduced circumstances, living in a bedsitter in South London.

He handed me a letter which I reproduce below. You will note from the date that it is some years old. He had no explanation for keeping it for so long. I did not ask him. I think he is very ill and perhaps unhinged by his experiences in his own country. I have taken the liberty of opening the letter and transmitting it by teleprinter to diminish any further delay.

Letter begins: Dear Scotsman, you were always so proud of being Scottish, as opposed to English, and remembering your national pride has helped me to maintain my own pride and sanity in all the lonely years since we parted.

I was told you had defaulted on a promise to send a shipload of grain to alleviate hunger, which was the reason I was put into what Party members call protective custody, but which I call prison.

I was several times assured that when this grain arrived, I would be free to join you in England. But it did not arrive, or if it did, the shipment was not ascribed to you, so I was not allowed to leave. Nor have I been permitted to return to my own home, so I must assume that everything there has been lost.

At first, I felt very sad that furniture and paintings I had grown up with – which in many cases had been in my family for hundreds of years – had probably been looted or just wantonly destroyed, as we saw for ourselves. What hurt me most was that my child would never see them. But then I realised that neither would I. So I have grown to accept what I cannot change.

I was sent to a 'camp of correction' where my baby was born. Each day I worked in the fields, picking root crops. When the earth was frozen, I had to sew shirts in a large building with other women.

This caused my eyesight to fail, and my general health deteriorated. I was allowed to keep my child for some years, but then a woman being released unexpectedly said she would take the child, claiming it as her own.

She had been a lady's maid to the Tsarina and had some liaison with Serov. I do not know why she was arrested – her husband was killed in the Great War – or why she was freed. We prisoners do not learn the reasons for many things.

I felt sad at losing my child, but yet relieved, since this seemed the only possible hope I would have of giving her any sort of freedom.

I kept your watch under a bandage, as you suggested, and gave it to this woman, telling her to take out stones for herself to cover her expenses and then to pass on the watch to my child – your child, Catherine.

Maybe you will never receive this letter. I can only hope. Even if you do, there is no way we can communicate. I do not have a name now, only a number. But sometimes, in the hut, where we huddle together for warmth at night, I try to imagine I am back on a summer lake in a boat with you. Or again, I dream of the ball where we danced together for the first and last time. Or of the night we spent in the city they now call Leningrad, as a result of which my daughter – *our* daughter – was born.

We may never meet again, dear Jamie, at least in this world. But we did meet and we did love each other. Love is not something everyone knows, but I knew it. And so, I hope, did you. I will remember you for the rest of my life. Please remember me. Not as I am now, but as I was, as we both were, Scotsman.

With my love always, Katharina.

Arabella put down the pages, took off her spectacles as her visitor came out on to the terrace. She was tall and dark, and moved with the grace of a wild creature.

'What will you have to drink, Catherine?' she asked her.

'An orange juice, please, Lady Doncaster.' She sat down.

'You must stay here as long as you like,' continued Arabella. 'Look on this as your home. When you arrived just after lunch, your story sounded extraordinary. But now I accept it all, every word. You are indeed the daughter of the Archduchess Katharina Sokolov, a member of one of the richest families in old Russia. Tell me, how did you get from what they now call Leningrad to Paris, where your grandmother brought you up?'

The girl smiled. 'More easily than you might think, Lady Doncaster.'

She took a small handkerchief from her pocket, unfolded it. In the centre lay a watch. The leather strap was cracked, the edge of the dial pitted with small holes. Each, Arabella knew, had once contained a diamond.

Arabella opened her handbag, took out the second diamond-studded wrist watch Colonel Dugdale had given to Jamie, held it side by side with Catherine's battered, scratched watch.

'They are the same,' said Catherine in surprise, 'except yours is smaller, a woman's watch.'

'Someone gave them both to my brother years ago,' Arabella explained.

'My mother kept this in the camp all the time, hidden by a bandage. Even I had no idea, until she gave it to me. I will never part with it now.'

'And now you have come all this way to find your father?'

Catherine nodded.

'But how did you find me? How did you know who I was?'

'A long story. But, briefly, in Paris, where an awful lot of refugees from the old days in Russia are living, one of them was a man called Serov. He said he had known my father in Petrograd. He told me his name. Then it was only a matter of looking him up in *Who's Who*. I tried to contact him through his office several times, but I could never reach him. I never even got a reply to my letters.'

'There's a reason for that, Catherine. When you are rich, so many people send you begging letters claiming relationship, friendship, anything, and asking for money, either for themselves, or to promote some mad scheme or other.

'We have a rule that our personal secretaries destroy them all and never reply. Yours must have been among them, I am sorry to say.'

'I'm sorry, too, as I could have found you so much sooner. Then I saw a mention of you and my father in a newspaper and I looked you up and found you had a house here. I sold the last of the diamonds in that watch to pay my fare – and here I am.

'Where is my father now? Is he staying here with you?'

'No. He is still in Lüderitz with his aeroplane. I tried to phone him earlier, but he was out. I will try again in a minute. But first, I would like you to read this.'

She handed Catherine the teleprinter message.

'I have just received it from the person who originally sent your father to Russia.'

As Arabella watched Catherine read the message with

mounting amazement, she suddenly remembered the picture on the cover of the magazine *Great Friends* she had bought at the bookstall on Exchange Station minutes before her father fell under the train.

Catherine's face, grave, intent, reminded her of the face of the girl in that picture, with a village church and a lawn behind her. At one time, to live in such a village had seemed the ultimate of Arabella's ambition. Now, she owned that village, and sometimes forgot just how many other possessions as well.

She also remembered the motto she had chosen for her crest: 'I pay all debts.' She had been so proud of this, felt that the words epitomised her own hardness of character, but now she was not so sure. In the light of what Catherine had told her, they seemed cheap and boastful. No one could ever pay all the debts they owed to others, not necessarily in money but in time, in help, encouragement, friendship. Only God paid all debts, and He never left a debt outstanding.

She wondered about this girl's mother, Katharina. She would like to have known her, to have been her sister by marriage. Katharina had inherited a fortune and lost everything except the most valuable treasure of all that no one could steal from her: the memory of love. Arabella had made her own fortune, but in doing so, how much of infinitely greater worth had she lost on the way?

Catherine put down the message, shaking her head in astonishment.

'I can hardly believe it,' she said at last.

Arabella smiled at her. 'That is what I felt when you first told me your story.' She stood up and went inside to the telephone, asked the operator to connect her to the Bay View Hotel, Lüderitz.

Jamie was swimming in the hotel pool when the call came through. He climbed out, put on a towelling dressing gown and

650

stood listening in amazement to his sister's voice over miles of wire, against a background of crackling static.

'Are you *certain* she is who she claims to be?' he asked her. He had heard how several young women had recently come forward, claiming to be the Tsar's youngest daughter Anastasia. There was some doubt whether the Bolsheviks had murdered her with the rest of the Russian royal family. Perhaps this girl Catherine was trying something similar.

'Positive,' Arabella replied. 'I have also just had a long message from General Brookes. Serov is in London. He has seen him. And Catherine has your watch. There's no doubt whatever she is who she says she is. Why, she's got your eyes!'

'I was flying north tomorrow,' said Jamie. 'I'll cancel that and fly back to Cape Town early in the morning. Be with you for a late breakfast.'

As he put down the receiver, he saw that his hand was trembling. It had never occurred to him that Katharina might have become pregnant. Now he was going to meet Catherine – her daughter, *his* daughter.

He could have spoken to her now. He wondered whether she had her mother's voice, soft and gentle. But it would be better not to know until he saw her face. He felt suddenly bashful, almost embarrassed at the prospect of meeting a daughter he did not know he possessed.

He picked up the telephone again and told his pilot to have the aircraft ready for a seven o'clock departure in the morning.

The car stopped behind the single-storey airport building at Lüderitz. Jamie looked up at the windsock; a slight breeze stirred it. If the weather held, they should have a quick and pleasant flight.

The cabin door of Jamie's plane was open. The pilot, in his shirt sleeves, walked towards the car as he saw Jamie arrive.

'Ready to move off, sir, whenever you wish,' he told him. 'We have all the clearances.'

Jamie followed the pilot to the aircraft. Inside, he sat down, strapped on his safety belt. Within a couple of hours he would be meeting his daughter for the first time. The thought stirred him. He could scarcely believe it; he felt Katharina was close to him. He closed his eyes for a moment and imagined her smiling at him.

The plane's radio crackled briefly as the pilot raced his engine. Then the aircraft surged forward and within seconds was airborne. Far beneath them, diminishing with every second as they climbed, the desert lay empty as a moonscape. The airport building shrank swiftly to the size of a matchbox, and was gone.

Jamie leaned back in the armchair seat, pondering on all the people who had lived and struggled and even died to possess diamonds buried in the sand beneath them, and in the hard blue ground of Kimberley.

Who had said that the whole earth is the sepulchre of famous men? He must ask Arabella; she would know. Certainly, the earth here and further north was also the tomb of as many dreams. Out of all the tens of thousands of men who had abandoned homes, families, security to dig for diamonds, only a handful had found even one stone of any real worth. Most had found nothing but disillusion or destitution. He and Arabella had been among the few lucky ones – and even then they had made their fortunes by subsidiary ventures, following Sun Tzu's advice: 'Make the devious route the most direct, and turn misfortune to advantage.'

Most of the diamond diggers had lived and died in obscurity. But of those few who had grown immensely rich in a matter of months, it seemed curious to Jamie that their resting places invariably reflected their often restless lives.

Cecil Rhodes died quietly, as he had lived, but was buried

with full imperial honours. His body was borne by special train on the five-day journey from Cape Town to Bulawayo. When the train stopped at stations on the way, crowded by blacks and whites, military bands played the Dead March. Finally, Rhodes was buried on top of a hill, the World's View, looking north towards the country to which he gave his name. He had kept faith with his dream. To the end, he had followed the metal arrow in Kimberley pointing north.

Barney Barnato, ever generous to friends of his childhood, even to strangers whose hard-luck stories touched his heart, was remembered by thousands of humble people at his death. Most had never even met Barney, but somehow they all identified with him. His wealth was proof to them that determination, courage – and a fortunate combination of time and chance – could bring success, no matter what a person's background might be.

Barney would have been amused to know that Johannesburg's Stock Exchange closed for the day to mark his passing. In London, two hundred carriages carried mourners from his sister-in-law's house at Marble Arch to the Jewish cemetery in Willesden. Along the Edgware Road, the drivers of horse buses dipped their whips, specially wrapped with black crepe, in salute as the coffin passed by. All his life, Barney had loved people; in death he was not divided from them.

Of all the men who found wealth through diamonds, Jamie felt that August Stauch had the saddest, most ironic and inopportune end. He had acquired the first diamond near the railway line outside Kolmanskop, and rewarded the native labourer who actually found it by appointing him his personal coachman.

Stauch, like the others, soon became a millionaire, and bought splendid properties in Germany and South Africa. He dispensed gifts on a lavish scale, without thought of their cost. But he invested unwisely and on a prodigal scale. He poured money into a scheme by which an inventor proposed to record speech and music on a wire, but the idea was before its time. Steadily, his millions melted away. When Stauch died, alone and after a long illness, a purse in his pocket contained all that was left: 2 marks 50 pfennigs.

The pilot turned towards Jamie. 'Sorry, sir,' he said. 'But I'm going to have to come down.'

'Why?'

'Oil pressure is fluctuating. I don't think it's anything serious. Probably only the pipe to the gauge fractured. If so, I can fix it quite easily. No problem. But I have to make sure.'

The plane began to descend, banking in a wide circle.

'There's a long hard patch of rock ahead, covered by a thin layer of sand,' the pilot explained. 'I'm landing on that.'

Through the window, Jamie saw the desert turn and rise, as it had done on his arrival at Lüderitz. Scrubby bushes, stunted shrubs rushed past his window, then the aircraft was down in a perfect three-point landing.

The cabin reverberated with noise as the pilot reversed the propeller blades. When he stopped the engine, silence seemed to sing like a violin string. Outside, a thin wraith of sand, disturbed by their progress, drifted past the windows, then settled.

The pilot opened the outer door, lowered the steps and jumped down. Jamie followed him. It was more pleasant to be in the open air than cooped up in the metal tube of the fuselage, warming rapidly under the sun.

The pilot walked round the aircraft with a box of tools, unscrewed an inspection plate on the engine. Jamie watched him; it was always instructive to see an expert at work. The pilot turned to him.

'As I thought, sir. Nothing serious. An oil leak in a join. Vibration must have cracked it. I'll seal it off. No problem.'

Ten minutes later, he was replacing the inspection plate. Then he wiped his hands on a rag.

'Ready when you are, sir,' he announced. 'Always better to be safe than sorry.'

'Always,' Jamie agreed, and climbed up the steps into the aircraft. The pilot followed him, closed the door, started the engine.

The plane began to move forward slowly. The pilot accelerated, and suddenly, instead of rising, the nose dipped.

Sand sprayed in an amber fog as the tips of the propeller blades bit into the desert. Quartz grains glittered like beads of glass. The engine backfired. A gout of blue smoke blew out of the exhaust, and the engine stopped.

'What's the matter?' Jamie asked.

'The rock we landed on just wasn't long enough for take-off. We hit the sand.'

Jamie peered over the pilot's shoulder, out through the tinted windscreen. He could see that the tips of the painted propeller were now bright metal, bent and twisted. Jamie controlled his irritation. His first inclination was to blame the pilot, but this would be unfair. People made errors of judgement every day. In a lifetime, he had made more than most. And the desert was notoriously treacherous. It would be impossible for the pilot to know how deep the sand was – or how far the rocky underbase extended.

'I'll call up Lüderitz on the radio,' the pilot continued. 'They'll send a truck to pick us up. Very likely they'll have a new propeller in their stores. Sorry about this, sir, but we'll be on our way as soon as possible, I assure you.'

'I hope so.' Jamie did not explain the depths of his eagerness to be away. Catherine was waiting to meet him, a whole new life lay ahead for both of them – and now this ridiculous, unheard-of delay. It was as unexpected and annoying as experiencing a puncture in a tyre when driving to a vital appointment, the sort of absurd mishap that should always happen to someone else, never to you.

The pilot pressed switches, spun dials, jigged the little control on his hand microphone up and down. Sweat began to varnish his face as he waited tensely for a reply.

'Tailpiece calling,' he said. 'Tailpiece calling. Over to you.'

From the wire-mesh speaker in front of him, only crackling atmospherics filled the cabin.

'Are you receiving me? Tailpiece calling. Over to you.'

The crackling continued.

'What's the matter?' Jamie asked him.

'I don't know, sir. They're either not receiving, or simply not replying.'

'That's unlikely, surely?'

The pilot frowned, did not reply. In the desert, the unlikely too often became likely, and the impossible seemed to him to be happening now.

'Wait five minutes and try again,' Jamie suggested.

They sat in silence, sweating in the increasing heat. But the pilot's second attempt to raise the airport was as unsuccessful as his first.

'It's no good, sir, I'll have to walk.'

'You can't walk to the airport. That's miles away.'

'I know, sir. But I've flown over this area many times. There's a road over to the right, barely half a mile away. I'll walk to that and stop a car. The diamond people have patrols going up and down all the time looking for trespassers. They'll stop all right. No problem.'

He produced a map; Jamie could see the road marked by a dotted line under the pilot's finger.

'Be back as soon as I can, sir.'

'Are you sure you can reach the road?'

'Of course. Got a compass.' He opened a bag, took out a sun hat, crammed it on his head. 'You may find it a bit cooler outside in the shade, under a wing, sir.'

Jamie nodded, watched the pilot set off across the powdery

sand; his feet sank in up to his ankles at every step. Jamie undid his safety belt, reached behind his seat for the ice-box. It always contained a selection of bottles of mineral water with an ice-pack. He opened it but to his astonishment and anger, the box was empty.

He went to the back of the aircraft to see whether someone, not knowing about the ice-box, had mistakenly stowed the bottles in the tail. It was the rule that every aircraft and every vehicle crossing the desert carried supplies of drinking water or mineral water. This was essential in conditions of such heat and distances. But although he found biscuits and chocolate bars in sealed tins, along with medical supplies, there was nothing to drink.

Who the devil had checked out the aircraft before it took off? Ultimately, that was the pilot's responsibility. He had personally reported he was ready to move off as soon as Jamie appeared at the airfield. Jamie never thought to ask him whether he had checked such obvious items as fuel and oil – or drinking water. He took that for granted. This slackness was inexcusable. The pilot would be looking for another job as soon as Jamie reached Cape Town.

He climbed down the steps, carrying a cushion from his seat. He put it on the sand beneath a wing, and sat on it, waiting. As the sun moved slowly above his head, the shadow of the wing moved with it. Jamie had to keep shifting his seat. Because he knew he had no water, his thirst increased. He felt his lips dry, then his mouth. His tongue grew hot and thick, like a piece of felt. Still, the pilot should not take too long to reach the road. He was probably already on his way back.

As Jamie sat, he began to imagine beakers of chilled water. He could hear ice tinkling like temple bells against the glass. He thought of foaming jugs of lager, misted with cold; of iced fruit juice, with chopped peaches and sliced apples floating among fresh sprigs of borage. He swallowed hard; his throat was unusually dry. He coughed and nearly choked.

He stood up, walked round the plane, to take his mind off these disturbing images, shading his eyes in the direction the pilot had taken. He found he was standing by the propeller, and ran his hand across the smooth hot metal. Then he glanced down at the shallow trench the tips had dug in the sand – and stared in astonishment.

The groove was thick with diamonds, glistening, winking, glittering at him in the pitiless glare of the sun.

Jamie went down on his hands and knees and scooped them up. He let them cascade slowly between his fingers, feeling a fortune in his hands, cold as ice and hard, diamond-hard.

He blinked, and when he looked again, the diamonds had disappeared. They were an illusion, a cruel mirage brought about by sun and sand and thirst. He was kneeling in the middle of the burnished empty desert, letting sand run through his hands, like a child on a holiday beach.

Jamie stood up, and as he did so he felt a breath of strangely chill wind blow briefly from the south. This was immediately followed by a hot blast, as though he had unexpectedly opened the door of a raging furnace.

Coming in from the north he could see a mistiness that had not been there moments before: a sandstorm, approaching very quickly. Soon, rising sand, twisted into grotesque dancing shapes by the fierceness of the burning wind, began to darken the sun. Jamie felt sand in his eyes, in his nostrils, at the corners of his mouth. He had better get inside the plane. Already, a haze of sand was beginning to obscure the outline of the aircraft; it looked vague and dim, like a photo out of focus.

He climbed up the steps hurriedly, shut the cabin door firmly behind him. The sun was shining only feebly now through swirling clouds. Mercifully, as the light grew weaker, the temperature inside the cabin dropped slightly.

He would be all right in here, he assured himself comfortingly. But the storm might last for minutes – or for days. How many days could he survive?

The level of the sand rose steadily. It reached and passed the bottom of the cabin windows, then began to creep on up the glass. Soon, it would completely block the windows and then cover the whole fuselage. He would be buried beneath a dune that barely an hour earlier had not even existed. The pilot would not be able to see the aircraft. It would be totally covered, like the ruined houses in Kolmanskop. How the devil could the man find him if he could not even see the plane?

Jamie realised he had to get out. It had seemed wise to shelter from the storm, but now he felt this had been foolish.

As he stood, uncharacteristically irresolute against the immeasurable forces raging outside, the cabin grew darker. The sand had almost reached the tops of the windows. He switched on the cabin lights, then switched them off. He must not waste the battery. If the battery was discharged, the pilot would never start the engine. But that assumed he could ever locate the aircraft – and this seemed more unlikely with every passing second. So many who had torn their wealth from the heart of the desert had found that, in the end, the desert sought something in return.

He spun the door handle, flung himself at the cabin door, trying to force it open. The thin padded metal moved a fraction of an inch, and then stopped. Tens of thousands of tons of hot sand on the other side kept it firmly shut. Jamie paused, streaming with sweat. Slowly, steadily, sand covered all the windows; he was trapped in the hot, airless dark, entombed at the heart of a growing mountain of sand.

Jamie started to shout. He beat with his fists on the cabin roof, seized an axe from the emergency equipment, ripped away the lining from the roof and began to hack at the metal fuselage. Then he stopped. This was useless. He was tiring himself needlessly – and who could hear him? Even if he cut a hole, there could be perhaps fifty feet of sand above the aircraft – or again there might only be inches. He did not know, he could not know, but in either case, weakened by thirst, he would be too exhausted to hack his way out. He remembered Yeung Lee quoting Sun Tzu: 'He who knows when he can fight – and when he cannot – will be victorious.' He must not fight his situation; instead he must make use of it.

He began to pull away the lining from the cabin roof, tore off a piece about five feet square, and suspended this like a crude bag under the bright metal roof in the tail of the aircraft. Then he lay down on the centre carpet. The less he moved, the less air he would need. Soon, overcome by reaction, he slept.

Far above Jamie's head, the storm ceased as suddenly as it had started. Morning merged with afternoon and moved on into night. The sun slid down the sky, and the desert lay cool and empty under a new moon.

In the cabin, Jamie stirred, sat up. A noise had awoken him, the tiny sound of dripping water. He switched on the light briefly. The metal fuselage now felt cold to his touch. Beads of moisture, condensing from Jamie's breath, had formed on the roof where he had removed the lining. They trickled down to the lowest point and then dropped like tears, one by one, into the bag he had made. Already this contained nearly two inches of water. Jamie plunged a beaker into it and drank the brackish water greedily. As he drank, he felt his hopes revive. This was not the end. This *must* be the beginning; time and chance were working for him at last.

He picked up the axe, and began to hack vigorously at the shining roof.

THIRTY-SEVEN

Coming Home

As Jamie's Rolls swept round the last bend in the Cape Town road, and the whole vast crescent sweep of Kleinmond's empty beach stretched ahead, he told his chauffeur to stop the car.

'I'll walk the rest,' he explained.

Jamie climbed out, stood for a moment thankfully breathing the fresh salty air. A heavy sea was running and surf thundered on the shining sand only feet away. It seemed almost unbelievable that, barely hours before, he had been buried in a metal cocoon beneath an immeasurable weight of sand like this farther along this same coast. If the wind had not changed, lifting that sand from the top of the aircraft's fuselage, by now he would undoubtedly have suffocated. Then, his body might have lain entombed in its metal cocoon for years until, perhaps, the wind blew again and revealed his bones, as it had bared the bones of Orlando and the Bushman.

If. A strange and tragic word, he thought as he began to walk slowly towards his sister's house. For some reason he could not properly analyse, he had not wished to arrive in his huge car. He felt somehow embarrassed by it. Now he was going to meet a grown-up daughter he had not realised he possessed, and he had no idea what she would be like.

She might be an indoctrinated Communist, resentful of wealth. She might hate him because she thought – or had been told – that he had abandoned her mother and her. Jamie wanted to meet her on as neutral terms as possible, simply person to person. He might have a lot of questions to answer, and he did not wish to risk clouding those answers by any show of material possessions.

He walked up the gravel drive, past palms rattling their fronds like castanets in the wind from the sea. Sprinklers played on barbered lawns. On the terrace, under a striped awning, three people were sitting around a white table. On this stood bottles of champagne in silver buckets and a tray of glasses.

He knew the three people had seen him, for they all stood up as he approached. His sister Arabella was smiling a welcome. Next to her, he could see Charles, grinning at his uncle's obvious shyness. Charles's right leg had not healed properly; he still walked with a stick. Now he waved this cheerfully in greeting.

The third person, a girl, was still in shadow, under the awning. As Jamie paused, she came out into the sunshine. For the first time, Jamie saw her young, grave, beautiful face and instantly felt his heart contract.

Time telescoped. The palms and the lawns and the other people vanished. He was not looking at a daughter he had never met, a stranger of whose existence he had been totally unaware until a few hours previously. He was looking at her mother, Katharina.

He was seeing her for the first time, as she stood on the edge of the lake at Tsarskoe-Selo. She was wearing a wide-brimmed hat, decorated with flowers. It shaded her face, just as the canvas awning now shaded her daughter's, heightening their extraordinary similarity.

Jamie was meeting Katharina again at the ball in the Winter Palace, asking hesitantly if he could have the first dance. He was leaving her in his room at the Hotel d'Angleterre, while he walked to the British Embassy, never for one moment imagining he could be leaving her for ever.

Jamie shook his head vigorously to push these disturbing memories from his mind, but they would not go. They had poured back from his past and they had come to stay. He was looking at Catherine and seeing Katharina. She must have been about the same age then as her daughter was now, he thought.

Time and the lonely years between had dissolved like sea mist in the sunshine. It was suddenly as though Katharina had never died, but was here smiling at him, not as she would be now if she had lived, but as she was then, as he would always remember her: young, beautiful, vulnerable and ageless. For him, she could never grow old.

Jamie took a slow step forward. He did not trust himself to speak, and in any case he could not think of anything to say. He felt drained of effort, emotion. What he had lost he had found again, and this was all he knew, all he cared to know. Words would come later, but not yet, not now.

Awkwardly, he held out his hand to Catherine. She ignored his hand and raced towards him, hugged him as though she would never let him go.

'Mama used to tell me that my father was shy and correct,' she said, drawing away at last, looking at him as though to convince herself that this was real, he was real. 'She often said he was everything she had ever thought an Englishman should be.'

'Scotsman.'

Jamie found his voice and corrected her.

'There you are!' Catherine cried delightedly. 'She told me about that, too. Now I *know* you are my father.'

Jamie sat down by his daughter's side. He felt weak, as though he had been running a great distance uphill. Now, at last, the long and lonely climb was over. Now he had reached the peak, and ahead the view shone diamond bright. Arabella poured champagne and Jamie's spirits soared like the bubbles in their glasses.

663

There was so much he wanted to say, and still it was as though momentarily he had lost the power of speech. He guessed this was also true of his daughter. They sat close together, smiling at each other, holding hands tightly, as if fearful that this meeting might somehow not be real but only an illusion, the shadow of a dream.

Catherine broke the silence first.

'There's so much to talk about,' she said practically. 'And yet the odd thing is I can't think of a single thing to say!'

'You will,' Arabella assured her. 'We all will.'

They laughed then and the tension vanished. Catherine opened her handbag. She took out the watch she had shown Arabella, handed this to her father.

Jamie examined the watch in amazement, seeing the small dark holes from which diamonds had been prised away over so many terrible years. He remembered giving it to Katharina as they stood together in her deserted, darkened palace, while the mob shouted angrily outside, coming closer every moment. Now the only sound was the empty boom of surf on a sunlit beach. Darkness was behind him at last. Now he was out in the sunshine.

'I never thought to see this again,' he said slowly, turning the watch with its cracked leather strap over in his hand, almost thinking aloud.

'Now at last it has come home.'

Catherine leant forward and kissed her father gently on the cheek.

'And so have I,' she said softly. 'And so have I.'